THE NEVER VEIL
COMPLETE SERIES

NOBODY'S GODDESS, NOBODY'S LADY, AND NOBODY'S PAWN

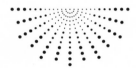

AMY MCNULTY

Snowy Wings
PUBLISHING

The Never Veil Series by Amy McNulty

First edition.

Published by Snowy Wings Publishing, PO Box 1035, Turner, OR 97392

Covers by Makeready Designs. Photography provided by Meet Cute Photography featuring Sakinah Caradine.

ISBN: 978-1-952667-47-3

❅ Created with Vellum

MORE YA BOOKS BY AMY MCNULTY

The Fall Far from the Tree Duology:

Fall Far from the Tree

Turn to Dust and Ashes

The Blood, Bloom, & Water Series:

Fangs & Fins

Salt & Venom

Iron & Aqua

Tears & Cruor

Vines & Florets

Tresses & Erubescence

Ballad of the Beanstalk

Josie's Coat

NOBODY'S GODDESS

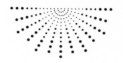

THE NEVER VEIL BOOK ONE

PROLOGUE

W hen I had real friends, I was the long-lost queen of the
elves.

A warrior queen who hitched up her skirt and wielded a
blade. Who held her retainers in thrall. Until they left me for their
goddesses.

Love. A curse that snatches friends away.

One day, when only two of my retainers remained, the old
crone who lived on the northern outskirts of the village was our
prey. It was twenty points if you spotted her. Fifty points if you
got her to look at you. A hundred points if she started screaming
at you.

You won for life if you got close enough to touch her.

"Noll, please don't do this," whispered Jurij from behind the
wooden kitten mask covering his face. Really, his mother still put
him in kitten masks, even though eleven was too old for a boy to
be wearing kittens and bunnies. Especially ones that looked likely
to get eaten for breakfast by as much as a weasel.

"Shut up, I want to see this!" cried Darwyn. Never a kitten,
Darwyn always wore a wolf mask. Yet behind the nasty tooth-
bearing wolf grin—one of my father's better masks—he was very
much a fraidycat.

Darwyn shoved Jurij aside so he could crouch behind the bush that was our threadbare cover. Jurij nearly toppled over, but I caught him and set him gently upright. Sometimes I didn't know if Jurij realized who was supposed to be serving whom. Queens shouldn't have to keep retainers from falling.

"Quiet, both of you." I scanned the horizon. Nothing. All was still against the northern mountains save for the old crone's musty shack with its weakly smoking chimney. The edges of my skirt had grazed the dusty road behind us, and I hitched it up some more so my mother wouldn't notice later. If she didn't want me to get the blasted thing dirty, she should have let me wear Jurij's trousers, like I had been that morning. That got me a rap on the back of the head with a wooden spoon, a common occurrence when I was queen. It made me look too much like a boy, she scolded, and that would cause a panic.

"Are you going or not?" Darwyn was not one for patience.

"If you're so eager, why don't *you* go?" I snapped back.

Darwyn shook his wolf-head. "Oh, no, not me."

I grinned. "That's because you're scared."

Darwyn's muffled voice grew louder. He stood beside me and puffed out his chest. "I am not! *I've* been in the commune."

I poked toward his chest with Elgar, my trusty elf-blade. "Liar! You have not."

Darwyn jumped back, evading my blow. "I have too! My uncle lives there!" He swatted his hand at Elgar. "Get that stick away from me."

"It's not a stick!" Darwyn never believed me when I said that Elgar was the blade of a warrior. It just happened to resemble a tree branch.

Jurij's quiet voice entered the fray. "Your uncle lives there? That's awful." I was afraid he might cry and the tears would get caught up in the black material that covered his eyes. I didn't want him to drown behind the wooden kitty face. He'd vanish into thin air like everyone else did when they died, and then we'd be staring down at Jurij's clothes and the little kitten mask on the ground, and I was afraid I wouldn't be able to stop myself from giggling. Some death for a warrior.

Darwyn shrugged and ran a hand over his elbow. "He moved in there before I was born. I think a weaver lady was his goddess. It's not so strange. Didn't your aunt send her man there, Jurij?"

Jurij was sniffling. *Sniffling*. He tried to rub at his nose, but every time he moved the back of his hand up to his face, it just clunked against the button that represented the kitten's nose.

I sighed and patted Jurij on the back. "A queen's retainer must never cry, Jurij."

Darwyn laughed. "Are you still playing that? You're no queen, Noll!"

I stopped patting Jurij and balled my hands into fists. "Be quiet, Darwyn! You used to play it, too!"

Darwyn put two fingers over his wolf-mask mouth, a gesture we had long ago decided would stand for the boys sticking out their tongues. Although Darwyn was the only one who ever did it as of late. "Like I'd want to do what some *girl* tells me! Girls aren't even blessed by love!"

"Of course they are!" It was my turn to put the two fingers over my mouth. I had a tongue, but a traitorous retainer like Darwyn wasn't worthy of the effort it took to stick it out. "Just wait until you find your goddess, and then we'll see! If she turns out to be me, I'll make sure you rot away in the commune with the rest of the unloved men."

Darwyn lunged forward and tackled me. My head dragged against the bush before it hit the ground, but it still hurt; I could feel the swelling underneath the tangled knots in my hair. Elgar snapped as I tried to get a grip on my attacker. I kicked and shoved him, and for a moment, I won the upper hand and rolled on top of him, almost punching him in the face. Remembering the mask, I settled for giving him a good smack in the side, but then he kicked upward and caught me in the chest, sending me backward.

"Stop!" pleaded Jurij. He was standing between us now, the little timid kitten watching first one friend and then the other, like we were a dangling string in motion.

"Stay out of this!" Darwyn jumped to his feet and pointed at me. "She thinks she's so high and mighty, and she's not even someone's goddess yet!"

"I'm only twelve, idiot! How many goddesses are younger than thirteen?" A few, but not many. I scrambled to my feet and sent my tongue out at him. It felt good knowing he couldn't do the same to me, after all. My head ached. I didn't want him to see the tears forming in my eyes, though, so I ground my teeth once I drew my tongue inward.

"Yeah, well, it'll be horrible for whoever finds the goddess in you!" Darwyn made to lunge at me again, but this time Jurij shoved both his hands at Darwyn's chest to stop him.

"Just stop," commanded Jurij. Finally. That was a good retainer.

My eyes wandered to the old crone's cottage. No sign of her. How could she fail to hear the epic struggle outside her door? Maybe she wasn't real. Maybe just seeing her was worth twenty points after all.

"Get out of my way, you baby!" shouted Darwyn. "So what happens if I pull off your mask when your *queen* is looking, huh? Will you die?"

His greedy fingers reached toward Jurij's wooden animal face. Even from behind, I could see the mask tip dangerously to one side, the strap holding it tightly against Jurij's dark curls shifting. The strap broke free, flying up over his head.

My mouth opened to scream. My hands reached up to cover my eyes. My eyelids strained to close, but it felt as if the moment had slowed and I could never save him in time. Such simple things. Close your eyes. Cover your eyes. Scream.

"DO NOT FOOL WITH SUCH THINGS, CHILD!"

A dark, dirty shawl went flying onto the bush that we had ruined during our fight.

I came back to life. My head and Darwyn's wolf mask spun toward the source of the sound. As my head turned, I saw—even though I knew better than to look—Jurij crumple to the ground, clinging both arms across his face desperately because his life depended on it.

"Your eyes better be closed, girl!" The old crone bellowed. Her own eyes were squeezed together.

I jumped and shut my eyes tightly.

"Hold that shawl tightly over your face, boy, until you can wear your mask properly!" screamed the old crone. "Off with you both, boys! Now! Off with you!"

I heard Jurij and Darwyn scrambling, the rustle of the bush

and the stomps of their boots as they fled, panting. I thought I heard a scream—not from Jurij, but from Darwyn. He was the real fraidycat. An old crone was no match for the elf queen's retainers. But the queen herself was far braver. So I told myself over and over in my head.

When the last of their footsteps faded away, and I was sure that Jurij was safe from my stare, I looked.

Eyes. Huge, bulbous, dark brown eyes. Staring directly into mine.

The crone's face was so close I could smell the shriveled decay from her mouth. She grabbed me by the shoulders, shaking me. "What were you thinking? You held that boy's life in your hands! Yet you stood there like a fool, just starin' as his mask came off."

My heart beat faster, and I gasped for more air, but I wanted to avoid inhaling her stench. "I'm sorry, Ingrith," I mumbled. I thought if I used her real name, if I let her lecture me like all the other adults, it would help me break free from her grasp. I twisted and pulled, but I couldn't bring myself to touch her. I had this notion that if I touched her, my fingers would decay.

"Sorry is just a word. Sorry changes nothing."

"Let me go." I could still feel her dirty nails on my skin.

"You watch yourself, girl."

"Let me go!"

The crone's lips grew tight and puckered. Her fingers relaxed ever so slightly. "You children don't realize. The lord is watching. Always watching—"

I knew what she was going to say, the words so familiar to me that I knew them as well as if they were my own. "And he will not abide villagers who forget the first goddess's teachings." The sentence seemed to loosen the crone's fingers. She opened her mouth to speak, but I broke free and ran.

My eyes fell to the grass below my feet as I cut across the fields to get away from the monster. On the borders of the eastern woods was a lone cottage, home of Gideon the woodcarver, a warm and comfortable place so much fuller of life than the shack I left behind me. When I was near the woods, I could look up freely since the trees blocked the eastern mountains from view. But until I got closer...

"Noll! Wait up!"

My eyes snapped upward on instinct. I saw the upper boughs of the trees and almost screamed, my gaze falling back to the grass beneath my feet. I stopped running and let the gentle rustlings of footsteps behind me catch up.

"Jurij, please." I sighed and turned around to face him, my eyes still on the grass and the pair of small dark boots that covered his feet. Somehow he managed to step delicately through the grass, not disturbing a single one of the lilies that covered the hilltops. "Don't scare me like that. I almost looked at the castle."

The toe of Jurij's boot dug a little into the dirt. "Oh. Sorry."

"Is your mask on?"

The boot stopped moving, and the tip of a black shawl dropped into my view. "Oh. Yeah."

I shook my head and raised my eyes. There was no need to fear looking up to the west. In the distance, the mountains that encircled our village soared far beyond the western fields of crops. I liked the mountains. From the north, the south, and the west, they embraced our village with their jagged peaks. In the south, they watched over our fields of livestock. In the north, they towered above a quarry for copper and stone. And in the east, they led home and to the woods. But no girl or woman could ever look up when facing the east. Like the faces of men and boys before their Returnings, just a glance at the castle that lay beyond the woods against the eastern mountains spelled doom. The earth would shake and threaten to consume whoever broke the commandment not to look.

It made walking home a bit of a pain, to say the least.

"Tell me something important like that before you sneak up on me."

Jurij's kitten mask was once again tight against his face, if askew. The strap was a bit tangled in his dark curls and the pointed tip of one of his ears. "Right. Sorry."

He held out the broken pieces of Elgar wrapped in the dirty black shawl. He seemed very retainer-like. I liked that. "I went to give this back to the—the lady. She wasn't there, but you left Elgar."

I snatched the pieces from Jurij's hands. "You went back to the shack? What were you going to say? 'Sorry we were spying on you pretending you were a monster, thanks for the dirty old rag?'"

"No." Jurij crumpled up the shawl and tucked it under his belt. A long trail of black cloth tumbled out immediately, making Jurij look like he had on half a skirt.

I laughed. "Where's Darwyn?"

"Home."

Of course. I found out later that Darwyn had whined straight to his mother that "nasty old Noll" almost knocked *his* mask off. It was a great way to get noticed when you had countless brothers and a smitten mother and father standing between you and any form of attention. But it didn't have the intended effect on me. I was used to lectures, and besides, there was something more important bothering me by then.

I picked up my feet to carry me back home.

Jurij skipped forward to join me. One of his boots stumbled as we left the grasses behind and hit the dirt path. "What happened with you and the crone?"

I gripped the pieces of Elgar tighter in my fist. "Nothing." I stopped, relieved that we'd finally gotten close enough to the woods that I could face forward. I put an arm on Jurij's shoulder to stop him. "But I touched her." Or she touched me. "That means I win forever."

The kitten face cocked a little sideways. "You always win."

"Of course. I'm the queen." I tucked the broken pieces of Elgar into my apron sash. Elgar was more of a title, bestowed on an endless number of worthy sticks, but in those days I wouldn't have admitted that to Jurij. "Come on. I'll give you a head start. Race you to the cavern!"

"The cavern? But it's—"

"Too late! Your head start's over!" I kicked my feet up and ran as if that was all my legs knew how to do. The cool breeze slapping across my face felt lovely as it flew inside my nostrils and mouth. I rushed past my home, not bothering to look inside the open door.

"Stop! Stop! Noll, you stop this instant!"

The words were something that could easily come out of a mother's mouth, but Mother had a little more patience than that.

And her voice didn't sound like a fragile little bird chirping at the sun's rising. "Noll!"

I was just an arm's length from the start of the trees, but I stopped, clutching the sharp pain that kicked me in the side.

"Oh dear!" Elfriede walked out of our house, the needle and thread she was no doubt using to embroider some useless pattern on one of the aprons still pinched between two fingers. My sister was a little less than a year older than me, but to my parents' delight (and disappointment with me), she was a hundred times more responsible.

"Boy, your mask!" Elfriede never did learn any of my friends' names. Not that I could tell her Roslyn from her Marden, either. One giggling, delicate bird was much like another.

She walked up to Jurij, who had just caught up behind me. She covered her eyes with her needle-less hand, but I could see her peeking between her fingers. I didn't think that would actually protect him if the situation were as dire as she seemed to think.

"It's crooked." Elfriede's voice was hoarse, almost trembling. I rolled my eyes.

Jurij patted his head with both hands until he found the bit of the strap stuck on one of his ears. He pulled it down and twisted the mask until it lined up evenly.

I could hear Elfriede's sigh of relief from where I was standing. She let her fingers fall from her face. "Thank the goddess." She considered Jurij for a moment. "There's a little tear in your strap."

Without asking, she closed the distance between them and began sewing the small tear even as the mask sat on his head. From how tall she stood above him, she might have been ten years older instead of only two.

I walked back toward them, letting my hands fall. "Don't you think that's a little stupid? What if the mask slips while you're doing that?"

Elfriede's cheeks darkened and she yanked the needle up, pulling her instrument free of the thread and tucking the extra bit into the mask strap. She stood back and glared at me. "Don't you talk to me about being stupid, Noll. All that running isn't safe when you're with boys. Look how his mask was moving."

His mask had moved for even more dangerous reasons than a little run, but I knew better than to tell tattletale Elfriede that. "How would *you* know what's safe when you're with boys? You're already thirteen, and no one has found the goddess in you!" Darwyn's taunt was worth reusing, especially since I knew my sister would be more upset about it than I ever was.

Elfriede bit her lip. "Go ahead and kill your friends, then, for all I care!" The bird wasn't so beautiful and fragile where I was concerned.

She retreated into the house and slammed the door behind her. I wrapped my hand around Jurij's arm, pulling him eastward. "Come on. Let's go. There're bound to be more monsters in the cavern."

Jurij didn't give beneath my pull. He wouldn't move.

"Jurij?"

I knew right then, somewhere in my mind, what had happened. But I was twelve. And Jurij was my last real friend. I knew he'd leave me one day like the others, but on some level, I didn't really believe it yet.

Jurij stood stock still, even as I wrenched my arm harder and harder to get him to move.

"Oh for—*Jurij!*" I yelled, dropping my hands from his arm in frustration. "Ugh. I wish I was your goddess just so I could get you to obey me. Even if that means I'd have to put up with all that—*yuck*—smooching." I shivered at the thought.

At last Jurij moved, if only to lift his other arm, to run his fingers across the strap that Elfriede had mended. She was gone from my sight, but Jurij would never see another.

It struck them all. Sometime around Jurij's age, the boys' voices cracked, shifting from high to deep and back again in a matter of a few words. They went from little wooden-faced animals always shorter than you to young men on their way to towering over you. And one day, at one moment, at some age, earlier for some and later for others, they looked at a girl they'd probably seen thousands of times before and simply ceased to be. At least, they weren't who I knew them to be ever again.

And as with so many of my friends before Jurij, in that moment all other girls ceased to matter. I was nothing to him now, an afterthought, a shadow, a memory.

11

No.

Not him.

My dearest, my most special friend of all, now doomed to live or die by the choice of the fragile little bird who'd stopped to mend his strap.

CHAPTER ONE

L ike most of the village, we couldn't afford a mirror, but if you asked me, that was a good thing. By the time Mother was done trying to make me appear half a lady, I was ready to smash anything easily breakable within five yards of where I sat. "I don't care how long you spend running the comb through my hair, it's never going to be soft and supple."

It'll never be as beautiful as Elfriede's.

Mother dipped the wooden comb in the bowl of water she'd brought to the kitchen-table-turned-rack-of-torture. It wasn't working too well. I could tell from the constant battle between my scalp and the roots of my hair that so badly wished to tear free of the skin. But it was either that or bacon grease, and I wasn't having any pig fat slathered over my hair in attempt to tame it, not today.

She gripped a chunk of hair like the tail on a dead squirrel and ran the wooden comb upward. "Oh!" came the shout, followed quickly by the snap of the wooden comb Father had carved for her upon their Returning years ago. The comb that was only really a last resort, a gift meant for Mother to treasure and run through her own silky, wavy golden hair. "We've broken the last of them," she sighed. "We can still use the grease."

"*No.*" I could just imagine myself smelling of dead pig on the first day I'd look upon the face of the man I loved. Not that he'd care even if I showed up smeared in mud with a live pig under each arm and missing a few teeth. He only had eyes for his goddess.

"Mother," interrupted Elfriede, the goddess who'd have his love with or without the mud and the pigs. She stood by the sink, perhaps hoping to see her reflection in the musty water collected there. One hand held a wavy lock of golden hair that had escaped from the bun at the back of her neck. "This keeps falling out."

Mother crossed the room and ran the broken half of the comb through Elfriede's loose tendril. I yanked and jostled the tangle at the top of my head until the other half of the comb came loose. "Can't I just cut it short?"

"*No*," said Mother and Elfriede at once, in the same tone I'd used moments before.

Elfriede patted the sides of her head as Mother crossed back over toward the bed my sister and I shared. "*Really*, Noll," said Elfriede, without turning her head. "You act like a young boy enough already. What if someone glanced over and thought you *were* a boy—*unmasked*—running around? You'd scare the women in the village to death!"

I drummed my fingers across the table. "As if anyone could mistake me for a boy." At sixteen, I wasn't as oak-pale as Mother and Elfriede, but my chestnut skin was lighter than any man's.

Mother appeared behind me to tuck a small clump of hair behind my lobe. She pinched the top of my ear playfully. "Yes, your ears are round and smooth, but you can't expect a woman to check for the pointed ears of a man when she's worried she's going to kill you just by glancing at your uncovered face."

I tucked a strand behind my other ear as Mother glided across the room with a silky deep violet dress over her arm. She grabbed Elfriede by the wrist and gently guided her into the shaft of sunlight spilling in from the open doorway. "Won't this look breathtaking on you?" said Mother, her face full of awe. She unfurled the dress and held it up before Elfriede. Its hem brushed the floor, kicking up a small flight of dust.

Elfriede beamed and stepped into the dress, sliding it over the slip she'd worn since Mother did her hair earlier. Mother grinned as she helped fasten the buttons at the back. "This was the dress I wore to my Returning," said Mother. She took Elfriede by the shoulders and spun her around. "And it's such a joy to see my dear girl wearing it for her own." She kissed Elfriede's temple and used a thumb to wipe a tear first from Elfriede's cheek and then her own. "What a fine color. It really brings out the blossom on your cheeks."

A dress the color of mud and vomit couldn't stop Elfriede's cheeks from blooming.

The goddess was stunning today, that was plain to see. I tried to imagine Jurij standing beside her, and the face I had never seen before. For some reason, the only male face I could picture for him was the one I'd seen every day of my life, a younger, leaner version of Father. Dark skin, the color of soil soaked in rain. Bold, sharp cheeks. Tall, pointed ears like daggers jumping out from his black, curly hair—hair that at least was familiar to me.

I longed to drink in Jurij's eyes, dark eyes that I knew carried flames within them, as did all men's, even when the only light for leagues was the smallest sliver of the moon. I'd known him for so long. But I could only see his face in my dreams.

I shook my head. "Have you ever seen a young boy's face?" I asked, more to Mother than to Elfriede. "I played with boys every day growing up, but I couldn't tell them from one another when I first saw them in the morning unless they said something." Jurij's tame masks an exception.

"Hmm? No. I didn't have any brothers or cousins my age, same as you, so how could I?" Mother left Elfriede and crossed the room to the chest at the edge of the bed once more, rummaging through the clothing inside. Elfriede stood patiently for what was no doubt something else to bring out the blossom in her cheeks. Her hands stayed clasped together, the corners of her mouth turned upward pleasantly.

"How do you know you're in love with Jurij, without ever seeing his face?" It was a silly question. I knew I loved him just the same. But it was different with me. Elfriede was always too dainty to battle with monsters; she hardly knew Jurij's name before he found the goddess in her.

Elfriede seemed a bit taken aback by the question. "What do you mean?"

"I knew you at thirteen. You and all of your girlfriends." I counted off the boys on my fingers. "There was the oldest baker's son. That one farmer boy. I think the candlemaker's son? You mooned over all of the handsome older boys in the village who had their love Returned and could take off their masks. Or that strong quarry worker. He takes his shirt off so much, it really doesn't matter what he looks like under his mask." I smiled as Elfriede blushed and wrung her hands together.

"All of you knew that none of those boys could ever love you, since they'd already found their goddesses, but surely they made for more entertaining daydreams than some scrawny eleven-year-old with dirt all over his kitten mask declaring his love for you."

Elfriede's face darkened. "I don't know what you mean."

"Oh come on, Friede! You cried when Jurij found the goddess in you! You were horrible to him for months, knowing he was the only one who'd ever love you—"

"Noll, stop teasing your sister." Mother plopped a neatly folded brown piece of clothing beside me on the table. "Jurij's a sweetheart. Elfriede was just scared and embarrassed, as most of us are when a man finds the goddess in us."

"I guess I'll have to take your word on that." I grabbed the folded clothing, and it tumbled over the table, the color of mud and vomit.

Mother didn't notice the frown that crossed my face as she slid in behind Elfriede, now fussing with loose tendrils of hair that didn't even exist. "Your man will find you someday, Noll. You're not the first late bloomer. Why, there was a woman my age whose man wound up being a number of years younger—you know, Vena, the tavern mistress. She was at least fifteen before her husband Elweard found the goddess in her."

"I'm sixteen."

I think Elfriede legitimately thought she was helping when she chimed in with, "There've been stories of women even older than sixteen—thirty, even. Roslyn told me her grandmother knew a woman whose man was seventeen years younger."

I could have puked right then. It would've blended into the color of the dress I slid over my head. "Let's not go there. And let's not forget those are only stories, and there's no woman living over the age of thirteen who has yet to have her man find her. That is, no woman except me, and..."

Her eyes. Huge, bulbous, dark brown eyes. Staring directly into mine.

"Hmm." Mother patted Elfriede's shoulders. "That reminds me. Ingrith is the only one who hasn't yet been invited to the Returning."

I rapped my fingers on the table. "Thanks, Mother. I love being compared to a crazy old woman who lives alone."

"I wasn't comparing you to anyone." Mother stepped over to the sink and picked up a dish from breakfast, wiping it with a cloth. Why she wasted her time washing dishes when she could just bat her eyes and Father would do anything for her was beyond me. "But someone has to invite her. The lord is always watching—"

"—And he will not abide villagers who forget the first goddess's teachings. I know." Although why the first goddess ever deemed that all should be invited to celebrate a Returning, I would never understand. "Why can't you or Father do it?"

Mother pushed aside a fallen bit of hair by rubbing the back of her forearm against her forehead. "The rest of us have been inviting people for weeks. We spoke to everyone else in the village. I think you could take the time to invite at least one person, Noll."

Nice of you to leave the crazy one for me.

Elfriede hugged her arms to her chest and tapped her elbow with her index finger. "You'd think my own sister could help with the invitations to the most important day of my life."

You'd think my own sister could have some sympathy for the fact that she was stealing my dearest friend from me.

"All right, all right." I stopped moving my restless fingers. "Goddess help us if the lord thinks we invited everyone but the old woman who would rather spit at people than talk to them." *Hope you like being wet on your Returning day.* "Anyway, it makes sense. Why not send one old loveless crone to fetch the other?"

"Noll." Mother shook a bowl over the sink, spreading water droplets, and Elfriede jumped back to get out of the fray. Elfriede held an arm out to examine her dress, and her nose wrinkled.

Mother didn't seem to notice. "I know your man will find you soon. It's just this feeling I have."

"I hope you're wrong." I sighed and stretched one arm above my head as far as it would go. The tight stitches in the shoulders of the dress made the movement uncomfortable. A seam ripped. *Great.* I plopped both hands on the table and dropped back into the chair. "Because if a man does ever find the goddess in me, I'm kicking him straight into the commune."

"How horrible!" came Elfriede's squeak from behind the delicate hand that covered her peach lips.

"Noll!" The bowl in Mother's hand dropped to the floor, clattering and echoing as it rocked back and forth. Luckily, it was made of wood. Another gift from Father, but this one for the wedding that occurred right after the Returning. At least Elfriede's and Jurij's wedding couldn't yet be held. It was Elfriede's seventeenth birthday, so she could perform a Returning, but Jurij was still only fifteen.

I sighed. "I'm not serious, Mother."

"I should hope so!" A look of rage spread across Elfriede's delicate features.

"Why?" I asked. "Because you never thought of doing the same to Jurij?"

"Oh!" Elfriede's hands clasped over her ears, her lips trembling. Tears started forming across her eyes.

Mother bent over to snatch the bowl off the ground. "Noll, hush now! Your father would be heartbroken to hear you talk like that!"

Speak of the man. A silhouette appeared in the open door, and Father stepped inside, closing the small gap between him and Mother with two huge strides and picking her up by the waist, wooden bowl and cloth and all. "What a beautiful day it is, my love!" said Father, oblivious to the tension in the room and the tears forming in his eldest daughter's eyes. He held Mother above him for a moment longer, craning his neck upwards to steal a kiss. "*Aubree...*" He practically moaned her name.

Mother smiled and flung the cloth down at him. "Gideon, stop that. You're not young anymore. You'll throw your back out."

Father gently put Mother's feet back on the ground, but his

hands remained firmly planted on her waist, his eyes locked intensely with hers. Mother was the first to look away. She searched Elfriede's face, but my sister bit her lip, unrelenting, not letting a single tear fall. "Elfriede, why don't you go visit Roslyn and Marden before the ceremony? You should be with your friends before the big day."

That's another thing I wouldn't be able to do even if I'd wanted.

Mother turned back to her sink full of dishes, sliding with difficulty even as Father still clung to her.

"What are you doing?" Father released Mother, only to scoop the bowl and cloth into his own hands. He scrubbed the bowl with fervor. "You should have the girls do that!"

I didn't think scrubbing dishes on your Returning day was a tradition, so that left me. I sighed and stood, but Mother waved me away. "The girls have other things to do today." She grabbed Father's hand in hers. "Honey, you're filthy. You were out there carving. Wash up first. Then you can do the dishes."

Father did as commanded, and Elfriede sent me a dejected look before stepping outside. "Bye, Mother. Bye, Father!" She left me out of her farewells.

"See you soon, dear!" called Mother. She faced me, her hands on her hips, her mouth poised to issue an order.

Watching Father wash up gave me an idea for how to deflect the next thing out of her mouth. "How come Father still obeys your orders?"

Father blushed and went back to pouring water over his hands in the sink and rubbing them together. "I don't." *Right.*

Mother raised a finger and walked over to the cupboard, removing a picnic basket. She rummaged through one of the clay pots and pulled out a roll. I heard it *clink* as she tossed it into the basket. She looked around at the counter next to the sink and plucked a wedge of cheese from a bowl. Someone—or maybe the mice—had started biting into it. Mother covered the top of the basket with a black cloth and dropped it on the table in front of me. "Why don't you bring these to Ingrith, and see if she wants to attend? We'll meet you at the Great Hall at dusk." She took my head and bent it gently forward to kiss the top. Good thing she hadn't smeared bacon grease into it.

I grabbed the handle of the basket gingerly with two fingers, almost feeling sorry for Ingrith if that was the extent of the gifts someone would offer her. It was little better than what the men in the commune got. Mother began to turn around but stopped suddenly, waving a hand at me. "And don't cut through the fields. Take the pathway. We don't want you getting your dress all dirty."

I think mud would blend right in with this monstrosity just fine. "Okay. Love you." I peered over her shoulder before I turned to leave. "Love you too, Father."

Elbow deep in water and plates, Father grunted.

CHAPTER TWO

S winging a basket around with two fingers was an excellent way to break those fingers, which was helpful if you were looking for an excuse to get out of working for a few days. But since the Returning had that covered for me, and my fingers were starting to stiffen in what looked a bit like a hook, I gave up and began to carry the thing properly. Having a hook hand was all I needed the next time someone made a comment about how no man would ever find the goddess in me.

Down and up and down and up again, among the violet lily-covered fields, I followed the dirt path that ran from the woods and the castle to the center of the village and out again in all directions. There were no houses between mine and the edge of the village, none but Jurij's, the Tailor Shop on the eastern outskirts.

Maybe if I hide my face behind the basket I could pretend I don't see it. Lifting the basket that high made my arms sore. But then again, it did house at least one rock-hard biscuit.

I stepped on the dog's paw before I even realized she'd run out of the Tailor Shop to greet me. We both yelped as I tumbled.

The basket went soaring out of my arms… and into the arms of a man with a male face carved from wood, complete with exaggerated pointy wooden ears that stuck out straight sideways.

It was the mask a man only wore on the morning of his Returning.

"Whoa!" The muffled voice was all too familiar. He bent forward to pick up the partially bitten cheese wedge, which had landed on the back of Bow, his golden dog. "Cheese is generally a fine gift for a Returning, but..." He held up the wedge with one hand like it was the carcass of some dead squirrel Bow had brought him. "The fur-covered, half-eaten variety is not quite to my taste."

I grinned and snatched the cheese from him, blowing on it to get rid of all of the hairs. "I don't know. I hear furry cheese is an excellent cure for missing eyes."

"Amusing." Jurij's creepy wooden face tilted to one side. "My eyes are here and ordinary, just like every other man's."

There was no way his eyes were ordinary. Not if I could have them locked on to my own, even just once.

Bow opened her mouth and panted, watching her master eagerly, probably smelling that weeks-old biscuit and actually deeming it fit for dog consumption. Jurij bent to set the basket on the ground, cooing as he grabbed Bow's muzzle and rubbed the sides gently, preventing her from attacking the basket. Elfriede wasn't the only golden-haired mongrel that got his attention. "You're going to be a cute little mama, aren't you?"

I glanced at Bow's bulging belly as I snatched up the basket. "She's pregnant?"

"Yup. I think it was the butcher's dog. Because you love your sausages, don't you? So who's eating the disgusting old cheese?" Jurij asked, still simpering in his high-pitched baby voice.

I dropped the cheese into the basket and moved the old black cloth around until it covered the travesty of a gift I was tasked with presenting. It took me a moment to figure out Jurij was talking to me and not his dog. "Our favorite village crazy person: Ingrith. Apparently everyone conveniently forgot to invite her to the Returning, so guess who gets to do it? In case the lord decides to prove that he actually exists and comes down from the castle to say that your Returning is canceled because one old loon wasn't asked to give her blessing."

"No!" Jurij stood and twisted his wooden face to look over and behind me.

"I was joking, Jurij." I rubbed my temples. His every movement let me know just how much in the way I was of who he hoped to see. "She's not with me. She's primping with her girlfriends in the village." Apparently he'd just missed her. Strange. Jurij would certainly have visited his goddess had he walked past her home. Elfriede was clearly more concerned with the occasion than with the young man who was the entire reason she was the focus of the village's attention. At least until the next Returning.

I couldn't see his face, but the way Jurij's shoulders slumped forward was visual cue enough to express his disappointment. Bow sensed her master's distress and nudged his hand with her nose. Jurij pet it absently.

The Returning would be meaningless to me. We could hold the ceremony alone in the cavern for all I'd care. All I'd want is to be with you.

I clutched the handle of the basket with both hands, running the toe of one shoe over the dirt in the road. "I'd ask why you aren't doing the same and primping and chatting with a bunch of excited young men, but you have no friends. Must be wonderful to be a guy. Soon as your buddy finds his goddess, he practically forgets anyone else exists."

"You're my friend, Noll." He said it with such conviction and so quickly, I didn't know whether to be delighted or let down. "I don't miss the other guys."

"I do."

Jurij pet the back of Bow's head absently, rustling her floppy ear like he might a curl of Elfriede's hair. "It's hard to explain. They're not important anymore."

"They are—they *were* to me."

Jurij shrugged. "I don't mean anything by it. I know they don't miss me, either."

I dug my heel sharply into the dirt. "Because your goddess is everything."

Jurij's wooden face bobbed up and down. "She is."

Unlike Mother, at least Jurij didn't try to soften the statement with assurance that some man would find the goddess in me one day. I was glad for it. "Nice face, by the way."

The smile carved onto the wooden face might have been genuine if it didn't look so freaky. "Looking forward to seeing what's under it?"

I forced myself to laugh. "Not as much as Elfriede, I'm sure." A lie.

The name of his goddess pulled Jurij into some dream state of mind. His wooden face looked off behind me again. I'd pretend to seek out what caught his attention, but if I chanced to look up and glance at the castle that lay flush against the eastern mountains, I'd have a bit of explaining to do to the village.

"Are you looking forward to today more or the wedding?" Sometimes it was easier to feed into his reverie than to try to snap him out of it entirely. Plus, today I was supposed to be happy for them.

Jurij tensed and rubbed Bow's head wildly. "I can't even think about the wedding yet."

"Why?"

He smacked Bow's back three times. She might have jumped, but her attention was focused on the basket in my hands. "It's just too much. Too much happiness to think about. I feel like I'm going to burst."

Hmph. I wonder if your father would agree if he had a mind of his own. "It's too bad you're not already over seventeen like my father was. He had his Returning and his wedding on the same day."

Jurij shrugged. "That doesn't matter. I can wait nineteen months and four days." Of course he had the exact days counted. "But today…"

Today he could finally kiss Elfriede.

Not that some clever couplings hadn't managed to before their Returnings by blindfolding the woman or making sure she kept her eyes shut tight when the man took his mask off. But Elfriede and Jurij were both too naive to try such things. "Today you get to walk around without a mask once and for all, never again fearing the eyes of women."

Jurij didn't respond. His mind was on the kisses, I feared, not the fact that he could finally let the skin on his face get acquainted with the sun.

"Well," I said, not wanting to keep the woman who would spit on me waiting. "I guess I should get going. I'll see you later. Congratulations."

"Thank you." Jurij stopped. "Do you want me to come with you?"

I felt the heat rush to my face. Of course, the only person in the entire village who could at all sense my discomfort was the one who was about to be lost to me forever. To a primping girl who had never fought a single monster with him.

"Sure. Thank you. I mean—" I shut my mouth, took a breath, and opened it again. "If you're not too busy. Today being what it is."

Jurij shrugged and made his way to the Tailor Shop door. "What more do I have to do? Swapped my mask, wore my cleanest clothing. I could use the distraction, actually. Every moment is proving to last forever." He opened the door and Bow bolted past him to get inside. "Luuk! Watch Bow, will you?"

A young boy poked his wooden face out of the door and nodded. As ever, Luuk wore his timidity on his face, his features obscured by a darling wooden puppy. Rather like a certain boy forever in a kitten or bunny mask who used to tag along with me.

"Where are you going?" asked Luuk. At least I think that's what he said. Thanks to his murmuring voice and the muffling veil over the puppy's mouth hole, he might have asked, "When is dew snowing?"

Jurij understood his brother better than I did. He patted his head. "Old lady Ingrith's." He leaned in to the house and reached for something that must have hung near the door.

Luuk pulled back shyly to allow Jurij more room. He tapped his two index fingers together, like he was waiting for a turn to speak. But no one else was speaking.

Jurij pulled a red apple out from the doorway and lifted it to his mouth hole. Laughing, he tossed the apple, unscathed, onto the top of the cloth covering the rest of the food in the basket. "Can't snack just now, I guess. I always forget you're not a guy, Noll."

Thanks so much for that.

"Mama…" Luuk coughed. "Mama says you and her are not to be bothered today."

Jurij scoffed. "Mother says not to bother her most every day."

That's especially true for her husband, I imagine.

25

Jurij grabbed the basket from me. He bobbed his wooden face toward the grassy fields. "Should we take the shortcut?"

I grinned, hitching up the bottom of my skirt. Dirt was sure to blend in. Who would notice a few grass stains? "I'll race you there!"

～

MY LEGS WEREN'T MADE for running anymore. About halfway between the Tailor Shop and Ingrith's, I gave up and started walking because there was no way I could run with the pain in my side. "Okay, you win, you win."

Jurij had managed to get several paces in front of me, even with the basket in tow. He strode confidently through the grasses like he didn't know the meaning of fatigue. But his body seemed to have noticed the exertion. By the time I caught up to him, I could hear his stomach rumbling.

"Do you need to eat?" I asked, thinking of the apple.

Jurij shook his wooden head. "No. Don't worry about it. Besides, we ought to present Ingrith with *something* edible." He stuck his hand into the basket and rummaged around. "What did you put in here? A stone?"

I tore the basket away from him and cradled it in my arms like a child. "I didn't pack it. Mother did."

Jurij nodded. "I suppose the gesture is all that's important. It's ill luck to have a Returning with the threat of the lord refusing to give the first goddess's blessing."

It's ill luck to hold a Returning when your "goddess" forced herself to love you. If Elfriede didn't love Jurij, he wouldn't live through the end of the day. Not if he still removed his mask. How could he be so confident that she loved him? After how she treated him?

I didn't know what to say. I didn't know how to even begin. But if his life was in danger... "Are you sure Elfriede loves you?" That was subtle.

From behind that contemptible mask, I heard what had to be a laugh. "Wow, Noll. Elfriede is lucky to have you as a sister."

My chest tightened. "I just meant..." What did I mean? I didn't think she'd kill him on purpose. She wasn't a bad person, really. But how did she know she wasn't just fooling herself into accepting the only man who'd ever love her? I couldn't see Elfriede taking up a trade and sending a man to the commune. To her, there was no other choice.

Jurij stopped walking, and I stopped too. "I know, I know. You're scared about today. But, Noll, I'm not going to die. Elfriede loves me." He squeezed my shoulder. "Have a little more faith in your sister. Sometimes I worry you don't realize how wonderful she is."

Jurij's faith in her stung. "She can be nice. I'm happy for you. Really." There was a sharp burning taste in my mouth. "But we're talking your life here."

The earth shook beneath us. I stumbled and Jurij, the fool, reached out to catch me. Even as the ground kept shaking, I wanted to fling his hands off my arm and shoulder. The touch was so intoxicating, my hands were trembling. From the quake or the contact, I couldn't tell. The basket I held, like everything about this awful village, kept the distance between us.

The shaking stopped. I looked up into the black holes in Jurij's mask, and he let me go, his face poring over the horizon. "That started nearby." Jurij rubbed his wooden chin. I'd have stopped to think about the ridiculousness of the gesture were it not for the seriousness of the situation.

I shook my head to clear it of the chaos under my feet and in my heart. "We should hurry."

Jurij nodded, and he sprinted. With the basket and my heavy heart weighing me down, I had no chance of catching up to him. My legs felt like they were caked in mud, and they were pulling me down, keeping me from him.

When at last I caught up to him in front of Ingrith's shack, Jurij was reaching out to the shriveled-up old woman, and the crone was batting his arms away, even as she stood on unsteady feet. The dirty black cloth she wore over her head tied her thick hair down and made her a bit less menacing than she'd seemed when I'd last seen her close up. When she was digging her claws into my shoulders.

Ingrith placed a hand on Jurij's chest and pushed him backward. "You just leave me alone. I've got no need for masked men 'round here."

"But Ma'am—"

"No buts. Get outta here." Ingrith tore her eyes from him and let her glare fall over me as I approached them. "Wonderful. Now there's a fine face I won't soon forget. Come to bother an old woman again with your fancy games, girl?"

Better to pretend I had no idea what she was talking about. "Did you cause the quake?"

Bad idea. Ingrith's face grew even more sour and puckered, and I wouldn't have thought that was even possible. "Yes, I did. And never you mind."

I glanced beyond the old woman to the rest of the northern dirt path. "But won't the quarry workers notice? They're close enough to have felt—"

Ingrith scoffed. "You let me worry about them workers."

There was no sign of movement from the quarry, but still. "It's got to be dangerous to look at the castle so near where there are men working." She couldn't have meant to kill the poor men, could she?

"Dangerous nothing, girl, I just made a mistake. A bird startled me. Can't blame an old woman for lookin' when something starts screeching at her." Ingrith's mouth clamped shut, and I could see the muscles tense in her jaw. She bent over to reach the walking stick she'd dropped.

Jurij tried to grab the stick for her. "Let me—"

"Oh, no." Ingrith slapped his arm, and Jurij pulled back, cradling his forearm and staring at the woman with his blank-eyed face. Ingrith snatched her stick and stood back up. "Didn't need no man's help then, don't need no man's help now."

Jurij turned his wooden mask toward me. The opened-mouth grin probably didn't match his real expression underneath as the ungrateful old woman smacked him. But that was the Returning mask, and that was the countenance he was stuck with for the day. Until dusk, anyway. *I hope I really do see his face. Surely Elfriede forcing herself to love him is enough. Surely...*

"Let me guess. Ol' Ingrith is the last to know. Ol' Ingrith just has to be invited, though there's no one who actually wants her to come, but goddess help us if the lord don' give his blessing. I take it you two are having a Returning today?" Her eyes rolled up and down, as she examined Jurij from head to toe. "You look too young to get married."

I didn't often ask the first goddess for anything, but I prayed that no one would notice the flush that I could feel spreading across my face.

"She's not my goddess." He said it in the same manner one might say, "Please pass the potatoes."

"Huh. If you say so." The way Ingrith stared at me, I had a feeling the first goddess had failed me. Again.

Jurij didn't seem to notice. "But I'm having my Returning today. This is my goddess's sister."

Ingrith's eyes narrowed as she looked up at the wooden face beaming down at her. "And let me guess. The goddess is too busy primpin' to bother with the likes of someone like me." Her gaze fell on the basket in my arms. "What's that? A collection for your blessed day? I haven't got no gifts left to give all these young'uns Returning every other week."

"No gift is necessary." Jurij uncovered the offerings within the basket. They looked even more pitiful strewn haphazardly among the old cloth, with plenty of empty space beside them. "We just brought you some food. We thought you might like something. And yes, we'd like to invite you to my Returning."

Ingrith stuck her head over the basket so fast I jumped backward, thinking she might be intending to ram her head into my chest. She leered up at me. "There's not a thing here worth havin', but for that apple." She snatched it out of the basket and took a bite. I might have heard her teeth crack. "You go take the rest of that garbage back where you came from." Bits of apple and spittle escaped from her mouth with each bite. "You invited me. The lord is satisfied. I'm not goin'. Now get out." She tossed the half-eaten apple on the ground, snatched the basket from me, and shoved it at Jurij so quickly he had no choice but to catch it before it fell to the ground. She started hobbling back to what she called a home.

Jurij sighed. It took a lot to make him sigh. Especially when you considered the mother he had. "Come on, Noll. We invited her."

Ingrith turned around as fast as someone a tenth her age. "No,

29

you go, boy. Girl, you come in here and help me. Time you make up for that foolin' around you did years ago."

Jurij's head tilted slightly. It was possible the only thing he remembered about that day four years prior were the parts with his golden-haired goddess.

Well, why not? What else was I going to do for the rest of the day? Find Elfriede and tuck that golden strand into her bun for the fiftieth time? I squeezed Jurij's shoulder. "It's all right, Jurij. Your mother might have noticed you went missing by now. I'll see you later."

I let his shoulder go and stepped forward. Ingrith nodded and went back to hobbling. In a few short hours, Jurij would be gone. He would vanish, or he would be hers. Either way, he was gone forever from me.

Goddess, if you hear my prayer, you'll make time stand still, just for a little while. Or take me back. Back before love could hurt me.

CHAPTER THREE

W e'd barely stepped inside when there was a pounding on the door. My chest squeezed in fright, but it didn't bother Ingrith. She hobbled over to the corner of her small shack, where a chest lay at the foot of the rotted wooden frame and the mildew-covered slab of hay she counted as a bed and mattress.

"Ingrith! Ingrith, you in there?"

The pounding wasn't stopping. Something thudded behind me. I pointed at the door. "Should I—"

Ingrith's dark, bulbous eyes were right in front of me. She was shorter than I remembered—or I was taller, I supposed—but she was no less frightening when viewed so close. "Should you nothing, girl. This is my house." She seemed to have lost a front tooth since the last time we'd had the pleasure of talking face to face. Or, rather, face *in* face.

"Ingrith! Why can't you open this door when I ask nicely?"

"I don't have to open my door for nobody but the lord's men." Ingrith leaned around me and cupped her free hand around her mouth. "You one of the lord's men? I suspect not, since I can hear you speak."

"Ingrith, we're coming in."

Ingrith pushed me aside and hobbled to the door, ripping it open with that one-tenth-her-age speed once again. A man stum-

31

bled inside, grabbing the door to steady himself. "You almost killed me, you crazy old—"

Ingrith shook her walking stick a little off the ground. "If I'd wanted to kill you, I'd've popped this under your mask and knocked it off. You're not welcome here."

She was right. He was still wearing a mask. And he didn't seem like one of the skinny, gangly teenagers running around the village. His face was that of a wooden fish, complete with a puckering set of lips over the black hole covering his mouth.

Behind him was a man whose face was uncovered. He had no reason to fear my eyes or Ingrith's. His love had been Returned.

Fish Face shook his vacant mask. "Did you cause that earthquake?"

Ingrith poked at his abdomen with her walking stick. "I did. What of it?"

Fish Face swatted the walking stick away with one hand and held his mask tighter with the other. "You keep that away from me, you old biddy!"

"Tayton, please." The unmasked man stepped inside and put a hand on Fish Face's chest. He turned to Ingrith. "There are men working in the quarry most days, Ingrith."

She sniffled and clasped both hands on top of her walking stick, which she lowered back to the ground. "I know. I can hear their racket. Makes my head ache and my ears ring."

Fish Face tapped his foot. "And crazy old crones looking up at the castle makes rocks fall on our heads."

She snorted. "Good. Then maybe I'll get a day of peace."

Fish Face nearly choked. "You senile, unloved woman—"

The unmasked man spoke as if he hadn't been interrupted. "I'm sure it was an accident."

"It wasn't," said Ingrith, as I said, "It was. She told me so."

Fish Face threw both hands into the air. "Who's this?"

"My guest." Ingrith poked at the floor near his feet. "Which *you* are not."

Fish Face scoffed. The unmasked man looked me up and down. I had to let my gaze fall. They were all so handsome when they were unmasked. And it was rare to have any take notice of me. And Jurij, he would be the same. Handsome, blind to me.

"Woodcarver's daughter," he said at last. So he actually knew of a woman besides his goddess?

Fish Face seemed as perplexed as his masked expression. "The one with a Returning today?"

"No," I admitted. "I'm her sister."

Fish Face started laughing. At least I thought it was a laugh. It sounded coincidentally like a fish flopping and gasping without water. "The only other unloved woman in the village. Figures."

My blood boiled. "Oh, like you have room to speak!"

"I'm married!" protested Fish Face.

I shook my head and gestured to his fishy face. "But your wife obviously doesn't love you, or you wouldn't still be wearing that ugly mask! Unless what's beneath is really much worse."

Ingrith cackled at that. I think she was actually happy.

Fish Face pointed at me. "Can you believe these women? If I had—goddess's blessings, whose mask is that?" I turned around to look at the chipped and cracked table behind me. There was a wooden mask there, all right. A snake. As chipped and cracked as the table on which it sat.

Fish Face might have been frothing at the mouth if he'd had one. As it was, his puckering fish lips looked oddly out of tune with the tone of his voice. "You murderer!"

The unmasked man put his hand on Fish Face's shoulder. "Enough, Tayton. That mask looks too old to be someone she might have killed recently."

"So you're saying it's all right; she must have killed that man years ago." Fish Face's expression perfectly matched his flabbergasted tone.

The unmasked man put his fingers to his temple. "No, Tayton. I'm just saying she's unlikely to have killed a man since we set out to work this morning. I think we would have heard if she'd killed anyone years ago."

Ingrith laughed and pounded her walking stick on the ground. "Shows what you know!"

"I need to get out of here," said Fish Face. "I can't stand to be around these crones one second longer."

These crones? As in the both of us?

Sighing, the unmasked man shook his head. "We're leaving. Ladies." He nodded first at me, then at Ingrith. I ignored him.

"Take care not to let it happen again, Ingrith," said the unmasked man as the two workers left. "It's dangerous for there to be earthquakes near the quarry."

Ingrith started muttering to herself and hobbled past me toward the table. I caught something like "useless, oblivious men" as she stepped past, leaving behind her scent of decay. With a groaning, scratching sound, she pulled a chair out from the table and plopped herself into it. She stared back at me. "Well? You goin' to stand there all day, like your mind has gone numb? Sit down!"

It was as if I were a man, and she were my goddess. A cloud of dust flew out from under my mud-colored skirt as I sat. The chair I was in was dustier than Ingrith's, but it seemed to be in much finer shape than the rest of the furniture. It was as if the chair had been sleeping, waiting for someone who never came to use it.

Ingrith pounded the walking stick, still in her hand even though it soared above her head while she was seated, making me sit taller in my chair. She pointed to the chipped and cracked snake mask on the table between us. "You know what that is?"

I raised an eyebrow. "A... mask?"

"*A... mask?*" Ingrith echoed my words as if they left a vile taste in her mouth. "Yes, we both have eyes, girl! I'm askin' if you know what that is!"

Okay, maybe hanging out with the crazy old crone to pass the time before I lost the only man I'd ever love was a bad idea after all. Then again, it did get me out of extra primping. "A snake?"

Ingrith pounded her stick on the floor again. "Oh, for the love of..." She grunted and reached across the table to snatch up the snake mask. She held it next to her face. "This was a man's face, girl! How do you reckon I got it and got no man for it to be wearin', eh?"

"I don't know. Your brother's or something?"

Ingrith sighed as if she needed to clear her lungs of all that dusty air in her house. She tossed the mask back onto the table, where it landed with a *thud*. "I never had no brothers, girl." She held up a finger. "Tut, tut. And before you go guessin' it was my father's, he was a loved man since the day my mama turned seventeen, so no, he had no need for another face when I knew him."

What did men do with their masks if they had their love Returned and could be rid of them? Smash them, break them, as I might do if I were them? No, they had other things on their mind. Like happiness and goddesses.

Ingrith sighed and shook her head. A white tendril broke free from the cloth covering her scalp, and I was reminded, with a jolt, of Elfriede. "You ever heard of a man called Haelan?"

I shook my head.

Ingrith heaved that weary sigh again. "Of course you haven't." She narrowed her eyes. "Your parents ever wonder how come there's no healer?"

What is she talking about? "Someone who... fixes boot heels?"

Ingrith pounded her walking stick not once, but three times. "No, I'm talkin' 'bout a *healer*, you damn fool! Someone who makes people who are sick or injured feel better."

"No." Wonderful. I was going to spend the rest of the day talking nonsense with this woman. "Mother tends to us when we're sick. I suppose women make their loved ones feel better."

"Some broth-and-huggin' home remedies aren't the same as sewing up a man to stop him from bleeding or blowing air into a girl's lungs if she stops breathin'." Ingrith let out a breath, and I could smell the sour scent across the table. "What do your parents think of me, then?"

That you're a crazy old crone, like the rest of us do. "They don't speak much of you."

"They think I never had a man to love me?"

"Yeah..." *They think that their daughter is probably going to do no better.*

Ingrith scoffed. "Bunkum! Every woman gets her man."

I cradled one arm against my chest and squeezed my elbow tightly. "I don't have one, either."

"Oh, sweet goddess. Can't be more than sixteen and she thinks no man will ever find her. Well, isn't that convenient?" Ingrith cupped her chin, pinching her lips together as she looked me over. "You in love with that boy you came here with?"

I bit my lip. "Why would you ask that?"

Ingrith shook her walking stick in the air. "'Cause you're a fool, girl, if you go lovin' where love is not needed! That boy's your sister's, he says? You get your *own* man. Love 'im or send him to the commune, don't matter to me. But if you get your heart so set on another, and your man come callin', don't you dare go pretendin' you're in love with that poor soul of his, you hear me?"

Don't pretend you're in love with him. Elfriede. "But... what happens if a girl convinces herself she's in love with her man? When she's really just—I don't know—in love with having her Returning? Or afraid to be alone?"

"Then she ought to delay the Returning until she's sure. No need to rush the day you turn seventeen. Don't know what's wrong with all these young fool girls, thinkin' they can't possibly wait any longer." Ingrith pointed the top of the walking stick in my direction. "I had my Returning when I was seventeen."

Something felt sour in my stomach. "But you have no man!"

Ingrith pounded her walking stick and her free palm on the table. "*Every* woman gets her man! You never heard that lord's blessing garbage at a Returning?"

I had, but—

Ingrith's large, round eyes grew even larger, even wider. "We invited them all, you see, we ought to have had the lord's blessing! *He* even came, that boy I truly fancied!" She laughed, but the laugh stuck in her throat like a fly caught in a spider's webbing. "Bernhard. Bernhold. Something. I don't even remember his name anymore! What a fool I was! He wasn't worth none of my love, no! He had *her*!"

My palms rested against the table. I pushed back, letting the chair move slowly away.

Ingrith leaped up, summoning that secret speed of hers. "But I *had* to have a Returning, you see! My man was good enough. Nice fellow. Did whatever I wanted, though that'd be no surprise, seeing as all men follow their goddess's orders when they're still wearin' those masks of theirs." Ingrith hobbled closer to me, and my palms pushed forward, my legs tensed, ready to jump as soon as she got too near.

She leaned forward and stuck those bulbous eyes in my face before I even had a chance to jump. "*Haelan.* Village healer. Yes, we had one of those back then. Lived right here. He had no family by then, so no one else could do what he did." She leaned back slightly and grinned, but it was a strange smile, a smile out of place on her sour, wrinkled face. "I promised to give him sons and daughters. Told 'im he could teach me and we'd all keep up the trade. Never seen a happier wood-faced man." The smile vanished. "Though I suppose I could have told 'im we'd be living in the quarry under rocks and mud spending our days eating insects and he'd've been just as happy."

Ingrith straightened as best she could, but she still looked hunched and twisted. "What made me happy is she'd once told me she liked Haelan." Ingrith nodded and stared off above my head, not even looking at me. "But after that, her man found the goddess in her, and just like that, she was so in love with him. With *him*. She was my dearest friend, and she knew how much he meant to me. She knew how much I loved Bernie."

Ingrith hobbled over to her door and pulled it open. She stood, staring out into the open, both hands clutching the top of her walking stick. Slowly, I moved as close to her as I dared, keeping her well in front of me.

A small gust of breeze blew in through the open door, rustling that free tendril of hair that covered the old crone's forehead. "But she loved Bernie. She proved it at her Returning. He took off his mask and clear as day, her love for him was made plain. He was still living, and they kissed each other as if their kisses were as necessary for them to breathe as air."

The wind blew a bit stronger. I shivered. We were too close to the mountains. It was cold.

Ingrith took a few small steps out into the open. "So I thought, why not hurt her as much as she hurt me? Why not share those kisses with her first love as she watched, watched as her soul wrapped 'round her heart and wouldn't stop squeezin'?" She paused, squeezing her fist as tight as it would go. Then she hobbled around the home and out of view, toward the east.

She'd forgotten I was even there. I could run, forget any of this nonsense ever happened. But I thought of Elfriede, and of Jurij. I hitched my skirt up and ran out the door.

Ingrith walked eastward a few paces in front of me, shouting to no one at all. "I was a fool to think I could hurt her! I was a fool to think that the love of little children meant anything to anyone but me!"

Or me.

Ingrith stepped into the lily-covered fields and tossed her walking stick aside. It vanished into the knee-high grasses. "The goddesses are all that matter! There's no room for love where love's not wanted! There's no room for hurt, for jealousy, for a love intended if not fully felt!"

I had no idea where she was going. Into the woods? Could she make such a long walk? Ingrith stopped and snapped around to face me, suddenly realizing I was still there.

"I looked before I loved, girl! I looked at the Returning!" Her eyes seemed about ready to roll out of her head. "He vanished, leavin' nothin' but his clothes and mask behind him!"

I stopped, and Ingrith closed the distance between us. She smiled. "And no one remembers. No one but me." She closed her eyes and started laughing. "They didn't even know what we'd all gathered for!" She put one hand on my shoulder to steady herself as she cradled her belly with the other hand. "I tried to hurt her by Returning with her first love, and she couldn't even remember he ever existed!"

I stepped back, trying to let Ingrith's hand fall, but she clutched harder, digging her yellowing nails into my dress. "Look!" She pointed behind her, upward—above the woods where I dared not look. I slapped a hand in front of my eyes.

"Look, girl!" She let my shoulder go, and her decaying old fingers pried at the hand I held tightly over my eyelids. "Look! There lives the heartless monster! The lord who gives the first goddess's blessing! Have you ever seen him? Does he even exist? Who eats the bread, who wears the clothes? What becomes of the things the men deliver there?"

I swatted at her with my free hand. "Stop! Let me go!"

"Who are the servants bathed in white? Where are their goddesses? Do none speak? Did they punish me? Why is some *man* ruling over this village and giving the blessings of the first goddess, a woman?"

I jumped back, my eyes clamped shut, but she was still gripping my arm, pulling it downward with a force not even a man could muster. "Let go, you crazy old—"

"Oh, *now* she remembers to shut her eyes! When it's not a life at stake, but a measly old earthquake. Well, I'm not afraid."

The ground began to shake. Ingrith laughed, and the ground beneath my feet shifted until I had no choice but to fall into the grasses. My eyes flew open, as wide as Ingrith's.

There it stood, dizzyingly high and regal, dark and dominant against the pale eastern mountains, ringed in verdant green trees from the woods before it. It was taller than I imagined, almost half the height of the mountain behind it. Its wide berth supported two great, jagged spires, so thin as to be impractical, but as menacing to me then as if they were actual swords, great daggers the building needed to defend itself against monsters. The castle. Forbidden to the eyes of all women.

The earthquake grew stronger, and my palms, scuffed and scratched already, clutched for the safety of the broken blades of grass and the fallen lilies, but the earth wouldn't stop moving. The old crone danced, somehow staying upright even as the ground shook around her.

"I'm not afraid, you heartless monster! Live forever, you will never die, but you'll never know love neither!" She grabbed her skirt and kicked her feet up high. "Punish me, lord! Strike me down and punish me!"

I didn't know what to do. "Ingrith!"

Her feet stopped moving, and a gasping, scratching sound came from her throat, as if she'd forgotten how to breathe.

Her clothing fell beside me, her body already gone. The ground stopped shaking. But my heart kept beating, strong and fast, as if the ground would never again be stable.

CHAPTER FOUR

I touched the dirty, dark shawl that had once covered her white head. It lay between a lily and an indentation in the grass, where Ingrith had once stood. Her clothing was now all that remained.

Had the lord actually killed her? But why? And how? He'd never executed anyone before.

No woman has ever looked at the castle for that long, either.

And no one ever really complained about him before. No one said what would happen if we went against the first goddess's teachings. They just asked his blessing, like he was some ever-watching shepherd spirit, like we were his mindless flock.

Someone has to eat the food, wear the clothes. Unless it's all the specters.

The lord's servants. Less reverently and more often called "the specters" in my mind. To a child they were too-real monsters, appearing without fanfare and dissipating into the mist once they were done with their errand. They showed up any time anyone had so much as a disagreement in Vena's tavern, not that there was much room for anything resembling an actual fight like those in the tales of queens and kings in the village of simpering men and goddesses. They also did the lord's shopping for him, silently handing merchants notes with the lord's orders. Clothed from head to toe entirely in white, the specters would have been hard not to spot even from leagues away. But their hair—each one had hair to his shoulders—was white. Their skin was white, as white as snow. It was as if they were men who'd had every bit of life, every bit of color drained out of them. They were like a walking death, if anything of our bodies was left behind once we died.

Only once had I gotten close enough to look at one's face. It was there that I saw the only hint of color: dark black eyes.

I shook my head clear of the image. In any case, at least we had an image to put to the specters—unlike the lord, whom no one had ever seen.

The heartless monster. She called him that. Was it all just Ingrith's delusion?

"Damn you, you crazy ol' crone! Ingrith!"

There was no mistaking that voice, muffled and angry and distant though it might have been. *Fish Face.* I wondered if this time someone in the quarry had gotten hurt—or worse. And they would come with their anger, itching to find Ingrith, and they would find me. Just me.

I released the shawl from my fingers and stood up, ignoring the soreness in my muscles. Before I could even stop to think, my feet kicked up the dress and flew farther into the fields. If I could just get out of sight before they came. If I could just pretend I'd been long gone before the second earthquake.

They knew you were with her beforehand. They'll see you running through the fields. There's no reason for them to keep their eyes down.

I ran, though, as if there were no other choice. I couldn't deal with all of the questions. I couldn't deal with the stares, the hatred. Not on this day.

Thanks to the hills, I might have gotten out of sight before they found her clothing. I made for the eastern dirt path as soon as I could, ready to insist I'd just been walking homeward. Home was so close. I was running at a speed I'd thought I'd lost, staring at the ground all the while, fighting through my body's struggle to breathe. Ready to pretend I'd never even cut through the fields.

My dress! There were tears and grass stains all over the skirt.

Home was right there. Mother and Father might still be inside; there had to be a little time before dusk yet. I could cover the skirt up with an apron. I could grab another dress when

Mother wasn't looking. *They'd notice. We don't have any other nice dresses.*

I kept running, straight past the house and into the woods. The trees kept the castle from view, so I looked up at last. I found the well-worn foliage to the side of the path and burst through the trees. I didn't care that stray branches scratched my arms and ripped at already-torn seams. I was going somewhere where I could rest and think, where I could quiet the insanity running through my head, where I could figure out what choices were left to me, if any at all.

A shriek, or more like a giggling squeal, tore through the air as something fast and hard slammed against my abdomen. I felt a sharp poke in my leg and heard a snap.

"Noll!" The little girl whose bushy, twig-filled head had just rammed into my abdomen stepped back and looked up, rubbing her forehead with one hand. In her other hand, she held a branch. The top of it dangled by a thread.

My pulse was still racing, and I shut my mouth, worried my heart might escape through my throat. I ran a palm over the pain in my side, swallowed my heart back inside me, and spoke, breathless. "Nissa." A farmer's daughter. A friend of Luuk's. We'd all played together before. "What are you doing here?"

It was a dumb question. I was the one who'd shown her the cavern in the first place.

Nissa tilted her head, pointing the branch at the cavern's dark mouth behind her. "Slaying monsters." Her mouth pinched. "It broke." She tossed the branch onto a nearby pile of moss and rocks.

I smiled, even despite everything. "Elgar's always broken. It'll mend next time you pick it up." *Pick it up somewhere else entirely.* My smile faded. "Were you in there alone?"

Nissa shrugged and clutched both hands behind her back. "Everyone else is getting ready for the Returning." Her gaze fell on my dress. "Aren't you going to get ready?"

I was ready. But maybe I'll never be ready, not really. "I will." I stood beside her and nudged her gently onward. "You go get ready, too."

Nissa walked a few paces, then stopped and turned around.

She stared at me quizzically with her large, brown eyes. "Aren't you coming?"

I shooed her onward. "Not just yet. I'll be there soon. Go on."

Nissa shrugged and skipped forward through the foliage, humming a tune as she went. I watched her until she blended into the trees and vanished from sight.

Vanished. Right in front of me.

I walked over to the broken branch Nissa had discarded and picked it up, turning the wood in my fingers. It'd been so long since I'd been the one to clutch Elgar. But there were monsters ahead; there were monsters behind.

～

WHEN THE QUEEN and her retainers were brave enough, they'd chase monsters into the blackest pits. The cavern off the main path in the woods held countless monsters and endless secrets, and the queen, who lost her retainers one by one, had never explored all its vast depths.

She'd tried to crown another generation of queen and retainers after her, to keep up the adventures, but good retainers were hard to find when they kept falling in love with goddesses one after the other. Nissa, in any case, just wanted to be her friends' equal, and although they battled monsters, she'd never called herself queen.

The queen was gone. It wasn't the same anymore. I swished the stick in front of me, not even bothering to pretend it was a blade, and certainly not screaming a battle cry.

This is stupid. I got bored and tossed the stick to the side. Because I'd had the wonderful idea of taking the stick instead of one of the candles the kids left by the entrance to light their way, I was marching forward in total darkness. But my eyes adjusted, and after all those years of playing as a child, and then watching after Nissa and Luuk and their friends, by now I knew the path well enough to navigate it in the dark.

If only there was somewhere I could go. But what was there, beyond the mountains, beyond the thick air that covered the edges of the land in mist? Nothing. There was no place for me to run and hide.

Nowhere but the "secret" cavern. The cold, dark, neglected cavern. Perfect for me.

~

I FOUND a stalagmite on which to lean my back and sat down on the floor of the cavern, hugging my knees against my chest. My mind was blissfully blank for a time, for how long, I didn't know. I shut my eyes and listened to the drip, drip, drop of some distant source of water that fell from the cavern ceiling and the dangling stalactites. I laughed quietly. We could never say those words as kids. We just called them "ground spears" and "ceiling spears."

"Hey."

I nearly tipped over. My palms shot out to steady me as my eyes flew open.

Jurij stood over me, his man-mask on, a lit candlestick in one hand. He slipped down beside me, carefully resting the candle atop a rock.

"Hey," came my brilliant reply. No "How did you find me?" "Why did you bother looking for me?" "Am I wanted for killing some quarry workers?" or "Don't you have a Returning to get to?" or "Tell me you won't die today!"

I went back to hugging my knees.

"It's beautiful, isn't it?" Jurij hugged his knees and looked up, where traces of his flickering candle caused shadows to dance on the ceiling. "I'd forgotten. I haven't been here in a while." Jurij stretched his arms and then his legs. "Luuk tells me you take him and his friends here on occasion, though."

The corner of my mouth twitched. "Probably not the safest thing to do, considering they could get hurt in here." I thought of Nissa, playing alone.

Jurij shrugged. "You and me had a lot of fun here."

I smiled, despite myself. "If by 'a lot of fun,' you mean I let you hold the candle while I did all of the sword-swinging, then yeah."

Jurij laughed. "Hey, the *queen* once told me that carrying a candle is an important job on any quest to the secret cavern. What was it? The candlelight keeps the monsters at bay?"

I pointed at the flickering shadows on the cavern ceiling.

"That's what I told you, but the candle actually made the monsters come out in the first place."

"I wasn't stupid, Noll. I knew that. I just let you believe otherwise."

I always thought I was ever so clever. "Sorry."

"Don't be." Jurij let his man-mask scan the dancing shadows on the ceiling. "I liked being told what to do."

"It got you ready for life with a goddess, I guess." That was low.

Jurij didn't seem hurt so much as amused by my statement. "Always so much hatred for goddesses. You won't feel the same when your man finds you." He laid a hand on my knee.

I tore my leg out of reach. "Oh, *please*, not you, too."

Jurij's arm was left awkwardly reaching toward me without anything to touch. He pulled it back and ran it through the top of his dark curls. "Sorry. What happened with Ingrith?"

So that was why he was here. Everyone thought I'd killed her, and Jurij knew right where to find me. "She's dead."

Jurij's man-mask bobbed up and down. "I know. She vanished after causing another earthquake. Luckily the men in the quarry were just leaving to get ready for my Returning and no one else was hurt, but they had no reason to believe Ingrith knew that. They ran to her cottage, but all they found were her clothes in the field. They figured she might have had a heart attack from the shock."

Or an always-watching lord punished her as she'd asked. At least no one else was hurt. Maybe they'd let me off with a lecture, after all. "What about me?"

Jurij's mask cocked slightly. "What do you mean? Nissa stopped by to talk to Luuk, and she told me you were headed into the cavern, which I found odd. So that's what I was asking. Did Ingrith tell you she was going to cause an earthquake again before you left her? I'm not too sure I believe her about the bird now that she went and caused such a tremor. We felt it halfway into the village this time."

No one saw me leave. "No. I..." I bit my lip. It wasn't like I'd killed her. And I'd barely looked. That crazy old crone did it to herself. "She was rambling about something awfully weird, so I left." *What if Ingrith wasn't completely crazy? What if a goddess who just thinks she's in love can still kill her man when he takes off his mask? Jurij's life could really be in danger.*

Jurij put his palms back on the cavern floor and leaned back. "You look worried."

I blushed. I'd gotten so used to never being able to see his expressions that I'd forgotten my face was as legible as an open book. "I'm worried about your Returning."

Jurij's mask bobbed slightly. I could almost picture his eyes rolling behind those soulless black eye holes. "Noll, I don't know how many times I have to tell you, I'll be fine." He sighed that rare and frustrated sigh. "Can we try focusing on how this is the greatest day of my life for once? Please?"

I bit the inside of my cheek as the heat rose to my face. "Of course you think it's the greatest day of your life. But you could die, Jurij! You just don't realize that because you don't have a mind of your own!"

Jurij sat up straighter. "You're some friend, Noll. You don't know anything about what it's like to have a goddess. So why don't you keep your opinion to yourself for once?"

I jumped up. Jurij wasn't like this. He wasn't bratty like the other boys had been. But he was blind, so blind. Blind to all of my suffering. "I'm only trying to make you think for once because I care about you!"

Jurij shook his mask-face and leaned on a stalagmite to stand up. "Do you think I don't realize that my life is in danger from the moment I open my eyes in the morning to the moment I shut them at night? Do you think I've never worried that some girl or woman not related to us will burst in one morning and kill me, my brother, and my father while we're eating together? Do you think I've never worried that Father's mask might fall off while he's sleeping, and Mother might look over and kill him where he lays?" He clenched his fist. "I know when love exists between a coupling, Noll, and when it doesn't. We men adjust. We're careful. We know what we're doing."

I grit my teeth. "You all spend so much time worshipping your goddesses, I doubt you know much of anything."

Jurij threw his hands into the air. "When has a man ever died at his Returning? When has a man ever died from a woman looking at his face at all?"

An excellent point. How did we even know men had to cover their faces? Maybe this was all some twisted game of the always-watching, never-present lord and his imaginary "first goddess."

Haelan. "Ingrith. She told me she killed her man at their Returning. And no one but her remembers the man ever existed."

Jurij tapped his fingers impatiently against his thigh. "You're using the ramblings of a crazy woman to try to delay the greatest day of my life?" He pointed at me. "With your own sister, I might add. Why do you hate Elfriede so much?"

Because she took the only thing that ever truly mattered to me. And she doesn't even realize what a treasure she stole. "I don't hate her!" *I don't. I don't.*

"Then why are you always talking as if she's lying about loving me and is going to kill me?"

"I don't think she's *lying.*" My throat felt parched, but there was no hope for the dryness to ever be quenched. "I just think she doesn't even know herself. She never knew you before you found the goddess in her."

Jurij waved a hand. "That's not important."

"*Yes,* it is! You were nothing to her! She only convinced herself she loved you because it was you or no one."

Jurij shrugged. "So? It's the same for me. It's her or no one. Her or the commune. Her or death."

"But you have no choice but to love her! You don't realize what it's like for a woman. We have the choice to love or not, to not even know if what we think we feel is real or just some crazy mixture of desire and filial affection." Tears formed at the edges of my eyes, and I bit my lip to keep it from trembling. "Jurij, I love you!"

Jurij sighed and shook his head. "I love you, too, but—"

"Not like that!" I dug my fingers as deeply into my arms as they would go. "I love you, like you love Elfriede."

Jurij ran a hand up and down his forearm. Before he spoke, there was nothing but the drip, drip, drop of the distant source of water. There was no horrible past, no terrible future. Time was standing still, and in my mind, an impossible future was still a possibility. *I love you, too. Say it.*

"Noll, I'm sorry. I don't know what to say. I don't know what you hoped to accomplish by telling me that. It's weird enough

47

that I still feel like being your friend after finding my goddess. Isn't that enough for you?"

The tears were rolling down my cheeks now, and I didn't know what made me angrier, him just standing there with that stupid wooden expression or the fact that he could see the tears streaming down my face. "Is that just to make Elfriede happy? What, did she command you to stay friends with me just because she didn't want me to lose all of my friends? Did you think—"

Jurij's hand stopped moving. "Yes."

My mouth snapped shut. "I'm sorry?"

"Elfriede commanded me to remain your friend, back when I first told her I loved her and she was overwhelmed by my confession. 'Go with Noll,' she told me. 'Keep being her friend. This is all so sudden. Please go.' She might have forgotten about it. Or not realized she was issuing a command when she stated it. But she hasn't told me to stop or said to forget that command, so I'm still bound by it."

Something bubbled up from my stomach and forced its way out of my mouth, like the simper of a dying wounded animal. It was quiet, but in the echo of the cavern, it grew louder and repeated, reflecting my pain back at me over and over again. I clenched my teeth as hard as possible, not caring about the pain in my jaw, doing everything I could to stop myself from making that sound again.

Jurij snapped up straighter and held his arms outward as if ready to embrace me. "Let me comfort you, Noll."

I could barely see through the torrent of tears building. "No! You're just saying that because the command is making you!"

Jurij shook his head and lowered his arms. "Look, Noll, after the Returning, a goddess's command isn't really so absolute."

Tears were spilling out. I thought of stupid Father and the stupid dishes. "What does that matter? You'll still do everything you can to make her happy."

"Yes, but…" He moved closer. "I'm just saying, I'll show you, I'll still be your friend. It won't be because Elfriede commanded it of me."

I jumped backward out of his reach. "Leave me alone!"

"Noll, I'm sorry!"

I stepped around the stalagmite and farther into the cavern, to

48

the very edge of the candle's glow. "Go away! You have a Returning to get to, don't you? Hope you live through it!"

Jurij lunged toward me, desperately grabbing for my arm, but I jumped back, back into the darkness. "Noll, I really do think of you as a friend. I didn't mean to hurt you. Please—"

I turned and ran, not caring that I stumbled over rocks and dips in the ground and whatever else was thrown out there to trip me. I ran as fast as I could, deep into the darkness, farther than I had ever been before. We'd been too afraid to go this far as children. But there was nothing in this cavern more terrifying than the future that lay outside of it.

"Noll!" His voice echoed and faded into the distance behind me.

I ran and ran. There was only darkness for yards. But then, there was a violet glow. It grew closer with each footstep. At last I neared it, putting my hand on the last stalagmite blocking my view as if I could tear it down with my fingers.

A pool, awash with bright violet. A light source, like a roaring, searing fire that burned underneath the depths of the waters. And something else. The laughter of children, the sound of Jurij calling my name. Only his voice was high-pitched, shy, and inviting. Like he'd not yet been corrupted by his goddess.

My feet flew forward across hard, slippery rock, at last puncturing the water's edge. I wasn't thinking. But there was no more reason to think. Just to find that laughter.

Though I'd never swum before, I dove. I started kicking and splashing as the water crushed me on all sides. But I was going forward. By all that I had in me, I would find some way to reach that happy sound. I bobbed up and down. Water streamed down my face, from the tips of that frizzy, wild bush of black hair I'd always despised, from the tears welling in my eyes.

The violet light grew blinding, positively blinding, shooting upward from beneath the water's surface. I closed my eyes to block it.

As I took one last breath of air, my nostrils filled with a scent so strong, my stomach turned wild with waves of nausea. A soaked animal, sopping from the sudden rain. An uncooked fish lying lifeless on a pond's grassy shore. Wet leather. I'd once spilled a mug at the Tailors' as they worked the material into clothing.

"Noll!" The sound of Jurij's voice—his deeper voice, his lost-to-me voice—was the last thing I heard as I tumbled below the water's surface.

But at the same time, almost an echo of Jurij's scream, another voice called me, a voice cold and far-flung, even though the emotion entrenched in it more than matched the intensity of Jurij's terror. "Olivière!"

There were none who truly knew me who would say my actual, feminine name aloud.

My eyes shot open, but the world was a blur around me. The violet light grew dull. The water threatened to fade to darkness, and I knew if I fell down there, I would never, ever get back to the surface.

Is that what you want? Part of me wasn't sure. I kicked and opened my mouth to scream, but I shut my mouth quickly when instead of sound escaping my lips, water started pouring inside, determined to consume me.

I heard a muffled sound beside me, but I couldn't make out the words. An arm wrapped around my chest, and I kicked once or twice more before I discovered that kicking wasn't going to do any good. I went limp in Jurij's arms, and with his more power-ful, focused kicks, we shot upward and broke the surface.

Only it wasn't Jurij.

There was a black leather glove resting on my shoulder, a bare and ghastly arm wrapped across my chest. In the violet light, I could see the pallor of the skin, an odd, creamy, soft rose, washed pale with white. *One of the specters? The lord's servants? No, not that pale.*

We'd come to the surface, but I couldn't breathe. My eyes drifted closed, and open again, my vision blurry. The black glove, the pale arm became a dark hand, a tan sleeve. *Jurij.*

Jurij kicked us toward the shore. My eyes closed, and opened. The black glove, the pale arm.

A hard smack against my back. "Do not fight the reflex," said an unfamiliar voice. Water spilled out of my guts. "You must purge yourself of the water."

My eyes shut again as the water spilled out once more. As I

struggled to keep them open, I tried to focus on the shoreline, and the tiny yellow flicker of candlelight I saw there. But the violet water stained my eyelashes and blurred my vision. Then I noticed the dark hand, the tan sleeve. My head twisted slightly to search for the wooden face.

"Close your eyes!" screamed Jurij.

Jurij grabbed the back of my head by the hair and shoved my head under water with a strength I didn't know his thin arms possessed.

"Close. Your. Eyes!" I struggled to breathe and started kicking and thrashing. For a moment, I thought Jurij meant to kill me, perhaps for another excuse to comfort my sister.

And then I knew what had happened. I nodded as hard as I could under the water, shut my eyes tight, and I felt Jurij's grip on my hair relax. He gently pulled me up, and I felt us reach the shore. He rolled me over onto my back. Perhaps not willing to trust me when it came to his life, I felt one of his hands clamp firmly over my eyelids.

"Are you all right?" he asked.

"Olivière. You could have died." The other voice was faded now, the strange glove and arm no longer in sight.

"Yes." I almost choked on another mouthful of water. *But I'll never really be all right again.*

"Keep them closed," said Jurij.

I nodded. I would never—not on purpose. Not even after we'd fought. I loved him.

Jurij decided to trust me. He lifted his hand from my face and helped me sit up, pounding on my back until I coughed up the last of the water that had tried to swallow me from the inside out. *The scent of wet leather. So sickening.*

I wiped my arm over my mouth to clean up the last of the spittle. My eyes were clamped so tightly shut I was afraid I would never be able to open them again.

"I'm going to go get my mask," said Jurij quietly. "It's floating on the pool's surface a few paces from here. Keep your eyes closed." Jurij's voice seemed wary.

I wouldn't risk your life, Jurij. Not like Elfriede would.

I heard him enter the water. Jurij was a natural swimmer, which I knew well from the times he and the other boys went swimming in the pond near the livestock fields, and this pool was even smaller in size. It was only complete idiots like me who could turn the thing into a death trap.

"You can open your eyes now."

I tentatively opened first one eye and then the other. Jurij stood above me in his man mask, looking wet, otherworldly, and beautiful in the deep purple glow. I embraced him, squeezing him more tightly than I thought possible, and he wrapped me in his arms, tapping my back lightly before pulling away.

I let the moment go.

I faced the source of candlelight. The candlestick was perched on a rock, with no one at all around it. "Where's the other man?"

"What other man?" asked Jurij.

"The other man." I turned my head this way and that, searching desperately for the stranger. "The pale one. Wearing leather."

Jurij squeezed my shoulder. "It's just you and me here."

"But—"

Jurij heaved a weary sigh. I supposed he'd had enough of dealing with me and my delusions, on what was the *greatest day of his life*. "Noll. We're both wet. It's cold. We need to get ready. It was already late when I came in here." He stood and walked over to the candlestick, picking it up and starting back down the way we came.

I stood, but I hesitated. The candlelight was shrinking before me. I looked once more at the pool. The violet glow still illuminated the surface of the water, although it was subdued and fading. Amongst the stalactites, the ceiling seemed to sparkle, like violet stars in the blue moonlight.

"Noll?" Jurij's voice echoed off the ceiling, almost like he was stuck there somewhere above me. "Are you coming?"

I shook my head to clear it of all its fantasies. There were no stars masquerading as violet lights in the ceiling. There were no laughing children deep in the cavern. No pale man calling me by my full name.

And no true love at all in the heart of the man I loved most.

CHAPTER FIVE

I n the Great Hall, all was quiet.

The two figures that drew everyone's attention held hands and stared into each other's eyes—or in Jurij's case, the black holes in his mask. Over his features was the Returning mask, only it wasn't wet and sopping, so I guessed perhaps he borrowed his father's. Not that his father had yet had a chance to use it himself, but he kept it on hand "just in case" the impossible suddenly happened. Jurij's new attire, red and bright and stunning, was a tad too large for him, so I guessed that was borrowed, too.

I could feel Mistress Tailor's gaze boring into me from the seat on the other side of Luuk. Father might have done the same from my other side—I was, after all, barely dried and still wearing a damp, torn, and grass-stained mud-and-vomit dress—but his eyes were forward, locked on the woman at the center of the stage behind the coupling, as if she were the only thing that mattered.

Mother stood behind Jurij and Elfriede, a black leather book in her hands. It was the book of the lord's blessing, the one kept at the Great Hall in a dark corner, layers of dust upon its sour pages, only touched when it was time for a woman to show to all that she was truly in love. *So come on, Elfriede. Prove that you're in love.* How was it possible to want and not want something all at once?

Mother smiled and stared out at the gathered crowd, waiting for the right moment.

Although there was a pit of worry buried deep in my stomach, I was almost falling asleep out of sheer exhaustion. It felt nice, having that land of dreams almost within reach. I hoped I would wake up and forget the day had ever happened.

Mother cleared her throat and held the book open, a bit of dust escaping from its crinkling yellow pages. The mother of the goddess didn't officiate her daughter's wedding. That occasion was less momentous and could be handled by some figurehead in the village. But at her daughter's Returning, the mother stood in ceremony, ready to do as her mother did for her and her mother's mother before her.

"In a dismal time, long ago, in our village enshrined in endless mountains gray and white, love was sparse, love was rare." Mother licked her fingertip and turned the page. What she saw there made her smile and glance at Elfriede, who looked away from Jurij in order to grin back at her. *"A mother's devotion to her child, a sister's loyalty to her siblings, might have been all one knew of love, of warmth and passion."*

I swallowed at the mention of a sister's loyalty, my mind lost in a mixture of guilt and revulsion. Without realizing, I'd clutched the skirt of my dress until my knuckles grew pale.

After a moment more of droning, Mother's voice grew louder, snapping me back to attention. *"But then the first goddess came down to touch the ground, from peaks unreachable, from nothingness beyond the endless mountains.*

"My children, I have heard your screams, seen your tears. You stirred my heart at the first cry, and so I leaped from the mountains and fell for ages, watching you suffer for years on end. At last my feet have touched the ground. You are no longer alone."

No longer alone. How wrong those words were. I couldn't focus on what other drivel Mother spouted from the lord's "blessing." The pain in my chest was too great.

Luckily, I was distracted by Mistress Tailor's sudden loud breathing, so deep I thought she must be snoring. Beside her, Master Tailor reached out a hand to touch her shoulder, and she shrugged it away.

Mother's voice grew stern. *"The goddess's words gave the women more than hope. She spoke and the women became goddesses themselves, goddesses with power to lock out the darkness. To keep it where it was deserved: across the faces of men."* I looked to Jurij, keeper of the darkness, but whatever he thought of this part of the story, his mask kept it from me.

Mother looked up from the book, the words seeming to come from her instead of the old and dusty pages. *"We mask our boys and men. Deserving of the love of mothers and sisters and aunts and cousins they may be, and to them they may show their faces. But to prove themselves truly worthy of love and of the first goddess's blessing, they must find the goddess in a woman of no blood relation when they grow from boy to man. They must treat her kindly, regard her with reverence, and win her affection. Should the goddess in turn love the man when she is at least seventeen years of age, she may Return her feelings to him and reveal his face to the light. From that day forward, he is free to walk unmasked, having proved himself worthy of love, never again to fear the power of a woman's gaze, no matter what the years may bring."*

Mother's eyes wandered back to the book, and she turned a page gently. *"Every goddess shall have her due. Every woman shall get her man. So spoke the goddess, and so it shall always be."*

With that, Mother shut the book. *Every woman?* That was proof enough that the first goddess wasn't as all-powerful as they claimed. *But Ingrith mentioned that line…*

My thoughts were racing, foolishly distracting me from the danger. Jurij let go of Elfriede's hand and ripped off his ceremonial Returning mask.

He's going to die!

And Elfriede's smile grew wider. She closed her eyes, leaned forward, and the two shared their first kiss, forever sealing their union.

She loves him. That can't be true! It can't be!

My mind was screaming at me. I wanted to run up and fling him back from her, guarding his face from her eyes, from the eyes of all of the women around me.

Mother put the book down on the table behind her and grasped both Elfriede's and Jurij's hands in her own, raising them high above her head. "The goddess has judged Jurij, her man, worthy of love!"

The crowd exploded. Shrieks and cries echoed throughout the space, hurting my ears.

Unmasked men and women melted into each other's embrace. Father jumped up and ran toward Mother, his arms outstretched. "Aubree!" called Father, devotion pouring into both syllables of Mother's name, over and over between kisses. I looked away. I bit my lip, willing myself not to cry.

As Luuk stood from the chair next to me to join the celebration, I squeezed his hand tightly. His puppy face met mine and he sat back down beside his owl-masked father and his sour-faced mother. But only a moment had passed when he stiffened. Summoning strength I didn't know he had, he ripped his hand free from mine, walked across to the room to the end of the row, and hugged a girl seated between her parents. *Nissa*. She was grinning as she hugged him back.

Mother unhooked herself from Father's embrace and laughed, pointing at Luuk and Nissa. "Look, everyone!" she shouted. "The Returned's brother has found his goddess!"

Laughter. Clapping. My hands clasped feebly together. *Another one. Another coupling. All because of the first goddess. All because of a woman who appeared out of nowhere, barking out orders and vanishing from sight. All because of the lord and his goddess's blessing.* My awful attempt at clapping ceased, my body flushed with rage.

There were two others who didn't bother to laugh with joy at the little boy who'd found his goddess. At last, I saw that stunning face I'd never seen before as it pulled away from Elfriede with great effort, its flame-filled eyes still mesmerized by her features.

CHAPTER SIX

"Half the village is here," observed Master Tailor. "How wonderful." Everything was "wonderful, wonderful" with that man. Must be great to live in a rosy, wonderful version of your awful life. *If only I could. But I'm a woman, with a woman's mind.*

After the Returning, everyone had filed up to the Returned to smile and pretend like they cared for the happiness of a man and goddess not their own. That left the families of the goddess and her man off to the side, waiting for the ceremony to be over. I stood as far away from Jurij and Elfriede as I could without leaving the area. But next to Master Tailor stood Luuk and Nissa, their hands clasped, and every so often, I heard them giggling. There was no escaping it.

"Do you remember Elweard and Vena's Returning? What, fifteen, twenty years ago?" asked Mother. She cradled a cup of wine in her hand. She'd offered me some, but I said no thanks. Wine, like the terrible laws of the village, made me nauseous. "The whole village was there."

Father had one arm around Mother's shoulder and the other stuck firmly across the front of her waist. "That one was a long time coming."

Master Tailor had neither food nor drink nor a wife who loved him to occupy his hands. No surprise. He couldn't eat with the mask on with all of the unrelated women about. But he could talk. "Didn't they marry before the Returning?" Mistress Tailor looked up between bites of the roll she was stuffing into her mouth.

"I believe they got wed *seven years* before the Returning." Alvilda, Master Tailor's sister, gulped down most of the contents in her cup, which I suspected to have some pretty strong liquor. She sloshed the little remaining. "Vena was nine-and-twenty when she Returned Elweard's love."

Luuk's puppy face actually tore away from Nissa, and he made a little choking noise. I wondered if he was gasping behind his mask. "So it's not too late for you, Papa!"

Master Tailor laughed. "Your mother's a bit older than nine-and-twenty, sweetheart."

Mistress Tailor, her jaw clenched, knocked against him as she made her way back to the buffet table.

My gaze followed her, even as Mother jumped to pick up the conversation with Master Tailor with some unimportant comment about the Great Hall's decorations. Mistress Tailor grabbed another roll and watched the crowd, her gaze resting on first one coupling, then the next. Although she was the mother of the Returned, although her other son had just found his goddess, no one spoke to her.

Alvilda was also watching. She nudged me with her elbow and lifted a finger off of her cup in Mistress Tailor's direction. "They shame her. Even more than they shame me."

"Is it really so bad not to Return love to your husband?" *At least* she *didn't risk killing him before she was sure.*

"Of course." Alvilda still hadn't finished the drink. She seemed fixated on creating little waves of turmoil within her cup. "It's expected for you to Return love to your husband. If you can't, you're supposed to be honest about it and refuse him."

"Dooming him to the commune? Isn't it worse for a man to live like he's dea—" I realized who I was talking to and clamped my mouth shut.

Alvilda laughed, and not out of mirth. There was something a little awkward about the way she spoke, and I wondered if she'd drunk too much. She wasn't normally the type who did. "I know, I know. I sent a man there." I noticed she didn't refer to him as *her* man. She sloshed her cup again. "Better that than being constantly reminded of my failure to love him."

"Then why do some women marry their men, if they don't love them?"

"Who knows?" Alvilda leaned her head back and poured the last of the drink down her throat. She looked around for a place to toss the cup and dropped it on the edge of a nearby pillar. "Maybe they just want children? No other man but theirs will help them with that. Maybe they feel guilty about dooming a man to the commune?" She squinted at Mistress Tailor picking up a cup and filling it from a flask of wine. "Or maybe… maybe they truly hope they'll love them someday, even though deep down they know it's just a lie they tell themselves?" She patted me on the back. "Well, take care, Noll." She gave one last pat on my shoulder. "I think I'm done celebrating for the day."

I glimpsed Jurij with his arm around Elfriede as they hugged yet another couple of almost strangers from the village who had come for the free wine and food. I was done celebrating for a lifetime.

As Alvilda hugged her brother goodbye and rubbed a hand in Luuk's mop of dark curls, Mother whispered something in Father's ear and the two broke apart, Father's face clearly full of the reluctance in his heart. He moved across the room to Jurij and Elfriede, and Mother came to visit me, sticking an arm through mine. She fanned a hand over her chest. "It's hot in here. I thought we might take a walk."

You mean perhaps I should explain to you in private what I'm doing here in a damp, torn, dirty dress. We made our way through the crowd, Mother smiling and nodding at the few who looked away from their beloveds long enough to offer congratulations. When we broke free of the Great Hall door, I saw that night had already fallen. It was quiet in the village center. For once.

"Is there anything you want to tell me?" asked Mother.

Do you want to know why I'm a mess on the outside or on the inside? I clenched my jaw, looking forward. We walked westward, a wise move for a pair of women who might want to scan the horizon from time to time.

"You know, your father wasn't the first man I loved."

That made me look at her. "I doubt that!" I wondered if I should point out that their mouths were practically sewn together most of the waking day. And the sleeping night.

Mother grinned. "No, it's true." The edges of her mouth drooped somewhat. "Of course, it was a doomed love. One man for every woman."

"Or no men for one woman."

Mother rubbed her shoulder into mine and tilted her head. "Come now, Noll, you know what I think about that."

I shrugged. "It's all right. I don't mind, I was just..." *Being angry*. "So. Tell me about this man of yours."

"He wasn't *my* man." She, of course, took what I said literally. "He was Alvilda's."

Oh. "But that means—"

Mother tipped her head forward a bit. Her fingers dug into my skin. "He's there."

By *there*, she didn't mean any of the rows of houses along the path we were walking, nor the fields of crops that went on for leagues until stopped by the western mountains. Certainly not Alvilda's home at the western edge of the village, where she peddled her woodcarvings as Father's only competitor.

No, between the fields and Alvilda's lay a small outcropping of dilapidated shacks. Their roofs had holes in them. Their flooring, I was told, was just dirt and rocks and filth. Each shack looked likely to topple over. It was lucky for the men who lived there that no woman bothered spending much time nearby because if one happened to look up to the castle in the east, surely the entire commune would fall over.

"That's sad. Still, if Alvilda didn't love him..." I knew I'd feel guilty in her place, but there was no avoiding it. "I mean, it doesn't seem fair that we can't love who we want to."

Mother kept the slow pace toward the west, silent for a while. Then she opened her mouth, her lips almost trembling. "Women are not forced by nature to love. When we love, we do so of our own will. Men have no choice. But we have three: love at once, learn to love, or never love at all."

60

"You forgot one. Love a man who will never love you."

Mother squeezed my arm closer to her bosom. "That's so poor a choice I wouldn't wish it on anyone."

We didn't speak for a moment more. At last, I moved my tongue. "But if it does happen?"

Mother stopped. "Then you do the best you can to forget him."

You don't know how I feel. You couldn't have loved that man like I love Jurij. I strained to read her light-brown eyes. In the dying light, I thought I saw the glisten of a forgotten choice. "Do you still love him?"

Mother let go of my arms and fanned a hand at me. "Don't be ridiculous. I was a child. That was long ago. Before your father found the goddess in me."

I sighed. Of course. There couldn't be anything to tarnish the sweet love between my parents. "So what was it about Father? The way he was bound to follow your every order?" *Useful for commanding a man to be a lonely loveless girl's friend, that.*

"*Noll.*" Mother shook her head, but there was a smile on her face. "To tell the truth, that part is sort of... disconcerting. Especially if you forget that anything you say that could possibly be construed as your direct command he does immediately. Even if you were joking."

"Do the commands and obeying really die down after the Returning like they say?" I snorted, thinking of this morning with Father. "It doesn't seem that way." *Great. Jurij is going to keep pretending to be my friend, even though I could never live down what happened in the cavern.*

"That takes a bit of the pressure off. If it doesn't appear that way to you, well, that's just the man acting out of love. But don't confuse it with pre-Returning commands. Those are absolute."

I thought of the little scene in the Great Hall. "I'm sure women like Mistress Tailor find that a benefit of not yet Returning their husbands' affections."

Mother rolled her eyes. "Yes, well, women like Siofra take advantage of it if you ask me. Maybe some little revenge for the poor men who had no choice but to love them in the first place."

"Is that why women whose husbands are still masked seem to

get more scorn than the women who send their men to the commune?"

"Well, at the very least, those women are honest with themselves. And by choosing to devote themselves to a profession or hobby, they have value in the community. Still, I wouldn't wish any woman to be in either position."

I forced myself to smile. "How lucky for you that it all worked out."

Mother paused before speaking. "Yes."

We stopped. We'd reached the western edge of the village. If we were going to go for a walk in the fields, we'd have to pass through the commune first. The stench was off-putting.

A man in a faded, cracked mask stumbled from one edge of the commune to the other. I couldn't tell what animal his face had once resembled. I figured he wouldn't remember, either.

He stopped and slumped over next to a basket. Dirt went flying as his rear hit the ground. The basket was full of bread and veggies, all of which were rotting. What didn't make it for mulch for the fields got dumped to feed the men in the commune. *At least the lord doesn't seem to care if these unloved men are not invited. Not that they'd go.*

The man's hand fumbled into the basket. He stuck the bread up beneath his mask, and I saw the mask bobbing. Between slow, slow bites of bread, he mumbled something, over and over and over.

"What's he saying?"

"The name of his goddess." Mother's lips puckered. I wondered if the name was Alvilda, or if seeing any man in this state would give her the same reaction. "Let's go." She pulled us away in the opposite direction. Her gaze immediately sank to the dirt path and the footsteps we'd left behind. Mine did the same.

"So what happens if a woman stops loving her man? I mean after she's already Returned to him?" *What happens if Elfriede wakes up tomorrow, her wonderful Returning day behind her, and gets bored with Jurij?*

Mother shook her head. The smile on her face seemed strained. "You ask every possible question, Noll."

"I just wondered if it's ever happened before."

Mother tilted her head one way and then the next. "He's safe once the Returning takes place. No woman's eyes can ever hurt him." She pressed her shoulder into mine. "Didn't you hear the lord's blessing? He proves his worthiness to his goddess, and his reward is a safe life thereafter, no matter how the goddess's feelings change."

It seemed strange to me. "But how do we know for sure? A man has no choice but to love, but a woman's heart..." *A woman's heart could love one day and hate the next. Couldn't it? Could I hate Jurij? Even after what he told me...*

"I know." Mother chewed the inside of her cheek. "That is, we know. We know the men stay safe after a Returning. It's happened before." She patted the back of my hand. "Not that there's anything for that woman to do, but to accept the man she's deemed worthy by then. No one else will ever love her anyway."

Something seemed off about what she said. Maybe I was supposed to be worrying about her and Father. *As if I didn't have enough to worry about.*

We stopped to let a cart pass onto the dirt road in front of us. I lifted my head up as much as I dared and saw the door to the bakery shut, a cart full of heaping hot loaves and sweet buns, and a man in a mask in front of us. "Darwyn?" I ventured a guess. The baker had many sons, but this one was of a height with Jurij.

He stopped pulling and turned. I couldn't look up at his mask, though; he was too tall, and the castle was off in the distance behind him. "Miss, Ma'am," he said, lifting up his cart handles and pulling his cart forward.

"Miss?" I muttered. "We were friends for twelve years, you—"

Mother stopped me. "You know they forget things like that once they find goddesses. What you and Jurij have is quite unusual."

What Jurij and I have was only at the command of his goddess. I wondered if in a few months we'd all be attending Darwyn's wonderful Returning. Roslyn would soon be old enough, and they seemed as in love as every other coupling in the village. In fact, I overheard one of Elfriede's sappy friends whisper that the two of them had even experimented a bit in the darkness. Guess the lips of one he used to find so girly and repulsive just couldn't be waited for.

"Where's he going?" I asked. The Returning ceremony was surely almost over, and I knew we hadn't ordered *that* much bread. There was enough to feed a hundred more guests at least.

"To the castle," replied Mother.

A cart or two passed by our house on the way to the path through the woods almost every day. Goods the lord ordered to feed him and his servants. The deliveries would keep the lord appeased, so he'd never have to venture out to see us himself. They'd continually make sure this village had the first goddess's blessing.

"Have you ever seen him?"

Mother laughed. "No woman is allowed to look at the castle, much less set foot in it. Why would I have seen him?" We didn't say anything for a moment more, listening to the wheels turning on the cart a short distance in front of us. "I heard you were with Ingrith right before she died today."

That was rather blunt. I stopped walking, pulling on Mother's arm to make her stop as well. "She was acting crazy, Mother. Even worse than usual." Did she suspect I'd witnessed it? "She... she scared me."

"I'm sorry I sent you alone." Mother took both of my hands in hers. "We were just all so busy." She looked up and down at my wreck of a dress. "I figured there might be some explanation for how your dress got to be so tattered. Did you fall into one of the ponds during the earthquake?"

Close enough. "Yeah. I didn't have time to change." Best to shift the focus elsewhere. "Mother, Ingrith called the lord a heartless monster."

Mother's lips puckered. "That's a rather rude way to address our benefactor, but I've heard the term before." She put her arm back through mine and gently tugged me forward.

"Who calls him that? And what does it mean?"

Mother shook her head. "No one who's properly grateful calls him that. And it doesn't mean anything. Not what you're expecting. Do you remember me telling you about kings and queens?"

The little elf queen. That's what I called myself. But kings and queens were just mythical figures in stories Mother used to tell Elfriede and me. "Yes."

"They make for wild tales." She pinched my shoulder playfully. "The type that keep little girls lost in their own little fantasies. But they're not real. They're just what some person thought of, to fantasize about a world where women and men might have once been equal."

I wasn't sure where she was heading with this. "So the lord isn't real?"

Mother snorted. "Of course he's real. He watches over us, and he pays us well for our wares."

I nodded. "The men leave the supplies in the castle foyer and pick up the copper pieces left there." Jurij had even gone once when he was smaller, to leave a few new sets of jerkins and trousers entirely in black. Odd, since the servants wore only white. "So even the men haven't seen him before?"

"No, they haven't." Mother heaved a deep sigh. "And when you don't lay your eyes upon something yourself, it's easy to make up stories, to fantasize about a man who doesn't die."

"What?" Forgetting myself, my gaze was a little higher up than it ought to have been. Darwyn and his cart were still ahead of us, heading through the eastern part of the village, but we'd arrived back at the center. I stopped and faced Mother. "The lord doesn't die?"

"Don't be silly." Mother smiled and started tugging me back toward the Great Hall, though it was hard for me to tear my eyes from the cart, even if it was off in the eastern direction. "The lord watches over the village from the shadows, but he must pass the job to his son when he's older, or maybe a child of one of the lord's servants. They're a secretive lot, never speaking, always just showing us the lord's requests on parchments—that's why we all learn to read. I refuse to believe that never finding your goddess makes you immortal. Every woman gets her man."

I couldn't believe what I was hearing. Did Mother even know of any women who'd been a lord's goddess? Who'd been a goddess of a specter? I never thought about it before. How were they going to have children without goddesses? Yet they were unmasked, so they must have had them at one point. When? "But does every man get his goddess?"

Mother stood in front of me, sliding her hands onto both of my shoulders. "I'm not sure I'm comfortable with all of these questions. The lord is good to us. He watches over us on behalf of the first goddess. His secrets are his own. There is but one thing we all know for certain: If a woman lays eyes upon the lord of the castle, the penalty is death."

CHAPTER SEVEN

I shivered. The night was young, but it was promising to be cold. And I was in a damp and tattered dress with no time to stop at home and change.

If Darwyn was making a late-night delivery, surely the lord would be awake and expecting his order. But would he be expecting me? Was he watching? Did he know? I'd fled the Great Hall almost as soon as Mother and I had arrived back, letting Father know I wanted to go home to change in case anyone missed me. He waved a hand and took his place at Mother's side without saying anything. I watched him go briefly, but my gaze soon fell on the face I ought to have known for ages, the face I'd never before seen. Jurij had the widest eyes that I had ever seen, almost perfectly spaced below the softest eyebrows and the longest eyelashes. His lips were curled into a smile that set off dimples in each of his cheeks. The cleft in his chin cried out for a finger's caress.

His beauty was more than I imagined, his face impossible to forget. But it was because of Elfriede's love that I was able to see him, and for that, the sight of his face made it so much harder. I tore my eyes from his beautiful features and turned to leave, quietly and unnoticed.

She needed only love him for today, and he's safe forever. That means he's free.

I shook my head to clear it. I'd been wrong about the Returning. But what would Jurij feel if he were actually free? I had a feeling that was something that only the goddess might be able to tell me. And since she was nowhere to be found, the lord was my only option. I trembled with expectation, with fear. *This is it. I have nowhere else to turn. I can't just go to bed and wake up, day after day, pretending my heart is still whole. I refuse to. The elf queen wouldn't.*

I was on the road home, out past the eastern edge of the village. I jogged a few steps and then walked briskly, jogging and brisk walking, whatever it took to get down the road quickly without drawing too much attention. Looking at the ground as I went made jogging decidedly more difficult.

I hesitated in front of the door to my house, then flung it open to check inside. I didn't have time to change, and I didn't care if the lord saw me in the ripped damp dress I was still wearing. It was my battle dress, a garment to show how hard I'd fought to make things right. Because if I was wrong and I wasn't able to free Jurij from this mess, it might be all I left behind.

I swallowed, but I was still determined. I couldn't yet face Jurij again after what had happened, after he sealed a pact with my sister. Not unless I had something to give him. Not unless his heart was finally set free. I grabbed a dirty apron Mother had hung off the back of one of the chairs and wrapped it around my shoulders, using one fist like a broach at my neck to hold it in place. Better than wasting time searching for a proper cloak.

I dashed off outside, not caring to properly close the door behind me. I jogged into the woods and heaved a great sigh of relief once I could look up safely again. It was then that I heard the turn of the cart, and I dived into the foliage. My heart just about jumped out of my throat when I glimpsed the wooden fox-face heading down the pathway in the western direction, the empty cart behind him. *So the delivery is done. It's time.* I waited for Darwyn to pass, not daring to move a muscle. Possibly not even breathing.

Once I heard the turn of the wheel fade away, I exhaled and jumped back onto the path. By then, the moon was so full that silver light poured from the sky and lit the way before me. Eventually the trees encroached upon the path so fully that I could no longer see the moon at all, but its silver light speckled through the leaves so softly I felt no reason to be afraid. I ventured on, pushing the occasional stray bough out of my way to go farther. And then the trees parted completely.

There were walls of dark stone as far as I could see. It took me a moment to realize that one layer of wall acted as a fence. Its gate swung open.

I braced myself. The ground shook.

Ancient, monstrously huge wooden doors beyond the outer wall parted slightly like I had seen Father's lips part when he longed for Mother's kiss. I stepped through, lifting one foot and then the other, willing myself to stay upright. A thin sliver of moonlight came with me and lit some of the way.

But even so, it was dark, darker than the cavern and the cloudiest of nights. I traced the shaking slit of moonlight with my feet as I continued to walk into the darkness, my gentle steps echoing like thunder in the empty space.

And then the shaking stopped. The door shut behind me.

"I've come to see the lord," I whispered, as loudly as I dared. Now that I was here, my courage faltered. There was no answer. My heart was racing. *What am I doing here? This is foolish, I still have time, I should go back—*

I thought I heard a trickle of water and paused. There was nothing but the stone floor and a pile of bread and buns at the door, and the more I stared at the moss-covered stones, the more apprehensive I felt. I closed my eyes, shutting out the only sliver of light, and listened for the noise. My hands out before me, I walked toward the soothing sound of the trickling water. I moved unheeded for some time until my hand brushed against a hard surface. Opening my eyes, I found another slit of moonlight pouring through another set of wooden doors.

Tentatively, I put one eye against the slit and saw a fountain surrounded by an empty space and then a circle of white rose bushes. The fountain resembled a little boy, his face unmasked, his arms and head raised towards the sky. In place of the eyes were two spouts of water that poured out and downward, sparkling deep blue in the moonlight.

I want to see his face. It was a stupid thought, considering what danger I had put myself in. But I was overcome by it. I tried to pull open the doors, but they moved only a hair's breadth even with all of my might. I threw my hands wildly over the doors to search for a better grip but found nothing amongst the rough surface of wood. Then I found the handle, but before I could grip it properly, my finger caressed a jagged sliver.

"Ow!" I sucked on my sore index finger and cursed a few times. It stung so much, I was tempted to rip it out with my teeth.

"Who goes there?"

The voice was haunting. Almost familiar.

I thrashed around to face it, but I couldn't see anything. The echo of gentle footsteps came toward me.

"A woman?" the voice remarked as it drew nearer. I could feel the air part to allow that smooth, tenor tone to reach me, and I shivered. *This was insane, he's going to report me, I'm going to die—*

The echoes paused, and the toe of a black boot settled on the edge of the arrow-shaped trail of silver light.

"What have we here?" It wasn't a threat, more like the indifferent curiosity I'd heard from Father when I was child, while he was tinkering with his latest woodcarving and I walked into the room carrying a slimy baby frog. It was a man, I knew, although the voice was nothing like Father's. It seemed younger, but older at the same time. Sweeter, but teetering on the edge of iciness.

"I..." The nipping air hurt my throat as I tried desperately to suck it in and clear out my mouth. The apron around my shoulders fell lightly from my fingers—a small breeze slid through the crack in the door behind me, and the cloth glided through the air. It settled in the trail of moonlight in front of me, just brushing the man's boot as it landed. "I'm looking for the lord."

The man laughed, whether joyfully or angrily, I wasn't sure. "You're shivering."

A black leather-gloved hand reached out into the silver arrow of light where I stood and grabbed my apron from the floor. I caught a glimpse of a lock of dark hair as he bent to retrieve it, but he retreated quickly into the shadows before I could make out more. Another gloved hand emerged beside the one clutching my apron and motioned for me to draw nearer.

"Come here," he said. "Do not be afraid."

My mind froze. A man in the castle. A man not all in white. Who could it be, but the lord? But if it were him, I'd be dead if the rumors were true. And yet here I was, and he didn't chastise me for my trespass.

"I, uh—" I started. Did the laws of the first goddess apply to the one who watched over the village for her? I looked away. "Do you need me to close my eyes?"

"Oh," he exclaimed. He pulled his hands back into the darkness with a start.

"Yes," he said. And, as an afterthought, "Thank you." I thought I heard him swallow uncomfortably in the silence that followed.

Good. Maybe he'll think favorably of me. Maybe he won't— I shut my eyes tightly. My quest seemed suddenly immensely stupid. *The penalty is death.*

Unlike with Jurij after the swim in the cave, there was no hesitation on this man's part. The moment my eyelids clamped shut, his boots echoed as he drew closer. I felt his presence overhead as he wrapped the apron back around my shoulders.

"Hmm," he said, perhaps lost in thought. "An apron for a cloak."

His breath glanced across the top of my head as he spoke. It ought to have been warm, but it was cool and refreshing somehow, even though I shivered from head to foot. I heard rustling and then felt a gust of cold air. I jumped a little as a heavy leather jacket came down atop the apron over my shoulders. Although the material was cold to the touch, warmth instantly flooded my body. "Do you feel warmer?"

"Yes, thank you."

The man began tying what I assumed was a cord of some kind around my right shoulder. I shifted uncomfortably from one foot to the next, as I had often seen Jurij do when he was around Elfriede and her attention was drawn elsewhere. I could feel the jacket slip a little as he let go, but it held in place, leaving only the area near my neck uncovered. "I need to speak with the lord of the village. It's… it's urgent."

The man scoffed. "I can tell. You seem to have rolled out of a muddy pond and caught your dress on a hundred branches.

Perhaps you also bumped into a fair maiden, making off with her apron."

I forced myself to smile. "Not far off. But the mud is just the color of the dress."

"Of course. It suits you."

"Thanks." It might not have been a compliment, but I couldn't possibly care less what his opinions were of my appearance at that moment, not when he held my life in his hands. My fingers poked around inside the too long arms of the jacket and gripped the soft seams nervously. "I have a request. Of the first goddess."

"Does not everyone? If only she could hear the voices calling her." He paused, his voice wavering. "Some more desperate than others." I jumped as leather brushed against my hand. He pulled on my sleeves and rolled them up so that my hands were free. He grabbed my palm and turned it over to separate my splintered finger from the rest. In my nervousness, I'd forgotten the slight pain that ebbed now from the tip of my finger.

"Can't you speak with her then?"

"You are injured," he said as if I hadn't spoken. My heart sank. What was I doing? I had a sinking feeling I was chasing a mythological woman, no more real than my queen and monsters.

The tips of a glove ran smoothly across my finger and reminded me of the delicate softness of bird down. When I'd played with my friends by the livestock, we'd often tickled one another with the down left behind by farmers' chickens, but this elicited so much more aching and none of the giggles. And there was something more, a warmth mixed in with the chill of the leather. *Leather.* Leather, like in the cavern pool.

I tried to pull my hand away, but his grip tightened and my palm was locked firmly in his grasp.

"It's fine, thank you," I said, a little more sternly than I'd intended.

He let my hand free. I stumbled, a bit off balance, and he steadied me at the shoulders.

"Let me get a needle," he said, "and I can remove the splinter for you."

"You needn't trouble yourself."

"It is no trouble at all, I assure you."

"I'm sure I can get it myself later, thank you." I cradled the finger protectively against my shoulder, lest he try to wrest it from me again.

"But you would not forbid me from treating it?" His voice seemed odd. Tentative.

"Uh, no," I mumbled. I didn't know whether or not giving in would end the embarrassment sooner.

"Wait here a moment."

The echoes of his footsteps reached my ears, and he was gone. I stood, wondering if it would be more foolish to stay or to go. *You came here for a reason. But you're risking your life! What is life without Jurij?* The dilemma was meaningless, as I hadn't made even a blind step forward when I heard his echoing footsteps again. A bottle clanged against the floor in front of me.

"I brought some ale to numb the area and bandages with which to wrap it."

I laughed before I could stop myself. "It's just a splinter."

He made a sound that I thought to be laughter as well, although it echoed throughout the chamber in a tone both sweet and melancholy. "Yes, well, I will do all I can to help you." The leather feathers cradled my injured hand that still rested atop my shoulder. "May I?" he asked. His speech was warmer and more confident.

"All right." It was my turn to speak tentatively.

He took my hand in his and pulled on it a little as he bent down to retrieve the bottle of ale. The cool liquid didn't sting as it should have and reminded me of nothing more than water. A rustle of leather and the hand touching mine became as cold as ice, as smooth as marble. He'd removed one of his gloves and now the icy fingertips grew warm. Somehow, I felt both comforted and violated. The pain from the splinter vanished.

"What is your request?" he asked as he began poking my fingertip with the needle. My heart soared a little at the idea that he might be able to ask the goddess to help me after all, that she might actually be out there somewhere, watching. My finger throbbed, but I felt that it should have hurt more than it did, that he was taking great pains to minimize my soreness. The needle pricked just a little harder than previously. I squeaked a little in shock.

"Did I hurt you?" The man's hand stiffened.

73

"Uh, no," I responded. *Better to finish this sooner rather than later.* Heat rose on my cheeks. "No more than anyone could help."

The man's grip loosened slightly. "But I should do better than anyone else."

My muscles weakened from being held aloft for so long, but I gritted my teeth and refused to let my limb waver. *Speak your mind, Noll. Tell him why you've come.* Now that the opportunity had presented itself, I couldn't make myself voice the foolish thoughts inside of me. The man went back to work, prodding the needle into my skin even more gently than before. At rare moments, the needle or the splinter made my finger ache considerably more, but I bit the inside of my bottom lip and made no more sudden movements.

"You must need something very important," said the man after a bit of silence. "You are aware of the penalty for a woman setting foot in the castle?" The man gave one final thrust with the needle. "I have it!"

This is it. I flinched. The splinter gone, I hoped I'd be free to pull my hand back, but the man gripped harder. "Wait a moment," he said. Then he added, "Please."

What choice did I have? I wasn't about to win a bout of strength against him. I relaxed my pull. "I..." I straightened my shoulders, doing my best to act the queen. "I was willing to risk death."

"Were you?" The trickle of the stingless ale fell over my fingertip again, and what followed was a gentle patting with what felt like cloth. Then the iciness of his fingers burned warmly again, and I felt no trace of pain. "That seems foolish. To risk such a treasure."

My face flushed, and I was almost glad that my eyes were closed so I could imagine he didn't notice. I felt exposed and vulnerable.

"I came to free my friend from the curse that binds him to a woman."

He laughed. The sound made me go cold. "Who has the power to do that?"

I bit my lip, but I couldn't give up now. "Who else would, but the first goddess?"

"And why would she ever break her own law?"

74

My lip trembled. My voice, when I could finally speak, was nothing but a hoarse whisper. "Is there nothing to be done?"

"Nothing." His voice was sharp, and I couldn't tell if it was my question or the answer to that question that had offended him. He sighed and let the sternness pass. "How strange of you to have a friend bound to a woman."

"He..." The admission caught in my throat. "She commanded him to remain my friend. Accidentally."

"In women there lies a careless sort of power." He patted my hand gently. "Why do you fear for him? Does she intend to send him to the commune?"

"No, it's not that. In fact, he's—" I stopped. I felt coddled and spoken down to, and my fear of punishment was overriding my desire for the impossible. "Never mind. I was foolish to think—" I wanted my hand free, with every bit of my desire. I felt strange, locked in this man's grasp, blind to what was going on before me. His fingers loosened, and I was finally able to pull my hand back.

His voice grew quiet. "You love this... friend?" He took such a sharp intake of breath I thought something must have hurt him. My blood went cold.

"Yes." I had said the words in haste and anger to Jurij in the cavern and spoken them in my heart a multitude of times before. But never had I admitted it to anyone else, and none but my mother knew to ask. And she at least had the pity not to.

My hand was enclosed in the gentle leather grip once more, and I let him take it, my muscles growing limp. Marble, as chilled as snow and as smooth and plush as satin, pushed gently against the back of my hand. I heard a light smacking noise upon its release, not unlike the noises Mother and Father made every time they met. *A kiss?*

"So you know," whispered the hollow voice. "Perhaps you understand now. Men have no choice but to love, for that is their curse. Women are free to love, for what good it does. You need not fear death here." He pulled me close to him, his body pressed against mine. I felt strange, revolted, but at the same time, an unbidden sense of exhilaration spread from my head to my toes. His hand stroked the back of my head, and I felt patches of his cold, thin arms sweep across my cheek. My other cheek brushed against the silken fabric covering his shoulder.

"That decree was my own doing, and I am delighted to at last be free from the order. For what would become of me had you not ventured here, against all counsel? What is your name?" he asked.

"Noll," I whispered. My lips froze as they brushed against the icy surface of his ear.

His hand stopped stroking my head and balled into a fist around some of my hair. It hurt a bit, but I couldn't express my alarm. My voice choked at the realization of what was happening.

"Olivière," his voice croaked through the darkness. Somehow he knew my full name, the girly name I couldn't stand to hear spoken. *Like the vision in the cavern.*

"Oh, Olivière," he spoke again, his voice trembling. He let go of my hair and wrapped both arms so tightly around me, I thought he must have worried that I would float away.

And then I knew he would never again let me go.

CHAPTER EIGHT

H e let me go home that night, but I could never truly be my own again, never truly be out of his embrace. Four months had passed since the lord of the village had found the goddess in me. I was only half a year away from turning seventeen.

And Mother was dying.

Before my thoughts were consumed with Mother's illness, I found myself bitterly thinking like Ingrith said she once did, hoping at the very least that the news of my foolish trespass might spark some jealousy in Elfriede—what was a scrawny, puppy-face boy compared to the lord of the village?—or some kind of regret in Jurij that I, too, had someone else to love me.

But I was lying to myself. A scrawny, puppy-face boy was everything. And Elfriede and Jurij were so dreadfully excited for me. It was the only time they bothered to spare me any thought as of late.

"Wasn't Mother right? We all knew your man would find you. And soon you can have your Returning and be as happy as me."

"Now you know the joys that exist between a man and his goddess! Now you know real love."

Their happiness was like the fangs of a monster, tearing into the defenseless flesh of the queen who'd foolishly set out to slay the beast, only to meet her own doom.

I couldn't get used to the idea that I was somebody's goddess. Not just anybody's goddess, either. But it was so far from what I'd wanted I didn't know what to do. Not only was Jurij's curse unbroken, but I left the castle that night knowing my future. Knowing I had someone to Return to.

Because no one seemed to consider that I might not want to Return to him.

My only refuge was Alvilda's workshop, as far west from the castle as one could get, short of living in the commune.

Alvilda's trade had once been secondary to Father's, considering she took it up only after refusing her Returning. However, since my mother's illness, Father was less inclined to work than ever and only did so when Mother was conscious enough to remind him. Alvilda stepped right up to fill in the void, and she got most of the real work these days. At least Father was too far gone to care. In fact, he helped her from time to time. Or just gave her a tool he no longer felt he needed. Mostly because he no longer felt like working.

I knocked and let myself in at the usual call of "No masked men here, come in!" Master Tailor sometimes visited his sister, and he could take his mask off in front of her.

But she failed to warn me that an unmasked man was there.

"Noll! What brings you here?" Alvilda looked up from her work—an ornate bed headboard, I believed. The smile that flashed over her features was genuine, although she couldn't be torn from her work for long.

Jurij and Elfriede were seated at the small dining table, eating. The table was covered with a thin layer of sawdust that belied how often Alvilda really used the table for its intended purpose.

Elfriede laid the rest of her crispel on the table and wrinkled her nose. "Good day, Noll." At least I think that was what she said. Elfriede's gentle voice and Alvilda's tools running across the wood made for a bad combination. *If I care to hear what she has to say, anyway.* I shook my head. I was being awful. It wasn't so bad when we were home without Jurij and she could tell me how *happy* she was that "my man" had found the goddess in me. But whenever Jurij showed up, I felt like there was nothing but frost in the air between us.

I'd spent the morning in the garden, trying not to think about anything, to little avail. I saw Elfriede leaving with a basket, and I figured she was off to fetch her man. I didn't figure on encountering them here.

It's almost like she knows what you told Jurij. She probably did.

"Good day," I said at last. "Didn't know you were here."

"Gideon sent us on a quest," said Jurij as he shoved the rest of the cheese in his mouth.

Alvilda laughed as she ran her file back and forth against the large rough edge that remained on the future headboard. "Not one of those monster-hunting quests, is it?"

It was my turn to smile. "No, we haven't been on one of those in a while."

Elfriede spoke at the same time, and rather loudly. "I always thought those games were rather stupid."

I opened my mouth to point out that her "beloved" enjoyed those games she found rather stupid, but I thought better.

Jurij looked first at Elfriede and then at me. I was surprised he was able to tear his eyes off her for someone as unimportant as me. He stretched and stood from the table, strolling over to examine some of the pieces of wooden art that lined Alvilda's walls from one side to the next. Jurij pointed to one of the pieces. "Have you ever seen this one, Noll?"

He's talking to me. I watched Elfriede out of the corner of my eye as I came up behind him. She seemed bored, more concerned with straightening imagined wrinkles in her skirt. But then I stood on my toes and put a hand on his shoulder in order to get a closer look. Elfriede got up at once and made her way to stand beside me.

I pulled my hand back immediately. *He's just your friend. He's her man. I thought you'd gotten used to that.* I focused on the carving. It showed a little girl smiling with a triumphant look on her face. She held a long tree branch—Elgar—high above her like it was the mightiest blade in the land. Beside her—but a little behind her, I took note—was a heroic-looking diminutive retainer wearing a kitten mask. I spun to face the artist. "Alvilda! Is that Jurij and me?"

She grinned. "It is indeed." She paused to wipe her brow with the back of her arm.

I laughed and exchanged a smile with Jurij, forgetting for just one moment that there was anyone else with us, that there was anything but happy feelings between us.

The chirping bird cleared her throat. "I've asked Auntie to do one of our Returning." *"Auntie." Of course. She'll be one of the family soon.*

My smile faded and I stepped back. Elfriede stepped in immediately to intertwine her arm with his. Jurij smiled peacefully and tilted his head so that Elfriede's golden curls caressed his cheek.

Alvilda appeared behind us, wiping sawdust from her hands with a rag that she carelessly tossed over the fireplace mantle once she finished. "I'm definitely looking forward to carving that." She focused her dark brown eyes on me, and I saw something in them that made me wonder just how much she meant her words. "But first, I'm a little busy with a special gift here."

She got between the coupling so she could grab Jurij by the shoulder and shake him playfully. The blush that covered Jurij's entire face said it all.

A bed headboard. An upcoming wedding. But Jurij wouldn't turn seventeen for a year. I forced myself to smile. "Are we thinking about wedding gifts already?"

Elfriede studied me a moment. She didn't seem to like what she found. "Headboards take a while, and Alvilda's too busy to spend all of her time on it." She smiled sweetly at me. "Of course, I know your Returning comes first, Noll. Just let me know what you'd like. I'm quite excited."

My Returning. A woman had the choice to send her man to the commune, but...

No one's ever been the goddess of the lord, not in my lifetime or my parents' lifetimes, either. It seemed to go without saying that I'd accept him.

Alvilda wiped her brow and slipped an arm around both Elfriede's and Jurij's shoulders as she stuck her head between them. She had a bit of sawdust in her hair. "Which tools did Gideon want now?"

I cocked my head. "Father wants to borrow tools?"

Alvilda nodded and stepped back. "More like he wants the tools I've borrowed back." She made her way to her toolbox and started picking through its contents.

"It's Mother, really." Elfriede hugged Jurij tighter. "She was doing a bit better this morning. She got mad that he'd given away so many of his tools when she was in and out over the past few days, and she asked that we get them back, so Father could start working again." Elfriede pinched her nose. "It'll make her happy."

But it won't make him work, she seemed poised to say. Alvilda laid out a number of tools on her workbench. "That seems a bit much to carry like that. You can borrow some baskets."

Elfriede walked to the cupboard and pulled out a basket like it was her home and she knew were everything was. She took out three and Jurij started filling them.

Alvilda crossed over to where Elfriede was standing. She smiled as she put one of the baskets back into the cupboard. "I think two baskets should be enough." Jurij finished loading the second basket as she spoke as if to prove her words true. "And I'd like to elicit Noll's opinion on that special gift I'm working on."

Beautiful. Now I'd be helping plan the décor resting over their wedding bed.

Elfriede's shoulders relaxed, and I suspected she was relieved not to have to fight for her man's attention on the trek back home. She stepped to the door without picking up either basket. "Thank you again for lunch, Auntie."

Alvilda nodded. "Sure thing. You're always welcome!"

Jurij slipped his arms around both baskets. I wondered if Elfriede knew that if she offered to carry one, he'd refuse, or if she didn't even bother to worry about him carrying all of that without assistance. Either way, he seemed delighted. "See you later!" he called, and then both were gone, Elfriede shutting the door behind them.

I turned back to the carving and sighed.

Alvilda left me to my thoughts for a few moments. I could hear her pick up the file and continue working. "I didn't really want to ask you about the headboard."

I jumped. Alvilda rested her file back on her workbench and grinned. "Come, now. Even I'm not that heartless."

Heartless. Ingrith had called the man who had found the goddess in me the heartless monster. I didn't know what it meant. I didn't understand anything about him, and I was so scared to find out more. So frightened to acknowledge that I had a big decision to make.

I snapped out of my daze just long enough to pull out one of the sawdust-covered chairs at the eating table. Alvilda followed suit.

"It's all right," I said, breaking a few tense moments of silence. I wanted to talk about everything. I wanted to ask her if there was a way to act as if I'd never gone to the castle. I wanted to ask her if it would be okay to delay the lord's courtship as much as possible, to pretend to be preparing my heart for the Returning day after day, year after year as I continued living as if nothing had changed.

But why is it different for me? Why do I have to Return at all? I'd rather live the rest of my own days in the commune.

Alvilda of all people should have been able to understand my feelings, but even she thought it a bad idea to reject the lord. "He's good to us. He pays the villagers well for their wares." But what did I care? If even Alvilda thought that I should sacrifice myself so the rest of the village could pocket a few more coppers, I couldn't betray any of my plan to delay the Returning. "Plus, he's—" Alvilda had dropped what she was going to say then, choosing to bite her lip instead. It was probably "always watching." The people in the village were worried he'd punish them for forgetting to invite someone to a Returning, so what would he do to them if his goddess refused to love him?

He's not always watching, though. He can't be. He's just a man.

So I couldn't ask any questions. Not questions that mattered anyway. Still, I figured it would be rude to pass up a rare invitation to get to know Alvilda better. She wasn't one for musings. "A waste of time, effort, and the brain our foremothers blessed you with," she often said.

"Why did you choose woodworking?" I asked. Maybe she'd mistake my intentions and tell me about the beauty of the craft; I could let it wash over me and retreat back to the emptiness in my heart.

"Well," said Alvilda softly. "Women have the right to choose what their hearts tell them. It's a gift from the first goddess."

My eyes welled again. "That's a lie! It's not a gift—and it's not even true!"

So much for sidestepping the issue.

Alvilda coughed. "It's not an easy gift, I know." She tapped her fingers over the table and looked thoughtful, a rarity on her features. "I know."

She let me cry a bit without saying anything more. I almost grabbed a rag with which to wipe my face, but I remembered the sawdust and spread my tears all over my sleeve instead. I no longer could stand to wear aprons.

Finally, I managed to compose myself. "Whatever it is, it's different for me." *I can't send the lord to the commune. I just can't. No one would let me.*

"I know, dear. I'm sorry."

What else was there to say?

Alvilda broke into the silence. "You know, I tried to love Jaron." So that was his name. Mother's first love. "I really did. I certainly didn't dislike him."

I scoffed. I hadn't intended to be rude to Alvilda, especially as she opened herself up to me. But even though I felt Alvilda was the closest person I had to someone who might understand, it wasn't the same.

Alvilda didn't notice or at least didn't comment. "Whenever I let my thoughts wander, I feel so ill at the idea of what my choice has done to him I want to retch."

I met Alvilda's eyes. They were strong, dark brown like mine, but I detected a glisten in them. Unlike me, though, she held it in, her throat making a gurgling noise as she steeled herself to speak further.

"I thought about marrying him even without the Returning. So many had done it before." She looked upward at the art carvings behind me. "But I couldn't decide if his muted happiness at being near me would be worth the torment of my own soul in his stead."

I nodded. "And people didn't urge you to marry him anyway? Tell you how sometimes the Returning is delayed years and that there could be a chance you would both one day be happy?" The words were not my own, but the echoes of voice after voice and lecture after lecture.

Alvilda bit her lip and didn't look away from the wall behind me. "Yes, they did. But no, I would never, ever be happy."

83

My gaze followed Alvilda's. She saw me looking and tore away, but I saw the carving in which she had been engrossed. Her family. Luuk as a toddler in his bunny rabbit mask, his mother holding him in her arms with a sour look carved deep and permanently into her features. Master Tailor stood next to Mistress Tailor, one hand on Jurij the puppy dog who stood in front of him, his other arm tightly around Mistress Tailor's shoulder, his demeanor projecting a sense of joviality that his face could not. Because Master Tailor still wore a mask, his face obscured by that of an owl's.

Of course. Alvilda had witnessed her brother marry without the Returning. As his blood relation, she knew his face, but she chose to carve him with his missing features. Perhaps to guard his secret from the wandering female eye. Or perhaps to remind herself of what could have been, had she chosen to marry Jaron against her heart's desire.

"In any case," Alvilda said, her tone calm but still trembling, "I'm sorry for my foolish ramblings. I know that your circumstances simply don't compare to mine. The lord is—well, in any case, you don't want to go through what I did." Alvilda walked across the room, rummaged through her toolbox, and came back to the eating table.

"Here," she said, tossing a small chunk of wood and a chisel on the table. "It's the most I can do for you. You're going to learn woodcarving."

CHAPTER NINE

W oodcarving was the only thing I had, the only thing that quieted my thoughts. When I worked, I was able to forget. I first took a tool in my hand and turned a rough piece of wood into a sphere. It wasn't much, but I controlled what the wood would be. And no one told me I didn't really get to choose.

I'd grown better in the past few weeks. Elfriede thought woodcarving was a wonderful idea—as a *hobby*, she emphasized. And then on further introspection, as a hobby *for now*, she would add. As if I could forget that I had so little time before I was expected to perform a miracle. I already had a miniature sculpture of Elfriede's new golden puppy, Arrow, to present to her as a gift. It was only after I had finished that my numbed mind remembered that Arrow himself had been an early wedding gift from Jurij, and I probably shouldn't have spent so much time carving his image into my mind before the happy coupling and I went our separate ways.

Father had little to say about my talent, or the tools I borrowed from him without asking. But I forgave him. I felt as numb as he did these days.

Mother was only sometimes with us.

Father was behind the house on a tree stump, whittling what looked to be a bowl or a cup. Mother sat beneath the shade of a tree on the edge of the woods, her hand clasping a small piece of wood. Mother should have known that if she was near Father when he worked, she'd wind up distracting him. But lately she was loath to part from him at all.

"How are you feeling today?" I nestled into the grass and leaned against the tree beside her. I clutched little wooden Arrow in my hands to work on the finishing touches, although my model was off somewhere with Elfriede and Jurij.

It took a moment for Mother to acknowledge me. She turned her head slowly. There were dark circles beneath her eyes, a sallow tinge to the once-beautiful oaken shade of her skin. "Better," she lied.

I looked up to watch Father's reaction. He held the bowl and chisel in his hands as if he were still carving, but his hands were frozen.

"Your father's working," Mother said. "He's making beautiful things."

Father's hands moved again, slowly.

I took a closer look at the wooden figure in Mother's grasp. "What's that?"

Mother turned it over and lifted her arms weakly to bring it closer to me. "It's a lily. Isn't it beautiful?"

Seeing the hint of a smile on Mother's face made me genuinely happy. I gestured to the fields behind Father. "It's lovelier than all the ones around us." It was getting colder, and those blooms were dying.

Mother leaned her head against the tree bark and shut her eyes. A moment passed and she began to breathe deeply.

I shifted the wooden flower that was slipping from her grasp to the center of her lap. I laid her hands across it. She didn't stir.

"She's getting worse every day." Father continued to carve his bowl. His interest in me was usually so decidedly little it took me a moment to realize he was speaking to me.

"The others in the village are still sick." I pulled my legs to my chest and wrapped my arms around my knees. A merchant's wife. The butcher's daughter. Even little Nissa's mother. All struck ill, the same day as Mother. The day after I visited the castle.

But Father had little interest in the rest of those ill in the village. He threw the bowl and chisel down into the grass, cradling his forehead. "I don't know what to do."

I swallowed. I didn't know what to say.

Father looked up from his hands. "Will you ask the lord if he can help us?"

"The lord?" I'd tried my best not to think about that night. Even though I always failed. "What could he do?" My voice faltered.

As if in response to my question, I heard the sound of a wooden wheel and the clip-clop, clip-clop of horses' hooves on the dirt path. It could have been perfectly timed, but the same thing had happened every evening since the specters brought me home the night I met the lord.

The black horses and the carriage burst through the trees and halted in front of our home. A specter sat atop the carriage, his back stiff, his hands clutching the reins. Two specters stepped out of the carriage and stood in front of it, their hands clasped behind their backs, as still as if there was no breath within them.

Now, as always since that first night, I was drawn to their eyes, all of them black like a hole in ice. As a child, the eyes had scared me a little. But then I noticed that there was no trace of flame there, and that too set them apart from other unmasked men. Somehow, this made the specters more sad than horrifying.

Father clasped his hands together and leaned his arms over his thighs. He tilted his head toward them. "Go with them. Ask."

I stood, quickly. "I can't." I couldn't. Going there in the first place had been a terrible mistake. But I couldn't possibly explain it to Father.

Mother's eyes fluttered open. She brushed a hand against the hem of my skirt. "Noll…"

"They're here again." I swallowed the sour taste in my throat. "The specters. His servants."

Father appeared beside Mother, kneeling beside her. "How are you feeling, darling?" He placed the back of his hand against her cheek. "Warm."

Mother laid a hand on Father's knee gently. "Gideon, I'm fine." She turned her head to look up at me. "Does he want you to visit him?"

"I… I think so." The specters appeared day after day at

twilight. If I walked near the carriage, they gestured inside. I'd never once stepped foot in it since that first night it had brought me home.

"She should go visit him," said Father. "It's rude of her not to. He ought to be able to see her."

"Gideon, no." Mother cupped Father's cheek in her hand. "How many times have I told you? You can't rush these things. Let her be."

It was odd how I'd finally gotten a man of my own as she wanted, and here she was, the only one to counsel patience. I ran the chisel over Arrow's wooden rump too hard, nicking it. Tossing the figure and the chisel down on the ground in frustration, I sighed and cradled my knees against my chest.

"Aubree—"

Mother put her finger over Father's mouth to stop him. "Go tell them she's not coming today."

He may not have been compelled to follow her orders, but he did anyway. I poked my head out from my knees. "Thank you."

Mother pulled one of my hands away from my knees to squeeze it. She cradled her wooden lily with her other fingers. "I just want you to be happy. I need to know you're happy."

Would I ever be happy again? "Don't." I squeezed her back and did my best to smile. "Don't talk like that."

Mother pulled her hand out of mine and placed it over her wooden flower. We sat quietly for a moment. The specters crawled back into the carriage, never once opening their mouths to respond to Father. The driver flicked his wrists, and the horses turned around by crossing the grass. They'd done that so often over the past few months, the lilies were crushed and broken in that small patch of grass in front of our home.

"Noll," said Mother, her voice quiet. She coughed a few times. "Let love find you."

"It did." I clutched my knees even tighter. "And I don't want it." *Not from anyone but Jurij.*

Mother patted the flower in her lap. "I won't rush you. It's not fair that it took so long for love to find you. You haven't had enough of a chance to get used to it."

"You mean like Elfriede got used to Jurij?" *Until she tires of him. If she hasn't already.*

Mother nodded weakly. "You were right, you know. She used to be so cold to him. One day, she stood inside the house, helping me wipe the dishes. She looked out the window in the kitchen, at you two running off to play beyond the hills. When she saw you whap him across the side with your tree branch—"

"Elgar."

Mother smiled. "Right. She asked me, 'What if I never Return Jurij's love? What if he's doomed to walk around with his face hidden forever? What if I send him to the commune?'"

So I was right. She only forced herself to fall in love so she wouldn't feel guilty.

With a grunt, Mother placed her wooden flower in my lap. "I told her that love, even when you didn't expect to find it, can prove a beautiful thing."

And what of the love that never came from where you hoped to find it?

Father kneeled down beside Mother, sliding his arm around her back. I carefully set the wooden lily beside my attempt at a dog and did the same, reaching across her shoulders to support her other side. Father grimaced as I did; he probably hoped to support his goddess all on his own. I wasn't sorry to disappoint him.

The three of us walked across the knoll and back into the house, a distance that might have taken either Father or I a tenth of the time on our own. Neither of us minded the pace, though, and for once, it was peaceful, with the tepid breeze that rustled the lilies all around us.

I tucked a strand of golden hair behind Mother's ear just as we reached the door. Father nodded toward it. "Open that, will you?"

As I did so, I got a fairly good view of the figure seated at our table, lit by the small lantern on the table before him. His hand, still clutching the lantern, trembled.

"Luuk? Jurij isn't here. He and Elfriede—"

"It's Nissa." Luuk's muffled voice was shakier than ever. "Her mother's dead."

~

MOTHER WAS the last one living. The illness had claimed the lives of three women in the village, one by one.

And because life without a goddess is apparently too much for men to handle, three men died shortly thereafter. Vanished, out of grief. Poor Nissa had no one left but Luuk, and because she was his goddess, Mistress Tailor decided to let her live with them.

Because she was his goddess. *I need to see him. I need to ask him to save Mother.* It was ridiculous. What would I do, command the lord to save her? Why would he be able to save her? *But you have to try.*

I let it go four more days after Luuk came looking for Jurij. Four more days of women and men dying. Four more days Mother moved closer to death.

Four days I'd clung to my woodcarving and felt sick to my stomach and let my stubbornness stop me from acting. *Ask him. And then you can tell Father how ridiculous it was to hope for anything.*

When the carriage came down the path as the fourth day shifted to evening, I was ready. When the specters opened the door and one extended a hand, I took it.

I clutched my shawl and felt the sweat pour off my palm in waves. The black leather seat beneath me felt hot. The air was stifling. But I had to try. I had to breathe.

Halfway through the woods I felt queasy—my mind playing tricks, that whisper of my full name in my ears—but it soon passed. I straightened my shoulders. *What am I so afraid of? He's my man. He'll be happy to see me.* But that was just it. By going, I was acknowledging he was my man.

You can't run away from this forever. I'd spent long enough trying.

The carriage ground to a halt too soon, the short trip made even shorter with the horses' assistance. The door opened and I took a specter's outstretched palm with my own trembling hand. It was cold, so cold, and I wondered not for the first time how these men could seem so lifeless and still be among the living.

The gates and then the castle doors opened as the specters approached, and I stumbled inside the thunderously shaking castle. Only once I was indoors did the earth settle. The castle wasn't dark this time. Torches lit the entryway, revealing an empty room, the scene of our first meeting. Even with the slight warmth of the air outside, it felt cold in the castle, like a gust of frigid wind encircled it forever.

I jumped as I felt a hand on my shoulder. Shivering, I turned, expecting to come face to mask with the lord at last, but it was one of the specters. He stepped back and gestured up the nearby staircase. Other specters lined the stairway, each gesturing upward. I cringed at the strange, inviting yet somehow unappealing sight. But I straightened my shoulders, clutched my shawl tighter around my throat, and ascended the stairs.

The line of specters continued on to the second floor and up another stairway to a third. I lost count of how many specters there were, perhaps a hundred, black eyes bearing down on me, black eyes watching from the edge of the light, each with one foot in the darkness. By the time I reached the top of the second flight of stairs, I exhaled, relieved there were no more steps awaiting me. Instead, a line of specters gestured down a hallway, their black eyes watching. I followed the path set out for me, stopping halfway when a line of specters blocked my way.

"I'm here to see the lord." *Who are these men?*

The four specters before me nodded and gestured to an open doorway. I let go of my shawl, rubbed my palms against my skirt to dry them, and stepped in.

The room was huge—far greater even than the cavernous entryway two floors below. But it was practically empty. I followed a long, thin, and threadbare black carpet thrown down over cobblestone flooring. At the edge of the carpet against the wall was a large black chair—a throne, no doubt, like something out of the myths about rulers called kings and queens, only they would have kept their throne rooms on the lower floors of their castles. Above the throne was a sword that glowed violet. A *sword*. Something I'd only seen in drawings for made-up tales about the kings and queens who wielded them. Something there was no use for in everyday life, so there simply was no need for our blacksmith to forge. Axes were for chopping wood. Knives were for butchering and cooking. But a sword? The kings and queens of tales used them to battle, and once men found their goddesses, they simply lost all interest in swordfights and adventure. And most women never had such interests to begin with.

Most women besides me.

This sword glowed brighter than the flames of the torches lighting the way. I'd never heard anyone mention that swords glowed in stories. There were no windows, so the glowing could hardly be a trick of the light. The only other thing in the room was a bookstand with a single, large tome closed atop it. *The book of Returning, perhaps? Always conveniently in the Great Hall on a Returning Day.*

"Well, Olivière. Welcome. I am glad to see you chose to make yourself so comfortable."

I dropped my hand immediately, not even realizing I was leaning against the throne, reaching up toward the sword. I didn't even remember walking those last few paces.

"Please. Do turn around. I assure you I am now prepared for your visits."

I turned, the sword somehow forgotten. His presence drew my eyes with such force I couldn't bear to look at anything else until I'd absorbed all of him.

He was cloaked entirely in black. Not only was his embossed leather jacket darker than a shadow, his folded hands were covered with what appeared to be smooth, black leather gloves. Instead of a mask or a beautiful face, a gauze veil dark as ink covered his head, the corners of the material tied closed with a somber broach on his left shoulder. Were it not for the wide-brimmed hat he wore atop the veil—which was just as dark as the rest of his attire, if perhaps a little more resplendent—he might have very well sucked all of the light from the room. As it was, the hat—a sort of metal, pointed hat—was glossy enough that it reflected the flicker of the torches' firelight in small, spectacular movements.

He walked past me before I could speak, his close stride rustling my skirt. I moved back to give him room, and he sank into the black throne, crossing one black boot over and resting it on his knee. He brought the tips of his gloves together, his elbows resting comfortably on the armrests. "I had hoped to see you again much sooner."

I swallowed and ran a shaky hand through my hair, tucking a chunk of it behind my ear. "I figured. I—I saw the carriages. I just needed some time."

"Time? Time for what?"

I clutched my shawl again, as if that would somehow save me from the chill that hung over every room of the castle. I formed my words carefully. "I'm not yet old enough for a Returning." It was true, and I wasn't saying there was going to be a Returning. Not the moment I turned seventeen, anyway.

The lord dropped his fingers and gestured around him to the empty room. "Since when does that stop a man from seeing his goddess?"

"It doesn't. Usually. But you didn't come to see me, either."

The lord scoffed. I could hear the sound clearly even through his veil. "You expect *me* to visit *you*?"

I blinked. This wasn't going at all how I expected. "No, I..." *I was quite happy not to have to think about you,* I wanted to say. But there was no need to tell him that. A man could crumble at even the slightest hint of harshness from his goddess. "It's just that... that's the way it's normally done. Men visiting their goddesses."

The lord tossed his head and cradled what must have been his chin with his thumb and forefinger. His face seemed turned a bit sideways, like he wasn't going to look at me, although I couldn't be sure. "I cannot leave the castle." His voice broke a little, and I was almost unsure I'd heard him right.

I didn't know what to say. It wasn't like I'd wanted him to come anyway. And arranging courtship was hardly the first thing on my mind. "Um, sir, Lordship..." The lord dropped his hand back to his lap. "My mother is unwell. Women have been ill these past four months, and they started dying this week. I thought... we all thought they'd get better, but now that doesn't seem to be the case, and..." I didn't know what else to say.

The lord tossed his hand in the air with a flourish, gesturing for me to go on. "And?"

I felt something snap in my chest, like the one word from him, the callous tone of his voice, was enough to stomp all hope I'd managed to muster. The hope that had gotten me to accept that carriage ride at last and face the fact that I was somebody's goddess, and that somebody wasn't who I wanted.

"And you're our lord. Isn't there something you can do?"

The lord drummed his fingers on one of the throne's armrests. "You have tried all the herbs?"

"Yes!" I regretted the tone of my voice the moment I said it. But it was obvious we'd tried that much, wasn't it? I tried to soften my voice. "I mean, of course. It seems to help with the pain a bit, but they're still—that is, my mother now, just her, she still has no strength."

The lord's fingers stopped tapping at once. "You say women have died?"

"Yes!" I squeezed my shawl tighter. Wasn't he listening? Wasn't he paying attention at all to the people he ruled over? *Why, then, do people say he's always watching?*

"There is no typical sign of illness? No rash? No sores?"

"No…" I bit my lip, thinking about Ingrith and her "healer" man. "I knew a woman, who… well." I swallowed, struggling to summon my courage to face this man. "She said there was once a family of healers in the village."

The lord's head snapped forward slightly. "Healers? I thought they had all been forgotten."

"They have. That is, if they existed at all in the first place."

"No matter. They are gone. They cannot help." The lord held a hand out to silence me before I could inquire further. He leaned his veiled face into his other palm. Neither of us spoke. Then he straightened in his throne. "Four months they have been ill?"

"About that, yes." I dropped my hand from my shawl and let my arms hang limply at my sides. Even without seeing his eyes, I felt them boring into me. I didn't know how very much I'd hate the attention. "They got ill the day after I first came here."

The lord jumped out of his throne so quickly I almost fell backward to the ground as my feet scrambled to give him ample room to pace. He walked to his bookstand and flung the heavy tome open, flipping through pages as if his life depended on it. Maybe my mother's actually did.

Can he read through his veil?

As if hearing my thoughts, the lord sighed and slammed the book shut with a grunt of frustration, sending dust into the air. "You will have to leave!"

I took a step back before I could even think. "Pardon?"

"Leave. Now." He gestured toward the door and flicked his fingers, summoning four specters from behind me. They held their arms out, leading me toward the door.

My head spun from one specter to the next, to the pacing lord before the throne. "What about my mother?"

The lord slowed his pace, but he didn't stop moving. He waved a hand absently at me. "I will do what I can, of course. She will live to perform our Returning."

If his first statement offered me a bit of comfort, his second was a kick to the stomach. "What do you mean? Is she going to die of this after that?"

The lord stopped and sighed, quite audibly. He positioned both hands on his hips. "I cannot tell you. I do not know."

"But you know *something*, obviously."

The lord took a few steps forward, closing the distance between us. "Olivière," he said, grabbing one of my hands. He squeezed it and brought it up between our chests. "I will do what I can. Please worry instead about preparing yourself for my Returning."

I ripped my hand out from his grip. "Your Returning? How can you speak to me about a Returning when my mother might be dead tomorrow?"

The lord leaned forward, trying to reach for me. I took a step back. "Olivière, the timing of your mother's illness is unfortunate, but—"

"The *timing*?"

"If you knew how long I waited. If you knew how hard this is for me, to accept your love."

"Accept *my* love?" I crossed my arms tight against my chest, all timidity forgotten. "What love? I don't even *know* you."

"A fact that could be remedied if only you would accept my invitation more often."

"And what do you mean, how hard it is for *you*? Do you think I want to be the lord's goddess?" I threw my hands in the air at him. "That I have any interest in this black void of a man who stays locked up inside this monstrosity of a castle, ignoring the needs of his people, a heartless monster who doesn't care if they're dying?"

The lord straightened his shoulders and clenched his hands into fists. "A *heartless monster*?"

"I was wondering what it meant. But now I know. You think nothing of your people."

"And whose fault is that?" His tone was so accusatory, I flinched. He started pacing again before his throne, back and forth, back and forth. "I cannot leave this castle, Olivière! I do not know one person in this village from the next. I blink and they die. I die and they would not know—they could not *imagine* the depth of the pain I feel."

I sighed heavily. He was making no sense. Leave it to me to wind up with the recluse with little grip on his sanity. "Don't talk to me about a Returning until my mother's health improves."

The lord stiffened, and I realized, far more clearly than I had the first time we'd met, that my words had power over him.

I decided to test it. I pointed above the throne. "And give me that sword."

CHAPTER TEN

I'd had to ask for the scabbard, too. And he gave them to me. Without a word. Thrusting them at me like he couldn't wait to be rid of them. Or of me.

The scabbard rested now around my waist. I hoped I wore it right; we'd used our sashes to hold our stick blades. I held the sword out in front of me like a violet torch that lit my way down the path that ran between the castle and my home.

I was stupid to think he could do anything. I bit the inside of my cheek. *That he would be helpful at all.*

I wouldn't have been comfortable with a simpering sycophant, true. That was part of the reason why I couldn't bear to see him again at first. The idea of a man weak at the knees and lost without me made me almost as ill as seeing Jurij acting just that way with Elfriede. Even if it might have been different if Jurij acted that way with me.

But this man wasn't at all sane. He was, impossibly, rude to his own goddess. He babbled on about things that made no sense. Cared about things that weren't anywhere near as important as my mother's illness.

But since when did a man care about anyone other than his goddess?

I shook my head. It may just have been because Mother's illness worried Elfriede, but Jurij was as worried about her as the

97

rest of us. If the lord truly loved me, he would have been worried sick.

If he loved me. He'd said it was hard to accept my love. For *him* to accept *me.*

I stopped my manic pacing halfway down the path and let out a roar of impatience.

The blade glowed even brighter. It seemed to pull at me, like if I let it go it would fly right out of my hands. But that was crazy.

"*Olivière...*"

That voice again.

I headed through the foliage, where the blade seemed keen to take me.

~

THE GLOWING LIGHT.

I stood before the violet pool in the cavern, Elgar's hilt clutched in both hands. Yes, Elgar. It seemed a fitting name for the blade. Elgar had taken me there, to the pool. And the pool still called to me.

Elgar drooped in my grasp, perhaps because of my faltering arms, weak from holding it aloft so long.

"*Olivière,*" called the pool. "*Olivière!*"

It was a chorus of voices, a hundred women and men, both familiar and unknown. What would I find if I finally went all the way down to the violet light?

The pool gave me its reply. "*Olivière.*"

I stood straight, snapping Elgar back upward in my grip. *This is stupid. Ridiculous. I should go home. I need to check on Mother.*

Elgar shot downward, yanking my arms more forcefully than anyone ever had before, pulling my body aloft briefly before we punctured the water and dived into the depths below. I hadn't had a chance to catch my breath. The toes of my boots had scraped against sediment for a moment, and then I felt nothing. It was as if I were floating, only I was flying downward, deeper and deeper into the light.

And then I stopped so suddenly it was as if my body had forgotten all movement. In my panic, the need for air ceased. There was nothing. There was no one. Nothing but me and the blade in my hand, the blade that spun and twirled round and round gently, slowly.

With every blink of my eye, I saw what I'd once seen. What I wanted to be again.

Jurij and Elfriede's Returning in reverse, coming undone. Little Jurij and me, battling unseen foes before we ventured outside, leaving the cavern behind. The old crone and Darwyn still with us. With every moment that passed, more friends came back to me.

But then friends became Mother, her face alight, bending down to the floor to pick me up and cradle me against her shoulders.

Then what I saw became unfamiliar. *Was that Mother as a child?* The images passed by faster and faster, and I spun so I could hardly bear to look. I squeezed my eyes shut and tried to shield my lids from the light.

I stopped turning with my arms tightly above my head.

No more vertigo. I opened my eyes. Nothing. Only violet light.

Is that what was to become of me, then? Would I float aloft in the light forever?

"*Olivière!*"

There was life outside the light, if I chose to seek it.

I clenched my jaw and nodded. Anywhere but home. Anywhere but that life. Somewhere I wasn't that man's goddess, if just for a little while.

Elgar shot upward, pulling me with it. This time, my arms didn't ache. This time, as we broke through the light and back into the waters, I felt as if I were swimming. As if I were in control.

I emerged from the cavern pool more skillfully than I had entered it. I had somewhere to go. So I went, following the familiar path through the woods and to the dirt road, trotting toward the village.

And I felt immediately disappointed. Even stupid. I was home. Of course I was. The lilies still dotted the hilltops. And my house was right there beside the—

No, my house wasn't there.

The hair on the back of my neck stood up. A chill swept the air, and a breeze rustled the tresses I could never tame. I turned.

My gaze fell on the castle, which towered over the land and threatened to make me cower.

You idiot. I squeezed my eyes shut. My knees buckled in anticipation of the fall.

But the ground didn't shake. I slowly opened one eye and then the next and openly stared at the castle, dumbfounded.

"Who goes there?"

That voice. So familiar, so scornful. But not entirely unwelcome. I could picture the voice now, asking me to wash dishes for Mother. To grab a chair for Mother.

My gaze darted from the castle to the dirt path through the woods behind me. A group of unmasked men covered in crisscrossing chainmail exited the woods behind me. They laid their hands lazily over the sheathed blades at their sides.

"You, boy," said one. What was that voice again? Fish Face? Had his wife unmasked him with a Returning?

Another slapped him across the chest. "That's no boy!" I didn't recognize him, either. But I guess I didn't know everyone in the village.

The men shook to life, some pulling their swords out and pointing them toward me, others jolting awake and staring at me with a look of utter confusion. Their faces, varying in their beauty, all had a degree of allure that stirred my heart. Yet I knew none of the faces. And none were masked. True, most men of that age were unmasked, but to find so many together at once? *And they have swords. Like out of made-up tales. This is clearly not real!*

"What are you doing here, woman?" demanded the one who had first spoken, the one whose voice I had mistaken for Father's. There actually was a bit of a resemblance, but the man had just a few different features, a bend to his nose, a sneer to his lips that Father didn't. The man hadn't drawn his blade.

There was something off about these men. Before I even realized I wasn't playing games with a stick blade, I'd pulled Elgar out of its sheath and fixed it readily in their direction. Both of my hands gripped the hilt. They'd come from the direction of the castle. "Who sent you?"

Some of the men burst out laughing, letting their blades fall. A few stuck them into the ground and leaned on them like walking sticks.

The leader took a few paces forward. I backed up uneasily, poking Elgar out in front of me.

The man dodged my awkward thrusts easily and knocked Elgar from my grip with the back of his hand. I cradled the sore spot without thinking, and the man slapped me across the cheek just as he had my wrist, with the back of his hand.

I cried out in shock. It was as if my own father had hit me. But he wouldn't have. No man would have. I mean, unless their goddesses asked them to, but then why would a woman ever do that?

The rest of the men laughed, and the leader gestured to where Elgar had fallen.

"Pick it up!" he ordered.

One of the men scrambled forward to do as instructed. He handed the blade with two hands to the leader, who picked it up and turned it around in the air, staring at the violet glow. The leader's brow furrowed and at last he lowered it.

"Take this back to His Lordship." He thrust it at the man, who nodded and turned back to the pack waiting behind him before disappearing into the woods.

His Lordship? Since when does the lord have a set of speaking servants?

The leader slapped me with the back of his other hand across my other cheek.

I jumped.

"Thief!" he cried. "How dare you walk around with a sword from His Lordship's castle?"

My tongue caught in my throat. "It's mine! He gave it to me!" Had he sent these men to get it back? Where had they come from?

But your house is missing, Noll. This can't be real. I rubbed my sore jaw. *But it sure feels real.*

The leader laughed, but his smile faded quickly. He grabbed me by the chin, and I winced from the pain of the pressure he exerted, a pain especially sharp in the cheeks that bore his blows. He turned my head back and forth, observing me like Mother often observed a piece of meat in the market.

He gasped. "Your ears! You mutilated your ears!" Despite the strangeness of the situation and the force exerted tightly over my face, my fingers instinctively brushed the tips of my ears. They were the same familiar, unwounded smooth edges as they were always.

I felt more lost now than I had before I entered the secret cavern.

The other men walked forward to join their leader in glaring at me.

"You're right!" said one, his voice cocky and assured.

"Whatever possessed this one?" said another.

They were puzzled and introspective. A flash of light burned in their eyes and then faded. But it was not the flame I expected to see, just a trick of the moonlight, an echo of a shadow. These men didn't carry flames in their eyes—and yet here they stood living before me.

The leader was confused, and he was angry. There was something about the way he looked at me, the way Father had always looked so longingly at Mother. Or Jurij at Elfriede. He let my face free and grabbed me tightly by the arm, yanking me forward down the dirt road and toward the village.

"Stop!" I screamed. The leader paused, looking over my head to address his compatriots.

"Let's go!" he said. "It's time we show those women exactly what happens when they disobey."

He pulled me forward. I started struggling, but another of the men appeared at my side and grabbed my free arm, yanking me forward just as forcefully. A third man appeared behind me, and a black cloth flew in front of my face, wrapping tightly across my mouth and digging hard into my teeth and tongue as it was knotted behind me.

The men dragged me down the path, away from the castle. Even the Tailors' home at the edge of the village was altered. My heartbeat echoed in my ears. Home, but not home. The village was much the same, but not entirely. *I'm drowning. I stupidly leaped into the pool again and this is my dying dream.*

The one place that seemed hardly changed was the commune, where the men stopped dragging me at last. A fire was burning in the center, and a few dark figures stood in front of it. The men in the commune could never bring themselves to bother building a fire.

"Come out!" screamed the leader of the pack. "All of you women, come out now and look at what we bring with us!"

The commune was changed after all. Women and girls stepped out from shacks. One after another, they surrounded the small roaring fire that was lit in the center. They huddled together in packs of threes and fours. Only occasionally did a woman stand apart—mostly the women who had been standing before the fire—her eyes narrowed.

And again, as with the men, I thought I saw women I knew, only to discover something that made their faces not quite familiar. I wasn't home, I knew that much. But I had no explanation for where I was. And why now, why when I had so much else to worry about, I found myself in this place.

"This *woman*," spat the leader, "dared to take a treasure from your lord! She violated her ears!"

Gasps and whispers broke out from the crowd before us. There were so many terrified faces and murmuring lips amongst the rare angry expression and the jaw clenched tightly. The women were thin and frail and looked defeated. Even the few who were with child looked malnourished. Though there were some lighter in skin tone and even a few as oak-tone fair as Elfriede with the same blond curls, quite a few were the same dark earth tone of the men.

And their ears. Every last one of them had the pointed ears of men. If this was a dream, I needed desperately to wake up. But I wasn't waking.

The leader let go of my arm, and the other man did the same. I barely had a moment to register my newfound freedom when a sharp kick on my back sent me hurtling forward.

"I don't know how many times we have to make this clear," said the leader. "You follow our orders! You never go against them! And don't you *ever* disrespect our Lord Elric!"

Elric? I couldn't remember if I'd ever heard someone say the lord's name.

The man grabbed at the small of his back and produced a whip. I raised my arms to defend myself, but two other men appeared at my side and flipped me back over.

The whip cracked fast, the snap echoing in my ears only after I felt the sting of pain shoot through my back. I tried to scream, but my tongue was bound. I tried to flinch, but the hands on me gripped tighter.

"This is what becomes of a disobedient woman!" He cracked the whip again.

My eyes rolled to the back of my head, a flash of light offering to let me flee with it into unconsciousness.

"Goncalo! Whatever is the ruckus here?"

A third crackle echoed and the whip lowered, hitting what I thought to be the ground behind me instead of my back.

"Lord Elric," said the leader, the man named Goncalo. "Only just punishment."

The men holding my arms let go and kneeled. The women before me crouched, their faces pushed tightly into the ground, while the men beside me remained more upright but still near the ground.

I rolled over and noticed with pleasure that Goncalo, like the other men, was kneeling. The whip was still clenched in his hands, its tips stained with blood. My blood.

"What has this woman done then?"

At the condescending tone, I looked up. A man sat atop a black horse, dressed entirely in black leather. He was bathed in the firelight, a glisten bouncing off of the metal on his pointed hat with the wide brim. My gaze was drawn to the hand clutching his horse's reins. The light bounced there, too, off a metallic bangle around his wrist. In the light of the fire, the bangle seemed golden, the sole sanctuary of color amongst the black silhouette.

His face was so alluring. His cheeks protruded so, I suspected the bones would cut my fingers should I touch them. His nose was so sharp and straight, it was almost unsettling. His fine brows were drawn together.

There wasn't a flame in his irises, yet they glistened strongly with a fire unseen.

The thought came to me at once: There was no curse over the men in this version of the village. If anything, it was the women who were cursed and tormented.

And this is "Lord Elric" unmasked, without a veil. But no, it can't be him. I just saw him, and he kept his face from me.

Pain shot through my fresh wounds, and I banished all thoughts of longing from my heart. *Why have I come here? What's the point of this?* A tear escaped from one of my eyes. I clenched my jaw and pressed my teeth into the grating muzzle tightly.

"Theft," said Goncalo. "Self-mutilation."

"Oh?" asked the lord. His voice, before so bored, carried with it some hint of interest. It reminded me of my recent conversation with the lord, when the things he said proved so callous, even if his words carried with them a slight trace of charm.

He jumped down off of his horse and crossed the short distance between us.

"And add 'failure to bow before me' to her list of trespasses," he said.

All eyes turned to me. Even the girls and women lifted their heads ever so slightly to get a look.

I felt the pressure exerted from all directions. Instead of succumbing to it, I stood and glared at the lord as he strode over toward me. He was taller than me. But only just.

Women and girls gasped and the men cried out, appalled. Goncalo moved one leg forward to stand, his whip shaking violently over his head.

"Kneel!" called the lord.

Goncalo instantly slid his leg back into position. I didn't move.

Still more whispers and gasps. A flash of anger shot across the lord's face. "Silence!"

All tongues halted. I remembered my muzzle and reached back, my muscles searing in pain with the simple movement. Even as my open flesh smeared against itself and the remnants of the dress I wore, I slid off the muzzle and tossed it on the ground.

The lord straightened his shoulders. He let a flicker of a smile grow on his face.

"Who is she?" he asked, looking straight down at me and not speaking to me at all.

"Was she not at the castle with you tonight, my lord?" asked Goncalo from behind me. "We found her coming out of the woods, holding the stolen blade."

"No, no," said the lord casually. "I would remember *her*. And besides, this blade is unfamiliar to me."

He pulled a short, glowing blade from a too-large sheath at his side. Elgar. So the men had brought it to him after all. He raised it into the air, turning it this way and that, letting the moonlight bounce off of the violet embers. I wanted to rip it out of his grasp.

"A strange blade," said the lord. "Smaller than I am used to, but somehow compelling nonetheless." He shifted his gaze from Elgar to my waist. "Ah. She wears the sheath still."

The man kneeling next to me grew alarmed and tore the sheath off of my waist. The movement stung against the wounds on my lower back, and I flinched.

The man held the sheath toward the lord with both hands. The lord seemed amused. He grabbed the sheath and slid Elgar into it, belting the sheath to his waist. Although his build was thin, the belt was just a bit too small for him; his face strained at the realization, but affix it in place he did, looping it tightly. He placed both hands on his waist as he finished, his elbows extended.

"Well?" he said. "Does the blade become me, girl?"

My leaking blood boiled over.

"My name is Noll," I said, my tongue bursting against fresh sores with each movement. "But only my friends call me that." I thought of the name that had drawn me there. "You will address me as Olivière."

The women and girls screamed. The men jumped to their feet, drawing their blades, shouting. The lord did not stir.

"Silence!" he said again. The women instantly went mute. The men stood beside me and behind their master. Never before then did they so remind me of the men of my village.

The lord tried to intimidate me with his stare, but I wouldn't let him. There was no flame within his dark eyes, and that fire that glistened unseen would not have power over me.

The lord broke the stare first and then laughed. He extended a black leather-gloved hand toward me and fingered the tips of my ears. The men relaxed slightly, and the grip on their hilts eased.

The golden bangle slid from his wrist to his forearm as he rubbed my ear tenderly. I shuddered at the touch and tried to draw back, but the lord seized my arm with his free hand and squeezed tightly.

"Olivière," he said. "I see what he meant about self-mutilation. What have you done to your beautiful ears?" A friendly smile beamed across his stunning features.

My stomach clenched. His face was just the mask of a heartless monster.

"Nothing," I said. "I was born this way."

Women and men alike whispered to their neighbors. The lord laughed, but the joy that spread across his face soon turned cold. He shoved me to the ground before remounting his horse.

"Lying to me gets her a day in the stocks."

He galloped off, leaving the men free to advance on me, their expressions twisted with both joy and fury. These were not the men of my village. They sheathed their swords, and I shut my eyes tight as dozens of hands set out to grab me.

CHAPTER ELEVEN

I couldn't wake from this dream. I was still living it. Hours had passed, and I was still here. *I'm home but not home. That lord, so pompous, so haughty.* I bit my lip. He was the lord I knew and not the lord I knew. But both versions made my blood boil.

The women wouldn't look at me. A young girl would sometimes glance as she passed, her face full of both curiosity and terror—*Nissa*, I'd think in my delirium—and then a woman standing next to her would shield her eyes and push her forward. *Not Nissa.* Nissa would be comforted by Luuk, not a mother.

My mother is dying, and I'm lost in a dream.

Most of the women went out to work in the fields or the quarry. Some piled crops into wheelbarrows and strained to push them into the heart of the village, toward the marketplace and the castle. Some of the women went into the village first thing in the morning, their arms full of tools. A rolling pin. A sewing box.

A gouge and a chisel. *Alvilda.*

Men would sometimes stumble their way into the commune, either intoxicated or merely bold and hungry. They'd enter a shack, or just grab the nearest woman and take off with her, back up the dirt path to the better homes within the village. Some of the men were laughing, some angry. Some were old, others could be no older than fifteen. Every woman looked terrified. Most of the men let their gaze fall over me in the stocks briefly, a few reaching out to caress my ear as they passed. Some would say things I couldn't hear. One licked his lips and smiled wickedly. I didn't fight back. I was too weak to care.

My throat burned with thirst. And my arms, tongue, and back ached with a feeling stronger than the ache of my heart all these past few months.

No one had attended to my wounds, and I felt my energy draining with each breath. From time to time, I would slip blissfully into unconsciousness, but I would wake again what seemed like moments later, my stomach growling and my head pounding. The sun felt hot and heavy over my head and at last, after what felt like days, I fell asleep and did not wake for quite some time.

~

MY EYELIDS FLUTTERED OPEN. It was nighttime and the full moon had begun waning, but light from moonbeams lit the commune. The dying embers of a fire cast shadows over the empty area in the center. No one stirred.

I heard a rustle behind me and realized that my back no longer stung. It felt warm and soothed as the ache was leeched from deep within me. My eyes grazed the ground and saw my shadow; I was being bathed in a violet glow.

A moan leaped from my lips, and I craned my neck as much as the stocks would let me. A small figure moved in the dark, the violet glow surging and receding with its movements.

"Who's there?" My lips cracked, and my tongue bled again.

The figure jumped.

After a moment, it crawled forward. A little boy.

Jurij.

No. I had never seen Jurij unmasked so young. I had never seen any boy so young unmasked. He was seven or eight years at the most. Unless it was a trick of the night, his skin was even darker than a grown man's.

The boy lifted his hands toward my face, and the violet light fled outward from his fingers. My tongue strengthened, my lips moistened, and the sting on my cheeks receded. I even stopped feeling thirst and was no longer bothered by hunger.

I closed my eyes and bathed in the warmth of the light, hesitant to open them even after I felt the light fade. And then I remembered. I was home, but not home. I'd seen this boy's face, and he was all right. No men hid in this place that was and was not my village. My eyes flew open.

"Thank you," I said. The words were not enough. He had ended all of my pain.

The boy nodded and fell backward to sit on the ground. He stared at me, questioning.

"What's your name?" I asked.

"His name is Ailill," said a woman's voice that stirred something joyous in my heart.

A tall, dark woman strode into my sight. I recognized her as one of the few women who had stood alone in front of the fire the night previous. Her features were unfamiliar, her face too young, but I saw a trace of my friend Alvilda in her expression.

"My name is Avery," she said. "And I want to know where you come from."

It was hurting my neck to look up at her from the stocks, so I let my head fall and focused instead on the boy on the ground. He tensed a bit at my gaze and pulled himself over to Avery, hugging her leg and burying his face within the folds of her apron.

"How did he heal me?" I asked.

Avery crouched in front of me, careful not to disturb Ailill much in her decent. She swept him into the crux of her arm.

"I'm the one asking questions," she said.

"I... I don't know how to explain where I come from. Other than I don't come from here."

"Obviously," scoffed Avery. "Despite what men think, we're not stupid. All of us knew immediately you had never been in the commune before, that you weren't one of our members who had run off, stolen a sword, and lopped off her ears. But few of the men care to remember our faces, so it's no surprise that not a single one noticed that you were new."

These were not men. At least, they weren't the men I knew. I tensed, thinking of the whip and the muzzle. The stocks and my stolen sword. And Lord Elric. "Will you alert them?"

Avery sighed. "Your secret is safe. For now. None of the women have spoken to the men about it, but I recommend you go easy on your revulsion, lest you draw even more attention to yourself. There are ways to work around a man's orders without defying him outright."

Ailill adjusted Avery's apron so that he could peek just a little over the material. I smiled at him. He ducked immediately back under the apron.

Avery watched our exchange and hugged Ailill closer. She kissed him atop his head and rustled her hand through his short black hair. She stood and pulled Ailill up with her.

"You'd better get home," she said. "It'll be sunrise soon, and they'll notice you're missing."

She tapped him on the back and pushed him forward toward the dirt path through the village. Ailill stopped a few paces from us, pausing to look back.

"Go on," encouraged Avery. She waved him forward.

Ailill did as bidden, walking up the path until he disappeared into the darkness.

Avery put a hand on each hip. My head fell and I stared at her legs, which stood slightly apart.

"Now listen," she said, every bit Alvilda again. "If there's anyone who understands hating men, it's me. But there's a way and a place for certain things, and I don't want you to ruin what we've started."

She sighed. "I'll show you around tomorrow after they free you. If you have any skill with a blade, you may be able to work with an ax. I'm the woodcarver, and tomorrow I'm heading to the woods to chop down a tree."

My heart ached, hopefully, for the ax, the chisel, and the gouge—for home.

~

"STAY QUIET," murmured Avery out of the corner of her mouth. "Keep your eyes on the ground and move forward quickly. Stick to the side of the path."

I found it hard to follow her orders, but I kept my head down, my hand clenched tightly on my ax. Disappointed I was no better at the thread and the needle than she was, and reluctant to speak to the other women about me, Avery had done a halfhearted job at sewing up the gashes in the back of my dress. They had few frocks to spare, and she thought it best I not attract attention with my healed back exposed. Even so, it was barely holding together, and I had to walk stiffly to keep it from popping open.

From time to time, my gaze wandered upward, and I caught a glimpse of men laughing and eating, drinking and dancing on the streets and through the building windows. And women and girls, their eyes always on the ground, serving food, sitting on laps, and being pulled and pushed and forced about among the revelry.

When we finally broke free of the village and started down the path toward the woods, I opened my mouth to speak.

Avery hushed me with a slight movement of her hand. "Not yet."

When we stepped into the woods, and I felt the cover of the trees hide us from view, I spoke. "What's—"

"Be quiet," murmured Avery.

I followed her down the path.

Some of the men in chainmail lined the path in the midst of the woods ahead of us. They chatted and leaned against trees or sat on the side of the dirt road. I remembered Avery's instructions and snapped my head back down.

"Off for more wood today, Carver-woman?"

"Yes, sir," replied Avery.

She set a foot off of the dirt path and into a familiar route through the trees. I followed after her.

"Don't go far," said one of the men.

"Yes, sir."

A hand reached out to grab my arm and pull me backward.

"It's her!" cried a man's voice. Instinctively, even against all I knew in my own version of the village, I looked up at him.

He seemed surprised to see my face. A look of anger and something far more salacious warped his features.

Avery appeared beside me, her eyes locked on to the ground around our feet. "I needed a sturdy hand to help with the chopping, sir," she said.

I dropped my eyes again.

"She's a feisty one," said the man. "Already up and moving. I can see why you'd think she was suited for hard labor."

"Yes, sir," replied Avery.

"Carry on," said the man. He let go of me, but as I turned, I felt a strong slap against my backside and heard the echo of the men's laughter. My face flushed red, and I bit my tongue so as not to scream.

Avery led me through the unmarked path that I knew led to my secret cavern. The farther we got from the dirt path, the faster she moved. Finally, just before the cave entrance, she gave a tremendous whack to the nearest tree, letting her ax rest in the trunk, and walked into the cave.

I gripped my ax tightly and followed Avery inside.

When we finally reached the pool and the violet glow, Avery faced me, one eyebrow slightly raised. "You walk through a dark cavern sightless with a sharp and deadly weapon in your grasp?"

I shrugged and laid the ax down on a nearby spike. My chest tightened for a moment as I looked at the pool. It could lead me home. But I couldn't jump in with her watching.

"I've been here before," I said.

"So I see." Avery sighed. "All right, no more games. Who are you and what are you doing here?"

"My name is Noll—Olivière, as I said, Woodcarver's daughter. I don't know why I'm here exactly."

Avery scoffed. "The woodcarver's daughter? I'm the woodcarver, and I have no children, much to my delight."

I cocked my head. "And Ailill?"

"He's my brother, not my son. Do I look old enough to have a child that grown?"

I looked her over, bathed in the violet light. I supposed, as much as I kept comparing her to Alvilda, she wasn't as old as my friend. She was perhaps more Elfriede's or my age, although her hardened stance and the muscles that rippled over her arms despite her small stature seemed to indicate a much more weighty life than ours.

"You didn't really answer my question," said Avery coldly.

"I'm a different woodcarver's daughter, obviously," I said,

113

trying to meet ice with ice. "I trained under Alvilda the lady carver and observed the work of Gideon, my father."

Avery tensed. "Your father works?"

The grip I had on my elbows loosened. "Yes. Doesn't yours?"

Avery cackled. "No man works. And my father, whom I thank the skies is now dead, was the most indolent of all."

I shifted from one foot to the other uncomfortably. "And your mother?"

Avery glared at me. "Dead as well. But in her case, I thank the skies for the end of her suffering. She wasn't sturdy enough for this world. And she was far too beautiful. That makes you stand out too much."

She thanks the skies, but not the goddess. But what love have I for the first goddess myself?

I nodded, thinking of the women grabbed by the men during my day in the stocks. Instinctively, I swept tendrils of hair over my ears, thinking of the hungry looks to which I had already been victim due to their discrepancy. I looked at Avery. She was pretty in her own way, but I wondered if she purposefully kept a sour look on her face to distort her features.

"My mother is not well," I said. "But even before her illness, she never had to work like the women here. And Father's always eager to help her with the housework."

Avery came a few paces closer, her gaze fixed down on me. "Then you are definitely not of this land," she said. "I don't know how you crossed the mountains or what exactly there is that lies beyond. All I want to know is if you can take us back with you."

I swallowed and glanced guiltily at the cavern pool behind her.

The chorus of voices calling my name was but a whisper now. *"Olivière."*

I watched Avery to see if she wondered why the cave echoed my name, but she didn't move. Her eyes betrayed hearing nothing but the undying echo of the trickle of water.

Can I, alone, hear it? Do the voices call only to me? The chorus of voices had led me here, and they were no longer shouting my name, demanding me to come. They whispered, letting me know I could go home, but the pool didn't want me to go just yet. *But I do. How can I stay here, when Mother is ill?*

"No," I replied.

Avery sighed and stared hungrily at the ax I had propped against the spike. "Then there's only one hope for us."

I followed her gaze and asked a question I had wondered since I first entered this dream version of the village. "Why don't the women fight back? The men seem open to a surprise attack." It felt appropriate to have a real battle here, a battle like that from stories, where there was such wrongdoing.

Avery scoffed and picked up my ax, turning it backward and forward in her hands. "I cannot rouse enough of them. The men seem lazy—and they are—but they have quick reflexes and brute strength. Our only advantages are in our numbers and the men's smugness. But most of the women will not even entertain the idea of revolution. They're too scared."

"But surely they can see that with enough of us and a directed attack, the men will fall."

Avery smiled. "*Us?* So you'll help us?"

"Of course!" I lied.

Avery put the ax down and leaned on it, much like the men did with their swords. "Perhaps you're not so bad, outsider. Then there is just one more thing you'll need to know. The men of this village have a gift in their blood."

"A gift?" I asked. "Like Ailill's healing?"

Avery nodded. "They all can heal. But you'll only find little boys willing to use it for our aid before they get too corrupted and their hearts turn black. In their lives of luxury, men have little need for healing for themselves. If you want a man to die, you need to take him by surprise so he and his companions won't be able to heal him in time."

She spoke of killing a person like it was a possibility, like people would ever think to do that outside of play and stories. *Perhaps I'm living a story right now.*

She sighed and leaned the ax back on the rock. "Let's go chop down a tree. I'm sure you'll find it relieves a lot of tension."

It probably would. But this wasn't my fight.

As soon as she disappeared into the darkness, I dove back into the pool.

CHAPTER TWELVE

My mind was blissfully blank as I walked back through the village—yes, this was my village, it had to be—and onto the path home. It was all a dream. My clothing, ripped and torn, dripped from the pond's water. Ripped mostly on the back. But that had to be a coincidence. I'd probably torn it on some sediment. Maybe I'd been sick under water, even unconscious. I could have died. I'd been stupid. I'd lost the sword I'd demanded from the lord in that water, but I had no desire to search for it. I needed badly to go home.

"*Olivière,*" the pool had whispered as I put it behind me. But I ignored it. To believe what I'd dreamed was real was more than I could bear. *Everyone already thinks I'm an oddity. First I'm nobody's goddess and then I'm the veiled lord's. I don't even want to think of what I could be after having such visions.*

I had to prove to myself I'd just been dreaming. If I closed my eyes, I could still feel the pain of the whip across my back. But my back was smooth now. Unhurt. There was no proof I was ever there.

At the edge of the woods, I breathed a sigh of relief. My home was there. I'd reached the flattened grass where the carriage had turned around day after day. I took note of a few broken lily petals that had floated across the dirt road, still vibrant and purple despite their pressing fate.

The door to the house was cracked open. "Mother? Father? Elfriede?"

I pushed on the door and heard the creak of the hinges echo against the silence inside. There was no light, and the fire was dead, but thanks to the moonlight that crept inside, I could just make out a figure in the chair at the table that faced the doorway.

"Mother?" I whispered.

Bit by bit, the lantern light revealed the figure. The eyes, dark with just a hint of the flames that ought to have burned brightly. The scowl on the lips of his strained face. And in one hand, on the table, the same blue dress I'd seen Mother wearing before I'd visited the lord. It felt like days ago, but I knew it to be just a few hours earlier.

"I hope you're happy, Noll," said Father. His voice cracked and strained with each syllable. "You wouldn't help her. And now she's gone."

Elfriede shrieked from where she sat atop the bed she and I shared; she buried her head into the shoulder of the man, *her* man, who comforted her.

I stumbled, the breath completely sucked out of me. There was no one there to catch me.

SIX MONTHS WENT by in a blur of numbness and woodcarving.

Every day the memory of the world in my drowning dream faded. Every day the memory of the lord doing nothing, caring only about his Returning, grew stronger. I told Father I'd tried to get the lord to help us. He didn't care. I didn't act soon enough. I wasn't there when she died and faded into nothingness—neither were Elfriede or Jurij, apparently, but they didn't merit Father's blame. So I didn't bother telling them about my dream. Why would they believe me? Why would they care? I hardly believed it myself.

The first thing I carved after Mother's death was my own interpretation of a heartless monster. It was a beast like the beasts of legend, a wolf, a bear, and a snake, all in one. I left an open cavity over the left side of its chest to show that there was no heart within it. Father didn't notice it. Elfriede gave me an uneasy smile and told me it may do some good scaring off rabbits from the garden. And that's where she put it, half-buried in leaves and dirt.

The day before my seventeenth birthday there wasn't enough scrap wood in the land for my trembling fingers. I finished the last few dozen projects I'd started—wooden animals, trees, and flowers—by adding a few more details than necessary. I ruined more than one, but my fingers wouldn't stop peeling away at the layers of wood. I started new projects I knew I would never finish, but it was just as well because the most I could think of carving was a blob of mud or a wooden rock.

My effort wasn't lost on Elfriede. Although, despite my better hopes, I thought she may have been more upset about the piles of sawdust all over her kitchen table than the reason for the mess. "Clean that off, will you? Father will be home soon."

"Here, let me help." Jurij released his hand from around Elfriede's shoulder and the one being became two. I didn't say anything as I set the carved pieces on the mantle, next to a wooden lily. Far better work than mine.

As Jurij wiped the dust into a rag, I numbly placed bowls and spoons for four people at our table. A brief jolt of pain brought me to life as I placed Jurij's setting down next to Elfriede's, and I thought of who had once sat there. "Ah. Good day, Jurij," came a slow, slurring voice, a croaking echo of what it had been. I glanced up to see Father in the doorway. He stumbled his way to his chair, a shade of the father I had known.

Father had the same features, but they were muted somehow. His strong, dark chin poked through a rough, unkempt black-and-gray beard. His curls drooped and stuck out in all directions, although somehow the pointed tips of his ears made a slight appearance through the wild tangle of knots. His eyes sparkled, but in a different way than they once had. The flame within them burned as lightly as a candle in its final few moments before the wick withered away.

Perhaps that described my father. He had lost his sunlight and was left only with the dimmer echoes in the children she left behind. What room was there for happiness with the sun's light gone forever? The moon alone could never be enough, not after years of dancing in the sun's delight. It was just a matter of time. Nissa's father had died the same evening as his wife. They rarely lasted beyond a year.

"Good day, Gideon," said Jurij. He tore himself from Elfriede long enough to put his hand on Father's shoulder. "How're Vena and Elweard?"

"Huh?" asked Father absently. Often these days you had to ask a question more than once.

"The tavern masters," I reminded him. Father practically kept them in business since Mother's death.

"Oh, fine, fine." Father's eyes glossed over.

"Father?" I asked, covering his trembling hand with mine. He looked at me, the smallest of smiles edging onto his lips. The light flickered in his eyes. It was still there. Of course it was. But only just.

Jurij picked up Father's and my bowls and brought them over to the fire. Jurij and Elfriede worked in perfect harmony, one ladling the stew and the other holding the bowls out to receive it.

"Vena asked about your wedding last night," said Father as he withdrew his hand from mine. For a moment, my heart nearly stopped.

"And what did she want to know?" asked Jurij jovially. He placed the stew bowls in front of Father and me.

I felt a rush of relief. Of course. *Their* wedding.

Father smiled, his face almost as warm as it had once been, his eyes growing brighter. "How much ale you'll need for the festivities, of course!"

Jurij shook his head as he grabbed the empty bowls for himself and Elfriede. "You know we only want a few bottles at the most." He paused a moment as he slid soundlessly next to Elfriede. Even from the table, I could see the lines burrowed deep between her brows.

"Or maybe none at all," muttered Elfriede. She plopped the stew into their bowls with a little less tenderness than was her custom.

My father's face fell. "I'll be on my best behavior. I promise you."

No one spoke.

Father and I sipped from our stew for a few moments longer, and Jurij sat down next to us, placing the bowls on the table and picking up his spoon.

Elfriede lingered back at the pot for a few minutes longer, stirring and stirring. Out of the corner of my eye, I saw her dab her cheek with her apron.

"Noll," she said tentatively. She stirred the stew with a little too much interest. "Would you be willing to help Darwyn deliver the bread to the castle?"

I drummed my fingers on the tabletop. "I didn't think the bakers were so busy they couldn't spare a few dozen members of their family to deliver bread to His Lordship."

"Noll. Help Darwyn deliver the bread," interrupted my father. He tried to take a sip of his stew, but his hand shook and the stew slid off the spoon, spilling onto the table. Whether because he had now gone a short while without his bottle or because he could barely contain his rage at me, I wasn't sure.

He only managed to truly seem among the living these days when it came to rejoicing in Elfriede's wedding and lamenting my unspoken opposition to my own.

I glanced out the window. Newly unmasked Darwyn stood in front of our house next to his cart full of bread. Father had no doubt come straight with him from the village and had let Elfriede know ahead of time.

"I promised I'd meet Alvilda after lunch."

"Noll, you need to stop with that woodworking—"

I didn't let Father finish. I grabbed a chisel and a block of half-carved wood and bolted out of the door, walking straight past Darwyn—no doubt fuming with impatience to be done with the task and back in his goddess's arms. I headed down the dirt path, my head held high in the western direction.

The wheels on the cart squealed. Darwyn had no interest in waiting for me to change my mind. Just as well. I wasn't going to.

Arrow bolted up the pathway from where he'd been playing nearby to lick me goodbye. I pulled the chisel out of his reach so he wouldn't hurt himself and kept marching forward. Arrow followed me for a bit, jumping and yipping and straining against all hope that the wood I carried would prove edible. Perhaps to him it was.

"Arrow! Here boy!"

As I came over the hill, Arrow's mistress echoed his name, and he went running. How like the master of the golden dog who'd birthed him.

Goodbye to you, too, Elfriede. I felt like a nuisance in my own home. Jurij had taken Mother's place. Mine was practically taken by a dog.

It took me longer than it should have to cross the small distance to the Tailor's. Weariness invaded my feet as the shop finally came into focus. My palm crushed against the uneven surface of the chisel handle, which showcased an elegant carving of a string of roses through which a series of butterflies fluttered their fair wings. It was one of my father's better works, from back when he loved woodworking so much he even carved his tool handles. I could probably carve handles. But I wouldn't forget the thorns on the vines and might include a few butterflies whose wings had ripped as they passed by them.

I stopped and took a closer look at the Tailors' sign, which Father had carved some years ago. I would have put the image of the thread and needle looping through the letters in the word "Tailor." I wondered if Alvilda would have a large piece of wood I could use to design my own sign for practice. If not, I could chop some down.

A shiver ran down my spine as the thought of the ax brought up faded memories of Avery from my dream. I'd left her before the dream had finished.

Anyway, signs take time. And you're out of time, Noll.

The door to the shop opened abruptly, revealing the tired face of Mistress Tailor. Bow scampered out past her feet and jumped up to greet me. I placed the chisel and wood on the ground so I could take her head in my hands and rub her ears.

"You're late," said Mistress Tailor, not even bothering to greet me. "Why didn't—" She glanced around and the corner of her mouth twitched ever so slightly. "Oh. Noll. I thought Jurij might have been coming home. For once."

"He's at my place," I said, although that was probably obvious. "If you'd like, I can tell him—"

She eyed the things I'd left on the ground and waved a hand. "No. Don't bother. If you're heading to Alvilda's, send my husband over. There's enough work around here for ten." She turned to Bow. "Come on, do your business. Clothes aren't going to sew themselves."

I tucked my tool and wood block into my sash and started down the village path, but as I passed her, Mistress Tailor had one more thing to say. "I wish you the best tomorrow. Whatever 'the best' may be."

I was taken aback. Mistress Tailor, the stout and surly woman of few words, had said what no one else would. And she seemed to honestly mean it.

"Thank you."

Mistress Tailor practically growled. "All right. No use crying over the broken thread. I'm sure Alvilda will have some nice words for you." With that, she and Bow went back into the Tailor Shop, and I was left to face the onslaught of people between one end of the village and the other alone.

If I thought I attracted attention before I became the lord's goddess, for being a rambunctious child or for having no man to call my own, I had no idea of the type of interest I would have to deal with as the day of my supposed Returning approached.

"Blessed be your birthday tomorrow!" An unmasked man next to a stand of produce tilted his hat at me, the grin on his lips a sign he had no idea how his words cut me to the quick.

I mumbled my thanks, spinning to get out of the way of the tanner and his cart of hides, itching to get away from the busy path that led to the center of the village.

"Watch where you're going, you foolish girl!"

The woman startled me and I nearly fell, flinging my hands out to steady myself. My fingers smacked against a wicker basket, my nails catching in a dark gauze laid over it. The gauze began to shift and I realized with horror what I'd done.

Not a basket. A bassinet.

"I'm so sorry, Ma'am!" I hurried to readjust the gauze, grabbing my finger with the other hand and carefully untangling the jagged nail from the thin material, all while not daring to look down. "Is he all right?"

"Oh. It's you." The woman struggled to balance a baby in the crook of her left arm with the handled bassinet slid across her right. The baby sucked its fist and leaned into her shoulder. She had powerfully dark brown eyes slightly covered by a mess of dark brown curls. "I apologize for yelling at you." The mother bent awkwardly to tighten the gauze over the baby in the bassinet.

"You needn't apologize," I said. "I should have looked where I was going. I put your baby in danger." I stared at the girl, the only type of baby I'd ever seen. "Twins?"

"Yes. The first goddess blessed me with both a girl and a boy, with a daughter to take care of me and my husband in our later years and a son to do the same for his goddess's family, to learn the value of love." She bounced her baby girl higher and shifted the bassinet onto her elbow once again. "It's fine. It was an accident." She smiled, falteringly. "We're so looking forward to tomorrow. My husband is one of the men playing the music. We've already gotten the copper for it." The baby on her left arm cried out suddenly, her face twisting in fury. "Shh, shh," said the woman, rocking her back and forth.

I didn't want to tell her there was nothing special "tomorrow." Besides, I hadn't gotten an invitation to my Returning. He must have assumed I'd go, but I had no plans to be there.

"Noll, praise the goddess!" A hand touched my shoulder. Elweard. He had a barrel under one arm and a grin that took up half his face. "Vena and I were just talking about you. We received so many coppers for the Returning—we're so looking forward to finally meeting him, and thanking him for all his orders—and the invitation asked us to provide enough for the whole village to drink." Elweard laughed, but he wasn't one to wait for responses, which was just as well. "But he paid us far more than that! The village couldn't possibly drink that much, even if there were enough wheat and grapes to make enough ale and wine, and we wondered if it would be wrong if we kept the copper and sent the two of you and his servants free drinks for life, or if the lord would need it back—"

Elweard droned on, and the woman curtseyed at me best she could with one screaming baby in her arms and the child's twin joining in the cacophony from beneath his veil. Stepping aside and putting the bassinet on a bench in front of a nearby shop, she tugged at the gauze gently, shifting it so slightly I could hardly believe it moved at all.

"Noll?" Elweard's voice drew me out of my reverie. "*Do* you need Vena to stand up for you and the lord? I know you probably have another in mind. Alvilda, maybe, since you've been helping her with carving, or your sister's man's mother—"

"No!" I gritted my teeth and fought hard to keep the anger buried within. The woman stood up, tightening the gauze over the bassinet, a deep breath visibly escaping her lips. I clutched my skirt with both hands as the woman disappeared into the crowd, that black gauze on the bassinet threatening to drown me in memories of the veiled lord, in images of me and him where Elfriede and Jurij had once stood, in him removing the veil, in what I would find beneath it... "No. Thank you, Elweard, but no."

Elweard scratched his head. "All right. Vena thought we ought to offer, that's all. But about the copper..."

"I have to go." I spun around, almost smacking into another woman. At least this one carried bread in her basket instead of babies.

"Oh my! Noll!" Mistress Baker placed a hand on her chest. "Just the woman I was about to go visit. I thought maybe I should ask which of these breads you want served at the ceremony and which we should just send home with everyone." She shifted the loaves aside in her basket, producing one roll after another. "The lord sent us enough copper to feed the village three times over, so we've been working hard and making everything, but we simply can't carry it all to the Great Hall tomorrow. My husband hasn't slept a wink in days, I swear—"

I swirled around as if in a dance and darted through the crowd, leaving poor Mistress Baker to her breads and probable confusion once she looked up to find me gone.

Relief flooded my body when I finally made it across town to Alvilda's. I almost tore the door open, but then I remembered her visitor and knocked before I entered. Alvilda told me to wait a moment, and then to let myself in.

"Good day, Noll!" called a cheerful voice as I entered. Master Tailor's worn down owl mask greeted me from Alvilda's ever-dusty eating table. "How goes the woodcarver's daughter?"

I sighed and slipped into the seat next to him, placing the chisel and the wood on the table, where they seemed right at home. Alvilda was by her workbench, lost in the task of whittling a chair leg. I could see the as-yet-unfinished headboard propped up against the wall in the corner. She said nothing.

"The same," I offered. I didn't bother to ask whether he was inquiring about the daughter in front of him or the one who made his son's life worth living.

Master Tailor answered for me. "I bet she's excited about her wedding in the spring!" Even though everyone in the village was excited for the Returning, the most important things remained the same. Their own men, their own goddesses. Their children and the goddesses and men belonging to their children. I was just an excuse to have a celebration. Copper in their pocket, a day off from work.

Alvilda dropped the chair leg she was carving and shook her head in disbelief. She threw her gouge on the workbench, marched across the room, and whacked Master Tailor on the back of his head. Sawdust went flying with each movement.

"Ow!" Master Tailor rubbed the back of his dark curls.

"Go home!" barked Alvilda.

"What?" asked Master Tailor quizzically. "I'm excited about Noll's Returning, too, of course. Nissa has been so helpful in making the lord's new garments. Not that they're much different than the usual garments he orders, but Nissa does such a good job, they look better than—"

Alvilda crossed her arms. "Out."

Master Tailor shook his owl head and stood up from the table. "Sometimes I wonder if you think you're my goddess instead of Siofra."

Alvilda tapped her foot. "That's a disturbing thought. At least you can choose whether or not to obey my orders. Although I do suggest you choose wisely."

Master Tailor waved his hand lazily in her direction. "I'm going, I'm going."

"Mistress Tailor asked me to tell you to come home," I interjected.

Master Tailor tensed and moved so quickly out the door that I could hardly believe he'd had time to cross the room.

Alvilda shook her head and filled the seat that Master Tailor had just emptied. "You have to watch how you word your orders from a goddess to her man. They're almost as effective as direct orders from the woman herself, so long as they have a basis in truth."

That was true. I felt a little guilty messing around with that kind of power, even if I hadn't intended to. "Sorry."

She shrugged and began playing with her fingers, concerned with picking out some of the sawdust stuck under her nails. "So," said Alvilda, finally giving up her futile quest to clean her nails and slapping her palms against the table. She picked up my half-block, half-rock piece of wood and examined it. "How goes the carving?"

I thought back to the ruined sculptures and other blobs of wood that looked no better than the piece Alvilda turned over in her hands. "Spectacularly," I lied.

Alvilda put the wood back on the table. "And how goes the carver?"

I waved a hand. "He's the same as always."

Alvilda shook her head and grabbed my hand that rested on the table. I flinched. "I meant the *other* carver in the family," she said.

I started bawling.

Alvilda got up from her seat and swooped in to embrace me, but that only made me cry harder. She let me cry a few moments more before she took my face in her hands and put on her most stunning smile. I wondered if this was how Jaron saw her when he first knew she was his goddess, and my heart ached for the pain he must be feeling even at that moment, to know that he would never hold her in his arms as I did.

"So, what would you like to do today?" asked Alvilda. I hadn't actually told her I was going to come over.

I glanced toward the work area of her home and the fallen chair leg. "Don't you have work to do?"

Alvilda shook her head and began shoving a few buns, some cheese, and a bottle into a picnic basket. "Nothing that can't wait another few days," she said. I noticed with some pleasure that her picnic basket's handle featured what I thought might be swords and daggers.

"A picnic sounds wonderful," I said.

CHAPTER THIRTEEN

Alvilda's choice spot for a picnic wasn't my own, but I imagined she didn't want me to head back home before I had to. We enjoyed the meager meal in silence under a tree just a ways from the commune. My eyes guiltily wandered over the moaning, wretched men sprawled out on the ground or walking about, lifting one foot after the other slowly, aimlessly. It was an odd choice for my last day of freedom, but I had no place else I'd be welcomed. After a little while, Alvilda went inside her home to grab my chisel. She gave me a new block of wood, and I'd started carving a flower. A lily.

It felt good to eat, to carve, and to not think. To feel less alone but to not have to answer to anyone.

The feeling didn't last beyond a few hours.

"Siofra sent me!"

I craned my head behind me lazily to see Master Tailor half jogging, half walking from the village toward our shady retreat. The closer he got, the louder his panting grew. The owl mask blocked his features from me, but I could almost imagine the strain on his face. He doubled over as he reached us, resting his hands on his thighs.

"What is it, Coll?" asked Alvilda. Her hand had tensed

around the picnic basket, and she looked ready to jump up and run.

Master Tailor waved impatiently in Alvilda's direction. "Siofra sent me…"

Alvilda rolled her eyes. "Yes, we got that part."

Master Tailor took a few more gasps of air through the horribly confining small hole that opened over his mouth. I wondered briefly if death superseded a goddess's commands or if a command gave a man the strength to overcome even death to see the order followed through.

"Take it easy," she said. "You can't follow your goddess's order if you're dead."

Master Tailor nearly choked on his breaths mixed with laughter. For a moment, my muscles relaxed, but Master Tailor's troubled laugh still made me nervous.

"Mistress Tailor sent you?" I asked, rather impatiently.

Master Tailor took a great swell of breath and stood erect. "There's been an earthquake."

My stomach churned. Alvilda looked as panicked as I felt. *With Ingrith gone, who would dare look at the castle?*

Master Tailor continued, oblivious of the discomfort of his audience. "We were sewing. The kids were helping out." He nodded his owl head. "That Nissa's going to be a fine tailor. I'm so happy Luuk found the goddess in her."

"Coll," said Alvilda. "The earthquake."

Master Tailor pointed east. "We heard a tremendous noise in the direction of the woods. It was like the earth was groaning, and we could feel it moving beneath our feet. It caused Siofra to drop the shirt she was sewing and tumble clear off her chair." Master Tailor paused, perhaps in pain at the idea of Mistress Tailor tumbling, even though he was under orders to continue speaking.

I had more pressing concerns. "Who looked at the castle?"

Master Tailor didn't respond to my question. "We went outside, and Siofra told me she saw a black carriage come out of the woods and stop in front of the woodcarver's home. I wanted to go check on Jurij and Elfriede, but Siofra stopped me. She said I had to explain what happened to Noll first, and then tell Noll to go." He directed his owl mask at me. "Go."

If Mistress Tailor hadn't worded her commands exactly right, he was liable to scream at me to go like a crazy person without any further explanation. If Alvilda thought it odd that her brother would turn into an unthinking being to speak Mistress Tailor's tale, she didn't indicate it. I wondered if Mistress Tailor often used her husband as a sort of messenger.

The black carriage. But it was too early in the day for it to come, waiting for its passenger.

Waiting for me.

But someone had caused the earth to shake. Elfriede wouldn't have been so foolish, would she?

Alvilda started gathering the basket and blanket. "Let's go." She shoved the items unceremoniously at Master Tailor, and he scrambled to catch them. "Drop these off at my home and then go comfort your wife. I'll send word as soon as we know that Jurij, Elfriede, and Gideon are well."

Master Tailor stood silent for a moment, shifting his weight from one foot to the other. He was finally free to do as he pleased, and he clearly seemed uncomfortable with the idea. Alvilda stepped up to fill the void that Mistress Tailor's fulfilled command had left behind in the man. "You've done as Siofra asked," said Alvilda, although she didn't turn to look at her brother. She grabbed me by the wrist and started dragging me toward the village. "Get going."

I wasn't entirely sure Alvilda didn't have as much power over him as his goddess because Master Tailor got his second wind and parted from us, jogging toward Alvilda's home.

As we entered the middle of town, Alvilda let go of my wrist and put an arm around my shoulders, pushing me slightly forward so that I could keep up the pace. The closer we got to the Tailors' at the east end of the village, the more people were out of their homes and shops and murmuring to one another. Almost every one of them would glare at us as we passed, a few whispering to their neighbors. I suddenly felt protected under Alvilda's tight grip on my shoulders.

"If someone looked at the castle by my house, why would the ground shake this far out?" I asked Alvilda quietly.

Alvilda shook her head. "I'm not sure. It seems that the farther east we get, the more people were affected."

129

She was right. The crowds grew larger as we moved on, and we had to fight our way through the center of the road, sometimes only able to shove our way through after a few curt exclamations of "Excuse us!" from Alvilda.

At last we broke free from the village horde, nearing the Tailor Shop at the very end of the line of houses. There stood Mistress Tailor in the open doorway with Luuk, Nissa, and Bow.

"Alvilda!" cried Mistress Tailor. Her voice had a frightening quality to it, one I wasn't used to hearing from the taciturn woman. She broke free from her grip on Luuk's hand and rushed forward, practically shoving me aside to embrace Alvilda.

Alvilda jumped, and her arms hung to her side limply. Her eyes flickered from left to right and then focused over Mistress Tailor's shoulders at the kids and Bow. She gave Mistress Tailor a quick pat on the back.

"Coll told us," she said. She gripped Mistress Tailor's shoulders, and she pushed her away so she could look at her. "He's on his way back."

Mistress Tailor's eyes glistened wet with tears. Her face seemed almost girlish. She stepped back and cradled one arm tightly against her chest. No sooner had she done this than Master Tailor's voice came booming from the crowd behind us. "Excuse me!"

Alvilda grabbed me by the wrist. "Come on!"

As we made our way up the first hill, Alvilda's ashen face turned a more sullen shade of olive-gray. I tugged my wrist free and ran in front of her.

My lungs, though ready to burst, inhaled the cool air imbued with an eerie fog that appeared as I came over the hill. The fog burned in my throat and likely kept the castle entirely from view. I was too afraid to check.

When my home emerged through the fog over one last little hill, I nearly stumbled forward. Arrow gave a low-toned growl from the mist beside me. The poor pup was tied to a tree at the very edge of the woods a few yards away, his muzzle wrapped in what appeared to be fine black silken twine. But more arresting than poor Arrow's plight was the black carriage blocking the doorway of my home.

On top of the carriage in the driver's seat sat one of the specters with his cloud-white hair tied neatly into a tail, a few curls framing his face, which at first glance appeared to be eerily alluring, but on closer inspection, was flawed and wrinkled. The men may have been much older than I had first guessed them to be. Still, his hair was not the gray, dirty white of the older men in the village. It was a pure, unblemished white hair that retained its youthful silkiness.

The specter looked forward, his hands tightly grasping black silken reins. He didn't so much as glance in my direction. The four pitch-black horses that stood erect in front of him were surprisingly silent. I hadn't seen many horses, not outside of the livestock, but I knew that I ought to hear snorts or whinnies, see them shuffling their feet or shaking their manes—*something* to indicate that they were bored just standing around. These horses gave me the impression that they were above showing such crassness, or perhaps they viewed it as weakness. *How have I never noticed before?*

Arrow let out a pitiful whine. For a moment, I thought of going to free him, but my heart was pounding, and I was eager to get inside.

I walked past the coachman without a word. Circling the horses, I stepped back as another specter appeared before me. The black in his eyes overwhelmed me, but just for a moment. I moved to step around him. The specter anticipated the movement and stepped to block me. I moved back to push through on my original path. The specter blocked me again. Daring him to try again, I stared into his black eyes.

"Let us through!"

Alvilda sprinted up behind me. I hadn't realized I'd put so much distance between us. Her face contorted in fury, and she breathed hard as she slipped in beside me. "What's going on here?" she snapped, taking a quick look at the carriage, the horses, and the specters in turn.

The specters said nothing. But I knew they wouldn't.

"They won't answer you," I said, as much to myself as to Alvilda. I didn't tear my gaze from the black eyes of the specter in front of me, waiting to see if he would prove me wrong. He didn't move. He didn't blink.

"This is the young lady's home," said Alvilda, slowly and with a hint of threat behind each word. "Let us in."

The lord's servant didn't move. Alvilda and I did the dance with him again, trying to move as one past him, but he blocked us. We gave each other a barely noticeable nod, split apart, and tried to pass by the specter via both sides at once. He moved to block me. Another specter appeared like a phantom from the mist at the side of the coach and blocked Alvilda.

"This is ridiculous!" shouted Alvilda, throwing her hands up in the air. She stood on her toes and attempted to shout over the specters' shoulders. "Jurij! Gideon! Elfriede!"

A lump formed in my throat. Somehow I knew Alvilda's impassioned screaming would prove useless. It was my words that were needed.

"Elfriede! Father!" I called, my voice trembling. "Jurij!" I stomped my foot. "Oh, let me through!"

The specters parted.

Facing each other inward, they extended their arms nearest the door to my home to point the way. The mist cleared in the pathway and the door parted slightly.

I stepped forward. The specters quickly took their places again behind me, blocking Alvilda's path.

"Let me through!" she snarled. She forewent all hope of decorum by launching herself at the specters, wrestling with them as best she could. Sadly, it looked about as effective as a kitten attacking a mountain. The specters barely moved in response to her attack, other than to continue to block her.

"It's all right," I told her, more confident than I felt. "Wait here."

Alvilda stopped struggling and grunted. "Just scream if you need me."

I laughed quietly. I didn't think she'd been able to reach me even if I was screaming as if my life depended upon it, but I didn't tell her that.

I stepped forward, willing strength into my legs to keep me steady. They still ached from the run, but there was more to my body's apprehension than mere exhaustion. The walk from the path to my doorway took an eternity, but eventually I found myself standing before the front door, my shaky hand on the surface. I pushed forward.

I didn't know what I expected to see inside my home, but it wasn't what I found. The fire roaring, the pot of stew still boiling. Elfriede stirring the pot, ready to serve the same stew for dinner that she had for lunch. I caught Jurij's eye as I entered. The knuckles of his hands atop Elfriede's shoulders were almost as white as the specters' skin.

Father sat at his usual place at the table, as if he hadn't moved since I'd last seen him. His hands were gripped tightly together atop the surface. His gaze was locked in front of him. Elfriede, even over her stirring, stared at the same place. Only Jurij would glance in my direction, but his eyes kept flickering back to the table.

A man sat there.

As if "sat there" were words enough to describe the effect of his presence. Two more specters stood at either corner of the man's chair, unblinking and unmoving.

"Olivière," spoke the lord. "I have been waiting for you."

He was as still as the specters around him at first. Eventually, he unfolded his hands and gave what appeared to be an attempt at a welcoming gesture, a diminutive open embrace meant to indicate that I sit in the chair across from him.

"Well?" The lord's hands tapped impatiently on the table.

I raised an eyebrow and looked from one person in the room to the next. Only Jurij's eyes would meet mine, albeit briefly. He seemed as puzzled as I.

Only I wasn't entirely puzzled. I hadn't gone to him in months. So he had come to me—even if he claimed he couldn't leave the castle. *Well, that was obviously a lie.*

A loud clang. Father, Jurij, and I all turned to look at Elfriede. Tears ran down her cheeks as she swooped down to pick up the ladle she had dropped, spilling bits of the stew across the floor. Jurij bent down quickly to join her.

The lord and the specters did not turn.

"That will not be necessary," said the lord. He raised one hand. "Please clean up that mess."

His voice was so arresting, I almost moved to help Elfriede clean the mess myself. But the words were not yet fully spoken before the two specters were bending down to mop up the mess with rags they pulled from within their jackets. Elfriede and Jurij stood up and backed away warily, clutching one another's hands for support, the ladle back in Elfriede's possession. One of the specters withdrew a miniscule broom and a small metal pan from his jacket and briskly brushed the floor once the stew chunks were missing. The other pulled out a black, silken sack and emptied his pan and the rags into the sack, almost soundlessly.

The first specter restored the broom and pan to his jacket and pulled out a new rag. He grabbed the ladle from Elfriede, eliciting a small whimper from her, wiped it clean, and handed it back to her. Elfriede took it but required Jurij to wrap his free hand around hers to support the ladle in her grip.

The specters glided back into place behind the lord. It had taken longer for me to understand what had happened than for the actual event to take place. The specters seemed unchanged from mere moments before; the only difference now was that one stood holding the silken bag slightly to his front as if it were a freshly caught rabbit. There were surprisingly no visible wrinkles to the bag's smooth surface.

"Olivière," repeated the lord, a force not unlike a blast of blizzard air behind his words, "be seated. Please."

I did as asked. The black hands shifted, intertwining the fingers lightly beneath the bottom of the veil.

"Thank you," he said. His head appeared to shift slightly and he waved an arm behind him. "Please, join us. Your stew smells wonderful, and I did not come to delay your dinner. My retainers will serve you."

Elfriede and Jurij exchanged a concerned look, perhaps a little surprised to be further noticed. An unspoken message passed between them and they shuffled over as one, Elfriede taking the remaining chair and Jurij standing protectively behind her.

"A chair," spoke the lord with another wave of his hand.

"No, that's all—" began Jurij, but the specters were already in and out of the home, returning with a cushion-laced stool instead of the black silken bag. *Did they bring that with them in the carriage?* They placed it down next to Elfriede, and one put his hands on Jurij's back in order to guide him to sit atop the stool. "—right." Jurij looked from Elfriede on one side to me on the other, as if hoping either one of us could explain what had just happened.

The specters were already gone, over by the stew pot, ladling stew into white glass bowls they seemed to have pulled out of their pockets.

No one said anything as they worked in fluid motions, setting out white bowls of stew and silver spoons before first me, then my father, and then Elfriede and Jurij. They went back to their guarded posts behind the lord.

Elfriede was the first to pick up her spoon, and Jurij soon followed. Elfriede's hand twitched. "Won't you dine with us?"

It was a silly question, considering the lord's veil. The lord didn't stir. "No, thank you, my dear. I am sure it tastes delightful, but your cooking is meant to enrapture a man other than me."

Elfriede blushed and turned her attention to a floating chunk of potato. Jurij spread his arm on the table, trying to hide his now empty bowl. Usually, he seemed to feel nothing but delight—or at the very most, indifference—to others noticing his love for his goddess. The small gesture of him hiding the bowl from view felt odd to me, like there was a part of him that had enough free will to think negatively of the lord. To think *anything* of the lord. My heart was a flurry at the idea that Jurij might dislike the lord because he'd steal me from him, like that were possible. But that just reminded me that I was expected to accept the lord.

I looked at my own overflowing bowl. I couldn't summon the will to lift the spoon. I shoved the bowl forward.

"I left Alvilda out front," I said, anxious to change the topic. "She was blocked from entering by..." My gaze traveled to the statue-still specters.

The lord waved his hand, cutting me off. "I will take but a moment of your time this evening. Are you feeling well, Olivière? You have not yet touched your food."

All eyes—visible and not black eyes, at least—fell on my full stew bowl and me. Even Father, I noticed, had finished at least half of his.

"I already dined with Alvilda." It was at least half-true.

Elfriede furrowed her brow and pursed her lips but said nothing.

"Alvilda?" asked the lord tensely. "She is?"

My father moved to open his mouth, but one of the specters bent down and perhaps murmured something where I imagined the lord's ear to be. *So they can* speak?

"Ah," said the lord. "The lady carver. I can see now why there are so many... interesting... wooden trinkets about." He motioned to the mantle above the fireplace, where I had haphazardly dumped this morning's creations.

Ugh. Those weren't my best work.

"Do you really think her a wise companion, Olivière?"

I felt a roar of fire grow in my stomach. "Alvilda has talent. She may get most of the village's carpentry and carving work these days instead of my father, but I assure you it's by his own deeds that he suffers in his trade as of late." I sent a pointed look to Father, but he did nothing more than pick up another spoonful of stew.

Another wave of a gloved hand. "I refer more to the detail that she refused her Returning."

My jaw dropped. "What business is it—"

"I've told her time and time again that I agree with you, my lord," interrupted Father.

My blood boiled. *Really.* I opened my mouth to speak.

"It matters not." The lord began to rise, and the specters slid smoothly behind him to make room. "The morrow is Olivière's Returning, and after the ceremony she will reside with me in the castle."

I shot up, sending my chair flying backward and crashing. "Excuse me?"

"Noll, listen." Father spoke quietly.

"I didn't agree to a Returning!"

There, I had said it. No one had asked my opinion before.

Elfriede dropped her spoon onto her bowl. The silver hitting the glass made a strange *clang*, not like the wood-on-wood of our usual dinnerware. Jurij seemed stunned, and I noticed his hand twitched nervously on his thigh, his chair half pushed backward, whether readying himself to jump up or forcing himself to stay seated, I couldn't be sure. Father's face glazed over, his eyes darting from corner to corner, probably looking for a bottle.

The lord stood unmoved a moment, towering about a head

over me. I tried to imagine where I might find his eyes behind the veil and I stared, daring him to correct me.

The lord's hat shifted, and he made a quick motion in my direction with a gloved hand. For a moment, I thought the specters might move to grab me. I tensed, ready to put up as fruitless a fight as Alvilda had. Instead, they righted my fallen chair and exited the house through the doorway behind me.

"I assumed you would be ready by the morrow," said the lord after a brief moment of silence. "I gave you time to prepare yourself. Even if you chose not to visit me. Besides, your father and sister assured me just now that you would be ready."

A pain shot through my chest. I glanced at Father and Elfriede in turn, but neither would meet my gaze. Jurij, at least, seemed in genuine shock at the revelation. Perhaps he'd been dreaming of Elfriede when they'd had the discussion.

"I can see now that I was mistaken. The ceremony should be canceled," continued the lord. He traced the table with the tip of a gloved finger as he made his way past my father to join Jurij and me at the other side. He held the finger up to his veil, examining the small traces of sawdust. Then he flicked away the dust with his thumb and grabbed my hand in his before I could stop him. His grip was harder than I remembered.

"But I will come for you on the morrow nonetheless."

He slid my hand under his veil and pressed those cold, damp lips of marble to the tips of my fingers.

CHAPTER FOURTEEN

I didn't speak for the rest of the evening. I couldn't look at my father or Elfriede, and it was just as well for Father, who used the opportunity to stay long into the night at Vena's. He didn't appear again, not even in the morning to bid me farewell.

Elfriede busied herself first with freeing and washing Arrow and then with all manner of outside chores until the chilly air forced her to enter the home and pull herself beneath the bed covers. It wasn't our shared bed that she entered, but our parents'. She needn't have bothered. I didn't use a bed. Instead, I curled up against Alvilda's side, and we shared a quilt wrapped around our shoulders on the ground before the dying fire. She said nothing, only ceasing her gentle squeeze on my shoulder to stroke my hair on occasion.

Jurij gave me a sorry look and a pat or two on the shoulder before he disappeared outside with Elfriede. *Some friend. But then, the command must have worn off after the Returning.* When she came back inside, he wasn't with her. I'd hoped to see him in the morning, but the carriage came bursting through the woods at the first fleck of light over the mountainous horizon. I felt the urge to flee, and I searched restlessly for some clue in Alvilda's expression that I should follow the urge to run, that I could still hope for the choice that was my gift. The choice that was my right.

Alvilda wouldn't meet my eyes.

Elfriede shuffled out of the house, her face red and puffy. She nervously embraced me. I didn't embrace her back. I half wondered if she was secretly happy to see me go, so I could no longer distract Jurij from his goddess. Because I had no doubt that Jurij had told her of how I begged for his love. He wouldn't have thought it mattered at all. And to him, it didn't.

"Good tidings," Elfriede whispered. "Joyous birthday."

I turned away.

Six specters appeared beside me, two grabbing my arms, the others before and behind me. They moved me toward the carriage as if I were a ragdoll.

"Wait!" called Alvilda. "I have to say goodbye!"

The carriage door shut behind me. I peered out the small window to watch as Alvilda chased after us for a bit, and Elfriede stood frozen in the doorway. Then they were swallowed by the trees, and the breaking light of dawn was replaced by the shades of darkness.

"*Olivière.*" I heard the whisper of my dream even then. Even when there was no hope for me to escape to it.

~

"Is the venison not to your liking?"

Since he had already noticed, I let my fork fall abruptly to the plate, taking a little perverse pleasure in the drop of gravy that spoiled the delicate roses embroidered into the too-white table-cloth. I tore at the trencher meant for scraping the plate of the meat's juices and swallowed a chunk of the white loaf. It crumbled too easily in my throat.

"Olivière?"

I continued chewing and stared across the far-too-long table at the speaker. My dining companion. A set of black-gloved hands attached to a hazy outline obscured by a sheer black curtain. Actual sunlight was allowed into this castle, even if it was only the orange tint of twilight and not the bright white of true sunbeams, but it could do little to help me make out the lord behind the curtain. So this was how the masked ate when their goddesses couldn't perform the Returning. At least this was how this one ate. I couldn't picture Master Tailor bothering with this elaborate set-up in his home. I believed he ate only with Jurij and Luuk, or maybe at the Great Hall with other men or with Alvilda. And never with his goddess.

But this masked lord wasn't one for propriety.

It was hard to decide when the lord looked most inhuman, walking around with a veil wrapped around his head showing me this or that room in the castle, or sitting leagues away from me at a dining room table, that long curtain hanging between us, for our first breakfast, lunch, and dinner together. The masks on the boys and the few masked men of the village seemed almost human in comparison, although they never actually resembled humans until the day of their Returnings.

I thought of the lord from my dream, and how he thrust his face in mine.

I nearly choked on my trencher.

The lord took great care to lay down his knife and fork so that the plate only clinked with the most dulcet of tones.

"Olivière? Are you all right?"

His hand motioned upward behind the veil, and one of the specters standing still at the far edge of the room came to life and arrived swiftly at my side to pour wine into a crystal goblet. I hated the foul taste of wine, but I grabbed it roughly from the specter and downed an entire glass until the bread worked its way free of my throat.

"Are you all right now?" The hands clutched the edge of the table. "Olivière? Answer me!"

"Yes!" I slammed down the goblet, hoping it would shatter, but it remained intact.

The hands let the tablecloth go and picked up the knife and fork again to cut the rest of the meat still on his plate.

I felt a bit light-headed. This was why I hated wine. I shoved the plate away from me. The flank of brownish meat was even more disgusting now that my nose was full of the stench of alcohol.

"Would you care for another dish for dinner?"

One hand stabbed at a piece of meat with the fork, and then the fork and the hand vanished behind the curtain.

I shook my head and used both hands to push against the table. "I'd like to be excused now." I stood up.

Half-a-dozen specters surrounded me on either side before I could take one step.

"Sit down," said the lord behind the black curtain. "Please."

I did not. "I'm not feeling well," I said through clenched teeth.

"You have not eaten enough. Food will improve your temper."

A few well-placed stabs from Elgar the Blade to his abdomen might "improve my temper." I took a deep breath. Just because I dreamed of a lord even more foul didn't mean this one deserved my anger. I moved to sit, but I caught myself halfway. And why wasn't he deserving? When I thought of how he'd acted when I'd begged for help, or how he assumed I'd perform the Returning... I had power over him. It was time he remembered that.

"Let. Me. Leave."

The fork fell to the floor with an echoing thud. One hand gripped the tablecloth again. I found it strange to observe the specters looking almost lifelike all around me. They didn't move to pick up their lord's fork. They didn't move to block me. In fact, a number of them stepped backward, clearing a roundabout way to the dining hall doorway. I smiled.

The lord loosened his grip on the tablecloth and picked up a napkin from beside his plate. "She means to let her retire from the dining hall for the night. And so shall I." The napkin disappeared behind the curtain.

The specters swept into a state of activity, having regained their composure. As expected, one swooped down by his lord to pick up the fallen fork. The others stood in two facing lines, forming an enclosed path between the doorway and myself.

But I wasn't satisfied.

"No, that's not the full extent of my wishes," I began, emphasizing each word with a strained attempt at Elfriede's own pretense of innocent sweetness. "Let—"

The lord flew into motion, knocking his chair backward into the waiting arms of one of the specters. The curtain in front of him shook rapidly with the movement.

"Do not speak further!" he bellowed.

141

The words echoed in the cavernous dining hall and died only after a series of repetitions.

I could see the two black-leathered hands clench into fists below the surface of the fluttering curtain.

I clenched my own fists. "I don't think you understand how this works—"

"Silence!"

"No! Who do you think you are? What do you think you're supposed to mean to me? I don't even know you. I don't want to be here, and you're expecting me to perform the Returning!"

The black fists pounded on the table. "Was it not *you* who first sought me out?"

I gestured at the ridiculously large, cold, and empty room around me. "Not for this! I never asked to be your goddess! I just wanted—" I bit my lip. There was never going to be any going back.

"You wished to free your friend so you could steal him from his goddess." He made a gesture toward the line of specters, and the two closest appeared at my side, their hands wrapped tightly against my arms. "How unfortunate that I was unable to help you with such a generous act." I struggled to break free, but I felt powerless in their tight grip.

The lord turned sharply. Before he took more than two steps, a series of specters appeared from the line, one to pick up his plate from the table and then one who fit the lord with his black veil and hat even as he walked. He appeared in mere moments from the side of the curtain.

"Come with me!" He exited the dining hall doorway.

The specters dragged me after him. I kicked and screamed, and, thinking of Alvilda, even tried to reach the specters' hands in order to bite them. They dragged me forward without hesitation, and other specters broke from the line to open the doors for the lord.

"Stop!" I screamed.

The lord stopped.

"Let me—"

"Silence her!" he ordered before walking again, and one of my pale captors produced a black veil-like material and wrapped it over my mouth, tying it at the back of my head. My eyes welled with tears. But not from sadness. No, this was a rage I'd felt only once before. *He's just like the men from my dream.*

Staring straight ahead into the back of that black-veiled head was no different than staring right into the front. It made me realize that there was no loss of honor to stab this man in the back if need be. The thought gave me comfort, and I let the specters drag me, soon willing my feet to keep up with their pace so that they wouldn't be so sore. But try as I might, I couldn't quite match my pace with them or with the lord in front of me.

He led us through the main entryway and up a flight of stairs. From there, we marched down the long hallway that contained an empty set of guest rooms—one of which the lord had shown me earlier and told me would be mine, an opulent room that retained the chill of the castle air despite the tremendous fire in the fireplace and the bear-skin rug spread before it. I had spent the afternoon after the "tour" and lunch nestled deep within the fur, and still the chill sliced down inside of me.

As we passed a hall window, I noticed that the sun had set. The dull torchlight and the slit of a moonbeam were all there was to light the way. But the lord moved through the near-darkness unheeded, as comfortable navigating the twists and turns of the path before us as I had been in my own dark secret cavern. Only I at least knew a violet glow awaited me at the end of that journey. What would await me now? A prison? A shackle for my arms and legs to match the muzzle over my mouth?

The lord led us up another flight of stairs and across a hallway. My heart sank at my speculations nearly proven. This had not been on the "tour." The specters had even blocked me from coming this far my first time to the third floor. The lord's shoulders twitched as we passed the throne room, its doors opened, the room darkened. But I'd never been past this point.

At the end of that hallway—the coldest place yet in the castle, a blast of icy air blowing in from the few windows—stood two more specters, immobile before a large wooden door.

"Let us in!" barked the lord. One of the guards pulled a set of keys out from his front coat pocket and turned the lock. He stood back and both specters pushed open the thick, heavy door; even they strained to do so at their usual rapid pace.

This was it. I was to rot in his prison the rest of my days. Probably "graced" on occasion by a visit from the lord, asking me if I would like some more wine or venison or if I found the cell cold enough or if I was ready to break down and perform the Returning.

Or why I'd "mutilated" my ears.

The nausea that spread over me was met halfway with something deeper. A force of sheer will lent steadiness to my shaky legs. I could let him think he had broken me. I would let him remove the muzzle with his leathery fingers, and with all of my might, even if they proved to be the last words I ever spoke, I could tell the lord to climb up to the roof of the castle or the tallest mountain and to jump to his death. I let the words form on my trapped tongue, ready to pounce the moment he removed the muzzle.

And then the specters dragged me into the room after the lord. He stood in our way for a moment before shifting to the side and pointing to a bed. There, in the middle of the room under a thick quilt, lay my mother.

CHAPTER FIFTEEN

I tried to scream, but the veil muzzle gripped too hard against my tongue. Its movements were heavy and impeded.

"Do you understand now? Do you understand what I am to you?"

My eyes darted around the room. I did not understand. I didn't understand at all.

My mother lay in a large wooden bed atop a plush mattress. Across her body, the thick quilt was tucked tightly below her neck and hid everything from view but her face. Aside from a roaring fire in the nearby stone fireplace, the room was empty. I wanted to know how she still remained visible after death and why he would have her.

She moved. I had to squeeze my eyes shut tightly for a moment to make sure I wasn't dreaming. But there it was. Ever so slightly, the area of the quilt over her abdomen rose and fell.

She was alive.

The mother I thought dead months prior had been alive all this time.

But why? How? Why had we held mourning? And why was she sleeping? Why didn't she wake after hearing all of the ruckus?

"Will you think twice about abusing your power now?"

My gaze shifted from my mother's peaceful shape to the harsh, black-covered lord. He stood beside the bed, his elbows akimbo, his legs slightly parted. He awaited an answer.

I had more than a few choice words to give him, but I couldn't speak. I did what I thought would rectify that situation and nodded.

My eyes still betrayed some of my intentions. The lord nodded, and one of the specters' hands released its grip on my arm and removed the muzzle. However, he stood holding it beside my head, ready to slap it back on at a moment's notice. And his other hand wouldn't release his painful grasp.

I said nothing. Nothing was to be gained yet until I knew what was going on.

The lord had no qualms about filling the silence. "We should have had the Returning today. And the wedding. I would have let your father and sister come to see her." He paused. "I gave you almost a year to get over that *boy* you thought you loved. But, as ever, you prove too stubborn."

It was difficult to bite my tongue and not respond to his comment about Jurij. I forced myself to remain calm. "What's going on? You said you wouldn't help me."

"I said I would do what I could." The lord stirred slightly, seeming to fight something within himself. Then he relaxed. "Her survival was to be a Returning present."

"What?" So much for calm.

The lord crossed both his arms tightly across his chest. "I would have told you, but only upon the Returning."

"But since I refuse the Returning, why did you tell me anyway?"

"Because you have acted so imprudently. You are taken with the power you have over me!"

"The power *I* have over *you*?" I gave a pointed look first to one of my trapped arms and then to the other before glaring in the lord's direction.

He must have nodded, if only slightly. His shiny metal hat tipped forward and caught a small sparkle from the firelight.

The specters released me but remained close. The one holding the muzzle tucked it into his front coat pocket. I had the feeling that even though they had set me free, it would take only a slight wave from the lord and I'd find myself ensnared again.

The lord's voice was hard and cold. "You know of what I speak."

I laughed. I was his goddess, but the thought didn't make me rejoice at my power over the lord. It was a mere illusion, like the power of my choice.

My mother was alive and the lord had her in his grasp.

I crossed over to her and felt her cheek. Ice cold, like the rest of this dreaded castle. I wished against all hope that I could turn back time and listen to her and the other villagers. That I had never so much as looked at this place.

I ran a finger across her golden hairline, noticing the touches of gray that framed her face, and watched the barely noticeable twitch of her nose as it took in and let out the frigid air around us.

I faced the lord, one hand still resting atop my mother's head. "How is she alive?"

The lord moved closer, the hollow echoes of his hard-tipped boots reverberating across the room. Without even thinking, I jumped up, sliding between the bed and the wall and clutching the headboard tightly with both hands. Although thin, the lord was more broad-shouldered than I. He wouldn't be able to follow me.

He almost tried it regardless, but he paused and walked slowly in the other direction. He ran a black-gloved hand along the length of the quilt covering my mother and stood opposite me at the foot of the bed.

"I expected to be thanked," he said.

Forget the lost blade Elgar. I wanted a few of my chisels and gouges. Perhaps I could carve him a new face so I could stop directing my anger at an empty black void.

"*Explain*," I uttered slowly, "why my mother is here."

"I had her brought here," replied the lord, "after you asked for my help."

So Father was right. He could have done something. But what had he done?

The specters snapped back into imitating statues.

He was careful with his words, this one, saying not a grain more than bidden. I had never seen a man not yet Returned so reluctant to obey his goddess. But he wasn't like the other men at all; the power he went great lengths to hold over me was more than enough to prove that.

I couldn't help but think the men I'd met in my dream were a warning, something my subconscious had picked up on the few times I'd met the lord.

The lord moved casually now toward the fireplace, the fingers on one hand running over the edges of the footboard.

"I would be careful," he said before pausing. "Just how freely you use that power."

He faced the fireplace now, folding his hands behind his back. One finger pointed outward briefly and the four specters flew in, two on each side of the bed. From their coat pockets, they each removed a small blade and held it out over my mother, ready to strike.

"No!" I screamed, my arms flinging forward, trying vainly through the holes in the headboard to block the nearest blades from my mother.

The lord stepped to my side at the edge of the headboard. He flicked his hand, and the specters put their blades back into their inner coat pockets. They remained hovering over her.

I fumed. "Don't hurt her!"

The lord shrugged. "I am not hurting her."

I pointed at the specters. "Don't let *them* hurt her."

"All right." He waved his hand.

The specters retreated through the doorway. Six more specters marched in. They were all so similar in appearance and in gait that I had yet to put my finger on whether they were identical or merely brethren.

The six shuffled in on either side of the bed, and each removed a blade from his inner coat pocket.

"Stop!" I yelled.

The lord tensed and didn't move, but the specters stirred just a little, glancing first at me and then at the lord. After a moment, the lord moved closer, running his hands slowly over the top of the headboard, almost within reach of me.

I clenched my jaw. "I can play this game all night."

"As can I."

I backed away from his encroaching fingers, not caring if that put me closer to one of the specters and his extended blade.

"I could think of a way to word it," I said, not bothering to pretend any longer, "so that I would *win*."

"And win you would," said the lord. He stood upright and made a slight wave of his fingers. The nearest specter grabbed me and pulled me out from behind my small sanctuary behind the headboard, the blade gone from his hand and both hands gripping tightly on each of my arms.

"But you would also lose."

The rest of the specters lowered their blades toward my mother and I screamed.

CHAPTER SIXTEEN

Don't look before love. *What if I agreed to the Returning and then he simply vanished at the unmasking? If Ingrith wasn't crazy, no one would even remember.*

No. It was too late for that. The lord knew I wasn't able to Return to him. And besides, what if he was needed to save my mother? There had to be a way to word it. To win the choice that was owed to me but to save my mother at the same time. Could the specters still respond to those little hand gestures if I commanded the lord to slice off his own fingers? Had they already been ordered to rush to my mother and kill her if I so much as dared? Would it end there? Would they go to the village and slaughter Father and Elfriede, Alvilda, the Tailors, and Nissa? And Jurij? Would it end with my own death or would they drop me in the commune, forcing me to live with the endless trail of blood my choice had wrought? Would the lord's death be worth it, when with his death, I'd lose all control over the one who held command over the specters?

You sound like a bloodthirsty monster. No different from the men in your dream.

I didn't have to kill the lord to come out on top. The specters gave me some hope. They seemed different when I gave my orders. They obeyed him, but in that brief moment, they at least appeared confused. That could prove to be my opening, if I could just figure out how to take advantage of it. But before I could risk my mother's safety, I would have to practice, to push and pull with inconsequential orders and figure out how I could stop the specters from acting, even as I prevented the lord from noticing what I was doing. But he noticed every order. He anticipated it. He must have spent all this time since he met me planning for my refusal, even as I lay ignorant in my bed beyond the woods. If the stories were to be believed, he could have spent a millennia preparing for my refused Returning.

The lord of our village. He who never stepped beyond the woods surrounding his castle. A lord whose birth and parents no one could remember. There were those whispers that he was proof of the tale—that men who couldn't find their goddesses among the village women would live forever until they did. For if no one remembered when he was born, was it possible that he was older than everyone who lived?

I shuddered to think of an old, wrinkled, spotted man taunting me behind that black veil. To unmask him upon a Returning might be more chilling than seeing him now hidden from view.

My mind swam with faded, unreal memories of the village that was and was not my own.

You said you would help them. And then you left them.

I shook my head. It wasn't real. My hands reached out for a phantom sheath at my waist. But even if it had been a dream, it lingered with me all these months later.

Because even if I'd seen that lord's face and not this one's, they seemed more and more alike the better I came to know him.

What if that was him in his youth?

An immortal man, whom I visited in the past in my dreams? Ridiculous, but my mind swarmed with questions. There had always been something eerie about our village lord. He was a man most of the village could hardly believe existed, but for the small but steady supply of food and other essentials the boys and men delivered to his castle—which, conveniently, had been stopped now that I had moved in. Until I performed the Returning, the lord's servants would go out into the village and bring home the necessary wares directly. No one—no woman, no man, no child—could set foot in the castle.

The villagers wouldn't object to dealing with the mute servants more often, especially since I heard nothing of the lord demanding his coppers back from what he paid for the Returning preparations. I'd seen the specters all my life. A hint of a white back turning around the corner here. A glimpse of the black carriage in front of the tavern there. There were actual monsters roaming about the village, and I was off fighting lambs.

Who were these servants? Why didn't they speak? Why were they unmasked? They couldn't be married. Or perhaps they had been or at least had been Returned to, but their goddesses lived elsewhere.

The women who lay beyond the cavern pool. A pool that was a path to the past.

Did it matter? I wasn't leaving the castle, that much I knew.

My mind grew tired with all of the thinking. For there was the question, too, of how much my friends and family knew about my mother. How much the entire village knew. Was I alone left in the dark, or did only a few of them know the truth of the matter? Did those closest to me know, and was that why they all seemed so anxious I perform my Returning? Had I broken my father's heart all over again by delaying his meeting with his one true sunlight? Did he truly believe I would experience the Returning with the lord without knowing what it was I put at risk—or that I could even do so once I had known all that was at stake?

That was the worst of it. Now that I knew, at least a part of me thought that it would be wise to give up the fight. But my heart would simply never be up to Returning to the lord. Even if all the will had gone out of me. I was cursed by the gift of choice.

What I would give to be Elfriede, whose heart shifted so freely from distaste to love after the initial shock of the confession. What I would give to be Elfriede, just to be with the one I loved.

But that was fine. I could live without love. I'd accepted that by now. I wasn't sure I could live without freedom.

YET ANOTHER DAY PASSED. I'd lost count.

At first, I filled my days with thoughts of my dilemma and ways to escape my trap. It made the time pass quickly, but it produced no results. Each idea ended with the lord's gruesome death, followed immediately by the equally horrific deaths of those I loved.

I began to resent the idea that my mother was alive after all, that she had not died from illness, and that the specters had stopped their blades a mere hair's breadth from touching her. And I hated myself for that. Especially since if it wasn't her, it would surely have been another loved one.

My mind went numb after a while.

I didn't see much of the lord. We dined together in the dining hall for breakfast, lunch, and dinner—at his orders. He tried to ask me about myself, about my thoughts on the castle, but he'd get frustrated at my silence and storm out. Eventually, he resigned himself to the same silence in which I had found refuge. We ate together, neither one of us saying a word.

I was given free reign of the castle, except I wasn't allowed to set foot on the third floor. The top of the second staircase was guarded by five specters anytime I thought myself alone and able to sneak up the stairs. Morning or night, they just stood there, staring above my head, their legs slightly parted and their hands clutched behind their backs. They moved only when I attempted to climb under their legs or fit between them—then all of a sudden they were fast as hares, blocking my path. At last, I gave up. The obstructed entryway meant I couldn't visit my mother, whose prison was the only place I could possibly wish to go in the dank and dreary castle. This made me even angrier and more eager not to please. I shut myself away in my room between meals.

When the snows came and blocked even the view of the village from my room's window, it felt fitting. I was trapped in a place from which I could reach no one I loved.

And even that dream world never came back to me. Without the blade, without the pool, I'd never know if I'd seen a vision of the past.

I saw the specters often. They brought me tea between meals and built a fire. At first they also brought things I assumed were meant to amuse me: old books, art supplies, and embroidery. All things to which I had never taken and had no desire to practice still. My mind was numb enough without drudgery. Several weeks into the snows, the servants saw to my fire, but they no longer brought me anything.

There were dresses in the chest at the foot of my bed. At first the specters would choose one—a different one each day—and lay it on my mattress. My hands dared to touch them and found them finer than anything I had seen on any woman, but rough and cold to the touch—and far too heavy. They also immediately brought to mind images of Master and Mistress Tailor, whom I assumed would have made them, as they were the only true tailors in the village. And thoughts of the Tailors brought up thoughts of Jurij. I wouldn't wear them.

Eventually, the specters delivered a strange package to my room that contained the clothing I'd left behind at home. I sorted through the pile, my heart nearly stopping when I came across the dress with the fine embroidery flowers on the back. I fingered it, familiar with the dress but the needlework new to me. It was the torn dress I'd worn that day I fell into the pool. She'd fixed it at some point, and I hadn't even noticed. It was clearly Elfriede's handiwork, done to mask the ripped material. The rips down the dress like the cracks of a whip. My finger stopped at a single crooked thread that Elfriede had failed to cover up.

This dress was first stitched by Avery. And that dream was no dream at all.

I burned with the stupid idea that this was more proof I'd met the lord in the past. In a past so long ago no one else even remembered it.

Not that it mattered. I wasn't allowed to leave the castle.

As soon as I slipped into the dress, the specters swooped into the room and took the dress I'd worn to the castle from the floor. I nearly screamed upon their sudden entrance.

The dress was given back to me later the same day, washed and folded.

For some reason, it felt like I had lost in a game I hadn't intended to play.

~

WHEN I WOKE up one morning, a surge of warmth hit my face. I lay in bed for a moment, picturing myself having risen from a nap on the hilltop where I'd often picnicked with Jurij. But I couldn't feel grass and dirt beneath my fingers, only cold silken plush.

I remembered where I was. My eyes opened reluctantly.

A sunbeam trickled onto my bed from the window. It actually warmed me, and I felt a stirring in my heart. Cautiously, I sat up and then took the few steps over to the window. I peered out and my heart soared, if but for a brief moment. The snow had melted. A gentle haze permeated the horizon, but I could still make out the village below. Perhaps spring had finally come.

Before I could be summoned for breakfast, I dressed, this time in the worn-down dress that I often wore when I'd been carving. It had been cleaned before it was presented to me and was cleaned every time I wore it since, but I still imagined it carried the scent of sawdust.

I bypassed the untouched vanity and the white hairbrush I knew would be lying out for me. Although I didn't brush my hair myself, the specters had started brushing it for me before meals. All the better reason to leave before they got there. Perhaps I would find a knife with which to chop it all off and leave them with nothing to make pretty.

Gently, I pushed the door open a crack. I sucked in my abdomen and squeezed through, quietly pushing the door shut behind me. No one was in the hallway, but I stood still for a moment anyway to see if anyone stirred. I knew from the "tour" that the lord's chambers were located on the floor above mine, but I wouldn't put it past the specters to be on guard. But no one came.

I slipped across the hallway to the staircase and took one step down at a time, cautiously peering through the banister for signs of the specters. There was no one.

I came upon the grand entryway and my heart skipped a beat. This was where I'd had my first encounter with the lord, more than a year prior. I could picture myself now, bathed in a moonbeam, following it to its source.

A sunbeam had replaced that moonbeam. The rays of dawn were peeking through the cracks in the door that led to the inner courtyard. I shuffled quietly over to it and peered through the space in the door as I had the first night I'd foolishly ventured to the castle. A garden. When I'd been shown the place on the "tour," it was but a drab collection of stone and branches. Now, almost overnight, the sun had breathed life into the place.

Feeling suffocated inside, I grabbed hold of both handles on the wide double door and pulled. I stood still for a moment and closed my eyes. They couldn't adjust to the brightness, and I felt blind, but the light that seeped in through my closed eyelids was enough to make my heart race and my mind come to life.

My thoughts flew instantly to the field of flowers that covered the hills near my home in the spring and how I'd run as a child, giggling with Jurij, Darwyn, and my other friends as we kicked up petals and rolled down the hills. I remembered looking up one day and seeing Elfriede sitting quietly atop the hill as she looked after us, careful not to disturb the passionate purple of the flowers that framed her peaceful little body. She weaved together lilies into a circlet for my hair, crowning me "the little elf queen." She'd first named me that, taking a title from one of Mother's stories, although I'm sure she didn't remember. There was no mistaking the vivacity of those hilltop blossoms, flowers that could both robustly cushion a tribe of lively little adventurers and still yield to the gentle movements of a weaver girl's fingers.

The garden in the castle featured only white roses on carefully manicured bright green bushes. Save for the large space immediately in front of the two large wooden doors that led back into the castle, the rose bushes linked together in an unbroken circle framing the entire garden. Cobblestones lined the rest of the garden ground, and there was sign of neither dirt nor grass.

It was no hilltop, but it would have to do.

I shivered. The winter air was retreating, but there was still a nip of cold in the spring morning. The closest thing I could find to a comfortable seat was on one of the two benches on either side of a stone table to the left of the entrance. I sat down on the bench that would give me a full view of the garden and stared again at the odd water fountain at the middle. Two streams of water still spurted from the eyes of the pointed-eared child, his arms outstretched towards the skies. My heart ached for his torment. He seemed to be reaching for something—and weeping because it would never be within his grasp. He and I, we shared much of the same feeling.

A tray with food appeared on the table before me.

I started. A specter stood next to me after dropping off the tray on the stone table, but I hadn't noticed him enter. Despite my best efforts, my movements in the castle hadn't gone unnoticed.

I felt ill.

But the specter soon retreated, leaving me alone in the garden. The empty feeling in my head and the rumbling in my stomach won out. I picked up the spoon on the tray and began eating. No one disturbed me. The sun rose ever farther over the horizon and the light made the water pouring from the child's eyes sparkle a brilliant blue. It was the first meal I'd enjoyed since my stay began.

CHAPTER SEVENTEEN

Whenever the sun was out over the next few weeks, I took my breakfasts and lunches in the garden. Even when it was overcast and a chill swept through the air, I went to the garden. Only rain disturbed my sanctuary. And dinner, for that was the one meal the lord ordered that I eat with him. He didn't tell me that—we still didn't speak—but the specters always appeared at dusk, their hands clenched tightly around my arms, and I was whisked away. I always knew it was coming shortly after they came to water the roses.

I began to feel. And that feeling, I was upset to find, was boredom. I almost wished for the books, the needles, and the paints again, if only to find some way to make each day pass by. But I didn't want them enough to break my vow of silence. I hardly wanted them at all. Instead, I took to staring at the fountain or pulling out the petals of a rose one by one.

As if hearing my thoughts, the specters started bringing things again. Paper, quill, and ink. A board decorated with black-and-white squares and thirty-two odd-shaped figures made of bone set on top. I laughed one time when they brought me a flute. I didn't touch it.

Once, they brought me a few blocks of wood and a set of gouges and chisels. I ached to pick up the items and numb my heart with them, but I refused to acknowledge the gift he got right. I didn't touch them, I wouldn't look at them, and they didn't appear again.

Drawing wasn't my strength, but I picked up the quill and ran it back and forth over the paper. I thought about writing a letter home, but I didn't know whether I would be allowed to send it, nor if I could even begin to express my feelings at their betrayal. There was no way I could write a letter to Jurij, and even if I could, I wasn't sure I wanted to. I held the different bone figures in my palms, running my fingers across the cold, smooth surfaces. I liked the one with the multi-pointed crown the best. It reminded me of the elf queen.

One afternoon, the specters brought a letter.

I looked at it warily where it sat on the stone table, at first afraid and then enraged that it might contain a message from the lord. But I felt a stirring in my heart that I hadn't known in ages as I looked at the script that wrote out my name: "Olivière, second daughter of Aubree and Gideon, Carvers." It was Elfriede's hand.

I turned it over and grew hot with fury to see the seal already broken.

I hope this letter finds you well. Jurij's birthday is next month. Enclosed is our wedding invitation. I hope you can come. His Lordship is welcome as well, if he would like.

I had to laugh at Elfriede's attempts to act as if all was well. To her, perhaps it was. I was gone and out of her hair, after all.

My fingers ran over the embossed edges of the invitation. A wedding in the hills beyond our home in the first full month of spring. So it was only a month until the wedding now.

I didn't know what to do. I didn't know what I wanted. At the very least, perhaps I could look out my bedroom window and watch the specks of people gathering in the hills that day. But what would be more painful, to watch or not to watch? To celebrate a sister's happiness or to keep pretending that happiness didn't exist for others because it never would again exist for me?

But a thought struck me. I didn't want to watch—I wanted to go. Not just to see if I could sneak to the pool and test my theory. Not just because any freedom, even for just a day, was better than whatever this was. A wedding may not be the best opportunity to air a deep and terrible secret, but Elfriede and Father at the very least owed me an explanation.

I would just have to do my best to pretend the groom wasn't the only person I knew who made life worth living.

But to go would be to open my mouth.

But would an order to let me go, even if just for the wedding, incite his anger? I knew that it would. I would just have to find some way to pretend that I had no power over him and to ask permission. Even if it meant locking my feelings away.

~

EVERY SECOND AT DINNER, my heart threatened to jump out my skin. From time to time, I would open my mouth to speak, only to quickly grab the goblet or fork and stuff wine or food in to silence myself. I couldn't let the opportunity pass. Still, it bothered me that he'd read the letter and still he didn't say a word. He wasn't the first to lapse into silence, but he wouldn't be the first to speak.

I cleared my throat. The air felt like knives in my raw airways.

"I assume you read my sister's invitation. The seal was broken."

I hadn't intended to start off so antagonistic, but I found the words and tone tumbling freely from my hibernated mouth. I stabbed at some meat and began chewing to cover some of my indignation.

A small cough came from behind the curtain, and a black glove reached for his goblet of wine. The goblet appeared again in view but remained cradled freely in one hand.

"Yes," he spoke at last. "Her wedding is next week."

The fork fell from my grip. "Next week? The letter says next month!"

"It is already the first full month of spring, Olivière."

I bit down on my lip. Hard. If I hadn't, I would have started screaming and said more than one thing I'd have regretted. Even if they would have satisfied me immensely before I later regretted them.

I grabbed my goblet from the table. After a large gulp of wine, I slammed it down.

"I would like to go."

160

"You may not."

My jaw dropped. Was the letter just to torture me, then? Why not just give it to me after it was over, and I had completely missed it? I tried to cover up my frustration by grabbing my napkin from my lap and wiping my face. At least the cover allowed my lips to turn freely into a sneer.

"And why not?" I asked.

The goblet disappeared behind the curtain for a while before reappearing, this time settling back on the table. The sip took far too long to be anything but intentional.

"You know why," said the lord. A finger ran across the jagged edges of the crystal goblet. "Unless you intend to order me to let you go?"

I forced my mouth into a thin line before putting the napkin back on my lap. My eyes fell to the napkin, suddenly interested in seeing that I smoothed it just right.

"I thought not," said the lord confidently.

"You may come with me," I said quietly. "If you like."

I didn't know how I would speak to my friends and family alone if he were with me, but the distraction of the lord of the castle out among his people might provide enough cover for an opportunity or two.

The lord behind the curtain laughed. It may have been as close to a joyful laugh as he could muster, but I heard it laced with traces of ridicule and contempt.

"How very gracious of you!" he said. "But I am afraid the answer is still no."

He stood up, his chair scraping backward. Some of the specters flew into motion, cleaning his dinnerware, putting on his veil and hat, and then settling against the wall as always.

"Good night, Olivière," he said as he came around the edge of the curtain. "It has been a pleasure speaking with you."

I stopped myself from saying something more explicit in response that would drip more venomously with that very same edge of disdain he displayed.

~

I TAPPED my fingers impatiently on the stone table as the specters cleared away my breakfast and brought out the board and figures. I snatched the white elf queen off of the board as soon as they set her there and started rubbing my hands over her smooth surface. If I rubbed hard enough, what would break first, the bone figure or my skin?

I could hardly see straight. The garden was spinning around me. Try as I might, I couldn't think of a way to get to the wedding that would leave my captor happy. The worst part was that I knew that was precisely why he tormented me with it in the first place. Because it was the first time in months that I felt anything more than boredom—and I felt powerless. And angry.

I began tapping the elf queen against the board in her vacated spot, watching the black elf queen, her mirror image, across the board in the same position. And then I was struck. Two queens. Two kings. Four... horses? Four castles. And other pieces I wasn't sure I knew. But this was a game, obviously. A game meant for white and black. A game meant for two.

I jumped up from the bench and ran into the castle entryway, looking for any specter within reach. A dozen appeared from the shadows at the edges of the room and lined up before me.

~

"YOU SEEM A QUICK LEARNER, Olivière. I have to admit myself surprised."

I did my best to smile. However, I knew from experience that my best attempt to smile when a smile was unearned could send livestock running. Still, I had to try.

"Well," I began, "I am when I actually *want* to learn something."

Surely I could get away with unspoken contempt. He wouldn't really have expected otherwise.

The figure in black sitting on the bench opposite me laughed. He began gathering the scattered pieces, dropping each one on its place on the board. Chess, he had told me, was his favorite game. But it was a bore since his servants always let him win.

I'd told him it would be my pleasure to make him lose. That had made him laugh, too.

"Are you ready then?" asked the lord.

I nodded.

The gloves gestured toward me. "Ladies first."

My hand gripped the white velvet of my skirt, and I fought to keep a surge of heat from reaching my face. I'd told the specters to help me dress in one of the fine ball gowns before I asked them to tell their master what I wanted. They had even gone so far as to intertwine white ribbons and roses throughout my dark locks.

When the lord appeared in the garden to join me, he stopped, nearly lost his balance, and then stood straight again. He laughed, and I could almost picture the amused look on his face. The face I imagined was alarmingly like Lord Elric's from my dream.

I was trying too hard. And I was ashamed to know that it fooled him not in the least.

I started with a pawn. The pawn, I'd learned, was practically powerlessness, a mere echo of the seven other identical pieces. It could only move forward, one slow step at a time, breaking its pattern to move diagonally only in the incredibly unlikely event that it was able to catch a more worthy piece off-guard and capture it. When there was enough action on the battlefield, the pawn might just get away with it. But to begin the game, the pawn's one-time ability of moving forward not one, but *two* spaces would have to be most I hoped for from the pathetic piece.

"So," I began as my fingers left the ivory pawn in the middle of the empty battlefield. "Why only white roses?"

The lord commanded a bolder first move, guiding one of his black knights to leap over the unbroken chain of black pawns guarding his king.

"Do flowers interest you?" he asked curiously as his leather glove retreated to the fold of his arms.

I gripped another pawn tightly as I guided it two steps forward. The pawns could only hold on to such bravado when the battlefield seemed relatively clear, so there was no sense in wasting the weak figure's unwarranted enthusiasm.

I shrugged. "Not really. But I like *color*."

He moved a black pawn one space forward lazily, forfeiting its one-time chance to leap forward double that amount. "What flowers do you imagine should live in my garden?"

Annoyed by his smugness, I moved my white king forward one space to where a pawn had just been. "Violet lilies grow on the hilltop by my *home*."

He didn't remark on my emphasis. "And where should we plant the lilies?" he asked, sending a black pawn one step forward again.

"Perhaps around the fountain." I took another white pawn and let it jump forward its first single space. "If pulling up some of the stones to allow the dirt in would be all right."

"Perhaps," he said casually, guiding a black bishop out on a long diagonal trek to the thrust of the battlefield and taking the life of one white pawn with no more guilt than a chicken devouring a worm.

"It would be a shame to lose any of the white roses," I said, flicking another white pawn two steps forward. "Which is why I suggested adding new space for flowers."

The lord nudged a black pawn forward two paces to match mine. "Perhaps we can pick some of the lilies for transplantation during the wedding. Is that what you would like me to say?"

I smiled sweetly. "Oh, but I'm not allowed to go to the wedding." I guided another white pawn two steps forward. "Apparently."

"You are, as you so rightly point out to me, a woman. You are free to come and go as you please." His favored black knight jumped from behind, slaying another white pawn.

"Let's not lie to each other." I sent another pawn two steps forward, not pausing to think of the danger it might face. "We are, after all, the only two people who can keep each other company in this castle. Since the rest are silent—or sleeping."

"It is not *my* speech that has the power to command *your* actions." His knight jumped again, pouncing on another white pawn that hadn't yet left the last line of defense. "You need only order me not to stop you from going, and you will find yourself able to walk out my front door."

"And I will also find a knife sent straight into my mother's chest." I sent another white pawn two spaces forward without much thought, eager to let it sacrifice itself and get the worthless piece out of my way.

He laughed and sent the black queen out into the battlefield to take the bold white pawn that had ventured too close on its own to the black army. "Well, well. It appears that you are not the only one in this coupling with power."

I bit down violently on my tongue for a moment. I moved a pawn one step closer to the black stronghold, sending it deeper into danger. "It's a pity you weren't born with yours."

"Was I not?" He sent a black pawn forward one space to take the white pawn head-on.

"I don't think even being born the lord of the castle equates to the power of the lowliest woman in the village." I suddenly noticed a white pawn with the opening to take a black pawn off-guard and slew the pawn before it could do any damage.

"Oh, I would have to disagree." The black pawn that had just recently entered the battlefield avenged its fallen ally by taking the white pawn that had dealt it such a swift blow. "After all, doesn't everyone in the village say the lord is always watching?"

I wrapped my hand around a white bishop in the last line of defense and paused, a chill running up my arm to my shoulder. I thought of how long my mother suffered, and he hadn't done a thing until I'd asked. "Watching, perhaps, when it strikes his fancy."

The lord shrugged and crossed his arms. He wouldn't take my bait. "In any case, I seem to be the only fool with the wherewithal and the means necessary to stand with his goddess as her equal."

"As her equal?" I lifted the bishop and moved it one careful step diagonally. "I'm surprised you give me that much credit."

"I have no choice but to admit your power." His black queen sped diagonally from one side of the battlefield to another, spearing a white rook without my ever noticing it had been in danger.

I yanked up a white knight and let it leap closer to the action. "And that bothers you, doesn't it?"

The black queen zipped horizontally and took out the white queen in one blow. How stupid I had been. I had lost my most powerful piece before she even set one foot upon the battlefield.

The lord laughed, but I knew he wasn't scoffing at my foolish move.

"I have to admit there was quite a lot to celebrate in being so long without my goddess," said the lord once his laughter subsided. "There was no need to concern myself so much with the needs of another." In the sunlight, I saw the embroidery on his jacket clearly for the first time. Roses and thorns. "Check."

So much for the lord's altruism and concern for the villagers. I picked up the white king and moved him one small, pathetic step forward out of harm's way. After the pawns, the king was actually the most useless piece, I was glad to notice. Why were all of the other pieces fighting so valiantly to protect this man too powerless to defend himself?

"Well, there was plenty *I* enjoyed before you found your goddess, too."

"Whether that is true or not, I am afraid you have lost far less than I." He left the black queen to hover dangerously close to the white king and entertained himself by sending a black bishop across the field. It felled the white knight that had so recently entered the fight without even one kill to its name.

"I find that hard to believe." I grinned. I'd nearly forgotten the pawns that managed to survive the brutal slaying by more powerful enemies actually had a hidden power that made their existence worthwhile after all. I moved one of the last white pawns forward one small space.

"You know nothing, you silly girl!" His black knight leaped again to slay an unsuspecting white bishop, a powerful casualty, but a piece I could do without now.

I pushed my pawn forward one more space. "I know that you leave behind no family, no friends to be with me. I know that it is *you* who demands I be here rather than setting me free and moving to the commune."

His hands clenched the edge of the table, like he dared to hope the stone would crumble underneath his pathetic grasp. "The lord of the village does not *move into the commune.*"

I drummed the fingers of my right hand on the stone table and cradled my cheek with my left. "That's right. Because you are a man with *power.*"

"Are you so selfish?" He slammed the table with the palm of his hand. "That you would rather see a man wither than simply be with him? I could give you anything you desire. You would not want for comforts. I do not need your heart, I just need you!"

I bit my tongue and let the sting of pain shoot through me for a moment before releasing it and gesturing toward the game board. "It's your move. I can't let you win without at least a proper fight."

A black-gloved hand grabbed that black knight again, and it jumped around the board searching for prey, landing in an empty patch of the battlefield. His voice grew quiet. "You were born to torment me."

"I think the same of you." I pushed the sluggish pawn one more space forward, passing up an opportunity to take out an overconfident knight that had yet to join the fray in order to make it to the edge of the board without notice.

I ground my teeth together until they hurt. "I'd like that pawn to become a queen now. And checkmate."

The lord stood, upturning the game board with both hands. The bone figures went flying across the garden, the captured white queen caught tightly between the roses' thorns.

CHAPTER EIGHTEEN

When the day of Elfriede and Jurij's wedding arrived, I expected nothing. The air was clear, and I thought I might be able to watch from my window at the very least. But I decided that would be more painful than not looking. If I was honest, it wasn't the wedding I truly wanted to see, but the groom, even if for just a short while.

I hadn't seen the lord since our chess game almost a week prior. He didn't show even for dinner. The specters brought food to me in the garden or in my room.

That morning, the specters didn't retreat from my room after they set down the tray. I asked them to leave me, but they didn't. I yanked the spoon off of the tray and ate my fill, watching the specters warily. Only once I finished did they stir, a couple cleaning the table of my breakfast, and a few more heading to my chest full of dresses. They withdrew a pale lavender gown that I hadn't remembered seeing before. But I'd paid such little attention to the fancy dresses.

A couple of specters appeared at my side, forced my arms up, and began to tug at my nightshirt.

"Stop! What are you doing?"

The specters shifted backward, and I thought I could see a

flicker of flame in the black pools of their eyes. Then the spark died out and they were back beside me, tugging on my shirt.

I slapped at the nearest hand. "All right! But I'll do that part myself, remember?"

The specters let go, and I walked behind the small screen where I could change into a slip in private. It was what I had done the week before, when I had asked them for help in dressing in that white gown.

I sighed and stepped out from around the screen, letting the specters fly into action. They slipped the gown over my head, then brushed my hair and worked in violet ribbons and lilies through the black tendrils. Purple lilies. Like the ones from the hilltops back home.

When they were finished with their work, two specters began tugging on my arms, and I struggled to break free. "Let me go!"

Both sets of hands loosened slightly. Then they tightened and started propelling me forward again.

"I'll follow you, I promise, just let me go!"

They stopped. After a moment, they began walking in front of me. I straightened out my sleeves and followed behind them.

We walked down the stairs, through the empty entryway, and out the front door. The black carriage waited for me, its doors wide open.

The specters paused before the carriage, spread to either side of the pathway, and gestured inside. I took a deep breath and propelled myself up the step, using one of the specters' extended hands to steady myself. A surge of panic implanted itself deep in my chest as I peered inside.

But the carriage was empty. He had let me attend the wedding, and he had not even spoiled the day by appearing himself. I didn't know what I'd done to "deserve" the courtesy of attending my own sister's wedding, but I was going to make the most of the opportunity as it was presented to me. I sat down, the doors shut, and I heard the quiet clop of the black horses as we headed down the dirt pathway.

∾

I HEARD REHEARSING MUSICIANS FIRST, followed by the chirping of birds. The smell of the baker's bread and something sweet tickled my nostrils. Quiet murmuring like a hive full of bees grew louder —and all of that noise suddenly snapped into silence.

The carriage stopped. The door opened. A white hand extended inside. I grabbed it and pulled myself out.

Nearly the entire village was gathered in the knolls among the lily-strewn hilltops. There were chairs, benches, and blankets arranged into rows along either side of the dirt road into the village. Of course, the ceremony took place in the opposite direction of the castle. Too many girls and women would be watching to chance one glancing upward if facing east. At the top of the westernmost hill stood a wooden arch and Elweard, Vena's unmasked husband and the tavern master, if only in name. He was the most popular choice for village witness to a union. It had to do with the discount you got on ale as a result. Vena liked to have Elweard feel important, as long as it didn't interfere in the running of her business.

At first I didn't see any of the faces I'd hoped to see. And then Alvilda, looking stunning in a red gown, jumped up from the front of the left row of chairs. "Noll!"

I saw a wooden duck-face and a beaming smile below a mop of bushy dark hair pop up on the chairs next to her. *Luuk. Nissa.*

Alvilda picked up her skirt slightly and ran down the hill toward me, not noticing or caring that she kicked up dirt in the nearest seated people's faces.

She crossed the distance in mere moments, almost as quick as any of the specters could, and wrapped me tightly in her embrace. She pulled back only to kiss me atop the head.

"I'm so glad to see you!" She grabbed my chin in her hand and turned my face to and fro. The calluses on her hand irritated my skin like sandpaper.

"You look well fed." She moved her hands down to meet mine and pulled my arms outward, observing my new garment. "You look like a lady. Elegant. Beautiful." She leaned in to whisper, "And not at all like yourself."

I smiled and squeezed her hands. "I'm so happy to see you, Alvilda. It's been a long winter."

Alvilda put her arm around my shoulder, guiding me up the

dirt path and toward the arch. I heard the specters and the black carriage move behind me, but when I turned to look, they had only moved to the side of the path and were still close enough to keep an eye on me. Alvilda propelled me forward and kept her voice low, but countless pairs of eyes—human and animal-masked ones alike—drank in every movement we made as we ascended the dirt road.

"I imagine you're anxious to see your father and your sister," she said. "And Jurij," she added in a lower tone. "But you've arrived mere moments before the ceremony is to begin. Come sit with Siofra, the kids, and me, and let's surprise them."

The kids jumped out of their seats and ran to hug me both at once, screaming, "Noll!" The duck beak on Luuk's face poked into my chest.

"Careful, Luuk," said Alvilda, gently pushing his shoulders back. "You'll stab Noll through the heart with that beak."

We laughed. I squeezed them both back, ignoring the poke. I tapped Nissa on the back of the head, and then bent one hand upward awkwardly to pat Luuk's curls that stuck up and out above the duck mask.

"You've certainly grown!" I let my hands fall, feeling sort of stupid for petting the kid atop the head. Another half a yard, and he'd be as tall as his brother.

"Thanks," said Luuk, tucking both hands into pockets in his fine dark trousers. Even through the muffled sound of his duck beak, I thought his voice sounded lower. And without so much as a hint of the quavering that used to accompany his every word.

Nissa, a little beauty in a cream-colored silken dress, put her arm through Luuk's. "Isn't he getting to be so handsome?" That made Alvilda laugh, but she was quick to bite her lip and cover it with the side of her hand, pretending she had a sudden itch beneath her nose.

"Yes, of course!" I'd have said I'd have to take her word on that, but I knew since he was still breathing that Nissa had never seen his face, either. Still, the way her young, dark eyes drank in the wooden duck, I might have been able to believe she saw beneath it to the wonder she thought lay inside. "And I love your dress, too."

Nissa blushed. "I made it with Siofra."

So they were on a first-name basis. I supposed it made sense since she was to be her future gooddaughter, the same as Elfriede. Nissa finally tore her eyes off of Luuk long enough to look at what I was wearing. "We made yours, too!"

"Did you?" I turned in place and let the skirt swish beneath me with a sudden appreciation for the fine skirts and dresses I'd refused before. "It's lovely. You're so talented."

Nissa beamed. "Thanks. We made it last month. The lord paid so well for it, too. We had enough copper left over to buy silk for my dress and for Siofra's, and for Alvilda's too."

At the sound of her name again, Mistress Tailor finally decided to join in the conversation in her own curt way. "Luuk, Nissa, be seated. It's about to begin."

Luuk and Nissa sat back down in their chairs at the end of the row, their hands clasped together. Alvilda guided me a tad forcefully into a seat between her and Mistress Tailor, who looked as pretty as I'd ever seen her in a muted green dress. Mistress Tailor didn't seem happy to see me, but I supposed I *was* unintentionally making a fuss at her elder son's wedding.

My stomach clenched. I'd been so happy to win this bit of freedom that I hadn't quite faced the fact that the man I loved would move beyond my grasp for a second time. But that was unfair. I already knew that he was long, long ago swept away out of my reach.

Alvilda squeezed my hand and pointed to the arch towering over Elweard. "How do you like my gift to the coupling?"

The arch looked familiar. "The headboard?"

Alvilda laughed. "It started off as one, but I had a burst of inspiration that told me this just had to be a wedding arch." She lowered her voice even further and whispered in my ear. "That and I love to tease Siofra. She hates useless gifts. When she saw it, she thought I wasn't going to make them a headboard at all, and I got an earful about always forgoing common sense to suit my poor choices. It was fun." She smiled, and I witnessed an odd flash of something I didn't recognize cross her features.

The music started, the dainty tune that heralded the bride and her parents' arrival at the ceremony. The bride's mother usually stood among them to emphasize the maternal cycle, an act the groom's mother did not share with her son. I thought of Mother lying in the castle for a moment and felt ill. Then I shook my head to clear the stirring of venom and turned with the rest of the villagers to watch as Elfriede and Father came down the first hill and ascended the second, being sure to keep my eyes downward, off the horizon. *I don't want to see the castle anyway.*

She looked beautiful, as fair as ever in a deep-violet gown I imagined to be the work of Mistress Tailor's. It was not unlike my own, although Elfriede's had real, live lily blooms woven into the material. Father stood beside her, a man-face mask hiding his face from me. Elfriede's features fell when she noticed me. Then she smiled, only a slight touch of pain remaining on her face.

They reached the top of the hill, and Father removed his mask and threw it at the ground. His eyes wandered in my direction briefly, his features as cold as stone, but his gaze was quickly drawn away to the hill.

The music switched to the hearty march that signaled the arrival of the groom and his father. Jurij and Master Tailor came over the lily-covered hill, both wearing masks. Jurij's was the man-face mask like the one he'd worn to his Returning, and Master Tailor's was also man in form, a mask I'd never before seen him wear.

When they arrived at the top of the second hill and took their places beside Elfriede and my father, Jurij removed his mask and tossed it on the ground, leaning in toward Elfriede for a quick kiss. Master Tailor removed his man-face mask to reveal his favorite owl mask underneath. The villagers laughed. Mistress Tailor shifted uncomfortably beside me.

Jurij, his back toward me, didn't seem to have noticed me. There was nothing in all of the land that could tear him from Elfriede. The happiness on his face slipped only slightly when he noticed the furrowed brow on Elfriede's expression. But she soon regarded her pain in his reflection and put on her best smile. Unlike me, she could genuinely and completely shift from pain to joy. But she had Jurij, and I had nothing.

I watched the ceremony and felt the pain of the Returning flood back. Once they exchanged the last of their vows and the final kiss of the ritual, they headed back down the dirt path together hand in hand. As their feet disappeared over the hilltop toward my home, my heart sank, and I wondered if he was watching. If this was indeed why I'd been able to go, if this was what he'd wanted me to see.

My clapping slowed, even as the rest of the crowd grew more jubilant. Alvilda's expression grew sour next to me, and she grabbed me gently by the hand. "Let's go," she whispered. She tugged me gently toward the back of the archway. I noticed Mistress Tailor's bitter expression as she watched us go; Luuk and Nissa leaned in toward one another, smiling girl forehead plastered against wooden duck crown. *It never ends, this wretched cycle.*

"Congratulations," Alvilda said softly to Master Tailor as we passed by him. She patted him on the back with her free hand. Master Tailor turned briefly and nodded. I thought I could hear him weeping, but the sound was hollow beneath the owl mask.

We walked around Elweard and stood behind my father. He saw us coming and pointedly turned back toward the jubilant crowd, digging into his front coat pocket and pulling out a small bottle. Before the bottle could quite reach his lips, Alvilda let me go and moved her hands to block it.

"Come, Gideon," she said. "Come and speak now with your daughter."

Father sighed and slid the bottle back into his pocket. The cheering crowd began to make its way toward us and the village.

"Let's go," said Alvilda, taking hold of Father and me, one in each arm. "We can talk at my place. We can pay our respects to the happy coupling later."

We headed down the hill and toward the village. The specters in the distance stirred and jumped atop the carriage.

"Tea?" asked Alvilda, already pouring the hot water into the mugs she'd placed before Father and me. She put down the kettle and went back to her cupboard. As she rummaged around for leaves, Father snuck a sip of ale out of his bottle. Alvilda dropped the tea leaves into the water and took a seat at her sawdust-covered table between us. She looked from one of us to the other. I grabbed hold of my mug.

"Gideon," said Alvilda, when no other voice was forthcoming. "I think it's time you have a heart-to-heart with Noll. It's actually high past time."

Father sighed and began fumbling at the outside of his coat pocket. "What does she know?"

I felt the heat of the tea almost singe my palm through the mug. "I know that my father is so ashamed to face me that he won't even speak directly to me."

Father wiped a tired hand across his gray and black hairline. "I'm sorry, Noll. When I saw you'd showed for the wedding... I just didn't know what to say."

"You should have started by asking how Mother was doing."

Alvilda gasped. Father's eyes widened. "She's well, then?"

I slapped my palms atop the table. Sawdust went flying, probably landing in my tea. "I can't say how well she's doing, fast asleep in the care of a monster!"

Father pulled his ale bottle out of his pocket and took a swig. Alvilda didn't stop him.

"I knew he had her," said Father at last. "I didn't know for certain if she was still living. I thought I'd feel it if she... well. I couldn't be sure."

My eyes couldn't meet his, couldn't stare into the budding ember of flame I knew I'd find there.

Alvilda looked from one of us to the next. "So you've seen her, Noll?"

I shifted in my seat uncomfortably. "Just once. My first night there, he took me to see her in a guarded room, sleeping. She didn't wake. And he made sure that I knew the consequences of abusing my power over him: Her death."

"The cheat!" Alvilda banged her hands across the table.

"That evening when you were gone, Aubree took a turn for the worse." Father gulped the ale for a moment, slamming down the empty bottle. "She was breathing so heavily. She could barely speak, but she couldn't stop moaning. Sweat poured off her like she'd just come in from a torrent of rain. Then she stopped moaning. That was scarier than when she *was* moaning. She was still breathing, but barely."

Father drummed the shaky fingers of his free hand on the table. "I heard a sound outdoors. I thought it might be you or

Elfriede come home at first, but it was louder than that. The door burst open. It was the lord's servants."

He picked up the bottle and tried to take another sip. When he came up empty, he leered at the bottle and put it back down. "I told them you weren't there, to be on their way to find you, that I had a dying wife to worry about. Then they came to the bed and picked her up, carried her right out the door without so much as a word to me. I jumped in and followed. 'This was all I wanted from Noll,' I told myself. Just to *ask* the man. Ask him if he could help us. Since he'd do anything for you."

"I *did* ask him. That same night. You wouldn't believe me. But that's probably why he finally sent for her."

Father shook his head. "The lord greeted us in the entryway to the castle, wearing his black veil and hat. I dropped right down to my knees, even as the pale servants lay Aubree on the floor before me. 'Have mercy, my lord,' I said. 'Do what you can to spare my wife. I'll do anything.' 'And where is Olivière?' he asked. 'Why has she not come with you?' Well, I wanted to say it was just that Noll is such a—" Father stopped suddenly, held the empty bottle to his lips and spat. He wagged a finger at me. "She's a *stubborn* girl, but I thought better than to insult a man's goddess right in front of him, so I said nothing."

But you don't think better than to insult your own daughter in front of her. Not that that was surprising. I took a sip of my tea. It tasted a bit of sawdust.

Father plopped his filthy spit-bottle down on the table. "The lord, he waited a bit for my answer. I suppose he finally figured I had nothing to say to him on the matter, so he bade me to rise. 'That woman continues to aggravate me,' he said, which is why I thought you hadn't visited him. I thought he'd tell me if you had. 'I can heal your wife. It will take time. Tell no one she is here, not even your daughters, and do not come here yourself. You can see your wife again on the day of Olivière's Returning.'"

If he could heal her, why wasn't he certain until he'd sent me away? "He told you not to tell me? How could he—"

Father cut me off, letting go of the bottle in order to wring his hands. "I dared to ask if he was certain he could save her. I regretted the words as soon as they were out of my mouth. He gave me a warning. 'The lord of the village does not make promises he cannot keep.' I begged his forgiveness. I just didn't know what to believe, what with the talk of immortality and how it was his lack of a goddess that had made him master of death. But I knew beyond a doubt that the lord had never found a goddess among all of the women in my lifetime, so maybe it was possible. I just worried that having found Noll, he'd have lost whatever it was that made him keep death at bay."

Of course. Another excuse to blame me.

Alvilda sighed and stretched her arms up over her head. "I hope you didn't say that part aloud."

Again, Father tried to drink from the empty bottle. "No, of course not."

"So you've heard it, too," I interrupted, putting the mug down. "The title the 'heartless monster.'"

Alvilda let her arms fall gently to the table. "People have never liked to talk much about the 'always watching' lord and his servants. A whisper here, a tale there—the things one could piece together are downright laughable." She sighed. "The 'heartless monster.' A strange way to put it, but it means that he's inhuman, an immortal whose heart never found its goddess and so he lives forever."

I felt something strange clutching my heart, like I could feel the man watching me. "Mother told me it was just a story." *But if that dream was real, and that was the lord when he was younger, it'd have to be long ago. So you're actually certain you went into the past. Through a pond.* I knew it was crazy, but it felt true. Maybe spending so long alone in the castle had made me lose my sense of reason.

"I have to admit," said Father, running a nervous finger over his palm, "it seems to be the only explanation. No one can remember when he came to be."

"Nonsense," said Alvilda, waving a hand. "All of this talk of immortality in our blood is merely an old wives' tale."

I cocked my head to the side. "And what of the men and the masks? And the power of their goddesses?"

Alvilda looked thoughtful for a moment but then shrugged. "That's just the way things are."

I mulled that over. What was in front of us was fact. What we couldn't prove was nonsense. But still I didn't understand why men and women were so different. Or why men and women were so different in such a very different way in my drowning dream.

"So you really don't know more about him than the whispers I've heard myself."

"Did you believe those whispers then?" asked Alvilda.

I shrugged. "Maybe. There are far too many things about the man in the castle that set him apart. You have no idea of the lengths to which he goes to offset the power I have over him. I wasn't exaggerating about his threat to kill Mother. It's like he can't stand that he loves me. I'm not even *sure* he loves me. Not that I *want him* to love me."

"Kill? A person? Like the animals we kill for meat?" Alvilda shook her head thoughtfully. "No. I'm sure not. But even so, I can't picture a man who had found his goddess who would do anything other than agonize and wish to please her. Younger boys can manage to engage themselves in different pursuits from time to time because their hearts haven't yet given up hope. But once a goddess turns seventeen, a man pretty much knows whether or not he'll ever have her—in one form or another."

She sighed. "For a man to actively plot against his own goddess seems something altogether new. I know men can be torn between their own desires and the desires to make their goddesses happy, on the rare occasion that those desires don't line up. But for one to grab hold of his own wishes while knowingly making his goddess so unhappy goes against everything we know. If that were true, maybe there could be hope for men without the Returning to find happiness in another form. But that simply is not so." She stared over my father's head at the art on the wall. It always came back to her brother.

"What if I told you I have reason to believe he's different? That he *has* lived a long time. Longer than he ought to have."

Alvilda seemed genuinely curious. "What do you mean?"

"I..." I bit my lip. "Did anyone—your grandparents, talking about their grandparents maybe—tell you of a time when men walked around without masking their faces?"

"No..." Despite the flush on Father's cheeks, he seemed to think I was the one who was drunk.

"You mean, like the tales of the first goddess?" Alvilda asked.

"That's just a story, Noll. A way to explain why thing are. But there's no proof things were ever any different."

Father shook his head. "Maybe they were. Long ago. But the legend of the first goddess must be a thousand years old."

We three sat silently for a while. I felt stupid. *A thousand years? You really think you traveled back in time a thousand years, and that the lord lived then and has lived to this day? How? It just can't be. It felt real then, but now it's just a memory.*

Finally, Father let out a deep breath. He didn't seem interested in my visions of the past. Not when his goddess's life hung in the balance.

"Whatever you think of the lord, Noll, he saved your mother's life."

Both Alvilda and I turned toward Father.

Father traced a pattern in the sawdust on the table with his finger. "Everyone who got sick from that illness died, Noll. Every single one. And I think all of her stress over your refusal to love your man made Aubree susceptible."

I grimaced. This revelation explained much of the unspoken strain between us after Mother's "death." My mother was his goddess, and whatever I was to him, nothing could match the worth he put on her health and happiness. He could feel free to blame me. I no longer cared. "Mother understood. She didn't want to rush me. She wanted me to be happy."

Father licked his dry, cracked lips. "But that's only because she assumed you'd eventually Return to him. Like decent women do."

Alvilda reached across the corner of the table and smacked Father on the back of the head. She sent me a satisfied smile.

Father rubbed his head and looked at Alvilda wearily. "That wasn't a comment on you, Alvilda."

Alvilda pounded her fist on the table. "I don't care. It's a darn careless thing to say about your daughter. What about a woman's *choice?*"

Father shook his head. "What worth is a woman's choice when it comes to the lord of the village? I'd hoped she would learn to love him. At the very least, that she wouldn't wish for him to be as wretched as those in the commune."

"The lord of the village does not *move into the commune,*" I said. Alvilda and Father both looked at me with puzzled expressions. I sighed. "And did Mother know what you had done?"

Father rubbed his cheek and stared at his empty bottle. "No, she was already beyond consciousness by then." A tear trickled out of the corner of his eye; that eye seemed dark and lifeless with its dying flicker. "I didn't know for certain until today that she truly still lived."

"And does Elfriede know?"

Father continued to scratch his chin. "I think she knows enough. She probably pieced some of it together. She spent more time around the house than you after I told you your mother died."

Probably because I spent most of my time outrunning carriages and deliverymen's carts. And because she was there, almost always with Jurij.

I'd had enough of the tiresome discussion. I would say my goodbyes and be on my way. Back to that chilling castle, the closest thing I had to a home now. I stood to leave when the door burst open. Jurij and Elfriede appeared in the doorway, and before anyone could speak, Jurij swept me into his arms and held me tightly.

"Noll," he whispered. "I didn't know you came. We missed you."

My hands moved numbly to squeeze him back. Elfriede, still in the doorway, wouldn't look at me. She stood there, her eyes on the floor, one arm cradling the other against her chest. She hadn't missed me at all. In fact, I imagined seeing her new husband in my arms was enough to make her wish she had seen the last of me when I rode off in the black carriage.

They never cared about me. Not Father, not Elfriede. They wanted me to stuff away all my hopes, all my feelings. I tried. I did. But if I'm going to accept that I'm the veiled lord's goddess, as they want me to, then at least I'll have one thing to remember before I lock all my happiness away.

I ran my fingers through the back of Jurij's hair and kissed him.

CHAPTER NINETEEN

The ground exploded. It cracked and groaned and roared to life. And I knew, just a moment too late, that it wasn't the euphoria of my first kiss that made me feel as if the earth moved beneath my feet. It was actually moving and I was sent flying.

"Alvilda! Are you all right?"

I looked up to see a masked man in the doorway. He crouched near Alvilda, who must have fallen off of her chair.

"I'm fine, Jaron." Alvilda pushed away at his chest even as he extended his hand to help her. "How is everyone else?"

I took in the shambles of Alvilda's home and shop. Furniture tipped over, carvings fell off the mantle, and some of the artwork was on the floor and split in two. Her tools lay scattered about the room. On the ground, Father rubbed his elbow. Jurij lay on Elfriede's lap beside the doorway. Elfriede wept. Jurij was moaning and a trickle of blood ran down his face.

And I was clear across the room, dazed but uninjured. It was as if the ground had moved solely to split Jurij and me apart.

And as I thought that, I knew that it had. That he had made it so.

Why did I do that? Goddess help me. I'm sorry, Jurij. I'm sorry, Elfriede.

But when I thought of how much the lord had overreacted to

my inability to Return to him, I wasn't very sorry to have hurt him.

Although only two specters had brought me to the wedding, half a dozen filed into the home now. I blinked and swore I saw even more of them piling into the road outside.

Alvilda scrambled to stand beside me, elbowing Jaron as he tried to restrain her. He didn't succeed, but he trailed after her, only one step behind.

"What's going on here?" Alvilda demanded of the specters. She still hadn't learned that she couldn't take them in a fight.

"Alvilda—" began Jaron.

"Be quiet until I tell you to speak again!" snapped Alvilda.

Jaron spoke no more.

The specters moved around Alvilda and seized me, propping me up. Alvilda launched herself at them, but the specters weren't bothered in the slightest. Jaron wrapped his arms around the kicking, snarling Alvilda but had no choice but to let her go when she ordered it. Two specters took Jaron's place and grabbed Alvilda to restrain her, if only to stop her from yipping at them.

"I apologize for being so late to the celebration."

Alvilda ceased struggling. Even Elfriede stopped weeping. All eyes but those of the specters turned toward the black figure that had entered the room.

"Congratulations, my dear," said the lord, extending his hand downward toward the weeping Elfriede. She looked back at him, confused, her eyes still swollen with tears.

The lord pulled his hand back, not bothered by Elfriede's lack of reaction. "What an accident!" said the lord. My gaze fled to the fallen Jurij on Elfriede's lap. The blood I'd noticed earlier extended clear across his left cheek. His left eye was swollen and clamped tightly shut. A bloodied gouge lay on the ground beside him.

The lord waved his hand in their direction and a few more specters entered the already crowded home to sweep Jurij from Elfriede's lap and carry him outside. Jurij moaned as he disappeared from view. Moments later, a black carriage passed by the open doorway, silently slipping away from sight.

What have I done?

"Fret not, my dear," said the lord to Elfriede. "My servants shall attend to him." He crouched down and cupped Elfriede's chin in one gloved hand. "There, there. You have to smile. Today is your wedding day. And was it not kind of me to allow your sister to attend?"

No. What has he done?

Elfriede's mouth cracked upward in a hollow echo of her smile. She opened her mouth to speak, but she bit down on her lip quickly. Was it the idea of our mother in the castle that kept her from asking the obvious?

Well, I wasn't afraid to ask the monster a question. "Where are you taking him?"

The lord released Elfriede and stood now, facing me. He adjusted first one glove and then the other, tugging on the leather cuffs.

"Well, well, good day, *my* goddess," he said. "Did you enjoy the wedding, Olivière? Or did you find the reception afterward more enticing?" His words gathered an extra edge toward the end of his latter question.

Heat swirled inside of me. "I enjoyed the reception very much."

The lord placed his hands on his hips and stood immobile for a moment. Then he motioned a hand toward me and turned to exit. "In any case, I can see I just missed the last of the festivities." He nodded at Elfriede, the tip of his hat bobbing down and up. "I dare say your sister will be glad to see us leave. The lord of the castle and his goddess alike. Wherever they go, no mere bride can compare. It seems we have stolen all that was owed to her this day. It is, after all, her wedding day."

"Noll, how could you?" Elfriede screamed as the specters pulled me toward the second black carriage. She was weeping, barely able to speak between heavy, quavering sobs. Her voice grew quieter, the words catching in her throat. "How could you be so selfish? You won't be happy until you have Jurij for yourself. You'd rather he die than be with me."

"Friede!" I shouted back, doing all I could to break free from the tight grips on my arms. I had more to say, but I wasn't sure what it was. I hadn't wanted this. I hadn't wanted her to hate me.

The lord seemed amused. "My, what a joyous family reunion." He nodded at the specters, who pulled me inside the carriage like they were lugging in a sack of grain. The lord grabbed hold of the sides of the carriage doorway and heaved himself inward. "You must be so delighted that you came."

~

MY FINGERS DUG into the black leather seat. It was my first time in the carriage with company.

The lord sat across from me, his hands folded tightly in his lap. I imagined his eyes attempting to bore through the veil to shoot daggers straight into me.

"That was not very nice," he said at last.

I gripped the leather harder, imagining that it was the arms of his leather jacket instead. "What have you done with him?"

"Are you going to order me to answer you?"

"Will you not answer me otherwise?"

The lord moved his hands up, stopping shortly below where the veil began.

"I feel compelled to answer you," he said. "I feel compelled to do anything I so much as think you want done. It is a battle within me not to slit my own throat at this very moment."

I smiled sweetly.

"But I will not let you have power over me."

I scoffed. "I don't think you have much of a choice."

"No, I do not," he said, his head tilting slightly toward the carriage window. "But still, I have the power to fight it. And I will fight it until my last breath."

Don't tempt me.

I bit my tongue and followed his gaze out of the window. We were entering the woods now. I had missed the chance to bid my childhood home one last farewell.

A surge of wickedness came over me. There was one place nearby that was still home. And it could save me, if but for a moment. *You promised them you would help. Dream or not, I've got to know.*

"Were you alive long ago? Say, a thousand years in the past?"

The lord's head snapped toward me. "How could you—"

"Answer me!"

The lord spoke before he could stop himself. "Yes."

I'm not crazy. It wasn't a dream! "Don't move," I said.

The lord tensed.

"Have them stop the carriage."

He knocked on the window and the carriage halted instantly. "Olivière, if you remember—"

"Stay still," I said. "Don't speak. Don't move."

If I can go back, I can stop him before Jurij was ever hurt. Before he ever took my mother. Before she ever fell ill. What if he caused the illness somehow? I didn't understand how or why, but it seemed to be too much of a coincidence since it happened right after I met him. *Maybe he planned to make me grateful to him from the start.*

I have to go back. Before this village ever became cursed with men and their goddesses.

I pushed the carriage door open and ran trembling off of the dirt path and deep into the woods.

My legs burned. My dress snagged on branches and tore. Lily petals fell from my hair, withered already by a day without earth and water. I hiked up my skirt and kept moving.

I reached the cavern and tore inside. I had no candle to light my way, and my feet stumbled from time to time over a rock or a spike I didn't fully remember, but I made my way through the darkness.

And it was the violet glow and the cavern pool that awaited me, called me home.

Even my wild and racing heartbeat seemed suddenly subdued, quiet, and calm. There was something in the pool that wanted me, a gentle vibration, an unrelenting reminder of life. It was as if until that moment I hadn't realized that even among the voluble pounding of my heart, there had been gaps every other beat. Moments of silence in which my heartbeat echoed here, in the pool, in the depths of the secret cavern.

Little droplets of purple rose up from the surface and spread out to banish the darkness trying to invade the corners of the cavern. I moved closer to the edge of the pool, dipping one hand into the water to grab a droplet of violet. But they were too quick.

Can I do this without Elgar? Was the blade the key?

The violet light came from a sphere, large as the pool, covering the bottom. I scrambled to my knees, shoving aside my skirt and scuffing my legs on the cold stone, and bent as close as I

185

could to the water's surface. The little droplets tore off from their shells and rose up to the surface, but as many droplets as there were, the sphere grew no smaller. It seemed to be contracting and expanding, like the beating of a heart.

I took a deep breath and submerged my head beneath the water. The violet droplets soared toward me, and I fell in. The sphere drew me in like a man to his goddess. I would swim to the heartbeat that called mine and embrace it.

I can do this. Even without Elgar.

I snapped awake. A familiar feeling. I felt the sudden shock of the water being disturbed and a moment later a strong arm pulled me violently upward. The figure next to me struggled. It thrashed with such force that eventually, I pulled away from the light. My heart ached as I saw it grow smaller in the distance.

Black leather gloves. A pale arm.

My lungs exploded to life again with a strong slap against my back. The watery violet blood of the beating sphere spilled from my mouth and burned my throat as it left my body. I hacked and choked and sputtered for air while that strong arm remained wrapped around my shoulder, my back to the man who supported me.

"Do not fight the reflex," said the lord from behind me. "You must purge yourself of the water."

I've been here before. Not just in this place. In this very moment. The first dream in the cavern, when Jurij saved me from drowning.

And now he has stopped me from going back to where I was needed. Where I wanted to go.

The hand slapped my back again, and my throat widened, letting the water flow out in a steady stream. Despite the part of me that was reluctant to see it go, still glowing violet even as it poured from within my body, it came easier with each blow.

The hand reaching across my chest slid softly to grasp onto my left shoulder just as I felt the hand that had struck me grasp hold of my right. The hands were wrapped tightly in gloves of black leather—wet leather. But I had already guessed as soon as I heard his voice. There was no one else to rescue me now.

"Olivière," he said. "You could have died."

I felt gentle pressure across the back of my head, the tickle of breath as it whisked past my ear.

"Do not try that again," he said. His hands squeezed my shoulders harder. "Please."

His arms wrapped tightly across my collarbone, his hands coming to rest on the opposite shoulder. He still wore his leather jacket. The smell of wet leather made my stomach rise with a sharp new wave of nausea.

He rustled slightly, thanks to the telltale squeak of his wet leather pants. I felt soft, damp feathers against my cheek and then a light pressure against my right ear. His hair, his lips... he wasn't wearing his veil. And he had kissed me!

I lurched forward, hacking again. I met some resistance from him at first. It annoyed me to find that even with all of my strength I couldn't push his arms off of me. But he let go of my shoulders and let me fall loosely forward. His hands caught me again around the chest before I could hit the ground. Nothing came out of my throat, but I couldn't stop retching.

"Let go... of... me!" I managed to sputter between hacking. Falling forward, I tried to use the small window of time my command afforded me to flip around, to turn my body to face him and let my eyes assault the sanctity of his face, but within moments, I felt a hand push hard against my shoulder, forcing me to lay face down.

"Don't!" His voice seemed all the more commanding as it echoed with the life force of the cavern.

We stayed still a moment longer, locked into our positions. With my cheek flat against the cavern floor, I faced the pool with my back to the darkness down the entry passage.

The hand released me. The cavern echoed with the steady pounding of his boots, which muted the sound of the rustling, wet leather.

"Rise," he said. His voice was once again composed, but there was an edge of iciness that conveyed everything.

I rolled over, fighting the pounding in my head. I sat up and stared at him. He'd retrieved his black veil from the darkness and had tied it around his head once more, placing the hat atop it. They were the only items of clothing he wore that weren't soaked. He towered over me, his arms akimbo, his legs slightly parted. I didn't see any of the specters.

I struggled to stand on my shaky legs. The lord's legs trembled slightly forward, but he stood his ground. Until I lost hold of mine.

He swooped in to steady me, and I pushed his chest, much like Alvilda had done with Jaron.

The sudden comparison brought fresh pain to the ache in my chest. Right after the kiss. Right before Jurij was taken by the heartless monster.

"Stand back," I told him, not bothering to disguise the bitter taste in my mouth. "The smell of wet leather is making me sick."

He let me go and took two steps backward.

I stumbled over to one of the spikes jutting from the ground and used its sharp edge as a grip with which to steady myself.

"You are nothing but ungrateful." Iciness.

I sneered. "Oh, I'm sorry. Thank you ever so much for injuring my dearest friend and then ripping him from my sister's arms on the day of their wedding."

The lord laughed coldly. "It seems to me that you and your *dearest friend* had done enough on your own to ruin the celebration before my arrival."

I scrambled to my knees and drew myself up to stand as tall as I could, trying to match his height and ignoring the wobbliness in my legs. "That's no concern of yours!"

"It is, my goddess, every concern of mine!" He started walking back and forth a few paces before the pool. "Have you no idea of the curse by which you have bound me?"

"I'm the one who's cursed," I shouted, "for I am denied a choice that was promised to me!"

He stopped walking and spun toward me. "You *never* had the choice to love the man who belongs to your sister."

"You're wrong! I'm a woman and I can love where I will, even where love will never find me!" I bit my lip. Even if it hurt others. Even if I was foolish. *I'm sorry, Elfriede. But I can't help but hurt you. Just like you can't help but hurt me.*

The lord started convulsing, his right fist struggling to find a place between pointing at me, resting on his waist, and being raised upward to the sky. "And I am a man! And I am *forced*, against my will, to love just the same!"

His fist unclenched, and he grabbed my left arm with a force I hadn't felt since his struggle against the violet glow's pull.

"Do not speak!" He echoed my words from the carriage. "Do not move against me, or I shall do more than wound your lover and safeguard your mother. I should have let you drown!"

I tried to tear my arm from him as he dragged me forward into the darkness, choosing the pain of struggling against his tight grasp over letting him have hold over me so easily.

"I should have *ordered* you to drown!"

He stopped. His grip tensed on my arm, and his weight shifted from one foot to another. I thought he might run past me and jump back into the water. Instead, he grabbed my other arm tightly with his free hand.

"I do not want to hear another word from you!" he said. "Every word that passes through those twisted lips is poison enough to break me."

"Good," I replied. He said nothing for a moment, and I stared right into where I guessed his eyes might be, a hungry smile curling the corners of my mouth.

"Is your heart so cold and closed to me?" he said at last. His grip slackened.

I clenched my jaw and gazed straight into the void that his veil created in the violet glow. I hoped my eyes, flameless though they may be, would burn straight through him. "I do not need my words in order to answer that."

He picked me up, slung me over his shoulder, and carried me into the shadows.

CHAPTER TWENTY

I could see by the leather-gloved hands just below the billowing black gauze of the curtain between us that the lord had little appetite. He picked at a piece of meat with his fork and had barely lifted any of the potatoes. My own appetite was surprisingly strong. I devoured every last crumb on my plate nearly as soon as a specter laid it in front of me.

A specter came to retrieve my plate the moment I put down the fork, and the black-gloved hands lifted slightly to call another specter to his side. The servant removed his plate and exited the room, but no one swooped in to place the veil and hat on their master. The lord remained seated, his palms resting atop the table.

He lifted the tips of his fingers again, and the specters filed out of the room, every last one.

The dining hall door closed. A gust of wind suddenly seized upon us through the open window, causing the curtain to flutter as if a giant hand had run itself across the gossamer surface.

"Speak now," spoke the lord. "They will not hear. They will not strike."

My tongue was struck dumb. It was impossible. I couldn't trust him. He was always two moves ahead of me.

Fine, I would play along. But he would be surprised to see

that I could play by his rules and still come out victorious in the end. *I'm going back to the pond. I have to stop him before it comes to this. I have to stop all the men.*

"Tell me where Jurij is," I said, my tongue suddenly snapping back into action.

"On the top floor," he replied. "In the room next to your mother's."

"What have you done to him?"

"I staunched and treated his wounds."

My lower jaw was grinding. "To the best of your ability?"

He didn't hesitate to answer. "No."

"What are you going to do with him now?"

"Nothing."

I sighed and rapped my fingers on the table impatiently. "Why did you bring him here?"

"To heal him."

I snorted. Really, he had been so eager to follow my orders for once that I had forgotten to actually form the words correctly. "Tell me why you brought him here."

"To heal him and to punish you."

There it was. I laughed and breathed a sigh of relief. "Release Jurij."

The black hands waved upward. So the specters were still able to follow his orders even when not within sight of their master. *Is this how he is always watching?* I wondered if somehow my wedding escorts had seen the kiss and had alerted their master from a great distance, or if it was the goddess curse that wreaked the pain of the kiss straight to his heart. I hoped it was the latter.

"Release my mother as well," I said.

Another wave of the black hand.

How simple. How dubious.

"Prove to me that they're going home."

A black glove gestured to the open window. I moved across the room, keeping a suspicious eye on his extended hand. I tore my eyes from the lord and let them fall outside the window, my body still facing the billowing curtain.

After a few moments, specters carried Jurij and my mother from the castle door to the two awaiting black carriages. Jurij, his face wrapped in bandages, shifted slightly, but my mother didn't stir. For a moment, I wondered if they were well enough to travel, but my instinct was to get them as far from the lord as possible.

Mother and Jurij were laid one after the other into the carriages. Without a sound, the black horses started moving, and the carriages disappeared down the dirt path through the middle of the woods. The specters who didn't drive the carriages walked in two steady lines after them. More and more specters poured from the castle door and out into the woods until finally, the last of the specters disappeared from view and into the trees. There had to have been a hundred at least, more than enough to keep watch over the entire village.

I faced the black curtain. There had to be a trick, a plan for the specters to strike when out of sight, or to wait perhaps, until they could capture Father and Elfriede, Alvilda, Nissa, and the Tailors, and everyone else within the village before they made their deathly blow.

"Command me to tell you if this is a trick," spoke the lord, as if reading my thoughts.

I wasn't willing to play the game just as he wished it. "Don't ever harm the people I love."

Something odd stirred in the lord. A black-gloved hand clutched the edges of the lace tablecloth, an unnatural dam causing ripples along its otherwise unblemished surface. "I will not harm the people you love."

"Don't ever let your servants harm the people I love."

"I will not let my retainers harm the people you love."

I clenched my fists together. "Tell me if you have already ordered harm to come to them."

"I have not."

He released his grip on the tablecloth. The ripples he'd made diverted seamlessly back into smooth waters of lace.

There had to be something I was missing, something he had planned to stay two paces ahead of me. Because now there was nothing holding me back.

"Tell me why you aren't fighting my orders."

"I never stood a chance against you, in the end." His voice was barely a whisper. His hands tugged carelessly at the bottom of the curtain.

My heart emboldened. Laughably, I felt that surge of pride

that I had once known as a girl, when I was the little elf queen defeating monsters in the shadows of the secret cavern.

And here sat a monster, hidden in the shadows of that black curtain.

I stepped forward. "You will not harm me."

"I would never harm you."

"You will not seize me or grip me by the hands or arms."

The lord tugged at the curtain, and I heard a small rip among the clattering of the curtain's rings. "I will not hold you."

I started, my tongue stumbling for a brief moment. It was off, but it would do. "You will keep no servants in this castle, and no one under your control will ever harm me."

"They are gone. They will not harm you."

I nodded. "You will do nothing to stop me from leaving."

"I will not stop you."

I paused mere paces from his side, only a thin layer of billowing curtain between us.

"Remove the curtain and show me your face."

The black gloves didn't hesitate. They took the bottom of the curtain in their grip and pulled. Rings the color of Elfriede's and Mother's hair, only brighter and shinier, fell like shattered glass all around us, to the floor and to the table. *I've seen a ring like that before—a bangle around Lord Elric's arm in my dream—in the past.* I didn't flinch as the curtain fell, letting the elf queen inside of me revel in her moment of glory. Nothing touched me. The curtain floated briefly before me as it made its leisurely descent.

My chest was an inferno, and I could feel the flame spark on the skin of my breast. My cheeks blazed, and the very blood that ran throughout my veins seemed ready to light my body aflame.

For he was beautiful. And he stabbed me through the heart with his beauty.

His dark hair came down to his shoulders. Like his hat had often done, the hair caught the flicker of the flame in the fireplace and showed me that it wasn't black like the men in the village's, but a dark, succulent brown that only masqueraded as black.

Just as I suspected, he did so look like Lord Elric. But he was paler, much paler. Almost like he was halfway to becoming a specter himself. His skin had an odd, creamy, rosy quality overlaying the soft white. His lips were dark red, as if they had been stained by blood. His nose was thin and straight—and familiar somehow. His brows came together in an almost perfectly straight line, and the bones in his cheeks practically burst through the strange, alluring skin.

His ears were as I expected. They poked through the dark tundra of his tresses and rose upward into jagged points. I stepped closer, my hand extended forward against my will to finger the sharp edges. I stopped and pulled my hand back before I touched him.

A timid smile slowly splintered his faultless face. His lips parted, and I could feel the warmth of his breath cross the few paces between us.

"And so you have made your choice at last, Olivière."

The fire in his eyes burst into red flames. And then he was gone.

CHAPTER TWENTY-ONE

E lgar must have proven essential to getting back to that place. Or it was all a dream after all, despite what I knew in my heart to be true. I tried jumping in again to no avail. Every time I came to the surface, I came back here.

Home and not home. But not at all that place I'd once been, that place with Avery and Ailill, with the darker lord and Goncalo.

So I'd given up. I lived among those who were lost among the living. I carved and I whittled, I sat and I stood, I walked and I lay. The few men who populated the commune did not disturb me, so lost were they in their own torment. We watched together daily as the farmers—men, women, girls, and boys alike— marched past from the village and into the fields beyond our heap of dilapidated shacks. They marched past again what felt like years later as the sun set, the women and the girls with their heads held high despite the fact they faced the east. They didn't look our way, and we didn't stir. And that was the most we could hope for of peace.

After the lord vanished, the earth trembled. My memory turned black, and then I woke up in a large field of dirt.

A field where the castle should have been.

I dragged my feet forward numbly, cradling my arms to my

chest in the chill of the moonlight down the dirt path back to the village. I paused at the edge of the trees where I usually broke off the path to visit the secret cavern. I'd try jumping into the violet sphere beneath the waters during the days that followed. But that day, I just wanted to be sure everyone was well.

I arrived at my home, recognizing the windows on the house on the horizon lit brightly by the flame of the fireplace.

When I opened the door, I was greeted first with surprise and then with warmth by Arrow, Elfriede, and Jurij. His face was untouched, not a scar or injury to be seen.

"Where's Father?" I croaked. "Was Mother brought home to him?"

The light fell from Elfriede's jovial face. "Mother and Father are dead, Noll."

She brushed her palm across my forehead. Jurij peered over her shoulder, his face full of concern.

"Were you out in that cavern again?" he asked. He touched my shoulder, and I shivered perceptibly. Still, Jurij didn't notice. "Did you swim? You don't appear to be wet from the pool."

Elfriede tugged gently on my elbow. The force was not one I couldn't fight against should I have wished to, but I had no such desires then.

She led me to the bed we shared and tucked me in.

"Rest now," she said.

She's forgiven me. I closed my eyes but didn't fall asleep.

Hushed voices held counsel over my questions.

"Why did she come back here?"

I should have known she was still angry.

"I don't know. She's acting delirious."

"Why did she ask for Mother and Father? How could she forget Mother died from her illness almost a year ago now?"

Impossible.

"Or that Gideon followed her shortly thereafter? I don't know. She doesn't seem... right." The way he spoke the last word made me wonder what the "right" me would be.

I flitted in and out of consciousness. A long time later, I heard the soft moans and rustles from behind me in my parents' bed, and I shuddered, pulling my quilt tightly over my head. In the morning, I glanced at the coupling intertwined in one another's arms, Arrow resting at their feet, breathing easily in their slumber. My gaze fell upon the delicate valley of lilies carved into the unfamiliar headboard. I left without a word, dragging my feet back down the dirt path and through the village.

I stopped in front of the Tailors', wondering if I might find shelter there. But I thought of Luuk and Nissa—the little Jurij and Elfriede in training. What room would there be for me? What place was there for me, among the sewing and the clothes? I walked westward.

I paused at Alvilda's door. *No. No, that wasn't home, either.*

The commune was just a few paces away. When the pool brought me nowhere, I had nowhere else to go.

And there it was that I sat now, carving life into a block of wood. At first, I left the commune only to speak with Alvilda, to borrow tools and to get supplies. She was as concerned for me as Elfriede and Jurij had been—perhaps more so because she wasn't lost in the bliss of Returned love as were those two. But she didn't pry.

I had but one question for her. "What became of the castle and the lord of the village?"

She ran her sawdust-covered palm over my forehead. I let the dust settle in my eyebrows. "What are you running your mouth on about now? What castle? What lord?"

There was no castle, no lord of the village. And there never had been.

I was nobody's goddess—odd, but not worth much notice in the village where all were concerned with their own exchanges of love and Returning. Maybe my man would be born a few decades later, they thought—it'd happened on occasion before. Old Ingrith didn't even have a man yet when she died, they said. Of course, I knew better.

She hadn't lied. She'd seen her man's face before she loved him, and with that, she killed him.

Pity she was gone now, too. She might have been the only one who could understand me.

For I knew now what she meant when she talked of killing a man no one else remembered. The fate worse than death that lurked around every corner for a masked man was that the eyes of a girl or woman upon his face would make him vanish not from life, but vanish completely from existence. It would be as if he never lived, forgotten to all but the woman who granted him that fate.

I had two visitors once, early on. And only once. Luuk and Nissa stopped by, the cart they dragged full of hides.

Nissa gasped when she saw me. "It's true! You're living *here!*"

Luuk's bear face tilted slightly. "Why?"

I looked up from my carving and opened my mouth only to find the airwaves cracked and coated with dust, my lips too dry to form words. The kids watched me expectantly. "I have no home," I said at last.

"That's not true!" said Nissa, her hands on her hips. "You were supposed to move in with Alvilda, the night of Jurij and Elfriede's wedding."

Alvilda told me that herself the first day I'd spoken to her. A new cot still took up a corner of her home, its quilt coated with sawdust.

Luuk pointed to the figure in my hand. "I thought you were going to become Auntie's apprentice. That you would take up a trade while you waited for your man to finally find you."

"My man did find me. I killed him. I killed him, and no one remembers."

One of the men from the commune tumbled out of a shack, his back slouched, his arms practically dragging against the ground. He moaned as he stumbled forward toward the bucket of water the farmers dropped off every few days for drinking, but his aim was off, and he bumped against the kids' cart, his outstretched arm brushing against Nissa's waist.

Nissa screamed, and Luuk jumped between her and the cause of her terror. "Let's go," he said, dragging her by the elbow toward the cart. The sight made me queasy—the thought of being pushed and pulled as I had been in another life—but Nissa let her man guide her without hesitation. As they pulled the cart away, she alone looked back at me.

Her expression reminded me of the look I'd given Ingrith when I thought she was just an old, crazy lady, before I realized the truth of what she said.

"Learned from Alvilda?" The voice was filtered and hoarse.

I turned my head slowly. The man scooping water up beneath his mask was Jaron, the only other commune resident whose name I had ever had cause to know. I recognized his worn-down animal mask from the quake at Alvilda's house, although I was certain he wouldn't remember the incident if I asked him, either in this life or my last. He stumbled forward and perched on a rock next to me, peering at my woodworking from behind his facial coverings. I couldn't make out what animal it was supposed to be.

I suddenly took notice of the shape of the wood in my palm. A rose. I ran the gouge brusquely over the petals, tearing them asunder.

"Yes," I said at last, not feeling that Jaron warranted my silence.

If he noticed that I now wrecked my creation, he didn't speak of it. Instead, he put a hand on my shoulder, his touch as light as a feather. "She will not come here."

She? Oh, Alvilda.

It was not Alvilda who was my torment. However, I knew instinctively that to this broken man, all torment was Alvilda. My heart tightened, and I wondered if Jaron and the other men in the commune had always felt this way. Even a tenth of my feelings for even a tenth of a second would be torture.

It was a wonder they did not die.

"That's good," I said. And it was true. I was in no mood for visitors.

Nevertheless, Jaron sat still beside me, his mask pointed toward the jagged wooden rose in my hand. I put the broken blossom on his lap and walked back to my shack in the middle of the commune.

AFTER A COUPLE OF WEEKS, they didn't feed us anymore.

There were supposed to be pity scraps, weren't there? The rotted produce that didn't sell in the market. And the buckets were supposed to be refilled because someone remembered the men didn't have the strength to pull their own from the nearest village well. Because someone cared enough that we didn't die of thirst. But the buckets ran out of water a few weeks after I joined the men in the commune.

I saw a man vanish one morning, his rotted dog mask clattering to the broken stone tiles in the middle of the commune. I felt compelled to trace the fading pattern on the mask, the nose, the mouth, the long, floppy ears, one half broken. I hoped it wasn't hunger or thirst that had killed him. How long were these men going without food or water? How could I have been so lost in myself that I hadn't noticed? I'd hardly eaten myself.

The men were lying in front of their shacks, moaning. One man was half in a shack, half out, rolling around and pawing for an empty bucket. He scooped imaginary water with the scoop beside it, lifted the empty ladle up under his mask, and grunted when the ladle fell from his grip, clattering to the ground. "Water..." It was the first word I'd heard him speak that wasn't the name of his goddess.

"Water," another man nearby joined in.

"Water," they all repeated.

I wanted to roll on the ground beside them. I wanted to not want water, to let myself vanish with the life I knew.

But thirst won out. As did the constant chorus of "water" punctuated by the names of women from around the village.

Those women couldn't care less if you starved. I knew it. What I once wouldn't have given for the problem of the lord to resolve itself without me. For him to suddenly vanish, for me to not know it was my fault.

I stood, fighting the weakness in my legs, and grabbed the nearest empty bucket. Without responding to any of the anguished cries, I headed toward the well at the center of the village, not caring if I drew everyone's notice as I dragged my feet through the crowd I knew I'd find there.

I drew no one's attention. And there was no crowd in the market.

Merchants' stalls were threadbare or empty. There was only a quarter of the amount of produce I expected to find and almost none of the cheese or fabric. The little things that no one needed, even if they were lovely, the gifts that men often bought their goddesses, were gone entirely. The rotting produce that would normally have gone to the commune was for sale at discounted prices, and it was only those cheaper items that the few villagers with baskets were buying.

"Come now," said one merchant. "Don't you have a young boy and girl at home? Don't you want to feed them the best? Look at the color on this tomato!"

A woman who seemed vaguely familiar grimaced and rifled through her basket for a single copper. "No. These." There was a pile of wilted vegetables in front of her, and she shoved them eagerly into her basket after the man accepted her coin, sighing as he tucked it into a pouch at his waist.

"I suppose no one can afford to pay for your husband's music no more." The man put his perfect tomato down gently with both hands in front of a sign that read, "High Quality Produce. Among the Last. 3 Coppers Each." He scratched his chin. "Why is that, you think? What went wrong? Seems just a few weeks ago, the farmers had more food for us than we knew what to do with."

The woman tucked a wilted head of lettuce on top of her basket. "I don't know." Her lips pinched into a thin line. "Maybe you merchants pay them too little for their crops because you charge too much and no one's buying. Now they don't have enough copper to feed themselves anything but what they manage to hoard from the rest of us."

The merchant yawned and stretched a hand over his head. "But the prices aren't so different, are they? I know we charged more than this for quality goods just a short time ago. And we had no need to sell this wilted trash."

I didn't think the woman cared. "Good day," she said, curtly. She met my eyes as she passed and looked at me from top to bottom, but she said nothing. I realized my bedraggled appearance wasn't as out of place as I expected. The woman's dress was coated in white dust, and I wondered what a musician's wife was doing to get that way, and who was watching those children the merchant mentioned if she worked.

"No one has enough copper." The merchant stared overhead, not paying me any mind. "How could so much copper just vanish into thin air? Goddess help us." He kept muttering to himself and I pushed forward down the path, my eyes widening as I took in the line in front of the well.

They *were* all tired. No one was quite as tired or hopeless as the men in the commune, but there was something different in the air. Men still had their arms around women, and women still laid their heads against their men's broad shoulders. But there were fewer smiles and less laughter.

"Thank the goddess water is always free," said the woman in front of me to her man.

"Yes, darling." He kissed her forehead. "I'm sorry."

"It's not your fault the payments at the quarry have decreased." The woman bit her lip and traced a finger over the man's chest. "How can the foreman *forget* where he got the copper to pay everyone from when people weren't buying stone for building materials? How does he expect to replenish it with more copper if he can't pay the men enough to dig it up?"

"We'll find more." The man took the woman's hand in his. "We all have our goddesses to take care of. So many of the men have children—"

"Thank the goddess we haven't yet had any." The woman smiled, but just barely. She didn't seem thankful at all. "I don't mean... Don't get it into your head that I don't want any. Because I do. It's just..." Her voice quieted as she played with her man's shirt. "I'd hate for them to be so hungry now, along with us. Someday it'll get better. We can welcome them then."

Someday it'll get better. It won't.

The bucket fell out of my hands and clattered to the ground. The coupling in front of me tore their gazes from each other just long enough to glower at me, but I didn't care. I crouched beside the bucket and hugged my knees to my chest.

They don't remember the lord. They don't realize it was him who kept this village running. I didn't even realize it was him, really. How could I? He never even came down to the village. He never spoke with the people directly. How could I have known he helped so many?

How could I have known what I was doing, when I yearned for my own freedom?

"Hey. *Hey.* Do you want some water or don't you?" The woman behind me kicked at my back lightly.

I saw the line that had formed behind me and realized I was some distance from the well and it was my turn. I didn't know how long I must have been lost in my thoughts. "Yes," I said, quietly, thinking of the men in the commune.

Every muscle ached as I dipped the bucket down with the rope to the well and pulled it back upward.

They all knew. Before they forgot him. They all wanted me to Return to him, to keep him happy because he was their best customer.

Because he kept this village going.

～

A COUPLE OF WEEKS LATER, I laid on the ground in my shack, telling my thoughts to quiet for once so that I might sleep and enjoy a brief moment of peace from my waking dream.

"Because you bring us water. And scraps. And for the rose."

A gruff voice. I struggled to open at least one eye, but my eyelids were heavy, and it strained me more than it should have. I blinked to bring the streaming moonlight into focus. A black figure stood in the doorway.

I shot up from my pile of hay on the ground. My heart beat harder, stronger.

And then I recognized Jaron standing before me.

It wasn't the lord. He was gone, and he'd taken everything I knew with him. My life was gone. I felt the violence of a torment that would not break, even across the jagged surface of my heart.

Jaron must have recognized the feeling in my face, for he was soon crouching before me with both hands extended.

He held a sheathed blade. *Does he even know what's in his hands?*

Before I could stop myself, I grabbed it from him, pulling it out of harm's way and removing the blade by the hilt. It sparkled with a violet glow that felt all too familiar. "Elgar? How…"

"Don't know what it is. Maybe a carving tool. Found it in a tree hollow in the woods," croaked Jaron tersely. "When cutting wood for Alvilda. Years ago. She would not take it."

Years ago? Of course. I just have to leave it there for him to find, all these countless years later.

I felt a stirring in my heart that wasn't quite like the pain it had known for the past month. It was mixed with great sorrow for Jaron and the truth of the longing I knew he felt even now for Alvilda.

I sheathed the sword and squeezed Jaron's shoulder. "Thank you."

Jaron's mask bobbed, and he stood up. He left the shack just as quietly as he had entered it.

I pulled out the sword, gripped my hair into a tail behind me, and sliced it off close to my scalp. Now that I was alone, I was free to be myself. There would be nothing about me for anyone to make pretty.

∾

I BRUSHED ASIDE the last of the branches that blocked the cavern's entrance from view. Elgar, my blade, had summoned me here. The sheath hung from my waist, and I rested my hand comfortably over Elgar's hilt. I couldn't walk through this life anymore. My parents were gone. My sister and the man I'd loved were lost in each other completely. The lord had vanished, but he left behind a feeling of emptiness in my chest each time I thought of his face—and I hated myself for that. I didn't want the burden of remembering him. If my heart was empty after I had slain the heartless monster, I would let the blade and the violet glow guide me to where I would stop him from hurting others in the first place.

I was the elf queen—and I was nobody's goddess.

CHAPTER TWENTY-TWO

Elgar proved the key to getting back through the violet sphere, as I'd guessed. This time when I resurfaced, I knew immediately it had worked, even though I had no reason to believe the cavern was any different.

But there was an ax against a nearby rock. As I grabbed it, I noticed Elgar and its sheath were missing from my waist. The memory of the lord taking the blade away with him to the castle surfaced, more real than I had let myself believe it to be all these long, long months.

There's no going back now. Not without getting the blade back. Somehow I knew this, even though the pool had taken me back once without it. But that was just as well. I had no place to go back to.

When I exited the cave, dripping wet with water, I came face to face with Avery. She looked at me like a piece of animal dung she had stepped in. "I almost went back in to see what was keeping you. Did you fall in that pool?"

"I…" I studied Avery's face. "How long was I gone?"

"What are you talking about?" Avery raised an eyebrow. "Just a few minutes. Did you lose consciousness?"

I shook my head.

"What did you do to your hair? Did you lop it off with the ax?"

I fingered my shorn tresses. *So that change made it through the journey.* To Avery, I'd walked into the cavern with long hair and walked out with short. It might have drawn attention away from the changes to my clothing—not that my dresses looked very different. But my back was missing the terrible sewing job Avery had done long ago. "Yeah… it was getting in the way."

"If you say so. The men will *love* that." Avery shrugged. "And maybe next time save the swim until after you've worked up a sweat."

We worked for hours. I felt almost as if I'd never been gone. As if my home was the dream. This felt so natural, so real. Like I didn't have anything terrible behind or before me, just the whack, whack, whack of the ax. I wondered how we were going to carry all of the wood back to the village without a wheelbarrow, and whether we'd bring it back to the commune or to a workshop I hadn't yet seen, but Avery said not to worry about it. Some days she just felled the tree and left the collecting for another day's labor. She was far enough ahead in her work that the men didn't care how she paced herself.

It took us most of the day, and my muscles ached for Ailill's touch by the end, but we brought a tree down with a thunderous crash and a surge of pride and exaltation. We hugged each other in triumph as the ground shook. For a moment, I remembered the times I looked at the castle in that other life. My spine tingled.

Back at the commune, Avery guided me into her shack, which she shared with more women and girls than ought to be able fit inside.

"Sorry," I said as I nearly fell onto a woman nursing an infant on the ground.

The woman looked as if she were staring into the eyes of a monster.

I crouched down to face her, and she backed up as far as she could, practically willing the strength to knock down the wall of the shack so she could back away even farther.

"She's darling." I tried my best to put on a smile and pointed to her baby. "What's her name?"

Avery grabbed me by the shoulder, pulling me upward. "It's a boy," she said. "He won't be named until he's weaned and sent home to his father. Only the girls stay with us and get our names."

I let Avery guide me to a small open corner of the shack across the way. The nursing woman sighed with relief as I left, letting a small smile work itself onto her face as she looked down at her baby.

Avery crossed her legs, sat down on the ground, and tugged at my hand for me to do the same. There was really only room enough for one of us, but I grabbed my knees tightly to my chest and did my best to cram onto the little free floor space anyway.

"You have to separate those likely to fight from the weak," she whispered. "The ones likely to fight have fire in their eyes."

That's right. You promised to help lead a rebellion, not take on the lord by yourself. But that was even better. I'd have help. I'd stop him for certain this time. Maybe life would be different when I got home. Maybe Jurij would never have found the goddess in anyone.

There was no flame in the eyes of the women and girls around me, not like in the men back home. But I soon understood what Avery meant. Most of the women and girls huddled together, crying softly, staring blankly, or looking ready to fall over dead. In the three other corners of the room were the biggest and the strongest—which meant nothing compared to a healthy woman back home—leaning or standing against the wall, nodding over at me as I looked.

"It's not enough," I whispered back. "We've got to get them all—or at least most of them—to fight."

Avery snorted. "We've been trying for years."

"But there are more willing, right? In the other shacks?"

Avery shrugged. "A fair few more. But not even a tenth of our total number."

Two women and a girl sitting on either side of us looked over uncomfortably. They tried to back away as best they could, but their space was limited. Avery shot each of them a look. "Cower and hide, like you always do! It won't change anything!"

The few whispers and moans in the room stopped. Avery stood, heated, looking down on all of the women gathered.

"You heard me," she said, her voice quiet, but her tone strong.

"We're the men's slaves and all of you—every last one of you—is the reason why the men think they own us."

"Don't give us trouble," croaked an older woman from across the room. "Just let us have peace."

It was my turn to jump upward. "You don't *have* peace!" Avery and the women in the corners seemed pleasantly surprised. The two who had been sitting stood to join us.

"I've come to help you!" I looked at some of the nearest faces, felt the pain and fear radiating from their eyes. "You called for me, in your hearts, I know it. You've suffered. Where I come from, it's the women who bring the men to their knees! It's the women who give the orders! Women don't have the power to heal, just the same as the women here—but we have something more powerful than that. We have a choice! And *you* have a choice! You can choose to be miserable, to give your daughters the same shoddy echo of a life that you enjoy, to labor and birth and die, or you can choose to fight!" I was lifting some of the sentiment from the lord's blessing. But what more suitable time was there than this?

The women gasped. Some hid their faces. The women standing in the corners gave a delighted cry, raising their fists into the air.

The euphoria spreading throughout my body came crashing to a halt.

"What is going on here, women?"

The sitting women screamed or buried their faces deeper into each other's bosoms. Those in the corners slunk back down to the ground. I faced the entryway and saw Goncalo. Behind him stood a few more men, their hands locked tightly on to a number of bedraggled women.

Avery cut in front of me and bowed, immediately lowering her head to the ground. "Just trying to liven spirits with a few stories, sir."

Goncalo scoffed. "No need to sharpen dull minds with stories in the commune, woman." He grunted and waved his hand forward. The other men pushed the women they were holding forward into the shack and let them go. Instead of catching one another, they tripped and fell and screamed, trying in vain to move out of each other's way.

"His Lordship is done with these," spoke Goncalo.

The men started moving about the commune, not caring if they stepped on a hand, foot, or leg. They shoved women over, grabbing their faces, slapping through their clothing at chests and backsides. Some molested women were ripped upward into the men's grasps.

Avery tensed in front of me. She crouched down and stuck her hands out behind her, grabbing at my bodice and trying to pull me down with her. I followed, but I hadn't yet reached the ground when Goncalo spoke.

"You cut your hair?" He spat. "How unseemly. But you won't hide that way." I dared to lift my head slightly and saw he was pointing directly at me. "That one's coming with us," he said.

Avery rolled around to face me, pretending she was falling forward against me in the ruckus of the men moving about the shack.

"Find Ailill," she whispered.

"Are you coming?" I asked.

"No, they can't take me to the lord," she replied. "He won't speak—Ailill. But find him."

Before I could ask why, two sets of hands seized me and dragged me across cowering women and out into the night.

CHAPTER TWENTY-THREE

I recognized the black carriages straight away. However, the black horses that pulled them shook their tails and stomped their feet, unlike the ghastly horses I had seen before. I thought that we would all be shoved inside the carriages as I'd always been, but the men instead dragged us to the back of the last carriage in the procession and bound our hands together before hooking the rope on the hitch. Then they piled into and on top of the carriages and cracked a whip. The horses trotted away. We stumbled after them.

Some of the women fell straight away.

"Keep up!" I whisper-shouted. "Keep up or the pain will be worse!"

The fallen women grimaced and pushed themselves up.

We continued to stumble as we headed up the dirt road and through the village. A few women fell, but I was never among them. I kept coaching the other women to stand up, to keep up, to ignore the leering eyes and the whistles of the men we passed along the way. By the time we broke free of the heart of the village, the other women and I had gotten used to each other's rhythms, and we trotted evenly in a straight line.

We continued over the hilltops, maintaining our grit and determination not to fall even then, and broke through the woods in a single formation. The central dirt road through the woods made for easy travel after the ups and downs of the hills. And before we knew it, we were there—at the castle. I was still not used to looking at it so freely. Its spires seemed less menacing now, even if I knew what lay ahead was sure to be worse than what was inside the castle when I'd lived there. But it was still so large, even larger so close. It loomed tall above us, threatening to swallow us up.

The carriages stopped before the large open doors. Fire and candlelight poured forth freely from inside. Roaring laughter and music filled our ears. Men came back to cut the rope loose from the carriage. Goncalo walked down the line, inspecting each of us. I noticed too late that it was I alone who still faced forward. He was drawn instantly to me.

"You all seem more sound than the women usually are after this journey." He grabbed me by the chin again and peered down at me. He needn't have bothered. I wouldn't have let his gaze intimidate me into looking away.

"I thought I heard you saying something to the others as we traveled," he said.

It wasn't a question, but I answered anyway. "I just told them to keep up, so we wouldn't all be dragged down by ones who fell."

Goncalo's lips trembled.

"Sir," I added, too late.

He smacked my cheek with the back of his hand.

"Good," he sneered. "Then you are all well enough to entertain us straight away this evening."

The women gasped, and more than one sent a surge of loathing in my direction.

Goncalo finally released my face. "Freshen them up!"

A series of women, old or scarred or altogether plain, came out from the castle. They bowed slightly and then grabbed our rope by the lead, like we were livestock to be pulled onward.

We were dragged upstairs, and more than one woman stumbled and fell this time, whether from exhaustion or just to spite me, I didn't know. But the women not bound by ropes didn't stop.

~

WITHOUT A WORD, the castle women freed our hands and got to work making us over. They washed us from head to foot, put us in slips and dresses, and combed and styled our hair. I was outfitted in a white gown, not unlike the one I had worn that day so, so long ago for the chess game in the garden. The one difference was the black shawl the old woman in charge of me draped over my shoulders.

I had a strange feeling about the old woman. She said nothing, did nothing that would make me think "crazy old crone," but her large, dark brown eyes had been burned into my memory. I couldn't help but think of Ingrith.

The woman made one perceptible noise, a disgruntled sigh when she picked up the brush and took hold of my cropped hair. Her hands went to work, brushing what little hair I had left. In the end, she managed to make my jumble of locks look presentable—even attractive—which defeated my purpose for cutting my hair in the first place. She finished the job by wetting the tendrils that caressed my cheeks and pulling them back, tucking a fresh red rose from a vase on the vanity behind my left ear.

Then she did something I didn't expect. She bent forward and whispered into my ear. "What sets you apart will be their undoing. Don't hide it."

I met her eyes in the vanity mirror and opened my mouth to speak, but she silenced me with a pinch to the cheek that was not still stinging from Goncalo's blow. It brought forth a rush of darker color. "This won't do," she said, lightly touching the bruise.

She nodded approvingly to the other castle women and the women made up like playthings. "Send them down," she said. "I need one of the boys to fix this one first."

The women did as bidden, exiting and leaving the old woman and me alone in the room, shutting the door behind them.

She met my gaze in the mirror and squeezed my shoulders.

"I'm Livia," she said quietly.

"My name is Olivière."

Livia nodded. "A nice strong name. A bit similar to mine, if I may say so."

"My friends call me Noll," I said.

Livia shook her head. "Women here do not need friends. They need a leader. They need Olivière."

To be needed... a leader. The women in my village needed no such thing, so complacent were they in how things were, how they perceived themselves to be in power. They couldn't even remember the leader they once had, the one who kept their lives so simple and easy.

The door opened just a crack, and a child squeezed his way through the opening.

"Excellent," said Livia, sweeping forward to greet the small figure. "They sent Ailill." She shoved the door closed quietly behind him and put her hands on his small shoulders, guiding him over to the vanity.

"Hello," I said, reaching my arms out to greet him. I hadn't seen him in so long, and he reminded me anew of Jurij as a boy. He may not have worn a mask, but he was just the same kitten in demeanor.

Ailill's eyes grew wide, and he buried his face in Livia's apron.

"He's a shy one," explained Livia. "But he's the most kind-hearted."

I smiled. "I've met him before. At the commune. He healed me after I was whipped."

Ailill rustled the edge of Livia's skirt and peeked over. Livia patted him on the back.

"Foolish child," she said. "Always off to visit his favorite sister."

I nodded. "Avery. She's the one who explained to me how things are run here."

Livia cocked her head. "So the whispers are true. You *are* an outsider."

"You didn't know? Avery said women knew who belonged to the commune."

Livia freed her skirt from Ailill's tight grip and gently pushed him forward. "Oh, no. I've spent most of my life here in the castle. I've never been a looker, but I can keep the place well in order. The present Lordship's father was the first to take advantage of that.

"Go on and heal her cheek, Ailill. Please."

Ailill looked cautiously first at Livia and then at me. At last, he extended both palms outward, and I felt that embracing, violet glow seep the sting out of my cheek. When he finished, Ailill stared at me and touched my ear cautiously, bringing some of the glow back to his fingers.

I took his hand in mine and pulled it gently away. "Those don't need to be healed." His eyes widened. "Thank you again, Ailill," I told him. "Avery told me to find you. I'm so glad I did. My name is Noll, by the way. But people here call me Olivière."

Ailill backed away, knocking into Livia behind him.

"Thank you, child." She patted his head. "You may go now."

Ailill nearly tripped over his feet in his rush to the door. It creaked open, and he disappeared, pulling the door closed behind him.

I turned to the vanity to see my unblemished cheek. Livia pinched it, bringing dark color to its surface. I wondered why she didn't just leave the slap mark.

"You don't speak to him with reverence," I said. "Ailill."

Livia sighed and placed her hands on my shoulders. "Not yet, anyway. It takes a while for the boys to learn to be heartless. For some, like his Lordship Elric, who made his father especially proud as a boy, it takes far less time than for others. Ailill is slower than most. He's been tormented, and like his father, he had such a fondness for his mother."

"Avery said she was very beautiful."

Livia nodded. "She was. She was a frequent 'guest' of the castle in her day. All the men were captivated by her, and she bore many children."

I cocked my head. "Many?"

Livia exerted pressure on my shoulders and directed me to stand. "Very few—only the hardiest—survived long. She bore more daughters than she did sons, and fathers care no more for daughters than they do for livestock. They only take special note of daughters and sisters to decrease the risk of inbreeding."

That's disgusting.

We walked across the room, toward the door. "Ailill was the

last she bore, and they say she saw something special in him—perhaps a human heart that no other boy could hold on to. It ripped her to pieces when they took him away. Ailill, unlike most boys, was drawn back to his mother. He started sneaking back into the commune for visits almost as soon as he could walk."

"And none of the men knew?"

We had reached the door now, and Livia spun me around to face her. "It was known but looked at as little more than an annoyance. A weak boy, a boy with too great a heart, a foolish boy—it led to a lot of torment that halted the boy's tongue. When his father died, he lost all special treatment he had in their shared fondness for that woman. When hearing of his father's death, His Lordship Elric rode straight into the commune, caught Ailill in the arms of his mother, and ordered her dead by morning. He made Ailill watch it happen."

I gasped. Livia nodded.

"Be wary how you deal with His Lordship," she said. "There are few women who do not wish his downfall, but there are none with the courage to play his game and win it. Perhaps you will be different."

I clenched my jaw. I would do it. I had won before, when I had everything to lose, and I would win again, when we had everything to gain.

CHAPTER TWENTY-FOUR

I stepped into the lit dining hall, easily willing each foot to move forward. It was a grand spectacle, and I was late to the festivities. Music blared from a corner in which several castle women plucked at their instruments grimly. Men danced, whipping their women partners to and fro. Other men sat around, eating and drinking, their arms wrapped tightly around one or two women. Castle women moved about, serving more food and wine. None of the women had food or drink. No woman had a smile on her face. There wasn't a man without one.

Except for the lord. He sat without his hat before the fireplace in a chair I recognized immediately. It was the chair in which he dined with me, although I had seen it only once, after the curtain fell, when so much of the color would be drained from the man who sat there now. Three women sat on the ground beside him, looking away. He cradled his cheek with his hand and tapped on the armrest impatiently.

There was no way to blend into the crowd, not with my late entrance, not with the rose in my shorn hair, and not with my exposed ears. Man after man turned from his women and companions to look upon me. The lord had not taken his eyes from the doorway the entire time; his gaze had been locked there before my entrance, as if he had been waiting for me.

He stood, not noticing or caring that he stepped on one of the women's hands as he did. The music stopped abruptly.

"Well, if it is not Olivière, the mutilated woman whose name I must use to address her. You made it to the celebration at last."

The men looked at one another and laughed. The lord held a palm out toward me.

Fighting the urge to flee or vomit, I pushed myself forward and let him take my hand. He brought it up to his lips and kissed it. A cold, dry kiss.

He cocked his head slightly. "What did you do to your hair? Short hair to match short ears?"

"What are we celebrating?" I asked, ignoring the question.

Men around the room whispered. A flicker of delight spread across the lord's face as he pulled my hand outward to the side, wrapping his other hand tightly around my waist. His golden bangle clashed against my wrist like a block of ice. I put my free hand on his shoulder.

"Why, your arrival, Olivière," he said. "And the end to all of my boredom."

He swept us both to the center of the room, and the music struck up again. Other men followed suit, dragging their partners to join us. I didn't let the lord drag me. Instead, I matched each of his steps with an echo, allowing us to dance as two, active and reactive partners.

It didn't go unnoticed. The lord leered at me, first concerned and then delighted. "You dance like no other, Olivière."

"You'll find I'm like no other," I said.

"That I can see. It is a wonder I did not notice you earlier." He freed his hand from my waist to run the coarse leather over the rounded edge of my left ear. "But perhaps it took your mutilation for me to notice your beauty." He gripped my waist again.

It would be mutilation that attracted your interest. I smiled sweetly, my gaze falling toward the lord's abdomen, where Elgar was sheathed. "The blade becomes you."

He laughed. "And yet I feel it drawn more to you—a woman, of all things. Would you care to delight me with the tale of how you procured it?"

"I'm afraid it's not much of a tale to tell. I was born to wield that blade against a heartless monster, and so it found its way to me."

The delight fell out of the lord's face, and we stopped dancing. "They say that each lord of this village finds a woman with whom he could not bear to part," he said. "I always thought it a weakness. I am not sure my mind is altered."

I made my best attempt at a grin. "But surely you, of all people, would delight in a change from the usual tedium?" I stopped myself from mentioning he would be less bored if he picked up a tool and worked once in a while.

The lord cocked his head. "I am no longer sure. What do you propose?"

His words shot through me like a kick to the stomach. Whatever he had in mind, I couldn't bear to give it, no matter what opportunities it might afford me. Besides, Elgar wasn't yet safely back within my grasp, and I felt that I couldn't properly confront a monster without it.

"The garden," I said, suddenly thinking of my old sanctuary.

~

WERE it not for the red roses that grew in place of the white ones, and the lack of a statue on the fountain, I would have thought I was back within my version of the garden. I could have sat down at the bench and table and awaited specters to bring me playthings and food. Perhaps some paper and ink. A block of wood. Or a game of chess.

The lord pulled me into his arms the moment we stepped onto the garden cobblestones, running his fingers through my hair, his lips over my face. I shuddered and convulsed and wanted to let him continue and also to scream and rip his eyes out all at the same time.

Instead, I put my palms gently on his chest and tried to push some space between us. "Do you enjoy chess, Your Lordship?"

The look of shock and anger on the lord's face at my gentle shoving was equal only to the joy that appeared now. He let me go and laughed, running a hand through his hair.

"Chess?" he said. "You bring me to the garden to play chess?"

I nodded. The lord's smile fell a moment, and he cradled his chin with his thumb and index finger.

"How do you know of chess?" he asked.

My heart raced. I'd said it without thinking, but a lifetime of labor wasn't suited to casual pursuits. That, and I was sure the lord didn't think a woman's mind capable of the intellect required to play.

"I taught her."

Both the lord and I faced the timid voice. It was Ailill, who stepped cautiously from behind a nearby rose bush to lie for me. I had to lift my hand to my face in order to stop my jaw from flying open.

The lord was not pleased. "What are you doing here, brat?"

He yanked Ailill's elbow, dragging him across the thorns and ripping small tears in his flesh.

"And you taught a *woman* chess? Are you stupid?" The lord laughed. "Of course you are."

He dragged Ailill past him, shoving him to the ground, so he could drop his boot on the small of Ailill's back. "Still looking for *Mama*, Ailill? Your sisters and the castle hags not enough to comfort you, so now you're spending time teaching games to deformed women?"

I rushed forward without thinking, collapsing to the floor and tugging on the lord's boot. "Get off of him!"

His boot lifted without resistance. He looked down at me, still as a statue, his anger transforming to confusion. My heart beat rapidly, and a familiar feeling swept over me.

I wrapped Ailill in my embrace. He looked up at my face, frightened, but I gave him a warm smile and pushed his head against my shoulder. He started chewing his thumbnail.

The lord placed his arms akimbo and laughed. He raised his head and laughed harder still, like the heartless monster I knew him to be.

"Looks like you found a new Mama after all," he said once his laughter died down.

"I'm not his mother!" I snapped. "I just can't believe you would treat him so cruelly."

The lord's smile vanished. "She is not a sister, is she?"

Ailill looked up slightly and shook his head no. The tension fled from the lord's body.

"All right, then," said the lord. "Let us play a game of chess. Ailill can help you."

~

WE SAT at the stone table, the chessboard between us. Once again, I played white to his black. Ailill sat tight against my thigh, watching the game intently, occasionally removing the mutilated thumbnail from his mouth to grab my hand and direct it to another piece. His choices were always right, and it was only with his watchful eye and guiding hand that I stood a chance of winning.

And winning I was. The lord's face soured.

"I tire of this," he said, when I stood but one or two moves from victory. He knocked his arm across the board, felling the rest of the bone figures and destroying my chances.

"You have a good teacher, Olivière." He stood and glared at Ailill, who buried his face in my side. "Too good. Although I admit it has been a pleasure playing against an opponent other than my feeble brother. Even if I think you owe more than a few of your small victories to him."

My heart skipped a beat. "Your brother?"

The lord gave me a look of bemusement. "You did not know?"

My jaw went slack. I couldn't form the words. "Then you… you ordered your own mother's death?"

Her own child killed her. I couldn't believe it. And here I'd been, thinking he was needed in the village, my heart half softening to him, even though I was still so angry with him. Until then, I'd pictured Ailill's mother as my own. Ailill nudged his face deeper into my side. The lord laughed.

"I did. She was nothing to me. I was rather annoyed by the hold she had over my father and this brat, to tell the truth, and once my father was dead, there was no reason to suffer her any further."

I choked. I couldn't find the words to speak the monstrous anger that spread throughout my blood.

"Get off of her," said the lord coldly. He reached a black-

220

gloved hand into Ailill's hair and tugged hard. "This one is mine."

Ailill moaned. His face pulled backward, tears lining his cheeks.

"Let go of him!" I shouted.

The black-gloved hands let go.

Ailill and the lord both stared at me, their faces reflecting the same puzzlement I felt. And then I knew. I knew for sure what my heart had been trying to tell me.

I shot upward. "Give me my sheath and blade!"

The lord unfastened the loop, removed the sheath from his belt, and handed it to me with both hands. I snatched Elgar from him and tied it back around my waist.

"Lord Elric. I want you to listen *very* carefully. Set all of the women free from the castle and send them to the commune inside of the carriages. Tell the men you tire of them and do not want a single woman here for the rest of the night. Speak to no one of these orders—in fact, forget them as soon as you have followed my instructions. Now go. Go!"

The lord, his face as empty and nearly as pale as a specter's, turned and left.

I looked down at Ailill and smiled. He breathed heavily, his face flooded with tears as he gazed up at me.

I grabbed his hand gently, but he tore it away.

"I think you should come with me," I said.

Ailill shook his head and stumbled back toward the rose bush from which he had first appeared in the garden.

I heard a loud ruckus coming from the entryway beyond the garden door. Voices, whispers, screams, and gasps. The thunderous clomping of the hooves of horses from outside.

"Ailill, come with me! Hurry!" I shouted.

Ailill shot out from the rose bush to my side. We joined the bewildered rush of fleeing women, the men still shoving and pulling them this way and that.

As we climbed into a black carriage, I caught a brief glimpse of Ailill's face in the moonlight. His eyes were wide with terror. He had seen a monster.

CHAPTER TWENTY-FIVE

"We strike tonight!" I shouted. "Before the rest of the men have time to think about what might happen with all of the women gathered here in the commune."

I stood before a roaring bonfire in the middle of the commune, still clad in my white gown and black shawl. All of the women and girls of the village crowded in a circle around me. Some still clung to each other, but quite a few more than usual now seemed ready to stand on their own.

Avery stood beside me with a few of the potential rebels. Ailill still wept into the folds of his sister's skirt, while one of his free hands clutched Livia's beside him.

"You have seen what I can do!" I said. "In my village, each woman commands the man who longs for her." I laughed. "But here, the men long for every woman! I can tell the men to do as we please!"

And I had. On the way back to the commune, I'd knocked on the carriage door and ordered the guard men to go door to door in the village, bringing forth any woman or girl taken for the night to be set free and sent back to the commune. Remembering Alvilda's words about my passed message to Master Tailor, I ordered the guards to tell any questioning man they encountered that I had ordered these women set free.

And they had been.

"So why don't you order the men to slit their throats now?" barked one of the standing women. "If your words carry such power?"

"I could..." To tell the truth, the idea was unsettling, even if these men were not the men I knew from my village.

Avery shook her head. "No. We do this with our own hands." She shot me a sideways glance. "And rely on Olivière only if things go sour."

I smiled and turned back to the crowd. "I know you're scared. But I heard your voices calling me. I came from beyond the mountains." It was true, after a fashion. "I'm here to show you that you can fight, that you have the power to end this nightmare! I know what it's like to live without love. I know better than any other could. Never more! Never more should you labor and birth and die!"

A number of women raised their fists and shouted.

"Who's with us?" I screamed.

More and more women raised their fists and shouted.

Avery cupped her hands over her mouth. "Just don't forget to leave a few for breeding!"

Laughter broke the last of the tension that held tightly on to the crowd.

Avery grinned and placed her hands on her hips, satisfied. "Let's go!"

The women shouted and screamed.

"Olivière," Livia spoke quietly beside me. "Not all of us are able to go."

I looked at Livia, her face covered in wrinkles. My gaze fell upon a few women still with child or nursing and the little girls in the crowd. Some were still scared and moved nervously to the outside of our circle.

"If you don't feel you can fight with us, do whatever will keep you safest during our battle."

Ailill dropped hold of Livia's hand and Avery's skirt and took off down the dirt path eastward.

"WHERE DID AILILL GO?" I asked Avery as she strode to a tool shed in the commune and ripped the doors open. She started pulling out axes, knives, pitchforks, and hoes and passed them down to her comrades, who spread them throughout the crowd of women.

She shrugged. The furor coursing throughout her body was too strong for her to bother with the safety of her brother, even if he was the only one of the two she could possibly love.

"If he's smart, he'll head to that cavern we went to earlier," she said. "I've shown it to him before."

I nodded, the nausea rising from my stomach slightly cooled. But still, I felt uneasy. "Why didn't Ailill heal your mother?"

Avery grimaced and picked up her ax and gouge from the tool shed, the last weapons that remained inside. She turned them over in her hand hungrily. "He tried. She was too far gone."

"Does their power not work on all wounds and illnesses?"

"The deeper the wound or illness, the longer it will take and the more power it requires to save someone. He would have had a better chance with a serious illness, but it would take all of his power, and it would take a long time. Tear a person into too many pieces too quickly, and no man has the power required to heal all the wounds in time to save them."

I felt sick at the thought of Ailill weeping before his fallen mother. What did she mean, too many pieces? Had he removed her hands and feet? Her arms and legs? Did her small, innocent child—a boy who still had a heart—stand there, watching the blood pooling around the last recognizable pieces of her body until she vanished, free of her pain at last?

I'll never forgive him. Never. I don't care what role he played in my village. I had the sudden urge to fight.

"That's useful to know." I pulled Elgar from its sheath and held it before me, allowing the moonlight to heighten its violet glow. "We'll have to make sure we don't leave behind too few pieces."

Avery grinned.

～

WE STRODE through the woods down the dirt path, my mob of women and I. Avery stood beside me, her ax raised high in the air, a battle cry escaping her lips every few moments. Every time we encountered a man between the commune and the castle, I ordered him to go inside a building and stay there until a woman came for him. I told him he was never to hurt a woman again. And I ordered him to pass along my message to any man or boy he came across in the future.

No, we would save our bloodlust for the castle. At least at first.

As we passed the area where I always broke off for the cavern, I sent my best wishes in that direction, hoping Ailill had done as Avery had said and that he was out of harm's way.

We left the last of the trees behind us, and Avery and I stepped forward. Avery lifted her gouge in the air to signal the mob to stop behind us.

Goncalo and his usual group of men snapped out of their lazy conversations and looked at us. They seemed surprised to meet with so many pairs of defiant eyes.

Goncalo fumbled with the back of his belt and pulled out his whip. As if a whip had a chance against a blade and an ax.

"What are you women doing?" he barked.

I smiled. "We're changing how things work around here."

Goncalo scoffed. "I'd like to see you try." He cracked his whip on the ground.

"Whip yourself," I said, devouring both words with my tongue.

Goncalo did as bidden, whipping the weapon across his legs. He yowled in pain. The men behind him murmured, pulling out their blades shakily and pointing them toward us.

"Settle down," Goncalo said to his men. "My fault. A rare mistake."

"Whip the man next to you," I said.

Goncalo did as bidden. The man jumped back and screamed. Blood dripped from an open wound on his arm. He lifted his other hand and pressed it over the wound, letting a violet glow pour forth. He looked at Goncalo with the confusion of an obedient dog kicked by its master. The crowd of women behind me burst into laughter.

225

Goncalo picked up his whip and strode toward me. The veins on his forehead throbbed to life, distorting his otherwise flawless features. "You insolent woman."

"Let us pass," I commanded. "All of you."

They could wait. It was time to say goodbye once and for all to the lord in black.

The men shuffled sideways, clearing the path before us to the castle door. More than one seemed lost in thought; others, like Goncalo, shook and trembled, doing their best to fight the orders given. But they couldn't move until my entire mob had passed through the door.

As the last woman stepped inside, Goncalo and the other men forced their way through the crowd, shoving women as they went.

I parted my lips to speak a command, but Avery thrust out her hand to cover my mouth.

"They'll get what's coming to them," she said coldly. "For now, let them think they have the upper hand."

I wondered how they would explain the whip and the way they let us pass. Perhaps they wouldn't be willing to admit that they had been dumbfounded and obedient at a woman's words.

"What is going on here?"

The lord entered the grand entryway from the inner garden door. I wondered briefly if he had been looking for me there. Had my orders muddled his memory, caused him to remember leaving me last at the end of our chess game? The door shut behind him, but that large crack I had noticed the first time I ventured inside the castle was present even then, and a trickle of moonlight fled into the foyer. The fire still burned brightly in the open dining room hall, but there was no longer any music, no longer any laughter.

"Lord Elric," spattered Goncalo. "There are women walking freely out of the commune, disrespecting men, waving around those playthings—"

The lord lifted a tired hand. "Enough, Goncalo. I can see."

Goncalo's face burned darker, and he took his place standing behind the lord. His hand still gripped the whip's handle and not the blade at his hips. He would regret the choice later.

The other men were not so sure of themselves. Many of them drew their swords as they gathered around the lord and Goncalo, and the rest tensed their hands on their hilts uncomfortably.

The lord put his hands on his hips. "The question is *why* are these women here?"

I put Elgar back into its sheath so that I could mimic his stance, the one that had always stirred rage inside of me.

"We come bearing a message," I said. "And it's for all men, not just for you, Elric."

The lord raised an eyebrow. "You have never been one for courtesy, Olivière. I believe you are addressing your lord."

"I have no reason to give courtesy where there is none owed."

The lord laughed. "As disdainful as ever, *woman*—Olivière."

He looked puzzled. I smiled. He hadn't intended to speak my name aloud. I had ordered him to address me by my name, after all, even if I didn't know at the time what I was doing. "One day you will surely beg to forget my name, *Elric*."

Goncalo surged forward, cracking his whip. "You insufferable woman—"

The lord halted him with a wave of his hand.

"No, please," said the lord. "Let her speak. She went to the trouble of bringing all of her friends for a visit. Let us hear their message, and then we can be done with this mess and punish the lot of them."

The last of the men who had not yet drawn their swords did so. The women shook their tools. I caught Avery's eye beside me. She nodded and began slinking away from me, between Goncalo and one of the other men.

I drew Elgar again and pointed it toward the lord, closing the space between us. It bothered me that he didn't move, and his guards didn't stir from their posts. I stopped just a few paces from the lord, Elgar looming dangerously close to his abdomen. He looked amused.

"In your arrogance," I began, "you have treated the women of the village as your slaves. You have worked them to the bone while the men sit on their asses. You have plucked them from the commune at will, treating them like your playthings, all of you— fathering children like it was no greater deal than siring cattle."

I turned my eyes from the lord and let them wander over the rest of the men in the castle. I recognized a few from my day in the stocks. Those last few words would be especially suited to them.

I continued. "But you will learn what love is, and you will respect the power women can have over you. For where I come from, it is women who have the freedom to do as they will, and the men have no choice but to follow them."

The lord tapped his fingers against his elbow impatiently. Behind me, the women started shouting and spreading throughout the room. Many stared straight into the guards' faces, willing them to melt.

Still the men didn't strike. My blood boiled.

"I will not let you forget what you have done!" I cried. "What I say will be done by any man who has ever felt longing toward me."

A flash of pain marred the lord's stunning features, but only for a moment. The women continued to circle the room.

I felt moved by the lord's sadness, as I had the only time I had seen him before all of this, when he was drained of color. But then I thought of Avery, Livia, and the other women of this village. I thought, too, of Ailill watching his mother die, using his healing in vain on a woman chopped into pieces. I thought of the lord's disdain and lust for me in my version of the village, the twisted game he played with my comatose mother, his plotting and planning to match his power over mine, blow for blow. I knew what I had to do. I would not let him die this day. He had to suffer, to know firsthand what he inflicted upon those around him. I only hoped I could word it so that I would win in the end, so I could enjoy watching him vanish that day in what I now knew to be his future—with one direct look from my eyes.

Yes. It's clear now. Things have to be this way. I felt as if a force unseen took over me.

"Men of this village!" The words flowed so easily. The curse that had shaped my life tumbled out of me. "Love only one woman each and treat her as the goddess she is. Leave no woman without a man to worship her. Obey your goddess's commands, pine for her heart and body and suffer if she will not Return her love to you. Win her heart with obedience and affection to enjoy a small reprieve from your torment. Fail to feel the Returning of her affections, and rot away for the rest of your wretched existence."

There was a strange stirring throughout the room. The men cocked their heads, as if lost in a dream. The already lax grips on their swords grew even laxer.

The lord's face flew into a fury. His expression contorted with something I guessed to be pain, his eyes rolling backward in his head.

I smiled. "But I have a special command for the lord of this castle. Do not find your goddess for a lifetime after a lifetime and more. Until then, keep no living company in your castle, not even the company of living, breathing horses with which to ease your loneliness. Live the lives of many men, leaving a mere shadow of each life behind to keep you company and to remind you of how long you have suffered.

"And don't think that a pretty face will abet you, Your *Lordship*, in your quest to win your goddess's heart. All of you men, lord and guards, villagers and tormentors, cover your faces now, cover your faces always, or crumble under the eyes of the women around you and vanish forever as if you had never existed. Find sanctuary from this command only in the blood relations who know you are no more than breeding stock and among all women only once you have earned the love of your goddess, no sooner than when she ages from girl to woman."

The last words had not yet left my mouth when I saw the tip of the gouge jutting through the lord's chest. It dripped with blood, spilling drops on the stone floor. Lord Elric fell forward without a sound. Before he could hit the ground, he vanished, and it was the leather clothing, wide-brimmed hat, and golden bangle that broke the silence, clattering like the crash of thunder that would start an avalanche.

Avery stood behind where the lord had been, her mouth contorted into a look of primal lust. She licked her lips, raised both her ax and her bloody gouge, and shouted out a cry that reverberated across the castle walls. The other women joined in, running forward while shaking their axes, hoes, and pitchforks at the ceiling.

Lord Elric had been stabbed, perhaps dead before I gave my command to the lord of the castle. But I had spoken all of the command aloud before I could stop my wayward tongue.

But this wasn't what I'd meant to do.

The spell was cast.

The castle roared to life. A halo of violet light spread across the land and the ground shook.

As I fought to stand steady, my eyes darted about the entryway frantically, falling at last upon the small figure peeking through the crack in the door to the garden. The dark eye that locked on to mine was wide and frightened.

Ailill. Who I could see so clearly now would grow up to be striking—perhaps more striking than his brother. Who was now the lord of the village and had been the moment Avery's gouge had struck the killing blow to their brother Elric. Who would now bear the brunt of my curse.

Who would one day love me.

No, he already loved me, in his childlike way. And that was all the more reason why my words would hold him prisoner, now and forever.

A flicker and then a flame burst to life in that small dark eye.

I felt ill.

I sheathed Elgar, knowing I would never draw blood with the blade. It was no more meant for slaying monsters than the tree branch I had once called by the same name. Full of pride at myself and my power, like I had been as a child, I was just pretending at battle. I hadn't meant for this to happen. The cavern pool had called me to a dismal time, and I was just following the example of the first goddess.

No. The truth was too plain.

I was the first goddess.

I dashed across the short distance between myself and the garden doorway, shoving aside women, dodging spears, watching as the guards screamed and fell and vanished one after another. A man who didn't fall prey to an ax, a hoe, or a pitchfork melted into thin air with no injury, banished from existence simply by the look of a woman's eyes upon his face. Goncalo stumbled and turned around to avoid one woman's stab only to come face to face with my stare. His eyes widened, the newfound flame within snuffed out, and he was gone.

A sour taste rose high within my throat. I ran through where Goncalo had been and ripped the shawl off of my shoulders. *I have to cover him. I have to teach him to keep his face from women who don't love him.*

I almost stopped right there, realizing what I was thinking. But I knew I had to move on, that covering him was the right thing to do.

That he would be safe from my eyes, if not safe from the eyes of anyone else but his sisters'.

After a lifetime, I reached the door, my hands running wildly over the coarse wood until I gripped the iron handle. Pulling it open the smallest amount I could afford, I slipped inside and slammed the door shut behind me.

Ailill stepped back from me as I entered, tears flowing freely from his firelit eyes, his hands shoved forward weakly to block me. Ignoring his attempt to keep me from him, I flung the black shawl over his head and dragged him behind the nearest rose bush. Squeezed tightly between the wall and the blooms, we both got pricked and scratched and gouged by the roses' pointed thorns.

I crouched down to my knees to match Ailill's small height and shifted the shawl so that I could see his face, which I cupped in both hands with as much force and tenderness as I could inject. His chest expanded and contracted rapidly. The look of terror on his face felt worse than any blow that had been inflicted to my body.

I smiled, although it broke my heart to think of what my words had done. I formed the next few words carefully. "For you, Ailill, lord of the village, for you alone, I have another command."

Ailill's shallow breathing slowed somewhat, and his face grew less terrified. His eyes dared not blink and would not move from mine.

My words meant for Lord Elric, backed by the ferocity of the abused women among my ancestors, had been too powerful to undo. I couldn't speak a countermand directly, for I had passed my power to all of the village's women, and they knew nothing but contempt for their abusers. I had forbidden the lord company in his castle, I knew, but I wondered if Ailill would still get around my words by seeking company elsewhere. Avery, her hands now so soaked in blood, would be unlikely to put much thought into saving Ailill so fresh after her victory. If he ran to someone like Livia, to whom he was not blood related, Ailill could vanish from existence. Long before I could meet him.

But how could I save him? I felt the hot sting of my foolishness, for even if I had intended the worst for Elric and the rest of the men, even those words rightfully placed would have harmed this poor, dear boy before me. I thought, too, of the men I knew from my time. I thought of Father and the shade he became following Mother's illness. I thought of Master Tailor and Jaron, stuck loving two women whose hearts would never Return to them—and also, by forcing them each to bear responsibility for a man's misery, what my words would do to rend Alvilda and Mistress Tailor unhappy. I thought of Mother and all of those who loved where love was not wanted. I thought of Nissa and Luuk and all the rest—children who grew up overnight because of the love I forced upon them. I thought of friends lost to love, and love lost to friends. I thought of Jurij, and all the lost hope of love I would come to know because I myself willed it.

There was no deep malice in my village's men. What disdain there was only existed because I had forced them to think of none other than their goddesses. Perhaps my words this day had made that happen, but they had doomed the men of my village, too. They had doomed us all.

"Ailill, though you may be bound by words already spoken, hide away and banish women and girls from your castle. Do not allow them even to look upon the castle, so that they may forget it and leave you alone. Treat the villagers well, but do not, if you can help it, walk among them—if you do, the earth will tremble, and the skies will rumble to scare the villagers away from you, to protect you from harm. The same will happen if a woman lays her eyes upon your abode. Await your goddess safely within your castle. She will find you."

The words came freely to me, but without the force I'd felt before. It was like these were my own words, and those others were someone else's.

The tears slowed their descent down Ailill's trembling cheeks. A snowflake appeared on his dark eyelashes, but the flame within his eyes couldn't melt it. Snow was falling, despite the previously temperate weather, threatening to blanket us in white.

"You will feel compelled to love your goddess, but do as your heart tells you. If you are ever to vanish at her direct gaze, you alone shall have the power to return."

I bent forward and kissed him atop the forehead. The frigid snow that peppered his scalp chilled my lips.

The roses beside us were blanketed in snow, hardly a trace of their red petals to be found. Letting go of Ailill's face, I yanked at a snow-covered blossom, not caring that a thorn poked my finger as I did. I tore out the thorn and placed the newly white rose in Ailill's open palm, giving his hand a tight squeeze with both of mine.

"Return back to life in your own time, if you alone will it. Return as if you had merely spent a time sleeping. And free yourself of woman's power upon your return." I bit my lip. "I command you to overcome the power of women at last upon your return."

I stood and pulled the shawl down over his face. A braver woman, a nobler woman, would stay and help the boy through the fate I had given him, but that woman was not me. There was no place for the kind of woman I was here, a pretender. The violet glow of the cavern was already calling for me.

Still, as I turned to go, I paused at the fountain, remembering the crying boy who would one day be entombed atop of its cascade of water. The more I thought about it, the more certain I was that the statue was of Ailill as a boy, now that I knew how he looked then. Had Ailill had that statue carved? Did it remind him of what I'd done to him, of what I'd done to all men, to women, too? What I wanted to do now was selfish, and I had been selfish enough to doom all of our kind. But still, my mouth opened.

"If, after your own Returning," I said, my back still to the shivering figure, "you can find it in your heart to forgive me, you, the last of the men whose blood runs with his own power, will free all men bound by my curse."

I clamped my mouth shut and marched forward. Through the door, past the torn and bloody piles of clothing, beyond the cheering women. I had played at leader, I had played at queen, and this is what my foolishness got me. I slipped away unnoticed into the secret cavern in the woods. I didn't look once behind me. My last act was to leave Elgar in the hollow of a tree I passed, waiting for Jaron to find it many, many lifetimes later.

CHAPTER TWENTY-SIX

Even without Elgar to guide me, the pool acted as before, but in reverse, its terrible purpose fulfilled. If the blade wasn't key to traveling, then I didn't know what was. I didn't know where the power came from, and it was just as much a mystery to me as the healing powers of the men. Had the suffering of women called me? Whatever the reason, I had answered pain with pain. I set in motion all of the misery that the men and women of my village suffered for generations. I had saved the women from torment, but the price was the free will of all men and the liar's choice of women.

All of that time I'd spent hating the laws of the first goddess—hating the very idea of goddesses—when I had made them all.

So lost was I in my thoughts that it took me a moment to realize the glowing cavern was lit up in red, not violet. I didn't test my theory, but I suspected it was a sign I was no longer welcome, that the past was forever closed to me. The beating orb at the bottom of the pool even seemed to cease, the silence seemingly pushing me away. So I left.

When I exited the woods, I expected to see the altered village on the horizon. I almost wanted to see it, to know that I couldn't go home, to have no choice but to devote myself to shielding the boy with a heart from the brunt of the pain I had caused him. It was a choice I wanted, a choice I should have had. But my feet carried me back to where I would live among those who suffered for my foolish tongue.

I headed toward my childhood home, not sure if my feet should instead take me straight back to the commune. But I was eager to at least see their faces. I didn't deserve comforting, and my heart hardened knowing that I would likely find little comfort awaiting me regardless. Little did they know, though, what real reason they had to hate me.

I halted a few steps from the front door. A chill brushed the back of my exposed neck and down throughout my soaked body.

The castle had returned.

My heart soared, my stomach hardened. But the ground didn't shake. They had worked, the words forming my final command. I'd given him permission to dispose of my power.

I pulled on the door in front of me.

"Noll?"

Jurij spoke my name. He stood next to the fireplace, his hand in Elfriede's, a stark scar across his cheek, his left eye wrapped in a bandage. Wounds from my kiss, as though the castle and the lord had never vanished.

Tears littered Elfriede's cheeks, her eyes neither on Jurij nor me but on the bed in the corner. Arrow sat alert by her side.

There sat my father, his arms thrown tightly across my mother.

My heart stopped. *Have I lost her a second—no, a third time?*

But her eyes were wide open, her pale oak face almost glowing.

"Noll?" she croaked hoarsely. "Come here, darling!"

I obeyed freely.

Tears shed down my cheeks, and I felt the moisture with my fingertips like it was something entirely new. I'd forgotten the feeling. I hadn't cried fully since the day before my seventeenth birthday.

We hugged and laughed and cried, my family and I, long into the evening that was already half-gone.

~

"F‌ROM WHAT G‌IDEON and Elfriede tell me, there's a strange gap in their memories that lasts about a month." Mother tilted her head to face me. "All they can agree upon is that there was suddenly a monstrous shake of the earth. Everything that happened since the wedding is in dispute. No one can remember clearly."

Including Elfriede's last words to me that day, I wonder?

Father slept soundly in the bed beside Mother. A few paces away, Elfriede and Jurij slept in the bed I once shared with my sister, Arrow comfortably nestled at their feet. Elfriede's breathing filled the air, as light and dainty as her speaking. The bed she shared with her husband, complete with a new head-board from Alvilda, no longer had room for me. There was no place for me in that house. But there I sat, at a chair pulled up next to the bed, my hand clutching Mother's.

"A strange thing." Mother picked up my hand and bounced it against her lap. "But there are stranger. Me sitting here, alive and well, for one. Aren't you tired?" she asked, her voice a whisper.

"I've spent enough time dreaming." I shifted a loose lock of Mother's golden and gray hair behind her smooth round ear. "I want to stay here and know that I'm finally truly awake."

In the last embers of firelight in the hearth, I could just make out Mother smiling, her head against the pillows stacked in a pile to support her back. "The past year. It all seems a dream to me."

You don't know the half of it.

Mother tapped the back of my hand with her free palm. "I wish you would tell me what's bothering you."

I did my best to smile and pulled my hand away so I could remove the rose from my hair. The petals crumbled nearly as soon as my fingers touched them. "I can't explain, not tonight. You're still weak, and it's been a long, long day."

"I'm feeling much better. Almost like I was never ill, just sleeping, and now I'm still getting used to the waking world." She stretched her arms above her head. Her face glowed in the dying firelight, and I knew she wasn't lying. "Do you know who healed me?"

I didn't dare to guess, not aloud.

Mother clasped her hands together over her lap. "It was your man. The lord."

I shook my head. "He's not my man."

Mother smiled. "So I hear. But he was unmasked. And quite handsome, I might say. Although rather strangely pale."

The corner of my mouth twitched. "Not as pale as his servants."

His "servants." The shades of all of his former lives. I shuddered to think just how many there were and how many years he had spent alone in his castle, only the shadows of his past selves to keep him company. I was surprised he wasn't driven completely mad. Or maybe he had been.

"No," Mother laughed, but then she bit her lip and looked pensive for a moment. "Noll, when I awoke, I found the lord sitting where you are now, his hands held over my head."

My instincts had been right; Ailill had finished healing my mother, even after all I'd done to him.

"There was a strange violet light shining everywhere. And then it was gone. I wasn't sure if I was still dreaming, so I tried to touch his arm, but he pulled away. I said, 'You're our lord, aren't you? You're Noll's man.'"

I leaned closer to my mother to hear his answer.

"But all he said was, 'Rest now. You're healed—I've given you all I had to heal you—but you still need rest.'"

I've given you all I had. His healing power was gone. He'd waited centuries for freedom, and his first act was to give up the last of his power. *For me?*

My mother continued. "I called after him as he headed for the door, two of those servants of his waiting to attend him. 'Wait! Let me thank you!'"

Don't go! Don't...

"The servants and the lord stopped suddenly, but he wouldn't face me. 'No thanks are necessary,' he said. 'But I do have one request.'"

The lord's words thundered through my mother's mouth, his distaste as clear as if he were next to me: "'Leave me be,' he said. 'Instruct all the village to leave me be. Send no women, send no men. My servants will come to the village for what is needed.'"

Stay away. The little boy trembling in the garden, a black shawl around his head. The veil, the veil... always the veil between us.

Mother shrugged. "And then he was gone. Gideon told me he

and his servants jumped into the black carriage that brought them here and were gone into the woods before he could even ask how he had healed me."

I'd listened to Mother's story without comment, mashing my tongue into my teeth when I heard of the lord's break from me. Those final words were meant for me, I was certain. He said to stay away so I would leave him be. I'd have to. It was the least I could do, after what I put him through.

Mother wrung her hands in her lap. "What happened between you two?"

"I..." I fumbled with the decaying rose petals in my hands. "I don't even know where to start." *Or if I could ever explain all that happened.*

"Well," said Mother, as she grabbed my hand in hers again. The petals fell to the ground, disappearing into the darkness at my feet. "May the first goddess watch over you and give you courage. You can tell me when you're ready."

I did my best to smile. "All right." I didn't think that day would ever come. Not if I had to rely on "the first goddess" to give me anything.

My eyes were just beginning to close when a pounding echoed across the house from the door, and I nearly fell out of my chair in fright. I jumped, my feet planted on the ground, my hands reaching desperately to pull it open. Who could it be at this time of night?

"Noll?" I heard Mother say. Father, Elfriede, Jurij, and Arrow stirred as the noise grew louder and louder, but I paid them all no mind. The door swung open, my hand clutching the handle, although I couldn't remember opening it so wide.

Before me stood a man and a boy unmasked, their grins truly as wide as their faces, one of the man's hands clutching a lantern above him, the other resting on the boy's shoulders. Beside them was Nissa, her face almost as happy, even though her eyes were puffy and tired.

"We don't need masks anymore!" screamed the boy. "The men in the commune started wandering around the village, telling people they didn't feel so sad anymore. That they didn't feel rejected by their goddesses. They didn't feel anything about their goddesses at all! They took off their masks, and no one vanished!"

"And the castle doesn't shake when we look at it!" added Nissa.

Of course. The rules of the village. Gone by the lord's remaining power.

The man lifted his hand from the boy's shoulder and extended it outward. I thought for a moment that he intended to hug me, but then Jurij brushed past me, and I spun to see Father and Elfriede behind me as well. Jurij and the man embraced, and the man sprinkled the top of Jurij's curls with his kisses while fingering the bandages on Jurij's face. A bit of the sparkle faded from his eyes. The eyes in which no flames were burning.

"Luuk!" Jurij picked the boy up and embraced him before setting him back on the ground. He mussed Nissa's hair. They were laughing, all four of them.

Elfriede pushed past me and hugged the man as well, kissing both of his cheeks. "Goodfather, it's a pleasure to finally see you."

My heart had been so distracted; I'd taken too long to see what was right before me. I smiled, and the feeling was foreign to me, something from a dream I had long, long ago.

I stepped backward, wondering if I was still dreaming, if I could fall back asleep and pick a different dream, or if this was the one I'd always wanted. Father and Master Tailor shook hands. Elfriede scooped up the children in her arms and kissed both Luuk and Nissa on the cheek.

Jurij's eyes fluttered from one to the other, and at last they rested on me. Those eyes seemed to understand that I was the one responsible for what they'd seen.

Eyes without flames. Each man's eyes had lost the flames that bound them.

And I felt a strange stirring in my heart over the next few days as I walked the village and saw, one by one, the masked boys and men encounter the laughing, smiling faces of their peers. To see the others so free inspired them to grab a hold of their masks, throw down their coverings, and smash them.

~

"MY FATHER AND MOTHER ARE SEPARATING," said Jurij. We lay together among the violet lilies atop my favorite picnic hill.

We could just make out the cottage at the edge of the woods from where we were sitting. The door opened and Elfriede stepped outside, one hand clutching a bucket and the other tucking a strand of fallen curls into the kerchief she wore on her head. She looked no larger than a mouse from where we were seated. She stared up at us for a moment, and I wondered what she thought, seeing her hated sister sitting on the hill with her husband while she worked, knowing her man wasn't there to take the task from her. I wondered if he was really her man anymore, even if he still was her husband. Then she walked away, disappearing around the back of the home with her bucket to collect water.

Jurij didn't run to her. He barely looked at her. He didn't even mention her name.

I ran my fingers over the smooth and silky petals of a bloom. There were no thorns to cut me. "I'm sorry." For his parents, for his goddess—for everything.

Jurij shrugged. "I'm not. It's not as if they hate each other. In fact, I think a different bond has formed between them, now that they're not bound by a love neither truly wanted. And Mother will still help Father daily with the sewing."

I raised an eyebrow. "Mistress Tailor not one for woodcarving?" I asked, now knowing full well where Mistress Tailor intended to live.

Jurij laughed. "No. Auntie may love her, but she's not blind with her passion. She knows her craft would suffer if Mother encroached upon it. Auntie likes to put too many 'wild and useless' details into her carvings, after all."

I was not shaken when Alvilda made her confession; she was a woman in love with another woman, and Mistress Tailor had loved her all of this time, too. Women had always had a choice to love, after all—since I gave them that freedom. Still, even if a part of her always dreamed of the day in which Mistress Tailor would be hers to love freely, surely Alvilda regretted the loss of her lonely life just a little. Mistress Tailor seemed to irritate her almost as much as she made her happy. I was sure Mistress Tailor would also find a hardheaded partner just as vexing as the eager-to-please one she left behind.

"What about the kids?" I tried to imagine Alvilda as a mother, and I wasn't sure the role suited her. Still, she made a rather fun aunt, and I could see her discouraging the kids from working.

Jurij was oblivious to the mischievous slant of my inner thoughts. "They'll live with both of them, spending their nights at one's home and then the other's as they wish."

"And Jaron?" I asked, thinking of Mother.

Jurij stroked a blade of grass. "He's not a bad looker, that Jaron, without his mask. I think he's having a hard time adjusting to a heart that's free." He leaned in to whisper. "They say he's been seen in the village with a *number* of women these past few nights already."

I grinned. Ah, well. Mother was married anyway.

Jurij hesitated. "He's not the only one having trouble adjusting to a heart that can now love freely."

Jurij's warm lips moved from my ear and to my brow, and he kissed me liberally.

I felt a strange sensation growing within me as Jurij pulled me tightly into his arms and moved his mouth from my brow to my cheeks and to my lips. I let my mind stop turning for just a moment, lost in crashes of pleasure I still felt in his embrace.

"Noll," whispered Jurij as he at last tore his lips from mine, "I love you."

For the second time in so many days, I cried. This time not from joy, but from the thought of how happy I would have been if Jurij had said that years ago. If he'd said that months ago. Weeks ago. Now I wasn't sure it was what I wanted.

I stared into his good eye for a moment, taking in the lack of flame within it. It was still so bright compared to the poor condition of his other eye, the eyelid drooping slightly, the scar down his cheek. I realized now all too well that the lord had had the power to heal—the deeper the malady, the longer it took. But he had Jurij in his castle a short while and had done nothing to heal his light injuries, other than to stop the bleeding. My chest hurt at what it might mean, but whatever my thoughts of Ailill's decision, I knew that all of the suffering could be traced back to me.

"I love you, too," I said, my hand running through his hair. "But I also love my sister. And so do you."

Jurij's grip on my back eased slightly.

"I'm torn," he spoke at last.

I felt a rush of relief. Even though he was no longer bound to love Elfriede, he loved her still. For I knew the heartbreak Elfriede would feel all too well if Jurij was torn from her side and thrust to her sister's.

I kissed Jurij's brow, and then I freed myself from his embrace. He went limp and let me tear away. My feet felt the call of the castle, the whispers of my true name on the chilling breeze that swept from the woods to the lily-covered hills surrounding my childhood home.

"Olivière..."

And I would let my feet take me. I saw his face in the past, and he hadn't vanished. It was confirmation of what I couldn't believe to be true, no matter how strong I felt it. I loved him. For in my village, women and men are free to love whom they will. And that is their curse.

"Ailill..."

BONUS SCENE FROM THE
LORD'S POV

Read a special scene from the pages of Nobody's Goddess from the enigmatic lord's point of view. This originally appeared during the blog tour, and on Wattpad and takes place in Chapter 14.

~

If this did not go well, there would never again be an opportunity to gaze upon her through anything but this veil before my face. I had been a fool during that first meeting all those months prior, and it was only by her kindness and determination to keep her eyes shut that I still breathed.

I was beginning to think it was a kindness I had imagined.

We were eating now, and I had removed the veil I usually wrapped around my face, instead relying on a curtain of the same material that separated my end of the table from hers. That kept my face safe from the scorn in her eyes. That kept her beauty swathed in a haze of material through which I could never truly see her.

She was not eating much. The food ought to have satisfied her. My servants were surely better cooks than her sister had been. I did not taste the stew the woman had offered, but I could tell from scent alone she had a long way to go before she could match the skill of one who had more years to perfect his art than she could imagine living. "Is the venison not to your liking?"

The clink of her fork on the plate was too loud for it to have been an accident. I waited for her reply. There was none. "Olivière?" I asked instead.

Still, she did not answer. The end of the table at which she sat was far from my own end, and I strained to hear what she might be doing. Damn this veil. I could not see clear enough. My own appetite unsettled, I carefully set my knife and fork on my plate. "Olivière? Are you all right?"

There was no response. By now, that did not astonish me. I was certain my voice carried well enough over the length of the table in the cavernous room. She would not make any of this easy for me.

I motioned for the nearest servant to refill her drink, hoping for some sort of response, even if it just be for her to refuse my hospitality. She did not. Even through the veil, I could see her snatch the goblet out of the servant's hand as she tossed her head back and downed the entire beverage at once.

Oh. She was choking. She was in danger. My goddess was...

"Are you all right now?" My hands clutched the edge of the table so tightly, I almost tore the delicate lace. I could not go to help her, even if she were dying. I had to go, but I could not. I wanted to—but I would not. I could not risk it. I had to... "Olivière? Answer me!"

"Yes!" It was the first word she had spoken all evening—all day, since the moment she had arrived in my castle. The sound of her dropping the goblet onto the table was loud enough to make me think the glass had broken.

She was fine. But she had nothing more to say. I picked up the knife and fork again and went back to cutting the meat on my plate. If she refused to enjoy the resplendent meal before her, there was no reason I had to do the same.

Her response was to push her plate away from her.

I had to take a deep breath to calm my beating heart and that cursed notion inside of me to satisfy her every whim. She could not think she ruled over me like all of the rest of the goddesses did over their men in the village. She could not know how hard it was for me to stay calm. "Would you care for another dish for dinner?" I speared the meat on my plate with a little too much vigor, shoving the piece inside of my mouth to force myself to remain focused on the task instead of on that voice inside me that wanted me to worship her. That foolish voice that had almost gotten me killed the moment I had seen her trespass into my castle.

"I'd like to be excused now." Olivière pushed her chair back and stood.

Six of my servants moved toward her without my having to order them. Their primary instruction was my safety, even above the quiet forcefulness of obligation they or I might feel toward her as my goddess.

"Sit down," I said. "Please."

Her response sounded strained. "I'm not feeling well."

I would not give in. I could not. If I let her know how easily she could harm me, if I gave her even the slightest indication that I valued her satisfaction over my own life—and damn it, there was a part of me that did just that, that cursed part of me, that cursed woman—she would never see me as her equal, as someone she could love. I attempted to keep eating, to diffuse the anger I knew she was feeling. The anger that seeped into my every pore, that cried out to be assuaged. "You have not eaten enough. Food will improve your temper."

I could hear her take a deep breath, and I knew, before she even spoke, that the words she would say next would challenge all of my strength to resist her every whim.

"Let. Me. Leave."

The fork fell from my hand and I held on to the table tightly if only to weigh myself down in my chair. I wanted to let her go. My servants were already complying without thinking, some making way for her to pass by. If she pushed it, she could walk outside the door and I would be powerless to stop her—and she would walk right past where I was seated, my face only protected by the veil that hung between us.

She could not know how much my every bone screamed out to gratify her. I would not have it.

I let go of the table, taking careful measures to draw in my bated breath quietly, so she would not hear the inner struggle. I picked up my napkin. "She means to let her retire from the dining hall for the night. And so shall I." I dabbed at my face and felt my muscles relaxing. Yes. I could do this. I could interpret her commands in such a way she might be satisfied but might not be tempted to use her power over me so often, so harshly. She wanted to leave, and I would let her. We could end this first dinner together pleasantly. There was hope for me. For us. For this village.

The servants sensed my calm and went back to their work attending to me. One picked up the fork I had let fall from my fingers, while the others formed a line between me and the doorway, keeping me from view should Olivière immediately exit.

She did not. "No, that's not the full extent of my wishes," she said, a strange falseness to her voice. "Let—"

"Do not speak further!" My hands shook. My legs would not support me. I leaned against the table with my fists, forgetting for a moment how I came to be standing, how the veil curtain wafted as if in a breeze. A servant righted my chair behind me. I must have knocked it down trying to stop her from speaking.

My words had been so loud, they continued to echo against the walls.

She would not let that be the end of it. "I don't think you understand how this works—"

"Silence!"

"No! Who do you think you are? What do you think you're supposed to mean to me? I don't even know you. I don't want to be here, and you're expecting me to perform the Returning!"

That felt like a rather low blow. When I had so foolishly thought today would be our Returning, that today I would be free of this curse, free of this veil, free of... I was blinded by these feelings I had for her. Feelings I never asked for. I pounded the table with both of my fists. "Was it not *you* who first sought me out?"

She flung her hands around her wildly. "Not for this! I never asked to be your goddess! I just wanted—" She stopped suddenly.

I knew what she had wanted. "You wished to free your friend

so you could steal him from his goddess." I summoned the nearest servants, and they went to her side, escorting her by the arms. I could not look at her. I could not stop my heart from pounding. It was maddening. She had not asked to be my goddess? I had not asked for it to be *her*. I was so tired of this. Of hope. Of everything. "How unfortunate that I was unable to help you with such a generous act."

I would have to show her. There seemed to be no other way to win her love, to get this wretched existence over with. I moved toward the doorway, knowing my servants would step in to protect my face from her if she did not think to stop them. They did, wrapping my veil over my head, pinning it at my shoulder and placing my hat atop it before I appeared around the other side of the curtain.

Now the whole world was veiled to me, but that was the price I had to pay for movement around the eyes of one who would not love me.

I exited the room first, leading the way. "Come with me!" I heard her struggling to escape from my servants' escort behind me, but I did not hesitate.

"Stop!" she screamed.

I stopped. I had no choice. There was such power and anger in that one word.

"Let me—"

She could kill me, if I let her.

"Silence her!" I ordered, and one of the servants holding her produced a piece of the veil material from his pocket and wrapped it around her mouth. She stared at me as it happened, and it was as if she were studying the veil keeping me from her, keeping her forever in a haze before my eyes, looking for a rip through which she could send me to my death.

The look pained me. My whole body hurt.

I walked forward again. I had stopped when she had asked me to stop, after all. I was under no obligation to stay that way.

My legs throbbed with the effort it took to move forward, knowing as I did, beneath my conscious thought, I was disobeying her desire.

Stop her from speaking, and I will not have to hear of her desire. Let me show her that she is not the only one here with desires. Let me show her that she has a reason to be grateful to me. Let me show her the gift I would have happily bestowed upon her today, if she had been willing to perform the Returning.

NOBODY'S LADY

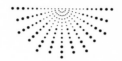

THE NEVER VEIL BOOK TWO

CHAPTER ONE

W hen I thought I understood real friendship, I was a long-lost queen. When I discovered there was so much more to my life than love and hate, that those around me were just pawns in a game whose rules I'd unwittingly put in place, I discovered I was a long-forgotten goddess. But goddess or not, powerless or powerful, my feet were taking me someplace I wasn't sure I wanted to go. What did I hope to find? Did I truly believe I could hear him call me—that he'd want to call me? Yes, I did. I wanted to see him again. I wanted to hope, even if I wasn't sure I was allowed. If I deserved to. I headed down the familiar dirt path beneath the lattice of trees overhead, pausing beside the bush with a partially snapped stem that jutted outward like a broken limb. The one that pointed to the secret cavern.

Only, it's not much of a secret anymore, is it?

My feet picked themselves up. Glowing pools would never again tempt me.

I reached the black, towering fortress that had for so long shaken and screamed at the power of my glance.

For the first time in this lifetime, I stared up at it, and nothing moved. My legs, unused to such steady footing while in the sight of the lord's castle, twitched in anticipation of a fall that never came.

There was no need. My feet dragged me forward.

At the grand wooden door, I raised a fist to knock.

But I stopped. I felt like if I touched it, the entire castle might crumble. It had done so once before. Not at my touch exactly. But I couldn't shake the feeling that I was responsible for whatever destruction I'd find in this place. But that was presumptuous of me. He was strong-willed, and he wouldn't crumble at the prospect of freedom. If anything, he'd be triumphant over it.

You can't stop now. I pulled my sleeves over my wrists and propped both elbows against the door, pushing until it gave way.

The darkness inside the foyer tried to deceive me into thinking night had fallen. The stream of light that trickled from the familiar crack in the garden door called the darkness a liar.

I gripped the small iron handles, the material of my sleeves guarding the cold metal from my touch, and pulled.

My touch had come to the garden before me.

The rose bushes that surrounded the enclosed circular area were torn, ripped, trodden, and plucked. The blooms lay withered, scattered and turned to dust, their once-white petals a sickly shade of yellowish brown, smooth blooms turned coarse and wrinkled.

The fountain at the center no longer trickled with water. Its shallow pool was stagnant, piles of brown festering in mildewing green liquid. Dotted amongst the brown was pallid stone rubble. The tears of the weeping elf child statue, which belonged at the top of the fountain, had ceased at last. But the gash across its face told me the child's tears had not been staunched by joy. I wondered if Ailill had had it carved to represent the pain I'd inflicted on him as a child. And I wondered if now he could no longer bear to remind himself of what I'd done.

I hadn't done this. But I felt as if I had. If Ailill had gone on a rampage after he came back to the castle, it was because of what I'd done to him. Everything I touched turned sour. I yanked and pulled, trying to draw my hands further into my sleeves, but there wasn't enough material to cover them entirely.

"Well, what a surprise."

I gazed into the shadow beside the doorway. How could I have not seen? The stone table was occupied. The place where I'd sat alone for hours, days, and months was littered with crumpled and decaying leaves, branches, and petals, obscuring the scars left by a dagger or knife striking time and time again across its surface. The matching bench that once nestled on the opposite side was toppled over, leaving only dark imprints in the dirt.

"A pity you could not make yourself at home here when you were welcome."

My breath caught in my throat.

The man at the table was clad entirely in black, as I knew he would be. The full-length jacket had been swapped for a jerkin, but I could see the embossing of roses hadn't been discarded in the exchange. He wore dark leather gloves, the fingers of which were crossed like the wings of a bird in flight. His pale elbows rested on the table amongst the leaves and branches and thorns. He wore the hat I was used to seeing him wear, a dark, pointed top resting on a wide brim. Its black metal band caught a ray of the sunlight almost imperceptibly. But I noticed. I always did.

His face was entirely uncovered. Those large and dark eyes, locked on me, demanded my attention. They were the same eyes of the boy I'd left alone to face my curse—not so long ago from my point of view. He was more frightened then, but there was no mistaking the hurt in those eyes both then and now.

"You are not welcome here, Olivière."

His words sliced daggers through my stomach.

"I... I thought I heard you call me."

He cocked his head to the side, his brown eyes moving askance. "You heard me call you?"

"Yes..." I realized how foolish it sounded. I was a fool to come. Why had I let myself fall for that sound again, for my name whispered on the wind? Why was I so certain it was he who'd said my name?

He smiled, not kindly. "And where, pray tell, have you been lurking? Under a rose bush? Behind the garden door? Or do those rounded female ears possess a far greater sense of hearing than my jagged male ones?"

I brushed the tips of my ears self-consciously. Elric had been so fascinated by them, by what he saw as a mutilation. This lord —*Ailill*—wasn't like that. He'd touched them once, as a child. He'd tried to heal them, thinking they were meant to be pointed.

The boy with a heart was the man sitting there before me.

Even after all we'd been through, he'd still done me a kindness by healing my mother. "No, I just thought—"

"No, you did *not* think, or you would not have come."

I clenched my jaw. My tongue was threatening to spew the vile anger that had gotten us into this mess to begin with.

He sighed and crossed his arms across his chest. "I gave explicit instructions that I not be disturbed." He leaned back against the wall behind him, his chin jutting outward slightly.

I wiped my sweaty fingertips on my skirt. I wouldn't let the rest of my hands out from the insides of my sleeves. The sweat had already soaked through them. "I needed to thank you."

He scoffed. "Thank me for what? For your prolonged captivity, or for not murdering both your mother and your lover when I had the chance?"

So you admit you took Jurij to punish me? You admit they were both in danger in your "care"? Quickly, I had to clench my jaw to keep down the words that threatened to spill over. *He's not who I thought he was. He wouldn't have harmed them.*

I loosened the muscles in my jaw one hair's breadth at a time.

"For healing me when you were a child. For accepting me into your castle instead of putting me to death for trespassing in it. For… For forgiving me for cursing you, even though you were innocent." My voice was quiet, but I was determined to make it grow louder. "For saving my mother's life."

He waved one hand lazily in the air. "Unfinished projects irk me."

"But you didn't have to."

A shrug. "The magic was nearly entirely spent on the churl anyway."

"I beg your pardon?"

He leaned forward and placed both palms across the rotted forest remnants on the table. "My apologies," he said, his lips curled into a sneer. "I simply meant that I wasted years and years and let the magic wither from my body to save a person of no consequence. You may thank me for that if you like. I would rather not be reminded of it."

How odd it was to see the face I'd imagined come to life. The mocking, the condescending—it was all there. I just hadn't known the canvas before.

And what a strange and beautiful canvas it was. That creamy peach skin, the brownish tint of his shoulder-length tresses. He was so much paler than any person I had ever seen. Save for the specters.

Despite the paleness, part of me felt I wasn't wrong to have mistaken one brother for another. Elric had been dark-skinned, but they seemed almost like reflections of the same person; they shared the same brows, the same lips, and even eyes of a similar shape if not color. Perhaps the face before me was a bit gaunter, the nose a bit longer. It was easier to focus on the differences. Thinking of the similarities made me want to punch the face in front of me all the more—and that would undermine everything I had set out to do when I made my way to him. *I wanted to see if you were really restored to life. Say it. I wanted to know if you really forgave me. Say it. I wanted to know why I... Why I feel this way about you, why I keep thinking about you, when I used to be unable to stand the sight of you. Say it, Noll!* I dug my nails into my palm and shook the thoughts from my head. He'd called my mother a "churl." I couldn't just tell him everything I was thinking. "Have you no sense of empathy?"

"What a coincidence that you should mention that. I am sending Ailill to the village with an edict. He can escort you there."

"Ailill?" *But aren't you him? Could I have been mistaken? Oh, goddess, help me, why do I do this to myself? Why do I think I know everything?*

He waved his hand, and one of the specters appeared beside me from the foyer.

The specters. There were about a hundred of them in the castle. Pale as snow in skin and hair with abysmal, black eyes. Mute servants who seemed to anticipate the lord's every command. Only now I knew who they really were.

Oh. "You call him by your own name?" I asked.

He raised an eyebrow. "I call them all by my name. They are me, remember?"

His icy stare sent another invisible dagger through my stomach. "Yes, but—"

"A shame you never cared to ask my name when you were

my guest," he said. "I have a feeling things might have turned out much differently—for all of us."

"You knew what would happen! Why didn't you warn me?" I had to squeeze my fists and teeth together to stop myself from screaming. This wasn't going at all like I had hoped. But what had I hoped? What could I have possibly expected? *I thought I'd be forgiven. I thought that Ailill and I might start over, that we could be friends, perhaps even... What a fool I've been.*

Ailill turned slightly, his attention suddenly absorbed in a single white petal that remained on a half-trodden bush beside him. "I was not entirely in control of my emotions," he said, "as you may well know."

"I tried to give you a way out!" My jaw wouldn't stay shut.

Ailill laughed and reached over to pluck the petal from its thorns. "Remind me exactly when that was? Perhaps between condemning me to an eternal life of solitude and wretchedness and providing yourself with a way to feel less guilty about the whole affair? And then you just popped right back to the present, I suppose, skipping over those endless years in a matter of moments." He crushed the petal in his hand.

"A way to let *myself* feel less guilty?" He wasn't entirely wrong. But it wasn't as if he had done nothing wrong.

Ailill bolted upright, slamming the fist that gripped the petal against the twigs and grass on the table. "Your last words to me were entirely for your own benefit, as well you know!"

If, after your own Returning, you can find it in your heart to forgive me, the last of the men whose blood runs with his own power will free all men bound by my curse.

"How is wishing to break the curse on the village for *my* benefit?"

"Perhaps because the curse was your doing? Perhaps because you only wanted the curse broken to free your lover from it in the first place?"

"Stop calling Jurij my 'lover.' He's not—"

"And you did free him with those words. You knew I would forgive you."

"How could I have known? I didn't think it possible you'd forgive me, not after all we've been through."

"You knew because you knew I wanted to be free myself. That

I would do anything—even forgive you for half a moment—to earn that freedom." His voice grew quieter. "You never wanted anything from me, not really. I was just a pawn in your game, a way to free the other men in your village, a way to punish the men from mine."

I fought back what I couldn't believe was threatening to spring to my eyes. No tears, not in front of him.

"The men of the old village deserved everything they got," I spat at last, knowing full well that wasn't the whole story.

Ailill scoffed and put both hands on his hips, his arms akimbo. Oh, how I tired of that pose. The crushed petal remained on the table. Its bright white added a bit of life to the decay.

"There were plenty of young boys not yet corrupted," he said. "And some that might have never been." He took a deep breath. "But, of course, you are not entirely to blame. I blame myself every day for ever taking a childish interest in you. That should not have counted as love."

I swallowed. Of course. Before the curse of the village had broken, a woman had absolute power over the one man who loved or yearned for her. When I visited the past through the pool in the secret cavern, I discovered a horde of lusty men who knew nothing of love but were overcome with desire. Since so many had lusted for any female who walked before them, and I had carried the power from my own version of the village with me, it had been child's play to control the men. But why had that power extended to Ailill? He had only been a boy then, broken, near silent—and kindhearted. He couldn't have regarded me with more than a simple crush on an older sisterly figure, but it had been enough.

"But you did forgive me." Why couldn't I stop the words from flowing?

Ailill shook his head and let a weary smile spread across his features. "Forgive *you*? I could never forgive you. No more than I could forgive myself for daring to think, if just for a moment, that I..." He stopped.

I shook my head. "The curse wouldn't have been broken. The men in the village wouldn't now be walking around without masks. Nor you without your veil. If you hadn't forgiven me."

Ailill tilted his head slightly. His dark eyes searched mine,

259

perhaps for some answer he thought could be found there. "I would still need the veil even now?" he asked, his voice quiet. "Are you certain?"

Removing the veil before the curse was broken would have required the Returning, a ritual in which I freely and earnestly bestowed my heart and affection to him. It would have never happened, not with the man I knew at the time to be mine. So yes, he would still need the veil to survive the gaze of women. I was sure of it. He'd been arrogant, erratic, and even cruel. Perhaps not so much as Elric, Ailill's even more volatile older brother, the one who wound up with a mob of angry, murderous women in his castle and a gouge through his heart. But even so.

It was my turn to cross my arms and sneer. "I said you could break the curse after your own Returning, and I specified that you didn't need my affection to have a Returning. All you needed to do was crawl out of whatever abyss I'd sent you to." I shifted uncomfortably in place. "And I suppose I should be grateful—for my mother's sake—that you did."

Ailill waved a hand at the specter beside me and brushed aside a pile of clippings on the table to reveal a hand-written letter. It was yellowed and a tad soggy. "Yes, well, the endless droning that made up your curse gets a bit foggy in my mind— assuming it even made sense in *your* mind to begin with. I am afraid I lack the ability to retain exact memories of an event that took place a hundred lifetimes ago when I was but a scarred child terrified of the monster before him." He looked up to face me as the specter retrieved the letter from his extended hand. "But I suppose it was not all that long ago for the monster, was it?" He turned again to the table, shuffling brush about aimlessly. "Take her with you to the market," he said.

The specter made to grab my arm as he passed. I slipped out of his reach only to back into another specter who had appeared quick as lightning from the foyer. He grabbed one arm, and the first specter seized the other.

"Let go of me!" I shouted as they began to drag me away.

The specters didn't pause, as they once would have.

"Stop!" called Ailill from behind me. The specters did as they were told.

Ailill spoke. "I forgot to inform you that my retainers lost all desire to follow your orders when I did." He waved his fingers in the air. "Carry on."

I struggled against the grip the specters had on my arms. *Again. He has me under his thumb again.* "I can walk by myself!" I screamed as my toes slid awkwardly against the dark foyer floor. "I don't need to go to the market!"

A black carriage awaited us outside the castle doorway. A third specter opened the carriage door, and my captors heaved me up into the seat like a sack of grain. The one with the letter slid in and took the seat across from me. He stared vacantly at the top of the seat behind me.

I leaned forward, whipping my hand out to stop the carriage door as one of the specters moved to close it. I didn't care what I touched in the castle anymore. Let the whole thing crumble.

A black-gloved hand covered mine. I jumped back. Ailill stuck his head inside the carriage. His face stopped right before mine, the brim of his hat practically shading me under it. The sight of his face so close to mine, unveiled and painted with disdain, caused a thunderous racing of my heart. It was as if I'd just run the length of the entire village.

"You kept your hair short," he said. He reached his free hand toward it, then pulled back.

I'd once let the bushy mess of black hair grow as long as it wanted, but once I cropped it closely to my scalp, I found it easier to deal with. "There hasn't been enough time for it to grow, anyway. Not for me."

He snorted. "Of course. But it makes me remember you as you were, long ago. When you cursed me and every man whether he deserved it or not." He leaned back a bit, putting more space between our faces. "I think you will be most interested in going with my servants to the market," he said. "But there will be no need to thank me in person afterward. I would rather not see you again." His eyes drifted upwards, thoughtfully. "In fact, remind the villagers that I am closed to all audiences. My servants will be out there to see that my edict is obeyed."

Before I could speak, he leaned back and let my hand fall from his. He reached around the door to close it.

"Wait—"

And slammed it in my face.

CHAPTER TWO

You fool.

You miserable, simpering fool.

If you let so much as one tear fall, I'll never forgive you.

I stared at the specter seated before me and laughed. I had been directing my thoughts to the raging idiot rattling around inside my heart, but I kind of liked the idea of pretending it had been the specter who had earned my ire. Him? Cry? I'd seen more life in that stone version of little Ailill that had spent all of those years sobbing atop the castle's garden fountain.

The specter really did look like Ailill. Paler, for certain, and with crow's feet around his eyes. This one was maybe in his forties or fifties. I had seen younger and older—mostly older. They were all versions of Ailill that had died, turned into ghastly shades to serve the new one.

I had a feeling I wouldn't have the opportunity to ask.

Not that I wanted the opportunity.

And he would probably just tell me I ought to know, since I was the one who cursed him to never die. Well, I used a myth I guessed to be true and commanded him not to meet his goddess —the one woman he would ever love—for many, many lifetimes. Apparently the men got to live long enough to meet their goddesses, no matter how long it took. Luckily for most men, it took far, far less time.

Luckily or unluckily? Eternal life had its advantages, I supposed, but it hadn't been meant as a blessing. And it hadn't even been meant for him. Not for the little boy I had befriended who had known nothing but pain.

And now that I thought about it, I always knew I would turn out to be his goddess, so I'd outright doomed myself, too. Put a sword, a weapon of tales of old, in my hands and I was bound to grow a little overly passionate and foolish. It was a lesson sorely learned. And a lesson I was foolish to think he would ever let me forget.

I sighed and rubbed my temples, tearing my eyes from the specter's face. I was used to the black eyes, but I wasn't yet used to the resemblance to Ailill. Odd that I spent so long wondering what was under the lord's veil when all the while his face was plastered across every servant in the castle.

I glanced out the carriage window just as we put the woods surrounding the castle behind us. I never used to be able to look up at the eastern mountains. Someone once decided that no woman or girl could look at the castle that soared up above the woods without causing the earth to shake. That someone, I was astonished to learn, was me. Ailill was right—I couldn't keep it all straight, even though I had done it.

We passed the small house on the edge of the woods belonging to my parents, Gideon the woodcarver and his wife, Aubree. We lived snug with the trees so Father wouldn't have to travel far for the wood he needed for his work. Of course, he had done very little work while my mother was held captive in Ailill's castle. I thought her dead, and Father didn't dare correct me. Ailill was healing her, but the road to recovery from her illness was nearly two years long.

The carriage dipped down and up the small series of lily-covered hills that separated my home from the heart of the village. Master and Mistress Tailor's—no, I'd forgotten. Master Tailor and *Siofra's* tailoring shop was the next home we passed. That was where Jurij had lived with his parents before he wed my sister. Now Master Tailor lived there alone, except when his younger son, Luuk, and Luuk's former goddess, Nissa, were visiting. Although his former wife still helped him run his business.

With Mother restored to us and newlywed Elfriede and Jurij living at home, it was getting rather crowded. I couldn't blame my sister, as she and her husband originally had the place to themselves. Mother and I had both been in the castle, and Father was a drunken lout more likely to be at the tavern than at home. It had only been a few weeks since I'd emerged from the glowing pool and all of these changes had taken place. I was pining for my own space. I had thought of the castle. How stupid. But there were those stolen moments in the garden and the food far finer than anything I'd eaten at home. Even the lovely dresses, although unsuited to me, had grown on me now that I'd spent weeks wearing the same old rags. But that was Ailill's place, not mine—and it was a prison once, even despite all the fine things. Once, I might have lived with Alvilda, the lady woodcarver in the village who had picked up all of the slack my father had left behind. But she was practically a newlywed herself, and I never quite felt comfortable around her lover, Siofra, even if she had shown me kindness from time to time. I still remembered her as I did as a child, a towering woman, gruff and surly.

We made our way through the heart of the village, and men and women, girls and boys alike jumped backward to make way for their lord's black carriage. I was still not used to seeing so many faces on display. Before the curse broke, only the men who had earned the love of their goddesses had been able to remove their masks. More than once, I'd shut my eyes quickly before reminding myself I could keep them open.

In the distance were the western mountains, bearing down over the crop fields. The commune beside the fields was now empty, devoid of the unloved and unmarried men who once called it their home. But the place carried too many unpleasant memories for me, too. I had lived briefly in two versions of the same wretched and fading spot.

The southern mountains served as a backdrop for the live-stock fields and farmers. The farmers had never been fond of me. As a child, I led a small group of boys around the village as their "elf queen" and attacked far too many cows and sheep with a tree branch sword I called Elgar.

That left the north. There was a quarry there, but more importantly, there was an empty shack. I might have accidentally killed the old crone who lived there a couple of years back. It wasn't really my fault—it was the earthquake's. But now that I knew I was responsible for the earthquakes, I guess it was my fault after all. My face flushed. One more black mark in my book.

The carriage ground to a sudden and sharp halt. Through the window, I saw the villagers who had been looking at the various stalls of goods for sale turn around to face us in wonder. More than one dropped the apple or blanket or whatever it was they were examining and stared slack-jawed, almost as still as the specters when they were awaiting orders. Did the lord of the village really still inspire such awe?

Their faces softened when one of the specters outside of the carriage opened the door and the specter inside the carriage disembarked before me. For all they knew, though, the other passenger could have been Ailill. His visits to the village were no longer unheard of.

I stepped outside, ignoring the proffered hand of the specter who had been driving the carriage. All around me, jaws slackened again. The villagers might have been just as scared to see me emerge from that carriage as they would have been to see Ailill.

Or perhaps they just didn't expect to see any evidence that I still carried their lord's favor. *Well, neither did I.*

"Noll!" cried a familiar voice. *Alvilda, shopping in the market?* She was wearing a golden, frilly dress, too, and carrying a basket across one elbow.

Alvilda swooped deftly through the crowd and stood beside me. She shot the specters a murderous look. *Ah, there she is.* They had a bit of history, although I'd never be able to say for certain whether it was these three specters in particular with whom she quarreled fruitlessly.

"Step aside," she grumbled to the nearest one. She had never learned that they would neither talk nor acknowledge her. Or perhaps it was her way of not acknowledging them not acknowledging her.

She looped her free arm through mine. "Watching you come out of his lordship's carriage has to be one of the last things I expected to see today."

The yellow monstrosity of a gown she wore was so bright, it almost blinded me. "And seeing you in such a lavish dress has to be the last thing I expected to see in my lifetime."

Alvilda pinched my arm and batted her long, dark eyelashes. "Oh, stop. You know I can't live with a tailor and not expect to be dressed up like a doll occasionally." She grinned. "Besides, we have a deal: she can dress me like a lady from time to time, and she has to shut her mouth for an hour or two that night."

I thought it best not to comment.

Alvilda watched the specters warily. The one who had ridden with me in the carriage approached the Great Hall door. As I had seen time and time before, he produced precisely what he needed from a pocket within his jacket. A nail appeared in one hand and a hammer in another, and he quickly posted the letter to the door.

Before anyone had a chance to read it, he was back in the carriage and the two others jumped up to the driver's seat. And then they were gone.

"That's... disturbing," remarked Alvilda. "Have any idea what they're up to now?"

I shook my head. "Ai—the lord said he was sending an edict to the village."

Villagers pulled away from their small clusters, and a few started shuffling over toward the Great Hall door.

Alvilda steered us both toward the growing crowd. "So you were visiting with him?" Her voice seemed too unconcerned, almost as if she was trying hard to seem nonchalant. But the slight grimace on her lips was unmistakable.

I bit my lip. "I had to thank him for what he did for my mother. And he was none too happy to see me."

Alvilda snorted. "That moron should thank *you* for putting up with his nonsense while letting him walk around with all of his limbs intact."

My eyes scanned the edge of the crowd uneasily. I still couldn't shake the feeling that he was always watching, that he had an eye to everything that went on around me.

"Don't—" I started. I could see Alvilda search my face skeptically. I turned my head away from her, staring intently at the crowd closest to the posted edict. "It's more complicated than that."

"If you say so," said Alvilda. Her tone made her disgust far clearer. Fat lot of help that was now. Where was her utter disgust with the man when I was looking for any way out of my coupling with him? I knew there were few places I could have hidden in our village wrapped in mountains, but surely she could have helped persuade someone to let me have my right as a woman to refuse him.

But it wasn't a matter of a woman's rights any longer. A man now had the right—no, he finally had the *ability*—to refuse love. As Ailill had so aptly demonstrated.

"I guess I shouldn't be so hard on the man. I'm upset with how he treated you, but I don't even know him. And I'm thankful I can watch the sunrise in the morning now. I suppose I have him to thank if he broke the curse like everyone's saying." Alvilda blew out a hard breath, which ruffled the hair that hung over her face. "Have you seen one yet? I always thought they must be like sunsets, only in reverse. Nothing special. But being able to look up at the eastern sky, not caring if you happen to see that castle, and watching the red light stretch out from the darkness over the mountaintops… Sunrises are so much more hopeful than sunsets."

"I never stopped to think about it," I admitted. "But you're right—"

"No!" screamed a woman in the crowd.

"That's ridiculous!"

The crowd turned into a mess of buzzing creatures. A gasp, a shout.

A woman slapped a man with her bare hand.

Everyone stilled for a moment.

"What are you doing, woman?" asked the man she'd hit. He cradled his cheek. "Have you gone mad?"

"I… I don't know." The woman stared at her hand like it was someone else's entirely. "But you…" She squeezed her hands into fists on either side of her. "How could you say such a thing?" Everyone began speaking at once again. Alvilda let go of my arm and shoved forward past the men and women toward the Great Hall door, clipping a boy on the head with her basket. It was easy enough to follow the path left in her wake, but once the people shoved aside had a moment to register their surprise,

I had to put up with a few accusing stares as I made my way past them.

"Huh," barked Alvilda brusquely as I at last returned to her side. "I suppose my brother and Siofra were the first in a new trend." She arched an eyebrow, indicating that she had never once cared that Siofra had been married when she moved in with Alvilda. Siofra and Master Tailor had announced they were separating, but there had been no formal way to break off the original union.

My eyes at last fell upon the yellowed and water-stained paper. How long had Ailill had it there, under the damp and dirty remnants of the garden I'd once treasured? Only to send it out as soon as I entered? It was like he'd been waiting for me to come, even despite his disdain at my arrival.

It read:

Read these words and obey the edict of your lord:

Due to the release of this village from the curse that plagued it for years eternal, I hereby release all men from their unions, formal and informal alike. As of today, there are no husbands and wives, there are no goddesses and their men. If a former coupling wishes to maintain their union, they will have to wed once more. My servants, acting in my stead, are the only people capable of blessing a new union.

I heard a few more palms hitting tender cheeks behind me.

CHAPTER THREE

Everything was chaos. Specters appeared out of the crowd to drag women away from men, and Alvilda and I soon discovered these women had all hit their men after they'd exclaimed joy at the edict. They'd *hit* them. Like the men had hit the women in this village long ago. Perhaps not so hard as that— they'd followed that lead woman's example and slapped their palms against the men's cheeks at first. But then one even started pounding her fists on a man's chest. He didn't seem very hurt. Just puzzled. We all were. I'd seen violence, but not here. And no one else had seen much violence at all.

People sometimes had whispered about a woman or two who had hurt her man, but so few claimed to have witnessed it. Alvilda said a young woman in her day—not her Siofra, despite how obviously unhappy she was—had treated her man coldly every time they were in public, and that man came to sport a bruise or two he never would explain. No one thought hard about it, considering the specters were sure to step in thanks to the "always-watching" lord if anything truly untoward had occurred. So they thought. If it was her, the man's silence made sense—his goddess could do no wrong, even if she hurt him.

These men got extremely angry.

"Leave me alone, you cow!" said the man being pummeled, grabbing her by both shoulders and shoving her backwards.

The specters swooped in to grab the fist-pounding woman by the arms before she fell, and two others pulled the man back, letting them both snarl fruitlessly until they calmed down.

No one was very calm for long. They screamed at each other, at the specters, at their neighbors, at their friends. Then someone's voice rang out loud over the others. "He should know what his edict is doing, shouldn't he? Isn't he always watching? Well, it's time he came out from that stinkin' castle and gave us some answers!"

I tried to warn the crowd that Ailill would have no visitors, but they wouldn't heed me. Still, I followed the castle-bound mob out of curiosity, hoping to see Ailill step out of his castle to address them. I dug my fingernails into my palm as I kicked myself for admitting, even if just in my mind, that I hoped to see him at all.

Following a horde of women up the dirt path through the village, up and down the hills and into the woods, brought up rather unpleasant memories of a previous mob, although that one hadn't included any men. Last time, I led them with a glowing sword held high above my head. This time, I dragged my feet at the back of the crowd and kept my arms crossed tightly across my chest.

What awaited us at the castle was an unbreakable line of specters, their legs spread slightly apart, their hands clutched tightly behind their backs.

"Let us through!" called one of the women at the front.

"We demand to speak to his lordship!" shouted another. *Oh, dear.* I was sure Ailill would appear to remind her that no one *demanded* anything of him. But he didn't.

The specters didn't move. One of the men pushed at the chest of the nearest specter, but he didn't waver. A few men and women followed suit.

"He can't cheapen our unions!" called Elweard, once he threw up his hands in disgust at the unmovable object that was Ailill's servant. "Why does he get to decide if our vows hold true?"

Vena, his wife—or, his former wife—slipped forward and tentatively put an arm around his waist. She didn't seem at all herself. She was known from the quarries to the fields of livestock to be the true tavern master, a woman who enjoyed bossing her husband around almost as much as he enjoyed letting her. But perhaps even in the face of his outspoken outrage at the situation, there was now room for doubts, even for her.

Because the men had all been compelled to love. With that taken away, with even their unions stripped from them, what was left to hold a coupling together?

"I love Vena!" shouted Elweard over the heads of the specters as he slipped an arm around her shoulders. "And I'd wed her a thousand times to prove it!"

Vena's eyes glistened, and she raised herself on her tiptoes to kiss him on the cheek. "My darling." Her voice shook. "I would wed you every day for the rest of my life."

The nearest specter pulled parchment, quill, and a bottle of ink from his pocket.

"And now what nonsense is this?" demanded Elweard, ripping the parchment from the specter's hands. "An arrest order for declaring my love against his lordship's wishes?"

While Elweard continued to wish for the nearest specter's death with his steady glare, Vena leaned over his shoulder and pored over the paper.

"Dearest," said Vena, "it's a declaration of our marriage!"

The crowd began whispering and pointing. Those nearest the coupling strained to read the parchment as well.

"It's true!" said one woman. "All we have to do is declare our love for one another, sign a paper, and the whole mess will be behind us!"

Elweard and Vena grinned as they gazed into each other's eyes. After a quick kiss, Elweard snatched the quill, and Vena grabbed the ink from the specter. They used the flat surface of a nearby rock to sign it.

So they were once again husband and wife, whatever that meant now. Did the specters producing the paper count as the lord's blessing? Why were we skipping over the wedding? Was it because Vena and Elweard had already had theirs? Or was that all meaningless now, as meaningless as the edicts of the first goddess? As far as Vena and Elweard were concerned, this new marriage would give them an excuse to throw yet another feast at

the Great Hall to celebrate, because that's just who they were—
simple people, happy with simple pleasures. Maybe they didn't
have to think about marriage too much—they just knew they
wanted to be the only one for each other. If only it were so simple
for everyone else.

The mob didn't make any headway after that. A few more
men and women came forth to proclaim their desire to be wed
once more, and a few more parchments were signed. I saw at
least two women pinch, prod, or poke their former husbands into
speaking up. When those men spoke their desire to be wed again,
their voices were unsteady, and the specters didn't pull anything
from their pockets. The couplings left the mob, former wives
stomping ahead of former husbands and former husbands
searching the mob for something. One's eyes rested a moment on
a woman near me, and she blushed.

THE VILLAGE HAD BECOME FAR TOO chaotic for my tastes—not that
it was ever a place that willingly drew me to it. I had to make my
way through it almost daily to help Alvilda with her woodworking, but most of the time, she let me escape to the woods right
away to chop wood for her future projects. I sometimes met my
father there, sitting on a tree stump, his shiny, unscratched axe
lying lifeless beside him. He'd nod at me and pick up a flask I
knew he often stashed inside his pocket. When I announced my
intention to move into the empty shack, it went somewhat unnoticed. Mother and Father were still together, but Father had made
no proclamations of undying love, and Mother had followed his
example. Frankly, I couldn't have left at a more suitable moment.
It made me yearn for the days when I had been so revolted by
the way they kissed and kissed and could only pull their arms
from each other's backs with a great and wretched show of
sadness.

Now that I was finally on my own, I preferred to work more
delicately with a chisel, a gouge, and a small block of wood to
felling a tree with my axe. Children especially seemed to enjoy
the little animals I crafted, so I called them toys and said they
were meant to be played with. I sold them around town a few

days a week. The first day I'd asked Master Tailor if I could sell some outside of the Tailor Shop.

Helping me gave Nissa some distraction. I think what she really wanted was an excuse to see Luuk, who always seemed to want to spend the night with whichever parent she wasn't currently staying with. It wasn't that Luuk didn't like Nissa, but he was no longer sure he was ready for romance. Nissa decided to break it off between them, although I was sure her heart wasn't in it. Theirs was just one of many messy partings, and theirs wasn't even that messy, considering how young they were.

So I avoided the messiness of the village whenever possible. I felt more comfortable staying at my lone cottage outside the quarry.

I was fully used to rejection, so there was no need for screaming and crying out with me. The few villagers who bothered to pass by were quarry workers, mostly men, the rest women who had rejected love before the curse had broken. There were few men in the village who would shed a tear over the lord's edict.

"Morning!" called one such tearless man. I looked up from the stool I'd set on my porch. One of the quarry workers, a pickaxe slung casually over his shoulder, waved as he walked by. His face had a familiar pattern to it. I'd probably met him when he came to chastise Ingrith, the woman who'd once lived in my cottage. Since I knew his face, that meant he had once been Returned. Not that that mattered any more. I nodded my greeting before turning back to work.

This morning, I was halfway through making a cat's rotund hindquarters out of a scrap block of oak left over from the new table Alvilda and I had finished crafting for Vena and Elweard at the tavern.

Alvilda had been on her way home from the market to work on that table when a specter appeared out of nowhere and—much to Alvilda's consternation—followed her home. The next time I saw her, she stood cross-armed and smirking in her shop's doorway with a piece of parchment stating that his lordship recognized Alvilda and Siofra as each other's wives. She said the confounded white creature had pulled it out of his inner jacket pocket as soon as Alvilda had explained the situation in the market and Siofra had expressed her desire to wed Alvilda as well. All it took was their signatures and they were united, on paper as they were at heart.

I wished I had been there to see it.

"It's a beautiful day, lady carver!"

My hand slipped. Now my wooden cat had a chunk missing out of its tail.

I looked up. Another of the quarry workers. I couldn't place his face. But he might not have had it out in the open until recently.

He took my curt nod as an invitation. His trousers brushed against the bushes separating my new home from the dirt road. I remembered those bushes as a safe place from which to get a good look at the old, husbandless crone who once lived in my shack. She had killed the one man who would ever love her. All it took was a look at his unmasked face. And no one else remembered he ever existed. I figured this out only after I had done the same.

The worker brushed the bush's fine needles off the front of his trousers with one hand and swung the pickaxe he had been carrying over his shoulder with the other. He put his free hand on his hip and spread his lips wide to reveal a set of perfectly white teeth. The effect it had on his richly dark face stirred something unexpected in my belly. I quickly looked back down at the damage his greeting had caused my cat.

"I hear you've been selling those in the village," he said.

His hand appeared in my narrowly focused range of vision.

"Do you mind?" he asked.

I looked up. And quickly looked back down, numbly putting the wooden cat into his outstretched hand and laying my tools beside me on the stool. What was wrong with me? I'd had enough of these feelings to last a lifetime, and I had only ever bothered with one man before. Or two.

"Let me see. A butt. But whose?"

I laughed despite myself. "There's no real-life model."

He grinned. "Oh, I don't know. Maybe you haven't seen my former wife's ass. If not for the tail, it might be a perfect match."

I shifted uncomfortably and stretched my smile into my cheeks as far as my lips would let me. It took an effort.

The worker handed the cat back to me and held his hand out to shake mine. "I'm Sindri, one of the baker's sons. Don't know if you remember me."

I felt the uneasiness in my stomach cease instantly. Sindri, one of the boys I used to play with as a girl. I shook his hand eagerly, a much easier smile on my face. "Sindri! I'm so sorry! Of course. How could I have forgotten?"

It was Sindri's turn to pull an uneasy smile onto his face. "Well, you've never seen my face, so I'm not that surprised."

Bile rose in my throat again. Another face I'd doomed to masking.

"Who was your goddess again?" I asked.

Sindri swung the pickaxe off his shoulder and let it scuff the ground by his feet. He leaned on it and glanced over my head, his eyes squinting at the promise of a still-brighter morning.

"Marden, Tanner's daughter."

One of Elfriede's friends. I'd never been that close to the girls. None of them wanted to swing sticks at pigs or roll on the hills and get their dresses caked in dirt. And Sindri had found his goddess early on in the process of maturing. I'd played with his brother Darwyn for far longer. I'd lost all track of Sindri and his goddess obsession soon after he stopped being one of the elf queen's loyal retainers.

"You got married?" I asked, picking up my chisel and going to work again. That was a rather stupid question, but I didn't remember the marriage.

"Yup," said Sindri, punctuating the end of the word sharply. "Never got Returned to. Not that I care now. When I think of how stupid I was, I want to strangle my past self. All of that trauma over that cold-hearted, selfish bi—"

He stopped. I thought of my recent bizarre feelings for Ailill and nodded. The chisel slipped awkwardly. Fur was starting to look more like scarring. Perhaps the fat cat would be a tomcat, complete with alleyway battle scars.

"You know," Sindri picked up again, "his lordship's edict has been a real blessing."

A dog barked sharply, cutting him short.

"Noll!"

My eyes snapped up at the dulcet, airy tones of my sister's

voice. It was a little off-tune and shaky. She was coming through the fields from the east, taking a shortcut from our childhood home to my new one. Skipping beside her to one side was Bow, Jurij's old, sandy-furred retriever, and on the other side was Arrow, Bow's perky and easily distracted golden-colored son. He stopped twice within a matter of moments to sniff the grassy field at his paws before galloping to catch up.

Elfriede hadn't visited me since I moved. I'd thought it best to stay away from whatever was going on with her and her husband. And that included staying away from knowing whether or not they had convinced a specter to produce a paper for them to sign from his ever-useful inner jacket pocket.

She was crying now, her golden hair limp against her flushed and fair oak-toned face. I felt a sharp pain slide into my stomach.

"What's wrong?" I stood, knocking the gouge off the stool. Arrow jumped in place, yapping.

Elfriede took first one deep breath and then another but, much to my impatience, didn't speak. Her gaze fell on Sindri, a cold blast of something I could only describe as annoyance sparking in her face. But this was Elfriede, my sweet and much-loved elder sister. She could hardly express that side of herself with witnesses.

"Uh, see you around, Noll," said Sindri, who had clearly picked up on something, too.

"Sure," I mumbled. He took off through the bushes and up the dirt path toward the quarry, jogging to join a pack of working men a few paces ahead of him.

Bow growled. I turned back to my sister, but not before putting the chisel and the half cat down on the stool behind me. Her wary eyes, puffed and darkened lids surrounding pale hazel, hadn't torn themselves from Sindri's back. Golden fur covered her wrinkled dress and apron. Her skin was perhaps in need of scrubbing. She looked as if she hadn't cared what she looked like for days at least.

"What is it?" I snapped at last. If I waited for her to open her mouth and stop sending death wishes after a young man she hardly knew, I was bound to waste all of the morning.

Elfriede's gaze turned reluctantly in my direction.

"Was that Marden's husband?" she asked.

"Former husband," I pointed out.

Now Elfriede's icy stare shot directly into me. "It won't do to be seen with a traitor like him."

"He just stopped to say hello." I could hardly believe the young woman before me was my sister. Had she spent the past few weeks locked up in a dark and desolate dungeon? No, my frail and carefree sister had not yet had the pleasure of that experience. I was sure my stay at the castle counted as something close enough.

"Well, don't say anything back," she barked.

I scoffed. Like I cared about the who-should-blame-whom of one of her giddy friend's couplings.

I put my hands on my hips. "I'll speak to whomever I like."

"Don't you have enough men after you?"

"What are you talking about?"

"Where's Jurij?" Elfriede asked the question with such volume and tenacity, I thought she imagined him in some crystal-encased cage around the back of my moldering shack. Arrow whimpered, even as Bow growled.

"How should I know?" I asked.

Elfriede stood on her toes to crane around my shoulders. *She really is looking for some cage!*

"He's been gone for days," she said, her voice cracking.

I plopped down on the stool, shoving the fat cat and the chisel to the ground beside the gouge. I cradled my face in my hands and heard the soft patter of paws. One of the dogs' noses brushed my knees.

Why did she have to involve me in this? Can't she see that I'm here to get away from all of this drama?

"Did you try his father's?" I mumbled through my palms.

"Yes. And his mother's place, too. Both were as surprised as I was that he had gone missing."

"His friends?"

"He doesn't have any friends," she spat. "Only you."

I rubbed my hands over my face. Arrow sat down beside me, looking upward expectantly. Odd. He could never be bothered with anyone but Elfriede before.

"Well, I haven't seen him, either." It was true. I hadn't seen him in weeks. Not since he kissed me and told me he loved me amongst the lilies on the hills. I thought it best not to mention that to his wife—former wife—who stood before me and was no doubt just waiting for an excuse to lurch forward and strangle me.

"Aren't you the least bit worried?" She paced back and forth, flailing her hands up and down. Up and down. Bow's head bobbed with her as she walked back and forth. All of the motion was making me ill.

"Should I be?" I asked. She stopped moving and shot me a look of pure and utter annoyance. "Look, whatever happened between you, he probably just needs some time to himself. I mean, how far could he go? There aren't a lot of places to hide."

"He should have told me!" she said, resuming her Bow-escorted back-and-forth trek to nowhere. "I would have let him be, but he should have told me!"

I sighed and reached out a hand to stroke Arrow's head. He actually let me touch him. His mouth opened, and his tongue spilled forth as I stroked him.

Did I dare ask what had happened? Clearly they had signed no paper blessing their second union. Perhaps that was all I needed to know. Thinking too much about it made my chest ache.

"Do you want me to help search?" I asked.

"No!" Elfriede snapped almost the same moment I asked the question. Arrow yelped and jumped backward out of my reach at the sound.

"Then what would you have me do?"

She marched onto the porch and shoved open the door to my shack, Bow and Arrow both at her heels. I hadn't known her capable of knocking over a small building with her bare hands, but I feared briefly for the welfare of my new home.

"Jurij!" came Elfriede's voice from inside the shack.

I jumped up and followed her.

"He's not here! What are you doing?"

Elfriede was on her hands and knees, leering into the area under my bed. Bow sniffed the ground beside her. Arrow had decided to lend his investigative ability to pinpointing my food stores. Elfriede jumped up almost as quickly as a specter and pasted herself against the wall, peeking behind my cupboard.

Arrow barked and pawed the door, perhaps hoping Elfriede would soon pull out a nice, long sausage.

"What? Are you looking for him back there? Behind about half a foot's length of space? Jurij is thin, Elfriede, but not so thin he might slide into nooks and crannies unnoticed."

Elfriede said nothing, her eyes darting frantically around the shack, but there were no more places he might be hiding. She let out a strange, shaky roar and plunked herself down in one of the two chairs around my small dining table. Bow sat down beside her and howled. Arrow's ears went back, and he lunged for the area beneath the table, pressing himself flat against the floor.

"Friede…"

She brought both hands up and then down, slamming them on her lap. Tears started flowing, and a series of chokes burst from her quivering lips.

I moved closer. She swung a hand wildly in my direction.

"Stay away from me!" She took a deep breath, choked with a sob. "You hussy!"

"*Hussy?*"

Elfriede sent me a cold, piercing look. "He told me he loved you. And you kissed him!" So she knew about that day on the hills after all. "And on my wedding day!"

Oh. *That* kiss. The one that had ended with an earthquake and Jurij getting a permanent gash over one of his eyes.

"Friede." *What can I say? I'm sorry? I am. I just…*

"I know you've always loved him," sobbed Elfriede. She rubbed her dripping nose on her sleeve. "You had no right!"

I threw my hands up in disgust. "I had no *right*? He was my friend before he was your man! And if I recall correctly, you didn't really want him at the start!"

That probably wasn't the best way to prove my innocence in the matter.

Elfriede jumped up from the table. "Don't blame me now for misgivings I entertained briefly as a child! He was *my* man, not yours!"

"Yes, *was*," I spat. "In case you haven't noticed, most of the town is in chaos. The past doesn't matter." I swallowed a lump forming in my throat. To me, the past was all that mattered, but she would never understand what I meant. "He loves you, too," I whispered.

Elfriede sniffled. "I know." She wiped first one eye and then the other with the heel of her palm. "But I don't want to share that love with you."

I turned away. What right did I have to deny any of it? "You're right. Once I would have given anything to steal him from you. I never wanted to hurt you. But I was tired of being the only one who felt a complete and utter mess inside. The only one whose feelings never mattered. But I feel fine now. I'm doing all right. Now you can all try dealing with those emotions I lived with for so long. Just leave me out of it."

Elfriede slipped past me, her sobs clogged, silent. Behind her trailed Bow, but it wasn't until Bow barked curtly that Arrow got up and followed. I twisted my body to watch Elfriede drag herself out my doorway and down my porch. She paused to look back at me, rubbing her hand over Bow's ear. Arrow started homeward without them.

"You know," Elfriede said, each word shaky, "I felt sorry for you then. But I don't think I can ever forgive you."

One after the other, she picked up the iron weights of her feet and left. Bow glanced at me but made no noise before following. Perhaps she didn't find me worthy even of a growl.

"I don't think I can ever forgive you." What a familiar line that was beginning to be. I wondered how many more I would wind up crossing off my ever-shortening list of loved ones. My decision to move to the old crone's shack was beginning to make more and more sense with each passing hour.

Still, I felt I should get going. Time to cross off one more.

CHAPTER FOUR

The person I used to be wouldn't have hesitated to cross the cavern threshold. She also wouldn't have come with a candle in hand.

Leave the candle. Make your way through darkness. You know the way by heart.

But I also knew now that there was more to this cavern than I ever would have imagined. Even when I was imagining sticks as swords and monsters flickering on the walls. Even when I fashioned myself an elf queen.

No, you're no queen. You're only *the first goddess.*

I shook my head and steadied the candle as I took note of my trembling hand. There were no goddesses anymore. It didn't matter if I was the first, or even the last. Everything was put right now.

So why does everything feel so wrong?

I lifted the candle higher to look for signs of Jurij, even though I was just guessing he came here. *Where else is there to go to be alone? Where else is there to go at all?*

I hoped the glowing light hadn't drawn him into the water. But maybe that was something it did only for me.

I told myself I'd never set foot in the cavern again. But if Jurij was in there, I had to know.

I stopped, bringing the candle closer to my chest. I heard the drip, drip, drop of the water trickling up ahead. And just at the edge of darkness, I saw a light. I was expecting that enticing violet glow, the light that always called me whenever I was near. The light that nearly drowned me more than once.

But the light I saw was red, dim and dark instead of bright.

I can't go there. A pain sheered through my chest. I swallowed. It didn't matter. There was nothing left for me there.

I blew out the candle and turned, forgetting why I came in the first place, focusing on nothing but getting out and pretending I was never there. My foot found a growth I didn't remember, and I stumbled.

"Whoa. I'm sorry."

A hand on my thigh and another on my ankle steadied me, the grip gentle but sturdy, enough to keep me from falling over without making it feel like I was caught against my will. I regained my feet, and the hands fell. I looked down, blinking to adjust to the darkness.

"Jurij?"

I wasn't sure how I hadn't noticed him as I passed.

"You found me," he said, a sheepish smile hidden in his voice. The sound of a scratch against a rock sent a shiver up my back, and Jurij's face alit with warm light. He smiled awkwardly as he placed a lit candle beside him on the ground and displayed the flint between his fingers. "You want me to light yours?"

I sat down on the ground beside him and slid my candle-stick over to him. "Thank you." I wasn't even sure why I blew it out in the first place. Like the red glow wouldn't be able to find me in the darkness. Like that pool ever needed to *see* me to call my name—or keep me away. I took a deep breath. *Enough. Enough of that pool and all that came with it. Remember why you're here.* "You could have said something when I passed by the first time."

Jurij guided his flint to the candle's wick. "I thought maybe you wouldn't notice I was here. You seemed pretty transfixed by the pool." He dropped the flint into the sediment to let the flame die out. "I thought maybe you weren't even here for me."

Because I have a habit of jumping in this pool. "Elfriede's looking for you."

"I know." Jurij set my candlestick down on the ground between us. "Why do you think I'm here?"

I shrugged and bit my lip to avoid stating the obvious. I didn't come to commiserate with him, or to encourage him to continue acting like a fool. I came to put an end to his estrangement, so I could get back to my cottage and live in peace. Because even though it was my curse that made Jurij love Elfriede in the first place, it was also my fault he wasn't blindly in love with her anymore. *And even though I once wanted him more than anything, I don't know what I want now.*

But I knew it wasn't this. "What's going on with you two?"

Jurij hugged his knees to his chest. "What's going on with anyone these days?" He continued talking to the ground, like it'd make for a better listener than me. "How is a man supposed to know what love is now?"

I knew the meaning behind his question, and the answer—the real answer—wasn't simple. But I wasn't there to discuss a man's choice to love. I still wasn't used to the idea that a man could *have* a choice. Regardless, I was here to set things right again. "You know what love is. You've experienced it."

"Have I?" Jurij's eyes met mine for the first time since I'd sat down beside him, and I looked away, unable to drink in the darkness without the flame that once danced there. I couldn't respond, so he continued. "The new edict has been a blessing in a way."

His words brought to mind other voices. *"His lordship's edict has been a real blessing."*

"You are not welcome here, Olivière."

I shook my head. No. No, Jurij wouldn't be like them. He had real reasons to love his goddess, not like Sindri and an unReturned love, not like Ailill.

"Yes," I said, interrupting Jurij before he could finish, "because now we know that those who marry truly love each other." I nudged Jurij's upper arm with my own. "And there's no doubt in my mind that you love Elfriede."

"I'm glad one of us has no doubts." Jurij laced his hands together around his knees.

"Jurij, I lived with choice in love my whole life." I took my knees in my arms, just so I could embrace something to stop the wild beating of my heart. "So has every woman. And if you think about it, the fact that Elfriede *chose* to love you is remarkable. It makes her more worthy of your love than many goddesses —*women*—were of their men's love."

My wandering eyes caught Jurij's, and my breath caught in my throat. I'd dreamed of days when he would look at me like that, albeit without the slightly drooping eyelid and the scar that ran over it, a reminder of the first time I kissed him. On his wedding day. His wedding to my sister. I coughed and turned away.

"*You* chose to love me, Noll."

Don't.

"And you knew there was no hope."

I don't want to remember.

"Yet you loved me. You refused the wealthiest, most powerful man in the village because you loved me."

Now hold on, it wasn't just about that.

"You looked for ways to break the curse. Noll, you *broke the curse* because you loved me."

"Stop!" I was on my feet, not even noticing when or how I got there. "Jurij, just *stop*." I held my hands out in front of me as if pushing against a force of air. "Who told you I broke the curse?"

Jurij gestured around the cavern like he was pointing out imaginary people. "Everyone! Everyone says it was because of you."

"It wasn't me." I clutched my elbows and stared at the flickering candle at my feet.

"Sure." Jurij didn't sound convinced. "You just happened to be one of the last goddesses to have her man find her, the never-dying, always-watching lord of the village no less, the same lord who now says that all marriages before the break of the curse are invalid, and you have nothing to do with the fact that now every man is as free as a woman to choose who he'll love."

His words bit. Jurij was the last person I expected to be so accusatory. It took a lot to make him angry—to make him feel anything other than love and meekness. "I didn't say I had nothing to do with it." I ran a hand up my arm to my shoulder. "But it wasn't me. It was him."

Jurij shifted on the ground, but I didn't look at him. The drops of distant water punctuated the silence. "Well, I *know* whatever you did played a large role in it."

I said nothing, but I could see Jurij's feet moving at the edge of the candlelight, his legs getting ready to stand.

"And I won't let you tell me it had nothing to do with me."

I'm in trouble. I took a step back, ready to flee, but I dug in my heels. *You're here for a reason.* "Jurij, that's rather egotistical. It's not like you." He was starting to really get on my nerves. *Jurij—* on my nerves. He'd never annoyed me quite like this before.

"How do you know what I'm like? Really? Considering I was obsessed with a woman for years and had no choice in the matter?" His hands clutched both of my shoulders. "Noll, you kissed me. On my wedding day."

I knew it would be easy to slide out of his grip, much easier than it might have been with Ailill, but I was frozen, unable to move. I swallowed. *I won't run from it then. I'll use it.* "I used you." It wasn't what I meant to say, but some part of me wondered if it was true.

Jurij didn't seem hurt or shocked like I'd hoped. If anything, he seemed amused. And I wasn't sure I liked the feelings his amusement stirred in me. "Used me?"

"I didn't like being forced to love the lord. I wanted to make him angry." It was true. I knew that now. I knew a lot of things now that I was too blind to see back then. Before I grew up.

"And making him angry would make him stop loving you?" Jurij didn't believe a word I said. "You are aware that because of the curse we had no choice but to love, so how…"

"He didn't love me. He never did. The curse just forced him to think he did." It hurt to speak the words aloud. I'd buried them so deeply amidst my peaceful day-to-day existence.

"That's what I've been saying. We were all forced, Noll. But you weren't. Not when it came to loving me." He leaned forward, and I had to make myself take a step back out of his reach. If I'd stayed put, I might have been on the receiving end of another kiss.

"My feelings for you made my sister unhappy."

Jurij took a step forward to close the distance between us. "And her loving me, and me loving her, made *you* unhappy."

I moved back in time with his steps, never letting him close the gap entirely, never letting myself enter his embrace. "I caused that injury to your face by kissing you."

"*He* caused my injury."

The tiny blaze of the candles grew dimmer, and the red glow of the distant cavern pool mocked me, warning me to stay away. I retreated into the darkness, knowing the light of day was nearby. "I was selfish, stubborn, focused only on my own desires."

"Sounds like just about everyone else in this village, Noll."

I kept retreating until my back slammed against the cavern wall. He grabbed my arms again, this time a little firmer, like he didn't ever want to let me go. I closed my eyes as his face drew nearer to mine. "All right! I loved you!" I said. His grip stiffened, and I opened first one eye and then the other. His face came to a stop near mine, but he was searching my expression, waiting for me to continue. I looked away. "But I don't now. Not like that." *Confused. We're both just confused.* I peeked up at him, waiting to see if my rejection would cause him the pain Elfriede's might have, had he still been in love with her.

Jurij's fingers unhooked from my arms. He turned and headed back to where we left the candles. Instead of blowing them out or picking them up, he sat back down on the ground beside them. I stood watching him for a moment, confused, still reeling from our almost-kiss. "Jurij?"

"Go." He wouldn't look at me as I approached, and I was certain I'd never before seen the shadow of anger on my Jurij's face like I did now. *Not* my *Jurij.*

"And leave you here?"

Jurij blew out a loud, slow breath. "For a while."

I placed my hands on my hips. "You've been here long enough."

"I can't go home. Not yet."

"To your parents'?"

"She'll find me at either one's. Tell me she hasn't looked for me there already."

"There and at my place."

Jurij laughed, and I saw something of his old, cheerful self dancing across his eyes, but there was no mistaking the bitterness there. "Of course she would assume I was there."

I didn't think she was that wrong in thinking so now, not after the way his eyes drank in mine just moments before. But I didn't think Jurij was in the mood to hear that. Not if I hoped to steer him through his confusion back to the right path. Back to Elfriede.

"It didn't seem like she'd be back to visit anytime soon." *Or ever.*

Jurij's grin reached his eyes, and I could have sworn I saw the flame flicker there once more. But no, it was just the reflection of the candles. "Looks like I've found a place to stay."

So much for convincing him to join the ever-growing list of people who hate me.

CHAPTER FIVE

"Let me get this straight. Jurij expects us to pretend we don't know where he is when Elfriede comes asking, yet somehow we're not supposed to be panicking that he's gone missing? Pass me some more nails, would you?" With one hand, Alvilda balanced two planks of wood for a large chest on which she'd asked me to carve a design. I rifled through her sawdust-covered workbench, found a couple of dusty iron nails, and dropped them into her extended hand.

"I know." It sounded even more ridiculous when someone else pointed out the flaw in the plan. "But if I don't let him stay with me, he'll go back to the cavern."

"You're seventeen, Noll—eighteen in a few months."

"Yeah…" I hadn't stopped to think about it, but come fall, it'd be a year since I moved into the castle. It felt like a lifetime ago.

"So you're a grown woman. And a grown woman has needs. I get that." Alvilda rolled the nails between her fingers. "Are you a coupling then?"

"No! *No!*" I sputtered. "I mean, I know why you might *think* that, but— No, I don't, now that I think about it. Why would you say that?"

"All right, all right. But a man moves in with a woman? What else are people supposed to think?" Alvilda placed one of the nails in her mouth like a piece of chewing straw. She stared me down out of the corner of her eye even as she took a hammer and pounded the first nail into place. "Schounds like..." Alvilda spat out a breath of air as she grabbed the nail from her mouth. "Sounds like he's taking you for a fool." She used her forearm to swat away a stray tendril of dark hair that fell across her face and went back to hammering.

I sat down on the bench beside Alvilda's worktable. My fingers drew circles through the sawdust as I stared across the room at the dining table. I still wasn't used to seeing that table dust-free. Mistress Tailor—no, Mistress *Carver*, or maybe now that I was on my own with my own profession I could start calling her Siofra—had taken over most of Alvilda's house and declared it an actual *home*. "There's work and there's home, and some of us need a little help differentiating between the two," she'd said to me when I first commented on how clean the place looked. "Alvilda can confine her work to the corner. No need to be dragging dust all over where the children are eating and sleeping."

And Alvilda had actually complied without putting up much of a fuss, as far as I knew. I noticed it didn't stop her from letting her work creep just a little bit beyond her "work corner" each and every day. It was why, at Siofra's insistence, building a workshop nearby was on Alvilda's to-do list. "Why not use the commune?" Siofra had suggested. "It's just sitting there, rotting, unused. Tearing down those filthy old shacks would do the village a lot of good."

But somehow, Alvilda had become "so busy" wrestling up projects from customers over the past few weeks that she'd barely done more than knock down the first couple of shacks, which I gladly helped with, feeling some of the painful memories fall away with each wall. Alvilda's lack of attention to the new work-space probably had something to do with the "waste of burning wood for two fires" she kept mumbling about. Not that it was so cold out yet that she'd absolutely need a fire, but she did work late most nights. She'd changed since Siofra moved in. She was gruffer, rougher around the edges. Like she had more annoyances to work out of her system with every swing of her hammer and every twist of a nail than she had back when she'd lived alone.

Alvilda must have noticed I hadn't responded to her remark that I was a fool. I didn't have anything to say; at this point, I probably agreed with it. Alvilda appeared beside me and took a swig from the mug she kept between a pile of filthy rags and a chisel on her worktable. "So how exactly does this living arrangement work?"

"He's sleeping on the floor. On some hay and blankets."

Alvilda peered down at me over the top of her mug. "And... doing what exactly?"

I shrugged. "Nothing. We haven't done anything."

Alvilda raised an eyebrow and put her mug back down. "No, *you* carved this box for me. And probably carved more of your toy animals, too." Alvilda leaned across me to grab a few more nails and went back to her box and hammer. "I want to know if Jurij is doing anything other than moping and trying to get you to make love to him."

"Alvilda! He isn't— We aren't—" I coughed and made a show of covering my mouth so I could hide the blush on my cheeks at the same time. "It's only been a few days."

"A few days becomes a few weeks becomes a few years in time." Alvilda whacked the hammer with probably a little more force than necessary. "Now that men don't need to be told what to do, they seem to need to be told what to do more than ever."

I thought about what she said for a moment, and what initially sounded like nonsense started to make sense. "Elweard still runs the tavern."

"*Vena* still runs the tavern. And Vena being bossy just happened to work out with Elweard looking for someone to boss him around, even without the curse driving him." Alvilda shook the hammer in my direction. "Elweard is about the only good worker left among the lot of them. Well, and Coll." Alvilda's brother—Jurij's father—had both sister and former wife to make sure he didn't slack any just because his whole life was turned upside down.

Alvilda picked up a nail. "Do you know what I had to go through to get an order of these? The blacksmith decided to use his newfound freedom to spend his days *lying in the fields.* Lying in the fields!" She shook her head and positioned the nail, taking a swing at it with her hammer. "I didn't even dare to ask who *with*. His wife—*former* wife—told me he could rot in the fields for all she cared. But I needed my nails, so I made sure to give him a reason or two to get up off his flower-covered ass." She swung the hammer back, resting it over her shoulder, and admired her hammering with a snarl, perhaps either intentionally or subconsciously showing me just how she convinced the man to get back to work. Then she placed the hammer down and snatched her mug up from the table like I might be tempted to steal it out of her hands. "And your father? What was his excuse to pack up shop in the last week? He's retiring?"

I shrugged and looked away. I hadn't been home in weeks. I wasn't really avoiding Father or Mother, but I knew I wouldn't be going home to a happy family reunion. Especially not with how things were with Elfriede.

Alvilda's rant was undeterred by my silence. She swung her arms around the room, sloshing a little of her drink onto the floor. "All this carving to do, and the other master carver in the village has retired?" She shook her head and took a sip. "No. No, I won't have it with my nephews." She slammed the mug down. "And Siofra and Coll won't have it, either."

"Luuk helps Master Tailor and Siofra."

Alvilda nodded. "He helps his father and mother and even me plenty. Nissa, too. They're young. We can still tell them they'd better help out." I didn't ask if youth helped them cope with Luuk's sudden lack of romantic devotion toward his former goddess. I didn't relish whoever was the one to have the discussion with Nissa that her former little love now thought of her as more of a sister. Alvilda pointed directly at me. "Jurij is the problem here."

I crumbled under Alvilda's stare, focusing instead on the circles my fingers keep tracing in the sawdust. I hated to admit what I already knew, that Jurij wasn't *my* Jurij. Even if this probably was the *real* Jurij, the one who'd have existed without the curse. Then again, the curse was the reason for his bitterness, so who knows who he would have been? "I'm working on fixing things."

"*Fixing things?*" I could hear Alvilda scoff. "And what does that entail exactly?"

I met Alvilda's gaze. "Jurij back home with Elfriede. With his wife."

"With his *former* wife." Alvilda sighed and threaded her arms across her chest. "Noll, you're just not getting it. Things aren't the same anymore. You can't influence Jurij now any more than you could when you wanted him to love you."

"That was different."

"Why? Because he *had* to love Elfriede, so there was no hope for you?"

"That's exactly why. Now, his feelings could go either way. Or another way entirely."

"Then wishing *your* will on him seems more hopeless than ever."

I stared, studying Alvilda. "But he can be convinced now."

"You can't shape him like one of your wooden toys, Noll!" Alvilda rolled her eyes. "He has his own feelings, his own desires. Let him figure out how he feels for himself."

"But I don't want him to love me. Not like that. Not now."

Alvilda tilted her head. "And why not?"

"Because." I stared back at my circles, surprised to find that I'd traced a blooming rosebud without meaning to. "It's just easier that way."

"Are you worried about Elfriede?" Alvilda waited for my response before continuing, but I said nothing. "Because she's stronger than you give her credit for, stronger maybe than even she realizes. She's beautiful and sweet, and there are dozens upon dozens of available men out there now. She doesn't need Jurij, even if she thinks she does. She just needs time."

She doesn't need him. And I don't need Ailill. "I need time, too," I said at last.

Alvilda didn't say anything for a moment. Then she picked up her hammer and went back to work. "Well, take it. You could all use a little time to stop obsessing over romance, if you ask me."

"Maybe." I took a deep breath and stood, gathering my tools into my work basket.

Alvilda pointed at me with the hammer again. "You tell Jurij his mother and I expect him here for dinner tomorrow. He's had enough time to mope."

"I don't think I can convince him."

Alvilda laughed and swung the hammer at a nail. "You tell him he can be convinced by you, or he can wait for me to come over and convince him." She gestured at the door with the hammer. "And he might want to spend tomorrow walking through the village, looking for someplace where some other man has slacked off. Because if he's going to relish being free, he's going to find something productive he likes doing. Or if he can't choose, I'll choose for him. He'll take over the tailor work and the carver work both." She slammed the hammer one more time. "And I can find plenty more work that needs doing."

I wouldn't doubt that, not even if the entire village were already carved from wood.

CHAPTER SIX

"How can Alvilda expect me to make up my mind in one day?" Jurij had asked that question so many times I was starting to bite my tongue. If he'd spent a little less time asking, he'd have had more time to think about it. The blanket he'd carried for me was slipping out from under his arm, its edges grazing the road to the heart of the village. I shifted the basket of wooden toys onto my arm, scrambled to pick up the blanket hem, and tucked it back tighter beneath Jurij's arm. He didn't seem to notice. "I haven't had time to think about it. I haven't had time to think about anything but..." He stopped speaking and gestured with his free hand. His eyebrows creased, his mouth pursed. "I mean, expecting me to help out with Mother and Father is one thing. When they're busy. I'd even help out Auntie if she *really* needed the help."

I halted at the crossroads, realizing Jurij was still ranting in an entirely different direction. "But that's what I don't get," Jurij was saying by the time I caught up with him again. I grabbed his upper arm to stop him.

"The baker's today, remember?" I tugged him back the way we were meant to turn.

Jurij followed my lead, letting himself be guided, not responding at all to what I'd said. "When I was El—*her* man, no one batted an eye that I went off to do nothing. Nothing but hand her cooking utensils and sweep floors and whatever else she demanded I do, even if it was just to stand there worshipping the ground she walked on."

I winced and readjusted the basket on my arm. Elfriede hadn't been *that* bad, surely. No worse than any other goddess. Probably better than some. Like Jurij's mother.

"No, *worshipping* a woman, doing whatever it took to make her life easier, *that* was a fine occupation of my time. But now that I can do whatever *I* want…"

I dropped the basket onto the ground, hoping the noise it made would snap Jurij out of his tirade. My toys were hardy; they could take the abuse. "We're here." I put my hands on my waist and looked at the little patch of ground in front of the baker's shop like it was something I'd built with my own two hands. Jurij had stopped speaking at least, but he wasn't thinking, either, apparently. "Blanket." I pointed to the bundle under his arm.

Jurij nodded and shook the blanket out, spreading it on the ground in the spot I'd asked Mistress Baker to let me borrow one day a week. She'd been so flustered when I'd asked, elbow-deep in flour and yeast, I wasn't sure she'd heard me. But she hadn't corrected me since, so I was content to keep setting up shop in front of one of the village's most popular stores. Everyone needed bread. And kids almost always tagged along to the baker's, hoping for something sweet.

I sat down on the blanket and opened the basket, setting out the wooden animals I'd brought along. Jurij stood there blankly. "Are you going to walk around the village?" I asked, placing a wooden doe next to the stag whose antlers had taken me half a day to get right. The broken-off one was just part of his appeal. "Look for some kind of work?"

Jurij scrambled to sit next to me, digging into the basket and grabbing a handful of animals. We didn't say anything for a moment. I finished emptying the basket, but Jurij was still staring at the animals in his hands, utterly unhelpful. He seemed to feel my stare and looked up with a smile. "These are nice, Noll."

I tore away, suddenly forgetting how annoyingly unhelpful he was being and remembering how attractive his face was. That cleft in his chin always had an effect on me. "Thanks." I tucked a little bit of hair behind my ears. It was short, but it still stuck out enough that it could get irritating if I swung my head around quickly.

Jurij put down the cat with the scarred rump and followed it with a dog and her puppy. He arranged and rearranged them until he must have decided they were shown off to their best angles. His hand lingered on the mother dog. "I don't suppose there's a way to get Bow. Tell El—your sister you need some company?"

I laughed, and not kindly. "I don't think she'd have much sympathy. Especially once she discovered I already had some company."

Jurij leaned back, resting his head against the bricks of the baker's shop. "Yeah, I guess that wouldn't work."

I reached into the basket and pulled out the last of its contents, a small wooden sign on which I'd carved "Wooden Playthings, 2 Coppers Each," and placed it in front of the eclectic little herd. "Well, if it's any comfort, she's bound to realize soon enough that you haven't gone off to die, and you'll get your dog back in the chaos that ensues."

Jurij pounded the back of his head against the baker's shop wall once, twice, and a third time. "That's not a comfort at all."

I shrugged. I knew that. But I didn't think he was helping things by hoping it never happened. "Why don't we invite her to your mother and aunt's tonight?"

Jurij tore his head away from the wall and stared at me. "Please tell me you're joking."

I ran a finger in a circle around a squirrel. "You might not find it so bad after all. You might..." *Just go back and make up with your wife already.*

"No." Jurij leaned his head back again and hugged his knees to his chest. He always did that when he was uncomfortable. I wondered if Elfriede knew that about him. Or if she'd ever seen him uncomfortable before the curse was broken.

"You know, Elfriede doesn't..." The giggles of children stopped me from continuing. I smiled at the boy and two girls standing in front of my makeshift shop. "Good day." The girl in the front held two copper coins between her fingers.

"Ask her!" The boy laughed and shoved the girl beside him.

"No, *you* ask her!" The girl he'd shoved dug her heels into the ground and pushed back against the boy's hands in her efforts to resist him, accidentally bumping into the girl with the coins in the exchange.

I pretended to cough and held up the cat. "Do you want to take a closer look? Go ahead. Pick them up."

The well-behaved girl with the coppers took the cat from me and examined it. The boy and girl behind her were undeterred, still pushing against one another. Jurij stared at them, one eyebrow raised. "What's up with those two?" he asked quietly.

I stuck out a hand to stop further inquiries on the subject. It wasn't the first time I'd gotten questions, and it was bound not to be the last. With any luck, they'd both prove too shy to ask, and that would be the end of it.

The little customer put the cat back on the blanket and picked up the squirrel, just as the girl behind her stumbled forward, her battle against the boy's persistence lost. "Um," she said, rubbing a hand over her forearm. "Wanted nolorloolike."

"What?" asked Jurij.

The children burst out laughing, the boy clutching his arms to his stomach, the girl covering her mouth as if she'd said something shameful. She hadn't said anything at all, really, except that I knew exactly what she meant, having heard it a number of times now.

I picked up the puppy figure and held it to the girl in front, who put the squirrel down and took the puppy from me. "They want to know," I answered Jurij, pausing to stop myself from grinding my teeth, "what the lord looks like."

The girl with her hand over her mouth squealed, and the boy stepped forward, practically shoving my customer aside. "Is he real?"

"Is he a person?" added the squealer. "Or a monster?"

"Is he all pale like them?" The boy nodded sideways. I hesitated to look, but out of the corner of my eye, I noticed a specter approaching.

Jurij turned his head to look, and his face soured. He put a finger to his lips. "Guys, calm down."

"This one." It was the first time the girl with the coppers spoke, and I had no idea which animal she'd picked.

I was torn between watching the specter and pretending that my sole focus was my customer. "Okay. Sure. Two coppers then." The cat after all. The one with the rather large rump. I held my hand out for the coppers, my gaze directed as much on the corner of my eye as possible, the giggles of the other children and the buzz of the villagers in the marketplace drowning out any hope of hearing his approaching footsteps.

The coppers landed in my palm. "Thank you." I turned my head just slightly, and for one fleeting second caught the black irises of the specter. It was almost like he was looking at me. But they'd rarely met my eyes before. They'd rarely done anything but fulfill the lord's orders with utmost efficiency.

But it was a fleeting moment. I'd only imagined it was longer. His face *did* so resemble Ailill's, if Ailill had aged to appear much older. His eyes fell, and he opened the door to the baker's shop, vanishing from sight.

"Noll?"

I shook my head to clear it and found Jurij's gaze fixed on me. He nodded sideways, and I followed his gesture to find the three children absolutely still, staring at me.

"She *knows* that servant, I bet!" cried the boy.

"Maybe she *likes* him!" I had no idea how the giggly girl came up with that idea. But then I realized my cheeks were hot, and I pocketed the coppers. I looked down at the array of wooden animals, straightening them back into order.

"Thank you for the purchase." I smiled, remembering what was more important. The girl cradling her wooden cat grinned.

"Oh! That *is* cute." The other girl grabbed the cat from my customer's hands. She seemed reluctant to part with it, but she had little choice in the matter. "I want one!"

"Two coppers," I said, pointing to the sign.

"Never mind." She sighed and handed the cat back to her friend, who gingerly pet it with one finger, like it was a miniature kitten.

The boy peeked his head over the two girls' shoulders, studying the blanket and all of my wares. "They're all right," he said, clearly not impressed. His gaze wandered to the shop window above my head, and I knew he was watching the specter conduct his business in there.

Jurij leaned over and picked up the squirrel. He pretended not to notice as the girl without coppers took in the figure hungrily, and he leaned back against the wall, turning the squirrel over in his lap. "You know, when I wanted coppers as a kid, I asked around to see if anyone had any work that needed doing."

Am I really hearing him say those words directed at someone else?

The girl scuffed her foot on the ground. "Papa used to give me coppers. Now he keeps them."

I didn't want to ask what he used them for. Thinking about how things had changed in the village with so many men refusing to work reminded me of that month no one remembered. When Ailill vanished—when I *made* him vanish—the whole village suffered without his purchases. If one man could make such an impact, albeit one man who spent a large amount in the village, surely dozens, if not hundreds, of men earning and spending less would, too. I grabbed the squirrel out of Jurij's hands and placed it back among the wooden animals. "Well, you earn some of your own, instead of asking your papa for them, and I may give you a discount."

That brought a smile to her face.

The boy was not so easy to appease. "You didn't tell us about the lord." His gaze was still focused on the window above me. "How come he never comes down himself? He must be monstrously ugly."

"He's not." The words were out of my mouth before I could stop myself.

I felt the eyes of all three children and Jurij bearing down on me. "She *likes* him!" whispered that girl again, although not very quietly.

"Then why won't he visit the village?" asked the boy.

"Because then children like you wouldn't have so much fun asking so many questions." Each of the kids responded with a blank stare. "He's more mysterious this way, isn't he? Who'd care about him at all if he wasn't hidden away?"

The door to the baker's shop opened, and I clamped my mouth shut. I busied myself fussing with the nearest row of animals, turning a perfectly fine display into something of a

299

mess. The specter had one of the baker's sons pushing a cart full of bread for him. I had to scoff despite my fear of being noticed. I knew the specters didn't eat anything. What did Ailill always need so much bread for? To make people think the specters were human? I wondered why I'd never seen a room full of rotting, moldy bread, but it could have very well been on the top floor, next to the tower prison. Where he'd kept my mother. And probably Jurij, for that one day he'd stolen him from me.

I shook my head. *From Elfriede.*

The cart stopped. "Oh. It's today."

Darwyn, Baker's son. One of my friends from childhood. A rather annoying friend from childhood. Looking down and clearly expecting me to say something.

"What's today?" I asked, tucking that too-long bit of hair behind my ear.

"Your shop." He let go of the cart handle to gesture at my blanket. "In front of ours."

"Oh. Your mother said it was okay."

Darwyn nodded. "Yeah, sure. I guess we don't mind. But if I knew you'd be here, I'd have..." He stopped, putting his hand back on the cart and turning to go.

I stopped fondling my carvings and stared up at him. "You'd have what?"

"Nothing." Darwyn started pushing the cart again. It carried more bread than would feed one man, but at least it wasn't overflowing like it used to be. Maybe Ailill was trying to be a little less wasteful. But how would such thoughts even occur to him in the middle of a long, brooding day?

The specter stepped out from the shop behind Darwyn, and I *knew* this time that his eyes met mine. I looked away, flustered. It wasn't like Ailill could read minds. Just get a report of all my actions. At least I hoped he couldn't read minds. But even if he could, it didn't matter. He'd already decided I still hated him, so he wouldn't bother reading mine.

The cricketing of the cart faded, the sound drowned out by the movements of villagers going about their business on the road.

"Let's follow him!" whispered the boy.

I looked up, for a foolish moment thinking the invitation

included me, the weird lone woman who'd rejected the lord and turned the whole village upside down. But the children were already lost in their own world, giggling and running down the road after Darwyn and the specter. My hand lingered on a wooden horse, thinking of the days when I led a group of boys around the village, always after the mysterious, always looking for adventure. At least, after everything, there were children now at play, children who might have forgotten one another in the days of the goddesses.

"Nothing?" echoed Jurij beside me, sometime after Darwyn had left. He snorted.

I leaned back against the wall beside him. "He probably meant he would have sent his brother."

"So he didn't have to see me?"

I studied Jurij, wondering where he came up with that idea. "Why would he care about seeing you? I was the one who always bothered him when we were kids."

Jurij let out a deep breath and shook his head. "I think everyone bothered him. To tell you the truth, I couldn't even stand the guy until he found his goddess."

I tilted my head and raised an eyebrow. "We barely saw him once he found his goddess."

Jurij shrugged. "Exactly."

I tsked. "So there's something to be said for goddesses after all?"

The laugh I heard from beside me couldn't have been more contemptuous if it had been Ailill's. "And what would that be?"

Jurij and I looked up. Darwyn had returned, the squeaky cart no longer with him to give us a hint of his approaching. I swallowed, wondering how much he'd heard. Not that I'd said anything beyond what he might be expecting. But if there was one thing I didn't miss from the days before my friends had found their goddesses, it was attempting to break up fights between them. *Even if I caused more than a few of them myself.*

"They gave you guys some sense of direction." An idea popped into my head as my gaze drifted between Darwyn and Jurij. "Say, Darwyn, your brother Sindri, he works in the quarry?"

I didn't have to look at Jurij to feel his accusing glare from beside me, but I purposefully ignored it. "Yeah?" Darwyn said after a moment's pause, clearly not following why I'd asked to begin with.

My eyes traveled to the baker's shop door. "And your mother could use some help these days, right? Since your father..." I cut myself short.

"Moved in with one of the farmer women. Sure. Lots of people doing strange things like that these days." Darwyn tried to state that fact as if it didn't matter, but his voice cracked as he did. He wiped his nose with one finger and crouched beside us, his gaze drifting quickly over my wooden figures and back again. "You looking for work, Noll? The shop, maybe, but I don't know if you have the heft for quarry work."

"I'm set with my woodworking, thank you." I nudged Jurij and looked at him for the first time since I started the conversation. His face seemed dejected, and he wouldn't return my gaze. "But Jurij needs something to do. And maybe it's time he asked some of his *friends* for help."

The look that Jurij gave me made me wonder if I'd finally added him to the list of people who once cared about me but didn't anymore.

CHAPTER SEVEN

"**A**gain? We just ate with them last week." Jurij wiped the sweat off his brow with his forearm and placed the pickaxe in its corner by the door. His scarred eyelid drooped heavily. "And where are we going to fit them all?" He shook his head. "Scratch that. You guys can eat here. I'll go to Elweard's with Sindri."

"Ha," I said, pulling open the cupboard and gripping the picnic basket handle on which I'd carved some flowers and thorns. "But is Sindri eating at the tavern? Why don't you invite him, too?"

Jurij regarded me as if I'd just asked him to marry his mother. But I supposed in this strange new life we'd been sharing for about two weeks, everything I asked of him would seem odd and new. I broke the silence. "Tell him he can bring any of his brothers, too."

Jurij glanced around the cottage, his eyes resting on the pork roasting in the fire. "You bought a pig."

I smiled and put my hands on my hips. "I bought a pig." My toys had been selling pretty well as of late—probably because they offered children in the midst of family turmoil a little comfort. Even fathers—or especially fathers—were buying them, despite the fact that they were the ones causing the turmoil in the first place. I wondered if they felt a little better distracting their children with baubles before they went off to the tavern. In any case, I had a sizeable stash of coins now, and it wasn't like I had anything else to save up for. The villagers needed people to spend more, so I wanted to lead by example.

"You knew we were having guests, and you didn't feel fit to tell me until I got home from the quarry." He scowled. "From a long, long day at the quarry."

I skirted the table and put my hands on Jurij's back, twisting him gently and guiding him to the door. "And a big feast will prove just the thing to make you feel better."

"Noll, you invited my parents. My brother. Nissa. *My aunt.*"

I smiled, feeling the sickening sweetness I poured into each muscle responsible for the movement. "Just be glad I didn't invite my family, too." I'd considered it. But since the Tailors had informed Elfriede that her former husband was safe and sound and living exactly where her own sister had sworn he'd never be found, I'd since realized they'd never reunite if Elfriede knew I was involved. "Now, go on. Invite our friends." I opened the cottage door.

"Yes, ma'am," mumbled Jurij. "Are you sure you didn't get a lot of practice being a goddess?"

"What was that?"

"Never mind." Jurij stepped onto the dirt leading to the road between the village and the quarry. "*Friends* is probably the wrong word anyway," he muttered.

He headed down the road toward the mass of men going home from the quarry. My gaze turned to the horizon. *Good. No rain.* The fire popped behind me. "Right. The pig." I rotated the animal on the spit, my mind racing with all of the preparations left to be done.

~

"I LIKE THIS ONE." Nissa probably meant it, but the extent of her enthusiasm made the comment seem about as genuine as Jurij's love for hard labor. She stroked the wooden rabbit in her lap like it was a live pet. It took a moment of studying her in the flicker of firelight to remember that Luuk had often worn a bunny mask, a hand-me-down from his brother.

I finished chewing my portion of meat. "You can have it." I nudged her. "No charge."

Nissa shook her head, and then, remembering herself, smiled ever so slightly at me. She placed the rabbit gently back into the basket I'd brought outside in order to show everyone gathered around the fire the new additions to my wares. "Let a child have it," she said quietly, failing to recognize that being thirteen hardly made her an adult. She observed the fire, and I noticed a hardness in her heart, maybe even harder than the hardness I'd felt at her age, when I saw the last of my friends leave me behind for my sister. Sure, Jurij had still been my friend, thanks to an unintended command from his goddess, but it wasn't the same. The secret hope I'd been harboring, that Jurij might love me when we grew older, was gone when I was Nissa's age. The way Nissa's eyes kept drifting to Luuk across the fire made me think she felt just as hopeless.

I'm sorry, Nissa. But you don't want a love like that anyway. I tossed the bone onto the fire. *It wasn't real. It didn't last.*

"Nice pig." For a moment, I thought Siofra might be complimenting the wooden pig I'd begun carving before they'd all arrived for dinner, but the block was still too formless for anyone to identify. Siofra was nodding at the tree stump on which I'd placed the roasted pig slices on a large platter and wiping her mouth with a scrap of cloth I'd gotten from the Tailors to serve as a napkin. "Good cut. Good buy. Good cooking."

I tucked the stray bit of hair behind my ear, still not used to compliments from the woman I'd grown up thinking was so surly. "Thanks."

Siofra held her plate out to Master Tailor beside her. "Coll, put another slice on my plate?" It wasn't a command exactly. But she'd already turned her attention to her mug, not even regarding the plate, which she must have assumed Master Tailor would take from her. It fell to the ground with a thunk.

Master Tailor stared at Siofra as he lifted his fork to his mouth and chewed slowly. You could practically hear every movement of his jaw between the crackling of the fire.

Siofra's face darkened as she snatched the plate. "Of course. I can do it myself," she said quietly. "I didn't mean anything by it."

As she stood to refill her plate herself, I cleared my throat, my gaze drifting to the large gaps between us I'd left for Jurij, Sindri, and whatever other Baker boy felt like joining us. My hand dug into Bow's fur. I'd been looking forward to seeing the look on Jurij's face when he saw our surprise canine guest, but now I wanted to grab him by the shoulders and shake him until the whiny, selfish man who'd moved in with me was replaced by the kind and caring boy who'd never spared a thought for himself.

But you were the one who felt it only right to give men their freedom.

"I like this ale," said Master Tailor, taking a swig from the mug I'd served Alvilda's and Siofra's gift in. "Alvilda, did you get this from Vena?"

Alvilda slammed her plate so hard on the ground beside her, I thought for a minute I'd served her meal on glass instead of wood. "All right. We've waited long enough." She bolted upright. "I'm going to search the entire village, I'm going to knock down doors, I'm going to find that lazy, ungrateful—"

"Alvilda!" Both Siofra and her former husband spoke the name at once, one pleading, even angry, the other so surprised, it was a wonder he was able to keep a grip on his mug.

Alvilda whipped around, first to face her wife and then to face her brother. She didn't seem to notice Luuk slinking down beside her as if hoping he could vanish entirely into the ground.

"No. This is ridiculous. I thought last week, when he dined at our house, that his plan to join the quarry workers would snap some sense into him, but that was just at Noll's urging, wasn't it? Leaving this entire meal to Noll, continuing to encroach upon her hospitality."

Despite my own irritation at the man who was the topic of her tirade, I started to feel protective, even defensive in the face of Alvilda's overreaction. "He hasn't been encroaching. He's been going to work every day."

Alvilda's boiling hot gaze fell on me. "Don't tell me he's been doing the minimum of what's expected of him like it's some accomplishment."

"It *is* an accomplishment." I jumped to my feet, staring her down across the fire. "Alvilda, don't you think you're being too hard on him? You didn't say a word against him for doing nothing with his days before the curse broke."

Alvilda thrust her arms across her chest. "Things are different."

"Things *are* different. You can't just expect men to pick up their lives like nothing's changed." My gaze fell on Master Tailor and Luuk. "Tell her," I said, as if my experiences put me in the position of acting like some translator between men and women. "Tell her things are different."

Siofra set her plate on the ground. "She knows that, Noll. She just wants what's best for our sons."

"*Our* sons?" The clatter of the plate on the ground beside me was enough to rival a dozen glass plates smashing. Master Tailor stood, his finger pointed at Alvilda. I'd never seen the man so angry. Granted, I'd never seen his face before the curse had broken, but I never imagined the features behind the owl mask he so often wore could contort so wildly. "Jurij and Luuk are *my* sons. Mine and Siofra's." He patted his chest with his fist. "And the two of you might have tried to forget I existed all of those years—"

Siofra gasped, standing. "We never!"

Alvilda put a hand out to stop her from crossing around the fire to get nearer to him.

"You *always*." Master Tailor's voice grew so deep and troubled, Bow woke from her nap emitting a low growl. Master Tailor paused, the lump on his throat shaking visibly as he swallowed. "It was always the two of you, from the start. I had my uses, but I was nothing to you."

"That's not true." I'd never heard Siofra's voice so unsure.

"No, it *is* true." Master Tailor shook his head. "I may have been too stupid to be hurt by it then, but it hurts thinking about it now." He sighed, his eyes darting between Alvilda and Siofra. Siofra couldn't meet his gaze, but Alvilda stared, daring him to say more. Master Tailor waved a defeated hand, dismissing them. "I don't mean I want Siofra back. I didn't have a choice to love her, you know." He tapped his fingers across his forehead as he paced back and forth before the fire. "But I can remember things. My *own sister*, Siofra, like I wanted to know what was going on between you. Like I was nothing but a messenger without a brain. But I remember what you had me say to her."

I clapped my hands together. "Okay, Nissa, why don't you help me clean up?" I looked across the fire. "Luuk?"

Luuk practically jumped up but stopped himself, his eyes wandering between Nissa, his mother and aunt, and his father, clearly trying to figure out who was least likely to cause him discomfort. And he wasn't having an easy time deciding.

Master Tailor seemed to notice the pause, and his attention drifted between Luuk and Nissa. He grabbed Luuk by the arm and pulled him upright. "No, Luuk's had enough of that. We're leaving." He looked at me. "Thank you for the dinner, Noll. It was great. Thank you for opening your home to Jurij, who is *a grown man* and can do as he damn well pleases." His extra emphasis was clearly not meant for me. "Tell him he can come home to me if he gets tired of the quarry." He looked back at Alvilda and Siofra. "Or of women in general."

I decided to let that last comment slide, given the situation, but some women couldn't.

"Coll!" Some of Siofra's usual stubbornness came through.

"No, let him go." Alvilda slipped an arm around Siofra and pulled her to her chest, roughly, more boldly than I'd ever seen her do before. "Let the man whine and see what good it does when the work still needs doing. Let him see that it's not so easy to think for himself and take on responsibility when someone isn't commanding him."

"So, Nissa," I spoke quietly, turning to see how the poor girl was handling it. She was clinging to Bow and trying to peer around my legs at the path Master Tailor and Luuk were cutting through the grasses, the shortcut that would take them to the Tailor Shop at the edge of the village.

"Oh, for—" Alvilda peered at the northern road to the village, tossing a hand in the air and then cradling her forehead.

Four figures ambled toward us, still some distance away. They were dancing. No, they stumbled every few steps, their arms swinging wildly up and down, their hands clutching mugs. In the quiet, all I heard was the crackling of the fire, Bow's heavy snoring, and the unskilled warbling of the four men.

Alvilda moved around the fire to grab Nissa by the forearm,

much as her brother had done to Luuk a moment beforehand. She looked at me. "Thank you for the dinner, Noll. It was great." *Wow, two barely-contained-rage-filled compliments for my cooking.* She peered over her shoulder. "Siofra?"

Siofra looked down the path, worry hidden behind the deep creases in her forehead. "He's drunk."

"He's a fool. And we'll have no part of it." Alvilda tugged Nissa along after her, and Siofra shuffled behind. "Tell him he can come home to us if he gets tired of acting like an idiot," Alvilda called to me over her shoulder. "Or like a man in general."

The three of them passed right by the dancing group, not even turning their heads to greet them.

CHAPTER EIGHT

The young man I wasn't too familiar with—the one with lips that seemed permanently puckered—poked Sindri in the chest, again and again. "Have I told you about my wife's mornings?" He had his arm around Sindri and was practically dragging him to the ground beside the fire.

"Former—*former* wives," slurred Sindri. His eyes were glazed, his attention focused on the ground.

"Former," repeated puckered-lips. "Every morning, she tooled me—"

"*Told*," interrupted Jurij beside him. He turned to Darwyn and started sniggering.

"Told me, Tayton, make the breakfast. Tayton, clean the house. Tayton, it's cold, chop more wool for the fire."

Darwyn and Jurij burst into laughter. "Wood!" shouted Darwyn.

"Wood." Tayton didn't seem to care that he couldn't get through a sentence without being corrected. He poked Sindri again and flailed his hand around. "Then I had to work in the quarry. And she just lay there, sleeping 'til lunchtime." He reached forward for the mug he'd set down on the ground beside him, completely oblivious to the fact that Sindri was now about a nose's length from the ground beneath Tayton's arm. Tayton let

310

Sindri go and sat back up, taking a swig from his mug. He wiped his mouth. "And *I* had to go home. Make her lunch." He made a spitting sound and widened his eyes, flicking his free hand before his face. "Whatta bibch."

"*Bitch*," said Jurij and Darwyn as one, their arms tight across their abdomens to keep themselves from falling over.

My fingers clutched Bow's fur as I regarded my new set of dinner guests around the fire, not a one of them interested in eating. Bow's head raised at the sound of Sindri's snoring. The baker's son lay there, face down, on the blanket where Tayton had dropped him. He was uncomfortably close to the fire.

I patted Bow to calm her and made my way toward Sindri to pull him back.

"Them's my wife's mornings. A whole lot of nothing." Tayton peered over the top of his mug at me as I rolled Sindri over.

Sindri's eyelids flittered open. "Wha? No, Marden, I'm too tired." He curled his legs against his abdomen and reached a hand out to grab my ankle, snuggling against my feet.

Tayton chuckled and spit back into his mug, swinging it side to side. "He thinks you're his wife."

"*Farmer* wife!" sang Darwyn and Jurij at once—a correction in need of correction—and they found them to be the funniest words ever spoken.

I ignored the cackling and reached down to peel Sindri's fingers from my leg. They proved harder to unfurl than expected, and I hesitated, concerned I might hurt him. In the end, I gave up and used my full strength to tear them away.

Tayton found the sight amusing, but his laughter suddenly stopped. "Hey! I know you."

I looked up only briefly to meet Tayton's eyes and turned back to the task at hand, grabbing Sindri by the upper arms and dragging him back a safe distance from the fire.

"'Course you know her, genius." Darwyn swayed a little where he sat. "She's Noll. Lord's goddess."

"No." Jurij slapped at Darwyn's shoulder lamely. "No goddess."

Darwyn and Jurij exchanged a glance, and they both grinned. "*Farmer goddess.*" They snickered. I couldn't guess if they knew what they were saying or not.

Tayton shook his head and brought his mug to his lips. "No. I know that. I know her 'fore that." He stared inside the mug with one eye open and one eye shut, tossing it onto the ground when he found nothing left in there.

I dropped Sindri and exhaled, wiping my brow with my arm. The fire was hot, which made dragging his heft all the more exhausting. I'd managed to get him rolled onto his back, but a terrible thought squeezed at my throat, an image of my father after one of his visits to Vena's, coughing and choking in his sleep.

"The elf queen!" Darwyn and Jurij shouted my *farmer* title, laughing as the sound echoed into the evening sky. They picked up forgotten mugs and toasted them into the air. "To our queen!" They clinked them together and choked down the contents, stopping to giggle between breaths.

Holding Sindri on his side, I grabbed the picnic basket full of rolls I'd brought out for the half-finished feast. I slid it against his back for support. He kept on snoring.

Tayton leaned over to grab his fallen mug, rolling it farther out of reach with his fingertips. At last he grabbed it and lifted it into the air for the "toast," too late, completely forgetting it was empty as he tried to slurp it again. He seemed puzzled as he tore the mug from his lips. "What's the elf queen?"

Darwyn and Jurij found the question hilarious, just like everything else that evening. I stood with a sigh, my hands on my hips. "All right, enough. I guess you can all sleep here tonight." *As long as I don't have to drag all four of them inside by their arms.* I looked at the cottage, calculating how tired I'd get dragging just Sindri over there. It wasn't too cold out. Maybe I could just toss some blankets over the lot of them and put out the fire so none of the idiots rolled into it.

"That's it!" Tayton dropped the mug back onto the ground. This time it rolled until it knocked against Sindri's fingers, but he barely stirred, murmuring something about being tired before drifting back into snoring. "You're the crone!"

Darwyn and Jurij's laughter was not something that should have surprised me, but it made my cheeks burn nonetheless.

"The little one," Tayton added, pointing at me. "The pretty one."

I tore my eyes from him and felt my cheeks grow even hotter. This bumbling drunk's compliment made me about as happy as any of his insults, and I could do without the leering that accompanied it.

I focused instead on those big, puffy lips, reminiscent of a mask I once saw. "Fish Face!"

Cue Jurij and Darwyn, who'd probably never run out of laughter. Tayton cocked his head and studied me, the words slow to reach him. "Fish?"

I pointed to my own face. "Your mask. The day of Elfriede and Jurij's..." My eyes darted to Jurij, but his head was lilting back and forth, not registering what I'd been about to say. "The day Ingrith died."

Tayton laughed, not an entirely appropriate reaction to the death of an old woman, even if he, like the rest of the village, couldn't have cared less about her. He waved his finger at me. "You were so nasty. So nasty." He started slinking backward, losing balance. "She was worse, but you called me unloved. Pointed me to the commune."

I crossed my arms. "You called *me* unloved."

His back slammed against the ground so suddenly I thought I felt the ground shake. I took a step closer to make sure he hadn't hit his head, but he was resting, eyes closed, a smooth rise and fall to his chest. His eyelids fluttered, his puckered lips parted, murmuring, "Unloved." The firelight glistened on a tear that streaked down his cheek.

I swallowed and looked away. Darwyn leaned against Jurij, snoring louder than his brother still curled at my feet. Jurij's eyes were open but glazed. The kind of glazed Father got after too many drinks. I could almost see the fire dancing in his eyes like it once did, could almost see the ghost of who he used to be in the way he stared. I wasn't so sure happy drinking was anything more than painful drinking under the mask of laughter. I wasn't so sure I could stand to watch Jurij wither away like Father had, not when he had so much to live for.

I turned the cuff of one of my sleeves and rolled it up to my forearm. *Okay. I don't need to get Elfriede and Jurij back together. It's probably best for both of them this way.*

I nodded to myself, watching Jurij's eyes flitter. *Screw love.*

These are my friends. Friends who need me—and each other. Friends who need to learn a thing or two about their own self-worth.

I picked up the bucket of water I'd kept beside the fire, then watched the flames burn for just a little while longer, relishing its choking cries as it flickered away to its death. The reflection of the flames vanished from Jurij's dark irises before he closed his eyes and fell asleep.

CHAPTER NINE

Poking and shouting didn't work. I tried to think of how we used to get Father up after Mother supposedly "died," but Elfriede and I just let him be most of the day. After all, what was he expected to do after his goddess was gone? To tell the truth, Elfriede and I kept thinking we'd wake up one day and he'd be gone, too, reduced to just an empty pile of clothes. Jostling him seemed like tempting fate.

Standing over the four sleeping forms, I weighed my options. Jurij was the only one I really had any business waking, even if the other three did fall asleep right outside my cabin. I dragged my bucket from the well, its contents sloshing over the rim.

"Holy goddess!" Jurij sat up so quickly, he nearly toppled over. His hand ran over his face, wiping off the water droplets.

I dropped the bucket on the ground beside him, letting it clang loudly, but it only stirred the slightest of groans from Darwyn. "I'd say you were late for the quarry. Or the bakery. And you are. But I thought today we might do something different anyway."

Jurij guided his palm through his short dark hair, shaking the water out and staring up at me. "We?"

"Yes, *we*. Or did you and your inebriated friends plan to spend the rest of your days drinking?"

Jurij shook his head and stared. "I don't remember you being this bossy."

As if on cue, Darwyn chuckled softly, but he gave no other sign of consciousness.

I crouched beside Jurij. "I was *always* this bossy." I was done making decisions for others, but I could still give them a push in the right direction. I nudged Jurij with my shoulder. "*You*, on the other hand, never used to put up such a fight."

Jurij cradled his forehead, shielding his eyes from the sunlight. "Noll, it's too early for this."

I stood, grabbing the bucket handle. "It's almost lunch time." I glanced between Darwyn, Sindri, and Tayton, choosing my next victim for after a quick trip to the well.

Jurij groaned. "Can you speak a little quieter?"

"You totally messed up my dinner." I glared at him until he opened his eyes. "You owe me." He grabbed my extended hand, and I strained to help him stand. "And you're going to make it up to me today." I shoved the bucket handle into his unsuspecting hand.

～

IT WAS warm enough that the four soaking boys—*men*—behind me were practically dried from the air just half an hour later, but you'd think that they were permanently soaked through to the bone from the way they still carried on about it.

"So let me get this straight." I didn't have to look behind me to recognize the sniveling voice of Tayton. "You four used to hang out in the livestock fields. Pretending sheep were monsters. And hitting them with sticks."

"We didn't actually hit them with sticks," I corrected. "That'd be cruel."

"No," snorted Darwyn. "We'd just give the poor things heart attacks by chasing them. Screaming and swinging until they started running."

"And then a few moments later, the farmers down the hill would start screaming and swinging their fists at us until *we* started running," added Sindri.

"Sounds fun." Tayton sounded entirely unconvinced.

"It wasn't just us four." Jurij sounded like he hoped he was making a rational argument to defend us. "Noll led a bunch of boys around the village back then."

Tayton scoffed. "Glad I was too old by then to be under her spell. Like I'd need to be bossed around by *two* women in my lifetime."

I twirled around and clapped my hands together. "We didn't just scare sheep. There's a pond south of the village."

Tayton raised an eyebrow. "You mean the livestock's watering hole."

I chewed my lip, biting back irritation. "Yes. Some of the boys would swim on a warm day. Like today."

"And you're suggesting we do that today?" Tayton pinched his damp jerkin with two fingers and pulled it away from his chest. "Because I'm not already soaked through."

I shrugged and turned back around, cutting through the grass east of the village and walking southward. "You can just sit beside the pond whining if that's more appealing."

"Considering our meat drinks out of that water, it probably is."

I ignored that comment. We'd reached the eastern path, and to my left I could just make out my cottage—my *family's* cottage—at the edge of the woods. Jurij brushed past me without pausing, leading the way southward. He didn't even glance at his father's home, let alone the one he'd shared with his former wife.

"Here, girl!" When Jurij turned his head, it was only to beckon Bow from the back of the group, where she'd stopped to sniff the familiar path between her two previous homes.

Bow barked and obeyed immediately, trotting up beside her master and sticking her nose under his hand.

Darwyn laughed. "Looks like *someone's* still under a curse."

"She's a girl," said Jurij, without a hint of teasing in his voice.

"Thus the 'here, *girl*,'" added Sindri.

Jurij paused, confusing Bow, who stopped a few yards ahead of him, whipping her head back to figure out why he'd stopped. "Why weren't animals affected?" asked Jurij. "Why only us?"

Jurij directed the question not at the group, but at me. I swallowed and kept walking.

"Why is it over now? Why anything, Jurij?" Darwyn clapped

317

him on the shoulder. I quickened my steps, eager to put a few more yards between us.

"… probably knows." It was muted, but there was no mistaking Jurij trying to whisper something behind me.

We traveled the rest of the way in silence. When we reached the top of the final hill, I peered down at the sheep grazing amongst the cows, the lilies gone from this field, probably eradicated by endless chewing. Bow didn't hesitate; she barked and charged down the hill.

"Bow! Stop!" Jurij ran past, a look of panic scrunching up his face.

Darwyn and Sindri followed, their faces contorted in laughter.

"Was this part of the game, back when you were smacking sheep with sticks?" Tayton appeared beside me, his hands tucked in his pockets. I nodded, looking up to take in the almost-smile he was fighting to keep from me.

The golden streak plowed toward the herd with three figures jogging after her, Jurij's arms flailing. "Sometimes. I'd forgotten she did that. We didn't always take her along."

Tayton seemed content to watch rather than participate. He nodded as Bow went one way, then zigzagged another, herding sheep and cows to block the men from reaching her. "Until yesterday, the dog was with Jurij's…" He paused, leaving the rest of the sentence unsaid.

"His wife. *Former* wife. My sister."

"I figured." Tayton scratched his chin. "He was complaining about missing her at the quarry the other day. I didn't ask, but I figured there was only one reason why he couldn't get her back."

Jurij managed to dodge a hopping sheep a few feet behind Bow. He held out his hands and took a small step forward. Bow stopped and sat upright, her tongue lolling.

"His parents got the dog back from my sister." I couldn't help but smile as Jurij lunged forward and Bow went flying in the opposite direction. Darwyn and Sindri caught up just in time to keep him from falling. "Since he was too scared to ask for her back himself."

I could feel Tayton's eyes boring into me. "He's not equipped to handle this, Noll. None of us are." He sighed. "I don't know how to explain it, but moving on, figuring out how to keep going forward, it's not simple. I don't know what I want for dinner. I don't know how to decide on what clothes to wear or what shoes to put on in the morning. I don't know when I should buy things or when I'm supposed to go to bed. I've forgotten how to choose."

"Tayton, I'm sorry you guys—"

"I know you are, Noll." He gestured at the sheep, the dog, and the three men running wildly after them. "I know this little trip to the sheep must be your way of distracting us. It's different for you, isn't it?"

I studied Tayton quizzically. "I know, since I'm a woman, that I never really felt what you all felt."

Tayton shook his head. "No, I mean... you're different from the other women." His eyes widened, and I followed his gaze to see Jurij had flung himself around Bow's torso and was rolling with her in the grass. He jumped up, unscathed, rubbing Bow's belly hard. I was so lost in the moment, so full of joy at seeing Jurij smile so freely, that it startled me when Tayton began speaking again. "Maybe it doesn't bother you as much. You don't have to see your former husband. And you never loved him."

"He wasn't my husband," I snapped. I lifted my skirt, some age-old instruction not to get my hem too dirty drilled into my mind, and started walking toward the flock. I should have said more—I *wanted* to say more—but I wasn't in the mood to discuss the details of my heart with Fish Face, whom I hardly even knew.

After half a minute, Tayton jogged down the hill beside me. "I'm sorry if I—"

"Never mind." I swallowed and tried to smile. "Let's just enjoy today, okay?" I let go of my skirt and ran, stumbling down the rest of the hill, frightening the nearest sheep who'd only just recently come to a rest.

Sindri's and Darwyn's brows sparkled with sweat in the brightness of the sun, and Darwyn was bent forward, clutching his thighs for support. "This... was a lot easier... as a kid," he sputtered between breaths.

Sindri patted Darwyn's back. "Life was much easier, little brother." He looked up, cupped his hands around his lips, and shouted, "Woo!" for no reason whatsoever.

The nearest sheep was probably four house lengths away by

now, but it likely felt much too close to this noisy band of too-old warriors. It bleated in protest and skipped a few steps farther. Everyone's eyes met, one after the other, and we all laughed. My eyes held Jurij's for a beat longer, until I had to look away. I collapsed onto the ground beside him, rubbing Bow's belly as she rolled over.

I caught Jurij's eyes again for just a moment. Long enough to remember the feeling I used to get when I imagined the eyes behind his mask, or when I first saw the flames that danced there.

"Noll, do you remember—" His head turned, his attention drawn behind me. Bow flipped over, her head cocked. A dog's bark slipped into the silence between us.

"Uh-oh." Darwyn shielded his face from the sun with his palm. "Tell me that's not some farmer's dog, come to chase us away from his sheep."

Bow jumped to her feet and barked back.

Sindri smirked. "What would a journey to the livestock fields be without being told to go away?"

"I was just hoping we could spend more than a minute here before it came to that," Darwyn replied.

Tayton craned his neck forward, as if the additional inch it gave him would make the barking dog coming over the top of the hill easier to see. "That's no sheepdog, it's—"

Bow barked and bolted, sending the sheep scattering once more. She whipped past one bleating sheep without so much as halting to round the bend, ruffling the sheep's wool with her tail.

Tayton shrugged. "I was gonna say it was a gold dog, like Bow, but I guess she figured that much out for herself."

Jurij stiffened on the grass beside me, his arm bending slightly to lower himself further down among the blades. I crawled up to get a better look at the commotion.

"The dog's with someone," said Tayton, his hands around his eyes to get a better look. "Two people."

Maybe it's Mother and Father. Or at least, if it's her, she's with Mother or Father. Might be a bit less awkward.

Sindri laughed so loud, I jumped. "It's Jaron!" He slapped Darwyn on the back, and they both followed after Bow. Tayton lifted a foot and then paused, looking at me and Jurij, who was now completely flat against the ground. "Did I miss something?"

I felt my cheeks crack as I forced a smile. "No. It's nothing. Jaron. I haven't seen him in a while. It'll be good to say hello. I just didn't know he'd gotten a dog."

"Ha, that man!" Tayton's attention was drawn back to the hill. "A different lady on his arm every time I see him!" He jogged after Sindri and Darwyn.

My mouth dried, and a surge of panic hit my stomach. *Mother?*

"It's Elfriede," spoke the grass at my feet, Jurij's head not so much as lifting up to confirm for certain.

CHAPTER TEN

"**N**ow, the black ones, their wool is harder to dye, so it doesn't go for as much." Jaron pointed at one of the black sheep with a fried leg of lamb, probably not realizing the irony. Elfriede had cooked all of the food Jaron pulled out of Father's carved picnic basket, I was sure of it. Jaron took a bite and gave himself half a minute to chew. "But the black ones have their uses."

"I can see that." Sindri laughed, staring at the voracious way Jaron attacked the leg of lamb. For a little while, it felt good to see him eating. He never ate much in the commune. True, I hadn't seen his face in those days, but he was a friend of sorts. And I could tell he was skinny—too skinny. He'd filled out rather nicely since, for an older man.

I blushed, my gaze accidentally catching Elfriede's as I looked away. *I can't exactly fault her for dating a man almost twenty years older.* I gripped a handful of grass, ripping it free of the dirt with such force, the roots popped out. The lord wasn't *my* man. But he was a thousand years old, thanks to me.

Darwyn extended his chin toward the towering black castle some distance behind me. I still always made a point of sitting with my back toward the east. Old habits. "He'll take black wool, won't he?" Darwyn posed the question to Jurij specifically.

Jurij shrugged, his expression the same stony look he had the moment Jaron and Elfriede joined us. He rubbed his hand over Arrow's head lazily. "Out of the tailoring business," he muttered under his breath.

Like he'd have forgotten the answer to that question just because he hadn't helped his mother and father for a few weeks. I let the blades of grass tumble from my fingers.

Jaron put down the remains of his lamb leg, scouring the picnic basket. "You're sure you're not hungry?" he asked. "We may not have enough for seven, but Friede packed plenty of rolls. She made them herself, and they're some of the best I've ever—"

"You work with livestock now?" I asked. The grass left a greenish stain on my palm that I rubbed with my fingers. "Did you do that before? Uh, that is..." I stopped, suddenly aware of Elfriede's pale eyes on my face.

Jaron didn't seem to mind. He laughed as he tossed a roll at Sindri, who caught it and started eating as if he wasn't sitting in a circle fraught with unspoken tension.

"I can barely remember what I did, Noll." Jaron shrugged. "Seriously. Maybe if I asked someone who knew me then. Life in the commune is pretty much all a useless blur in my mind. For the most part. There are a few things I remember, but..." He tossed another roll, this one to Darwyn, who fumbled but caught it before it fell on the ground. Too bad for Arrow, who seemed to be watching with interest.

"What about your parents?" Darwyn asked, too curious to start eating.

"Gone. Probably." Jaron passed a roll to Tayton and offered one to me. "Noll?"

I shook my head. "No, thank you."

Elfriede stopped glaring at me and dug into the basket, unwrapping a wedge of cheese she didn't offer to share with anyone. Jaron bit into the roll, pointedly forgetting Jurij.

Sindri spoke with his mouth still half full of bread. "What do you mean *probably*?"

Jaron cocked his head, as if Sindri was the one making the strange statement. "They were farmers, I think. I forget which kind. I didn't get any social calls from them when I wound up in the commune. I kind of forgot what they looked like after all that bleakness."

Tayton chewed his roll slowly. "But surely they would remember you? If your father didn't care, then your mother?"

I flinched with guilt at the idea that a man could be so enamored with his goddess he barely cared about his own children. *It's not always true. Remember Master Tailor. Your own father. Sort of.*

Jaron raised a hand to stop him. "I really couldn't tell you." He popped the rest of the roll into his mouth and waited to finish chewing. "Maybe she did visit me early on. Maybe she commanded my father to do so, too. I wouldn't have been able to focus on anyone in the commune, especially not with *her* living so close."

Without being asked, Elfriede uncorked the bottle she'd carried along with the basket and filled Jaron's wooden cup with ale. There were no cups for the rest of us. They'd clearly planned a picnic for two.

"Thank you, dear," said Jaron as he took the mug from her. The "dear" sent a shiver down my spine, and Elfriede seemed to notice. She smiled at me—actually *smiled*—perversely as she placed the bottle back on the grass beside her. *Bet you didn't know that Mother used to love that same man beside you, did you?* I smiled back at her. I felt dirty doing it. But still. Of all the men she could have used to taunt Jurij and show she was moving on, why Jaron? Why a man so much older, someone who spent years pining for Jurij's aunt? Unless that was exactly why. Someone who'd moved on from Jurij's family, just as she would. Someone older because she used to be embarrassed her man was a little younger.

I grabbed another handful of grass. Not *her* man any longer.

Jaron nudged Tayton with his elbow before taking a sip from his mug. "So why is it the one time I see you young men at the tavern, you get so drunk you can hardly stand straight?" He leaned his head back and swallowed the rest of his mug's contents. "You scared all the young ladies away. Not a great impression, if you're looking for companions."

Elfriede's eyes widened, and her head whipped immediately toward Jurij, but Jurij didn't so much as flinch. He continued his slow, methodical stroking of Arrow's head, his focus on the grass in front of him.

Tayton stuffed the rest of his roll into his mouth. "Who faid we were wooking for wommm?"

"No one *said* anything." Jaron extended his mug out to Elfriede, who uncorked the bottle and poured more without a word. Jaron had had little experience serving a goddess himself, so he might not have thought anything of it, but it still felt strange to see a woman serve a man. The liquid sloshed as Elfriede's eyes darted back to Jurij every few seconds. Jaron pulled the mug back to his chest, not seeming to notice that Elfriede was still pouring. "Thank you, dear." He turned back to Tayton. "But a man knows. You're all young, hardly with your goddesses before—well, *before*." He took a sip as Elfriede hastily corked the bottle, her eyes darting to the wasted liquid on the ground. Knowing her, she was probably considering ripping off her apron and sponging the spill, even though it was on the dirt and grass. "Love is so different without being forced into it, lads. It's fun."

"I wouldn't have guessed that, from your behavior." Darwyn's words were coated in sarcasm, and he and Sindri both burst into muffled giggles as they probably imagined Jaron seen each night in town with some different woman on his arm. I wondered if this was Elfriede's first chance to be so honored, and if so, what were the chances of the two of them deciding on a picnic the same day I decided to take the guys out for a day of relaxing in the fields.

Jaron was undeterred. If anything, he seemed flattered as he took a sip from his mug. "Women are beautiful, lads, kind and lovely, if you let them be. If you can just put everything else behind you—"

"I think we've had enough of women." It was the first thing Jurij had said in ages, and everyone in the circle stopped to stare at him. "At least *I* have."

Jaron set his mug down on the ground beside the basket. "And that explains why the first place you ran to after the lord's decree was into the arms of his own lovely goddess." He raised his eyebrows at me.

I swallowed and focused on the grass in my hand, squeezing the blades so hard they bled wet green juice into my palm.

"I didn't *run into* Noll's arms."

"Really? Could have fooled me, and half the village while you were at it." Jaron's hands were intertwined, his weight against his elbow as he leaned a little too casually against the grass. "I'm surprised the black carriage doesn't ride up to the door of that shack the two of you share and give you another puffed eye to go with the first one."

"Jaron!" I dropped the blades of grass, and some of them stuck to the wetness on my hand. I'd forgotten Jaron, a shade of the man sitting before me, had been there to witness that debacle.

Darwyn gasped. "A bit harsh, my good man. Jurij is just as much a victim as any of us."

Jaron stared at the ground. "If you count breaking not one but two sisters' hearts over the course of his young life, then fine."

It wasn't like that, I wanted to say. If Jaron thought my time at the commune was because of Jurij, he was mistaken. I looked between him and Elfriede for any sign of shame at what he'd just said, but I found none. Her eyes were on the ground, as if pretending we weren't there would somehow make it a reality.

Jurij stood up, walking past me with both Bow and Arrow trailing after him. Jurij's lips trembled into a semblance of a smile. He rubbed behind Arrow's ears. "Stay, boy. Just your mama and me are going."

"Take him, too."

Elfriede hadn't said a word since she came down the hill. It had been so long since I'd heard that delicate voice, and it'd been even longer since I heard it approaching anything near composed and refined.

It was enough to finally get Jurij to look at her.

She didn't return the favor. "Take the dog," she said, her nose scrunched up and her gaze locked on Jurij's knees. "He's too much work. And he was just something from *you* anyway."

Jurij scoffed. Then he did something really strange. He bowed toward Elfriede. "Goddess forbid you have *too much work* to do by yourself, Elfriede. Fine. *Thank you.* He was the last thing I regretted leaving behind." He turned on his heel and pushed past Tayton and Jaron, weaving through sheep, with Bow at his heels.

"Here, boy!" he called, turning back just once to wave Arrow toward him.

Jumping to my feet, my cheeks burning with anger, I opened my mouth to say something, then snapped it shut. Elfriede's lips trembled, and a glossy shine enveloped her eyes.

CHAPTER ELEVEN

I could hardly make out his silhouette in the darkness beside
me. The fire long extinguished, the two of us settling in earlier
and earlier each night. "To sleep," I'd said. "Exhausted," he'd told
me. Since encountering Jaron and Elfriede at the livestock fields,
Jurij had done nothing but work and sleep, eat and think.

I couldn't see him clearly in the pile of hay and blankets we'd
used to fashion a mattress on the floor, but I could hear his
breathing, the wavering inhale and exhale just barely audible
beneath the dogs' snoring.

I couldn't sleep. I never could sleep that early. If I'd been
alone, I'd have stayed up later, carving another animal. If I'd been
at my former home, Mother would have found something for me
to do. The only time I could remember closing my eyes and
wishing for sleep to come this early was during that silent time in
the castle. The time when I had no one and nothing to keep me
company. Nothing but thoughts that hurt and festered, and no
promise that the next day would be any better.

*If I had known then what I know now, would those days have been
different?*

*If I had apologized for dooming him to that fate from the start, would
he have ever been cold and cruel? He was kind during our first meeting.*

The memory of him tending to my hand in the darkness

brought a raging heat to my face. I wasn't angry at him—I had no cause to be angry at him then.

What if I'd tended to that kindness and learned to love him before my seventeenth birthday?

What if I'd been able to push Jurij out of my heart back then? At least Jurij and Elfriede would have been happier. Ailill would have been happier—if he'd never gotten to know that stubborn side of me. I would have been...

"What shall we do for dinner this evening?" Ailill's knight would have snagged my rook when I wasn't paying attention. I'd have been focused instead on those pale brown eyes.

"Mother invited us to dine with her and Father. Friede wants to ask my opinion about her gown for her wedding."

"A lovely idea! We shall invite them here. It is far roomier." Ailill would have signaled to a specter at that and relayed his instructions. He would have grinned as his attention turned back toward me and I moved my queen diagonally across the board. "Perhaps you should put on the gown you wore for our wedding for the occasion."

"It's just a dinner, not the wedding. Besides, it's not our wedding day. We already had that with the Returning." I would have been blushing then—I could feel the heat in my cheeks even now. Ailill would have caught my queen with a pawn. I wouldn't be able to believe how distracted I was, how I couldn't have seen the danger I'd just put the poor piece in. "Thank you again, for saving my mother..." I would have to say something sobering, otherwise I would never have been able to tear my eyes from him. "I still wonder, at that miracle."

"You need not thank me." Ailill would have leaned over the board, his elbows knocking over the pieces, neither of us caring. "I would do anything for you." His face would have been mere inches from mine, his breath like a surge of fire across my cheek. "Thank you, for loving me. That is the true wonder..."

This is ridiculous. My fantasies couldn't capture Ailill properly. He was cold, not warm. He was stubborn, not agreeable. The whole thing rang false. My dreams could never capture happiness—whatever that was like.

Of course, if I'd been happy, I'd have had no reason to leave, voices calling me or not. I'd have had no reason to cause Ailill to break the curse. But then I'd also have had no reason to create the curse to begin with, and Ailill wouldn't have loved me, and Jurij wouldn't have loved Elfriede, and Elfriede wouldn't have loved Jurij.

It was all so confusing. I couldn't lay there a moment longer, lost in my thoughts.

I flung back the blankets and swung my legs over the side of the bed, my toes scuffing the rough wood floor. In the dark, I could just make out Arrow's head lifting. "Shh," I whispered, wrapping my cloak around my shoulders. It was still summer, but the season was waning and the nights had grown colder. I slid on my boots and tiptoed to the door. Arrow clopped toward the moonlight, his toenails scuffing the floor with each step.

I patted his head. "Stay." He nudged his nose past my hand, determined to fit his entire body under my arm and out the door. He never did respond to me that well. I let him go and followed. As I shut the door behind me, I spared one last glance at the pile of hay. Dog and master were blissfully breathing, lost in the respite of their dreams.

"Arrow!" I shout-whispered. "Here! Don't go too far!"

Arrow clearly hadn't insisted on coming out to do his business. Or if he had, he'd forgotten the task entirely and taken to frolicking in the fields of flowers like it was the perfectly natural thing to do when the rest of the village was sleeping. "Arrow!" But he took off even farther.

I'd planned to get a taste of fresh air. Maybe take a moment away from the man I'd once loved—perhaps still loved—sleeping there in the shack beside me. To remind myself that I was finally free to walk away from my problems, to push aside the anger in my head. Regardless, it was clear I was following Arrow's plan now.

"Arrow! Come!" My voice grew louder farther from the cottage, where I wasn't concerned about waking Jurij and having him interrupt my escape. "Arrow!" But he wasn't listening. He ran straight through the fields as if chasing something only he could see.

The moonlight was just bright enough that I could make my way after him. He was heading home—to Mother and Father's home, to Elfriede. If I could just grab him before he whined too loud outside their door, I could go back without them ever being any wiser.

But damn, that dog was fast.

I gave up on calling after him and headed for the eastern path, not because I cared about getting my dress and cloak stained with the dew forming on the grass, but because I thought I had a better shot of running fast on the dirt path. It worked, but there was still no hope for catching up to him before he got there. By the time I came over the last hill, he was already there panting outside my parents' door. The slightly *cracked* door.

I froze. Elfriede seemed to be smiling as she rubbed her hands over his head. I wondered if I should turn back, leave it to her to give Arrow back or to keep him, pretend I never knew he'd run off. But Arrow gave me away, and Elfriede saw me.

I swallowed and pulled the cloak tighter at my neck. "He ran off," I said, taking a few careful steps closer.

Elfriede's lips soured, and she wiped her cheeks with the palm of one hand, the other still digging in behind Arrow's ear, which made him melt in joy beside her. She looked back over her shoulder—a fire was still going, albeit a dying one—and shut the door behind her. "Take him." She glared down at Arrow, as if he were the one she was talking to.

I stepped closer, running a hand atop Arrow's head. He looked back up at his former mistress, his tail wagging like he had no sense that he wasn't wanted. But I didn't feel that from her, either. "You can keep him if you want."

Elfriede sniffled. "No."

"He's *your* dog." I patted Arrow's head. "He's always been your dog. It doesn't matter if he was born from Bow."

"It matters to me." Elfriede inhaled a long, tortured sniff, fighting the mucous her pinched tears wanted to let loose from her nose. "Mother and Father are asleep already. I don't want him waking them up. Go."

"Sure." I turned, laying pressure on Arrow's neck to guide him away, but he wouldn't budge. I pinched my lips together as Elfriede stared at Arrow. Her eyes sparkled too fiercely in the moonlight. "Why were you with Jaron?" I'd meant to think it, but I was asking it, even though I had an idea of what kind of answer was in store for me.

Elfriede's eyebrows arched slightly, and she used the back of

331

her hand to wipe furiously at each eye. "I don't see how that's any of your business."

I nodded. "Maybe not. But he's not exactly known for his faithfulness these days."

Elfriede glowered at me. "Maybe I don't expect faithfulness from men anymore. Aren't you the one insisting women need to start treating men differently?"

"Where did you hear that?" Arrow slid down, throwing his front legs over my feet, as if deciding he and I were going to be standing there indefinitely. "Before today, you hadn't said a word to me in weeks!"

Elfriede took another ragged breath, too proud and dainty to blow her nose into her sleeve in front of me. "I don't need to speak to you. Everyone knows you're going around with all the young men these days, giving them ideas about how they're finally free from women."

"What are you talking about?"

Elfriede jutted her chin out, either to appear standoffish or to keep the snot from flowing. "I *saw* you with four men."

I flung my hands up in the air. "I wasn't *courting* them!"

Elfriede seemed as oblivious to my words as she was to common sense. "Not only my husband, no. You couldn't just keep it in the family. But Marden's and Roslyn's, too!"

Of course. Her friends. The ones I wouldn't touch with a three-foot stick, although as a child I did swat at them with Elgar, which was basically the same thing. "And you're spending time with Jurij's *aunt's* former man."

She seemed to hear *that*. "It's not the same." She squeezed her arms tightly across her chest. "Alvilda never had the slightest interest in Jaron, and you *know* it."

"Maybe not, but Mother did!"

Elfriede stopped speaking, but her jaw hung open a moment before she snapped it shut. "That's a lie!"

"No, it's not!" I pointed to the door behind her. "Ask her!"

Elfriede threw her arms into the air and sniffed loudly. "Sure, let me wake both Mother *and* Father and ask if Father wasn't the only man Mother ever—"

The door opened behind Elfriede. A cold sweat formed on my forehead, and my cheeks flushed. I hadn't spoken to my parents in so long. It was Father, looking every bit as disheveled and empty as when he was first parted from Mother. "What is going on—Noll? Is something wrong?"

I stared into my father's bloodshot eyes, a haze of fatigue over his face that seemed to have no hope of lifting. I swallowed. I'd barely seen him the past few weeks—no, months now. I'd run from the castle, but I'd also run from everything else. I'd tried to put it all behind me, thinking things would get better in my absence. "No," I said, too late, after a moment of staring. "No, Arrow just ran away, and I came back to get him."

Father grunted and turned his attention to the dog at my feet. A flicker of a smile lit up his face and even made his tired eyes brighter. "Aw, there he is! Missed you, boy!" He crouched and ruffled Arrow playfully behind the ears. Arrow lapped up the affection, rolling over onto his back.

I raised an eyebrow. Elfriede's lips were pinched as she turned to go back in. "If you like him so much, Father, he can stay." She glared at me. "But I better not see you here tomorrow, demanding I let you take him back."

I scoffed. "Wouldn't dream of it. But if I do miss him, I'll just send *one of my men* along to pick him up."

Elfriede went inside without another word.

Father murmured in an infantile voice from my feet. "Good boy. Good boy, that's a sweet little boy!" He finally seemed to notice I was still standing there and looked up, his eyes hopeful. "So the dog is staying?"

"If that's what Elfriede wants," I said. "I don't really have a say in anything anymore."

Father patted Arrow absentmindedly, looking back into the open cottage door behind him. "I have a feeling nobody does, Noll. Not anymore."

I searched for the moon, wincing as I realized just what it hovered over in the eastern sky. "If we ever did." Was he watching now, the lord who was "always watching"? I tore my gaze from the silhouette of the castle in the night and nodded at Father. "Good night, Father."

He didn't look up from Arrow, but his patting of the dog's stomach slowed. "Good night, Noll."

Arrow flipped over and turned toward a sound in the woods beside us that only he could hear.

But then I heard it, too. The turning of the wheels enveloped me with the feelings of nostalgia and dread I'd experienced when I'd heard them every day for months after I refused to visit the lord. My eyes fixed on the path to the woods, my body aflutter with anticipation and revulsion, my mind spinning and as conflicted as ever.

The black carriage emerged from the edge of the woods, the moonlight glistening off its roof. My heart beat so fast, I could barely make out the pounding of the horses' hooves. Not quickly, no, never quickly with him. He had nowhere to be in such a hurry. But then again, I couldn't be sure. Not with the way the moment slowed down impossibly so, cutting me off from every-thing else, from all my other senses.

White seemed to shine as bright as the sun in the dark carriage window. I thought of his paleness, how his brown hair framed his face, so lacking in color. But my eyes caught his—just for a moment, but a moment that lasted—and they were black. Of course. One of the specters. An Ailill. Him but not him at all.

The specter turned his head and looked forward. I felt dismissed, ignored. Nothing to a ghost of a man. Time resumed its normal pace, and the carriage fled west down the dirt road, fading into dust and darkness.

"What are they up to so late?" I'd almost forgotten Father was still behind me.

I clutched my forearm. "I don't know." I shivered from the cool breeze. "But it's none of my business."

And it wouldn't be ever again.

CHAPTER TWELVE

"You thought we were *what?*" Darwyn rolled a wooden wolf in his palm, dropping a few crumbs from the bread he was chewing atop the wolf's nose.

I yanked the wolf from his hand so he could devote himself to properly eating and flicked it to send the crumbs onto the blanket. Annoyed with the way the yellow crumbs stood out amongst my forest of animals, I slapped the wolf down next to a doe and picked the crumbs up between my fingers. "Courting women. At the tavern."

Darwyn laughed and stuffed another bite of the roll into his mouth, oblivious to the spray of crumbs flying from his open jaw. "Just how many women do you think visit the tavern?" The question was partially muffled by the bread, but his tone made it all rather clear.

"I don't know. Dozens?"

Darwyn swallowed and shook his head. "Most women are pretty angry about the whole former-husbands-leaving-them thing."

I dropped the crumbs to the side of the blanket, resisting the urge to brush the rest of them from where they'd settled across Darwyn's tunic and trousers. "Then what *have* you been doing since we met with Jaron?"

Darwyn shrugged as a woman dragging her young son behind her entered the bakery door beside us. "Working. Sleeping. Eating."

"Eating *at the tavern*."

Darwyn raised an eyebrow and popped the last of his roll into his mouth. He chewed a few times before speaking. "You must really be interested in what goes on at this tavern." He swallowed. "I'd love to visit this place you've invented. Sounds like the women fawn all over you there. Might be interesting to see how it feels the other way around." He stared off into the passing crowd contemplatively, but I could see the mischievous glint in his eye.

I hugged my knees to my chest, not bothering to fix the skirt that bunched up as I did. "If you're not courting women, then why hasn't Jurij gone off with you?"

Darwyn studied me. "Probably because I haven't been up to much lately. I mean, I've gone to the tavern a few times."

"I knew it!"

"For drinks." He coughed, and his cheeks darkened slightly. "With friends."

"Have you seen Jaron there?"

"Yeah, sure. I guess *he's* courting women. But there haven't really been that many there to court. If you care about that sort of thing." He genuinely seemed like he didn't. "You think Jurij is avoiding Jaron?"

"Of course he is!"

"Even though he left his goddess—his former wife—of his own free will?"

I buried my nose in my knees. "It's complicated." I knew full well it was possible to feel disgust and affection at the same time.

Darwyn nudged my arm with his elbow. "It's only as complicated as you make it, Noll."

His gaze traveled from one passing villager to the next, a grin lightly touching his lips. He seemed happy. Happier than I'd ever seen him, though I couldn't recall ever seeing his face, even after his Returning. I was otherwise occupied at the time, being trapped in the castle.

The door to the bakery swung open, and Darwyn's mother stuck out her head. "Darwyn, how long does it take you to eat?"

She had flour mixed between her black and gray tresses, and more than one lock of hair had fallen out of her bun. The flour reminded me of Alvilda's sawdust, but I'd never seen so flustered an expression on the woodcarver's face.

"Yeah. I'm coming." He rolled his eyes at me as he stood. And he was certainly taking his time to stand.

"Just as useless as your father," mumbled Darwyn's mother as she turned to go back into the bakery. "I wish you hadn't chased Roslyn away." The rest of her rant went unheard as the door shut behind her.

Darwyn winced at his former wife's name. The bit of happiness I'd seen was gone, replaced with as much seriousness as Jurij usually wore these days. He wove his fingers together and stared at them. "Roslyn was good at baking," he said, answering a question I didn't ask. "Me? Not so much. Even if I was raised by bakers. That's why I get stuck with the delivering most of the time."

"She lived here?" I hadn't known. Maybe Elfriede or someone had said it, but I hadn't paid attention to my friends' love lives after they found their goddesses. Most goddesses wanted their men to move in with them. To help their parents with their professions, or just because it was what they were used to, and men would have no complaints.

Darwyn nodded. "Mother asked her. She'd only had sons, and they were all leaving. Roslyn's parents already had Marden and Sindri to help with the tanning."

Oh, right. Roslyn and Marden. Darwyn and Sindri. Two sisters paired with two brothers.

Darwyn loosed his fingers and ran one hand over his hair. "She liked it, so she said that was fine. She wasn't here long. We'd only been married a short while before... well, *before*."

I studied him, cupping a hand over my eyes to shield them from the bits of sunlight that trickled across the tops of the buildings. "You don't hate her."

Darwyn blinked. "Why would I?"

I blinked back tears from the sun. "She bossed you around? You resented being forced to love her in the first place?"

Darwyn cleared his throat. "Well, sure, maybe. But she wasn't so bad. And it wasn't her fault."

The door to the bakery opened and Darwyn flinched, but it wasn't his mother. Two customers, the mother and son. The child's arms were wrapped around a basket full of bread, but he stared at my carvings as he passed. His mother, oblivious to his slowed pace, put a hand on his back, guiding him in front of her.

"Darwyn! Now!" Mistress Baker's voice made him flinch again, but the door closed and his shoulders loosened.

He grabbed the wolf he'd been playing with and tossed two coppers on the blanket beside me. Holding his purchase out in front of him, he turned the wolf this way and that. "This is good work, Noll. I like it. Reminds me of my favorite mask."

I tucked that too-long bit of hair behind my ear and grabbed the coppers. I could feel my face flushing as I thought about all the fighting I did with the boy in that wolf mask. "Thanks. You didn't have to."

Darwyn gazed over the wolf he rolled between his hands to meet my eyes. "I don't hate Roslyn. I don't even dislike her."

"You're not at all the Darwyn I remember. I'd have thought you'd be, I don't know—"

"More agitated?" He grinned, and I wondered if that was the grin he wore as a child, if this was the boy who was once my friend and annoying rival. He glanced back at his wolf before tucking it into his pocket. "I just don't have feelings for her. Not like that. Staying with her wouldn't be fair, don't you think?"

I chewed my lip. "But how can you be sure you won't fall in love with her again? What if all you needed was to spend more time with her, to learn to love her?" I sounded like the villagers back when they used to say the same things to me. Only now I felt like I knew what they meant.

"I would do anything for you."

Now I was remembering my daydreams as if they were real memories.

Darwyn coughed. "Are you really counseling couplings to get back together now? Or are you wishing they'd stay apart? I'm not entirely clear on that."

"I'm not *counseling* anything. It's not really my business."

"Right. But since you're curious, I'm sure." He laughed. "I'm *very* sure."

Certainty was written all over his face, and I flinched, remembering something similar on Ailill's face the last time I saw him.

Darwyn crouched beside me, balancing on the balls of his feet. "This thing with you and Jurij and your sister, it's not really my business. But I think you were right to get Jurij out in the fields, get his mind off things."

Two little girls squealed with excitement as they pattered up to my blanket, one bouncing up and down, her hand clutching something tightly. "Looks like you've got customers." Darwyn stood and reached for the door as the girls crouched before my display of animals. "Get him to the tavern, Noll. You come too. Keep them both from drowning in ale and sorrows." He saluted me and went inside.

Both?

"You have another squirrel! She has another squirrel!"

One of the girls shoved the squirrel in my face, interrupting my thoughts on what Darwyn might have meant. "Can I have him?"

"Sure. Two coppers." It was the girl from a month or so ago, the one who'd wanted to buy something when her friend did, that same friend now digging through her pocket to hold up a wooden cat.

My new customer grinned sheepishly and held out her other hand, the one she'd clutched into a fist. "Can I pay with this?"

In her hand she held a yellow coin. *Golden.* Like the bangle Elric wore and the rings that held up the veiled curtain.

Metal a color I'd only seen with the lord and his brother.

My blood ran cold, and I swallowed, unable to speak, my heartbeat thundering in my head. I wrapped my fingers around the coin she held out to me and nodded.

CHAPTER THIRTEEN

"You and me." Jurij pointed at me and then himself. "You want to go with me to Elweard's tavern." Buried beneath the exhaustion of a long day at the quarry, the look on his face was pained disbelief.

I rolled the golden coin between my fingers and the table. I didn't make supper, or even start a fire. I was hoping that might be enough to convince him. "Fine. Let's not go, then. There's some bread in the cupboard. It'll have to do for supper."

Jurij patted Bow's head and climbed over her to reach the table. He pulled the chair out and sat down beside me. "No, it's fine. It's just... why?"

"Why what?"

"Why the sudden invitation to the tavern? The tavern you've yet to set foot in since you went through all of that with your father." He took a deep breath, and the skin between his eyebrows furrowed. "Is *she* going to be there?"

"What?" My thoughts were so far from Elfriede, it actually took me a moment to figure out who he was talking about. But there could be no other. Jurij might not have known the pain of the commune, but his watered-down version of those men's torture centered pretty clearly on my sister, the woman who supposedly *used to* have a hold over him. I tapped the coin on the table. "I doubt it."

"But you don't *know*."

"Do you want me to ask her?"

"No!" He eyed me suspiciously. "But you didn't tell her we'd be there at the livestock fields that day, did you? You didn't tell her we'd be at the tavern tonight?"

"Of course not!" The accusations stung, but I knew he was thinking about how I tried to convince him to go home when I found him in the cavern. "Jurij, are you going to live your whole life in hiding? Or are you going to learn to put this awkwardness behind you?" The coin slipped between my index and middle fingers, and the last of the day's sunlight streaming through the window caused the coin to sparkle. "You're not the only one who feels awkward, you know."

Jurij snorted and slapped a palm on the table. "I don't think Sindri or Darwyn or Tayton seem to run into their former wives as much as I run into mine."

"You've seen her *one time* since you left."

"And that was more than enough. She teased me about Arrow and then stole him back right after."

I leaned back in my chair, tapping the coin on the table. "You act like your feelings are her fault."

"Of course they're not. But they're not exactly my fault, either." His gaze wandered across the table, catching sight of the coin I rolled beneath my fingers. "What's that?"

My hand froze, my mind racing over the possibilities. A part of me wanted to keep it secret, as well as what it might mean. But the other part of me was rolling it on the table in plain sight, and I could hardly pretend I didn't know what he was talking about. I slid the coin across the table to him. "I got this as payment today for one of my carvings."

Jurij took the coin between his fingers and held it up to the last rays of sunlight. "It's not copper."

I leaned over and snatched it back from him. "I know that."

"But what is it? It's hard like copper."

I examined the coin again. Whenever I moved it, the fiery glint of the sun sparkled. "Golden copper."

Jurij looked as skeptical as he did when I first invited him to the tavern. "Who gave that to you?"

"A little girl. I don't know whose daughter."

"And you didn't think to ask where she'd gotten it?" Jurij dragged the coin across the table for a closer look.

"I *did* ask," I corrected him. "She said she found it in the village, on the ground. But I might know where it really came from."

"There's a golden copper source, and you're keeping it a secret."

"Not a *source* exactly."

"The cavern?" Jurij picked up the coin, examining its smooth, unadorned surface.

"No."

Jurij froze, and the coin slipped from his fingers and bounced onto the floor, rolling away.

"*Jurij!*" I jumped to my feet, stepping over Bow to stop it just before it disappeared beneath the cupboard.

"You mean it's from *him*, don't you?"

I held up the coin to get a look in the dying light for dents or scratches. But the coin was flawless, except for a speck of dust. "How would a random village girl find a coin from the lord?"

Jurij scoffed. "Why don't you ask him?"

I rubbed the coin against my sleeve, buffing away the dirt and restoring the impeccable surface. "Maybe I don't really want to know," I mumbled quietly.

"You don't want to know anything."

I gripped the coin in my fist. "And what's that supposed to mean?"

Jurij pushed his chair back and pointed east. "There's a man there who, if rumors be true, has lived since before our parents were born. Before *their* parents were born."

I said nothing as I clutched my fist to my chest, my focus on Bow, who'd put her head down, satisfied what I held was nothing she wanted.

"The village exists one way for generation after generation. No one was complaining," he continued. "Well, practically no one." We shared a pointed look. "And then one day, for no discernible reason, it just stops. Everything we know, our entire way of life just... stops."

"And you're upset about that?" I asked. "I thought you were happy to finally have your freedom."

"This isn't about me being happy or unhappy." He stared at me like he was waiting to study my reaction. "This is about you." He pointed to the wall again. "And him. Isn't it?"

I couldn't look at him. I opened my fist and rubbed the coin with my fingers.

"Noll, do you know why the curse broke?"

I didn't answer.

"Do you know how the lord was able to heal your mother?"

I still said nothing.

Jurij sighed, and I heard him push his chair back. "All right. Keep your secrets. Keep your weird golden copper and your weird former husband."

"We never got married."

"Right." He grabbed his cloak from the stand Alvilda and I made together. "You're right. It's a nice night for the tavern."

He slammed the door behind him, waking Bow from her nap. She stood and looked at me, the door, and back again.

I closed my fist over the golden coin until it dug into my palm. *A nice night for the tavern?* "I know, girl," I said to Bow. "I'm going."

But I'm not walking there with him. Let him stew a bit.

I THOUGHT I'd gotten used to the stares. In a village where nobody seemed to care about anyone other than their goddess or their man, it had taken a lot to be noticed. But between the kinds of trouble my friends and I would get into, being so long without a man, and the lord finding the goddess in me, I'd managed it. And then there was the fact that my father, who'd somehow managed to live while his goddess was "dead," had practically moved into the tavern, and on more than one occasion, I'd had to go collect the man before he drank our last copper. I'd walked this path down the village many times before, feeling all the stares.

But I thought those days were behind me. Everyone else had their own problems now. I wasn't just a thorn in their sides, disrupting their blissful couplings with my oddness. We were all odd now. So why did I swear every head turned my way as I passed by?

I stopped in front of Vena's tavern door and took a deep breath. No, I was imagining it. I sold my own carvings now, and no one batted an eye. I bought bread and cheeses. Delivered Alvilda's carvings. I thought I'd finally earned the right to disappear into the crowd. Even if it was past sunset and the crowd had significantly dwindled.

The door opened, and the laughter from inside spilled out into the alleyway. The man who stepped out was grinning from one ear to the next, a dark flush over his cheeks. He barely noticed me as he passed, and for once, I felt validated. I was just imagining the prying eyes. The sound of laughter grew muffled as the door swung shut behind him.

I could do this. I put my hand on the door handle and pulled.

No one looked up as I entered, even with the bells on the door chiming to signal my arrival. I pulled the hood of my cloak back and scanned the tavern for familiar faces in the muted light of the fire. The place was bustling, far more packed than I'd ever seen it when I'd come to get Father. There wasn't a free table in sight, and there were only a couple of small spaces at the counter if you felt like wedging shoulder to shoulder with men on either side. And almost every table was full of men. I recognized one young woman, maybe one of Elfriede's friends, on the lap of a man at the table nearest the fire, and I nearly choked in surprise. No. That couldn't possibly be one of Elfriede's friends. Those girls were always too reserved. They were all supposedly devastated by their husbands' departures. Not exactly the type of woman I expected to sit with her arms around a man's neck, her lips brushing the tips of his ears.

"Oop. Careful now!"

I stepped back just in time to avoid the slosh of ale that escaped one of the mugs Vena held in a single hand. Her other hand held a platter of meat arranged hastily with some wilting parsley leaves for garnish. She put it all down at a table several paces away, her intrusion not even noticed among the men doubled over in laughter. Rubbing her face with the back of her wrist, she smiled. "Haven't seen you here in ages! You looking for your father, dear?"

She passed by me again, slipped into a small opening between two men at the counter, and tapped the countertop. "Two more, honey!"

I could just make out tall Elweard on the other side of the counter over the heads of the men in front of him. "Sure thing!"

"Hey, there, sweetheart!" A man from a nearby table sloshed his mug toward me. "I know who you are!" He raised his mug higher. "To your man. No. To the lord!"

"To the lord!" said the two others at his table. They clinked their mugs together and took large gulps, laughing as they slammed their mugs down.

One of the men winked at me. "Nice of you to drive him mad enough to decide he'd had enough of all this goddess business."

"She can't have been any worse than my wife," scoffed his tablemate. He eyed me over the rim of his mug. "She's a fair sight better to look at, too."

I stared at a grain in the wood on the counter, determined to ignore him. The look in his eyes reminded me painfully of the men from the past who'd set me down the path I'd regretted to begin with.

"All right, all right," said Vena. "You leave Noll here alone."

"Aw, Vena, you're no fun!" said one. He raised his mug. "One more!"

"Not for you! I'm not stupid. I've learned my lesson: You show the coppers you have for the night upfront. You only had enough for three mugs. You want more? You bring more coppers."

The man and his nearest tablemate started snickering. One quietly said something like, "… can mine some more tomorrow," but Vena didn't notice. Was Ailill keeping watch over the quarry workers? Along with the stone for buildings, the workers used to mine copper not just for use for all of our metals, but for coins on occasion, too, which the blacksmith made and the specters collected for… Quarry worker wages? I'd never thought about it before, and it would have never occurred to those men to make coppers for themselves back then. But I just realized I was staring at two quarry workers and the rarely working blacksmith, and it didn't seem so impossible anymore.

Vena leaned her elbows atop the counter and sized me up.

"Don't mind them. They've been doing that for weeks. Toasting the lord for, well, their newfound freedom, I guess you'd call it. But you don't care about that." I think I was starting to. Who was running this village if Ailill allowed the men to spend their days doing nothing? Toasting him indeed.

"Your father hasn't been here since…" Vena looked at the ceiling and took her time thinking, so I answered for her.

"Many months ago."

"Two nights ago," finished Vena at the same time. She turned back to grab the mugs Elweard plopped down behind her. "Don't think he's been here tonight."

She brushed past me, again holding the mugs in the air as she squeezed through the small walkway between me and the parade of men walking back and forth from the counter. *The both of them.* I stepped up behind Vena. "My father still drinks here?"

Vena jumped slightly but tapped my shoulder as she managed to squeeze back past me. "Honey, *everyone* drinks here. Every man anyway." She gazed around her crowded tavern and put her hands on her hips, something approaching pride on her face. I could almost hear the gratitude for the freedom of men on the tip of her tongue, but maybe considering her man didn't use it as an excuse to leave her, she knew better than to be grateful for something that few other women would count as a blessing.

Vena pulled a wrinkled rag off of her shoulder and dashed across the room. I followed, my gaze darting from one smiling man to the next, not recognizing anyone I'd come for. Vena stopped at a table that had just emptied, her rag a flurry of action across the tabletop.

"I'm looking for—" I stepped back to let one of the table's recent occupants pass, the stench of alcohol foul in the air as he let out a belch. "I'm looking for Jurij."

Vena's hands didn't stop moving, one dragging the rag around, the other stacking the mugs and plates together. Her eyes, though, moved up to meet mine, and the firelight sparkled off of them mischievously. "Is it true what they say then? You and the tailor's son living together?"

I gripped my cloak with one hand. "It's not like that."

"Uh-huh." Vena paused to wipe her forehead with her wrist again. "I haven't seen him, but it's hard to keep track with all the business. His father and brother are upstairs, if you want to ask them."

"His *brother*?"

Vena swung her rag over her shoulder and gathered all of the dishes. "Let me know if you want to order anything," she said, passing by with a tune on her lips.

I spotted a staircase at the back corner, a dozen or so men milling about between me and it. Sighing, I made my way through. "Excuse me," I mumbled, but I couldn't tear the men— and women entwined between the men as if carved from their bodies—away from each other for more than a moment. I had to squeeze myself through some uncomfortably tight spaces, and when I made it to the corner, I practically somersaulted forward as I broke free from the crowd. My hand rested on the wall as I caught my breath. Candlelight flickered at the top of the stairs. I'd never been up there, and I wasn't sure what to expect, nor how Vena was expected to serve a second crowd equal in number up top.

Only there wasn't a crowd at the top at all. The noise from below was audible but faded. Lit torches hung from the wall every few feet, but it was still dim. There were rooms, maybe nine or ten of them, with closed doors on either side of the curving hallway. Of course. I'd heard Vena had the idea of making extra rooms out of her and Elweard's living quarters on the second floor. Alvilda had even carved doors for rooms they must have previously left open. "Lodgings," Vena had called it. Some men didn't have a home to go back to if they weren't staying with their wives any longer. The commune men never had a home to begin with. Vena's new "lodgings" wouldn't come close to providing enough space for all of them. It made me wonder where the rest of those men were now hiding. *With new loves? In the fields? In the commune?*

But Master Tailor wasn't one of those men. He had his own home. His former wife had been the one to move out. So why would he need a room?

As I approached the nearest door, I heard the murmur of voices. The reddish glow of fire protruded from beneath the door. I knocked loud enough to be heard over all of the voices. Then I realized this wasn't the room they were coming from. And I heard *groaning*.

I took a few steps back and tried to disappear down the darkened stairs, but the door opened before I could get there. A man emerged, his shirt missing, his dark chest slick with sweat that shined in the dim firelight. He covered his bottom half with a sheet. I tore my face away. "I'm sorry, I was looking—"

"Noll? Is that you?"

I looked back up despite myself. It was Darwyn, running his hand through his hair. Darwyn's half-naked body was covered in sweat. My cheeks burned. *I'm very sure.* I didn't dare peek to see who lay in the room behind him.

"I didn't think you'd actually come!" He reached back awkwardly to close the door with one hand, the other clutching the sheet in front of his lower body. "I'm sorry. I didn't expect you."

I stepped back as he stepped forward, until my boot hit the wall behind me. "No, I wasn't… I didn't mean to bother you."

Darwyn laughed and turned away, beckoning me to follow him down the hallway. He took small, careful steps so as not to send the thin sheet wrapped around his waist falling. "Let me show you where Jaron's been staying."

My foot froze mid-step. "Vena told me the Tailors were up here."

Darwyn nodded. "They're with Jaron. It's better when it's a private party." He pointed to a door around the corner. "But you probably don't want to go knocking on all of the doors around here." I blushed as I caught up to him, the murmur of voices—the muffled *noises*—growing louder.

"I'll be there in a minute." He smirked and pulled his sheet a little higher. "Just need to freshen up a bit."

I stood still, cringing as his shuffling footsteps faded behind me. I wasn't sure I could look him in the face again so soon after that. *Then you better get inside so you don't have to walk in with him. Or with whoever he's got with him.*

I straightened my shoulders, tucked the too-long piece of hair behind my ear, and raised my fist, ready to knock.

The door spilled open, and my fist hung suspended over the chest of a specter.

CHAPTER FOURTEEN

"A ilill?" It felt like someone else was speaking. I didn't realize the name had passed my tongue until the thunder of my heartbeat quieted.

"Need something else, my good man?" Someone from behind the specter spoke. I didn't know who. My senses were dulled, and I couldn't stop myself from staring up into those black, unblinking eyes. Like all the life had been drained out of him.

I cursed under my breath and looked away. *Since when have you called them by that name?* But this one was younger than many of the rest. He looked so like him, I'd nearly forgotten I didn't care anymore. I stepped back to let him pass, watching as his white, shiny shoes scuffed the wooden floor and disappeared into the darkness of the hall.

The ghost of a past life. But how does it work? Does he die, become a shell, and then appear out of thin air as a baby? The thought of a castle of specters silently attending an infant not yet knowing he was fated to join them sent a chill down my back. I thought of Ailill, the *real* Ailill, the young boy I'd known who became the first shade. He'd had no one. No one at all for years and years after I'd left him.

And now, after a thousand years, there was the man who'd been mine at the castle. Ailill but not Ailill. Some muted copy, twisted and unused to company that didn't do everything he wanted.

"Noll? I'll be!"

In the firelight, Jaron, Sindri, Jurij, and a young woman I barely knew were gathered around a table, mugs and half-empty plates scattered across its surface. Each gazed at me expectantly.

Jurij was the only one less curious to see me and more flabbergasted. Like he couldn't believe I had the gall to show my face.

Jaron didn't seem to share the same sentiment. "Did you come to join us? A bit late for dinner, I'm afraid." He pointed to an empty chair beside Jurij. "Have a seat. Next time Vena comes up, we'll order another round."

"I'm not sure Vena will ever have a spare moment." I shuffled to the chair, taking in the room. Beside the fireplace was a small bed in the corner, but nothing else of note. A single window looked out into the night, the pointed roofs of the homes and shops across the way just barely visible. The silhouette of the tall spires of the castle beneath the mountain was but a conspicuous fleck in the background.

Jaron chuckled. "Well, it probably doesn't help that we've been keeping Roslyn so long." He patted the shoulder of the woman beside him gently. "Thanks for wasting your short break with this old man, darling."

The corner of Roslyn's lips twitched, but she settled into an easy smile. "No waste at all." Her dark eyes roved over the table, meeting mine. I flushed, thinking of Darwyn in the room down the hall. "Besides, you have Noll now. You won't have to be alone."

Jaron sniffed and leaned back in his chair. He failed to contain his smirk. "Now don't you go spreading rumors, sweetheart."

"I wouldn't dream of it." Roslyn's smile grew uneasy as she passed behind Sindri to the open door.

Jaron leaned over the table. "You have to excuse her, Noll. There's this rumor that I'm just about the only man in town who welcomes the company of women these days. That I can't be seen without one." He took a sip of his drink, and I watched what impact his words had on his companions. Jurij stared down at the table blankly, but Sindri hardly seemed to be paying attention. His eyes followed Roslyn hungrily.

350

"Oh!" Roslyn jumped as (a fully clothed) Darwyn appeared out of the darkness of the hallway. She clutched her chest as if to keep her heart from beating right out of it.

Darwyn nodded and tried to speak, but his voice caught. I noticed the lump bobbing at his throat. "Roslyn," he said at last.

Tayton stepped up behind Darwyn, giving Roslyn someone else to look at. Her gaze fell to the ground, and she pushed past them both, careful not to brush against them.

Darwyn took a deep breath and smiled at me. "I see you found your way, Your Majesty."

Tayton grimaced and stepped around Darwyn to sit in the open chair beside me. "Is this another one of those things from your childhood I don't get to know about?"

Darwyn nudged Tayton's shoulder playfully with his fist and tugged on the back of his brother's chair. "The elf queen, remember? I told you about that."

Sindri got up from his chair and sat in the one Roslyn had vacated so Darwyn could slip in beside Tayton.

"Oh. Right," muttered Tayton. He did his best to stay grumpy, but I thought I saw his pouted fishy lips almost straighten into a smile.

"Did he leave out the part where he found the whole elf queen thing obnoxious?" I asked.

Tayton shook his head. "Nope. Got that part pretty clear. He probably fancied himself someone who'd eventually usurp you."

I appreciated the conversation, if only because I was still shaking from my encounter with the specter. "A retainer usurp the queen? He had no chance. Not when love proved such an easy distraction for him." I regretted the word *love* as soon as I said it. "Or passion. Whatever you'd call it. At least he's over that."

"Hmm? Over love and passion?" Tayton rubbed his fingers under his chin as if pretending to think hard and then exchanged a sly glance with Darwyn. "I'm not sure. So I doubt he'll ever get a chance to usurp you."

Now I felt like the one being left out of something that seemed to make perfect sense to those around me.

"All right, all right." Jaron clinked his finger against his mug. "Nobody came here to discuss what goes on betwixt the bed sheets, right?" Jaron pointed at me. "Have anything to tell us?"

I looked from one face to the next, surprised to see all but Jurij staring expectantly. "What are we talking about?"

Jaron tapped Jurij's shoulder. "What was it? A golden copper?"

My head whipped instantly to Jurij. "You told them?"

Jurij shrugged. "Was it a secret?"

"No, but…" I reached into the band at my waist in which I'd tucked the golden copper. "I don't see why it should matter."

Jaron reached out his hand, and I hesitated, running my fingers over the golden surface. He seemed undeterred, so I dropped it into his palm. He held it out above him, a little bit of the firelight flickering off of its surface. "Well, I'll be. It *is* yellow."

"Let me see." Sindri snagged the coin from Jaron's loosened fingers and held it out just as he had. His face soured. "What is this?"

Darwyn grabbed it from him and leaned over to show Tayton. Their fingers brushed each other's lightly as they stroked the surface. "It feels like copper." Tayton took it in his fist and shook his hand up and down. "Maybe a little heavier."

He opened his fist, and I snatched it back before the coin kept passing from man to man indefinitely. "Okay. So I have a golden copper. Care to let me know why you all seem so interested? Or why one of the lord's servants came out of this room before I did, for that matter?"

If I hadn't been so flustered, or so determined to convince everyone—and myself—that I wasn't bothered, it would have been the first thing out of my mouth as soon as the specter had left. Instead, I posed the question now, ready to know why they hadn't thought fit to bring it up earlier. *Push me, and I'll push back.*

Sindri's eyes immediately fell downward, and if I'd hoped Jurij was going to start looking at me now, I was mistaken. Darwyn and Tayton seemed puzzled, curious—but it wasn't to me that they turned their attention. It was to Jaron, who leaned back in his chair with a sigh. "What do you think of us, Noll?"

Jaron stared relentlessly, and I had to stop myself from turning away. "What do I think?"

Jaron ran a hand over his face. "Are we the men you knew before? Is any man?"

I studied each of my friends in turn, but none would return my gaze. "What's this about?"

"It's not enough for some of us, just to move on." Jaron scratched the stubble under his chin. I wondered briefly if when he wore his mask in the commune, he'd grown a thick beard beneath. "It's not enough for most of us."

"What do you mean, not enough?"

Jaron opened his mouth, but Jurij snapped to attention, cutting him off. "We want to know why, Noll. Why things changed. Why they were ever the way they were. Don't you?"

I felt the weight of the golden coin in my palm.

"She *does* know something!" Sindri pounded his palms the table. "You told us she did, but I wasn't sure."

"Who's *sure* I know anything?" I glared at Jurij, finding none of the easy demeanor that used to dominate his features. "Jurij, what have you told them?"

He shrugged. "That you might have broken the curse."

"Me?" I swallowed, glancing out of the corner of my eye to see if anyone was reading the guilt flushed all over my face. "But how—"

"You love him, don't you?"

The words were like Elgar slashed across my chest. The real Elgar.

Jurij didn't seem to notice. Or maybe he did and didn't care. "You Returned to the lord of the village, and then everything changed."

"If I Returned to him, why am I here and not with him? Why would my Returning be any different than any other woman's?"

"Maybe he didn't love you back." The harsh tone in Darwyn's voice was enough to stop my assault. He fumbled with his hands on his lap, like he was trying to pretend he wasn't the one who'd spoken.

I threw my hands up in the air. "If he didn't love me, why did he find the goddess in me in the first place?"

"That wasn't love." Tayton put a hand on Darwyn's shoulder. "Maybe once you Returned to him, he broke free from the spell. Maybe we all did."

I dropped the golden copper on the middle of the table, crossing my arms against my chest as the coin wobbled slowly into silence. "I wasn't aware that you'd been conferring with the lord of the village about his opinion on love."

"We don't have to," started Sindri. "We know from *our* experiences."

"Your experiences don't come close to that man's." I tilted my chin at Jaron, surprised at my own defensiveness. "Answer my questions, and I may answer yours." I tapped the coin with my finger. "What did you want from one of the lord's servants?"

The corner of Jaron's lips twisted just slightly. "You know, you may not be asking the right question."

"What do you expect me to do? Walk up to the castle gates, invite myself in, and ask if oh, maybe, the gold copper a child gave me was his indirect way of saying we need to talk?" I slid the golden copper off of the table, tucking it back into the band around my waist. "If he wanted to talk to me, he could come himself."

Jurij scoffed. "You claim the lord won't explain what happened to us, but asking him directly isn't exactly what we had in mind."

Jaron got on his hands and knees, reached beneath the bed, and pulled out a small, carved keepsake box. I recognized it as one Father had made—old and a bit worn, probably not without a previous owner or two—and wondered if Jaron had made a point of avoiding Alvilda's carvings. He returned to his seat, shoving aside his mug to put the box on the table. He opened it. "He'd come himself if he wanted to talk?" He pulled out the single item inside the box, a yellowed piece of paper that crinkled at his touch. It was a drawing of a room much like this one, with a man in the bed and a child in a chair beside him, focusing on something in his hands. There was a single jagged edge to the parchment, as if it'd been torn from bindings. "Think you could make him want to come see you? It might give us the time we need to explore where he keeps more of these."

Jaron nodded, and Darwyn got up from the table. He knocked on the wall and leaned against it, then, seeing my gaze on him, pointed to Jaron.

"Me and the man staying next door do each other favors on

occasion," explained Jaron, and I wondered briefly if it was rented to one of the other men from the commune. "He's downstairs enjoying the raucous company, so I asked some friends to stay in his room, out of sight, until the lord's servant left." Jaron held the paper closer toward me. The boy had gotten up, leaving a shirt and a needle on the chair where he'd sat. He leaned over the form of the sleeping man and shook him awake.

The drawing. Shook the man awake. On the paper.

The man sat up. And somehow, even though he was drawn in plain black ink, I saw it clearly: Master Tailor in the bed, little Luuk beside him. Both moving on paper.

Jaron tapped a finger on the paper. "So what you should have asked is, what did one of the lord's servants want from us?"

The door to the room opened, and in stepped Master Tailor and Luuk.

CHAPTER FIFTEEN

"Where did you get this?" I asked. "*How* did you get this? And why, if the specter wanted it, do you still have it?"

Jaron flipped the paper over, and there was writing on the back:

We have no need for so much bread. Send enough for one. The payment will remain the same. Distribute the food or pocket the payment as you see fit.

I scoffed, turning to Darwyn. "The specter gave your mother a note. On the back of a moving piece of paper?"

Darwyn shrugged. "Mother is so harried, she didn't bother to flip it over. But I did, when she was scrambling in the kitchen. I didn't know what to do with it, who to tell. It wasn't until after we met Jaron that day that I wound up spending time here and unloading the burden. I gave it to Jaron—and now that pale man keeps dogging him, probably wanting it back." He shuddered at the "pale man."

Jaron flipped the paper over. The image had changed to the very table at which we sat, down to the detail of Jaron holding a piece of paper over the mugs and plates on the table. My drawing self stared at the paper in Jaron's hands, my hair longer and thicker in the back than I pictured. I was afraid to move. Afraid to see the change in the picture.

"It follows Luuk." The drawing of Jurij turned to the drawing of me. And as if to prove his point, Luuk walked to the fire, grabbing the poker to turn over the log. My drawing disappeared from view as just Jaron at the edge of the table remained in focus, the image echoing Luuk's steps across the room.

I gripped the golden copper through the band at my waist. "Why is the lord watching Luuk?"

No one had an answer.

∼

JURIJ DIDN'T COME HOME—DIDN'T come back to *my* home—that night. Or the night after. For the second morning in a row, I carved at the table in my shack, my blade moving too fast without my attention. I sliced the tip of my finger, cursing as I dropped the half-formed wooden cow on the table. Rushing to the basin, I tipped a bit of the water out of the nearby bucket to wash the blood away. My finger stung as I washed it clean of the blood, only for it to ooze out in red again seconds later.

Blood on the chest of Elric, the man who so looked like Ailill. There was nothing, and then there was a pool of blood.

I grabbed a rag and twisted it around my finger, pulling it tight and wincing at the pain. I clearly had no idea how to fix this. Ingrith once told me, right here in this room, about a man who'd been a "healer." Only she didn't mean "healer" like the men from Ailill's village, who had a power I still couldn't explain. She meant someone who fixed your wounds and tended to your illnesses, but without the violet glow. Without the assistance of something I didn't understand pouring out from his fingers.

Little Ailill cradling my face to remove the bruise from the slap. Little Ailill taking my pain away after the stocks.

When I was so cold to him during my first night in the castle, what was going through that same person's head?

"This will be your room." He nodded toward the nearest specter, who seemed to read his intent as he went to the window and pulled back the drapes. I expected to see dust flying, but it was annoyingly pristine. "You may let the light in as you please."

Thank you for the instruction on how to push aside drapes. *I scoffed loudly. But I was determined not to speak to him.*

Ailill stiffened just slightly, but I was too concerned with seeing the prison hidden beneath the extravagantly plush bed and the shimmering baubles before the mirror. A mirror. I'd even have my own mirror! I squashed that feeling of gratitude and wonder as soon as I felt it.

He took you from your home. Against your will. Isn't he supposed to do what you want him to do? He refused to help your mother when you needed help the most.

I pushed past the specters and back into the hallway.

"Are you hungry?" Ailill asked, appearing at my side. "I have instructed a meal to be ready as soon as we have finished our tour."

I stopped in my tracks, not sure what would be worse, dining with him or continuing on this tour of his extravagances. Probably the former. I'd never eaten with a masked man before, let alone one who was so good at getting my blood boiling. Besides, I wasn't hungry. I couldn't imagine being hungry ever again. I shrugged.

Ailill joined his hands behind his back. "This castle... displeases you?"

You displease me, not the castle. *I didn't say it, but it was almost like he'd heard me anyway. He flinched. I didn't say anything.*

"Is there anything I can do... to make you more comfortable?"

I clenched my jaw, knowing I couldn't ask him to let me go. Knowing everyone expected me to just accept him. Just live forever with this man I didn't even know. With this man who'd done nothing to help my mother!

The tour continued after that in near silence, and the disastrous meal together—followed by the truth about my mother. *No, not the truth. Not the whole truth. Just enough for me to despise him even more without realizing...*

Without realizing it was that scared little boy beneath it all. He'd been so eager to please me. He'd pushed down all the anger he'd felt about what I'd done to him, and he'd tried to be friends again. He'd hoped I was the "Olivière" he'd gotten to know as a child. He'd hoped I'd come to free him, that I would reward his efforts with, at the very least, a tender smile.

It's no wonder he treated you cruelly after that. I leaned against the table with my good hand, drumming my fingers across the surface. Two days I'd been alone. Two days I'd finally been back to the solitude I'd enjoyed at the start of the summer, and peace was still unattainable. My mind clouded freely with thoughts and images I'd done such a good job of suppressing until now.

"Doesn't everyone in the village say the lord is always watching?"

"Watching, perhaps, when it strikes his fancy."

Ailill had been so smug, then, as if daring me to guess what exactly in the village might have captured his interest.

I felt my chest tighten at the memory and almost lost my balance. I'd clutched the injured hand to my breast but reached out to steady myself, wincing at the pressure. The rag was dyed red, the blood dripping out onto the table.

What was it Mother had taught me? What kind of leaves would make a poultice? My head swam, flashes of memories searing into my mind. I ran back to the basin, leaning over, almost sure I was going to throw up. Darkness danced at the edges of my sight as I stared at the puddle of water dyed red.

So Luuk had "struck his fancy." A child would have been my last guess. He was Jurij's brother, and Ailill was sensitive about how I'd once felt about Jurij. But why Luuk, then, and not Jurij himself? Of course, this was me seeking a message in every coded action, a message meant for myself when I knew he was no longer in love with me. If he ever truly was.

What was I supposed to tell Jaron and the others? I'd never seen moving pictures on a page and could only guess that was how Ailill was "always watching." But I'd seen things—I'd *lived* things—that couldn't be explained. That would turn everything upside down far more than their piece of paper.

I dry-heaved over the red-dyed basin. My blood soaked through the rag, dropping one crimson pearl after the other onto the water's surface.

I thought of the time I'd spent in the castle. Of how Ailill had taken Jurij after his wedding, held my mother in a room to which I had no access. I'd worried then that he'd have his revenge on everyone I cared about, no matter how thin the connection. Luuk and Nissa. The Tailors. Alvilda. Father and Elfriede. And I was right to worry. He *was* watching them. He was watching us. He was *still* watching us. He had to be. If he had paper like this, then it only made sense.

But what made little sense was why he'd send the paper. He

359

wouldn't have *accidentally* written the note on an enchanted piece of paper and ordered it to be given to one of my friends.

I fumbled at my sash for the golden copper with my good hand. *But then why all the indirect messages? Why bother me now, after he told me to leave him alone?*

My finger stung, and I felt the pressure of tears stirring under my eyelids, the pounding of the crying I refused to do weighing on my head. *What was the poultice Mother used for cuts?* I wondered again. *Why am I so helpless? Why won't my thoughts leave me alone?*

I took a deep breath, rubbing my good hand across my cheekbone and trying to soak up the moisture that had escaped against my will. *Alone. Alone.* Even when I wasn't alone, I felt alone. There was no one who could even begin to understand. No one but Ailill. And I wasn't in the mood for any of his games.

After staring at the blood pooling on the rag over my finger, I straightened my back and grabbed my cloak, swinging it awkwardly over my shoulder with one hand. *You lost her for well over a year. You thought you'd never get her back again. Why haven't you gone to her?*

I may not have been able to tell her everything. But I sure as rain could ask Mother for help.

~

WHEN ELFRIEDE OPENED THE DOOR, I almost turned right around and walked away without a word. *It's not like you didn't expect to find her here. Seeing as how her new man has plenty of other women to share his time with.*

Elfriede's lips soured just slightly, but she didn't study me long. Arrow barked from behind her. I could just make out the swish of his golden tail.

"Shh, Arrow. It's fine." She looked at me. "Have you been *crying*?"

I rubbed my cheek again with my good hand, clutching the injured hand tighter against my chest. "No." I tried peering over her shoulder. "Is Mother in?"

Elfriede chewed her lip, as if considering refusing to answer me. Her gaze fell on the wrapped hand against my chest, and a flicker of something, maybe pity, passed across her pale eyes. She nodded. "Out back." Then she slammed the door in my face.

I took a deep breath and stepped around the house to the small yard we—they—kept behind the cottage. It's where we grew our potatoes and other vegetables, just to save a few coppers on the stuff we had to buy from the market. We got most of our daily eggs from the chicken coop. *Their daily eggs.* With how long Father had been not working—since before the rest of the men lost interest in their work, thanks to Mother's illness—I was certain Mother and Elfriede had been relying on their own crops as much as possible. I wasn't sure what they would do now that summer was winding to a close.

As I passed the window over the basin, I heard laughter. Elfriede's delicate peals punctuated by a gaggle of hens. She had company. There was so much work to be done in the village, and Elfriede and her brood had nothing better to do than monopolize my family's home and whisper about her outcast of a sister with the bloody hand.

"Mother?" I called. I felt lightheaded. Warm, sticky blood crawled down my forearm from beneath the rag.

Mother appeared from around the chicken coop, wiping her hands on her apron. "Noll?" She smiled and reached her arms out for an embrace. "Why haven't you come by earlier?" She stopped, her face and arms falling. "What happened to your hand?"

I winced as I unwrapped the blood-soaked rag. "I cut it while carving. It won't stop bleeding." The rag fell to the ground, soaked and useless.

Mother examined my hand. My finger stung as she turned it over, dyeing her own palms red. "It's bad, but not too deep. We need a poultice." She tugged on my elbow and led me back toward the cottage.

I froze, thinking of the women in there.

Mother stopped. "What is it?"

"Elfriede has company."

Mother nodded. "I invited the girls for dinner. We do that a lot now. Pool our coppers to afford a cut of meat once a week or so. Although I wonder if more of us should follow Roslyn's example and look for work in the village. There's plenty of it to be had now."

I hadn't thought about how quickly Mother and Father's savings might deplete, considering how we'd spent so much of it even before the curse broke. And at least back then, Jurij was so concerned with Elfriede's health and happiness that he gave her all of his earnings from the Tailor Shop so we could afford more food. Now, with neither Father nor Mother nor Elfriede working…

"I'm sorry I haven't been more help." Guilt squeezed at my chest. "I haven't been drowning in riches, but my work is paying off. There's still enough for me to buy bread and vegetables." It helped that both were cheaper than they had been in years, to attract more customers, since everyone I knew seemed to be economizing. Every woman, anyway. "I should have brought something."

"Nonsense. You have your own hearth to heat." She paused. "But today, you should stay, once we've gotten this taken care of."

"No, I ought to get back."

"Noll, you live a short walk from here, but I haven't seen you in months. I've tried giving you your space. I just assumed, at some point, you'd finally have enough of it. You're staying."

I swallowed, nodding. Even if I was unwelcome, the hostility might prove a distraction.

Mother guided me gently to the door and opened it. "Friede, grind some yarrow."

Elfriede picked up a bowl from the counter on which she prepared the roast. She pulled a pestle out of the bowl and walked across the room toward us, Arrow's eyes on her the whole time. "I've already prepared it, Mother."

Mother smiled, and I could almost hear the "what a perfect, helpful daughter" oozing out from between her lips. "Thank you, dear." She took the bowl and continued dragging me along, only letting me go long enough to pour some water from the bucket into the basin before dunking my hand into it.

Mother added a little water to the bowl and picked up the pestle. I waited, unmoving. Even though I couldn't see them, I could feel the eyes burning at my back. I'd only spared the women the briefest of glances before being dragged over to the basin. If I knew Elfriede, Marden had to be among their number. I couldn't for the life of me think of any of her friends I hoped would be there. Somehow, all of Elfriede's good friends seemed to have been paired with mine. I supposed it only made sense. Most goddesses weren't a thousand years younger than their men, after all.

Mother spread the poultice over my wound. It stung, but she grabbed harder so I wouldn't have a chance to pull away.

Someone cleared her throat from the table behind me. "Perhaps we should get back."

Mother patted my hand dry with her apron, taking care not to touch the goopy mixture at my fingertip. "Marden, dear," she said without looking up. "You told me you'd stay for dinner."

I took in the women at the table out of the corner of my eye. Marden twirled her fingers through a curly, dark tendril. "I don't think we should impose. I didn't realize you'd have company."

"It's just my daughter, dear. My husband's out for the evening, so there's plenty of space." Mother smiled and let the apron fall, patting my hand gently. "It'll be just us women." She squeezed my hand as if to emphasize I belonged with the group.

"Roslyn's got an early shift tomorrow."

"I can stay."

I turned to face the table and saw the beauty who'd been with Jaron and the other men at the tavern a few days before. The one who'd left almost the moment I sat down to join them. She struggled to smile at me when I caught her eye. But she seemed to put in the effort—so much so, I felt compelled to smile back. Just a little.

"Wonderful." Mother clasped her hands together and crossed the room to the cupboard, pulling out the plates. "How's the roast, dear?"

I hadn't noticed Elfriede standing beside the fire, turning over a hunk of well-charred meat. "It's ready," she said, reaching out for a set of tongs behind her.

I grabbed a handful of skirt in my good hand and shuffled my feet, trying to decide whether it was better to run for the door or remain standing beneath the assault of the Tanner daughters' gazes.

"Noll, for goddess's sake, help me set the table."

I jumped at the word "goddess," immediately shuffling over to where Mother held out the wooden plates.

"Let me," said Roslyn, standing. "Noll is injured." She smiled tightly again. "Why don't you have a seat?"

I took one look at the thin, hard line of Marden's lips and immediately cut my own struggling smile short.

CHAPTER SIXTEEN

"Does Alvilda still give you her surplus of work?" Mother put her fork down beside her plate. She hadn't taken very big portions, and she'd barely touched what little she'd taken.

I coughed, feeling the silence hanging over the table, remembering the day we'd first brought home the stool on which I sat. The day Elfriede first invited Jurij for dinner. "She does. I mean, she *did*. I haven't seen her much the past few weeks."

Marden snorted and stabbed a chunk of meat with her fork. "Why doesn't that surprise me?"

Elfriede stifled a laugh, making a great show of getting up from the table to bring over another pitcher of water.

I tapped my plate with my fork. "She's not upset with me, if that's what you think. Things have just been... awkward. All around."

Roslyn watched me carefully over her forkful of potato. Even while Elfriede and Marden had spoken to one another and to Mother, Roslyn had yet to say a word since we'd started eating.

"Awkward," Marden spat as Elfriede filled her mug and sat down beside her. "That's a mild way of putting it."

Mother seemed about to say something but instead took a sip from her mug. I wanted to ask if Father was at the tavern—if Father was *frequently* at the tavern—but I didn't think it right to ask the question in front of an audience ready to jump down my throat.

"Some people seem to have adjusted." I picked at a potato on my plate. I didn't mean for my eyes to flit accusingly toward Elfriede and Roslyn, but they did. Roslyn hadn't done anything to make me unwelcome, and I'd already sort of hashed things out with Friede. I quickly turned to Mother. "Jaron is about as happy as I've ever seen any man."

Mother's shoulders stiffened at the name, and I couldn't help but watch for Elfriede's reaction. She cupped her hand in front of her face and whispered something to Marden that caused both of them to dissolve into stifled laughter. Not what I'd expected.

Roslyn set down her fork. "I think you'd have to be a man to be happy with how things are now."

I shoved a too-large piece of potato into my mouth in an attempt to stop the feelings that threatened to swell up through my chest.

Mother stroked her mug with her finger. "Women like Alvilda." A corner of her lips turned up. "Siofra. They're probably happier than anyone."

Marden raised her eyebrows. "Because they each fell in love with another woman?"

"Because they no longer have the burden of what to do with the love of men." Mother reached across the table to grab Elfriede's pitcher of water and poured herself a glass. "Men whose love they never wanted anyway."

I lowered my fork. There was something about her tone that made the rest of the food on my plate suddenly unappetizing.

"I'm glad you've all been trying to move on." Mother cradled her mug, not overly concerned with drinking from it. "Girls, it's time we stopped feeling sorry for ourselves. It's time we stopped waiting around for men to worship us. It's not going to happen anymore."

"Mother, is there something wrong with you and—"

She held out a hand to stop me, lowering her mug without even having a sip. "Things with your father are right where we both want them to be."

"But you never got remarried."

Mother snorted. "Who needs a piece of paper?" She grimaced.

"We're... working through some things. We both need some space. Time to reevaluate who we are. And there's no room for bitterness in this. Things are different. We just have to accept that."

Roslyn burst into tears. She sobbed so hard her shoulders shook. Marden wrapped an arm around her and pulled her into an embrace. Elfriede jumped up to stand behind her, tucking Roslyn's hair behind her shoulders. Mother touched her elbow. I froze.

"It's just..." Roslyn pulled away from her sister and wiped her cheeks with the heel of her hand. "I lost *everything*. Not just Darwyn, but my way of life. The feeling that someone was there for me, no matter what happened. Knowing I meant everything to someone, even if I meant nothing to anyone else. The things that got me through the day, the reasons I woke up in the morning."

Elfriede stroked her hair. "*We're* here for you, Roslyn. We feel the same way."

"And you're not *nothing* to us, Lyn. We're family," Marden added, her own eyes glistening.

"I know. I know." Roslyn hiccupped as she took a deep breath. "It's not that I'm not grateful to have the job at the tavern. Or to be back home. But the tavern work is so different, nothing like the bakery, and things are so tense between Mother and Father at the tannery. And you're just as miserable as I am, Mar."

Marden snorted. "I'm *over* being miserable. Sindri can take a jump off the mountainside for all I care."

"*Marden*. You don't mean that." Elfriede was crying, too. She let go of Roslyn's shoulder just for a moment to wipe a tear from her own eye. Then she and Marden stared at one another and laughed, choking on hiccups.

"No, I *do* mean it." Marden threw her shoulders back and tossed her dark hair over her shoulder. "I mean, I wouldn't be *happy* if he jumped off the mountainside."

Roslyn's voice was quieter. "But what if there was never any hope of you getting back with Sindri?" She craned her head up to look behind her. "Or Jurij?"

Elfriede's smile vanished, and she patted Roslyn's shoulder lightly. "There *isn't* any hope."

I grabbed my mug of water with a shaking hand and brought it to my lips, dying for a way to occupy myself.

Marden shook her head. "It's not a matter of hope. I'm not hoping for that." She leaned back in her chair. "Why would I want this man I hardly know back? He's not the man who worshipped me. He's not *my* Sindri. That man's gone."

Roslyn wiped her nose on her sleeve. "But my Darwyn really *is* gone." She heaved a great sob and buried her head in her arms on the table. Mother carefully leaned forward to pull the plate out of her way. "He's in love with another *man!*"

I spit out my water, immediately drawing the attention of every other person in the room—and the dog for that matter.

Marden rolled her eyes. "Don't tell me *you* didn't know. I thought you were *one of the boys.*"

I nearly tipped the mug over as I clumsily put it back on the table. "I've seen them a few times. I don't know *everything* they've been up to." Darwyn wrapped in a sheet, walking into the room a few minutes later with Tayton, the looks and light touches that passed between them that night—all of a sudden everything took on a very different meaning. I wiped my mouth with the back of my sleeve.

Roslyn was only fleetingly deterred by my outburst. "And they meet *at the tavern!* I'm working tables and practically passing out from exhaustion, and he's upstairs with that big-lipped, obtuse fool that Rosalba never really liked in the first place." She burst into louder sobs and slammed her head against her arms once more.

I opened my mouth, ready to defend Tayton. Not that we were really good friends. Or that I'd forgotten how he'd acted toward me and Ingrith a few years back. I was at least a little amused by the fact that I wasn't the only one who'd noticed his resemblance to a fish, even with the wooden fish mask removed. But Elfriede seemed to read my mind, and the glare that she gave me before I could move my tongue was enough to shut my mouth again.

Mother grabbed a fresh rag from the basin, dipping it in the clean bucket of water before wringing it out. She slid back into her chair and patted Roslyn's elbow gently, rousing her and offering the cloth. "It's good to let it out sometimes, dear." She nodded as Roslyn took the rag and began tapping it against her cheeks. "So long as you know that tears won't change anything."

Roslyn nodded sullenly, and even Marden let out a great sigh. The fire seemed to have left her, if just for a moment. Roslyn held the damp cloth in both hands, staring at it. "It's not that I'm jealous." She grinned as Marden nudged her. "Okay, I'm a *little* jealous. But like Marden said, I miss *my* Darwyn. I don't care what *this* Darwyn does. I just miss what we once had." She gently put the rag down on the table. "I hate working at the tavern."

"Mother and Father could use your help with the tanning," said Marden.

Roslyn interrupted her. "No. I was so glad to be done with that the first time."

Marden shrugged. "It's not *that* bad. I guess. A little tiresome now that I have to do it without Sindri..." She smiled sheepishly. "*Okay*, without him to boss around. I said it. I miss bossing my husband around."

Roslyn laughed and rubbed some of the moisture off of her face with the back of her hand. "*You* would."

Marden grinned. "What did we need a man for, if not for someone to support us?" She looked at her sister, Elfriede, and Mother in turn. "I'm serious! What do you miss so badly?"

Roslyn tried her faltering smile. "The bakery."

Mother tossed her head back. "His arms around me."

Elfriede pinched her lips. "His eyes. And the flame within them. It seemed to light up the world around us, like it burned just for the two of us, and the love we shared."

The four of them fell into silence. Even Marden lost some of her fire.

I cleared my throat, bringing their drifting attention back to the fact that there was someone else left in the room. "I think I can help at least one of you." I nodded at Roslyn. "Darwyn's mother really misses you. Why can't you keep working at the bakery?"

Roslyn seemed to light up for just a moment, but a shadow fell quickly back over her face. "I can't."

"Why not?" I reached for the golden copper I kept tucked in the band at my waist, finding comfort in the solid shape. "I get it.

369

I get it more than any of you might believe. It's not a great feeling when your entire world is ripped out from underneath you."

Marden's nose crinkled. "I thought *you* were happy with the way things turned out. Since it freed your sister's husband to move in with you."

"Oh, but consider how much she lost, too!" Roslyn covered her mouth at the outburst, clearly embarrassed. "I just meant... the castle. You could have been not just his wife, but his *lady*. Lady of the entire village."

"I'm not cut out to be anybody's wife. And I'm nobody's lady."

I glanced at Elfriede to see what she thought of the comment. Her usually plush lips were thin, unmoving. "Imagine what it's like for the men," I said. "They went from knowing exactly what they wanted—from knowing *all* they'd ever want, experiencing bliss or despair because of it—to suddenly having the freedom we've had all along. How can you expect them to trust their own hearts, after years of their hearts misleading them?"

I let go of the coin and put my hand flat against my leg, willing myself to forget Ailill. "The power we had over men was dangerous. But at least if we loved the men back, everyone knew that love to be true." I locked eyes with Elfriede. "The love the men gave us—it was never true. It was never their choice."

I stood up from the table. "But that doesn't mean we have to just curl up in the corner and wait for the men to sort out their messes. We have our own lives. We should be finding what *we* can do to make ourselves happy, instead of lamenting that there isn't a man who's a slave to our whims anymore." I threw back my shoulders. "I'll go with you, Roslyn. Let's get your job back. Darwyn's mother said you were good. It'd be a shame to waste your talent."

Roslyn regarded her sister for a moment, and Marden simply shrugged and looked pointedly away. "But I can't deal with Darwyn," said Roslyn. "He hates me."

"He doesn't hate you. I promise you." I moved around the table and held my hand out to Roslyn. "But if you want someone to hate, hate the first goddess, not him. She caused all this to happen in the first place. She didn't really think things through."

Roslyn studied me, and I wondered what kind of pain was

written on my face. Perhaps some part of me wanted to give it all away, to tell them who I was really blaming. But then Roslyn took my hand and stood up slowly. "If you really think they'll take me back."

Mother smiled and nodded, encouraging me to continue.

"I *know* they will," I said, squeezing Roslyn's hand. "And if working there makes *you* happy, the rest will follow."

Roslyn smiled and squeezed back.

CHAPTER SEVENTEEN

It was getting dark by the time Roslyn and I reached the middle of the village, and people were shuffling out of their shops to light the torches that illuminated their doorways. Roslyn looked happier than any woman had ever looked on her Returning day. She looked happier than I'd ever seen her with Darwyn—although, to tell the truth, I'd hardly paid attention in those days. Darwyn's mother burst into tears and embraced Roslyn the moment the request to move back in and keep working at the bakery was out of her mouth.

"My sweet girl, you dearest!" Darwyn's mother kissed her atop her head over and over. "You'll always be a daughter to me. You don't even have to ask."

The next half hour was filled with both women laughing and crying, and Mistress Baker assuring Roslyn she was doing her the greater favor, and Roslyn insisting the opposite. Finally they both just agreed to disagree and continue to think they owed each other everything. If it weren't for what I wanted to ask Roslyn, I might have left, leaving the two women to have their endless moment.

Now all that was left was for Roslyn to work one last shift at the tavern and tell Vena and Elweard she was moving on. And to tell Darwyn she was moving in. Just not into the room they'd shared.

"You really don't think Darwyn will mind?" Roslyn's ecstasy was interrupted every few moments with a wrinkled brow as she kept asking the same question over and over.

"No, I don't."

"I mean, it'll be awkward for me regardless. But I *know* he's moved on. And baking will keep me busy." She cocked her head. "It might actually go smoother without having to tell him to do one task after another. I always thought he kind of got underfoot when he was my husband. I'm not like some women. I don't need kisses every few seconds to keep me going." She nodded and kept walking, jauntily placing one foot in front of the other. I decided not to let my curiosity about which women she might have meant distract me.

I grabbed her arm gently. "Roslyn."

She hugged me before I could stop her. "Oh, *thank you,* Olivière!"

I felt my cheeks burn and my throat grow dry, both at the hug and the sound of the name only one person still called me. "Noll," I corrected. I patted her gently on the back, not used to embracing other women my age. Other than Elfriede, that is, and we were out of practice.

Roslyn laughed and pulled back. "Of course! I know. Sorry. I just think your full name is so pretty. And it's a very pretty evening, isn't it?" She turned on her heel and started walking back toward the tavern.

"Wait!" I called, jogging a few steps to catch up to her. "Before you go in, can I ask you something?"

Roslyn still seemed to be floating in her bliss, her smile only faltering slightly when a man's shoulder shoved against her back as he went ahead to enter the tavern. "Is this about Friede?"

"No." I opened my mouth to speak again, only to feel a lump forming in my throat at the way Roslyn's face fell. "Is there something I should know about Elfriede?"

Roslyn threaded her fingers together. "She's not happy."

"I know that." I took a deep breath. "She's far from the only one."

This time it was my turn to be jostled from behind as another group of men found their way into the tavern. "Hello, sweetheart!" one called out to Roslyn. His smile and wink reminded me distastefully of the men who'd spurred me to start this whole mess long ago.

Roslyn waved halfheartedly and tucked a strand of hair behind her ear, shrugging at me. "I definitely won't miss all the attention from the tavern."

I nodded. I wasn't going to be distracted again. "The other night, when I visited Jaron's room—"

"He's just a friend. I don't like him the way the other girls do. I wasn't seeing him or anything."

I gripped the coin in my sash with my poultice-free hand, resisting the temptation to cut her off with my hand over her lips. "I just want to know what happened between them and the spec —the lord's servant."

Roslyn cocked her head, her joy completely erased by bewilderment. "The lord's servant? He usually sends one or two a night to collect ale and wine."

I wondered what a man who'd reduced his bread intake to skip the appearances of feeding a hundred still had to do with daily shipments of alcohol. And ale as well as wine. I shook my head. "But why was one in Jaron's room then?"

Roslyn hugged her arm against her side. "I don't know. They don't speak, you know?"

"I know."

She looked over her shoulder at the tavern door, as if eager to step away from the conversation. Instead, she turned back and kept her voice low. "But Jaron seemed to know he wanted something. He teased him and told him to join them for some food and ale, but the lord's servant didn't budge from right inside the doorway." She covered her mouth and sneezed, and I just about shouted out in frustration at the delay. She sniffed. "He stood there for a quarter of an hour. It made for an awkward meal. Then Jaron told the servant he could either take 'it' himself or stand there all night, but he wasn't about to hand 'it' over 'just because some wide-eyed vacant man stood there staring at him.' And then the servant left."

So Roslyn didn't know anything about the page with the

moving drawing. "Does the servant often stop by Jaron's room when he comes to the tavern?"

"I don't know. I don't spend all my breaks up there, but Vena said it'd be quieter than it was on the ground floor, so I kind of got used to it." She looked over her shoulder again. "I should really go tell Vena this will be my last night." She turned on her heel and then stopped. "Do you mind breaking the news to Darwyn for me?"

I let go of the coin in my sash. "That you're moving back in?"

Roslyn nodded.

"I can go with you to tell him if you like, but it really should come from you."

Roslyn put her hand on my shoulder. "Great, thank you! I'll be upstairs after I talk with Vena. You can just ease him into it."

She was gone inside the tavern before I could say anything more. I squeezed my fists together, almost forgetting about the slight jab of pain it would cause in my poultice-covered fingertip. *She's given you an excuse to talk to them again. Just take it.*

I pulled open the door. The tavern was as crowded as it had been the other night, and I wondered why setting men free from the curse of love meant they all felt the need to gravitate toward more ale than was good for them. *Don't any of them eat at home with their wives anymore? Do any of them* have *wives anymore?*

I caught sight of Roslyn leaning over the counter, talking to Vena and Elweard as they scrambled to fill up mugs. Vena's mouth was slightly puckered, and Elweard nodded solemnly. I hoped Roslyn left my name out of it.

I slid between two tables to reach the staircase, stretching my hand out to grab hold of the railing like it was the ledge of a cliff in the suffocating noise and warmth of the crowded tavern.

"Noll?"

If I hadn't been half expecting to see another specter or a half-naked friend, I might have jumped more at the sound of someone calling my name. As it was, it wasn't the presence that startled me, but the identity of the person who'd spoken. "Father?"

His eyes were glazed, his cheeks slightly darker than they ought to have been. But then again, my memories of him anything but flushed with ale were starting to fade. I'd been home so seldom after Mother returned, and it didn't look like being reunited with her was improving his health, now that there was nothing left to tie them together but history and two daughters.

Father stumbled a little and on reflex, I reached out to catch him. He threw a hand out to stop me and caught himself on the rail, slapping his feet down the last two stairs. "They say you won't help."

I pulled my arms back. "Won't help?"

"Jaron said he and the others might be close to getting some answers, but they need your help." He brushed his face with his forearm as if to clear his eyes of the cloudiness. "But you wouldn't help them. Just like you wouldn't help me."

The laughter in the tavern grew louder, buzzing in my ears. "Help you? I did nothing but help you in all the time Mother was at the castle."

Father let go of the railing and pointed at me. "You and that castle. You won't have anything to do with that castle. No matter how many people must suffer for it."

He was wrong. I'd *gone* there. Even though I hadn't wanted to, I'd done it for him and Mother and Elfriede. But it wasn't enough for him. It never was. I backed up as much as I could to get out of the way of his trembling finger, but there wasn't enough space to move. "What's this about, Father?"

There were tears welling around his dark, lifeless irises. "I don't love her anymore." He wiped his nose with his wrist and hiccupped. "And I don't like it."

Although I half expected it, my stomach clenched at his admission. "If you don't like it, then change it. *Choose* to love Mother." I reached back to grab the railing, tapping my fingers atop it.

"I don't know how." Father took a deep breath and clutched his shirt. "I don't know how to deal with these feelings. Like wanting to be alone, but feeling anger at the idea of her with someone else. Like having this *hole* in my chest and not knowing how to fill it." He stared at me accusingly. "But *he* might have the answers. And you won't get them from him."

He hobbled off, almost tumbling against a man seated at a nearby table. The man laughed. "Little too much to drink, hey, Master Carver?" He turned back to his companions, chuckling away. Father kept walking, undisturbed, vanishing into a crowd of men and mugs and plates.

I watched him pityingly, then squared my shoulders and walked up the stairs. I had enough to think about without Father blaming me for his problems. That wasn't anything new anyway.

I paused in front of the door to Jaron's room, about to knock. I couldn't think of what I wanted to say, if I should go in on the pretense of speaking with Darwyn, or if I should just come out and ask what they wanted from me.

The door creaked open at my knock. I poked my head in, but there was no fire roaring, no man in sight.

"Hello? Jaron? Darwyn? Sindri?"

The room was a mess, with plates scattered on the ground and clothing and bed sheets tossed about like someone had been looking for something in a hurry. I noticed the box in which Jaron kept the page open and upside down atop the bed.

"Hello?" *Maybe someone found something in a hurry.*

I took a step into the room and felt a pair of arms embrace me from behind, pulling me roughly backward into the hallway.

CHAPTER EIGHTEEN

My assailant wanted to drag me into the neighboring room, but I reached out for the doorframe and pulled hard, kicking back at his shins. "Let me—"

A hand covered my mouth, even as he muttered, "Ow. Noll, it's me. Be quiet and come in here."

I let go of the doorframe and stomped my foot. Jurij tugged me inside by the elbow and closed the door behind us. The room resembled Jaron's, only there was a fire roaring and the room wasn't torn to pieces. I tapped my foot. "Well?"

Jurij put a finger in front of his lips as he shook one of his legs. Probably the one I'd kicked. He walked over to the table and pointed to a piece of paper. *The* piece of paper. My good hand trembled as I stepped forward, leaning on the table for support. The drawings were moving, little Luuk walking in place—or that's what it seemed at first. The trees in the background kept disappearing off the edge, and I realized he was walking forward.

Trees. "He's in the woods."

Jurij placed a hand on my shoulder, stopping me. "One of *them* is in the next room over," he whispered.

I frowned. "One of the lord's servants? Jaron's room was empty. Ransacked, but empty."

Jurij's lips twitched. He pointed to the wall. Not the wall bordering Jaron's, the other one.

I studied Jurij's face but realized I was about as likely to get him to explain what was going on as I was to find Ailill himself in the next room. I looked back at the piece of paper and watched Luuk walk down the path that ran through the woods. His lips were drawn in a tight line. He shivered. The sun had set, and the nights were getting cooler.

"What's he *doing*?" Lowering my voice seemed to be the only thing that would make Jurij willing to talk. I wasn't in the mood to explain the volume of our voices probably didn't make any difference. It wasn't like someone had *stolen* the piece of paper. Ailill had clearly wanted us to have it.

Jurij ignored my question. "What if he has pages for all of us?"

I thought about that. Paper Luuk flinched and crouched, only to see a rabbit burst out of the line of trees in front of him. He breathed easier, stood, and kept on his way. "Maybe he does," I admitted.

Jurij tapped the paper. "Well, he at least doesn't have Luuk's anymore."

"What are you saying?"

I didn't think it was possible, but Jurij lowered his voice even further. "Then Luuk's the only one he won't see coming."

"You sent a child to the castle alone?"

Jurij shushed me again. This was beginning to feel a bit ridiculous.

"*Okay*," I whispered, pointing at the paper. "What is he going to do?"

Jurij shrugged. "Just look around a little."

I crossed my arms, not caring that I scraped off some of the hardened poultice as I did. "Luuk. The kid whose hand Nissa had to hold every time they strayed too far in the cavern."

"You wouldn't help us."

"So I keep hearing." Luuk arrived at the castle gates. At least they were bound to stop this foolish plan, since I doubted they'd open. "Does your father know? Or your mother?"

"Father does." Jurij pulled the paper closer to him. Luuk was pushing on the gates to no avail. "We haven't spoken to Mother in days. It's not really easy between Father and Mother at the moment."

"Of course." I imagined Siofra or Alvilda would have tried to knock some sense into them. Maybe literally. Luuk was running his hand over the wall now. Looking for a secret entrance? "So why is a spec—*servant* in the room next door? Is he looking for this?" I pointed to the paper and gasped when I saw Luuk grab on to a protruding stone and haul himself up. He dangled on the wall, his feet a short distance from the ground.

"We think we convinced him it was stolen. Maybe." Jurij seemed unconcerned with the little drawing of his brother, who swung his arm out a few times until he finally found another stone to grab. "We ransacked Jaron's room ourselves before the servant got here."

"He's going to hurt himself." My face snapped up from the paper. "*You* guys did that? Why?"

Jurij stepped closer, one finger in front of his lips to quiet me, the other reaching out to touch my shoulder. "The servant in the room next door can hear you."

I tore my eyes away from Jurij to make sure Luuk was okay. He'd reached the top of the wall. "How is he going to get down?" I whispered. Luuk answered my question for me by swinging his legs over to the other side and dangling from the top. He slipped, falling the few feet straight to the ground. I flinched, but Luuk stood up and brushed off his pants.

I let out a breath I didn't realize I was holding as Luuk slinked away from the wall. I tapped the paper. "You think *he* has pages like this to watch everyone?"

Jurij nodded.

"So he could be watching us watching Luuk right now."

Jurij nodded again.

"So what was the point of the ransacking if he can see us looking at the paper?"

"We just wanted to make sure we kept the servant nearby. Jaron and the others are explaining that it was stolen."

"What's the point of keeping one servant nearby? There are at least a hundred servants at the castle! Where you sent Luuk!"

"We know. We just figured that if the lord's watching, he'll be watching the servant in the village. The one with us."

I touched my forehead with my fingertips, shaking my head and not caring about the tiny prick of pain in my sore finger. "I wish I *had* offered to help you. I could have told you that the man's not as stupid as you seem to think."

Jurij reached for the hand that was tapping my forehead, tugging it gently downward. "What happened to you?" He cradled my hand, running a fingertip across my skin so lightly I couldn't help but picture a flower petal swaying gently across the back of my hand. Lying down in the warm grass. Jurij at my side. Right there, yet so out of reach. *Ailill.* Of all the people to think about now, I had to think about Ailill, holding my hand just like this the night I first met him. *Were they so different, now that I knew Jurij capable of anger, and Ailill capable of compassion? Was it the curse that made them seem so different to me at first, or was it... Ailill had been alone for so long. Jurij didn't understand how fortunate he'd been, having a family to love him. Having Elfriede accept and love him.*

"A small cut." I pulled my hand away and forced my breathing to slow. "Jurij, you need to tell me what's going on, or I'm about to march to that castle to find Luuk." The drawing of Luuk paused. There were no windows on the ground floor at the front of the castle. He gave the door a tug with both hands. I whipped my head back to Jurij. "What is the point of all of this? If he gets caught, he could—"

Jurij grabbed hold of both of my shoulders and pulled me toward him, his lips pressing hard against mine.

I don't know how long we stayed like that. I don't even remember if I had adequate time to step back and didn't—out of shock, maybe. Or because some part of me wanted the kiss.

Fool.

Our door burst open, and I finally came to my senses. I was just about to release his lips and pull back, when Jurij took charge and ended the kiss for me. "You must have felt us calling for you," he said, smiling. It was a hollow echo of the smile he used to give Elfriede at one of her kisses.

A specter stared at us—stared at *me*. Behind him, the firelight just barely flickered over the forms of Jaron, Master Tailor, Sindri, Darwyn, and Tayton in the hallway.

381

Jurij grabbed my hand, threading his fingers through mine. He brushed against the poultice, and the skin beneath it stung. I watched him warily out of the corner of my eye, but he looked straight ahead, facing the specter.

He grinned. "Noll and I would like to get married."

CHAPTER NINETEEN

T he specter stood perfectly still. I lost my sense of time, only awakening when I noticed the group gathered in the hall disappearing into the darkness of the stairway.

Jurij squeezed my hand, and I studied him. The lump in his throat wobbled, but he still looked straight ahead. "Don't you need to bring out a piece of paper for us to sign?"

At the word "paper," Jurij seemed to remember what he'd left clear as day on the table. He guided me by the hand to block the view, his free hand extended toward the specter as if expecting him to produce one of those marriage certificates from his pocket.

The specter didn't respond, his black irises locked on me. Then he reached into his pocket and pulled out an ink well, quill, and piece of paper.

I tugged on Jurij's hand and whispered, "What. Are. You. Doing?"

The specter crossed to the table in a few strides. Jurij reached back and grabbed Luuk's paper, crumpling it into a ball in his fist. I almost gasped, wondering if such a thing could be broken.

"Jurij," I whispered. I didn't know whether to expose Jurij's audacity in full view of one of the lord's servants. This had to be a distraction so Luuk—and the others now too?—could explore the castle unimpeded. They'd wanted me to summon Ailill out of the castle, and I'd refused, but they'd gone ahead and figured out a way they just might do it on their own. Only it still relied on me, and without my consent. I ground my teeth together. "*Darling*," I said, in my best impression of Elfriede at her finest. Jurij's hand twitched at the word, his palm moist and sweaty against mine. "I know we've discussed marriage, but perhaps we should wait until our parents can attend."

"Marriage is just a piece of paper now," he snapped. "And I've had enough overdone ceremonies to last me a lifetime."

The specter dipped the quill in the open ink well and began writing.

"We've discussed this, too. *You've* had ceremonies. I never loved anyone else enough to even have a Returning."

The specter's arm stiffened, halting his writing. Then he dipped his pen again and wrote even more furiously.

"Yes, but it has to be tonight, sweetheart." Jurij squeezed my hand hard, as if to emphasize his point. I squeezed back to emphasize that I was going to slap him for using me this way the moment it was all over. I didn't think he got my message. "You agreed, just moments ago. We can't keep living a lie. It's time we were husband and wife."

"Noll? Darwyn—oh, sorry. Am I interrupting?" Roslyn poked her head in through the open door. She glanced at the specter hunched over the table and took him in from head to foot. She didn't comment, just pointed behind her. "I tried the room that Tayton stays in. And I was about to try Jaron's when I saw this door open." She shook her head. "Never mind, I'll just tell him later."

"No!" The volume of my voice made Jurij jump. His grip slackened, and I pulled my hand away, wiping it on the front of my skirt. I'd worn the poultice down and felt my skin rip a little again. I rushed across the room and slid my arm through Roslyn's. She cocked her head as if to ask what had come over me, but I pulled her toward Jurij and the specter as if it were only natural, as if Roslyn and I had been friendly for years instead of just the past few hours. I patted her arm. She was going to be my excuse to stop this whole mess without admitting in front of the specter that my friends were idiots. "Seeing Roslyn reminds me, Jurij. I'd really prefer we had some witnesses. It will be tonight, of course, but you have to do this for me. It's my first and only time, after all. *Please*."

Jurij's eyes darted from the hunched over specter, to Roslyn, to me. The specter didn't react at all. I frowned. Had anyone ever seen a specter write anything? All the notes I assumed came from Ailill himself, written ahead of time. The marriage certificates for Vena and Elweard or Alvilda and Siofra were already written, without names, when the specters brought them out of their pockets. They just required signatures. No one had ever gotten one of these silent spirits to respond in any way—no one besides Ailill, in any case. The only way we knew they could understand us was because they acted differently when we spoke to them.

I could feel Roslyn shrink back just a little in my grip. "Are you two getting *married*?" She pointed at the specter. "Right now?"

"*Yes*—" started Jurij.

"No!" I shook my head and swallowed, feeling Jurij's expectations boring through me along with his pointed gaze. "I mean, not right *now*, we were just discussing that."

Roslyn pulled her arm out from mine and, although I expected her to flee or get angry, considering her relationship with my sister, she took my hand in both of hers. "Noll, it's really none of my business. I won't try to stop you from getting married. If you're both happy, I have no reason to stop you."

Jurij and I exchanged a glance as Roslyn dropped one hand and guided me gently toward him. She placed my hand atop his, shackling me back to the man I once loved—maybe *still* loved—who'd just tried to force me to marry him because of a stupid plan. He hadn't even asked if I was willing to participate. I felt the crinkle of paper in Jurij's fist and slipped it out into my hand, hopefully without either Roslyn or the specter noticing. But the specter wasn't looking. He stood straight now and put the stopper back on the ink. Jurij gripped my wrist before I could pull my hand away.

Roslyn's lips quivered. "It's just—Elfriede's awfully unhappy."

Jurij's face soured. "Things aren't the same as they were."

"I know! Believe me, I know." Roslyn spoke quietly as she

broke into a shy smile. "And things being different doesn't mean they have to be unhappy."

I tried returning her smile, but my focus was drawn to the specter. He tapped the quill on the jar of ink to shake out the remaining droplets and laid it down beside the certificate, straightening his jacket.

"I just think—I mean, Noll and Friede are sisters. They may not have a lot in common, but they love each other, right?" Roslyn's voice quavered at the end of the sentence, perhaps not as sure about her statement as she pretended to be.

I hesitated but nodded. "Yes, but—"

Roslyn held out a hand to stop me. "I understand things between the three of you are complicated. But I do think Elfriede can be happy without Jurij. I *know* it. Only…"

Jurij's hand on my wrist slackened at the same time his back stiffened. "Then what's the problem?"

Roslyn tilted her head toward me, as if waiting for me to speak. The specter stepped around Jurij and walked toward the doorway, the ink well, quill, and certificate left behind on the table. I leaned around Jurij, trying to get a better look at the certificate. "I think Roslyn is saying we need to make peace with Elfriede."

Roslyn clapped her hands. "Yes!" She reached forward and wrapped her arms around my shoulders for a hug. "I told Friede she just needed to talk to you!" She pulled back to look me in the eyes. "That there's no way her sister could be doing anything to hurt her on purpose!"

Jurij had let my wrist go in the confusion, and I patted Roslyn's back awkwardly. Even with the paper in my fist, I figured it was better than to pat her with my hand that had started bleeding again. "Roslyn's right," I said, glaring at Jurij pointedly. "We shouldn't say we're getting married before *discussing it* with the people most affected."

Jurij furrowed his brow and refused to return my look. I followed his eyes to the doorway and noticed the specter had left us. Before we'd had a chance to sign anything.

Roslyn noticed now too and pulled away from me, covering her mouth with one hand. "Oh! Sorry. Did I make you reconsider?"

I scowled. Agreeing to talk to Elfriede first wasn't the same as telling the specter we'd changed our minds. "What do you mean?"

Roslyn stood on her toes and tried to peer over Jurij's and my shoulders at the table behind us. "Well, they're not supposed to pull out a marriage certificate unless they know both parties want to get married, right?"

I felt a twitch at the pit of my stomach. She was probably right. But I'd been taken aback. I'd tried to play along, but was that the same as accepting the marriage? How did the specters judge that anyway? The piece of paper showing Luuk felt heavy in my hand, and I tucked it into my sash beside the golden copper.

"So I figured if he left before you signed it, he must be waiting for you to make peace first." She smiled.

I gave her a faltering smile in return. "You're right." Jurij turned and peered over the table. Roslyn seemed eager to get a look, too, so I grabbed her hand gently and led her to the door. "Thank you," I cooed, trying again to sound like Elfriede. "You've given us a lot to talk over. Um…"

"I'll give you some privacy," said Roslyn. I almost laughed at that, considering what we'd discovered about moving drawings on pages. She squeezed my hand. "And thank *you*, Noll." She pulled the door shut behind her.

I had a feeling that might be the last time I'd hear those words from anyone for quite a while.

"Noll, Luuk's page! Quickly!"

I was across the room with my hand digging into my sash for the crumpled wad before I could think about how embarrassed and angry I was. He sounded *that* worried. Jurij peered over my shoulder as I unfurled the paper.

It took me a moment to orient myself to the drawing. But Luuk was crying, tears clearly visible on his ink face. His hands gripped iron bars, and he shook them. His mouth was open, and I could almost hear the cry for help passing across his silent lips.

"Damn it." I shoved the paper at Jurij's chest. He caught it with trembling hands. "I could have told you there was no way he'd get away with it. What were you thinking?"

Jurij pulled the page away from his chest and examined it.

"They're on their way. They'll find some way to help him. And *you* wouldn't help us."

"Well, you pretty much forced me to help anyway, didn't you? You might have told me what you were planning."

Jurij paused. "We thought he might be watching you too closely."

I threw my hands up in the air. "Well, in that case, he would have already seen me meeting the lot of you and being shown this page."

"That's why we stalled the one servant. To keep his attention on him."

I exhaled a deep breath. "Do you think the man's an idiot?"

The lump at Jurij's throat bobbed, and he laid Luuk's page on the table, absently smoothing it with one hand. "I don't know anything about the man. Other than he changed you."

"He changed *me*?" I crossed my arms. "Don't talk to me about change. I haven't changed. *You* have!"

"You *have* changed," Jurij said. "The Noll I love *loved* me. The only thing I can think of that might have changed your mind is him!"

I snorted. "Not falling in love with my sister, having a Returning with her, flaunting your sickeningly sweet affection in front of me day after day, and marrying her?"

"You loved me even so. You kissed me on my wedding day."

He had a point. I'd assumed that hadn't meant anything to him because he didn't have a will of his own. "It wasn't him who changed me."

Jurij let out a breath. "Then what did?"

I almost told him. He'd probably swear I imagined the whole thing or call me a liar. Yes, this new and changed Jurij would probably never believe me, but staring into his eyes and remembering the flames I once saw there, I felt the tension release from my neck and shoulders. I wanted to burst out crying. I wanted to hug him, to tell him everything. I took a step forward. But the marriage certificate on the table caught my eye.

If you think I am about to give my blessing to your happiness...

This is what the specter had written while we'd been trying to distract him. He hadn't been distracted at all.

If you think I am about to give my blessing to your happiness, you are mistaken. I cannot stop you from spending your nights beside the former husband of your own sister, but I am lord of this village, and under my new law, only my Ailills give permission to wed. There is no will of the first goddess in this village now. She foolishly gave me permission to crush her power into dust.

But it does not matter. I cannot hear you when not around my retainers, but I can see you, as I assume you and your cohorts might have learned. I allowed you this knowledge. I do not understand why they seem to think they can enter my castle unseen when they know what I can do. But I must forgive them for being foolish; they are quite new to the freedom of will that you and the other women have so long enjoyed.

This proposed marriage is a falsehood, a distraction meant to send me running to you. I have seen you. You push away this boy for whom you once risked everything because now he has free will. You do not like men with free will. You never have. You may stumble over your feelings for him now, but you will never commit to marrying him, or any other. Men are no longer docile enough for you.

Nothing you could do would make me come running. If your cohorts want answers, they should have asked you. You played a larger role in all of this than I ever could. As it is, they trespass without permission in my castle, and here they will stay.

Perhaps you will bring my pages back to me when you stop by for a visit, as I no doubt expect you to soon.

I flipped the paper over, dreading what I might see on the other side. A drawing burst to life of Master Tailor in a cell, his legs crossed on the stone floor. Beside him sat Sindri, his shoulder against the iron bars, and Darwyn and Tayton, who held hands even as Darwyn seemed to be shouting something and gripping his hair in anger. A pair of legs paced on and off the page, boots I guessed belonged to Jaron.

"He got them all," I said. Since it hadn't been that long since the men had left the tavern, I could only imagine Ailill had sent out his specters and a carriage to bring the rest of them to his cells that much quicker.

Jurij growled and began pacing back and forth across the room in echo of Jaron. "Now what?"

I folded the second moving drawing and tucked it in my sash. "Now we walk in through the front gates."

CHAPTER TWENTY

W e didn't speak until we'd reached the outskirts of the village, past the Tailor Shop. Seeing the empty, darkened windows emphasized where we were going like a punch to the stomach. I spared a moment's regret for not racing to tell Siofra and Alvilda. But then we'd be headed to the castle trailing behind a raging, screaming woman who probably wouldn't make it past the first set of specters.

"What did he mean, you played a larger role? And that we should have asked you?"

I was so distracted by my thoughts I flinched at hearing Jurij speak beside me. The timid smile that had formed at the thought of Alvilda in a rage faded, replaced by the cold hardness of the reality I'd created by going through the cavern pool.

The moon was bright, but I kept my eyes fixed on the path. I shivered as we neared my childhood home. Not just because of the cold nip in the air, or even due to the sister who slept behind closed doors. But because of the memories of another night I ventured down this path, cold and damp, determined to free the man who now walked beside me, the one I now pushed away.

He sighed and ran a hand through his hair. "Of course you wouldn't answer." He gave the home in which his former wife lived the briefest of glances and led the way into the woods. "How about this then: What did he mean, the Ailills?"

"That's his name. The lord's, I mean. Ailill."

A twig snapped loudly beneath Jurij's foot. "Huh. I guess no one ever bothered to ask his name before."

I tucked the pesky too-long piece of hair behind my ear, feeling guilty for so long not caring to know his name. "No one cared about anything outside of their men and goddesses before." *Or, in my case at least, other people's men.*

Jurij pushed aside a branch hanging across the path. "So the Ailills? Plural?"

"It's what he calls the specters."

"The what?"

"His servants."

"Why?"

"Long story."

"I'd like to know."

"I'm not sure we have time." The beaten shrubbery ahead marked the path to the cavern.

We were quiet then, but soon Jurij interrupted the silence. "You know, you never asked."

"Asked what?"

Jurij nodded toward the path ahead. "What it felt like the last time I was here. What it felt like to have my wedding day turned upside down."

I stopped. We didn't talk much about *my* time there. I didn't even think to ask about his. "You remember?"

"Not much. My whole life until things changed seems like a haze." He paused beside me. "But I remember… the shaking. Then waking in a strange place. The blur of white figures, the dark void at my bedside."

"The servants. And Ailill," I said. "Wearing his veil."

"I asked for Elfriede." Jurij traced the line of the scar on his cheek. "I remember the pain on my face, I remember how much it hurt, but it was nothing compared to how I felt being apart from Elfriede."

And he was parted from her because of me.

"But that was stupid of me," he said, his fist tightening around the paper in his hand. "I know that now."

Neither of us said anything for a moment, a moment we shouldn't have wasted just then.

"I was so consumed with thoughts of Elfriede," said Jurij, breaking the silence, "I didn't stop to think about it at first, but the lord, he was... a mess. He was wet. His veil and hat were uneven."

That was after he saved me from the pond. I shuddered thinking about what happened then, and how we'd fought in the cavern—how I'd almost killed him then and would go on to "kill" him for a time shortly thereafter. In the time between then, we'd parted as soon as the carriage door opened. Before he'd joined me in the dining room, he'd stormed upstairs—probably to treat Jurij. Although not to the "best of his ability," as I remembered asking.

"He took his gloves off, and I remember thinking how *pale* he was. How ghastly pale. Like one of his servants dressed in black."

"He's not quite so pale as that," I said, realizing Jurij had never seen Ailill without his mask. "But yes, he's fair."

Jurij didn't comment on it. I was glad. I didn't want to explain how I came to know Ailill's face so well.

"There was warmth on my face, then," continued Jurij, "and for a moment... I saw things with a clarity I'd never felt before then. The pain on my face lifted. The pain in my heart eased. I wasn't thinking of Elfriede. I wasn't thinking about anything."

He did *try to heal him with his magic.*

"Then it all stopped. The lord pulled his hand away and tugged on his glove roughly, like he'd burnt his hand. He said, 'I suppose you felt nothing then. When my goddess's lips touched yours.'"

My goddess? I'd forgotten he would call me that from time to time. I knew I was his goddess once, but I'd bristled every time he said it. Now...

"I was so confused. I remembered you kissed me." He chanced a glance my way. "But it meant nothing to me when it happened. It wasn't the first thing on my mind even until he asked, but as that warmth faded away, I saw it clearly. Just for a moment. I *felt* something for you. Something greater than I'd ever felt for you, something like what I'd thought I could only feel for Elfriede."

Did his healing powers "heal" the curse right off a man? Could he have freed him when I asked and he chose not to, or did Ailill himself remain unaware of that fact? I never even thought about it!

"But it was just a moment. I remember... the lord said something more, something quieter then. 'If only you knew what you took from me. It was not even your fault. But I confess I cannot help myself even still.' As the pain rolled back over me, so did my longing for Elfriede. I was growing delirious, blind to everything about me. I asked for help, for some explanation, but they ignored me. I don't really remember what happened after that. I don't remember what happened for a *long* time after that."

"It wasn't just you, Jurij. Ailill didn't make you forget the next month. That was the month that no one seems to remember."

"But you do, don't you?"

I picked up my skirts. "We should go."

Jurij crumpled the paper in his hand, then seemed to notice what he was doing and smoothed it out. "The two of you keep so many secrets from the rest of us. And you wonder why I was so reluctant to ask you to play your role in this plan." Jurij held the paper showing Luuk up above him, trying to get the filtering effects of the moonlight to show him his brother. "What would he lock them up for?"

I rolled my eyes. "Breaking into his castle against his edict might have had something to do with it." I clutched Master Tailor's page in my hand, the paper with the message written so coldly for me on its reverse side. Some of the men in the image stood, and others sat. There wasn't much change. "We'll get it straightened out. He won't hurt them."

Jurij laughed, but there wasn't any joy in the sound. "You mean like how he didn't hurt me?" He pointed to his scarred eye.

"I don't think he meant to do that."

Jurij stuffed Luuk's paper into his pocket. "Well, I'm glad you don't *think* he meant to slice a gash down my face. Or take me captive thereafter."

"It was the earthquake!" I grabbed Jurij's hand, and he stopped, stiffening. "Before the curse broke, Ailill was doomed to cause the ground to shake if he left the castle. And he was trying to treat you when you woke up."

Jurij's features softened. I could just make out a glint in his

393

irises in the silver light that trickled through the leaves above us. "So he didn't cause the earthquake on purpose?"

"No. Yes." I shook my head. "Whenever he left the castle back then, he'd cause an earthquake. He knew that, but he didn't control the tool that cut you."

"Why just him? The rest of us may have been cursed, but I don't recall any other man making the ground shake just because a woman looked at his home. Or because he stepped out of it."

"To protect him."

Jurij's gaze drifted over my head. The cavern lay behind me. I wondered if for some reason it was calling him too. "I have a feeling you know more, but you won't tell me if I ask."

I dropped Jurij's hand and moved forward, pushing the call of the cavern away with each step. "You wouldn't believe me if I told you."

"Tell me anyway." Jurij's hand gripped my shoulder, pulling me back to face him.

I faltered a moment. The castle gates were there, just in sight at the edge of the path. The cavern still called me in some way I couldn't explain. I could run away to either of them to avoid answering him, to avoid thinking about my past—but both were the places I was most likely to remember. "I'm the first goddess."

Jurij's hand slackened. "What?" He was almost laughing.

I drew a deep breath. "The one from the legend. The one who balanced inequality and cursed the men."

"Huh." Jurij dropped his hand from my shoulder. He looked about to say something more, and then he shut his mouth again. "Are you sure he wasn't deceiving you?"

I sighed and kept marching forward, crumpling my message tighter in my fist. "Never mind."

"I'm serious!" Jurij said. "What if he gave you visions while you were with him? Why else did I feel those things I felt while in his castle?"

"Visions?" I repeated. We'd reached the castle gates, and I didn't even blink when they drew open. I'd yet to approach the castle walls and find them slammed shut. To me, anyway.

Jurij stepped between me and the open gate, suddenly forgetting his haste to rescue his friends and family. "If you go in there, will you see visions again?"

I clenched my fists at my sides. "Jurij! I'm not seeing, nor have I ever seen, visions!" I thought about my experiences in the pool and shook my head. No need to explain the things the pool showed me. I pointed back down the path. "You know the cavern?"

"The cavern?"

"*Our* cavern! The one with the glowing pool."

"The one you almost drowned in."

"Yes." *The one where you rejected me, then tried to force me into your arms.* "I traveled to... well, I guess I traveled to the past there."

"In the cavern." Jurij looked at me as if worried I was unwell. I remembered too vividly his looks in that alternate time he didn't remember, the time when the lord never was, and my parents were gone.

"Through the pool," I corrected. He stared at me blankly, and I threw up my hands. "Ugh! Never mind! I knew you wouldn't believe me."

Jurij glanced over his shoulder and held his hands out as if to stop me. "All right, all right. Let's say I believe you."

"Sure. *Let's say.*"

"How did *you* have the power to curse all of the men?"

"I just used the power I was born with."

"Which was?"

"Being able to control any man who found the goddess in me."

I could tell Jurij desperately wanted to check over his shoulder again, but he also didn't want to let me out of his sight. A bead of sweat trickled down his forehead. "So in *the past*, and we're talking a long time ago, the lord was there?"

This was hardly the time or place to get into this. "Yes. But I didn't mean he was the one who found the goddess in me. Not *just* him anyway." Jurij let me lower his arm without resistance, and I walked past him.

"There's only *one* man for every woman," Jurij said as he stepped beside me. "At least before..." His gaze fell over the darkened room, and his jaw opened. "What happened here?"

I'd spent so long thinking of the castle as some sort of prison for just me, the lord, and the specters, I'd forgotten

395

that Jurij had been here a few times himself to deliver clothing.

The place was a mess. The door to the inner garden was open and swinging in time with a gentle breeze, slamming against the wall every other moment. Moonlight illuminated the rest of the room, even if the torches went unlit. There were barrels lying on their sides throughout the foyer, small puddles of liquid seeping out through a number of them. A pile of rumpled black clothing lay scattered between the entranceway and the stairway, boot prints clearly visible on the fabric, like someone had kicked and stomped on them rather than picking them up and moving them out of the way. I could see why the specters had asked for less bread to be delivered. There was a stack of green, rotting bread near the foot of the stairs, knocked over like a mountain after a landslide.

What has that man been up to?

"So where is he?" asked Jurij. "Hello?"

"Shh!" I put a finger to my lips, not even sure why. He was here, obviously. Our friends were here. But the place was too quiet, and I was reluctant to make a sound. I reached for the slip of paper in my sash. "Let's just get the guys and go," I whispered, not at all convinced it was going to be that easy. "If they're where my Mother was being kept—"

"What is *that?*"

I turned around. "Jurij?" He was walking toward the dining hall. "Jurij, it's not that way." But he went into the room without a moment's pause. Satisfied the men remained holed up in their pen, I stuffed Master Tailor's page back into my sash and followed. "Jurij?" There wasn't much light in the room. It was almost like he'd vanished.

"What are these?"

I walked toward the noise and knocked into Jurij as he stood up, his hand gripping something he'd picked off the floor.

I blinked. "A bangle. It used to keep a veil up over the table."

"A veil?"

I bent down to grab another bangle that glistened in the dark. My fingers brushed the fallen veil. Had it laid there since that day he'd vanished?

"Did you used to dine together? Before he could remove his mask?" Jurij cleared his throat. "I mean, his veil?"

"Yes. Sometimes." I reached into my sash and pulled out my gold coin. It also glistened in the slivers of moonlight.

"The gold in the castle, like you told us about."

The gold on Elric's arm. The bangle he wore that glistened in the firelight.

"Where'd he get it?" Jurij asked.

"I don't know." I swallowed and tucked the gold coin and bangle into my sash. I grabbed Jurij's arm. "The prison cells are upstairs. On the third floor."

Jurij wrenched his arm away, like he thought I would grab for his bangle. For the first time in this conversation, his voice didn't sound incredulous. "If you're the first goddess, why did you curse the men?"

I clutched at my chest, unable to contain the pain I felt there. "I was trying to save the women. I meant to punish *some* men. The men who deserved it."

"How would men *deserve* it? For loving the wrong women? For not obeying their goddesses quickly enough?"

"You think I'd punish helpless men over something so trivial as that?"

"I don't know what I think. You—"

"They hurt women." That caused Jurij to shut his jaw quickly. "Really *hurt* them. I don't know if you've ever even thought about it, but men are physically stronger than women for the most part, and these men... Their actions..."

The door to the foyer slammed shut, and the air hissed with the scrape of steel on firestone.

"And you made the innocent men suffer for it."

The wood in the dining hall's fireplace roared to life.

Ailill stood gazing at the flames, his forearm pressed against the mantel.

CHAPTER TWENTY-ONE

"Did you come for your marriage certificate?" Ailill stood back from the flickering fireplace and gave Jurij and me a faltering smile. "I suppose it is unfair that I denied you one when asked. But then, I could not be sure you both felt ready."

Jurij, all fire and flame when he first sprung the marriage announcement on me, took a step backward, fading into the darkness.

I straightened my shoulders and took a step toward the fire-light, my rapid heartbeat be damned. "How do you know when someone is ready?" I pulled Master Tailor's crumpled page out of my sash. "Would this have something to do with it?"

Ailill laughed. "I see you got my message."

I shook the paper in the air. "You see a lot of things."

"Yes, well, since there is no sound, I have to imagine the rest of the story."

I tore my eyes from Ailill's face, not sure if the gaunt features were a trick of the dim firelight or a sign of poor nutrition. If it was the latter, he had no one to blame but himself. The specters did all the cooking and cleaning, so—

Where were the specters?

"Our friends. Are they in the prison cells?"

Ailill nodded toward the paper. "What does it look like?"

"*Why* have you imprisoned them?" Behind Ailill, a speck of light danced among the shadows. The glistening of Jurij's golden bangle.

If Ailill heard the door to the entryway cracking open behind him, he didn't show a sign of it. Only, I didn't believe he was that stupid. "I said that no one was to set foot in my home, and I have had half a dozen visitors tonight already. Would you really blame me for enforcing my edicts?"

I lowered my hand and bent the paper slightly, keeping it out of Ailill's sight so he wouldn't notice me checking it for signs of a specter near Master Tailor. Or a foolish Jurij. But it was too soon for that. "Your home is a mess."

Ailill raised an eyebrow and stood straighter, dropping his elbow off the mantelpiece. "Am I to believe these boys are on a cleaning mission?"

"*Boys?*"

He crossed his arms and shrugged. "They are all boys to me."

Then am I nothing but a little girl to you? "What happened to the spec—the Ailills?"

"You just saw one tonight."

"Why haven't they cleaned up after you?" I looked him over, head to foot, noticing the way his usually tight clothing seemed to bunch and hang loose here and there. It was dirty, too, no longer the sharp, dark black he once wore. "Or cleaned *you?*"

Ailill tossed his head back and started pacing the room, taking a step away from the fireplace and me. "I am grateful, as ever, for your apparent concern."

I scoffed. "I'm sorry I asked. If you want to rot away in this castle when you're finally free to go where you please, that's your business. But my friends—"

"Free to go where I please?" Ailill stopped pacing, his back to the door and the sliver of moonlight let in when Jurij had opened it. He scuffed a boot against the floor. "And where would I go, pray tell? To the tavern to fill myself with drink? To the fields to whack sheep with sticks?" He shook his head. "No. I am quite trapped in this place. Same as you, or any other of the oblivious people here, but it feels worse when you know just how trapped we all are."

I pretended to pay attention as I cautiously flipped the page open just enough to see a new set of feet in front of the bars. Master Tailor stood, shaking Jaron beside him. I tucked the paper quickly into my sash and made a show of tossing the too-long bit of hair over my shoulder, even though it swung right back into place. "A little company might do you some good. Even if it is just some sheep."

"I have tried company," Ailill sneered as he looked away. "I did not find it worth the trouble. And I do not think you have found company much worth the trouble, either."

I resisted the urge to cross my arms and instead pulled the coin out of my sash, leaving the gold bangle tucked in beside it. I tossed the coin onto the table, kicking up a small cloud of dust. "Did you send this to me?"

Ailill seemed hesitant to move, but he looked back over his shoulder, keen to see what I'd tossed on the table. It glistened in the dark, just like his veiled curtain's rings. He frowned and dropped his arms, crossing the room to step beside me before I could blink. "Where did you get this?" he asked, holding it up to the firelight.

"From you, I thought."

Ailill pinched his lips into a thin line, his eyes mesmerized by the flicker of flame over the golden coin. "Is this the coin you have been playing with? The one you got from that girl and showed to your consorts?"

I snatched the coin from his fingers, a shiver running down my back as his leather-coated fingertips scuffed against mine. My wounded finger stung. "You've been watching me. On that paper."

Ailill's gaze darted down to my hand, to the coin that glistened there. "Yes. It gets rather boring."

I tucked the coin back into my sash, not sure I wanted to part with it now if it wasn't some part of his scheme. "So why are you surprised I have it?"

"Because I do not see the goings-on in full color, now do I?" He reached forward, and I stepped back, determined not to let him touch my hand. But he was after the paper tucked in my sash. I felt almost faint from embarrassment, thinking he'd noticed my injured fingertip and wanted to fix it, like he did that first time we met. Or the first time *I* met *him*. He unfolded the paper and examined it thoughtfully. "I wondered why you paid such close attention to the coin, but I did not dream it was anything but a copper."

I tried pulling the paper from his hands—*Jurij*—but Ailill lifted the paper higher, out of my reach, still examining it. "No. No color." I paused in my attempt to grab the paper, my heart stilling. *Of course. Jurij would have had to find a key to unlock the cells. They're probably still in there, waiting.* "See?"

Ailill held the paper up so I could see the moving drawing. Master Tailor was no longer in his cell. He and the rest of the men —even Luuk—were in a place I didn't recognize at first. A sparse room on the third floor that contained the lord's throne. It hadn't had a hole in the back wall when I'd last seen it.

Ailill turned the paper back around and studied it, his face hardly registering any surprise. *He's not that stupid. He planned to let Jurij free them.* "Ah," he said at last, his eyebrows raised. "You were wondering about the Ailills? Here they come. Just in time to stop them." He turned the paper back to the other side, and I saw Master Tailor jolt as a score of specters circled around him. The men drew near each other, back to back, and Jaron's fists went up like he expected a fight. Several specters pushed the throne back over the hole, sliding it perfectly in place beneath the sole decoration on the wall, a blade hanging downward, its tip pointed to whoever dared sit in the chair below it.

Elgar. Back above the throne. But how?

Ailill nodded and crumpled the paper, tossing it into the flame beside him. I jumped as the fire sparked outward. "Well, that is that," he said, putting his hands on his waist, his elbows akimbo. "A night in my cells for trespassing just became a life-time sentence."

"What?"

"I do not make all the laws, Olivière." He raised a finger to stop me from speaking. "I do not wish to hear it, considering the laws you passed yourself. Just be content I had the Ailills stop them from proceeding. A step into that hole carries the penalty of death." He turned and walked out of the room.

CHAPTER TWENTY-TWO

Even though I rushed after him, Ailill was nowhere to be found. "Ailill!" I hadn't addressed him by his name in perhaps a thousand years. "Ailill! I'm not done with you."

A blast of cold air flew into the entryway through the open garden door. I had to hold my skirt down. "Ailill?" He wasn't to be found in the garden. "Ailill!"

Forget it. Ailill had an annoying habit of making himself vanish or appear whenever you wanted the exact opposite. I stood on my tiptoes to grab one of the unused torches from the wall. If the entryway was an example, I'd have to expect the rest of the castle to be equally dark. The fire from the dining hall breathed life into the torch. I stared at it, remembering the fire in the men's eyes before I'd uttered my curse. *The men may have explored the castle in darkness. But I'm not concealing my presence here.*

Let him come.

Ailill clearly had no intention of stopping me, as not a single specter appeared to block my path. I climbed first one set of stairs and then the next to the third floor. The disarray continued as I climbed. Open doors creaking in the cold dampness of the hallway were the only obstacles in my path.

He won't frighten me. It was as much a message to myself as it was to him. *If he does mean to frighten me.* There was more to this darkness, this disarray, than Ailill let on. It was almost like he'd lost all fire, all fight—all reason to carry on and live.

I stopped as I reached the third floor. Elgar was there, just a few steps away. How? It should have been gone, lost to time. How did Ailill... ? I shook my head. It wasn't the time. My friends were at the end of the hallway.

No sense in going in unarmed. The blade is more mine than his.

I strode into the darkened throne room. A blast of absolutely frigid air turned my breath into puffs of white smoke. I resisted the urge to shiver and held the torch higher.

The faintest violet light glowed from behind the throne, now that I knew to look for it. I wasn't sure if the shiver that ran down my back was due to the cold or the familiar glow.

Pushing aside the throne got my friends sentenced to his dungeon for life. But whose life? Theirs or his? What if he died first?

I shook my head. *You're not going to hurt him again. You've seen what fighting can do.* I swallowed, too embarrassed to dwell on my thoughts any further.

I strode up the patched carpet to the throne, my hand already outstretched for the blade, when I heard a rustle beside me. I swung the torch in that direction. There was nothing. Nothing but that book on the stand Ailill kept, open and yellowed.

The book. I strode over to the stand. It was open to the page I'd so recently held, the wrinkled page Ailill had tossed into the fire. Impossibly, it was there in that book, bound within it, showing Master Tailor back in the cell. The writing was still there on the back. I shivered and flipped forward more pages, each with a drawing of a person. My eyes quickly darted from one to the next until I found an ink silhouette of my sister, lying in bed, her eyes wide open. Almost as if she knew I was watching her.

I jumped back. So this was the source of the pages. The lord who was "always watching." *Where did he get this book?*

I felt a burning at my waist, and I reached inside my sash, withdrawing the golden bangle. The coin grew hot as well, but I left it there. Once I held the golden bangle over the book, the metal burned my hand, and I cried out, dropping it. I bent over, about to pick it up.

"You ought to have kept hold of that. It could have saved you from prison." Ailill, the ever-watching lord, stepped out from the shadows. He snatched the bangle up from the floor before I could grab it. "But as you are so keen to find your friends, I would be glad to let you join them."

He waved a hand at the doorway, and a dozen specters entered the throne room. He turned his attention to the bangle in his hand, dismissing me as a dozen pale hands reached out to take hold of me.

～

"HE EXPECTS us to stay here for life?" Tayton paced back and forth, back and forth, his footsteps on the cold stone floor echoing miserably in my head. "And he doesn't have the guts to tell us that? Just pass a message along through you, and we just accept that?" He gripped the bars of our shared cell and did his best to shake them. They barely moved, but they made a terrible clatter.

I cradled my forehead. "Tayton. Stop that. Please."

"Ugh!" screamed Tayton. He kicked the bars, causing more of a racket. The specter guarding us didn't even flinch. Tayton had already tried sticking his hand through to grab him, but of course, he was just out of reach.

"Tayton, you're not helping." Jaron's voice was recognizable from the cell beside ours, even if I couldn't see anything more than his arm sticking through the bars. I found out he'd been locked up with Luuk and Darwyn, and that the specters had to pry Darwyn and Tayton apart. "Quiet down. Some of us are trying to think."

Tayton kicked the bars one more time for good measure before plopping down on the pile of hay beside me. He scowled, as if daring me to comment on the last kick.

Jaron cleared his throat. "Thank you. Noll, please explain again. Without outbursts from the audience this time."

I threw my hands up in the air. "I don't *know*. He's being stubborn. And secretive. And frustrating. As he *often* is. He knew you were coming. He knew Jurij had left to go free you. He let it all happen so he could catch you in his throne room."

Jurij's frustrated snort came from the other side of my cell's wall, where he, Sindri, and Master Tailor were imprisoned together. "For what?"

I crawled closer to the bars to make my voice carry more clearly. "You tell me. You somehow knew to move the throne." I eyed the specter in front of my cell as I spoke, but he continued to stare straight ahead, oblivious to the prisoners in front of him. Some of Ailill's contempt was etched deeply into his wrinkled face.

"That book." Jurij's hand appeared out from his cell, as if to confirm I was speaking with him. "We found the source of those moving pages."

"I saw." I didn't mention I'd seen Elfriede. "It looks like everyone in the village has his or her own page."

"Yeah, well, we flipped through it. We found what must have been one of our pages because we saw ourselves there in the throne room, looking at the book."

Another hand appeared out of the cell with Jurij's. "Only, on the page, there was something strange about the throne in the throne room." Sindri. "There was a hole in the wall behind it. We could see it on the page, clear as day."

"And what about that... it was a sword, wasn't it?" asked Tayton. "Above the throne? I didn't think those things were real."

I wondered if Jaron remembered giving me the same blade, in a time that did and didn't exist.

"It was all suspicious," added Darwyn. "So I thought we should see if the hole was really there behind the throne. Some of his servants were waiting behind it." He laughed miserably. "I didn't think... that is, I'm sorry if that's why we're here."

Tayton plastered himself against the opposite wall, holding out his hand toward Darwyn's cell. "It's not your fault! You couldn't have known." Another hand appeared in place of Jaron's. After stretching and bending awkwardly, their fingers grazed one another's.

"It's my fault!" The trembling wail from Darwyn's and Jaron's cell reminded me that Luuk was still half a child, even if he'd grown taller and spoke deeper. "I shouldn't have come alone. I knew I'd mess it up." Despite his physical differences, Luuk really seemed the least changed by the curse's breaking.

"Enough!" thundered Jaron. "We all agreed to this risk. Let's just figure out why the lord let us get as far as we did, and what exactly we did to get thrown in here."

"You mean besides entering his castle against his edict?" Master Tailor asked.

I shook my head, even if he couldn't see it. "That wasn't going to be a lifelong offense. He purposely baited you to the throne room."

"Not because of the book," added Sindri. "I mean, he gave us pages from it. That can't have been something he'd jail us for."

"Then the throne. And the hole," said Jurij.

I gripped the nearest bar. I'd seen the hole, and he hadn't stepped out of the shadows until I'd read the book. No, until I'd dropped the golden bangle. I patted my sash, looking for my golden coin. I panicked. There was nothing there. I shot up and removed my sash, shaking it out.

"What are you doing?" Tayton twisted away from his attempted handhold with Darwyn to stare at me. "Is there a mouse in your clothing?"

"What's she doing?" Jurij's voice sounded panicked. "Is she undressing?" I can't say if he was panicked or angry about that.

"*No.*" I kept shaking the sash. "My golden coin is gone."

Jurij sighed. Definitely anger this time. "Oh, no. How will we be able to buy anything now? Oh, wait. We'll never need to buy anything again because we're never leaving this castle."

"What if he doesn't feed us?" Luuk's voice shook.

"We'll be noticed! The women won't stand for us suddenly disappearing." Jaron spoke with calm confidence.

Master Tailor snapped. "Speak for yourself! My former wife and sister aren't speaking to me. Even Luuk's former goddess won't help."

"Coll," interrupted Jaron, "we'll be fine. You know that. We didn't come here without realizing the risk."

"Elfriede! Or Nissa!" I stomped my foot. "Luuk, Nissa isn't angry with you."

"But my mother and Auntie are, and she's with them."

"I know, but Nissa feels different." I stared at Tayton. "And maybe not all of the wives care, but Roslyn does, Darwyn. They'll notice we're missing. They'll come."

"Sure. If we're not dead before then." Sindri coughed.

"Why did you mention Elfriede?" Jurij's question was quiet under all the comments, but I heard it clearly.

"I saw her in the book. She was wide awake in bed. Almost like she knew something was wrong."

"How would she know?" interrupted Sindri.

Master Tailor spoke next. "Does it matter? If there's a chance someone knows we're here—"

"How is a woman who happens to be awake at night a sign that she knows we're here?" Darwyn dropped Tayton's hand. His voice had a little edge of that gruffness I expected from him as a child. "Does it surprise you a woman would be so upset about things she'd be unable—"

"Enough!" Jaron spat. "Okay, everyone? Enough." The dungeons fell silent, but for the crackling of the torches. "We haven't even spent a full night here. No need to panic. People will notice we're missing."

"And know to look for us in the lord's castle?" Tayton ran a hand through the short, thick hair atop his forehead. "It's hopeless. Why did we even come here?"

"We wanted answers!" Something clanged in Jaron's cell, and I just made out the sole of a boot kicking against the bars. "And goddess help me, we at least deserve that!"

My eyes flicked guiltily to the ground, even though only Tayton was there to witness it.

Jaron continued unabated. "A lifetime in this prison? After the commune? He hopes to threaten *me* with a lifetime in this prison?" He scoffed, and I could practically hear him spit. "With my friends here? With someone to talk to? With endless things to want and wish for, with something else to think of other than the bitch who sent me to my torment?"

"Jaron," Master Tailor's voice wavered.

Jaron seemed to catch himself. "Coll, I'm sorry. I don't blame Alvilda. Now I know how she feels. I'm not in love with her. Not in the slightest. If someone asked me to be with her now, I'd be just as repulsed at the idea as she was." He paused. "No. You know what? She gets just a *tiny* bit of blame. Maybe a whole lot of blame. She could have just ordered me to sit in the corner, and I'd have been fine. She could have carved me a little hovel outside of her door and told me to lay in it like a dog, and I'd have felt better than I did in that commune."

Darwyn must have seen something on Jaron's face that the rest of us weren't privy to. He sounded alarmed. "Jaron, please. This isn't helping."

"This isn't *helping*? It's helping me just fine!" I heard Jaron's boots pound over the cell floor. "So she loved someone else. I get that. Oh, boy, do I understand what it's like to love someone you can't have." He paused again for a few paces. "But it wasn't the same for her, was it? The one she loved also loved her back. And she could go more than a breath without thinking about her."

"Jaron. Stop." Master Tailor's voice was firm. Louder than I'd ever heard him speak before. "You think it would have been better being at her side with that feeling she'd never love you back? It wasn't."

A lump at Tayton's throat bobbed noticeably. He seemed to be straining to contain himself.

"Ha!" Jaron's laugh was anything but genuine. "You had a roof over your head without holes in it. You had warm food in your belly. Sons to call your own." Jaron's voice wavered so, I could almost see the tears forming in his eyes. "You had someone to love you."

"But that someone wasn't her." Master Tailor sighed. "Now I know just how important my sons' love was. But it didn't matter then. Everything was so messed up for us. The important things didn't matter."

"Jaron." It was my voice that called his name. "You weren't unloved. I know someone who didn't forget you."

I had no idea if Jaron could even guess at my mother's affections, if his childhood memories were wiped out after years of suffering for Alvilda.

Jaron's voice came closer, and I saw his hands wrap around the bars of his cell. "Noll! Goddess, Noll. How could I have forgotten? You spent a time in the commune with me."

Tayton's head shot up, his eyes wide with wonder.

Jaron's voice drifted, like he was searching his memory. "I remembered thinking you were nice. You talked, unlike the other men..." He stopped. "Why? Why would I think you were there with me?"

I stared at Tayton. "I was. For a month before the curse broke. I just didn't think you'd be able to remember."

"That month that no one can clearly remember." It was Master Taylor who spoke. "What happened then?"

"You wanted answers?" It'd been so long since he'd participated in the conversation, I'd almost forgotten that Jurij was in the cell behind the wall I leaned on. "Then you should have asked Noll."

It was time I shared what they needed to know. It was time I shared everything.

"I'm the first goddess."

CHAPTER TWENTY-THREE

E verything was silent in the cells on either side of me. Tayton stared. Even Luuk had stopped sniffling.

Jaron was the first to respond. "The *first* goddess?"

"Yes," I admitted. "I placed the curse on men."

"How?" asked Tayton. "Why?"

I felt my heart thumping hard against my ribs. "I think it had to do with my powers as a woman. I don't know why or how exactly, but I was there. In the past."

"You're making this up!" Darwyn sounded angry, angrier than I'd heard him in years. "Noll, this isn't helping."

"She's not making it up." Jurij seemed strangely confident for someone who'd just been arguing the opposite a few hours before. "Why else would our curse suddenly be broken? Why is everyone unclear on what exactly happened the month before?"

Darwyn wasn't deterred. "Because *Noll* is the first goddess? The woman from the tales at the Returnings? The one who cursed men long before we were born?" He snorted. "Yeah."

"He has a point," added Sindri. "How is that even possible?"

Luuk piped up. "Noll said she was the elf queen!"

Darwyn laughed, and it wasn't very nice. "Don't tell me you actually believed that."

"Hey!" I jumped to my feet. "Quiet! Do you want me to explain things or not?"

Even though Tayton was the only one I could see, I could feel the furious energy vanish from the air.

Jaron spoke loudly over the others. "Go on, Noll. And no one interrupt her."

My gaze flicked quickly to the specter standing across from my cell. *Ailill can't hear what I say on those strange book pages. But the specters can hear, right? Does he somehow hear through their ears?* I opened my mouth. "Some of you already know about this, but there's a cavern—"

The door to my cell opened, the specter producing a key from his inner coat pocket and pushing his way in before I could finish my sentence. Tayton stood, eyeing the specter warily. "Now wait a minute."

The specter grabbed my forearm and dragged me out of the cell.

"Where are you taking her?" asked Tayton.

I could finally see into the cells on either side of me, the line of worried faces pressed up against the bars. I had only an instant to meet each of their eyes as the specter locked the door to my cell behind us and placed the key back in his coat pocket.

"What are you doing?" demanded Darwyn. "Don't tell me she's forbidden to talk about this!"

"Well, if that isn't proof that Noll speaks the truth," added Master Tailor, "I don't know what is."

"No!" Jaron gripped the bars and shook them wildly in vain. "Not when we're so close. Not when—"

But I had just enough time to send Jurij a warning glance amidst all the shouting and cursing letting loose from the cells. *Don't talk about what I told you. At least not yet.* I was dragged out the door and back into the chillingly cold third-floor hall.

I tugged against the specter's grip on my arm, but I had no hope of resisting. "Ailill!" I dug my heels into the floor. "I mean *you*, not him! Let me go!"

The specter hesitated, and I saw something strange flicker across the void of his eyes. He was old, this one. Older than many of them, now that I looked closely. Washed pale with time. A shade of a long-forgotten man.

"I'm sorry," I said, and I meant it.

His fingers loosened, and I recognized something of the lord in his quieter moments. Regret. Longing.

His mouth opened.

"Leave us."

It wasn't the specter Ailill who'd spoken. The specter dropped his hand from my arm and turned, retreating into the darkness at the other end of the hallway, not even sparing me one last glance. He passed the current lord in black, pale but still breathing. Ailill stood, his arms crossed, in front of the throne room. He looked me over from head to toe and nodded. "Come in here." He vanished inside the throne room, leaving me alone in the hallway.

He gives an order, and I'm to obey? He once had to do the same when I spoke, but he did everything he could to resist me. He should have known I could do the same. He'd left me completely on my own in the castle. I could just walk right by, go after that specter about to speak, or walk out the front door, come back with an army.

But no. I'd tried that once before and wasn't pleased with the results. Besides, I had no doubt the specters would appear from the shadows to stop me if I tried.

I tossed my shoulders back and followed Ailill into the throne room. He had let all but one torch extinguish, so I could barely make him out atop the throne. If not for the glisten of the golden bangle he let dance over his fingers, I might not have known he was there at all.

"I tried sparing your friends the harshest of punishments. I truly did."

I hadn't spent all of this time with Ailill—*parrying* with Ailill —not to be able to divine the meaning hidden beneath those words. "Of course. That's why we were unceremoniously dumped into your cells for life." I marched toward the throne, closing the distance between us. "And now? What harsher punishments await us?"

The golden bangle stopped twirling on Ailill's fingers. "Us? No, you are exempt from any further punishment, I gather."

"You gather?"

Ailill let the golden bangle slide over his hand to his arm. I was reminded revoltingly of his brother Elric. "This is not a game, Noll. I spared your friends from death, and then you try to condemn them to it."

"I didn't think it was a game. It never is that simple between us." I jutted my chin out and climbed the step to the raised platform so I could look down on him as I spoke. Elgar glistened faintly as I did. I pointed at it. "Where did you find that?"

Ailill looked up at it briefly, then turned away. "I cannot tell you."

Convenient. "All right. Keep your secrets. But may I ask what would have condemned them to death?"

He rolled his eyes and looked away. "You told them you were the first goddess."

I dug my nails into the palm of my injured hand, ignoring the pain. "But... wasn't I?"

He rested his elbows on the throne's armrests and placed his fingertips together. "I suppose you were. In this village, at least."

"In *this* village?" I thought about the village in the past, how I felt like it both was and was not my own.

"And then you were going to give them a map to the heart of the village, let them find their way there if I ever felt gracious enough to let them out of here."

I didn't really think he was planning to let them out, but I let that comment slide. "The cavern?" I decided not to point out that Jurij and Luuk already knew about it, although he must have known as much.

"The pool there." He tilted his head slightly. "Surely you remember the beat of the heart beneath its waters? You rode its heartbeats to the past. I was as sure of that as I was that you were the first goddess returned, that day you first trespassed in my castle."

"So why didn't you tell me?"

"Tell you what? That you had doomed the entire village to its wretched existence? You clearly had not yet traveled to the past. Would you have believed me?"

"No. Maybe not," I admitted. "But it would have been better to hear that than be pushed and pulled around, thinking you were nothing more than a heartless monster."

Ailill threw his hands in the air. "Again, back to that.

Certainly. You would have just considered me a ranting madman. One who kept entirely to himself and then droned on about a past long ago where you cursed mankind. Would you have fallen in love with that?"

In love? "Were you ever concerned about me falling in love with you?"

Ailill slapped the armrest with one hand. "You doubt that? After all you now know about me?" My heart felt almost like it'd stopped beating. Then the hope that lingered there in that breath between beats floated away as Ailill shook his head and turned away. "After a hundred or more lifetimes, I was ready to be done with this curse. And I would not get there by vanishing the moment you saw my face."

Of course. He wanted me to love him to free his own soul. Not because he loved me. "But that's what happened anyway in the end, isn't it?"

Ailill shrugged. "I had given up by then. It was not the first time I had. But I had hoped it would be the last."

I felt a sharp pain in my chest, even if I couldn't stop the anger that invaded my body every time I stood near him. "You lived this long only to give up? It shouldn't have mattered what I thought of you! That's no reason to give up on living."

Ailill laughed harshly, but I knew it wasn't because I'd said anything amusing. "I am surprised to hear you talk so! You, who became a shell of herself at the idea of her beloved marrying her sister. A beloved you were not even compelled to love, a beloved you had hope of one day no longer desiring."

I squeezed my arms tight across my chest, swallowing back tears. "How would you know how I was before Jurij and Elfriede's Returning? I thought you weren't 'always watching' after all. You seemed surprised when I first arrived in the castle."

Ailill pointed to the book on the stand and nodded. Without waiting for his instructions, I walked over and flipped it open. A man sat beside the fire in his home, a woman at his side, a child at his feet. Whether one of the few remaining families from the curse or a new one formed in the days after, I couldn't say. I flipped again to a random page, seeing Darwyn's mother sweeping out her bakery, a smile on her face, her lips moving. She must have been talking to someone off page. *Roslyn.* The two had found happiness in their new arrangement, as friends and baker-women. It seemed like weeks ago, but it was really just earlier that evening.

"I did look," said Ailill from behind me. "I watched this village evolve for countless years on those pages. A mere echo of what was going on out there, but all I would be able to see."

I didn't say anything. I turned a page again and saw a man sleeping in a bed. Another page had a man and woman clinking their mugs together and drinking a toast. After a few moments, Vena appeared on the page, dropping off more mugs on the table between them.

"I saw my sister on those pages," continued Ailill. "Silently, she worked. Organizing the village after the curse. Guiding the women to gain more confidence. Blessing newfound families." I heard him sigh. "She never created one of her own. Not that it surprised me. She did not seem the type to forget, and there would be no man worthy of her forgiveness, even if he was altered."

I turned the page again, trying not to think about Avery's bloodlust and trying to imagine her settling down as a leader. I couldn't picture her with her own children, either.

"She never came for me." Something in Ailill's voice seemed about to crack. "I wondered if she even knew I was alive. Or if she even cared."

I stopped. "But they must have known they were left with a lord?"

Ailill waved a hand. "They knew the castle shook when they looked at it. They were scared. Or maybe they did not think they had left behind anything worth going back for."

"But your servants—"

"Did not yet exist." He drummed his fingers on the throne's armrest and smiled, haltingly. "I had not died yet. They could have sent their men after me, but no one thought to. They could have come even if the ground shook, but Avery did not try."

"I added the earthquakes to protect you. I was worried after Avery stabbed your—stabbed *him*. I thought she might hurt you."

"Who knows? To me, that would have been preferable to isolation. Even if she had killed me, I would have sprung to life once more."

"I... I'm sorry." I turned back to the book, more out of shame than a real need to flip through its pages.

"Sorry for the earthquakes that kept my sister from me, or sorry for the whole appalling mess you made of things?"

I flipped to another page. My mother. Alone in bed. Her brows furrowed even in slumber. Alive because of him. "Both," I said at last.

"Of course—" Ailill stopped himself. It was as if he had expected me to say "neither" and had readied himself for the argument we almost always had. "Well. I do not expect Avery would have sought me out regardless."

Mother tossed and turned in bed. I felt bad that even her dreams couldn't offer her peace. I saw the foot of Elfriede's bed in the image. Her sheets were all crumpled.

Ailill continued his story. "I grew older, clinging to that book, living for a time off food stores my brother and father had prepared for some unknown purpose. And when it ran out, I had the food they gave—well... I had food at least. I saw my sister die. I watched as everyone I ever knew faded into thin air. And when the day at last came for me to join them..." He stopped, and his leather attire squeaked uncomfortably in the silence behind me. "Well. I came back. This time with a pale old man for company."

I traced my finger across the dancing ink on the page, wondering what it'd be like to only see those you love on its pages, to watch them fading away until you were left with nothing but strangers. I wanted to ask so many questions, but I wasn't sure if dredging up memories of what I'd done would set my friends free. I wasn't even sure what was so important about keeping the cavern's "heart" a secret that he would summon me to stand beside him even after all our fighting.

Ailill's voice was closer when he spoke again. "In any case. The story repeated itself, only with strangers filling that book's pages. And repeated itself. And repeated itself, only, the women fell into a comfortable routine of being objects of worship after a few ages. There was no need for anyone to organize the village. 'The lord' was the leader. The leader they hardly needed or cared about. But their lack of caring emboldened me. I stopped relying on food from the same sources and sent the servants out shop-

416

ping. I had no lack of copper with which to pay for it. My father had stockpiled quite a bit, and his father and grandfather before him." An arm clothed in black reached over my shoulder, and a dark-gloved hand rested a mere hair's breadth from mine. He turned the page. "I had the servants collect all the weapons, tossed aside in trunks and sheds, forgotten generations earlier. Nobody alive recognized their purpose or cared that we took them. I made sure the idea of swords faded into the realm of myth, so person would never harm person again. An ideal world for all, in a way. Just take the free will of all men away and imprison me. Life was very peaceful."

I thought of Elgar, guiltily, and wondered how he'd found the blade at all, when I'd left it in a tree for Jaron to find for me. The sword seemed to exist outside of reason, like there were two in the village at once, one over Ailill's throne and the other in the tree.

Before I could ask, Ailill spoke again. "Eventually, I stopped caring." He turned the page. This one showed the crowded tavern, Vena running across the book, men's heads thrown back in laughter. The page followed a man with his arm around a woman's waist, his other hand holding hers as they swung around the crowded room dancing, tripping, and nearly tumbling over with laughter. "I would open the book on occasion, but I tended to find it hurt too much to look. To pretend I meant anything to the people in these pages."

It was my father. My *father* dancing with some other woman. Who was she? I couldn't put a name to her face, but I really didn't care. To see the look of delight on my father's features when he held a woman besides my mother made me gasp and turn away.

By turning, I found myself perfectly positioned in Ailill's arms. The torchlight danced and flickered across his brown hair. His dark eyes bore into mine, and I felt his arm shift behind me, move ever closer to the center of my back.

"Do you blame me for so seldom looking?"

"No." I swallowed and tore my eyes away. My hands gripped the sides of my skirt. I was unsure what to do with them. How to move away—or if I even wanted to. Ailill dropped his arm and took a step back, taking with him a raging blaze of something powerful between us I hadn't even realized he'd brought with him.

A glint of light caught my attention on the floor just beside the stand. I bent down and picked it up—it was the coin I'd lost. I held it out between Ailill and me, letting the firelight dance off its luster. "When you took that bangle away," I said, nodding at the bangle around his arm, "you said it would have saved me from a lifetime in prison. So what does this coin, or any golden copper, mean?"

Ailill ran a hand over his bangle. "It means you have the right to know. To see. To rule over this village."

I twisted the coin this way and that, not believing that even something so bright and beautiful could give me the right to that. "Like your bangle?" I asked, thinking of the one Elric wore.

The corner of Ailill's lips twitched. "And the dozens of others like it." He removed the bangle and held it out in front of him in echo of my stance with the coin. "I got so bored with receiving them, I started to use them for practical purposes." He smiled, and I thought of how the golden rings held the veil over the table aloft, how they clattered as they fell to the ground when I ordered him to rip it. "And then I began to leave the remainder behind. I thought it dangerous to populate one village with over a hundred such tokens, solely because I was sent back time after time after time."

I gripped the coin tightly in my palm and lowered my hand. "You keep talking about our village as if there are others."

Ailill smiled again, and it didn't feel like he was mocking me. More like he was impressed his pet could perform new tricks. He slid the bangle back over his arm and gestured around with both hands. "We are surrounded by mountains, Olivière. Everywhere you look, there are mountains." He stepped back, walking toward his throne. "And people are born, and live, and die in this village, and they never seem to think about what is on the other side of them."

"But..." I frowned. "How can there be? The mountains end? And other people live there?"

Ailill sat back on his throne, crossing his legs so one ankle rested on the other knee. "Not quite, but close enough."

"So why haven't any of these people noticed us?"

"Who says they have not?" Ailill gestured at the book behind me. "Where do you think I came by such a tome, a book that shows the people of this village at play?"

"*At play*? Is that what our lives are to someone like you? Just a game?"

Ailill rested his fingertips together, always looking somehow both bored and in charge whenever he sat there. "There are greater forces than a simple lord in a single village, Olivière. Even one who frustratingly will not die." His eyes seemed to search the ceiling, as if looking for a person who might be listening. "And whether my vexing immortality is still in place remains to be seen."

"What do you mean? Because you found your goddess, you..." I stopped. It was only my not being born yet that had kept him alive.

Ailill shook his head and waved a hand. "Do not worry yourself. I might be freed from the curse at last. It is exactly what I wanted for many, many years."

I gripped the coin harder and felt its smooth edges push into my skin. "But you can't die!"

Ailill raised his eyebrows. "I am touched you care." His voice betrayed his meaning, his sarcasm back in full force, dripping over the sentiment.

"I *do* care!" I stomped a foot, feeling like the little elf queen not getting her way. "Must you continue to be so frustrating?"

Ailill stood and stepped down the platform. "My sentiments exactly."

"I caused this. I caused all of this, I know." I looked up as Ailill stopped moving, the surprise clearly written on his face. "I want you to have a chance to live this time."

Ailill froze but said nothing.

"I want all of the men to have a chance to choose what makes them happy. And the women understand that the happiness they had before was never *really* happiness. Not when there wasn't a choice. Although I don't want things to go back to the way they were, either. *Everyone* in the village deserves to be treated well."

"Olivière—"

"No, let me speak! For once, just let me talk without misunderstanding and berating me. Give me some answers!" I threw my hands up. "The hole behind the throne. That leads to this place beyond the mountains?"

Ailill took a step closer, his hand outstretched. "Yes, but—"

"And knowing about that is the danger?" I held out my coin again. "Unless you hold a golden copper, knowing that there's a world beyond the mountains somehow justifies imprisonment? For *life*?"

"Olivière, *yes*, but not now." Ailill brushed past, laying his hand on my shoulder for the gentlest of shoves.

My eyebrows furrowed at his look of concern. "What is..." The last word died on my tongue.

The moving ink drawing of the tavern had erupted into chaos. Man after man came to blows with each other, some with bare fists, others with broken glasses or even chairs raised over their heads. Things moved so quickly, tables turning, plates crashing, the silent fury screaming across the page, and I couldn't find my father. The page was supposed to be centered on him.

Ailill furrowed his brow, one hand marking his place while his other raced through the pages. "I was afraid something like this might happen."

"Like what?" I asked stupidly. "A fight in the tavern?" It looked worrying, but it was nothing like the battle I'd caused in the village of the past.

Ailill continued to scan the pages. "Too much freedom. Sometimes men cannot be trusted with it." He grunted. "As you have seen." He stopped flipping the pages, and his eyes widened.

"What is it?" I asked, leaning in beside him for a better look.

A man I didn't recognize plunged a shard of glass into another man's back. The second man crumbled, his head lolling forward and then his body vanishing, only his clothing cluttering the floor.

I gasped. "Someone might have *died*! We have to stop them! Find whose page that was! Find out if he was killed or hurt or..."

Ailill let the pages fall back, leaving the page he'd held open, the page belonging to my father. Bright red burst onto the paper, the first shade of color I'd seen on any of the pages. It dripped down, like spilled ink. Like blood. And then the page went blank before vanishing in a surge of bright violet.

"FATHER!" I screamed, clawing at the book. It was he who was stabbed on that other man's page. He who crumpled. Ailill's arms slipped around me, his hands clutched together at my abdomen. Tears streamed down my face. Endless, white-hot tears.

Ailill's cheek pressed against my temple. It was warm, not at all like the cold marble I remembered. "They watch us now," he whispered, barely audible over the sobs choking out past my throat. His lips brushed close against my skin, like the flutter of petals in a breeze against my cheek as I lay in the lily fields. *Lily fields.* I'd associated those, that feeling of serenity, with Jurij for so long.

"They are always watching." He took a deep breath. "But we cannot let them win."

CHAPTER TWENTY-FOUR

I strode out of the throne room before I could even think.

"Olivière, where are you going?" Ailill grabbed me by the shoulder and spun me around. He cradled the book in which I'd watched my father. I'd watched his page burn.

Father's not dead. He's not! But I couldn't just stand there. I had to know.

Ailill frowned. "Do you intend to run all the way to the tavern?"

My stomach hurt, and my throat felt dry. I didn't know what I intended. I was going to head down the stairs and just run until I got there. Until I could prove to myself it wasn't true. My eyes wandered over Ailill's shoulder to the door leading to the cells.

I spun out of Ailill's grip toward my friends. "I have to go!"

"Now what are you planning?" asked Ailill as he walked quickly along beside me. "The door is that way."

"Aren't we going to free them?" I gestured at the door to the cells. "They could help. They know the crowd at the tavern."

Ailill didn't respond to my question. "We will take the carriage. It will prove faster."

I started. "You'll come with me?"

There was a slight bob to Ailill's throat. "Of course."

"But you never leave the castle." I frowned. "Hardly ever, that is."

"This is too important." He muttered something to himself about how "the Ailills would restrain them" and disappeared down the staircase to the second floor.

Several specters appeared from the dungeon and walked past me at a brisk pace, following after him. I may as well have been invisible. One bumped into me with an echoing clatter as he passed and didn't even slow down.

I stood there a moment longer, staring at the dungeon door they hadn't even closed behind them.

My father needed me. Because he couldn't be dead. It had to be some mistake. But he wasn't the only one who needed me.

Something glistened from the floor beside my feet, and I bent to pick it up. The specter who'd brushed past me had dropped the cell key. It was almost like he was asking me to free them while Ailill was distracted.

~

THE BOOK on my lap jostled with the bump of the carriage, and I was afraid my tight grip on its edges would make the thing crumble beneath my fingers. Up close, it wasn't really in the best of shape—although when I considered how old it was, I was surprised it hadn't faded to dust years before. My fingers traced over the scene of the tavern men fighting, from Vena's point of view, as she and Elweard cowered behind the counter, their arms wrapped tightly around one another.

I wanted to throw up. My mind was racing. I hadn't felt this anxious, this *awake*, since the day I'd led Avery and the other women to Elric in the castle. And thinking about that, I realized no one in this village—in this present-day village—had seen physical fighting before.

Ailill tapped his knee with his fingers, displaying worry for the first time in all the time I'd known him as an adult. "The Ailills can restrain them," he said, for the tenth time at least. "They will have to."

I flipped the pages until I found one with a better view of the brawl. It followed a man I didn't know as he threw a punch and then received one.

Ailill had been talking to himself since we'd left the throne room. He touched the fingers on one hand as if he were counting. "There are a 104 of them. Some more frail and older than others." The specters, I assumed. Even though some certainly looked older than others, I hadn't suspected any were "frail." "There are 564 men in the village, minus the seven currently in the cells."

I stopped flipping through the book to glare at him. His knowledge of exactly how many men were in his village would have impressed me—assuming it was right—if it wasn't compounded by the fact that he still intended to keep my friends in his prison.

"I will not have them bring swords," continued Ailill. "The longer the people go without thinking about those, the better." He ran a gloved hand over his face. "But just because I secured all the swords in the fifth life does not mean they cannot turn their tools into instruments of death." He laughed sourly. "I seem to remember women made great use of pitchforks and axes at one point."

I swallowed, too distraught to think of the mob of violent women, instead thinking of the glass shard in Father's back. I turned the book back to where Father's page had been. I felt the page that had been behind it, the tanner's wife, asleep in her bed. Completely free of the pain and worries that filled my chest.

Because I couldn't quite believe Father was dead. Page or no page, I had to be mistaken. Or if not, then I'd just have to undo it. Somehow. Someway. I'd been into the past before.

"Olivière?"

His voice brought me back to the moment. "Does this mean my father is dead?" I tapped the woman's page.

"Olivière," said Ailill, softer than was his usual custom. "The book shows the truth of the village. When a page burns, that means the villager has vanished into… Well, he moves on from this life."

"*No!*" I slammed a palm against the book. "You burnt Master Tailor's page, and he didn't die."

"Burning the page is not the same as the page burning itself. My act only returned the page to its bindings."

"I know! I saw it. I..." I didn't know what I was going to say. The next word caught in my throat, suffocating me. Breathing hurt. Thinking hurt. I'd lost my mother once, and that pain had numbed me for months. Father and I had never been as close, but that brought its own kind of pain. We'd never properly talked since men became free. What kind of man was he really? All I'd have to remember him—the *real* him not bound by devotion to Mother—was that night I brought Arrow back and our chance meeting in the tavern, when he'd reminded me of the father who'd blamed me for Mother's illness.

"Olivière." Ailill's soothing voice melted the cold panic and confusion ringing in my ears. He got up from where he sat across from me, his back hunched, his arms out to steady himself as the carriage flew down the path. He slid in beside me, our thighs pressed close together on the too-small seat. His arm flew around me, and before I knew it, I was cradling the book to my chest and pressing my head against his shoulder. It took me a moment to realize the great heaving sobs I heard were coming from my own throat, that my tears were dyeing his black jerkin even darker with dampness.

"He can't be dead." My voice cracked. "I just saw him. And I thought my mother dead once, and she wasn't."

"She was in my care." Ailill's gloved fingers ran through the back of my hair. "And I have no such power left. He has already vanished."

I leaned away and took his hand in mine, dropping the book to my lap. He swallowed, perhaps hurt that I'd pulled back from him yet again. But I took the glove off and gripped his hand tighter, running my finger—the injured finger now almost entirely without poultice—over his smooth, pale skin. I wanted to feel that healing touch. He'd used it once on me, on a splintered finger. He could use it again. He could fix my hand and save my father. But even if he couldn't...

"I could save him," I said, determined. "The pond will have to accept me and take me back in time. I'll make it." My eyes burned as tears continued falling.

Ailill threaded his fingers through mine. "Olivière, you cannot let your thoughts take you to such dark places. You cannot turn to that power. Please. You do not understand what you were dealing with when you fell through that pond before. They toyed with you."

I wanted to scream. "Who are *they*?"

"I… cannot tell you."

"Fine." This whole exchange reminded me of how frustrated Jurij must have been when he was the one asking questions and I was the one not giving answers. "Then what do you mean, they toyed with me? By sending me into the past?"

He didn't answer. I clutched the book again to my chest with one hand. It was a wonder Jurij hadn't taken me by the shoulders and *shaken* the answer out of me, because that's what I was considering doing now.

Is this what those women who assaulted their men after the edict dissolving marriages felt? The desire to hurt even those you love just because they don't act exactly how you want them to? Violence is a scary thing. The little elf queen knew nothing of it. "Ailill," I said, willing my heartbeat to slow, "what happened to you during that month you were gone? Why does no one seem to remember it but me?"

"Does a dreamer remember his dream after he has finally wakened from it?" An echo of a smile glinted across Ailill's face briefly, but it was hollow. "They toy with me, too. With all of us."

"Is it these people who are really the ones 'always watching'? Are we nothing but—" The carriage ground to a halt, and I flew forward. With the book cradled to my chest, I couldn't stop myself from falling.

But Ailill was there to catch me. He gripped my shoulders, saying nothing of it as he tore his eyes from me to look out the carriage window. "It is too soon. I told them not to stop but for any injured parties we come across." Alarm colored his face as he gently pushed me back upright and swung the carriage door open, jumping to the ground without even waiting for a specter to assist him.

I pulled the book away from my chest. I'd bent a page, and now Mother's face was halfway revealed. I pulled it out and smoothed down the creases, realizing with a jolt that I saw an ink figure I'd never seen before—Ailill—running across her page. I left the book on the seat and jumped out of the carriage after him.

"Where have they taken her?" Mother looked up. "Noll!" She

ran past Ailill to pull me against her chest, choking back sobs. Did she know about Father? "Elfriede's missing." She pulled back and wiped her eyes with a shaking hand. "Forgive me, your lordship." She curtsied unsteadily. "I should have greeted you. I've just been so frantic." Lines had deepened across her face. The past few hours had aged her.

Ailill nodded curtly, his hands behind his back. What I once would have taken for rudeness I understood now was simply his mask for discomfort. He was so unused to interacting with others, now that I thought about it.

"Since when?" I asked, thinking about how I'd seen my sister in bed on the book's page just a short while earlier. No, hours earlier. And she'd been awake, looking worried or frightened.

"I don't know!" Mom threw her hands out as her eyes clenched, tears running down her face. "A few hours maybe. I was asleep. Or, I was trying to sleep. I should have heard her leave. But I just woke up, and she wasn't there." She cradled her face in her hands. "I came out here to find her, and then I saw the carriage and—oh, *goddess*." Her gaze ran over the two lines of specters at rest behind the carriage, and she sobbed. "Something has happened, hasn't it?"

"Yes," I said, unsure of how to tell her. "But not with Elfriede." I swallowed. I didn't really know she wasn't involved. The pages showed such a mess of chaos at the tavern.

The pages.

Ailill gestured to the specters and pointed toward the village. The servants continued their march toward the tavern, splitting to walk around the carriage, my mother, and me. I let go of Mother, eager to slip back to the carriage. *Why now? Why did Elfriede have to go tonight, of all nights?* I tapped my foot anxiously, willing the men to hurry up so I could get back to the book in the carriage.

I heard Ailill speak from behind me. "Why do you think your daughter has gone against her will?"

I'd forgotten she said something about people taking her.

"It's not that she'd go against her will. It's just…" She grabbed me by the shoulders, pulling me away from the line of specters between me and the carriage. "I've tried to help her get over things, Noll. It's been so hard. She took it so much harder than I thought she would." She hiccupped. "And all this time, I had my own problems to worry about with your father."

I met Ailill's gaze at that, and his eyes fell immediately to the ground. The last of the specters filed past, leaving only one atop the carriage, his hands gripping the black horses' reins. Ailill slipped inside the carriage, and I felt relieved that someone was going to get the book to find Elfriede.

"And I was worried about *you*, Noll." Mother sniffed. "It's just I thought you might be doing all right. Handling the change better than anyone. Maybe even finding some happiness with Jurij." She broke down again. "I'm sorry, your lordship, I shouldn't speak in front of you so. It's just been so hard keeping this family together. I thought maybe just *one* of us would find some happiness. But perhaps it wasn't with him after all. Noll, are you and the lord a coupling again? I didn't even stop to think what you were doing together. I…"

I wondered if Mother would be happy at the thought, or if she'd come to understand what had passed between us, how she'd been his hostage while lost in slumber. But he'd healed her… I had to clench Mother's arms tightly to keep her from falling to the ground. I looked to see if Ailill had heard what Mother had said—especially how everyone assumed I would run right back to Jurij despite all I'd been through—but his attention was on the open book in his hands as he stepped out of the carriage, his brow furrowed.

"We should go," he said, his voice fraught with tension.

"What is it?" I asked, suddenly scared that I'd lost my sister and my father in the same evening. *She couldn't be at the tavern, could she? Looking for Jaron? For Father? Did it matter?* I was going to set it right. Somehow.

Ailill flipped a few pages, not bothering to explain anything to Mother, who could barely contain her sobs. "The fight has gotten worse."

Mother's jaw hung open. "A fight?"

I shook her gently, snapping her back to reality. "Not with Elfriede. Right?" I looked to Ailill for confirmation, and he just nodded, scanning one page after the other. "Is Elfriede all right? Ailill?"

His head snapped up at the sound of his name. The crease

between his eyebrows softened as he took a step closer to me. If things weren't so chaotic, if I weren't so mad at him over my friends, if I weren't so angry about my father, so determined to get to the cavern to undo everything, I'd have melted under the softness of his gaze.

"Your sister is with her friends," he said, snapping the book shut and pulling it back just as I reached out to grab it from him. I'd wanted to see for myself. He stared earnestly at me. "Noll, go back inside and wait with your mother. I will return for you when I have finished with the fight at the tavern. Then we will go fetch your sister and put your mother's mind at ease together."

"The tavern?" interrupted Mother. "What do you mean *fight*?"

I grimaced. The only fights she knew were ones people fought with words alone, or from stories about legendary kings and queens who fought with swords that were just imaginary items.

Ailill replied to her for me. "People have gotten hurt." He stepped back toward the carriage, gesturing up at the sole specter that remained. He twisted around to face us again. "Stay here."

Mother wrenched out of my grip. "No! Your father's probably there. I thought Elfriede might be there, too. She... that is, many of the girls like to visit... someone."

"Jaron was with me. He's back at the castle." I took a deep breath, not ready to explain all of that just yet.

"With you? Oh, Noll." Mother's irises glistened with moisture. "Not you too. What about... ?" She eyed Ailill warily, perhaps afraid to finish the sentence with a name. Unsure which name to finish it with.

Ailill nodded toward her, ignoring Mother's train of thought. "Elfriede is not at the tavern. Please. Go inside."

"Then where is she?" I demanded. I tried to snatch the book from his hand, but he tossed it into the carriage. "Why aren't you letting me—"

"Olivière, I will explain everything upon my return." One of his hands gripped the edge of the open carriage door, and the other, the hand still missing a glove, reached out to cradle my head. "I must go. Promise me you will stay."

I shook my head. "I'll go with you."

Mother latched on to my arm, pulling me farther away from

Ailill's soft hold. "How does he know this? What's going on? And what about your father?"

I swallowed.

"Olivière!" called Ailill, reaching out to shut the door. "I will go ahead. You escort your mother to safety indoors."

"No, wait! Ailill!" I looked between my hysterical mother and the closed carriage door as it drove by. My eyes met the specter's briefly, pleading. He returned the gaze but continued onward.

I wanted to run after him and make sure no one else got hurt. But wasn't this the opportunity I'd wanted? Ailill had been against me entering the pool again. If Mother hadn't flagged down the carriage, I wouldn't have had this chance.

But Mother was crumpled into a heap on the ground beside me. I couldn't take her with me to the cavern. And I couldn't risk her running to the tavern and putting herself in harm's way. Not after everything. Not after Father.

"Come on," I said, crouching down and lifting Mother's arm to drape it around my shoulders. "You have to tell me what's going on with Elfriede."

～

THE CHAOS WASN'T CONTAINED to the tavern alone. Out of old, rusty habit, I thanked the first goddess there weren't people stabbing each other in the village streets—remembering then, that I was thanking myself, and a whole lot of good that would do. Men and women alike were running to and fro, shouting at one another. Man pushing aside woman, woman pushing aside man, children ducking into doorways. What had spurred them all out of their homes to compound the problem, I wasn't sure—but then I realized. The parade of specters. The hermit lord's black carriage. That kind of sight was bound to attract notice.

Please, Ailill, let us not have made it all worse.

There was at least enough room on the roads to push through the village's center and make my way toward the old commune, and from there to Alvilda's and Siofra's home nearby. But dragging my reluctant mother along made the journey far too slow.

"Why?" she sobbed, mumbling that word to herself for the hundredth time. "Why did it all come to this?"

"Mother," I spat at last, frustrated with trying to maneuver her around a small crowd of children who'd come out to see what was happening. One cradled a wooden squirrel to her chest, and my heart warmed, despite the state of the village. "You have it wrong about me and Jaron. I'm not coupling with Jurij, either." I couldn't bring myself to mention Ailill.

"Why did you let him move in with you then?" asked Mother quietly, as if she'd barely heard me.

"That doesn't mean we were a coupling!" It seemed like the older women in the village couldn't let go of that idea. "I know how I once felt, but he's not even the same man anymore. I'm not the same woman. But we're still friends." I sighed, relieved as Mother stopped resisting. "I wanted him back with Elfriede."

Mother stopped and pulled away. "I didn't."

"Why?" I backed into the wall of the nearest building as two frightened women passed by.

"I wanted her to find love. Real love." Mother cradled her arms against her chest. "Love that kept on going, even against all odds. Even against all hope. I thought what you had with Jurij was a good example of that."

"Mother, you were the one counseling me to wait for my own man."

Mother shook her head and raised her voice. "That was before all this!" She threw her arms out at the people wandering the streets, many hurrying toward the commotion. "Before the lord set the men's hearts free!"

"Ailill didn't..." But he *did* in a way. Though only because I'd let him. I sighed, remembering Ailill's warning that knowing I was the first goddess, or at least knowing *how* I was the first goddess, could condemn someone to death. I wasn't even sure he meant death by his own hands anymore. All of that talk about the world beyond the mountains, and *they*, and the golden copper somehow connecting it all. I couldn't tell Mother, even if it *were* an appropriate time.

I'd told Jurij. I hadn't given him all the details, but I'd told him more than the others. And maybe he'd told the rest of them since. But even if he hadn't, Jurij knew.

I had to get to the cavern and undo tonight. All of it. Those small moments with Ailill were nothing in comparison. My own desires were nothing.

Still, he held my hand.

"Mother." I grabbed her by the hand and dragged her forward. "Now's not the time. Please come with me to Alvilda's. I'll look for Elfriede," I lied. "But I have to go."

The door to the nearest building burst open, and I had to drag Mother back to avoid her getting hit. Darwyn's mother came out. We were standing in front of the bakery.

"Aubree! Noll!"

My grip slipped from my mother's hand. Mistress Baker looked terrified. "I can't find them! Any of them!"

Mother slid in beside the hysterical woman, dropping her own panic with the appearance of someone else in need of comfort. "What is it? Who?"

Mistress Baker pointed down the road. "People are talking about something going on at the tavern. I couldn't get close enough to get in there. Some of my boys have been spending a lot of time there." Tears streamed down her cheeks. "I thought I'd at least wake Roslyn, to help me get in there. But she's gone, too!"

My stomach lurched. *"She is with her friends."* What could the girls be up to? Why tonight of all nights? Ailill hadn't seemed as concerned about them as he was about the tavern. *But why did he refuse to show me?* "Darwyn and Sindri are all right," I told her. "They're not at the tavern."

Mistress Baker laid a hand on her chest, exhaling a deep sigh of relief, even if her lips still wavered. "You're sure?"

"Yes." I dug my nails into my palm. I felt I'd made a terrible mistake, even if it seemed the best choice at the time. *Please, do what I told you.*

Mistress Baker took me at my word and ran her fingers over Mother's arm. "But Roslyn! And my other boys. I can't be sure they were at the tavern. I know they didn't visit it as often as Darwyn and Sindri." She swallowed. "I know Merek at least would be with his wife. They stayed together after all of that."

Mother took Mistress Baker's hand in hers. "Roslyn must be with Elfriede. The lord said she was with her friends."

"The lord?" Mistress Baker seemed confused, then relieved,

until she read the distress across Mother's features. "And where are they?"

"Noll!"

Alvilda and Siofra ran toward us, not from the direction of their home, where I'd hoped to drop off Mother, but from the center of the village.

"We can't find Nissa!" sputtered Siofra as they ground to a halt beside us. She doubled over slightly, fighting to catch her breath.

"We thought maybe she'd gone to be with Coll and Luuk," added Alvilda. "But they weren't home." She glanced back at the chaos behind us. "And now we hear there was some problem at the tavern."

Here I go again. "Master Tailor and Luuk weren't there. And neither was Jurij. They were all with me—at the castle, before this all started. But I don't know where any of the girls are."

If any of the women had questions about what I was doing with such a large group of men at the forbidden castle, they likely didn't think it the right time to ask. The relief that loosened some of the furrows on their faces was temporary, filled with a new worry about the women whom I couldn't vouch for.

Siofra pinched her lips. "Nissa might be with Roslyn."

"I didn't know Roslyn and Nissa were friends."

Mother looked embarrassed. "They are. Elfriede felt sorry for her after Luuk left her, and she and the others just sort of took to her. The girls have been spending a lot of time at our house. A sort of gathering for young rejected women."

The women all exchanged glances, and I felt pointedly left out. I'd felt that way longer than any of them imagined. Well, besides Alvilda and Siofra, perhaps. But that had worked out for them in the end.

Alvilda wrapped an arm around Siofra and pulled her closer. Siofra's head lulled gently onto the taller woman's shoulder. She looked about to pass out. "Nissa's been saying something recently," said Siofra quietly. She rotated her head to look up at Alvilda. "A place to battle monsters?"

Alvilda nodded, mulling over what she'd said. "She was too young to get along with those girls the way she wanted. She kept wanting to show them something. A place she used to battle monsters."

"With a pool!" added Mother as she slammed her fist into her other palm. "That shined with red, glowing light! I thought she'd made it up. Noll often did the same at that age."

My heart practically stopped. I didn't know Nissa had gone that far into the cavern. But the cavern. Where I was headed. Where Ailill was not keen to let me go.

It makes perfect sense now why he wouldn't let me see her page. But if the place was such a danger for me, why so little concern for my sister?

Mistress Baker frowned. "Roslyn mentioned... No, but why? She at least had reason to be happy now! Even without that no-good son of mine."

"Thea, what is it?" asked Mother, more concerned than ever.

Mistress Baker's eyes widened. "When I offered to take her back, she cried. She said she and her friends had almost given up hope—that they'd considered succumbing to the glow, and just letting it all go! I didn't know." She choked. "I didn't think that meant they'd drown themselves!"

And even if that wasn't what they'd intended, they might very well find themselves the recipients of a death sentence. Ailill's mysterious "they" who lived far beyond the mountains. Always watching. Toying with me.

Please, let the pool have closed its heart.

CHAPTER TWENTY-FIVE

erding a group of hysterical women to a secret, dark cavern wasn't the best idea. But there was no way I was going to convince Mother and Mistress Baker to stay behind now. Alvilda or even Siofra might prove helpful in talking some sense into Elfriede and her friends, but I was sure Mother and Mistress Baker were just a breath away from losing themselves completely.

So how am I going to dive into the pool without them noticing? How will I get the glow to accept me? I'd just have to figure it out once I got there. If I successfully changed the past, then none of it would matter. I'd make sure to stop Elfriede from even leaving the house, and none of us would be in the cavern this evening.

At least with Mistress Baker to care for and a goal in mind, Mother seemed to steel herself a little better. Her tight grip around Mistress Baker's shoulders kept them both steady as we marched back out of the city and into the woods. Away from the tavern. Away from Ailill and the danger he thought more pressing than the cavern.

He's got over a hundred specters to help him calm things down. He can do it. But even if he couldn't, I could. I could save Father and stop Elfriede. Maybe save Jurij, too. And never put Ailill in danger in the first place.

"This way," I said, pointing to the bush bent from all the times we'd pushed past it to get to the cavern a short distance ahead. The women followed me with only Mistress Baker's occasional sobs to punctuate the chirps and hoots of the animals in the darkness. Mistress Baker could only find two candles to light our way, and she tried to light them with shaking hands before Alvilda took over. I tapped my foot impatiently. I just wanted to be there and make sure it was all just a misunderstanding. And take them all away from the cavern so I could do what I needed to do.

It was unsettling, leaving the murmurs and shouts of the chaotic village behind us. But something about what Ailill had told me, the threat of someone other than him "always watching," made me certain Elfriede, Roslyn, and Nissa were the more pressing matter.

"Here it is." I held my candle up to give them a better look at the mouth of the cavern. "Watch your step. There are stalagmites all over the ground." I nodded at Alvilda as she followed behind me. "Take the back. Light as much of the ground as you can with your candle."

We didn't speak for several more minutes as we made our way slowly through the cavern. More than once, one of the women stumbled, but there were no complaints, no suggestions we stop to rest as we plowed forward. The whistling emptiness was invaded by a faint trickle of water.

"The pool's up ahead," I said, clearing my throat. The light that should have been violet poked into the darkness, as red as the blood on Father's page. There was no way the page had been lying. Father was dead. And I couldn't tell Mother. I wouldn't need to, if I could change the past.

Father. Part of me worried I couldn't do this. That I'd never get to know the real him. I'd failed to thus far. I'd just seen glimpses of him, been reminded of the time he drank to forget the pain of Mother being trapped in Ailill's castle, and turned away.

Darwyn had even asked you to save him. To save "both" of them. I frowned. I never knew who else he'd been referring to. Jurij? Or was it the lord? But why would he care about the lord? It had to have been Jurij. But my mind had gone instantly to Ailill, my thoughts never more than a step away from him. Somehow, that had become the case.

My chest clenched at the image of Ailill's castle in my mind. Rotten and in disarray. And he'd been taking so many deliveries of wine and ale from the tavern.

He'd looked thin when I saw him. Almost like he was trying to wither away.

The trickle was drowned out by a splash, and Mother screamed. She let go of Mistress Baker's arms and pushed past, running forward.

"Mother, wait!" I couldn't reach her. Even when she tripped and stumbled, the brightening red glow was enough to give her confidence in her steps.

I picked up my skirt with one hand and ran after her, not caring that the candle extinguished as I did. Not thinking of the women I left behind.

As the pool came into view, I gasped. The useless candle slipped to the ground.

"What are you *doing* here?" I shrieked, running toward the large gathering of people at the water's edge. "I told you to hide in my shack!"

Jaron turned his head, not moving from where he stood, casually leaning on a stick. "We discussed it and thought it might get a little crowded in there. Best make use of our freedom while we have it, right? It's not like we'll be able to effectively hide from him anywhere."

I frowned, my gaze falling over the men I'd freed from the castle's cells just before I'd joined Ailill in the carriage.

I'd wanted them to hide. To stay away from the tavern and just get out of there, so I could reason with Ailill once the whole thing blew over. I should have warned them to stay away from this place.

Mother bent down by the water. "Get out of there!" She tugged on Nissa until they both fell on the sediment. Nissa laughed as she rolled over, dripping wet. Mother was furious.

"Darwyn! Sindri!" Mistress Baker reached out to hug them both. Before they could even process that their mother stood beside them or think to reciprocate the hug, she pulled back. "Roslyn!" She pushed past them to draw the young woman into her arms.

Roslyn smiled and hugged her, twittering like a sweet little bird. "Goodmother!" She laughed and pulled away, covering her mouth. "I suppose it's just Thea now, isn't it?"

Mistress Baker's lips grew taut, and she stuck a finger in Roslyn's face. "I was worried sick about you! I thought you were in the tavern—and then I was sure you'd drowned yourself!"

"*Drowned* herself?" Nissa stood, brushing off the front of her skirt. Siofra brushed past Master Tailor with a spiteful glance, as if he had anything to do with Nissa being there. Finding Luuk a short distance away, she led Nissa to him and put her arms around them both. Luuk looked embarrassed and shifted away, patting the side of his leg.

Mistress Baker looked at all of the faces around her, perhaps more confused than I was. "What's going on here then?"

"Nothing!" said Sindri. He also looked uncomfortable, and he'd spoken his protestation of innocence too quickly. "Jurij said we should see something here. And when we got here, we found the women. Swimming."

Elfriede and Marden sat at the edge of the water, whispering to each other. Their clothes were damp, as if they'd slipped them on hastily and they'd gotten soaked due to the wet undergarments beneath. Mother joined them.

I just about jumped out of my skin as someone's arm entwined through mine. I turned, expecting Jurij or Ailill, but it was Roslyn, smiling. "We've been here a few times, swimming."

I wanted to rip my arm away from hers, but I couldn't blame her oblivious peacefulness if she truly didn't know what was happening. "At night?"

Roslyn shrugged. "Sure. Why not? Everyone expects so much of us during the day." She dropped my arm and motioned for Jurij. "And I wanted to celebrate today. And maybe just help ease the pain of your happiness a bit for your sister."

Jurij didn't take the cue to stand beside me. His glare was cold, and he dropped his eyes, focusing on his side, at which he clutched something.

"Well, that was stupid," said Alvilda, stopping beside her brother and looking him once over. "And dangerous. Especially tonight."

"We didn't know they were here," protested Master Tailor.

"Tonight?" cut in Roslyn, her sweet voice wavering. "What's going on tonight?"

Every man's eyes dropped down to his side. Every man's but Jaron's. *But I didn't tell them about the tavern. I didn't want to put them in harm's way.* Jaron stood straighter, no longer leaning on his stick. He lifted it up in the air, letting the red light of the pool bounce off it.

It was a sword! All of the men had scabbards tied around their waists. Every one of them. Even Luuk.

"Tonight the men decided it was time to get some answers," said Jaron. I couldn't sense malice in his words, but the sword he held aloft gave me dreadful feelings of nostalgia. There was a time when men acted much like he was acting, not even realizing the menace of their actions. Jaron slid his sword back into the scabbard at his side and nodded. Roslyn screamed as Darwyn and Tayton shoved her aside and slipped their arms through mine, gripping me tightly.

Jaron smiled. He looked almost friendly. "And Noll here has some answers."

CHAPTER TWENTY-SIX

I struggled to be free of Darwyn and Tayton, sending them both my angriest glare. Neither looked down, and neither caved much to my resistance, so I went slack.

It wasn't like I wanted to keep it all secret. But I'd have to find a way to explain my hesitation.

"What is the meaning of this?" demanded Alvilda, striding toward me.

But before she could get much closer, Master Tailor stepped around her, pushing his hands against her chest. "Stand back, Alvilda."

Alvilda's eyebrows furrowed, and her face soured, like she'd eaten something rotten. "No! Step aside, Coll, or so help me, I'll—"

"You'll what?" interrupted Jaron, his casual stride to stand beside Master Tailor belying any ill intent. "Command him to stand down? Send him to the commune to rot?" The corner of his mouth twitched. "You don't have any power here, Alvilda. Not anymore."

Alvilda spat at the ground near his feet. "You think I was any happier knowing I couldn't be with Siofra thanks to you meddling men? Don't blame *me* for the rules of this village."

"Blame Noll." Jurij's voice was quiet. Elfriede lifted her head as he stood beside me. It was the first time I'd seen her move at all since we'd arrived.

All eyes were on me. Even the women's, and they looked more surprised than angry.

I glanced warily at the glow of the red pool beside us. "This isn't the time."

"You had weeks, *months*, to pick a better time." Jaron stepped closer. "We waited long enough for Jurij to get the truth out of you. His way didn't work."

I eyed Jurij curiously. "His way?"

The lump at the base of Jurij's throat bobbed, and he looked away. "I thought if you loved me, you'd tell me everything you knew."

I supposed it was lucky Darwyn and Tayton had such tight grips on me because I imagined myself punching him across the face. "You liar! All you've ever done is lie to me! You pretended to be my friend! You pretended to love me. You no-good—"

Jurij spun around, bringing his face closer than ever. "I wasn't lying! I loved you. You gave me my freedom, and then you pushed me away." He turned away and wouldn't look at me again.

"*She* gave you your freedom?" echoed Mistress Baker, oblivious to the intensity of the conversation.

"People are hurt at the tavern!" I shouted, drowning out Mistress Baker's question. "There's been a fight—a *real* fight, in which people spill each other's blood—and the lord and his servants had to rush out to stop it." I gulped, not expecting the sudden wave of emotion that slammed into me. I had to stop myself from letting tears fall. "And I... I've got to take care of it. I told you all to wait out of harm's way." I eyed Roslyn and Elfriede. "And then *you* all had to have this little pity gathering at the worst time."

"*Pity* gathering?" Elfriede shot up, practically knocking Mother down as she did. "How dare you belittle us?" She marched toward me, clenching her fists.

"Oh. Because you've been through so much just because your men left you," I growled. "Excuse me while I reserve my sympathy."

"Enough!" Jurij's voice reverberated off the cavern ceiling. He

441

looked from Elfriede to me and back again. "Both of you." He sighed and ran a hand through his short hair. "I'm tired of being the cause of fights between you."

I rolled my eyes. Since when had he cared about that? Maybe he couldn't help it before, but he could now.

Jaron stepped between us sisters, nudging Jurij aside. "We know about the fight at the tavern." Jaron nodded at Darwyn and Tayton, and they let me go, even if they still stood within easy reach. I pulled my arms away to make the point that I didn't appreciate being held in place. What was the point of holding me down anyway? Were they worried I'd run, or a specter would step out from the shadows to whisk me away?

I stopped. "You *knew* about the tavern?"

Jaron looked smug and patted the sword at his side. "The boys told me about those games you used to play. A queen and her retainers battling monsters with tools called swords meant to destroy your foes. We realized people could fight each other with or without these tools." He gestured toward the scabbard at his waist, which I noticed was slightly askew and over his stomach, not at all the tight and practiced way the men of the distant past had worn them over their hips. "Of course we didn't expect to find a whole stash of these things in the castle after you let us free. But we didn't need them for our fellow village men, anyway. Fists would do."

"What are you saying?" asked Mistress Baker, her voice wavering.

Jaron shrugged. "We planned the fight in the tavern. If we failed to return after we investigated the castle, Gideon agreed to provide a distraction that might summon the lord and his men away."

"You *planned* that?" I felt hot tears burning my cheeks, but I couldn't stop them. "Father's dead because of your plans!"

The air went still, the stifling thickness of the cavern with so many people in it threatening to suffocate us all. Even Jaron's smugness slipped just a bit. "How do you—"

"No!" Mother screamed. She broke down into sobs, far worse than when she feared Elfriede had gone missing.

I took a step toward her, but Darwyn and Tayton clutched my forearms to stop me. I glared at them and by the time I turned back, Jaron was crouched beside Mother, patting her back. "Aubree, she must be mistaken. Don't get yourself so worked up."

"The pages!" I screamed, roaring to life. "Father died in ink and silhouette before my eyes. And more men and women could too." I strained my shoulders, struggling to free myself. "What were you thinking? You figured out men could harm one another, but you didn't consider how easy it would be for that harm to become permanent? Even fatal?"

Jurij rubbed his scar and watched as Elfriede crouched beside Mother and took her into her arms. The red of the pool flickered across the tears streaming down my sister's face. Jaron backed away, watching the two sobbing women like they were some monster he'd unleashed upon the world. Perhaps their tears were.

Alvilda frowned. "What are you talking about? Pages?"

I stopped fighting, and I felt my captors relax. They still didn't let me go. "Ailill watches us through pages in a book."

Alvilda raised an eyebrow. "Okay…"

"Well, if *you* had shared what you knew with us earlier, it wouldn't have come to this!" Jaron took the distraction from my weeping family as an excuse to wag a finger in my direction. I felt a sudden wave of anger for this stupid man and his stupid plan, which put my father and so many more in danger. And now he wouldn't even let me be with my family. Marden took my place patting Elfriede on the back, and Roslyn brushed past Jaron to join them, Mistress Baker trembling and following after her. Even Siofra let go of the children's hands and directed them over toward Mother and Elfriede.

"Don't blame this on me!" I snarled. None of the men but Jaron would look at me. That said all I needed to know; they did indeed blame me. *But how much has Jurij told them?* I swallowed, wondering if I was just imagining the red of the pool growing brighter and deeper in color. Was it time? Could I go back? Could I stop myself from even hinting to Jurij while I was at it? "The lot of you schemed without me, trying to drag me into your foolish plans, coming up with the stupidest of ways to find out something you don't even need to know!"

"Don't need to know?" Jaron practically spat as he grunted in frustration.

"Why can't it be enough for you that you're free? Do you really need to know why?"

Jaron patted the hilt of the sword at his side. "That's easy for you to say since you know everything!"

"I *don't* know everything!" The water seethed red, echoing my anger. "And if I told you what I know, I could put you all in danger!"

Jurij snapped back to the moment, tearing his focus from the huddle of grieving women. "Danger?" he asked, anxious, disbelieving. "From whom?"

"Who else?"

Ailill.

The specters that filed into the cavern from the darkness were so silent, not a single person had noticed them approaching. They split into two lines, settling in behind the group on either side, blocking us all from the path back to the entrance.

Falling into place at the center of the half circle of specters, Ailill stepped out from the darkness, tugging at the bottom of his glove as if he were just slipping it back on.

He's all right! I couldn't believe how relieved I felt. There were tears in his clothing. His boots were scuffed and dirty. His hair was a bit mussed and out of place. There was a dark bruise on his cheek, and a thin line, no thicker or deeper than a cat's scratch, across part of his throat that smeared red across the delicate paleness of his skin.

He didn't seem to notice me studying him as he forced a smile. "I had wondered where you all slipped off to." He gestured slightly, and the specters moved forward, each reaching for the nearest person. "Perhaps you can find the answers you seek in the life beyond." The specters lifted their arms and reached forward as one, easily tearing the swords from the scabbards the men wore too loosely at their hips.

The specters raised the swords above their heads with both hands, all pointed down at the men.

Ailill crossed his arms and nodded. "Proceed."

"No!" I screeched.

CHAPTER TWENTY-SEVEN

The specters stopped as one, the blades hovering dangerously over the men's heads and backs.

Their sudden hesitation gave the men enough time to pull away. Sindri, Darwyn, Tayton, and Master Tailor formed a half circle with their backs to the water. Even Alvilda stood beside her brother, her hands clenched at her sides. Siofra pulled Luuk out of the way, and she and the rest of the women, my mother and Elfriede included, stood in a half circle around Luuk and Nissa, whom they pushed toward the water's edge.

I was worried they were making a mistake, trusting in that water to save them. I didn't want them anywhere near it. I had no idea how I could go back through time with so many people around.

Now that Darwyn and Tayton had abandoned their posts at my sides to form their protective barrier, I was free. Jaron stood at the center of that group, his blade clumsily drawn. The specters hadn't disarmed him or Jurij, who'd been further inward when they arrived. I scanned the statue-like crowd of ghastly pale figures. There should have been enough of them to take the blades from Jaron and Jurij. But there weren't. Not in the cavern anyway.

"What happened to the rest of the specters?" My heart thundered wildly at the idea of vanished specters and dead men, more lives to go back and save.

"Specters?" Ailill echoed my word as he stepped forward, hands clutched behind his back. "Oh. I keep forgetting what you call us."

Us? I supposed Ailill considered himself as one with them in a way. Although he seemed convinced with the curse broken, he wouldn't find himself joining them.

"They are detaining the rabble-rousers from what is left of the tavern."

"What's *left* of it?" repeated Alvilda. "What did you do to it?" I was afraid she'd launch herself at the nearest specter, but Master Tailor grabbed her forearm and pulled her back with a warning glance.

Ailill cocked his head. "*I* did not do anything. It was the men of this village who started the fire."

"Fire?" spat Jaron. "I never told them to start a fire!"

Ailill raised an eyebrow and nodded at the nearest specter. They all lowered their weapons, holding them at their sides. "But you told them to start a fight, I assume?" He chuckled darkly. "I should have guessed. I only wonder how you managed to get out of the cells while I was distracted."

I shifted uncomfortably and decided to stand beside Jurij. We alone were between the specters and the line of villagers. "I let them out." I eyed the nearest specter, as if I really had a hope of identifying which of them had dropped the key or which had almost spoken to me. *Are the specters truly one and the same?* "One of the Ailills dropped the key."

Ailill scanned his specters, struggling to contain a smile, my comment eliciting amusement when I expected anger. "Interesting," he said, almost as if expecting the culprit to speak up. For, now that I thought about it, the idea of these perfectly trained statues doing anything on accident was absurd. I'd either found a rogue specter—and the thought that one had tried to speak to me led credence to that theory—or I'd played right into Ailill's plans, which his lack of utter anger and disgust might attest to.

Both ideas seemed wrong. Possible, but wrong. I'd never known a specter to act without Ailill's instruction, or at least a general sense of what he'd wanted. But it made so little sense to me that this would be what he wanted.

Ailill gave up on his fruitless search for the suspect and clasped his hands together in front of him. He studied us, staring over my head at the line of people behind me. Or at the deep red glow of the pond he insisted they should know nothing about.

I used the silence as an opportunity to ask what I'd been dreading. "Ailill." His head snapped toward me, a mixture of surprise and delight on his face. "My father?"

"Olivière, you knew from the pages…" He stopped, his eyes drawn back to the pool. "He was gone. I asked the tavern masters. He was one among a dozen or so who vanished in the battle. I am sorry."

As I thought. All the more reason I had to make this work.

A scream of rage echoed around the cavern as Mother launched herself at the specter who had threatened Luuk, her arms flailing.

"Mother, no!" I shouted.

"Aubree!" I heard again and again.

I pushed past Jurij, determined to stop her, afraid of her getting anywhere near a specter with a blade. But Mother turned sharply, running right toward me. I stopped, surprised, but Mother kept advancing, tears running down her cheeks. She was going to try to punish somebody for this. If she somehow thought I was to blame, if she, like everyone else, just wanted to lay the blame on me without giving me the chance to fix it, then I'd let her. I'd tried. I tried staying away from everyone. I tried letting solitude be my penance for my sin. I was tired of trying.

An arm clamped down across my chest, dragging me backward. I tried to turn, but the force was too great. I kicked.

"Now, hold on, Aubree!" Jaron! Jaron the flirt, the instigator, the all-around troublemaker I'd considered more of a friend when he hadn't an original thought in his head. His left arm was clenched tight across my chest, his right hand still holding the sword awkwardly at his side. The tip of the blade poked into my skirt, ruffling it as he fought to hold me.

Mother kept running, and Jaron did the unthinkable. He raised his sword so the tip pointed at my neck. "Aubree, stop!"

Mother froze just a short distance from us. "Jaron, let her go!

How could you?" She choked on her sobs. Like a coward, he'd used me as a shield. As though my mother's fists could possibly harm him as much as he and the rest of the men had harmed the people in the tavern.

"I'll let her go," he panted, but I didn't feel at all comforted. I struggled to keep my feet firmly planted, but he was dragging me so that I rested on my toes. "I just want you to calm down and listen."

Mother shrieked. *"Listen?* Your foolishness killed my husband!"

"Your *former* husband," pointed out Jaron, a correction not at all appropriate given the circumstances.

Mother's face grew dark as her eyes widened. "I don't care! I loved him even still!" She looked like she was barely restraining herself from leaping at him. "I wish I'd never loved you! I hate you!"

Jaron's grip slackened somewhat, and I almost twisted away, feeling the prick of the blade on my throat. But he tightened his grip again and backed up, turning his head to and fro. Everyone around him was suddenly an enemy, even if no one else had made a move. He turned us both so I could see Ailill again, but he was gone. *Gone.* Impossibly gone. In desperation, my eyes darted to Jurij. He looked from me, to Jaron, to my mother, and back. Frozen in place. His hand on his sword's hilt.

The specters were just a blur of white at the edge of the darkness. Not a single one moved forward to stop him.

Jaron dragged us back through the circle, even as Alvilda swooped out to lay a hand on Mother's shoulder. "What are you doing?" she sneered. "Jaron, let Noll go right now!"

"Ha!" spat Jaron. "You can't order me around, Alvilda! Not anymore!"

"This isn't about that, Jaron!" Master Tailor stepped beside his sister. "Great goddess, man! What are you doing? Let the girl go!"

"I'm not doing anything!" He swung his sword out, pointing it at everyone in sight. "I just want you to listen. Calmly."

"You're the one who's not calm!" said Tayton. He took a step forward, swinging his clenched fist. "We didn't want to hurt her!"

"Tayton, *no!*" shouted Darwyn, grabbing on to his shoulder.

"No one move." Jaron flicked the sword back to my throat. It hurt. I could feel the warmth trickling down my skin. I didn't dare breathe.

"All right," said Jaron after a moment of silence. He dragged me slowly backward until I felt the water lapping at my feet, and he froze, probably realizing he couldn't retreat any farther without falling into the pool.

"All right," repeated Jaron. His breath fluttered across the top of my head. "Start talking, Noll. Tell us everything. Explain to them why I had to go to such lengths. And then we'll all go home. We'll be fine."

"My father is *dead*, Jaron." I expected my voice to be strengthened by anger, but I practically choked on the words. "And so are a number of others."

"No," said Jaron, in denial. "He's lying. You hear me?" He waved his sword away from me, pointing it across the crowd. "The lord just doesn't want us to know the truth."

I brought my heel down as hard as I could on his toes.

"Gargh!" He bounced back, trying to maintain a grip on me, his sword hand wobbling.

I kicked back again, aiming for his shin, twisting my leg around his to drag us both down. I fumbled, and he brought the sword toward me, but I squirmed away and eventually wound my leg through his, using my fall to take him with me.

I heard a man's guttural scream from some distance away as I fell, but it was drowned out by the splash of the water, and then the thud of my head against the sediment. The roar of the movement in the water made everything else impossible to hear.

Everything else but the beat of the heart. I twisted free of Jaron, who flailed beside me, and set out for deeper waters, to the point where neither of us could stand up. My head throbbed, and my vision blurred. I was overwhelmed by the red. The burning, fiery red from the heart in the water. The thump of the heartbeat. The threat of drowning.

Time seemed to stop, and I reached out for it. I wanted that red to go away, and I tried willing back the violet light that had been more inviting. I floated in place close to the sediment, telling the orb I needed to go to the past.

And then, whether I imagined it or not, I heard my name whispered. *"Olivière."*

The red bled into a dark violet. *Yes! Take me back. Let me undo this!*

I reached out again, but it was gone, the red drowning out the violet once more, a pair of hands grabbing my wrists and tugging me upward.

I tried to scream, to shout "No!" But when I opened my mouth, I invited in the water. It tasted sour, like the scent of copper. I closed my mouth and kicked, feeling the pressure of the water in my chest.

"Olivière!" This time my name wasn't so clear, but I felt a tugging at my wrists. I floated right up beside my captor.

My eyes were blurry, thanks to the water and my throbbing head. But he was dressed all in black, his pale face inches from mine.

I opened my mouth, "Ailill" spilling out across my tongue but sounding like only a gurgle of water. Why was he stopping me? I knew he hadn't wanted me to use the pool, but couldn't he see I had to? I wasn't going to let this evening happen.

I panicked, throwing my head back, and Ailill kicked, bringing us back to the surface after what seemed like forever but couldn't have been more than a moment.

We broke through the surface, and I vomited water. Ailill hugged me close to him, resting my chin over his shoulder and pounding on my back so I could throw up the rest of the water I'd swallowed. What should have been the quiet trickling of the cavern walls was filled with splashing and shouting. I couldn't focus. I concentrated on breathing, on the way I felt so close to Ailill. I felt warm. Safe. Even though my head told me I was neither of those things.

I had barely started breathing again when Ailill dropped his hand and swam backward, dragging me with him. "No!" he barked. "Stay back."

A mess of bodies slammed into us, almost knocking me under.

"Leave her alone!"

"Damn you!"

The words were halted between splashes and gasps of breath

450

as two—no, three, four—men splashed through the water, a tumble of limbs.

"Just stop!"

A glint of red reflected off a gilded blade. The tip poked out from the water, driven upward with a powerful swimming kick. There was no way I could avoid it. I froze, telling myself to swim away, to duck under, anything. *Get out of the way!*

But as my eyes fixated on the blade, liquid red wrapped around my legs like a rope of solid blood. All the shouting died in my ears, and I heard only the echoing heartbeat of the water below. I couldn't move. The red of the pool had restrained me. *"Olivière!"* It wasn't calling me. It was angry with me. *Why? Because I'd tried to order it? Because of what I'd done the last time I went through it?* Whatever the reason, it would drown me, one way or the other.

"Olivi—gah!"

The tip of the blade shot up, stopping a hair's breadth from the base of my throat, and I lurched away. The blade had come through Ailill's chest, and now it dripped, dripped, dripped blood into the glowing red water.

"Ailill!" I grabbed his upper arms, struggling to keep him from sinking. The squeeze of the red light on my legs faded, for what good it did now. I had to kick to stay afloat, but I was panicked. I couldn't let him move, not with the blade still struck through his chest.

Struck through his chest from behind, just like Elric had been when I led the rebellion to stop the men of the old village. And then I'd decided that I was a fool for playing at battle. That I never wanted to see bloodshed again.

Ailill's lips oozed with blood, but he tried to smile. It wasn't a cruel smile. No, it was the most genuine smile I'd ever seen across his face. "I love... when you say... my name." He spat out a river of blood, his head lurching forward.

"Ailill!" I screamed again, not sure what to do. Lift him off the blade? Swim to the sediment? *What can I do? How can I save him?* "No, no, no, no, you can't—"

Though I clenched his arms so hard I might have left bruises, his body collapsed, leaving me holding nothing but black leather.

"No!" I shouted again, but he was gone. Vanished into death. The very last death.

And behind where he'd been, still clutching the hilt of the blade that dripped red with blood, was Jurij, his mouth agape.

CHAPTER TWENTY-EIGHT

"**Y**ou!" I screamed. "How could you? How could..." I swam
forward, screaming nonsense, ignoring the blade that hung
limply from Jurij's grip. I pounded my fists into the water, one
hand still clutching Ailill's jerkin.

Jurij pulled the blade out of my path and then tossed it, letting
it succumb to the heartbeat of the water. He swam backward,
holding his hands out to stop my approach. "Noll, wait! Noll,
listen! I didn't mean to."

"You didn't mean to? You were swinging around a weapon,
and you didn't *mean* to?" I reached him, snarling, and tried to
clobber him, but I faltered when I hiccupped and choked on the
flowing streams of tears. I could barely keep myself afloat. "Who
were you *trying* to kill then, *me*?"

Jurij swam backward out of my reach, the coward, and I just
got my second wind to surge after him when Darwyn and Tayton
appeared on either side of me, holding me in place.

"Calm down, Noll!" shouted Darwyn, but he got a splash of
water from my foot in his face.

"Let's get to the sediment," said Tayton. He leaned his head
back to avoid another flurry of kicks. "Noll, *Noll*. Let's go."

"No!" I said, determined to dive back under, but they over-

453

powered me. I reached out toward the red glow, willing it to turn violet, but it refused. It burned.

You are not welcome here. The echoing voice in my mind was so harsh, so final, I knew at once that my last chance to go back to the past was beyond me. There would be no undoing this night, no matter how hard I tried. It was like Ailill's death was final not just for him, but for all hope of miracles.

The water surged like a great gust of wind shot through it, and I flew back, hearing screams echo throughout the cavern. When hands grabbed my arms again, I stopped resisting and was dragged out of the water toward the sediment.

"What was that?" Alvilda's voice rang out.

The surge calmed into ripples behind me. But my heart sank. If I dove in, the pool would send me right back out. But maybe once I got clear of all of these people, I could try. And try. As many times as necessary.

You're a fool. Father and Ailill are gone, and all your power to stop it is gone with them.

As soon as I broke free of the blood-stained water, Mother and —to my surprise—Elfriede swooped in on either side of me, wrapping me in their embraces.

"Oh, Noll!" Mother rubbed my head and cradled me, her tears falling onto my forehead. "Noll, I was so worried."

I pushed her away, and fury that shouldn't have been directed at her must have been plain on my face. She nodded at Elfriede, and they gave me space. I pounded the sediment as they moved back and stared at the jerkin in my raw and bleeding fist.

"Where are they?" I stood on wobbly legs, gently shoving Elfriede when she swooped in to help me stand. "Jaron! Jurij!"

I blinked, clearing the drops of water that still clung to my lashes and ignoring the pain that throbbed at the back of my head. I looked around, trying to bring the many—too many— figures into focus. And then I noticed the piles of white clothing in a half circle around the length of the pool's sediment.

"No!" I screamed again, walking toward the nearest pile, shoving aside several people who tried to stop me, who let me go despite my weak pushes and faltering steps. I collapsed, laying Ailill's black jerkin next to the white jacket.

I traced my fingers over both. Even though the black one was dark and wet, they had the same embroidery of roses and thorns. My fingers stopped on one of the white jacket's blooms. On the black one, there was a hole framed in dark, dark blood.

"Where are they?" I snarled again, turning around to face the group. Master Tailor stood beside Alvilda, and between them Jaron sat cross-legged on the ground, his arms tied behind him with his own scabbard belt. Siofra stood off to the side with Luuk and Nissa, her arm around Jurij's shoulders.

"Why?" I asked, leaping to my feet so ferociously I almost fell over. "Why did you kill him?" I didn't know where to direct my anger, who was more to blame. But I stepped toward Jurij, passing by Jaron to beg for answers from the man I'd once loved more than anything.

He was reluctant to look at me, and Siofra let go of him to stand between us. "Now, Noll, you couldn't see what was going on."

I gripped the jerkin to my chest. "I don't care! He killed him."

Jurij's head snapped up. "Is that such an awful thing? He was going to imprison us for life. And you said yourself you didn't want to be with him before the curse broke, and he forced you to be with him anyway."

"I was working on the imprisonment! And it wasn't all his fault. You don't understand!"

"Apparently not." Jurij looked down. "I thought you loved *me*."

"I told you—"

He waved a hand. "I know. You don't. Not like that. Not anymore. Well, maybe I'm tired of loving where love isn't wanted."

"So you killed Ailill? Because I didn't love you?"

He didn't answer.

Siofra placed a hand on my shoulder. "He didn't mean to, Noll. It was such a mess. They were all trying to get Jaron away from you. To rescue you. You weren't coming up, and we were worried you'd hit your head."

I choked. "But why did you bring your sword into the water?"

Jurij's eyes narrowed. "I wasn't thinking. I just saw a chance to save you. I dove in."

I shook my head. "You launched up with the blade extended. Were you trying to kill me? Jaron?" I paused. "Why did all of you get swords at all? Who were you going to harm with them?"

Jurij clenched his jaw. The flames may have been gone, but his eyes burned with their own fire, glistening from the red glow of the pool. "The lord and his servants," he answered after a moment's hesitation. "If it came to that."

He brushed past his mother and me, moving down the path to the entrance and disappearing into the darkness.

∿

THERE WAS no sign of Jurij, the Tailors, or any of my friends. Everyone's plan to calm me down by keeping me back in the cavern a while longer, while the lot of them ran away with their tails between their legs, seemed to have worked.

But they couldn't hide from me forever. Not if they didn't know there was a place beyond the mountains. Besides, they never got the answers they sacrificed so much to find.

And if some "they" watching us beyond the mountains wanted to punish people who knew about their existence, then that was fine with me. Ailill had told me the gold coin saved me, marked me as one fit for ruling. But I wasn't imagining things when the red light in the pool held me paralyzed as the blade approached. I was done trying to protect them. I was done trying to protect myself.

As Marden and Roslyn broke through the last of the trees and bushes to the path that ran through the forest, I fingered my sash. The golden coin was still there.

"Noll?" asked Mother, her arm around my back. I took another step forward.

"His carriage is still here!" exclaimed Marden. "No horses, though."

I froze.

Elfriede stopped at my side, reaching out a hand. "Noll—"

"I'll be fine," I said, waving her away. "Just leave me be."

Elfriede looked hesitant, but Mother let me go and wove her arm through Elfriede's, gently tugging her away. "Come see us when you're ready, Noll. We have... mournings to arrange."

456

They joined Roslyn and Marden on the path toward the village, leaving me beside the carriage. The first light of dawn trickled through the leaves above me.

As if I could forget that I'd lost both Father and Ailill. As if I could forget the lord's smile as he vanished from my arms, leaving me before I could say what it was I truly wanted to say.

But this time, at least, he hadn't vanished from existence. The clothes. The carriage. Even the castle might still be standing. This time, I wouldn't be the only one who knew him.

I lurched forward, leaning against the open carriage doorframe to keep from collapsing. I looked at the emptiness inside for what felt like forever, taking in the blackness of everything, the memories both painful and longing. There was one thing that wasn't black. A book with open pages.

I dragged myself inside the carriage, crawling on hands and knees. I held on to the jerkin even as I picked up the book, dragging it over my lap.

I saw myself, sitting on a carriage seat, looking down at a book on my lap. My fist still clutched the jerkin to my chest.

The ink smeared as tears dripped onto the page. But the water quickly dried and the ink was smooth, only to be drowned again and again.

The book grew hot in my lap, and the back glowed bright with violet light.

With wavering fingers, I turned the pages to the source of the light. My other hand clutched the leather so hard my wound reopened and my finger bled. But I kept clutching. I kept willing myself to breathe.

A half-formed page wound out of nothingness, fibers in the paper as clear as thread stitching, only without the needles. When at last the page was complete, the light faded, and I was left staring at a blank, yellowing page, one that seemed as old as the rest of them, even if I'd just witnessed its creation.

It was the castle throne room, complete with that hole in the wall where the throne should have been. The throne was already pushed aside.

Out stepped man after man after man. Their hands clutched behind their backs, their faces so similar, their ages varied, although most were older, far older-looking than one would think could walk so upright. They filed out of the hole and off the page. I counted. A hundred and four... a hundred and five.

And that last specter's face was young, perhaps in his twenties. He paused, and I saw Ailill, *my* Ailill staring out at me.

My fingers traced over his form. His jerkin wasn't colored in black ink. It had to be white. My Ailill was a specter.

He stepped aside, and behind him came another specter. No. His face was dark, shaded lightly with ink that only gave an impression of color against the yellow of the page. His clothing was even darker, the blackness of night, like the jerkin I held tight in my hand. And he looked younger. Not as young as the Ailill I'd known many years in the past. But a man newly grown. Seventeen, perhaps, just a little more life to his eyes, just a little more roundness to his cheeks.

And on his arm, he wore a bangle.

NOBODY'S PAWN

THE NEVER VEIL BOOK THREE

CHAPTER ONE

I clutched the book to my chest, the open page crinkling as I moved. I was afraid to look at it, afraid to see that I'd just imagined the throne room exploding to life. My damp dress raised bumps on my skin, which the cool morning breeze of an autumn day did nothing to alleviate. Even as the sunlight trickled through the leaves overhead, there was no hope of warming. No hope of going back to how things were just a day before.

My first thought had been to run to my friends, to run to Jurij when I saw the movement on the pages—but then my breath caught. Jurij had *killed* him. He might have returned—at least, that was what I wanted to see, to confirm with my own eyes—but that wouldn't change the fact that Jurij had driven his sword clear through his back. No, I couldn't go to Jurij. I couldn't go to any of the men, to those fools who'd destroyed the tavern and my father along with it.

I'd considered telling Mother at least what I'd seen. In my hazy thoughts of the previous few hours, I didn't remember if I'd have to explain to her what the book was, and how I'd known what had happened. But she had Father's death to come to terms with, and as I'd flipped through the book to find her page—my hand keeping my place on that last page, I couldn't risk losing that page—I saw her standing in our home besides

461

the wood, Elfriede at her side, their faces both contorted as the full awareness of what we'd lost sunk over them. I could see the tears even in the black ink, see the puzzlement on Arrow's face as he looked up at them, but my eyes weren't drawn to their tears for long. Jurij walked onto the page and flung his arms around my sister.

I slammed the book shut, losing my place. Panicked, I flung it back open to the last page, and it was still there. It still followed the drawing of the young man who was and was not Ailill.

"Ailill." I said his name to the dawn, to the empty path through the woods before me. "Ailill, you didn't die for the last time. You came back. I know it." I squeezed the book harder to my chest, afraid to check, afraid to see if the page would turn red with blood and fire, like it had with my father's. I tried not to think of how it was selfish of me to want that. How he'd practically said he was ready to die at last after this life, how I was the one who'd doomed him to all his many lives.

My boot squished into the soft dirt, and I felt the sash around my waist loosen. I was prepared to trod on it as it flitted to the ground, but the heavy weight that hit my foot drew my attention. I paused as a trickle of sunlight glinted off the ground and caught my eye. The golden copper. It had stayed in my sash through all that time in the cavern pool, through almost drowning.

Still clutching the book, I crouched to pick the copper up. I held it out above my head and it caught the light. Before I'd realized it, I'd arrived at the black castle that nestled against the eastern mountains. Fear spread throughout my body at the thought that the gate doors might not open for me. I clenched the coin in my fist, feeling the weight of carrying the book with one hand but refusing to let the coin go. *Let me in*, I thought, and the gates parted quietly.

They hadn't even finished opening before I squeezed through them and stepped inside. "Ailill?" I called out, not caring how hollow the echo of my voice sounded in the entryway. *The throne room*, I thought, heading toward the stairway and coming face-to-face with a specter.

"I..." The sentence caught in my throat. I wanted to embrace the specter, but it would be too strange. They were back. It was proof he was, too. I studied the specter, the weak light pouring into the room through the open door not enough to fully make out his face. "I need to see Ailill," I said at last.

The specter said nothing. He was joined by a wave of other specters descending the staircase. They fanned out on either side of me, ignoring me, some even bumping me aside.

"Where are you going?" I asked, fully aware that none of them would answer. I stepped back, letting the specter who had blocked my path join the group, and I found myself tracing my steps back toward the doorway to make room for the flurry of movement. The sunlight from the doorway wasn't enough to make the entryway light up entirely, and no torches were lit, making the already usually dark room difficult to navigate. Yet the group of specters knew exactly what they were doing as they lined up in two parallel lines between the exit and the doorway at the back. They stilled all at once, their hands behind their backs, their legs slightly parted.

Sunlight streamed in from the doorway to the garden at the center of the castle, the place that had been my sanctuary all those months before. The dueling sunbeams from that door and from the open doorway behind me lit up the line of specters just enough that I could make out their stern, unmoving faces. My eyes roved over them and came to a halt at the end of the line.

"Ailill...?" I asked, my throat parched. "Ailill?" I crossed the room, ignoring the line of specters to reach the one who'd caught my attention.

I knew they were all "Ailill" in one way or another, but this specter—this young face, this disheveled hair—was mine. I was sure of it. "Ailill," I said again, reaching out to touch the white hair that cascaded off his shoulder with two fingers, leaving the coin clutched in the remaining three. "You're a specter now." I shook my head, remembering he never called them that.

"You're one of them. A servant." The hair that ought to have been deep brown was brittle in my hand. The eyes that ought to have been dark brown were black, and they focused over my head, not looking at me even as I fondled him. I gripped the hair harder, and the book dropped from my other hand to the floor. It echoed loudly in the entryway as I grabbed hold of Ailill's shoulders.

"Talk to me!" I said, my cheeks burning. Tears I hadn't even noticed cascaded down my face. "Say something!" I pounded his chest, determined to get a reaction out of him, not caring when the coin fell to the ground beside the book with a clatter. I'd never outright assaulted one of them. Surely there came a point at which they reacted. "Ailill—"

I felt a tap on my shoulder, and I turned. One of the specters had broken the line, and he held his hand out to me, his palm open.

"What?" I snapped, rubbing a haze of tears out of my eyes. This specter seemed familiar—what a farce, they *all* seemed familiar, and since they were all shades of the same man, I knew why. I couldn't shake the feeling that I knew this one more personally than the others. He was older than my Ailill, but not too old, perhaps a couple of decades older. This specter was looking at me, his black eyes boring through me. I hesitated and took his hand, which was holding the golden copper I'd dropped. "Thanks," I muttered. I reached for the book tucked beneath the specter's arm, and he drew back. I stared at him in shock. "I need that."

He fell back in line, carrying the book with him.

"Ailill," I started, not knowing what else to call him, "give that back! I only dropped it a moment—"

"May I ask how many times you are going to call me before you come inside the garden? Surely it has not escaped your notice that these men are clearly leading you here."

I froze, my hand still extended toward the specter who had taken the book from me. My ears picked up the trickle of the water fountain from the garden. I *knew* that voice. It felt a little off, perhaps, too calm, too blithe, but he had spoken.

"Ailill!"

A young man—perhaps a year or two older or younger than me—leaned against the door frame to the garden, his arms crossed against his chest, one leg crossed in front of the other.

"As you have said. Many times now." He nodded at me. "Come join me. I believe you have a lot to tell me."

He turned, crossing past the rose bushes—the bushes no longer withering, no longer dying, even with the chill of winter soon upon us—and sitting at the nearest stone bench. My eyes flitted over the rest of the garden. The entire place looked so much more cared-for than it had the last time I'd seen it, months before when I'd first sought out Ailill after the curse had broken. The benches were upright, and there wasn't a speck of brush out of place to litter the walkway or the table. Even the fountain spurted clear water, and the broken statue of the boy crying was conspicuously missing.

"Come," repeated the young man, gesturing to the bench on the other side of him. On the table was a chess game, and I remembered the matches I'd had with Ailill, and the brother I'd mistaken for him. I clutched the coin harder.

"Do not bother to hide that," said the young man, nodding. "You bring gold into my castle, and you stand there, your mouth agape, as if you do not know what it means."

"Gold?" I repeated, opening my hand to look at the coin I held there tightly. "The golden coin?" Some instinct compelled me not to betray my ignorance. *Ailill told me this token gave me the right to know...* I straightened my back and stepped in farther.

"Of course I know," I lied, trying to put that confidence into my shaky, soggy steps. I stopped suddenly, my eyes scanning the man's face. Of course. This was why he was shaded darker in the book; he came back, but he was no longer faded. He was born again, but younger—only slightly younger—but how? Why at this age? This was Ailill, as dark and as beautiful as any man in the village—no, even more so. I gasped. "Ailill!"

He shook his head, and the corner of his lips upturned into a smile that set my body on fire. "As you have said," he repeated. He gestured to the chess board. "Then come. Join me. I should enjoy a game with a lady in on the bet, my future bride."

CHAPTER TWO

I nearly dropped the coin from my clammy fingers. "Your bride?" I sputtered, unable to stop myself. The look on Ailill's face was almost convincing enough to make me think he was genuinely surprised.

"I assumed you knew." He studied me. I saw something in his expression I could hardly remember ever seeing before: uncertainty.

I tucked a piece of hair behind my ear; it was nearly dry now, although I still felt soaked to the bone. *"A lady in on the bet."* I'd been so flustered by the "bride" part that I hadn't even stopped to think about the first thing he'd called me. I closed the distance between us and sat down on the bench, keeping the coin clutched tightly in my palm. I reached out and lifted one of the chess pieces, a pawn.

"You are soaked," he said, regarding me.

I put the piece down in entirely the wrong place. "Yes... The pool, in the cavern. That was merely an hour ago, even less. How long has it been for you?"

Ailill had his hand on the pawn piece I'd moved, but he froze as he lifted it off the board. "How long... has it been?"

"Since you..." I shook my head. "Ailill, what happened to you?"

Ailill frowned slightly, putting the pawn back where it had been to begin with. "You moved that piece incorrectly," he said. "I would have thought you would know how to play, if you were in on the bet."

I yanked the board to the side of the table, not caring that the pieces tumbled as a result. The white queen rolled off the board and to the dirt beside the nearest rose bush. "I *do* know how to play," I snapped. I stopped myself from reminding him *he* taught me. There was something off about him, something more than the fact that he was younger and altered. "I'm not in the mood for games."

Ailill's eyebrows arched as he regarded the mess I'd made of the game board. "I see that." He leaned back in his seat, supporting his back against the castle wall. "Then what *have* you come for?"

"Answers."

"Answers? To what questions?"

I took a deep breath and watched Ailill, thinking through what I was about to say. I wanted to ask him about the "they" he kept bringing up before everything got out of hand, the "always-watching" people he barely spoke of above a whispered hush. But I couldn't disavow my feeling that something more than just physical appearance had changed with him.

"What happened to you?" I repeated.

Ailill looked down at me over his nose. "You know me," he said after a moment's silence.

"Of course I—" The words caught in my throat. "You don't know me?"

"I do," Ailill said as he leaned forward and put his arms on the table. "I think. There's something about you... But no. It can't be."

"Can't be *what*?"

Ailill waved a hand in the air dismissively. "You remind me of someone I knew as a boy. But I have not *been* a boy in so many years, you are sure not to believe it. Unless...?" He stared at me again, and I looked away. "You might believe it. If you knew me in my last life. If you carry that gold with purpose."

I cocked my head slightly, staring at Ailill's black-gloved hands on the table, careful to avoid his eyes. "I know you die and are reborn," I said. "You died not very long ago." I gestured at myself. "So little time has passed, I haven't even bothered to throw on a fresh pair of clothes."

"Drowning?"

My eyes snapped back up to meet his. "Pardon?"

"Did I drown this time?" Ailill asked. He seemed drawn to the dampness of my clothing. "I cannot say I know how, unless I left the castle..."

"You *did* leave!" I decided not to correct his assumption that he'd drowned, not just yet, not just now. "Are you telling me you remember nothing from your past life?"

Ailill frowned and looked away. His gaze was drawn to the rose bush, and he plucked a withering bloom from the leaves and branches. "I do. I remember all of them. But none so clear as my first." He turned the dying rose in his hand, examining it closer. "I remember the pain, mostly. The never-ending pain. The always-enduring loneliness."

"Don't tell me your last life isn't *clear* to you! You seemed perfectly aware of your other lives before that..." I stopped, biting my lip. He hadn't said anything specific about any of those other lives beyond the first one. Nothing beyond watching the villagers in the book, sending servants out to get food and clothing. "You *have to* remember. You're sitting here right now without covering your face—"

Panicked, Ailill dropped the rose bud onto the table and put his hands toward his face, as if feeling for something. He laughed at my surprised reaction and dropped his hands, reaching for the rose bud again to twirl between his fingers. "That is no surprise," he said, and I had to wonder why he made a show of panicking. Ailill didn't joke. Did he? "They told me the curse was broken before they sent me back. I had to wonder why I *was* being sent back, then, but—say." He smiled awkwardly. "You haven't met them, have you?"

"No, I haven't." I took a deep breath, trying to bite back my annoyance. "Maybe you'll introduce me."

Ailill laughed and let the remnants of the petals fall from his gloved fingers. "How did you come across that gold then?"

"*They* sent it to me," I replied. It may not have been fact, but for all I knew, it wasn't a lie, either. Who else could get their hands on this color metal, if Ailill insisted it wasn't him?

Ailill shrugged. "Then you should know how to find them."

I cleared my throat. "I do. The hole behind the throne room."

Ailill frowned, but his attention was drawn to something behind me. "Ah. So that is where it was."

I flinched as a specter appeared from behind me and placed the book he'd stolen from me on the table. I reached out for it, but Ailill grabbed it first, raising an eyebrow as my hands landed on his.

"This belongs in the castle," he said. "How did you come to have it with you?"

"*You* brought it with us when we left yesterday evening. To deal with the tavern fight."

"Fight...?" Ailill's brow furrowed as he flipped through the pages. He gasped. "Dear goddess! How has this village come to this?"

I couldn't stop the blush that flitted across my cheeks at Ailill still invoking the deity we both knew—at least I *thought* we both knew—was just a foolish girl. Namely, me. "There was a fight at the tavern last night. And a fire, you told me."

"A fight? But how?" Ailill scowled and stopped leafing through the book to stare at one page in particular. "The game has changed," he said, and I didn't understand his meaning. He slapped the book shut and stood. He looked me over. "You had best put on warmer clothes."

"Why?" I asked, not taking his meaning. I needed him to explain to me what was going on, to take me to "them"—but I hadn't even been back to Mother and Elfriede, even if Jurij was with them. I hadn't seen who else might have been hurt in the fight and the fire, or how else my world had fallen apart since the night before.

Ailill passed by me and headed toward the door, the book tucked beneath his arm. He paused just for a second to favor me with an incredulous look. "You say they sent you that gold. Then you should know we have work to do."

CHAPTER THREE

There was still a stash of those dresses Ailill had had made for me in the room that used to be mine. I was hesitant to bother changing—there was so much I kept thinking about, so many questions I wanted answered. But before I could go after this new, forgetful Ailill, before I could even figure out where he went, two specters blocked me at the garden doorway. One was the one who'd stolen the book from me, and I was just about to let him have it for that, when I realized the other was *my* Ailill, the one who'd been stabbed through the back to save me. I clamped my mouth shut.

They led me to my room, where I rummaged through the chest of clothes until I found the least ostentatious dress in there. The drabber clothing that had been mine since before I became the lord's goddess, the kind of dresses most women in the village wore, had been sent back to my house shortly after the curse was broken. So I was stuck with silkier dresses covered with little flourishes that had no business being on something someone was going to wear to do anything more than sit there like an orna-ment. I chose a dark red one, as it seemed the closest color I could find to the browns and tans I usually wore. It also had a little pocket in the material behind a flower that was perfect for my coin.

I glanced at the two specters who'd followed me into the room and ducked behind the changing screen, peeking back out again to grab a lovely yellow dress, which I turned into a rag and used to dry myself off after I'd peeled off the soaked outfit. I cringed a little to use a dress as a rag that I was sure Siofra, and perhaps Nissa, had made after Ailill paid them, but I never would have worn it anyway.

By the time I stepped out, drier, a bit warmer, but still clammy, the specter who had stolen my book stepped up to greet me, a hair brush in hand.

"No, thank you. I remember a specter's skills with a hair brush quite well," I said, fluffing my hair with my fingers. It was wet and could probably use a good brushing. I ducked over to the mirror and saw it had grown longer since I last looked in a mirror—not as long as it once was, but longer than I thought it was—I didn't exactly have access to many mirrors. I cringed when I saw how lovely the dress looked, after I'd gone out of my way to find one that wouldn't make me stand out too much. I placed a hand atop the brush as the specter held it out toward me. "Let's not bother with that," I said, looking into his eyes, speaking to him as a person. Something unsettled me as I held his gaze, and I felt the tug of something familiar beyond his similar appearance to a somewhat-older Ailill.

"You—" I started, but I felt a brush run through my hair and jumped, ripping my head backward. "Ailill!" The most recently-created specter had snuck up behind me to brush my hair. I cradled my head in my hands. I couldn't keep thinking of them all as "Ailill," even if that's what Ailill—*my* Ailill and the new Ailill—called them. I snatched the brush from the most recently-created specter and began running it through my hair, gasping as it ripped through knots. "Fine. If it must be done, I'll do it." I turned to the mirror and cringed as the brush caught on another knot.

I flung the brush down on the small vanity after I finished and gripped the table, taking a deep breath. "You," I said, turning and facing the most recently-created specter. "You're the one I knew. The one who hated me. The one I sort of disliked, too." A cloud of something flashed over that Ailill's face and I stopped, surprised to see anything resembling emotion on those pure-white features.

"I didn't hate you, though. Not in the end." I straightened my shoulders and tugged at my dress, smoothing out the wrinkles. "You'll be 'Scorn' when I talk to you, all right?"

The cloud of emotion that had passed over "Scorn's" face dispelled, and I couldn't tell whether this hurt or pleased him or made no difference at all. I turned to the other specter. "And you. I'm sure I recognize you. You dropped the prison key for me, didn't you? And you were going to speak to me, I know it. You opened your mouth that one time…" I paused, waiting to see if my words had any effect on him. He just kept looking at me, though. That in and of itself was odd, as they usually looked over my head when they didn't want something from me. I threw my hands up in the air.

"Fine, don't speak. Keep pretending you can't, even though I've seen you all whisper to your lord from time to time." I pulled out a pair of new shoes from the chest, comfortable shoes but shoes not as practical as my soggy boots were. I slipped them on and swept past the specters, pointing to the one I was addressing as I passed. "You'll be 'Spurn.'" I stopped and looked from Scorn to Spurn and back and then nodded. "Well, gentlemen, let's get moving." I held out both arms apart from my torso, inviting them to slip in on either side. They stood there a moment and then the strangest thing happened. They exchanged a look with one another, just the slightest of nods, and moved forward as one to slide in on either side of me.

~

"AILILL!" I called as I arrived outside the castle, dropping my escorts' arms and gathering my too-long skirt in my hands. I stepped up the black carriage steps and swept into the open door, ignoring the hands the other specters on either side offered up for assistance. "You waited for me!"

"Of course," replied the darker, younger lord of the village. The door of the carriage shut behind me and Ailill tapped on the roof of the carriage, signaling the specter driver to let us be off. "The Ailills had to go get the carriage anyway. They found it halfway along the path in the woods for some reason."

I grimaced and said nothing.

Ailill smiled. "There is no need to explain. I assume it has something to do with the state of your previous attire," he said. "And the fate of my last incarnation."

"Yes," I admitted, my eyes dropping to my hands, which I held together in my lap. I thought of the last time we shared a ride in this carriage, just the night before, and how close we'd come to... Well, how close we'd come to something. I eyed the book that Ailill kept on the seat beside him. "You should know at least, if you're going to investigate the tavern fight and the fire... Some of my friends were responsible."

"Your friends?" Ailill leaned back into his chair.

"Not directly," I said. "Although they were the ones who came up with the idea. They thought a fight might distract you, and things got..." I stopped, choking on my words, remembering the fate of my father. The thought was like a fresh knife, tearing apart a barely-scabbed wound. "Things got out of hand," I added quietly.

Ailill sighed. "Need I ask why your friends intended to 'distract' me?"

"I can tell you, but right now—"

"Right now we have other things that require our attention." Ailill smiled, although it seemed to require some effort. "You look lovely."

"What?" The comment was so off topic, so completely unexpected, that I momentarily lost my train of thought. I tucked my hair behind my ears, unable to take his comment in stride, not when my stomach was already a wave of so many other emotions. I could feel his eyes burning into me, so I looked away, out the window. "Stop—" I started.

"I apologize. Now is hardly the time for that, either. I couldn't help myself. You—"

"No, stop! Stop the carriage!" I knocked on the roof, and the carriage ground to a halt. Ailill hardly had time to register his surprise before he had to fling his hands out, grabbing hold of the walls to stop himself from falling.

"Where are you—" Ailill began as I thrust open the carriage door.

But I was already down the steps and running toward the cottage at the end of the woods, the home of Gideon Woodcarver and his family—*my* family. The home of Gideon Woodcarver's widow. "Mother!" I shouted as I clutched my skirt higher; that insufferable dress was simply too long to be practical. "Mother," I called again, flinging open the cottage door. "Elfriede," I said, quieter. My gaze fell over the room, and I saw Mother sitting at the edge of her bed, clutching something to her chest, with Elfriede beside her, her arm around her.

"Noll?" Mother's voice croaked as she looked up to see me.

I glanced around. "Where's Jurij?" I asked, thinking of the scene out of the book.

Elfriede's water-filled eyes narrowed. "Not here." Her tone seemed too hostile, considering the tragedy that should have bound us.

"You just missed him," said Mother, oblivious. She paused to catch her breath between sobs. "He went to the site of the tavern after... After that. And he found this." She held out the cloth she'd been cradling.

I couldn't place it, but I knew it was a jerkin. Whether because it was covered in soot or because I hadn't seen him enough the past few months—the past year or more—to recognize it, I couldn't say for sure I knew whose it was. But I did. Just from the way Mother gazed at, I knew it was Father's.

I rushed over to her and put a hand on her knee, sitting on the other side of her. "So he's gone," I said, after a moment of silence.

"*Of course* he's gone!" Elfriede let go of Mother as I reached out to hug her myself. She stood and paced the room. "I thought... I thought maybe he got out. It was *burned down*, how would they know so quickly who survived?" Elfriede's eyes flitted accusingly toward me. "But Jurij—but *he* said he heard it from Vena herself. Father was the first to die before the fire even started. Stabbed through the back with a broken glass. Vena was so shocked, she was still clutching the clothes he'd left behind as she made her way out of there." She spat, an act so strange I found myself leaning back away from her instinctively. "What could he have been *thinking*?"

"Elfriede, please," said Mother quietly. "You'll just upset yourself—"

"I've reason to be upset!" Elfriede whirled on Mother and me, the tears in her eyes hardly hiding the anger. "Mother, Father participated in this plan of Jaron's. He *started* that commotion at the tavern—"

Mother squeezed the clothing tighter. "We don't know that!"

"We do! Even he—even Jurij admitted as much!" Elfriede pointed at me accusingly. "And you, Noll? What was your part in all of this?"

"My... part?"

Elfriede flung her hands in my direction. "Just look at yourself! Our father just died, and here you are, sitting there in a pretty dress like it's your wedding day!" She took a deep breath, gathering more energy for her tirade. "You have to know something!"

"No more than you. Not about that fight at the tavern, or the tavern fire—"

"You *lived with* Jurij. You spent time with these men, you have to know something!" She sat back down beside Mother, the volume of her voice lowering. "You have to know what to do."

What to do? My fingers clutched the fabric of my dress, so silky and fine, so out of place on me and in the middle of this grief.

"Elfriede, please. Settle down. Your father wasn't the only loss Noll has dealt with today." Mother scoffed at herself, her eyes drawn to her lap. "Today. It must be yesterday by now. But we haven't slept, and this day just keeps on going..." She stopped, suddenly choking on a sob. Elfriede rushed in to wrap her arms around her as Mother pressed the sooty jerkin to her lips. No one said anything for a while longer, and even Elfriede's sadness seemed to have won out against her anger, as her sobs joined Mother's. I froze, suddenly incapable of feeling. It was like I was dreaming, like my grief belonged to another person. I'd lost a parent before and she sat there now, right beside me. Could I go through that again? Could I convince myself it was real this time, that there would never come a day in which I'd see Father again?

"I feel terrible," came a voice after a moment. Mother, Elfriede and I all lifted our heads in tandem toward the open doorway.

Ailill stepped in, but he stopped when he saw the expressions on Mother's and Elfriede's faces. Elfriede's jaw dropped open.

"I overheard your exchange. I was curious to know why you suddenly leapt out of the carriage." Ailill clenched his hands into fists at his side. "I did not realize you had lost your father. And then, I realized… I do not even know your name."

Elfriede glanced at Mother and then me, the puzzlement clear on her features. *Does he mean me?* she seemed to be asking me. *Or Mother?* Why he'd care to ask either name right now was probably just as bizarre a question as why he was standing there breathing, a bit younger and far darker than he was the only time she'd really seen him before.

I stood and fixed the fabric of the dress that caught at my thighs, smoothing out the dark red material. I knew exactly what he meant, and, looking into his eyes, and seeing how they searched me, *really* searched me, I fully believed it finally. This was and was not the Ailill I knew. And he didn't remember me— well, he didn't remember anything that could tie the two of us together. Anything that would make us enemies. Anything that would make us friends.

Or more than that.

I extended my hand so he could take it. "I'm Noll," I said, as he took the hand and raised it toward his lips. "But you once knew me as Olivière."

Ailill's eyes widened and he dropped my hand before he managed to kiss it.

CHAPTER FOUR

The next few days were a blur. Mother, Elfriede and I hardly slept and could barely eat, and I had more than just Father's passing and the mourning arrangements to fret about. There was work to be done in the village to get us all past this and to introduce Ailill to his people. Thinking back on it, so few people had actually seen him—and those few who had had seen him die in the cavern—that no one questioned his new appearance, not at first. No one even knew he'd been killed. My former friends and Elfriede's friends must have been so in shock, they didn't have the chance to spread the rumor before Ailill showed up in the middle of the village the next day to introduce himself.

I wasn't there, not then. I heard later from Alvilda how Ailill had exited the carriage, stunned an already-stunned crowd into silence, and walked over to Elweard and Vena, his arms extended. He'd embraced them both, but they didn't embrace him back. Their faces got more astonished, if anything. Even Alvilda was too tongue-tied to ask just who he was, and why he was claiming to be the lord, when she knew for a fact he was dead. Yet she saw the resemblance regardless.

I'd been so shocked about Ailill's return, so numb about Father's death, it hadn't occurred to me to consider how the fire had eventually stopped and kept from spreading too far. It had rained in the night, while we were in the cavern. That rain had saved most of the village, but there were already too many who were lost. There was something no one in the village would ever be able to get back: their sense of safety.

First men started realizing the freedom of their hearts, and that freedom lead most of them away from their goddesses—only there weren't any "goddesses," not really. No woman was worthy of worship anymore, not in men's eyes. And so went the safety and security of love, of family.

Then the men discovered there was more to life than love, and they wandered freely from their jobs, leaving behind the things that needed to be done. Too many wandered into the tavern, and too much drink and too much freedom led them to that day when they discovered violence. "Rediscovered" violence, I should say. I knew that long ago, the men who were their ancestors knew it all too well.

Violence led to destruction and death and astonishment. It died down in the dawn of the new day, as the smell of burnt wood floated away with the after-rain breeze. It was gone for now, as people mourned the twelve men and two women who'd perished in that fight or in the blaze thereafter. I didn't trust it to be gone forever. Not now that I knew what even the men I loved and trusted were capable of.

But those were thoughts for another day.

"What do you think about these?" asked Alvilda, for probably the second or third time. I spent far too long gazing at the wall and thinking about other things the past week. I counted on Alvilda to remind me I had a job to do. Apparently.

I pulled the drawing of small cottages closer to where I sat at Mother's table. Arrow lifted his head at the movement, no doubt hoping it was something to eat. I hadn't been back to my own cottage since this whole mess had begun. I wound up asking Nissa to go and fetch some of the clothes I'd left there. Elfriede seemed more subdued now that I wore less noticeable clothing. "It's fine," I said, quickly pushing the drawing back to Alvilda. Disappointed, Arrow let his head droop. "Whatever you want."

"Whatever *I* want?" Alvilda sighed and put the drawing back on the top of her stack of similar images. "Noll, the quarry workers can help with the stone foundations, but you're the only

one I can count on to help me with the wood parts, now that..."
She bit her lip as I met her eye. "I'm sorry. I wasn't thinking. I
didn't even mean your father, although that's part of it. I just
meant... The village is in even worse shape than it has been the
past few months."

"I'm the only other skilled woodcarver left," I admitted. Not
that we could have counted on my father to help out these past
few years regardless. *That's not fair. Who's to say? Maybe he would
have stepped up. If he wasn't one of the ones who caused this problem in
the first place.* "You need my help, and I can't fully focus. I'm
sorry."

"I didn't mean it like that." Alvilda shuffled her papers,
looking for one in particular. "You have other responsibilities. I
can't really expect you to be out there, rolling your sleeves back
and building a new commune for the men displaced by the
tavern fire, all things considered."

"Maybe not, but I should be. I'd *like* to be." It was true that I'd
grown fond of carving animals—little wooden toys for the kids in
the village—in the past few months. My woodcarving skills
leaned more toward the little details than the practical, but I'd
helped Alvilda fill orders before, and she'd even started building
her own workshop on the outskirts of the abandoned commune
with a little of my input. I could help her do something productive, something I knew would help the village, and there was a
selfish reason I wanted to help, too. Working with the wood just
might keep my mind off of everything else.

Alvilda stopped her flutter of movement and reached out to
grab my hand. "Are you really going to be the 'lady' of the
village?"

I swallowed. "That's what he seems to think. Although... I'm
not sure that's what he wants."

"Who *is* he exactly? He resembles the lord we saw in the
cavern, but—"

"It's him. Just... reborn."

"Reborn?" Alvilda pulled her hand from mine so she could
lean back. "Are you telling me when he dies he's just... reborn?
As a young, but grown, man?"

"I guess so." I grabbed the drawing sticking out from the rest
of the pile and looked it over, bending a corner of the page.

"Those servants you hate?" I said, hesitating. "They're his former lives."

"You *must* be joking!" Alvilda scoffed, but then she studied me, and the smile vanished from her face. "You're serious."

I nodded. "Don't ask me to explain how—or why—it happens to him."

"But—"

I glowered at her. "No, *don't*. Please."

She sighed and straightened her pile. "All right. *I'll* let it go. For now. But you know I'm not the only one who saw him before this—"

"But you're one of the only ones who might make a fuss about it right now." I stared at the drawing of the cottage on the page. It seemed comfortable, inviting. I ran my fingers over it subconsciously. "The men who were involved in that have been cowering, their tails between their legs—"

"I'd hardly count going back to their daily lives 'cowering.'" Alvilda sounded skeptical. "Actually, they're being more productive than they have been in weeks. Months. All of a sudden, blacksmiths are actually smithing. Quarry workers are digging. Luuk and Jurij are actually interested in woodworking—"

The page fell out of my hands. "What about Jurij's job at the quarry?"

Alvilda tossed her head to flick her hair over her shoulders. "He moved back in with Siofra and me. I had to make sure he was doing *something*. Lo and behold, the woodwork he was so reluctant to help out with actually suits him."

I reached for my sash, gripping the coin through the soft material. Holding it calmed me, even if I still had so many questions about it. "I'm glad *someone's* with him."

"Noll—"

"No, I mean it. If he was alone, I just might track him down and—"

"*Noll!*"

I jammed my finger on the drawing. "This one," I said. I'd been staring at it for so long, maybe my mind was playing tricks on me, but it seemed so inviting. "Make them look like this."

Alvilda frowned, clearly not happy to let my comment slide, but she did so anyway, reaching for the drawing I'd taken. She nodded, studying it, and some of the tension in her forehead dissipated. "Hmm. Sturdy but small. We could build these quickly. They're not too complicated. I'll have to ask for help."

"Take what labor you need," I said, pushing back from the table. "Any able-bodied person not busy with work—man, woman, or older child. And there's plenty of other help for you." I stood and went to the door, opening it. "Spurn!" I called, ignoring Scorn on the other side of the door. It unnerved me to look at him for too long, and Spurn had shown more signs of life even before Scorn came to be. "Alvilda and her builders need plenty of wood for the commune project. Can you and some of the other specters handle it?" I didn't care that I called them "specters" when Ailill left them to attend to me as "servants." It was a hard habit for me to break.

Spurn met my eyes and nodded, and he was off, down the road that led through the woods to the castle. I stared at Scorn, who kept looking dully forward, ignoring me, not bothering to fulfill the task I'd asked of them. I shrugged and turned around.

"Olivière!" If the voice weren't so high pitched and friendly, hearing my full name right then might have made my heart ache terribly. Instead, I turned back around and did my best to smile as Roslyn came over the hill from the direction of the village. I returned her wave and took note of Mother's haggard appearance as she came into view, leaning into Elfriede on one side, Mistress Baker holding her arm on the other. I took a deep breath and turned back in, leaving the door open.

"Who is it?" asked Alvilda, a little leery.

"Just Mother and Elfriede returned. With Mistress Baker and Roslyn." I sat down again and straightened my shoulders, grabbing the chosen drawing from where it lay on top of the pile of other ideas. "I've asked the servants to get you ample wood for the project. Work with what labor you can on crafting the homes until then. When they've finished chopping, you can rely on their help for the building."

Out of the corner of my eye, I saw Alvilda smile smugly. "And here I thought if anything *you'd* request to chop down the wood."

"All by myself?" The thought actually comforted me for a bit. Just me, an axe, the woods and nothing but silence to accompany me. I laughed. "There's too much else to do. Vena and Elweard lost their tools for ale making in the fire—not that I'm sure that's a bad thing—so I have to see about getting the blacksmith to craft hoops for new kegs and all the other things they'll have to describe to me. And then we have to make sure enough of the men have gone back to farming so we can get the last of the autumn crop in before winter—"

"You know," interrupted Alvilda, "you don't have to do *that* by yourself, either."

I stiffened. "I don't mind." I nodded toward the door. "And I have them to help when you can spare them."

"Good day, Alvilda, Olivière." Although I hadn't meant that group at all, Roslyn entered the cottage just then, a basket on her arm, followed by Mother, Elfriede and Mistress Baker. "Olivière, you should have seen your mother this morning. She was so helpful in helping us fill our excess order..." Roslyn kept talking, but she turned to the women behind her, fussing with trying to cheer up my mother.

Alvilda leaned over and whispered to me. "I didn't mean the labor. You're not the only one leading the village."

"We've delegated the tasks," I answered quietly. "I'm... not sure he's ready to see me again just yet."

"*Olivi...*" *Ailill clutched his hands behind his back, leaving my own hand out and hanging. I lowered it to my side, awkwardly, as Ailill cleared his throat. "Olivière?" he repeated. "Like the—"*

"*Woman you knew as a child," I finished for him.*

His eyes darted to Mother and Elfriede behind me, but I didn't turn to look, though I could feel them staring at us. I wanted to see Ailill's reaction. It was like I'd stabbed him and robbed him of all that new vigor he seemed to have in this new life.

Ailill clicked his heels together and nodded, struggling to smile. "Yes, well. There is so much work to do." He turned, and I walked after him, but he stopped, looking back over his shoulder. "Stay," he said, softly. "You have your own mourning to arrange."

"*Yes, but I want to help—"*

"*You shall." Ailill snapped his fingers, and two specters entered my home. I blinked. They were clearly Scorn and Spurn, the two I'd named to keep them separate from the others in my mind. "I'll leave them with you," continued Ailill, as the two men filed quietly into the room. "No, they better wait outside." He nodded and they followed him out.*

I was too steps behind, ignoring Scorn and Spurn as they took their posts on either side of my family home's door. "I can help," I repeated. "If you'll wait for me."

Ailill paused with one foot on the first step leading to the carriage. "You shall," he repeated, and he turned around, lowering his foot back to the ground. He stared at me for a moment and seemed at war with himself. In the end, though, he reached out quickly, taking my hand in his. He didn't raise it to his lips but instead squeezed it lightly with both hands. "The people know you are to rule beside me, I assume?"

"No," I admitted. "That is... They knew I was your goddess, but now there are no—"

Ailill dropped my hand, cutting me off. "It matters not. I will make sure they are aware, so they can turn to you as well as me in the upcoming weeks." He climbed into the carriage and poked his head out as he reached for the carriage door. "Rest. Mourn. I will send word with my plans for settling this unrest as soon as I can."

He shut the door before I could say more, and the carriage moved down the road toward the heart of the village.

I hadn't seen him since. He was apologetic in his letters, always citing the work to be done in rebuilding and setting up temporary housing for those displaced, in settling the villagers' fears. But I'd seen his carriage drive back and forth between the castle and the village at least twice a day and he'd yet to do more than send a specter to look in on me. Even during the memorial we'd had for Father in our backyard. I couldn't bring myself to send word, but with Spurn and Scorn there, always watching, and with the book left behind, I knew he must have seen me in one of my darkest hours, and he hadn't come.

He barely knew me now, but he knew enough to detest me again.

"Well," said Alvilda, oblivious to the dark turn of my thoughts, "I suppose you're right. He seems to be efficiently running things. Men who can't stand to go back home have been staying with friends until the commune is ready. Vena and Elweard may not have ale, but they're cooking and serving what they can inside the Great Hall."

I stood with Alvilda to show her out the door. I smiled best I could in reaction to her news, but I felt like it was more like a grimace. "Give my best to Siofra and Nissa," I told her. "And to

Luuk." I decided he was young enough to get a pass on his part in it all. His father and brother had practically forced him into it.

Roslyn and Mistress Baker added logs to the fire as Elfriede brought out the iron pot she'd cleaned the night before. *Stew again*, I thought. That meant she'd need some help peeling potatoes.

"You can tell them yourself," said Alvilda, distracting me. "If you're going to speak to Vena and Elweard, you're bound to run into us at the Great Hall one of these days. There's been so much work to be done, we haven't had time for cooking. We've been relying entirely on what Vena's been providing."

"I can eat here," I snapped, harsher than I meant to. "I don't need to go there, I mean." I rolled back my sleeves, prepping for Elfriede's rather disdainful call to potato-peeling duty, but Mother surprised me by getting up from her chair by the fire and offering to peel the vegetables instead.

"Farewell, Alvilda," Mother said, doing her best to smile. Her smile was beautiful, even if it didn't reach her eyes.

"Take care," said Mistress Baker, and Elfriede and Roslyn added their farewells as well, and Alvilda returned in kind.

I was left with nothing else to do other than to escort Alvilda outside for a bit, doing my best to ignore Scorn posted beside the doorway.

"You know, Noll," said Alvilda as she adjusted the piles of papers she'd tucked beneath her arms. "Rebuilding a village after this…. this *tragedy* is more than simply constructing new cottages and figuring out how to make ale."

"I realize that," I said. "I'm just not sure I'm the one most suited to, well, to anything other than fixing the things that are broken."

Alvilda squeezed the pile of parchments tightly against her chest so she could take both my hands in hers. "The people *are* what's broken, Noll. The damage to them could last far longer than the damage to the buildings and the things."

"I know." I couldn't look into her eyes for long, but I made the mistake of looking away. My eyes caught Scorn's, if only for a second. He still seemed like he was looking past me. *He's not him*, I reminded myself. *Not anymore. That new Ailill, he's the one who's living. Even if he doesn't remember you. That's... probably for the best anyway.* "I'm not good at... fixing people."

"You don't have to be," said Alvilda, squeezing my hands. "You just have to show them how to fix themselves." She took a deep breath. "Well, I'd best be off." She turned to go but stopped to look at me one more time over her shoulder. "Drop by for dinner at the Great Hall one of these evenings," she added. "If you're afraid to go alone, then bring a friend."

I grunted, not in the mood for her to give me some lecture if I pointed out that all of the friends I'd gained in the past few months after losing them as a child were the ones I was sure were most broken of all.

I turned to go back inside, my chest strangely tightening as I heard the sound of laughter. *You should be glad they're laughing. We need some laughter in this household.* I found myself gazing at Scorn and I realized my twinge of jealousy at the sound was because I was outside the cottage when it happened. Because I was always outside, even when I thought I was in. If my "friends" had cared enough about me, they would have told me what they were planning. And I could have stopped them. Maybe. At the very least, I could have warned him.

"Olivière?" said Roslyn, tearing my eyes from the statue-still reminder of my failure to save him. "Care for a roll?"

I stepped inside, taking the roll she held out to me.

CHAPTER FIVE

"There's a pin coming out of your hair," said Roslyn, and she reached over, making me stop. My hair was growing longer, but I wasn't in the mood to cut it. Roslyn had urged Elfriede to (reluctantly, and only with Roslyn watching) teach me how to pin back the pieces that would have otherwise kept whapping across my face. Evidently, I still had a ways to go in my lessons.

Roslyn slipped her arm back through mine when she finished adjusting my loose tendril. "It's sweet of you to ask me to come," she said, not for the first time. "But wouldn't you rather ask Elfriede?"

"She's eating at home. With Mother and Marden." We had a string of visitors in the weeks since Father's memorial, all kind and concerned for Mother and Elfriede. But that wasn't the real reason I hadn't asked Elfriede. The truth was, I'd be just as awkward with her at my side as I would be going alone—or more awkward. We were on speaking terms, but we only seemed united in making sure Mother didn't slip too far beyond where we could reach her. There was still something that hung in the air between us, something that existed many years before for a very different reason than it did now, but something that only worsened over time and never went away. I thought after what we'd seen, we could at least be united in our dislike of Jurij, but his

486

name never passed either of our lips. His visit that first day after the fire and the cavern, from what I could gather, was only half welcome.

"That's right. Marden did tell me she was going over there." Roslyn's skirt swished almost annoyingly close to mine, practically tangling the two together. So this was what it was like to have a female friend—friend?—other than the decidedly masculine Alvilda. Roslyn lowered her voice, bringing her head in toward mine. "Did you know she has a new man?"

I faltered, practically tripping over some empty baskets next to a marketplace stall. The stand was pretty bare. The influx of farmers after the fire roused some of the men back to work was still not enough to get us enough vegetables to eat for the present, considering we were more concerned about storing what we had for winter. "Marden?" I asked, suddenly feeling very stupid that my first instinct had been that she was referring to Elfriede.

"Yup," said Roslyn, pulling back and breaking into a smile. She winked. "You wouldn't have guessed it, right? Not after all those sour things she had to say about Sindri. But Mother and Father invited some of the displaced men over to stay at the Tannery, and one took to the work real fast." She jabbed me with her elbow, almost sending me toppling over. "And took to Marden even faster."

I smiled, not sure if I was supposed to laugh. "She didn't seem to want a new husband—"

Roslyn waved a hand. "Well, I wouldn't say she's grooming him to be a husband or anything. I don't think women are too eager to jump right back into that." She paused, thinking a moment. "But she likes him, and he makes her happy. And she's much nicer to be around when she's happy."

I just hoped she learned that this time she'd have to keep being "nicer" if she wanted him to keep making her happy. Still, it wasn't my business. I barely knew Roslyn's sister, and in any case, from what little I knew, I at least understood she wasn't thrilled to be around me. "That's good," I said, patting Roslyn's forearm awkwardly. "I'm happy for her." I felt the strain of the effort, but I knew it was the right thing to do. I'd asked her to join me for dinner at the Great Hall when she finished work at the bakery for the afternoon and I'd touched base both with Alvilda in the commune construction area and the farmers in the crop fields. The least I could do was try to *be* a friend to someone I hoped could be mine. Even if the last time I'd spent so much time with other girls my age, I was running at them and threatening to strike them with a wooden stick.

"And you?" I thought, wondering if that's what Elfriede or one of the other young women would do. Continue talking about men and love, wanting to know every detail of each other's feelings.

"Me?" asked Roslyn, incredulous. "I have no time for men with all the baking I have to do. Besides…" She grew quiet, her face a little grave. "I didn't really have the best of luck last time."

"No one did. Not really. None of us can hope to find that kind of love again." Still, I felt foolish for asking her, and bringing up the sore spot that was her former husband, Darwyn, my former friend. In the past few months, he somehow discovered a passion for another man, another former friend, Tayton. I supposed if Alvilda and Siofra could love one another with free hearts, it only made sense that some men would feel the same for others of their gender as soon as their hearts were set free. Roslyn and Darwyn got on well enough shortly before that night, but what she'd witnessed in the cavern might have changed that… Darwyn was no longer even living at home with his mother, instead staying at his older brother's family's house with Tayton, from what Roslyn told me.

"Yes, well…" Roslyn turned over her shoulder, and I knew exactly who she was staring at. "Some of us have a lot more hope than others, don't we?" She smiled and nudged me. I knew she was teasing, and she meant well, but I couldn't even begin to explain how wrong she was.

"What's it like?" asked Roslyn, not picking up on my discomfort. "Having them follow you all over? Do they ever leave you to run messages between you and his lordship?"

Without thinking, I gazed over my shoulder to find Scorn and Spurn a few steps behind me, silent, faithful pets always keeping an eye on me—to protect me (from what?) or to see what I was up to, I couldn't be sure. Spurn had done well in gathering more specters to supply Alvilda and the men and women helping her with the wood she'd need to finish the new commune. She hadn't been thrilled with the idea of them helping her build it, though, and she'd shooed them away, and now Spurn took his place beside Scorn always at my beck and call.

"Yes," I said, at last remembering Roslyn's question. "But just about getting the village back on its feet."

"Sure," said Roslyn, and she nudged me. She laughed. "Keep your secrets."

You have no idea.

"You know, Elfriede still thinks—watch it!" Roslyn pulled me back, just in time to keep me out of the way of three children who ran past us to get into the Great Hall. Laughing and screaming, they paid us no mind. Roslyn shook her head. "Someone ought to be watching them."

I smiled, taking a very different lesson from the children who'd nearly run us down. "I think it's good they're happy," I said, my eyes following them as we stepped into the crowded room. "These past few weeks, I wasn't sure any of us were going to be happy again. Even those not directly affected by the fire seemed to have..." I stopped as the murmur of voices died down only moments after we entered the echoing room. People nudged those beside them, and soon, nearly every set of eyes in the building was on us as we made our way toward the back of the hall. This was where mothers once performed Returnings, and it was now occupied with a makeshift fire pit and tables for all the meal fixings.

Roslyn nodded at the villagers who stared at us sheepishly, clutching my arm tighter like I might prove some protection from all of the glowering. That was a mistake, of course. If she wanted to escape the staring, she'd never be safe at my side. She should have stood farther apart, not closer.

We approached Elweard and Vena, and I took a deep breath as I remembered the reason for my visit and the things I hoped to accomplish while there. "Good evening, Elweard. Vena." I gently shrugged out of Roslyn's grasp to bend over the karge table and examine the roast the former tavern masters had made. "I came to see how you're getting on. It smells divine," I added, weaving my fingers together.

"Noll! Good of you to drop by and see us." Vena smiled and reached for a wooden plate. Hers had all burnt up in the fire, but she'd salvaged a new collection from donations from the villagers. The set hardly matched anymore, but it could be argued that the mismatched dinnerware was more appropriate for the awkward new tavern settings. The place couldn't be used for Returnings any more, after all, and there were no unmasked men and boys who needed the space for socializing away from women's eyes. Why not let it become the site of the new tavern, as large and oversized as it was? Vena could make a welcoming tavern out of a stump and tree clearing. "Can I get you and Roslyn something?" she asked, already scooping some mashed potatoes onto the plate. Elweard hummed a tune behind her as he spun a roast over the fire at the back of the hall.

"Yes, thank you," I said, reaching for my sash, only to fumble and reach again for the new pocket Elfriede had sewn into my dresses. Nissa had suggested it, after seeing me subconsciously reach for the golden coin I kept in the sash I tied around my waist, and suggesting a more secure way of keeping my things with me. Nissa started the project one afternoon she visited but encouraged Elfriede and me to work on the rest together, claiming she had far too much sewing to do for Siofra and Master Tailor. She was probably just trying to get Elfriede and me to bond over work, but I was no more skilled at that as I was with hair pins and hairdos. It didn't take long for Elfriede to snatch the dress I'd been working on and claim she'd finish the rest since I had enough to take care of. It sounded almost like she *blamed* me for that, but I wasn't about to argue with her.

"Oh, no, your copper's no good with us," said Vena, eyeing the small collection of coins I withdrew from my pocket. I caught just a glint of gold and quickly cupped my hand around the pile of coins, eyeing Vena to see if she'd noticed it. She didn't seem to have as she handed me a plate piled with sliced beef, potatoes, a sharp knife and a wooden fork and spoon. "We owe you thanks for getting us back into business and letting us use this Great Hall. And *you*, Roslyn, for giving us a hand when we were in over our heads with diners and drinkers."

I passed the plate to Roslyn behind me, and Roslyn thanked her former boss, and there seemed to be no ill will at all between them.

"Speaking of drinkers," I said, tucking the coins back into my pocket. "How is everything working out for making new ale?"

"Fine, thank you," said Vena, pointing to the back of the Great Hall. "It'll take us some time to get up and running, but your *friends* have been quite helpful." She peered over my shoulder as she handed me my plate. "Will they be needing anything?"

I followed her gaze to see Spurn and Scorn standing stock still behind Roslyn. They drew most of the stares now, which I found strange, considering how far and wide Ailill had sent the specters to help the people settle in. Still, many of the villagers had gone back to eating and talking amongst themselves, which helped relieve some of the tension in my shoulders.

"No," I answered Vena, not tearing my eyes from Spurn. He was the one who'd shown some signs of life previously. I kept hoping he'd start talking, but then I might stop accepting that Scorn, the Ailill I knew, was gone for good, this young stranger who couldn't stand to be near me left in his place. Not that Scorn could stand to be near me when he was the lord. It was different with the new Ailill, more like he found out something unflattering about a stranger he had business with, and he'd do his best to keep his distance without outright cursing her. Actually, that was exactly true. "They don't eat."

"Really? Well, I suppose so." Vena wiped her hands on her apron. "I guess I've never seen one eat in public. They used to ask for such large amounts of food in the castle..."

I grimaced.

Vena stopped wiping her brow with the back of her forearm, examining me curiously. "I mean, they *do* eat, don't they?" She frowned. "Although the lord has decreased the amount of food he has delivered. He did that even before the fire—"

"Watch it!" Roslyn raised her plate over her head as that same trio of children ran past us again, squealing. "Honestly, if I were their mother—"

"Let's sit," I said, putting a hand on Roslyn's back to guide her to the upturned crate that made up the nearest empty table back in the corner. "Thank you for the food!" I called to Vena as we retreated from her questioning, but she was back to being a flurry, taking an empty mug from a man and rushing to fill it with water from the barrel behind the table.

Roslyn followed my lead, pinching her lips and clutching her plate tightly with both hands, determined not to let any of the crowd jostle the food off of it. We arrived at the empty crate-table, the seats used for Great Hall functions towering well over the "table" surface, and I put my plate down on one end.

"Hey!" I turned and saw the three running children come to a sudden halt between Roslyn and me, almost causing her to drop her plate. She looked annoyed as she waited for them to move. But they didn't.

"Are you going to make the animals again?" asked a boy.

"Not anytime soon," I admitted, but I did my best to smile. Roslyn rolled her eyes and stepped around them, placing her plate beside mine and taking a seat.

"Aw," said one of the girls. She unclenched her fist to show me what was inside and I immediately recognized one of my carvings, a squirrel. "We wanted another one."

"I do have some I haven't sold yet," I said. "But I'll have to go back and get them." I studied the animal the girl held out in front of her. "Didn't you buy that when you were alone, sometime after your friend bought one?"

"Yup!" She smiled at her friend, who pulled a wooden cat out of the sash around her waist. They clicked them together, giggling.

I rummaged around in my pocket and found the golden coin. I hesitated, looking to see if Roslyn was watching me, but she seemed bored, and her gaze wandered around the room as she started eating potatoes.

"Did you use this to buy it?" I whispered as I placed the golden copper on my lap.

The girl bent over to inspect it and she grinned. "Yup!"

"Who gave it to you?" I asked, which I should have done immediately. I just assumed I'd known. But if he wasn't lying, it wasn't Ailill.

The girl shrugged and leaned back. "I just found it." She cocked her head and pointed behind me. "He might have dropped it." She scuffed her toe on the floor, sheepish. "Okay. It fell out of one of his pockets. Finders keepers and all..."

"His?" I turned around and saw her looking at Spurn and Scorn behind me. Scorn, of course, hadn't existed yet, so that left

Spurn, but surely she couldn't tell one from the other. Still, it was definitely one of the specters. Did that mean Ailill had been lying to me?

The shrieks of the kids snapped my attention back to them.

"Show us the ones that are left!" called the boy, as the girls started running again.

"I'll bring them here," I promised. "And you won't have to pay for them. Every kid who wants one can get one. Until I run out anyway!"

"Really?" The boy seemed incredibly pleased. "Thank you!" He ran after the girls, shouting something about how he was "getting one of them."

Roslyn eyed me over a spoonful of potatoes. "That's nice of you," she said as I tucked the golden copper into my pocket, grateful she didn't seem to notice it.

I shrugged and picked up my own spoon. "I have other things to worry about just now. Besides, I guess I don't need the copper to live on my own. At least not until Elfriede tells me to get out of there."

Roslyn scoffed, shaking her head. "You really don't get along with your sister, do you?" I opened my mouth, but she put her spoon down and pointed at me. "Don't answer that." Her eyes flitted up as she watched Spurn and Scorn stand against the wall behind me. "I didn't want to say anything while those kids were nearby, but did you just tell Vena that the servants don't *eat?*"

I took a bite of my potatoes. "No. She must have misunderstood me."

Roslyn leaned forward, putting her elbows on her knees, not at all interested in her dinner. "Ah. So it's a secret, is it?" she asked, her voice a hushed whisper. "I understand." She leaned back in her chair and grinned. "Does that have something to do with why *someone else* seems so changed—"

"Scorn!" I said, perhaps a little too loudly. I felt my face flush as the man in white stepped beside me. "Get us both a mug of water, would you?" He left to do my bidding, and I felt like merging into the wall and never resurfacing. I shouldn't have asked *him* of the two if I was going to ask either of them.

"Sorry," said Roslyn, her head sinking into her shoulders. "I know with everything going on, we haven't really had a chance to talk about… about that night. But you have to know, we're all curious—ah. Thank you." She grabbed the mug that Scorn extended out to her, and I did the same, only I downed half of it in one gulp. Roslyn took a dainty sip and cradled her mug. "I could get used to that."

I stabbed a piece of beef with my fork and raised an eyebrow. "Having someone follow your orders?"

Roslyn sighed and put her mug down next to mine. We were running out of room on the table. "No, of course not. You're right. I don't want normal men to act like that again. Not now that we know how they really felt about it." We ate in silence for a moment, the buzzing of tavern talk the only thing hanging in the air between us. "Still, that makes me wonder. Are *they* like the rest of the men? Do you think they resent being servants?"

"I don't know," I said, realizing until Scorn had come into existence, I hadn't really thought of them as former people. "If they're like people at all, I suppose they resent a lot of things." I paused. "Like the person who cursed them in the first place."

Roslyn gasped, but she kept the noise quiet, quickly covering her mouth. "Cursed? Olivière, I know you have your secrets, but you can't exactly expect me to let that pass without asking—"

"Noll. Roslyn." I'd been so ashamed of all the information that kept leaking past my lips, I hadn't even noticed someone approaching the table. "I'm surprised to see you."

CHAPTER SIX

I looked up and saw Sindri, Darwyn's brother, and a friend I once had as a child. A friend I had as of late until he followed in his brother's footsteps to do something incredibly foolhardy and reckless. Sindri tried to smile, and I could almost see the sweat glistening on his brow in the dim light of the wall torches.

"Oh. Good evening, Sindri," said Roslyn, but her eyes dropped immediately to her lap, where her hands smoothed out the wrinkles in her skirt.

That's right. Not only is he her former husband's brother, but Sindri was married to her sister Marden. And Marden never unmasked him, never had their Returning.

"Does our presence bother you?" I asked, picking up my knife and fork and coolly avoiding looking at him.

"No." I could see out of the corner of my eye that Sindri ran a hand over the back of his head. "That is, it's a good surprise. I'm glad to see you, I mean."

I silently continued eating, determined to keep my strength up even if I'd suddenly lost my appetite. It wasn't like I didn't expect to run into any of them here—that was why I'd dragged Roslyn along, after all, so I wouldn't have to face them alone or tempt them to have too private a conversation—and I'd decided to come anyway. I might not be sure I was going to be Ailill's bride, despite what he'd said—and I wasn't sure that even mattered to me. He wasn't the same, and in fact, if he'd forgotten me, well... He was better off without me. Still, I was willing to try to undo this mess, as far as those who were innocent in the matter were concerned. I couldn't retreat back to my lonesome cottage and ignore it all, not after I'd seen what this village could become if men became too comfortable in their freedom and boredom.

Roslyn didn't have as personal a qualm with Sindri as her sister did, and maybe that dislike for extended periods of silence I'd observed in her drove her to speak. "Why don't you grab a chair and join us?" she asked.

I nearly choked on the last slice of meat on my plate, but it went unnoticed. Sindri grabbed a chair from the excess behind me and brought it to our tiny table. At least he didn't bring any food or drink because there wasn't room for it.

Sindri took no cue from my silence and skipped over the social graces that would have required him to thank Roslyn for the invite. He put the chair down, backwards, so he could lean his arms across the top of it. "I've wanted to speak with you for weeks," he said, staring at me uncomfortably, "but I know you've had a lot to deal with. I should have come to your father's memorial—"

"I'm glad you didn't. That none of you did." Actually, their absence had hurt a little, even though I didn't want to see them. But to see Alvilda, Siofra and Nissa come without the rest of their family, not even young Luuk, seemed awfully insensitive considering the role they played in Father's passing.

"We wanted to," said Sindri, undeterred. "We all did. We talked about it, though, and we thought it wasn't the best place to see you for the first time since that night. We wanted to talk, but it wasn't the right moment."

Our table fell into silence for a few moments, but Roslyn interrupted it. "You were missed," she said, laying her spoon down, the somber mood making her as done with her dinner as I was despite the half portion remaining on the plate.

The corner of Sindri's mouth twitched upward. "That's kind of you to say, Roslyn. I don't think everyone missed me, though." Whether he was talking about his former wife, who'd been there for Elfriede, or me or most of us, I didn't bother to ask.

"It would have been nice of Jurij to show," said Roslyn, surprising both Sindri and me at the mention of his name. Roslyn seemed to notice our distaste for the name, although why Sindri should feel the same, I had no idea. "For Elfriede," Roslyn added, as if that explained everything.

It might explain why I saw Jurij with his arms around Elfriede in a half embrace in the book mere moments after the cavern.

"Jurij misses you," said Sindri, turning to me. "*And* Elfriede. He's such a mess these days, easily the worst off of all of us—"

"Good," I said, interrupting him.

Sindri sighed. "Noll, we didn't mean for this to happen. It was never supposed to lead to all of this destruction, all of these deaths."

"What did you expect would happen?" I demanded. "Didn't you fully understand the consequences of fighting, of waving around swords like they were toys?"

"No, I don't think we did!" Sindri raised his voice and a nearby table of people stopped talking to stare at us curiously. Sindri glared back at them, and I wasn't comfortable seeing the flash of anger there. Men had never been so quick to anger before the curse was broken, not usually, and I worried that it was the first step in a process that might lead to men like those in the village from Ailill's childhood. Sindri turned back after the gaping people returned to their conversation and drummed his fingers atop the back of his chair in front of him. "Swords and fighting—that was just a game to us. Something we played with *you* as children."

"Don't blame *me* for this—"

"I *don't*. Of course I don't." Sindri paused as Roslyn stood, gathering her plate and mine, and bringing them back to Vena without a word. *So much for using her presence for protection from this sort of confrontation.* "I'm just trying to explain to you that we didn't have such bad intentions. When Jaron and Jurij came up with the idea—"

"*Jurij* was responsible for all of that?"

Sindri shook his head. "It was mostly Jaron. I mean, Jurij thought he could use a marriage to you as a means of distracting the lord, but—"

"Yeah. I remember that brilliant idea." I sighed and watched

Roslyn deposit the plates on the table by Vena, hoping she'd wander back. Instead, she seemed to notice how busy Vena was and took our plates and the whole stack of them to a bin in the back filled with soap and water, earning Vena's overwhelming adoration.

You're on your own. Be thankful it's just Sindri and not one of the ones who came up with the idea or one of the muscle-bound brutes who kept you pinned and unable to move.

Sindri's gaze followed my own. "She's doing well, it seems," he said. "I don't remember her ever looking so rosy. She's far more beautiful than her sister, and kinder. I can't believe I didn't notice back then. That I was *incapable* of noticing."

I threw my hands up in the air, not in the mood to foster new romance. "So what *did* you hope would happen, Sindri, when you all concocted this elaborate plan?"

Sindri rubbed the back of his neck sheepishly. "We wanted answers, Noll. Answers you seemed to have but weren't up to sharing with us."

"I didn't realize they were that important to you," I admitted, thinking back to every time Jurij or anyone else had asked me to explain something I only half understood myself. It hadn't happened *that* often. They were all consumed with moping about their former wives and goddesses more than anything, and that was something I assumed they'd soon get over.

"They were. They *are*. Wouldn't you want to know? Why you were born one way, and then suddenly had everything you knew pulled out from under you?"

"Ha," I laughed, not hiding my sarcasm. "You don't even know how much everything changed for me. Much more than everything changed for you."

"I'd like to know," Sindri said, not really convincing me he cared that much about my own suffering. To be fair, we were only newly friends again over the summer, and even then, I spent less time interacting with him than I had the others. "That's why we agreed we wouldn't be idiots this time. We'd ask you—*beg* you—to just share what you know with us—"

"I can't." I shook my head. "Even if I wanted to—and I'm not exactly in the mood for it, I have to say—I really can't. I'm sorry." I stood and pushed my chair back, remembering what I came for, what I risked seeing any of my former friends for. I passed Sindri, intending to walk to the nearest table and talk to the people seated there to see how everything was affecting them and ask them if they needed anything to feel safe and comfortable, when Sindri grabbed me by the wrist, stopping me from moving forward.

"Is what Jurij told us true?" he asked, and I shuddered, thinking of how much I had told Jurij that night on the way to the castle, how Ailill had said that anyone who knew as much without a golden ring or coin was in danger.

I yanked my elbow out of Sindri's grip and tossed my head. "And what did Jurij tell you?"

Sindri's gaze darted from me to Scorn and Spurn, who had taken their places behind me. His hand lowered slowly. His voice was quiet, hushed. "That you're key to everything. That you know how this curse got started. That you're responsible for it ending."

I pinched my lips together. So he hadn't told them the details. I wondered if he knew telling them I was the first goddess—that the pool in the cavern had thrust me into the past—would endanger them, or if he had other reasons to keep what I'd told him secret. If he even believed me, despite all he had seen. And why, if knowing was putting oneself in danger, he hadn't been killed or taken away.

Sindri raised an eyebrow. "Noll, you can tell me. You have to admit that I at least know the lord's been replaced—"

Scorn stepped between us and wrapped his hands around Sindri's neck.

CHAPTER SEVEN

"What are you doing?" I shrieked. "Let him go! Let him go, let him go, let him go!" I started slapping Scorn's arms as hard as I could, trying to grip those cold white gloves and pry them off of Sindri's neck. Sindri slapped at Scorn's arms as well, pushing back his chair and kicking his legs out as he thrashed around.

"Scorn, stop!" I screamed. "*Stop!*" I turned to Spurn helplessly. "Stop him!" I commanded.

Spurn didn't move at all, his hands tucked behind his back, his legs slightly apart like he was merely watching over me. There might have been a quick flicker of his eyes, but I didn't care. If he wasn't going to help me, he was absolutely useless.

"STOP!" I started kicking at Scorn's legs. Sindri's face was darkening, and there was foam spurting out from his lips. "Someone help me!" I turned around to see the entire Great Hall gawking, not a single person moving, not a single person willing to help.

I lunged at Scorn, wrapping my hands around his torso and throwing my entire body weight at him, trying to drag him to the ground with me. "AILILL!" I screeched. "AILILL, STOP THIS RIGHT NOW!"

Scorn barely flinched even despite all of my efforts. Sindri had stopped sputtering, and his limbs weren't moving. He was limp, and that could only mean...

"No!" I looked up at Spurn, even as I still had my arms around Scorn, even as I tried and tried to get him off of Sindri. "Please," I begged. "*Please!*"

Spurn moved at once, stepping in behind Scorn and placing his hands on both of his arms. I tumbled backward to give him more room and fell to the floor, my eyes unable to tear themselves away from the struggle. They both strained, their arms twitching, their hair becoming untidy, their jackets undone. I'd never seen a specter so disheveled. What felt like ages later, Spurn won, pulling Scorn's hands from Sindri's throat and tackling him to the ground, the two rolling away from us.

In shock, I almost joined the crowd of useless villagers murmuring and staring at us. Then I regained my senses and crawled over toward Sindri, where he'd collapsed to the ground, knocking into the crate-table.

I grabbed him and pulled his head onto my lap, shaking him. There was blood from where his head had struck the table, and it smeared against my skirt and spilled onto the floor. "Sindri! Sindri!" He was bleeding, but more importantly, he wasn't breathing. That seemed more pressing, even as the blood soaked through to my legs. I turned back to the crowd. "Someone *help!*"

Roslyn dropped the plate she'd held in her hands, the clattering practically the only sound in the hall. She raised her skirt so it didn't trail on the floor and ran over, taking a longer route only to avoid the still-tumbling specters. She slid in beside me, her face ghastly, her hands cradling her head. "What do we do?" She seemed too panicked to do anything.

"We have to get him breathing!" I said. "And *fast!* How? How?"

Roslyn beat her head with her hands. "There's a way, there's a way." The words tumbled out of her. "You remember that girl who nearly drowned in the pond in the fields when we were kids?"

"What?" I said, confused and angry and panicked. Girls playing in the pond? When was this? Girls couldn't be bothered to get off of their butts to do anything when we were kids. "What? No."

"You weren't playing with us." Roslyn grabbed Sindri by the temples, gently moving his head so it rested on the ground. The squish of the blood almost made me vomit. "That old crone came out of nowhere, and she said—she said we have to breathe the life back into her!" She pinched Sindri's nose and bent down to give Sindri a kiss.

"What are you *doing*?" I demanded. How in the name of the goddess did she think *that* was an appropriate thing to do just now?

Roslyn came up from the kiss and grabbed me by the front of my dress. "I'm saving him!" She looked angry and determined, more serious than I'd ever seen her before. "You go the other side! Start pressing hard on his chest!"

"*What*?"

"Do it!"

I did as Roslyn asked, crawling through the pooling blood and pressing hard on his chest with my fists every time Roslyn came up from a kiss. It couldn't have been long, surely if time had passed, *someone* else would have come to help us, but it felt like forever. Kiss and pound. Kiss and pound. Until eventually...

"It worked!" Roslyn beamed.

Sindri's eyes popped open and he started sputtering and choking. She helped him up and I immediately rushed in behind him to steady him.

"Hold him still," Roslyn said, and she let go. She shifted to bring the fabric of the back of her skirt forward a little. It was less stained with blood. She brought the edge of the skirt to her mouth and ripped it, swooping in to wrap it around Sindri's head even as she kept talking.

"It's less serious than it looks." Roslyn tied the fabric tight. "It's a pretty small gash. There's a bump, but—did I hurt you?" she asked as Sindri winced.

Sindri stared at her as his coughs died down. He kept staring and staring and staring.

Roslyn didn't seem to notice. She looked at me, as she stood and wiped her cheek with the back of her wrist, not noticing the blood she smeared all over her lovely complexion. She looked around at the crowd. "We should get him out of here," she said under her breath. "Let's bring him to the Bakers'. His mother will want to know what happened—"

A shriek cut her short. It sounded like Vena.

"Watch him," I said, nodding at her to support his head as I had before. I scrambled to my feet, nearly slipping on the puddle of blood. *I hope she was right about the wound*, I thought. *There's so much blood.*

My entire mind went blank as I pushed aside the last of the useless villagers and approached the table where Vena had been serving.

Spurn staggered to his feet from where he crouched, nearly toppling over. I pushed aside a woman, leaving blood on her shoulder, not caring, diving in to catch him and stop him from falling.

"He *killed* him!" shrieked Vena from somewhere behind him.

Spurn wouldn't look at me, and white hair tumbled across his forehead to dangle over his eyes. If he could breathe—they didn't breathe, did they?—he would be panting, but he just appeared exhausted, and there was no air coming out of his mouth to blow the tresses away.

My gaze fell to his hand, which held the knife Vena had used to cut the beef. It was stained dark and dripping—with juice from the meat?—and my eyes moved past that to the ground, where a set of white rumpled clothing lay. There was no other specter. Scorn—the ghost of Ailill, *my* Ailill—was gone. Vanished. They couldn't die a second time, could they?

"…must go…" The voice was so quiet, so soft, I didn't at first realize I was hearing it. Spurn spoke in my ear. He *spoke*. His lips parted again. "*Now.*"

CHAPTER EIGHT

"**B**ut I can't... Sindri..." The words were hard to get past my lips, but the stares of everyone in the Great Hall quickly silenced me. I looked at Spurn, and I saw something like *life* in his eyes, which made what had just happened even more terrifying. *Ailill is gone. He's really gone. But he tried to kill Sindri!* I checked to be sure Roslyn was still with Sindri, and that he still seemed awake and moving.

Please let him be all right. I grabbed Spurn's arm. "Drop it," I hissed, and he let go of the knife. It fell to the floor with a thud, and I started dragging him out, happy to see the group of onlookers parting as we made our way past.

"Noll, what are we to do with th-the clothing?" I could hear Vena ask behind me.

"Burn it," I said, still dragging Spurn behind. We were almost to the door.

A man stepped in front of me, blocking our way. "There's been death in this village for weeks now," he said, scowling. "We thought *you* were going to help us get past that, and now your own servants act like *monsters*."

"I know. Please, step aside. I need to speak with the lord."

"He told us you were to be 'the lady'! To rule beside him, to guide us through all of these troubles—"

"I will," I sputtered, surprised at my own lie. "I'm trying. Please step aside."

Spurn escaped from my grip and stood between us, pushing me back with a hand on my chest.

"Spurn, don't!"

He didn't have to do anything. The man looked up into his black eyes and stood in our way for just a breath longer, stepping aside without any violence between them. As I passed him, though, I could see more of that anger on his face, and the thought of what condition I was leaving these villagers in scared me. Spurn had been so insistent we leave, and I really had no idea what to do, anyway. It was a relief to get out into the crisp, chilled air of the early evening, to leave the chaos of the Great Hall behind.

Spurn wasn't following me. He was leading, and I felt stranger and stranger seeing him act like he was human. Like he was a man, suddenly no longer cursed, suddenly given freedom.

I grabbed him by the arm again, and he spun around. "We have to talk!"

His face didn't have the same range of emotions as I'd expect from a man who'd just stabbed someone to death, but there was something a little more there than I was used to seeing in specters. His black eyes moved too much—they searched me. He didn't open his mouth, instead cocking his head behind him and turning around, as if to tell me to follow him.

"No," I said, grabbing his arm and dragging him down a dark alleyway. There was just enough moonlight to see where we were going, but not too much that we might be seen. At least I hoped not. Dressed all in white, he reflected what little light there was.

Even though he'd had the strength to resist me, he'd allowed me to drag him down here. "Talk," I said. "I *know* you can. Don't pretend you can't."

He said nothing and tucked his hands behind his back, standing with his feet slightly apart, in almost-perfect imitation of a specter at the ready. He hadn't fixed his white hair, which hung limply over one of his eyes, his nose and mouth.

"You've talked to Ailill," I said. "Or at least another few of you have—you whisper in his ear—and you just talked to *me* in there." I dug into my pocket and withdrew my handful of coins.

Sorting through them in my palm, I quickly latched on to the golden one. "See?" I said, putting the copper coins back and holding the golden one between my thumb and forefinger. "Ailill said I have a right to know because of this."

Spurn's shoulders twitched just slightly. Holding on to the coin tightly, I tucked it out of sight. "But you made sure I got this, didn't you?"

"Yes," said Spurn, and I was struck again by the hollowness of his voice.

It's frightening.

"You wanted me to have this? To have the right to know about everything?"

Spurn didn't move, but his mouth opened up just enough to say, "No."

"It was Ailill, then, who asked you to make sure I got it?"

"No."

I bit my lip. "Not the current Ailill, the one before, I mean?"

"No."

I threw my hands in the air, my fingers still clenched around the coin. "Make no sense, then! Why not? You know, I didn't want to know more about this village. I was content to make a life of my own in a quiet place, away from everything. I could close my eyes and forget." I did close my eyes, and I didn't forget. The image of the violet pool, the sensation of traveling through water, was replaced with the suffocating pull of the red one. I opened my eyes. *You're asking the wrong questions.*

"Who wanted you to make sure I got this coin?"

Spurn opened his mouth slightly, hesitating, but then he spoke, every word causing him pain, like there were shards of glass on his tongue. "*They* did. They lost… strength in this village after… curse was broken. They are at war. They should not… have been able to compel me. But they did."

"Who are *they*?" I asked. He didn't answer.

I grabbed Spurn's arm and pulled it out from behind him, clutching his hand. "You're different from the rest of the servants, aren't you?"

"Yes."

"Can other servants speak to me?"

"Yes. But will not."

"Even though they speak to Ailill?"

"Different. He is lord first, and he is part of us all."

I sighed. "You dropped the key for me, didn't you? That night when the fight at the tavern started? So I could let my friends go."

"Yes."

"Why?"

"Two reasons."

I waited for him to elaborate. When he didn't, I spoke again. "Two?"

"I know... you."

"I know you know me. You all know me."

"No... I *know* you. I was the... first."

"First?" It was going to take me forever to get him to speak enough to start making sense. "You were the first to know me, so you were one of the specters who kept visiting my house after I met Ailill..." I trailed off, searching his eyes. I'd been about to ask why that made a difference, why that could possibly be important, but all of a sudden, it dawned on me. "You were the first Ailill! You're the grown-up shadow of the child I met, all those years ago."

Ever so slightly, Spurn nodded.

I threw myself at him and hugged him, and it was like hugging ice, both cold and unresponsive, as he didn't so much as twitch beneath my embrace. "I'm sorry," I whispered. He said nothing. "You look so much older. You spent all those years alone, not knowing what was going on, not understanding... You must have been so frightened."

After a moment, I pulled back, wiping the trail of tears that still stuck to my cheek. "I know it's little solace, but... I didn't mean to do that to you. I didn't mean to make you suffer like that."

Spurn's gaze slipped slightly above my head, like he was just remembering he wasn't supposed to look me in the eye, and I could have sworn I saw the lump at this throat move—but he didn't swallow. The specters had no need for such things.

I cleared my throat and clutched my skirt with both hands. "You said two reasons. What was the other?"

This alone induced Spurn to speak again. "They... wanted."

I shook my head, not about to frustrate myself by demanding to know who "they" were. I changed topics. "Why did Scorn attack Sindri?"

Spurn looked pitiful, like a wayward dog on its last breaths. I took his hand again and squeezed it in encouragement.

"He knows."

"About the lord being reborn?" I fought to stop myself from losing patience. "But... Everyone there that night knows. And they've been left in peace until now."

"He... spoke of it. Others in danger, too."

I felt like someone had kicked me—not Spurn, not poor pitiful Spurn, but someone unseen. "But the others... How can no one else have spoken about it? Things have been hectic since, but you can't expect them all to remain silent. They might not have quite come right out and asked me, but I know they're all curious."

"Spoke... to you. In front of us." Spurn dropped his hand, and it fell limply to his side, not joining the other one behind his back. "Always watching. But cannot hear. We can."

I clenched my fist tightly around the coin. "So even if *they* observe someone talking, they can't say for certain what it is they're talking about. But if all the people in the cavern that night need to keep silent around the specters, with so many out and about these past few weeks..." I bit my lip, a horrifying thought entering my head. "It's only a matter of time before any of them are at risk again! I have to speak to Ailill!" I don't know why I hoped he'd be able to—he'd even *care* to—save the people I cared about. At the very least, he could take me to these annoyingly mysterious "they" so I could put an end to it all.

I started walking back to the village road, but I stopped, spinning around to face Spurn. "The specters—the servants—you can die?"

Spurn nodded, slowly.

"Aren't you already dead?"

"Yes."

I shook my head incredulously. That would have to be a secret for another time. "Let's go," I barked, leading the way to the castle.

∾

WE MADE it as far as my family's cottage before we ran into anyone who might speak to us, considering news of what had happened at the Great Hall hadn't quite spread yet. Unfortunately, the sight of Alvilda, Siofra, Nissa, Luuk, and even Master Tailor outside of my family's door did little to assuage me. I couldn't rush past them, hoping to get my answers from Ailill.

"What's happened?" I asked as Spurn and I climbed the last hill to join them.

Siofra turned away from looking through my open door. I peered inside quickly to find Mother and Elfriede at the door talking to them, Marden behind them at the table, half-eaten dishes in front of her.

"Jurij is missing," said Siofra plainly. Her voice wavered, and I thought I might be about to see the stern woman cry.

My stomach jumped up into my throat as I studied each of the faces in front of me. Most were screwed up with worry, and I couldn't imagine any of them knew anything—I wondered if Jurij's family had mistakenly assumed he'd come to see Elfriede or me—until my gaze rested on Master Tailor. He never struck me as much of a thinker, but I knew he'd been involved with what had happened. He'd even risked his youngest son's safety by having him play a part.

"Coll," I said, remembering that at almost eighteen, I was a year past being a grown woman and I could dispense with giving my friends' parents the respect of addressing them by their titles. He hadn't really earned it anyway. "Do you have any idea where he could have gone?"

Coll shook his head banefully and stared at his feet. "I haven't seen him in a couple of days. Siofra and Alvilda said he'd been with them—"

"He *was* until yesterday evening," interrupted Alvilda. "He left after we'd had dinner at the Great Hall, and he told us he was going to spend the night with *you*."

"He didn't come over," snapped Coll. "I didn't see him at all."

That gnawing feeling in my stomach was growing worse and worse. "There's something you must know." As if everyone expected me to tell them I'd found Jurij's empty clothing, the color drained almost immediately out of every face. What I had to tell them might not be much different, but *no*. I refused to believe there'd been more deaths until I could confirm it. *What a fine time to go missing, though, Jurij.*

I told them what had happened with Sindri and Scorn in the Great Hall, leaving out the exact words Sindri had said to earn the death sentence.

"That's terrible!" Mother's voice warbled. "Why, then, he's still in danger. I have to tell Thea—"

I raised a hand to cut her off. "He's with Roslyn, and they're going back to Mistress Baker's." I paused, reminding myself to call the woman "Thea." "Actually, if you could go visit them," I said, looking to Elfriede, too, and hoping she'd join her, "and explain that they should stay away from the lord and his servants. At least until I've been able to talk with Ailill."

"What... do you mean?" asked Alvilda. I'd never heard her sound so uncertain. She was clearly eyeing Spurn over my shoulder, and I wondered if his haggard appearance fed into her alarm.

"This one's okay." I glanced at Spurn for confirmation, but he was doing his best to seem as immobile and unaffected as any other specter. "But I wouldn't expect you to spot him from any other, so best to steer clear of any of them for a bit. I hope not for long. Still, you must all be careful what you say around any of them." I looked over Mother's shoulder to see if Marden was listening. "This applies to you, too, Marden. Please come here."

Marden cocked an eyebrow but stood, probably biting her tongue to stand behind Elfriede.

"All right," I said, looking at each in turn. "Listen to me, and say nothing. Don't respond at all, no matter what you may want to know. You never know when a servant might be around the corner. They're so quiet, they might catch you unawares." I looked above Siofra's and Alvilda's heads to the path that cut through the woods. There was no sign of movement, other than the slight rusting of the bright orange and red leaves. "What you witnessed that night in the cavern has left you with a lot of questions, I know that." I glanced at Coll accusingly. "You may think I'm hiding all of the answers from you, but I have a lot of questions, too.

"You may also have noticed that... not everyone looks the same since that night."

"I'll say," began Alvilda, "the lord—"

Siofra nudged her quiet as I lifted a hand. Raising my voice, I spoke over her. "It was Sindri commenting on that difference, specifically mentioning *the lord* that made one of the servants reach out and choke him."

Alvilda immediately clamped her mouth shut. I took a deep breath and continued. "It's incredible it hasn't happened to anyone who was there in the cavern so far, but speak of what you noticed that night within the earshot of a servant, and he will attack you."

Mother gasped as Alvilda threw her hands up in the air. "That's appalling! The lord talks about rebuilding the village, about rebuilding that feeling of safety lost after the fight and the fire, and then he orders that we're to be killed for asking questions?"

"It's not him. Please don't ask. Just don't blame him."

Siofra looked from Alvilda to me and back. "All right," she said. "We'll trust you." Alvilda scowled, but Siofra kept speaking. "We'll trust Noll to take care of it," she said, commandingly. It was almost like when she used to order Coll around. "But…" She stopped and put a hand on Luuk's shoulder, dragging him close to her. He looked awkward and uncomfortable, but he didn't escape from her grip.

"Are you saying Jurij was attacked by a servant?" asked Coll quietly.

"Maybe." My eyes darted guiltily to the ground. I was still so angry with Jurij, but I didn't want him to die. Still, the thought of his fate being unknown should have bothered me more. A dark part of me thought that maybe he deserved it. And that thought made me want to cry. *How far we've come since those days when I could think of little but him.* "I don't know," I added to mollify them. "He would have left clothing behind, surely."

"If we don't know where he went, how could we find them?" said Elfriede, speaking up for the first time since the conversation had begun. "Or what was to stop the servant from disposing of the clothes afterward to keep us from knowing?"

I frowned. She was right. Would Ailill know? I knew *they* would know, though, and Ailill could at least let me speak with them.

"What about Darwyn and Tayton?" asked Mother. She

stepped out from the doorway and Siofra and Luuk moved aside to let her pass. She had her shawl on, and she seemed determined. The look suited her well.

Alvilda spoke. "I saw them not two hours ago. They're taking one of the new cottages in the commune, and they've been helping with the rebuilding."

Mother's eyes widened. "They're surrounded by servants; they could be in danger."

Alvilda shook her head. "The servants brought the firewood, but I said we could do without them for the construction. Looks like my instinct was right."

I nodded. "Still. Mother, perhaps you and Thea should warn them. Elfriede? Marden? If you set out with Mother and start looking, you'll find them sooner. I think they're staying with Malek."

Marden shrugged and stepped out, but Elfriede shook her head. "They're probably with Sindri. Thea would have sent for Malek at least, as he's her oldest—if not all of her sons. She gets really upset when one of them is ill or injured."

Marden's lips curled into a sneer. "I wonder if she'd even tell his father. *I* wouldn't, after he left her for some tavern drunkard. In fact, I'd hardly care about Sindri being injured if I weren't so done with fretting about him—"

"Willard's new love died," interrupted Coll. We all turned to look at him. "Willard, the former baker. Sindri and Darwyn's father. She was with him in the tavern during the fight."

"Hmph," mumbled Marden. She crossed her arms, almost as if to say "she deserved it."

"All right," I said, not about to let the conversation wander. "I have to speak with Ailill. I'll see if he knows anything about Jurij."

"What about Jaron?" Elfriede asked, turning back into the house. She reappeared at the door quickly, a shawl around her shoulders. "Someone has to warn him."

My gaze flit between Mother and Elfriede. Mother stared off at the village, refusing to acknowledge the man. I understood entirely. He was as much, if not more to blame, than Jurij. And he'd once meant something more to Mother. Something like Jurij had meant to me.

"Look for him, too," I said, raising my chin defiantly. "He's the most likely to talk of any of them." I hadn't asked where Jaron was staying now that his room in the tavern was gone. I hadn't wanted to think about him, but I should have. I should have told Ailill what he had done even if I hadn't wanted to.

"Noll, let us go with you," said Siofra. "You can't go alone to the castle."

"I'm afraid I must." I took her free hand, the one not bitterly clutching her son to her. I did my best to smile. *I'm going to reassure someone. I may not have been able to do anything in the Great Hall but make things worse, but I'm going to do this. I'm going to make this village safe again.* "I promise you. I'll find him."

"You'll find out what *happened* to him," said Luuk, almost too quiet. He looked devastated, like he knew more than he let on. Maybe he just assumed that Jurij was gone, that he'd spoken and a servant had heard him. I dropped his mother's hand, entirely unsure of myself again.

"Noll will *find* him," said Nissa, stepping forward. "The elf queen can always find her retainers."

I laughed, all doubt forgotten. *It'll be fine. Ailill has that book. With a flip of the page, I'll find him hiding somewhere they haven't thought to look.*

Spurn stepped closer, his elbow brushing mine. He still appeared docile, but I knew he was trying to tell me something without others noticing.

"Spread out!" I said, heading back toward the path. "Search the village for the rest of them! I know how to find them, but if you get to them sooner and speak to them, all the better. Be careful, though, how you explain things." I took my first steps into the woods that stood between me and the castle, Spurn close behind me.

The elf queen and her retainer are off to confront some monsters.

CHAPTER NINE

No one was in the entryway to the castle when Spurn and I arrived. The door to the garden was shut, but I opened it anyway to make sure no one was hiding. "Ailill?" I called. "We need to talk. It's important!"

The chilly autumn wind rustled through the rose bushes, scattering leaves and grass.

I turned around and bumped into Spurn. He was following far too closely behind me. I backed up and rubbed my sore forehead. "Is he upstairs? Do you know?"

Spurn's lips twitched in what might be considered his version of a frown.

"Never mind," I said, too impatient for an answer. "Let's go."

I poked my head into the dining room as we passed, but there was no fire burning, and no sign of life—or whatever it was that could describe the specters. I took the stairs nearly two at a time, pausing at the second floor landing where Ailill's bedroom and the other rooms were, but something told me I wouldn't find him in any of them. I continued up the stairs to the third floor, heading for the throne room.

The moment I reached the landing, I knew my instinct had served me well. The third floor hallway was the only hallway lit up with torches, and both walls were lined with specters at attention, their hands clutched behind their back, their feet slightly apart. *I guess I never thought about where they rested when not doing their work*, I thought as I passed the first few in silence. *Ailill forbade me from coming to this floor when I stayed here because my mother was in that room by the prison. Perhaps they all stood here, silently, waiting for Ailill's call.*

I passed an open door I'd never bothered exploring before—there were a number of rooms on the third floor I'd never seen, including one of them that must have held a cache of weapons my former friends found during their escape—and I stopped suddenly, noticing the light pouring into the hallway. I looked up, the throne room forgotten.

"...does not need that much seasoning. What is it?" Ailill, addressing a specter, had his back to me. The specter, bent over a table near a roaring fire, had paused in his work over a pot to stare at me. Ailill followed suit. He quickly masked his surprise with a stilted smile.

"My... lady," he said, putting his hands behind his back like a specter and bowing his head slightly. "What brings you here?" He gestured behind him. "I had not instructed enough food to be prepared for us both, but if you have not yet eaten—"

I cut him off with a gesture. "I have." *Come to think of it, I never saw where the food for our meals was prepared, either. Why are so many important rooms on the third floor? The throne room, the prison, and even the kitchen—wasn't it a pain for the specters to bring it down two floors to the dining room for serving?*

"I see," said Ailill, looking around the room awkwardly. "Just as well. I have not yet used the dining hall this rebirth. I found it rather large and drafty for one person." He crossed the room and sat at a small table.

I followed him, not taking the sole other seat at the table, instead wringing my hands nervously. *Spit it out, for the love of the goddess! This is an emergency. And you're not leaving this time until you have answers.*

Ailill studied me, his face puzzled. "May I ask to what do I owe this visit?" The specter who'd been cooking stepped between us, laying down a cloth napkin, a bowl and a spoon in front of his master.

I watched the specter nervously as he went back to the table to grab the pot. He used no cloth to shield his hands from the heat, and I had to wonder again how a specter could feel no pain and didn't even breathe, and yet I'd seen one die. Or others had seen him die, anyway.

"There's been a problem," I said, fascinated by the way the specter poured the stew into the bowl silently. Truly silently, without producing even a clink.

Ailill picked up his spoon and eyed me curiously, his gaze shifting to somewhere up over my shoulder. I turned around and saw Spurn there, doing his best to seem immobile, but he couldn't hide the way his hair and clothes were disheveled. "Apparently," said Ailill, but he didn't seem concerned. Instead, he started eating, not bothering to look up again.

"One of the spec—the servants is dead." Ailill's hand froze with the spoon halfway to his mouth, but only for a moment. He went back to eating.

"A shame," he said at last, putting the spoon down and wiping his lips with the napkin. "Still, you know they are not truly living."

"I know that," I snapped. "Which makes me wonder how one can truly *die*."

"They can vanish, just like people." Ailill lifted his head and nodded at the specter who'd served him, and the specter came over with a glass full of wine. "Whether you choose to believe that means they are dead depends on your point of view."

That was about the last thing I expected him to say. My knees weakened, and despite the gravity of the situation at hand, I sat down in the seat across from Ailill. At least that way, he'd have no choice but to look at me.

"When people vanish," I said, "they die. They're no longer with us—what did *you* mean?"

"Yes, I know," said Ailill flippantly. "They are dead. I did not mean to imply otherwise for the villagers. They no longer appear in this village, so they are dead, gone, and vanished." Before I could ask him to elaborate, he put his glass down and picked up his spoon again. "As for the Ailills, I wouldn't consider one of them *dying* to be a problem. They're already dead." His eyes flickered just slightly to Spurn, who stood behind me.

I clutched the edge of the table. "It was Scorn—that is, it was the latest Ailill. The one before you. The one I knew."

Ailill shrugged and took some more stew. "He wouldn't remember you any more than I would. They have no more feelings left, these shades."

I studied Spurn at that, questioning that assessment of them. He may not have explicitly said so, but he had memories, whatever Ailill said. And while his reactions were muted, he certainly didn't seem devoid of feelings. Unless there was something special about Spurn that made him different from all the others... I actually had to believe he was different because I didn't want to think about the Ailill I knew, *my* Ailill, attempting murder like that. He *wasn't* capable of that. It was maddening to think about.

I switched tracks. "That servant tried to kill my fr—one of the villagers." I lifted my chin and studied Ailill's reaction haughtily. "And I know why."

Ailill put his spoon down and wiped his fingers. "You know why? May I ask then if you killed him?"

"Who? The specter?" I shook my head. "It wasn't me—"

"It was the other Ailill I left you with." He nodded his head at Spurn. "Him."

I waited to see if Spurn would react, but he hardly moved. "Yes, but I didn't ask him to. I wanted him to stop the other specter from killing Sindri, but—"

"He responded to your orders," interrupted Ailill. "He must have thought the only way to stop him was to kill him."

"They're not *that* loyal! If they were, Scorn would have responded to my orders to stop."

Ailill raised his eyebrows. "'Scorn'? No, do not bother to explain that." He sighed and gestured at the serving specter, who came over with the bottle of wine for a refill. Ailill held his full glass for a moment, swishing its contents and staring somewhere off at the wall behind me. "You say an Ailill—a servant—tried to kill your friend." *Sort of friend*, I thought to myself. "And that wasn't at your own order?"

"Of course not! Who in the name of the first goddess would ever order *that*?"

"The name of the first goddess?" repeated Ailill, his brow furrowed. "You mean your own name?" So he knew. I suspected

517

as much. He could remember his childhood, but the rest of his lives still were unclear? Then it shouldn't have bothered the last Ailill so much that he'd been reborn over and over, if he didn't *feel* the length of all those lives.

"Never mind that. A slip of the tongue, a careless expression."

"So," said Ailill, taking a sip and ignoring me. "you are certain. You did not even *think* you wanted that man dead."

"*No*, I certainly did not!" If specters acted even at my thoughts, then Jurij wouldn't have lasted more than a day.

"Then whose orders would supersede your own?" The glass almost tumbled from his fingers. He stood, slamming the glass down and staring at me accusingly. "What was he talking about when the servant attacked him?"

I pulled the gold coin out of my pocket and clutched it tightly. "*You*. He wanted to know why you were back, younger, darker— how you could be back after he saw you die."

Ailill swallowed uncomfortably and rapped his knuckles against the table. "He does not have the sign of a ruler," he said, quietly, rubbing his arm. He was wearing one of the golden bangles. "He is not supposed to know."

I nodded, thinking about how this wouldn't have been a problem before. No one bothered about the lord, not when they had their own affairs to attend to. When I'd spoken about my theories with Alvilda after Elfriede and Jurij's wedding, nothing ill had happened to us. Maybe speculation was different than actually *witnessing* it, and then speaking of it.

"You say he witnessed my last death," said Ailill, and he let go of his bangle to raise his hand to silence me. "Do not bother to relay the details at this moment. He was not the only witness, I gather?"

"No. But I spoke with most of them right before I came here and told them to watch what they said, and to warn the others."

"Good." Ailill ran a hand over his chin in thought. "Yet… Will it be enough? Never before have so many been privy to even a *hint* at what lies beyond the mountains, I am sure of it."

"All right," I said, standing. "We shall ask your mysterious *them*. I need you to take me 'beyond the mountains.'"

"You have never been to see them before?"

"No." I wasn't sure if I should admit I didn't even know who "they" were. Other than some people who lived beyond the mountains, always watching us. A version of the lord himself, only farther away. "I have never had the pleasure."

Ailill cocked his head. "I would hardly call it a pleasure." He looked up at the ceiling. "You have to grant me at least that much honesty," he said, almost as if speaking to someone.

But I thought "they" couldn't hear us. Just like Ailill can't hear through the pages of his book.

The book. "Even so, I must see them, but I need to check on Jurij's welfare first."

"Jurij?" asked Ailill, curious.

If I weren't so certain he was telling the truth about not remembering his last life in detail, I would roll my eyes at his display of ignorance.

"He was... a friend. Married to my sister, before the end of the curse."

"I admit I am still curious as to how the curse ended," said Ailill. "They told me little this time, but I could tell something was different. They were not pleased."

Again. "They."

I brushed past Spurn to exit to the hallway. "Is the book on its stand in the throne room?" I asked Ailill over my shoulder.

Ailill caught up in a few strides, joining me as I walked toward the throne room a few doors over. "You certainly know your way around." He seemed amused.

"I do," I quipped tersely. "Perhaps too well."

"Wait!" Ailill grabbed hold of my hand just before I took my first step into the throne room. "If it is a friend you inquire after, one who claims responsibility for the events of that evening, then I may already know where you will find him."

I felt the weight of Ailill's hand on mine, the coldness of his black leather gloves. Before I lost him last time, we'd held each other's hands without the leather between us. It felt different then. There was heat even despite the cold. "Where?" I asked, not willing to let his hand go.

But Ailill dropped it first and pointed down the hallway. "In my prison."

CHAPTER TEN

"Step aside!" I waved my hand at the specter standing outside of the door leading to the prison, and he actually did what I asked of him. I looked over my shoulder to find both Ailill and Spurn behind me, and I wondered if they gave some signal that I was to be obeyed, or if the coin I clutched in my fist was really enough to get the specter to bother with me.

Since Ailill was initially convinced Scorn acted on my orders, I'll choose to believe the latter.

I grabbed hold of the door handle with the hand not clinging to the golden piece and pulled, but it didn't budge. I had no choice but to put the coin back into my pocket and use both hands, but I still struggled with the effort.

"Let me," said Ailill, stepping behind me. "It is probably a poor design for a prison, but it is much easier to push open from the other side than pull open from this one."

I looked over my shoulder to glare at him, but I immediately dropped my head, my cheeks burning. He was *right* behind me, and he put one arm on either side of me to put his hands above and below mine on the door. I could feel his chest behind my shoulders, his arms against mine.

"Pull," he said, and it took me a moment to reconsider the

task at hand. I faltered, but I went back to pulling, and the door gave way much easier.

Ailill stepped back to make room, and I examined him, biting my lip. Should I thank him? When he imprisoned Jurij?

It's not like Jurij didn't deserve it.

I settled for grunting at him, and I brushed my hands on my skirt. They were wet with sweat from the effort. I refused to believe it was from nervousness.

"Jurij!" I called, walking into the hallway lining the prison cells. When Ailill had kept my mother in his castle, he'd put her in the room next to these. Unconscious, she wasn't at risk for escape, I supposed. But I hadn't even known these actual cells existed until he'd thrown my friends and me into them that evening the mess of the fight and the fire all started. "Jurij!" I called again, passing the second empty cell. "Your parents are looking for you—"

"Good evening, Noll," came the casual voice from the third cell. It sounded bored and a touch depressed—and extremely familiar.

"Jaron." I peered into his cell and found no one else, so I kept walking to check the last cell, but I didn't see anyone else in that, either.

"He's not here," said Jaron. "Not unless his lordship brought in a second prisoner while I slumbered."

I chose to ignore Jaron for the moment and confronted Ailill. "You told me you had Jurij in your prison."

"I told you I had a *friend*," responded Ailill. "He claimed to be a friend of yours, anyway. Can you blame me for forgetting the name he gave me?"

If it didn't also mean a clean slate for all of those problems between us, I'd blame you for forgetting a lot of things.

"He didn't seem much interested in my name," interjected Jaron. "Just took me at my word that I was responsible for the fight that started the fire."

"I'm looking for someone else," I said, raising my voice to be heard over Jaron.

"What's this?" asked Jaron, clearly hurt. "No shred of forgiveness for a man who's owned up to his stupidity but still desperately seeking a man who hurt you more than I did?"

"I didn't say anything about forgiveness," I snapped at Jaron, forgetting my attempts to ignore him. I tapped my foot. "His parents are worried."

"Have they cause to be?" Jaron looked from me to Ailill and back. His eyes rested curiously on the untidy appearance of Spurn behind Ailill.

"Yes," I said, watching for Ailill's reaction. "Everyone who witnessed what happened in the cavern that evening is in danger."

"You mean everyone who has a clue that the lord standing there isn't—"

I strode over to the cell and kicked through the space between bars, slamming the toe of my boot into Jaron's shin as hard as I could.

"Ow! Damn it!" Jaron cradled his shin and bounced a little, losing his balance and leaning against the cell bars. "What in the name of the first goddess is wrong with you?" He put his foot down again, tentatively. "That's you, though, right? That's what Jurij said."

I chose to ignore the comment and focused on telling the man to shut up before he put himself at risk any further.

"You have no proof of that," I said, swiftly realizing that the difference between Sindri talking about the lord being replaced by a younger, darker version and Jaron or Alvilda or anyone conjecturing about the strange things that were part of this village was that Sindri had witnessed what he saw. Still, I'd rather Jaron refrain from speaking of such things. "And I'll have you know I did you a favor. Sindri was attacked not long ago, for speaking in front of a lord's servant about what he saw that evening."

Jaron turned around and stuck one arm back through the cell bars, gripping the bars with his other. "I talked about that night in front of plenty of servants when I walked in here."

"What exactly *are* you doing in here?"

Jaron shrugged and looked at the ground. "Where else would I be? I couldn't stop thinking about how my plan had failed."

"So you decided to exile yourself to the prison?"

"It was only a matter of time."

I shook my head. "No one was going to come and arrest you. I hadn't even thought about it, and Ailill didn't remember—" I cut myself short, biting my lip.

"You knew this man was responsible for the fight?" asked Ailill, curiously. "And you did not think fit to tell me?"

"I've barely *seen* you since that night," I answered. "And it was hard for me to think about what happened then. I just didn't consider that the men responsible should be locked up."

"The *men*? How many men came up with this idea?" demanded Ailill.

"I was the leader," said Jaron. "It was my idea, really. That's all that's important."

Ailill didn't seem convinced. I was wondering why Jaron was still breathing. "What exactly did you tell Ailill then? When you turned yourself in?"

Jaron leaned back from the cells and crossed his arms, resting his back against the wall. "That I told your father—'a man,' I said, that is, didn't want to sully his name—to cause trouble that night at the tavern."

I waited for him to continue, but he didn't. "That's it?" I looked from Jaron to Ailill and back. "Well, that explains why you're still breathing. The details put you in danger. The details about..." I stopped, studying Ailill.

Jaron seemed to catch on. "Ah." He nodded. "All right, then, I won't talk about it."

"He would not give his reasons," interjected Ailill. "For causing a fight. I gathered that he and others were 'at the cavern,' as you so often say, but he would not tell me more."

I watched Jaron, taking note of his placid reaction. I started wondering if more than just a sense of guilt had led Jaron to the castle. "Did he return the sword he took from your castle?"

"No," said Ailill, rubbing his chin with his hand and studying Jaron carefully. "Are there more of those missing?"

"There are," I said, before Jaron could come up with some lie. "They weren't used in the fight in the tavern, but Jaron and a number of others took swords with them that night."

"Noll—" started Jaron, but I ignored him.

"And you know who else has them?" asked Ailill, also turning away from Jaron. His mouth turned into a frown and he reached out to grab me by the elbow. "Perhaps we can finish this conversation elsewhere."

"Aw, come on," said Jaron, exasperated. "What are you so afraid of? I'm not going anywhere. I won't tell anybody."

I let Ailill guide me past the other empty cells and out of the prison. He and Spurn shut the door tight behind us, and Ailill didn't grab my arm again.

"Is he actually locked up?" I asked. "I have to wonder if the only reason he brought himself here willingly was to snoop around for answers."

"Yes, he is confined." Ailill nodded at the specter standing watch at the door as we passed him. "I was not sure I ought to confine him based on his confession alone. But he was so insistent, and I was sure that isolating the instigator of the violence might prove beneficial for the village, at least for a short while."

I stopped. "You plan to let him go?"

Ailill paused, realizing I was no longer walking with him. "Should I not?"

"No. I… I don't know." I looked over my shoulder, as if expecting Jaron to be there, but all I found was Spurn. I gritted my teeth. "He can stay for now. I need to use the book to look for Jurij."

We arrived at the throne room before Ailill began speaking. "This Jurij? Is he one of the friends who took the swords I had sequestered?"

"Yes," I admitted, although I was reluctant to explain just what he'd done with the one he'd stolen. "I should have asked for them back immediately. I'm sorry, I…" I shook my head. "I haven't been thinking clearly."

I stopped in the middle of the room, uncomfortable moving farther into the pitch black. There was a scratch of flint and Spurn appeared in the darkness, lighting one of the torches. He took it off the wall, shook the dying embers off of the flint and immediately set to lighting the next torch.

As the room came into better view, I found Ailill already at the book on the stand, poring over the pages. I approached him, eyeing the throne warily as I did. *This is how we'll find "them,"* I thought. *Through the hole behind that throne.*

"How many years ago was he born?" asked Ailill. "Around your birth?"

"Jurij's a year younger." I tucked some hair behind my ear and watched as Ailill flipped the pages. Something hit me suddenly. "The pages are organized by when we're born?"

"Yes." Ailill stopped, studying me. "I would have thought you would know. Was the book not in your possession until recently?"

"Briefly," I said, ignoring the implied accusations. I flipped through the pages, recognizing some of my contemporaries. Roslyn sat in a chair beside Sindri on a bed, Thea nearby. Their faces were serious, their frowns evident, as they spoke to people whose backs were to the page. They were my mother and Marden, likely come to warn them as I requested. I hoped Sindri was recuperating.

I kept flipping. "Jurij should be somewhere around here." I frowned. "He has to be. One of these." I froze. I'd come to an entirely blank page. I thought there was some mistake, so I flipped it again and I saw a moving drawing. My heart racing, I realized the image was of Darwyn. Tayton was walking somewhere with him, and they looked concerned. They stopped in front of the bakery door, and Alvilda, Siofra and the half figure of someone—probably Coll—came into view as the door opened and the former Master Baker appeared. *So they tracked them down and warned them, and they were off to visit Sindri.*

I flipped the page back to the blank one, but it hadn't changed.

Ailill slammed the book shut, nearly smashing my hands in with it.

"Hey!" I said, but the look on Ailill's face stopped me cold.

Ailill stared at the throne. "Does he know about this entryway?" he asked quietly. "Your friend?"

I stared at the throne, too. The longer I looked, the more I swore I could feel the chilly air and hear subtle whispers. "He does, but... What are you saying?"

Ailill pursed his lips. "The *only* way the page turns blank is if the person is on the other side of the mountains."

The other side... Why had no one else considered a world beyond the mountains? Unless they couldn't?

"If the person dies," continued Ailill, "the page burns and—"

"—vanishes," I finished for him. I frowned. "But that doesn't explain how Jurij would be allowed to cross over." I reached into my pocket and clutched my golden coin tightly. "If someone who's witnessed peculiarities so much as mentions it, they're attacked, so then how can someone without a piece of gold…" I felt like someone had kicked me in the stomach. "He has a golden bangle!" The memory hit me like a gale. "I saw him take one that night, when they were lying on the dining room floor."

"I thought they were rather ill-placed when I found the excess of them there." Ailill scowled and moved closer to the throne, studying it. He raised a hand and Spurn hung his torch back on the wall to join him. Together they pushed it aside. Ailill took a deep breath and wiped his brow after they'd finished.

I stepped up the dais and joined them, staring into the void.

Olivière, spoke the whispers. When Ailill reacted, I knew I wasn't imagining it.

"You're saying Jurij went in there?" I asked. "But how? Wouldn't he need help to push the throne? And how did he push it back into place after he passed through it?"

"Not through here exactly." Ailill bit his lip. It was strangely alluring, and I shook myself, focusing on what was important. "There is another way, if they desire to open it to someone."

"The cavern pool," I said, and I could feel Ailill's curiosity burn beside me. "Which Jurij also knows about. He's the only one of the group of witnesses whom I told about the magic of the pool."

"Then he has gone to see them," said Ailill. "Although why they should let him pass, I cannot say."

I clutched Ailill's arm nervously and he gave me a strange look, an almost embarrassed look, but I was too nervous to think on it. "Then he's in danger! And you and I are the only ones who even know how to find him."

The lump at Ailill's throat bobbed perceptively. He gently removed himself from my grip. "Then we shall have to step through the mountains and confront them."

CHAPTER ELEVEN

"**Y**ou will not need that. It will not show you what he is up to, even if you bring it with you."

I hesitated, my hand on the book on the stand. It wasn't just Jurij I hoped the book would show me, but if we were going there, wherever *there* might be, I felt like I needed to keep an eye on the village we would be leaving behind. Especially considering what I'd just seen Scorn do.

Still, it was awfully bulky, and I had no idea how long we'd be gone. "What should we take with us?" I placed my hand back in my pocket to clutch the coin.

"Nothing but the proof of your status." Ailill tapped the bangle around his wrist. He hesitated. "But keep it out of sight."

Spurn approached the dais again, a torch in hand. Ailill took it and looked at me, his face awash in the ember light. "Since it is your first time through, we shall bring a torch to light the way." He reached back to take my hand in his. His touch through the leather was cold and formal. "You need not be afraid. It is but a short trip, and once we pass the veil, we will be at our destination."

"The veil?" I asked, as he took the first step into the cavern.

"Yes," he replied, and with one last look over my shoulder at

Spurn—who stood still and at attention, but whose frown was hard to miss—I stepped through.

I expected the shadows and the chill. The dark, hollow space of the cavern prepared me for the emptiness of these harsh, stone places. Subconsciously, I'd come to associate them with an echo and the trickle of water, quiet small noises in an otherwise near-empty void.

Instead, I was treated to the loudest sound that had ever passed through my ears. "Argh!" I screamed, dropping Ailill's hand to cover my ears with both hands. "What is that?"

Ailill didn't respond, and I could see the puzzlement clear on his face in the flicker of his torch light.

The echoing boom—far worse than any cave-in at the quarry, almost like the mountains themselves were tumbling down—continued, and a wash of red glowing light appeared from deep within the darkness, like it was approaching us on a gust of wind.

Ailill dropped the torch, which I could hardly hear clatter, and grabbed my hand again in his, urgently, squeezing hard. "Run!" he shouted, pulling me.

I ran, clutching my skirt with my other hand to keep from tripping. The light was growing larger, that sense of coldness drawing closer, but Ailill kept us running, faster than I had in months, harder than I had in years. I wanted to ask why we were running toward the light and not away from it, but there was no time. I had no breath.

"We are almost there!" encouraged Ailill, his own breaths short and staggered.

I wanted to shield my ears from the boom that pierced my head—the sound I swore I could feel in my bones—but I couldn't. I just had to keep running and running toward the red light.

We dashed through it before I even realized it was before us: a long, thin sheet of dark material. Gauze-like, the material let the red light through but filtered it, and it was only once we were entangled in the material that I noticed it: the material was a veil much like the one Ailill once wore, and the one he hung in his dining room to keep my eyes from him.

There was no end to it, but Ailill kept pulling me through. I felt the veil wrap around me and I tried to scream, but no sound came out over the sound of the booming, and I felt the wispy material caress my lips. I tried tugging his arm to make him slow, but he kept pulling and I got more and more entwined in it until we broke through, and the booming sound ended without fading, just like someone had reached out and silenced the mountain with a hand. We fell.

Ailill grabbed me at once, slamming my body against his, putting a hand on my back and the other on the back of my head to clutch me to him tightly. We both rolled down, and I felt the unevenness of the surface with every sharp jab, every aching poke to my body.

We couldn't have fallen long, but it felt like such a long time, I was almost becoming numb to it. When we stopped rolling at last, Ailill didn't immediately let me go, and I knew he must be feeling the same aches and bruises and the same swimming headache I did.

Ailill breathed hard above my ear, and I felt the race of his heartbeat against my chin. We stayed like that, silently, for some time until he finally relaxed his grip and shifted apart from me.

"Are you... hurt?" he asked between deep breaths.

I slammed my palms against the ground and noticed the dry dust that flew into the air with the movement. I ignored it and pushed myself up, groaning involuntarily as I adjusted myself to sit beside Ailill. The light was dull but blinding after having been inside the dark castle and mountainside. It was sunlight—at dusk. We were outside.

"What is it?" asked Ailill at once, all of his fatigue wiped away by worry.

"My foot." I winced as I readjusted myself and ripped my boot off, annoyed by the layers of skirt in my way.

"It is not bruised." Ailill lifted my foot before I could even drop the boot to the ground, stunning me into silence. "At least not yet." He raised one hand to his mouth, ripping off his leather glove with his teeth and spitting the glove onto the ground beside him. He switched hands and repeated the process before proceeding to touch my foot lightly, pushing and prodding. "Can you put weight on it?" he asked.

I finally got my wits about me and blushed, pulling my leg

back to get my foot out of his hands. I put it down and felt no discomfort, but all the movement caused a rattling in the boot in my hands. I turned it over and a large, dark rock fell out, with a pointy edge that had probably stabbed my sole. "I'm fine." I scrambled to put the boot back on, not looking at him.

Ailill sighed. "That is good news. We both seem to have survived intact, albeit a little worse for wear." He stood, and I studied him, noting the dirt all over his clothing that matched my own, the occasional tears to the material and the disarray of his hair.

"We did not fall far," he said. "But it is too far of a climb to go back, I am afraid to say. Not with that incline."

I stood, almost losing my balance and accepting Ailill's help reluctantly as I steadied myself on two feet. He let me go and I followed his gaze upward, where a large hole, the size of the hole behind the throne, appeared on the side of a—mountain?

I studied the brown, small flat mountain and felt unnerved. I twirled around, taking note of more smaller mountains, even some far in the distance, each with a flat peak. The ground was dry and brown and barren but for a few small strange green plants with needles protruding from them. The only thing that looked at all familiar was the sky above it, all awash in the great orange glow of a sunset. It wasn't the red light we'd seen in the tunnel. No, that was too much like the light that had replaced the violet glow in the cavern.

"Those are called cliffs," said Ailill, perhaps thinking my thoughts dwelled on the flat, small mountains. He looked around. "We appear to be in the canyon, outside the castle."

"This… is on the other side of the castle? This is what lies beyond the mountains?" I stepped forward, my body trembling. I didn't want to be afraid. I hadn't come here to turn back.

"Yes." Ailill let out a deep breath and put his hands on his hips, turning back to look up at the hole in the cliff. "In a way. But I was not referring to our castle, but the castle we came to visit. The Never Veil usually takes me directly to them, right out through their own hole behind their middle throne."

"That was the 'Never Veil'? That hanging veil we passed through to get here?"

"Like the pool in the cavern, as you seem to be familiar with, the hole behind my throne can lead to various places. It is not until you pass through the veil that you know just where you will go. The Never Veil lies between us and them, a curtain to shield us from the truth as it shields them from the *intrusion* of us." He bit his lip. "Still, they have never found cause to send me anywhere but right to them."

So I wasn't to see "them" right away or find out what any of these cryptic messages meant. Ailill took a few steps one way and then another, shading his eyes with a hand as he looked off into the horizon.

I bent down to grab the black leather gloves where he'd left them and clutched them tightly between both palms. *Should I ask him? Should I admit just how entirely unknowledgeable I am, that I'm no "lady in on the bet"? Clearly he knows something is already off about me, but to what extent? If he only remembered his last life, he'd already know all of that, but he also would never have taken me here.*

I swallowed back the questions I wanted to ask. He knew I'd never been here, but he couldn't know I'd never even spoken to any of them. He couldn't know I didn't fully realize who "they" are. "So what do we do next?" I asked. I was here to meet them, and I would. I needed his help, not his scorn. The less he knew about our history, the better. What he knew was already damaging enough.

Ailill nodded at me. "Well, I know we are in the right place, but the question is how far we are from the castle." He grabbed the gloves from me and tucked one under his arm while he pulled the other over his right hand. "If the queens were responsible for sending that red light to stop us, they would have resorted to sending us the farthest possible distance once they realized we had already breached the veil."

The queens? My heart fluttered. Here was the answer already, and I didn't even ask for it.

"But if the kings intervened," continued Ailill, tugging the second glove over his left hand. "They would have tried to stop them, bringing us much closer to the castle than the queens would like."

The kings? Kings and queens? Which are "they," or are they both the ones who watch over us?

"In any case, we have no choice but to walk there." He

pointed one way, opposite of the setting sun. "The castles are always in the east," he said, as if that made any sense to me. "So east we must go."

He set off before I could say anything more.

CHAPTER TWELVE

I'd hardly had time to notice the temperature before, but as the sunlight grew dimmer, I couldn't help but shiver. I wondered if it was already winter here, but I didn't remember it being abnormally cold when we first broke through the veil.

Probably noticing my distress, Ailill stopped, removed his black jacket, and swung it behind me.

I put a hand out to stop him. "You don't have to—"

"Nonsense. You are clearly cold." He let the jacket rest on my shoulders as I crossed my arms tightly against my chest.

I grabbed hold of the jacket and frowned, staring at Ailill's dark, exposed arms. His shirt seemed to be missing sleeves. "But what about you?"

He shrugged. "What do I have to fear? Freezing to death? Clearly, there is no end to the number of times I am able come back to life."

I hesitated, but then I slid my arms through the jacket, wrapping myself in his warmth, in his scent. I remembered vividly the first time he wrapped his jacket around me, when I first met him, my eyes closed.

Ailill continued walking onward, and I jogged a few paces to catch up. "But you won't be the same person if you die and come back," I said. *He's not the same person at all. There's no rage, no bitterness.*

"Does that matter?" Ailill kicked a rock with his foot. He glanced at the twilight sky and sighed before leading me to the edge of one of the cliffs. "We had better build a fire. It gets cold in a canyon after the sun sets."

"I think it does matter," I said, trying not to dwell on my disappointment in not meeting these kings and queens immediately. *Who knows what Jurij is up to. Or if all of the people back home have managed to stay out of danger.* "You're leaving the castle this life. You're leading the village in person. Maybe this life will be worth living."

Ailill paused mid-movement as he picked up a dusty ball of twigs and weeds that got caught against the cliff side and a rock. "Were my previous lives not worth living then?"

I watched as he broke the ball up into a flatter pile of brush and wiped his hands on his jerkin. He smiled awkwardly and took a few steps closer. "Pardon me," he said, reaching toward my chest. "May I? I left my flint in my inner lining."

I flushed and dug inside the jacket flaps, too nervous to let him reach inside himself. I withdrew the flint and handed it to him. He picked up a rock and struck the flint against it. "You cannot completely not remember," I said, trying to make sense of the new Ailill before me. It was true that it was only his first life he told me in detail, but he did mention subsequent lives. Getting food for himself from "sources"—these kings and queens?—and watching as every last person he knew died and faded away.

Ailill kept striking his flint with no success. He crouched beside the pile of brush and looked up before striking it again, smiling slightly. "I remember my first life clearly, but if you are wondering why my previous incarnation knew of his previous lives, the answer is quite simple: The other Ailills told him." He blew on the rock, and small bits of flint went flying. "And the one who knew the most about my previous life is gone, you told me." He struck again, this time causing the flint to set fire. "Ah!" He touched it to the brush over and over again until the little spark went out. "This is so much easier when they are here to help us, is it not?" He started pacing around the small campfire, picking up any twig he found and tossing it in to keep the fire burning. But there were few twigs and sticks in this barren place.

I helped him, searching for what little scraps I could find. I wished I'd brought some of the spare chunks of wood I used to carve with me. The fire wasn't going to last all evening.

Ailill settled down facing the fire, his back against the cliff side. I hesitated with my twigs over the small fire, observing as his eyes flickered with the reflection of the firelight. Why did the men ever have fire in their eyes? There were so many things I hoped to ask these kings and queens, not least of which was why they'd allowed Jurij to find them but had tried to stop me from coming.

I threw the small pile into the burning brush and sat down beside Ailill. "Your previous incarnation talked of infinite pain," I said, watching Ailill's reaction carefully. "He seemed to *feel* the torment of being alone for every one of his lives. You'd have me believe he'd been alone for just a few years, reborn as a young man like you, grown and faded no more than a decade before his life ended?"

I thought I noticed Ailill's lips twitch just slightly, but he masked any reaction by gathering his legs together in front of him and hugging them close to his chest. I didn't know what to believe. Part of me felt like he was lying, that he could remember everything, but I really knew nothing about this process, and there was no way this younger man, this happier, kinder man sitting so casually beside me, was the same man who hated me with every breath he took not so very long ago.

"Being alone for any period of time can be a torment," said Ailill at last, not meeting my eyes. "Especially if I could not walk among the people I looked after."

"Looked after" was a generous way of describing it. Did he even give his blessing to the Returnings, like so many people thought he was doing? Did he even care if we invited everyone in the village to attend? What was the meaning of all those stale traditions?

Nothing more than the curse you weaved with your very own mouth, I reminded myself.

"And what of you?" asked Ailill, breaking into my thoughts.

"Why do you not tell me more about my previous life, if you are so eager that I know it?"

"You don't have to know about your previous life." I ran my fingers nervously over one of the arms of the jacket. The embroidery on this jacket was different than the previous one's. Instead of roses and thorns, the flowers were clearly lilies. "I just can't believe... I can't believe how much you've changed."

Ailill shifted beside me and lowered his legs to the ground. "Change is a good thing, is it not?"

"It can be," I admitted. "But not always."

"What about now?" Ailill gestured to himself. "Have I changed for the better?"

"I suppose so. You're more..." I struggled to find a word that wouldn't offend him, or make him think I hated him previously. "You're more relaxed," I said at last.

"Relaxed?" Ailill cocked his head. "How so?"

I looked over to find him practically lying against the cliff side, so relaxed he was practically asleep. I stifled a laugh. "In almost every way! Although I have to ask... Why do you speak so formally?"

"Formally?" Ailill frowned slightly. The flickering fire made shadows dance across his jaw and neckline, shadows that drew my gaze to his tight jerkin and the tight form beneath it.

I tore my eyes away. "You spoke that way in the previous life, too. Still, I'm surprised if you're so much more *relaxed* now that you still speak like no other."

Ailill nodded, and I peeked over to see realization wash over his face. "You speak of words like 'I'm' and 'you're.' Taking less time to speak."

I screamed giddily, making him flinch, and grabbed his arm lightly. "You said them! You can actually say them!"

Ailill's cheeks darkened slightly and he rolled his eyes and looked away, but I didn't miss the smile playing on his lips. "Of course I can say them. I understand you, do I not?"

I let go of his arm and pointed at him. "Uh huh. Right there! Right there, anyone but *you* would have said 'don't I'!"

Ailill removed one of his gloves, making a point of being consumed by the task. I noticed his jaw twitch just slightly. "It is a habit passed down from lord to lord, or from lady to lady, an imitation of those who rule over all of us. I knew immediately you were only a new lady, one who must have been allowed to be such through marriage, when you spoke to me like a common villager."

I frowned, not entirely sure what he meant. From "lady to lady"? "Allowed to be"? Were there other lady rulers of the village, and who allowed a marriage? The kings and queens? Had they *allowed* Ailill's father to force himself on that poor woman in the commune who was Ailill's mother? Or did she not count as a lady because she had no gold of her own?

"Here." Ailill took my hand in his and slipped his glove over it. "When you touched my arm, your hand was like ice." He took off his second glove.

"Don't," I said, only just understanding I'd let him dress me like one of the dolls Elfriede had had as a child. I started peeling the other glove off. "You'll freeze for certain at this rate. You can't just strip everything off and—" I choked on my words, a startling image appearing in my head. *Strip everything off.* Like a goddess and her man did. *Elfriede and Jurij. There are no goddesses anymore.* Like a husband and wife, then. *But what of Alvilda and Siofra?* Or a wife and a wife. *And Darwyn and Tayton.* Or just two people who chose each other... I was so flustered, I couldn't keep my thoughts straight.

"I see your point," said Ailill, grinning slightly. He slid his glove back on and put his bare hand on my gloved one, stopping me from removing it. "Keep that one. We shall share." He turned his attention to the fire and picked up a small handful of twigs to throw into it. It was dwindling, and I feared there wasn't enough material to keep the fire going.

I tried to suppress a shiver as I looked at my hands, one gloved and one not, and remembered my first meeting with Ailill. I was so scared and taken aback, so unprepared to become his goddess, I never realized how nice his concern for me had been. True, it was a bit excessive—what man's wasn't for his goddess?—but I wondered if he hadn't been so cold and dismissive the next time I'd seen him, if I could have learned to be happy. Would he have been so maddening the following time if I'd been able to accept that I was no longer nobody's goddess much sooner? If I'd given up on my feelings for Jurij?

I laughed spitefully to myself. My feelings for Jurij. How much things had changed.

"Does something amuse you?" asked Ailill, tearing me from my thoughts.

I tucked my hands beneath my arms and hugged them tight. I looked at Ailill, prepared to talk, and the words caught in my throat. When had I come to feel this way about him? Because I *did* feel something for him, something different, but somehow better than what I'd ever felt for Jurij. There had been so much hate between us—and while I certainly wouldn't count him blameless, despite everything I now knew—and I regretted clinging so desperately to my stubbornness. I hadn't known Jurij, not really, not like I came to know Ailill. And now Ailill barely knew me.

Maybe that was for the best. Maybe... I could teach him to love me this time. Actually *love* me.

I want him to choose *to love me.*

I pushed that too-long strand of hair out of my face. "It's nothing. What do you think the..." I hesitated, but then I decided to throw myself into everything that puzzled me. "The kings and queens want with Jurij?" Part of me wanted not to care, but I did. I wasn't yet ready to forgive him for his act of violence, intentional or unintentional, but I felt bad for the way he'd wound up in that position. I felt bad that he thought he loved me when he didn't, not really. We were best friends once, whether he'd chosen that or not.

"I cannot say." Ailill frowned as our tiny fire died out, leaving us drenched in nothing but night and starlight. "Stolen golden token or not, no other man from our village should have the right to meet them."

"No other *man*?" I asked, noticing the emphasis.

"Well, yes," said Ailill, standing. He stomped the life out of the last few embers. "Each village has either one man or one woman in charge of it—or on occasion, one of both."

"*Each* village?" I practically screamed it into the darkness.

Even in the dim light, I could see Ailill pause and study me. "Are you certain you were given the token from the queens, and that you haven't stolen—" His question was interrupted by the sound of something strange and hollow, like a dog crooning at the moonlight. Only it was higher pitched than that. More soulless.

"A coyote," said Ailill, sitting back on the ground. "They are relatively harmless."

Relatively?

Ailill stretched his bare arms above his head and lay down. "We should rest," he said. "We will continue walking at first light. It cannot be much farther."

My stomach growled, releasing some of the tension I felt at the echoing howl. I was thirsty and my feet ached, and I felt the throbbing of bruises forming all over my body from the tumble.

"There will be food there," said Ailill, reading my thoughts. "And once we are inside, they will not be able to help but welcome us. They have kept me fed in the past." I could hear his leather clothing rustling as he tried to make himself comfortable. "During that first life," he added. *Because he can't remember the other ones?*

So these kings and queens were his original sources of food. Even so, after what little he'd told me of them, I couldn't see why he trusted them.

I was too tired to think. If I stayed up much longer, I was sure to dwell on my thirst and hunger. I moved to lie down, my head at Ailill's feet.

Ailill stirred in the darkness. "Lie up here. Beside me." He gestured out toward the small space he'd left between himself and the cliff side. "It will be warmer. And we will be better able to react together should a coyote come wandering over."

I scrambled over to the space he indicated, a jolt of energy at his words giving me the strength to make the movement. I lay down on the painfully hard ground, using one of my hands as a bony, uncomfortable pillow.

I stared at Ailill's back in front of me. Blinking, letting my eyes adjust to the darkness, I saw the gentle rhythm of his shoulders move just slightly with each breath.

I've never seen him sleeping, I thought. *It makes him feel more... amenable.*

I ran the soothing softness of the glove he'd lent me against my cheek.

"We shall share," he'd said. Only that wasn't what we were doing at all.

I sat up slowly, doing my best not to disturb him. Removing my arms from the jacket he'd given me, I draped half of it over my side and lay down again, gently laying the other half across his side like a blanket. My bare hand lingered on his bicep as I let go of the jacket, and I had to stop myself from leaving it there and feeling the cold of his skin transform into warmth.

His hand shot out to grab mine. Bare skin on bare skin, he squeezed it, and the iciness of his touch gave way to heat that made my heart pound faster. I was so tired, I couldn't say for sure whether or not that last part was just me dreaming. I think I tried to squeeze it back, but I soon lost touch with everything but the enveloping darkness of sleep.

CHAPTER THIRTEEN

L ight had just broken over the horizon when I next opened
my eyes, but that wasn't even the first thing I noticed.

Ailill had turned over to face me, the jacket we shared as a
blanket pushed down off his shoulder. He held a finger over his
lips.

I was still fatigued, and it took me a moment more to sense
what was bothering him. There was a rustle of movement from
somewhere above our heads.

"What is—" I whispered, but Ailill covered my mouth with
his palm until I quieted. He let go, craning his head over his
shoulder and pushing himself up.

A coyote? I wondered, thinking of the wild animals back home.
There was nothing so frightening-sounding in the woods by my
home, nothing that sent chills down my spine in the darkness.

Ailill shifted his feet beneath him, carefully and quietly, and
rose slowly. He took a few steps eastward, and I sat up, scrambling to pick up the jacket as it fell, my hands trembling.

"I don't mean any harm, I just—oh, you."

I flinched at the sound of the familiar voice and stood quickly,
clutching the jacket to my chest. *"Jurij!"*

Jurij stood in front of Ailill, the two young men about even in
height. Jurij looked exhausted, and there were puffy circles under

his eyes. I noticed his clothes were dusty but intact, and as the aches in my thighs, arm, and head began pounding, I couldn't help but wonder if he was spared Ailill's and my rather dramatic entrance into this dusty, forsaken land.

Ailill kept a wary eye on Jurij but shifted his head just slightly to address me. "This is the man you sought, then?"

"Yes." I stepped up to stand beside Ailill, watching Jurij warily. "How in the name of the first goddess did you come here? *Why* did you come here?"

"The first goddess?" said Jurij, a sad smile playing on his lips. "Do you mean—"

"Me, yes, thank you. It's a force of habit. You're avoiding my questions."

"I don't know." Jurij shrugged. "I felt compelled to go back to the cavern and I fell in and…" He put a hand to his waist as if lost in thought, calling attention to the sword in a scabbard at his side, and the golden bangle around the wrist of the hand that patted it.

"You still have that sword? And you stole that golden bangle, too! Give them back!" I dropped Ailill's jacket and lashed out to grab the sword's hilt. Jurij leaned back out of my reach.

"They weren't *yours*, though, were they?" Jurij's face soured.

I bent over to grab Ailill's jacket, huffing. "They're not *yours*, either! And you clearly have no right to them."

I folded the jacket over my arm as Jurij and Ailill stared each other down, the tension palatable.

"You never formally introduced me to the lord," said Jurij, smirking. "If this is even the same lord."

"I could use a proper introduction to this man myself," added Ailill, and I felt like there was more than just an introduction at stake.

I sighed. "Ailill, this is Jurij, the fri—the man everyone was looking for. Jurij, this is the lord, albeit altered, and his name is Ailill."

"Altered?" snorted Jurij. "I'll say."

Ailill broke the eye contact at last and turned to me, puzzled. "Does this man bear some ill will toward me?"

"If anything," I said, before Jurij could answer himself, "you ought to bear ill will toward *him*."

Jurij scoffed. "I'd say the feeling was mutual, considering how he treated his villagers like play things."

"He didn't treat us all like *play things!*" I protested. "And who put *that* nonsense in your head? I don't think what you *did* to him is equal to that."

"I *told* you it was an accident, and I was *trying* to save you, no matter how ungrateful you've been about it—"

"You also *told* me that you'd pictured yourself doing something like that regardless—"

Ailill raised a hand. "I see there is clearly something I am missing that happened between you two, but if I might ask that we put any further discussion on hold? The sun has risen, and we best make haste. The castle cannot be much farther, but we cannot afford to spend another night out here without arriving at our destination."

Jurij looked like he had plenty more to say, but he settled for scratching his arm. The bangle jostled against his wrist as he did. *It's because I led him to the dining room that he got his hands on that. It's because of that that he's here.*

"All right," I said. "I'll wait to discuss that. But I want to know why he's here to begin with."

"I told you," started Jurij, "I went to the cavern and fell in—"

"I guessed that." I turned to Ailill, ignoring Jurij. "Yet he shouldn't be here, right? What use could *they* have for him?" It was nice being on the other side of the mystery for once, even though I was no more sure who the "kings and queens" were than I'd been just the day before.

"We shall have to ask them." Ailill took the coat from my arms and draped it over his forearm. It was hotter now that the sun had risen, and I didn't think either of us would need it. I removed the one glove from my hand sheepishly as I noticed Jurij watching us, and Ailill took it from me silently, slipping it back over his own hand. "Shall we be off then?" He didn't await either of our answers and strode forward past Jurij to lead the way.

Jurij and I exchanged a wary glance before we both picked up our feet and followed him.

~

543

I OPENED MY DRY LIPS, desperate to fill what must have now been an hour or two of silence with something. "I hear you've taken to woodworking."

Jurij's shoulders shook perceptively from what must have been surprise at my willingness to talk.

"I suppose I owe Alvilda for that compliment." He peered down at me from beneath his hand, which he used to shield his eyes from the sun overhead. "I couldn't tell you, not really. After the cav—well, after that night, I felt too numb to work. I didn't go back to the quarry. I didn't go back to your cottage. So at some point my aunt must have been tired of me sitting there like a lump of wood and sought to correct that by putting a lump of wood in my idle hands."

Ailill was a few paces ahead of us, leading the way without stopping for a rest. He'd claimed it couldn't be much farther, but all I saw were a maze of cliff sides blocking out the skyline.

It was strange to hear Jurij so jovial, like the night in the cavern was just a dream. "You said the cavern called to you, like it did to me once," I said.

"Yes," said Jurij after a moment. "It was in that instant that everything made sense. It's not that I didn't believe you, but I fully believed you when I went into the cavern and saw the violet glow. It was red before, wasn't it?"

"Yeah," I admitted. "It has been since I traveled through it."

"I should have realized that." Jurij took a deep breath. "I should have realized it'd changed colors. I'd seen it before, after all, the day of Elfriede's and my Returning." He frowned.

That day used to be a painful day for me because it was then I'd realized that Jurij was only compelled to be my friend through an accidental command of Elfriede's. I didn't think the day had any painful significance for Jurij, but maybe now that he was free to think for himself, he finally saw the injustice in it. I'd gotten over that pain already. The night I thought I'd lost Ailill in the cavern was far fresher for me.

"Your family is worried about you," I said, switching topics. "We were all... Well, it was a fine time to go missing, as I'd just realized everyone who was in the cavern that night was in danger."

Jurij stopped in his tracks, but Ailill didn't, and I kept moving. Jurij jogged a few paces to catch up to me. "What do you mean?"

I lowered my voice. Ailill already knew this, but I didn't want to invite any discussion between the two of them. "One of the servants attacked Sindri because he mentioned the lord's altered appearance."

Jurij grabbed my arm, stopping me. I noticed he used the hand with the golden bangle. "Is he all right?"

"Yes," I said. Ailill seemed to have noticed our absence and stopped just ahead, right as the cliff side began curving outward. "Everyone's all right. I warned them not to discuss what they saw in the cavern within earshot of any servants."

"But why?" Jurij's grip tightened on my arm.

"I don't know. Ailill said these people called the kings and queens know. They live here, watching over us."

Jurij ran his head across his sweat-caked forehead. "If I weren't already astounded by jumping into a pool and coming out through a curtain on the side of one of these flat mountains, I would hardly believe you. Kings and queens. Like the rulers in stories..."

"You didn't come out in water?" I asked, confused. When I'd swum through the pool, I'd come right back up through the top of it, albeit in a different time.

"No," said Jurij, turning his attention back to me. "Or maybe I just dreamt it all. I don't know. I remember the violet glow, the cavern pond, my name being called by whispering voices... I jumped in, but instead of water, all I can remember is breaking through a gauze black curtain, and then I was here."

"It's a veil," I said. I doubted it would have the same significance to him, considering he never stared at the veiled lord for as long as I had. "Still, I don't understand. How? Could you go back through it?"

Jurij shook his head. "No. I tried, but when I walked back into the small cave opening, there was only stone wall, no 'veil' as you called it."

"But if the kings and queens wanted you here, and they didn't want me here, why not at least bring you directly to the castle?"

"You keep mentioning a castle."

I ignored him. "Unless... Ailill said the queens don't want me here, but the kings would be fighting back? Are the two in some sort of conflict?" My surmises didn't matter. As Ailill said, the answers awaited ahead of us. "Where were you going, Jurij, with that sword on your hip last night? I assume you hadn't planned on jumping through the cavern pool to find yourself lost in a land unfamiliar to you."

"No," admitted Jurij. His eyes darted nervously over to where Ailill stood, his back to the cliff and one of his feet resting flat against it. "I was on my way to see him."

"Why?"

"Jaron and I... came to an agreement." He put his hands out in front of him. "It was nothing nefarious, I swear to you! We decided to turn ourselves in."

I bit my lip. Jaron *had* turned himself in, but he hadn't mentioned Jurij supposedly coming to join him, even though he knew I'd been looking for him. My eyes darted to the sword at Jurij's side, which he touched nervously as he watched Ailill.

"You wanted to be put in prison?" I asked. *And you prepared to go with a sword?* I wanted to add, but I wanted Jurij to tell me about that himself.

Jurij looked at his feet. "No, not really, of course. But we felt the pain of what we'd done every day. Those men and women gone. The tavern fire. Even if he was back, I knew it wasn't the same man, and I knew, deep down, I'd killed someone with my own two hands." He sighed. "And for what? We had more questions than ever—and very few answers."

"But *you* had some answers. Jaron hinted he knew more than he should have. How much did you tell him—tell anyone? About me being the first goddess, about the power of the cavern?"

"I didn't say anything. I told you I didn't believe you entirely myself until I traveled through the Never Veil."

My blood ran cold. Out of the corner of my eye, I kept checking to see if Ailill was watching, but to my horror, he'd vanished. Had he gone around the corner to scout ahead? I picked up my skirt and darted after him.

"Noll, wait—"

"I have to find him!" I called, not bothering to look back over my shoulder. "He's the only one who knows where he's going."

And to tell the truth, I felt uncomfortable at the prospect of being left alone with Jurij.

"Noll! Slow down! I haven't finished talking to you!"

I was almost there, and I was sure to find Ailill just around the corner. *Keep going. Keep going!*

"Noll!"

I'm almost there. "Ailill! Where did you go? AILILL!"

Jurij seized me by the shoulders, spinning me back to face him. I nearly collapsed, I was so out of breath, but I was determined to get away from him. "Relax!" Jurij said, and he smiled awkwardly. "He's just around the corner. I saw him peek ahead while we were talking."

"Let go of me!" I said, and I gripped both of his arms tightly. I tried to tear them away, but I didn't have the strength.

"Noll, what's wrong with you? I know we've had our issues, but you're acting like I want to kill you—"

I gave up trying to get his arms off of me, but I stood my ground defensively. "How did you know it was called the Never Veil?"

Jurij frowned. "You told me. You said it wasn't a curtain—"

"—it was a veil. But I didn't tell you the name of it."

Jurij sighed and he looked over my head. "That was stupid of me. I wanted this to go another way." He shifted his grip to one of my arms and tugged me back down the path behind him.

Even though I dug my heels into the ground, I couldn't stop him from pulling me. "AILILL!" *Help me!*

Jurij tugged harder. "Noll, please don't make this any harder. Come with me, or I'll have to—"

"You'll have to what?" I demanded. "Use that sword on me?"

Jurij frowned and gripped the hilt with his free hand. "If I must." He drew it out from the scabbard slowly and raised it above his head. "I'm sorry."

I turned and started to run. Everything went black.

CHAPTER FOURTEEN

Before I even opened my eyes, I could feel his arms under my knees and around my back, and my face pressed against his chest. The back of my head throbbed.

I was still for half a moment longer before I screamed, not caring that it made my head hurt so much worse. "Let me go!"

I pushed against his chest and tried to get my eyes all the way open. The light was blinding.

"Olivi—Noll! Noll, wait, please! It is I."

I stilled instantly. The sound of my name was foreign with that voice's timbre, but there was no way Jurij could imitate Ailill down to the stilted speech. I blinked away tears until I could see.

Ailill's deep brown eyes looked straight into mine, and even without the flames, I found them mesmerizing. We didn't stay that way long, though, before he broke away and slowly crouched, so he could set me down on the coarse and barren ground.

I ran a hand to the back of my head and winced. Instead of my hair, I found a strip of cloth there. "What happened?" I asked groggily. "Where's Jurij?"

Ailill scoffed and gently grabbed my forearm, pulling it away from my head. His other hand still supported my back. "Your *friend* hit you on the back of the head with the hilt of that sword."

How had it come to this? How was Jurij so lost to me? Was it my fault? Should I never have loved him, never have stopped loving him? What was it like to finally return the affections of someone you thought loved you, only to find that person no longer in your reach?

I stared at Ailill as I considered those questions. My eyes darted to his abdomen, which was bare, the shirt he wore beneath his open jacket torn hastily above the navel. I felt heat rush to my face as I took note of the edge of his hip bones, so sharp and defined around the top of his thighs before they vanished out of sight beneath his trousers.

"Where were you?" I asked, the question surprising me, as well as the shaky voice with which I delivered it. "I searched for you, and you were gone."

"I had just gone around the corner," said Ailill, his face clearly pained. "I had a feeling we were near, and I wanted to be certain. I... I apologize. I should never have left you alone with him."

I frowned, considering everything. Never have left me alone with Jurij? That was once all I had longed for. And now... Now I didn't even know who he was anymore.

"What happened?" I repeated. "Where is he now?"

A slight breeze stroked Ailill's face, dancing through the hair that framed his sharp cheekbones. Every sharp bone in his body called out to be touched. "I do not know where he is. Only that I heard you screaming, and I ran back. I saw you coming toward me, your *friend* with that sword you say he stole raised above your head, both hands on the hilt, and he hit you with the bottom of it."

"He could have *killed* me!" I'd been determined not to be so angry with him, to remember what was once between us, but it seemed all he did was make things worse.

"Yes," said Ailill. "I cannot say for certain whether he realized that, but despite it all, I will grant him the benefit of the doubt. When you fell to the ground, he looked like death. He was afraid he had killed you."

I scoffed and winced at the movement. My head throbbed, and my side was still sore. "What did he expect?"

"He was incoherent," said Ailill flatly. "By the time I got to you both, he had flung the sword to the ground and was cradling you, repeating your name over and over." He pinched his lips. "He said he only wanted you to 'go with' him."

"I got that part." I took a deep breath, doing my best to ignore the pain. "What I don't get is why he would hurt me to get me to go with him."

"I do not think he understands what he does."

I thought of Jurij's sword through Ailill's chest and how cruel he seemed at my anger over it. "He understands enough."

"He let you go as soon as I got there. I worked quickly to staunch your wound." He bit his lip. "If only I still had my power…"

"Don't blame yourself," I said. "You used the last of it to save my mother. I couldn't be more grateful." I wished the words had flown so easily after he did it, that I could go back and thank him properly when he truly understood.

"Well, they will be able to treat you, if they prove welcoming." Again with the *they*, but it no longer felt as ominous now that I had an inkling of who they were. Although considering how little I truly knew, perhaps it still should be.

"So where is he?"

"Gone." The tips of Ailill's gloves brushed my cheek and he gestured in the air as if he was letting a bug he caught go. "I could hardly question him or accuse him before he ran, leaving that sword behind in the dust beside you. I could not carry it without its sheath as well as you, so I left it behind."

"I can't believe this." I started to shake my head but had to stop when I felt the pain reverberate in my skull. "I know he's changed, but I never imagined Jurij capable of hurting *anyone*, let alone me."

Ailill swallowed visibly. "Freedom can be a difficult burden. One most men would ask for nonetheless, but one not suited for everyone." Even after a night spent out here, the faint tumble of the weeds through the empty landscape between beats in our conversations was a strange sound to get used to, like we were lying in the midst of a dance of wool. "In any case, your friend's panic set us on the right path."

I slowly turned my head to get a look.

"He retreated down a path between cliffs I had hardly noticed, and I picked you up and followed soon after to confront him. He was out of sight once I turned the corner, but he led us straight here."

I blinked, sure the pain in my head was causing me to see falsely. Because off in the distance, less than an hour's walk away, were two castles that looked just like Ailill's. Joined in the middle with a single doorway, it was almost like Ailill's castle was reflected in a mirror. Instead of mountains, they were surrounded by cliffs. Instead of being dark and black and ominous, they glowed softly in violet.

And I could almost hear my name spoken on that desolate wind.

～

AILILL QUICKLY RELENTED when I protested at the idea of him bringing me to these queens and kings in his arms like an infant. It was more than just the fact that the memory of waking up in his arms like that made my face hot and my head dizzy. I didn't understand most of this, but I did remember that feeling of being dragged beneath the water in the cavern. These people may have tried to kill me, and I knew I wasn't about to like what I found in their castle, but I had to go. I had to know. And I needed to start off with as much strength in my corner as I could get.

Unfortunately, the pain in my head and the aches all over wouldn't let me walk upright with my shoulders thrown back. When Ailill suggested I at least let him wrap his arm around my shoulders to settle me against him as we walked, I had to oblige. We only took a few steps before I slipped my arm around his back.

"For better balance," I said. He didn't say anything.

There was no outer wall in front of these twin castles, no outer door to swing open at our approach. The land was so barren, it was little wonder. These people surely expected no visitors—at least none who would walk through their front doors. Ailill had made it clear the Never Veil usually brought him straight inside this place when he stepped through.

Still, I thought we might be expected. Especially if this was where Jurij was headed—and where else could he have gone?

The doors to the joined castles swung open slowly at our approach.

The lovely coolness of Ailill's jacket—returned to me after I insisted on walking myself—caressed my cheek as I lifted my head back slightly. "Is that a good thing?"

The lump at his throat moved subtly. "It is rarely the fate of pawns to encounter a 'good thing' at the hand of more powerful pieces."

And to think, I thought. *I used to believe he was one of the more powerful pieces.*

We stepped inside together, our feet crossing the threshold at the same time. It was like coming home.

The entryway looked exactly like Ailill's castle, only brighter, as the sunlight filtered in from every open doorway. Some part of me felt like it was more than the light, though, it was the fact that I was walking through here, leaning on Ailill, feeling his supportive hand on my shoulder. The open door straight across from us led to a garden, and I could hear the trickle of a water fountain. Through another doorway I spotted a long dining table. And there was the stairway at our right, and to the left—

A second stairway. A mirror image of the first.

Of course. You're not home. You saw two castles. There have to be two stairways.

Ailill paused halfway inside. His lips were pursed, his brow furrowed, as his eyes darted back and forth between the stairway, but his gaze landed on the garden ahead of us.

I blinked, trying to adjust to the light stairways. H. The flowers on the bushes—the roses?—weren't just white as they were in Ailill's garden. They weren't hibernating for the upcoming winter, either. The bushes were verdant and lively, the blooms bright and colorful. Each seemed to be a different shape, every bloom was a different color.

"Should we go in?" I asked, already letting my hand fall from Ailill's back and stepping away, toward the open garden.

"Halt! Olivière Woodcarver."

It wasn't Ailill's voice, although the stilted, affected delivery reminded me of him. It wasn't even a single voice. It was a multitude of them, both male and female.

I turned slowly. Ailill was already turned around and backing toward me, his hands out behind his back as if to stop me from pushing past him.

Three men descended from my left, which I supposed was the south castle, in perfect tandem with three women from my right and the northern castle. They were spaced evenly apart and moved almost as one, the one side a mirror image of the other in movement.

They wore clothing, but they may as well not have, as it clung so tightly to their skin, they could have been naked. I saw every curve, every bulge of their bodies, and although they differed in height and weight—even among their own gender—they were all an example of the form of the body at its finest. The golden material of the tight suits shined and glimmered in the rays of the sunlight as they filed into a half circle, as did the identical golden crowns they each wore upon their heads.

I don't know how long they stood there before speaking. I was too entranced by their appearances. I noticed they each had rounded ears—even the men—and my hands moved subconsciously to caress my own. But that was practically where what was similar about their appearances stopped.

The tallest man was the most familiar to my eyes, not that he reminded me of anyone in particular, but because his appearance was the least surprising, as he resembled the men in my village. His face, neck, and hands were as dark as wet soil, as was the short but voluminous hair that peeked out from beneath the crown. His shoulders were broad, and he carried himself with an air of power and beauty.

The shortest woman, still taller than I and quite imposing, shared the look somewhat of Ailill's paler form, that creamy rose complexion almost but not quite as pale as a specter. Her hips were wide, her chest buxom, and her gorgeous long hair was almost the color of copper—*red*—and curly as it tumbled over her shoulders.

The man of middle height looked like no one I'd ever seen before. Slim, but still with greater muscle than Ailill, his skin was almost golden in tone to match his golden outfit. His dark, black hair reached his shoulders in almost perfectly straight lines, and his eyes, dark and powerful even from where I was standing, were slightly smaller than I'd expect, more blended into his lovely features.

The woman of middle height was as light in skin as Elfriede, but the richness of her long, wavy brown hair made her beauty something else entirely. Her nose was straighter, thinner than I expected, her dark eyes penetrating. She was the only one of them who stood with a hand on her hip, the others content to let their arms hang beside them.

The shortest man shared the light oak skin tone of this woman and of Elfriede, and his handsome, sharply defined features looked bold against the long black braid that rested over his shoulders. His eyes were wide, his nose sharp and pointed, and his lips came together in a long, thin line.

The tallest woman—the one who stood at the middle beside the tallest man—commanded my gaze as soon as I laid eyes on her. She wore her hair short, but I saw it was shiny and black and straight from where it peeked out beneath her crown. Her skin tone was about as fair as the man with startlingly different eyes. Her eyes were even similar to his but wider, more distinctive than his. Her face was fuller than his too, the tip of her nose rounder. She was thin, almost one straight line, the curves where I expected them just slightly prominent. She studied me across the top of her nose, her chin jutted just a bit forward.

"You have done wrong, Ailill, and you forget yourself." It was the tall, dark man who spoke, and it was only by his speaking that I could tear myself from the tallest woman's gaze.

Ailill grabbed my hand in his and I let him, but he still wouldn't move from where he stood in front of me. Ailill spoke, loudly, his voice cracking. "I am surprised you lecture me so, Your Majesty Adeyemi. Was it not you and the other kings who stopped the queens from sending us even farther from the castles?"

The tall woman laughed, glancing at the women beside her. "You are mistaken. It was we who stopped *them*."

"You, Your Majesty Jangmi?" asked Ailill. He frowned. "You have never helped me—"

"We had no intention of helping *you*, foolish child." It was the middle woman who spoke. "It was her." Her eyes fell immediately on me.

The quiet, calm room exploded as the men started shouting, the women turning to them and shouting back in response. I couldn't make sense of the argument, but I heard my name, my full name, over and over, spoken with both distaste and triumph, but spoken coldly regardless.

"Enough!" called Adeyemi, and everyone fell calmly back into lines. They stared at us.

I opened my mouth to speak, but Ailill dropped my hand and crossed his hand over his chest, bending forward. "I apologize if I have done wrongly," he said. He straightened from his bow. "She has a token, though."

"A token?" sneered the middle man. "What token? I see no token on her arm."

I rubbed my wrist absently, knowing there would be no golden bangle there. The pressure of the eyes on me made me reach into my pocket and bring out my golden coin. "This," I said, my voice catching in my throat.

The shortest man stepped forward and studied my open palm. He asked me to turn it over and I did, grateful he didn't just snatch it out of my hands. He turned back to his companion. "How does she come by this—this mockery of a token?"

"That is no mockery!" said the shortest woman, and she stepped up to examine it. She nodded. "It is made of gold, and so it belongs here. That is what we agreed to."

"It is not a bangle," said the man.

"What does the shape of it matter?" said the middle woman. "Nowhere in the rules does it say it has to be a bangle!"

"You seem remarkably familiar with this object," said the middle man, stepping forward. "If you are found to have sent it—"

"It will be no different than you letting that boy through the veil with the stolen bangle!" shouted the middle woman.

"The two incidents are not even comparable," said the shortest man. "You know who this girl is—"

"Silence!" said Jangmi, holding a hand up, and the others fell mute, walking back into place. "Ailill," she said more calmly. "Let us at least start with introductions."

"She has no right to be here!" called the middle man.

"Kin, be still," spoke Adeyemi.

Ailill put an arm behind my back and guided me slightly forward. "These are the kings and queens of the realm," he said, as if "the realm" would make any sense to me. "They watch over us and all of our villages, ever playing games to win their bet."

I was speechless. I wanted to say something—*anything*—but nothing could make it past my lips. *A fine show of strength you're giving them.*

"I am Jangmi," spoke the tallest woman. She cupped her hands in front of her waist.

"I am, as you may have observed, Adeyemi," said the tallest man.

"Chrysilla," said the middle woman.

"Kin," echoed the middle man.

"Marigold," spoke the shortest woman.

"And Estavan," finished the shortest man.

Their names were as strange as their faces to me. It took all of my effort to keep each of them straight.

"You must have many questions," said Jangmi, "but I am afraid we cannot answer them as of yet. We must consult on how you came into possession of that coin."

"We know *full well* it was you who sent it," interrupted Estavan. "You have thought of her as your champion pawn piece ever since she altered the purpose of that pathway."

"And we know *full well* it was you who attempted to bar her entrance from the castles," said Marigold, "even though we let that boy with the stolen bangle through without interference. And that pawn was simply a cheat."

The argument moved so fast, I could hardly keep up with which of the shorter kings and queens were speaking. "It is not a cheat if we were not the ones who sent him the bangle!" said a king.

"There should not have *been* excess bangles in that village!" said a queen.

"Do not blame *us* for that!" said a king. "It was *her* who made that village so strange!"

"It worked out very well for you with your never-dying lord

there, has it not?" said a queen. "Why are you then complaining?"

"I will tell you why," said one of the kings. "Because we did not attempt to stop her. If it was not *you*, it had to be the girl herself! Every time she passes through an entryway, things do not go as expected. She did not even cross paths with the Never Veil the first time. Instead she somehow *turned back time* without our consent."

"*We* did not give her consent," snapped a queen. "Restarting a village without permission from both sides is such an affront to the rules—"

"Be careful what you say to them," whispered Ailill beside me, startling me. "They do not take kindly to lack of respect."

Jangmi's eyes were strangely on Ailill as he pulled away from me. She turned back to Adeyemi. "Might we settle this argument more peacefully?"

The rest of the kings and queens fell silent. Adeyemi cradled his chin with his hand. "Yes, perhaps we better. Let us retreat to the gardens to discuss their punishment. Ailill and Olivière's both."

They moved as one, circling around us to head to the open doorway.

"Wait," I said, and they actually paused. I tried to ignore Ailill's panicked face, and I clenched my fists, feeling the coin press into my palm. "You can't just..." I grimaced. "Whatever you decide, I'd like some answers first." I thought of Ailill's whispered warning. "Please."

Their faces went aghast, except for Jangmi's. She smiled coolly. "Then come with us to the garden, child." And they all went through the door.

Ailill spun on me as the last king stepped through, grabbing my shoulders and quietly shouting in a strained whisper, "What did I just tell you?"

"What are we here for then?"

Ailill ran a hand through his hair, his voice dropping. "We will get answers for you. I promise. But please, follow my lead. You have to be careful."

"Children!" called Adeyemi from the garden door. He

gestured behind him. "Come and join us. We have agreed. We will heal you, refresh you—and then discuss your punishment."

Ailill held his palm out to me and gave me a weak smile. I took his hand in mine and squeezed it, and we stepped forward into the sunlight, our footsteps in tandem.

CHAPTER FIFTEEN

The green light coming from Jangmi's fingers felt warm and comforting. I closed my eyes, and I could picture a little boy healing my wounds in the stocks, running that warmth over a bruise on my face. I opened one eye carefully, reminding myself that the "little boy" was sitting right next to me on a garden bench, getting his bumps and scratches healed by Adeyemi.

It was hard to remember Ailill as a little boy. It hadn't been anywhere near as long for me as it had been for him, but for the little time I knew him, I never imagined he would grow up to be the man who would find the goddess in me. I never imagined I would set that into motion.

In any case, though, it wouldn't have felt that long ago to Ailill, either, if he only remembered his first life. Every time I thought about the paler Ailill whom I'd fought with, pleaded with, even loved... I couldn't believe he hadn't remembered his previous lives. He seemed to live the pain of a hundred or more lives in isolation. It couldn't have all been the specters telling him about their own lifetimes.

"There," said Jangmi, drawing me out of my reverie. She crossed one leg over the other and folded her hands upon her lap. "I have restored your health completely."

"Thank you," I said, quieter than I meant to. I rubbed the back of my head absently, searching for evidence of the bump. There was none, other than the matting of my hair. I looked down at the strip of black cloth Ailill had used to wrap my head wound. It was soaked with a dark stain.

"We have finished here as well," spoke Adeyemi. "And just in time."

Marigold and Kin brought two trays of charred meat with roasted potatoes and carrots and set them in front of Ailill and me. I watched him tentatively and only picked up my fork to start eating once he did.

"Thank you." Ailill kept his head down. He was strangely meek beyond measure around these kings and queens, even if it was true that I'd yet to see him overly stubborn this rebirth at all.

"Thank you," I echoed, but I didn't put my head down. Instead, I let my gaze wander over the garden. I'd been right about the bushes. They weren't just different colored roses; they were different colored flowers. Flowers that had no business being on what I thought of as rose bushes to begin with—like the violet lily-covered bush a short distance in front of me.

"Now that that is settled," said Adeyemi, standing. "We must discuss what is to be done."

I laid down my spoon—golden, as was so much in this place —and opened my mouth to speak. I stopped when I felt Ailill's hand on my knee. He squeezed it but didn't tear his eyes from his plate. *Wait*, he seemed to be saying. *Listen*. His eyes weren't focused on his food. Instead, he was actually paying close attention to the kings' and queens' movements. I took a drink of unnaturally clear water from the golden goblet on my plate.

"Very well," said Jangmi. She stood as well, joining Chrysilla and Marigold in facing the kings. She looked at both of the women in turn, took note of their slight nods, and proceeded. "We think we should keep Olivière here, for study."

I choked on my sip, but the kings and queens paid me no mind. Ailill's hand squeezed harder.

"What is there to study?" demanded Estavan. "She is an anomaly. She should be removed from the game immediately!"

"Keeping her here for study *would* remove her from the game," said Chrysilla. She tossed her head back and clutched her hands together in front of her abdomen, the image of elegance.

"So would eliminating her," said Kin. He was the first to tear his eyes from the other rulers in order to look at me, and I felt a chilling menace in his gaze. I put my goblet down overly carefully.

"That is poor sport!" scoffed Marigold, whipping her hands to her hips. "After what we allowed for you, this man who never fully dies—"

Estavan stepped forward to meet her. "You *allowed* it because it was a woman who made it happen!"

Jangmi moved between them. "It is only fair, then. If Olivière is to die, then Ailill must too."

"Hold on!" I said, ignoring Ailill's pleading glance. "You can't heal us and feed us, just to kill us!" I pushed the tray forward, most of it untouched. My appetite was gone.

Adeyemi raised an eyebrow in my direction but soon turned back to Jangmi, my outburst unremarked upon. "Ailill cannot die. He has not fathered a child. We have yet to see if a lord or lady will replace him as that village's guardian."

"Oh?" said Jangmi, as if humoring him. "I thought you planned to anoint a new lord of that village. Is that not what you promised the interloper who stumbled upon a golden bangle and found his way here?"

Jurij. He wanted to be lord of the village? What in the name of the goddess for? What kinds of aspirations could he possibly have to lead the village, to live in the castle—

To get rid of Ailill.

"Where is Jurij?" I stood, ignoring Ailill's tug on my arm to sit down. "What have you promised him?"

Kin shook his head. "You see what I mean about her? She must be eliminated."

"She must be *studied*," said Marigold fiercely. "You really want to eliminate this anomaly, this pawn who has been able to affect the rules of the game, before we even know why or how she does it?"

"She puts us all in danger," insisted Estavan.

"Danger?" Chrysilla snorted. "Maybe if you are so weak that a pawn might pose a threat."

Estavan pointed a finger at her. "You only say that because she's a woman and her advantages are an advantage for you!"

"Enough!" I said, raising my voice. I ignored Ailill's whispers of my name—"Noll" again; I cringed—and pounded my palms against the table. "Where is Jurij?"

I finally had all of their attention. Jangmi exchanged a look with Adeyemi, and then nodded at Chrysilla. "Perhaps you best fetch the Lily Book," she told her, and Chrysilla left the garden.

Jangmi turned back to Adeyemi. "Your Majesty," she began, strangely addressing another ruler with the same title she might earn herself. "Perhaps we can agree at least that the village that produced these two is a win for both genders."

"*Your Majesty!*" said Marigold, appalled.

Jangmi lifted a finger in the air to stop her. "No. It is. Freewill led to gender equality in that village."

"But—" began Marigold.

Adeyemi jutted his chin outward. "You would dispense with the idea that it was a woman's power that caused the most impact in that village?"

Jangmi nodded. "If you will give up any conviction that it is your man who never dies who allows you sovereignty over that village."

I felt Ailill's hand grab mine. At some point he'd removed his gloves when Adeyemi had healed him, and his palm was cold and clammy. I tore my eyes from the bickering kings and queens to look at his face, and he looked paler than I'd seen him since this rebirth, almost like some of the life was draining right out of him. I didn't want to sit, but seeing him like that scared me, so I did.

"What is it?" I whispered.

Ailill simply shook his head and kept watching the scene unfolding, all pretense of eating his meal forgotten.

Then I realized. It was these kings and queens who allowed him to rebirth, somehow, even if it was me who'd ordered it. They held Ailill's fate in their hands even now.

"*I grow weary of this life.*" He hadn't wanted to come back, but he had. How did I reconcile that with this kinder, younger man who held my hand now?

"Your Majesty," said Estavan. "We have never had such an advantage in any village. If we concede defeat here…"

Adeyemi shook his head. "We will still have other villages. It

has been so long since we have found one where there is equality
—where a lord and lady both have a golden token. It is just one
battle."

"It only takes one battle to turn the tide of the game," said
Kin. "To allow *them* this advantage."

"They are sacrificing their very obvious advantage in this
woman at the same time." Adeyemi's eyes fell on me. "It will be
worth it."

"Good," said Jangmi, just as Chrysilla appeared through the
doorway, a large book in hand. I knew immediately it was like
the book we left back home on Ailill's stand, the book that
showed what every villager was up to. Marigold and Estavan
broke rank to sweep away the trays as Chrysilla laid the book
down on the table in front of us. She flipped it open silently,
pushing past pages of moving pictures until she reached one. She
pushed the book closer to Ailill and me.

We both peered at the page. Jurij, back home in the village.
Jurij... with Jaron in the castle, each with enough sheathed
swords trundled under their arms to give half the village a
weapon to fight with. To fight *who* with? What were those two
up to?

I gasped, covering my mouth with my free hand. "What's he
doing?"

"You asked where that pawn was," said Adeyemi. "We sent
him back through the Never Veil, back to your village."

"Why does he have so many swords?" I demanded. I looked
at Ailill. "You didn't dispose of them, even after what happened
that night in the cavern?" I shook my head, exasperated at
myself. "No, I should have done it. I should have told you. You
didn't even remember the danger the men put us in, grabbing
those relics from the village's past, swinging them around
wildly—"

"Does not remember?" It was Kin who spoke, and he said it
so condescendingly, I looked up immediately to glare at him.
"Who does not remember?"

"Ailill," I said. "He doesn't remember his last life, and the
specter of that life vanished before he told him about it."

Kin laughed, and it was the first time I saw a smile on his lips.
It wasn't convivial. "He suffers no loss of memory at rebirth. I

suppose it is not possible for a mere pawn's mind to recall everything in a lifetime, let alone over a hundred, but his last life would certainly be prominent in his mind. Especially one so eventful as that one."

My hand dropped Ailill's as a chill ran through my body. I looked at his face, ready for him to dispute what the smug king had told me. He said nothing, and he wouldn't even look at me. He stared ahead at the open book, watching the village. Always watching. Never forgetting.

And always lying to me.

CHAPTER SIXTEEN

Everything I thought to be true over the past few weeks was a lie. Everything I thought I could count on, everything that seemed to give me some semblance of hope, was stolen from me. Jurij had turned into someone else entirely, someone far beyond what his newfound freedom justified. And Ailill—this kinder, gentler Ailill, the one who seemed to forgive me for what I'd done to him as a child, the one who wasn't tainted by all that time we spent together in his castle… didn't exist.

He was *playing* with me.

I didn't know if my discomfort gave Kin or any of the others any more pleasure. I couldn't look up at them. I was too busy trying to bite back the tears that were forming in my eyes as I stared down at my hands, which I clutched together in my lap.

"If we are agreed," said Jangmi, "that this village is a tie, there is still the issue of what is to be done with them."

"I move we adjourn to the dining room," said Adeyemi. "We could use some food, and in any case, we shall not be able to discuss this in front of them without interruption."

I was too hurt just then to interrupt or to care what they did with me. What a stupid thing to think when my life could very well be in jeopardy, when the lives of the people I left behind were in danger in so many ways.

Ailill finally found it fit to break his silence. "Your Majesties," he said, rising, "if you would but permit us to go home…"

I shook my head. A tear fell and I used the back of my hand to wipe it away. "I haven't asked—"

Ailill held a hand out in front of my face to quiet me. "I did not realize our presence would be so unwelcome. Please."

The kings and queens moved to the garden door and filed through it without comment. Adeyemi was the last to exit, and he turned to Ailill. "You two will stay here. I will do what I can to save you."

"Save *her*," Ailill said, startling me. He walked over toward Adeyemi. "I know I do service to the kings, but please, consider her life. She has yet to live one, and I have had so many—"

"Stay put," said Adeyemi, and he shut the door. I heard what may have been a bolt closing on the other side of it—I didn't notice any lock beforehand, but the door had been open. It didn't matter. I wasn't foolish enough to think we could sneak out of the castles and get home. There was no way to get back there unless these people allowed it.

Ailill and I were left alone, the only sound the trickling of the water fountain, the only real movement Jurij and Jaron on the page in front of me. Ailill didn't join me again at the table, instead deciding it was the perfect time to stroll through the garden. I watched through blurry tears. My head ached with the effort of hiding them.

"Why," I started, feeling the word croak in my throat. "Why did you lie to me?"

Ailill acted as if he hadn't heard me. I might have believed him if it weren't so quiet.

The longer I stared at him, the more I saw the Ailill I knew. How could I have ever doubted it? How could I have not seen?

Ailill stopped beside a bush covered with violet lilies. He put his hands behind his back. "Come here, would you?"

As if he deserved to order me about. As if I was going to stand beside him and patiently wait for him to say whatever it was he had to say, what little he felt fit to tell me. I was so tired of these games between us.

"I hope you're not going to ignore my question." I stood and crossed the garden. "Although I doubt there's anything you could say that would make me..." Ailill pushed aside a few branches on the bush covered in lilies to reveal a smaller bush inside of it. It was almost like the impossible bush with the lilies was just the outer wrappings to a regular rose bush with white roses beneath it. I gritted my teeth. There was plenty about this place I didn't understand, but what I didn't understand the most was why Ailill had lied to me. After all we'd been through.

I grabbed his wrist and tugged it away from the bush, letting the lilies fall back into place. "Tell me!" I said, dropping his arm.

Ailill pushed aside the branches again and plucked a single white rose petal from a bloom. He held it out in his palm carefully and walked back to the table and benches, flipping through the pages.

I could feel the anger boiling over inside me. "What are you *doing*?" I demanded, approaching him. My eyes flitted to the open page, and I felt my breath hitch in my throat. My anger toward Ailill forgotten—at least for that moment—I pushed in beside him, my arm brushing against his, to get a better look.

It was Elfriede's page. And she wasn't with Mother or any of her friends, as I'd asked her to be. *She wanted to look for Jaron*, I remembered. Although now I had to wonder if she'd really wanted to look for Jurij. No matter. She'd found them both.

Elfriede was waiting in front of the cavern pool. I could see the ripples in the outlines of the water. She had her back to the pool, and she sat on a rock, her hands folded across her lap. She stared up at the two men, a tangle of swords on the ground beside her. I stared at the scene, trying to make sense of it. Had she seen Jurij go through the pool or come back from it? Had she helped Jaron and Jurij this whole time? Was she helping them now, or had she simply come across the scene, her intention of looking for one or either more innocently motivated? Oh, why couldn't we *hear* what they were saying?

"That is… actually not what I meant to show you," said Ailill, snapping me out of my reverie. "Not just yet. We have problems of our own here."

He thrust his hand, palm up, over the page. Then he grabbed the petal from his palm with the other hand and crushed it.

I didn't know what he meant to show me at first, but soon my attention was caught by the flutter of movement on the page below. Elfriede, her face frozen in horror, fell off the rock on which she was sitting, and Jurij dove forward to catch her. She landed on his torso. Jaron's knees buckled as he attempted to stay standing, his hands reaching out for the nearest stalagmite to steady him. The swords began spreading out on the ground, as if someone was tilting the entire book, and the village along with it. The ripples on the water became splashes, like someone had jumped into the surface, even though no one had.

Then it stopped. The three figures stared at each other, each more perplexed than the next. Jurij, frozen in place, lingered with his arms around Elfriede's shoulders for a moment before she pushed him away and stood, slapping her skirt, and sending little specks of dust flying.

I pulled the book closer and began flipping the pages. Every page showed a mess: pots and pans on the ground; spilled bowls of stew; tables and chairs turned over. Every face had the same expression of shock and wonder.

"Did you do this?" I demanded, glaring at Ailill.

He recoiled at my stare. "Ye-Yes," he said, regaining composure. He tossed the crumpled petal on the table beside the book. "That is how the earthquakes were created," he added. "Whenever I left the castle."

"You could have hurt somebody!" I flipped through the pages quickly, but I saw none that were burning up like my father's had. None that showed anyone with any alarming injuries. I frowned as I reached my mother's page and saw the group around Sindri. Darwyn and Tayton were no longer among them.

"You are right. I did not think—"

"No, you didn't. After all our village has been through, the last thing it needs is more grief and danger." I kept flipping toward the back, looking for Darwyn or Tayton.

"You would make a better lady than I do a lord, despite the best of my efforts in the past few weeks," said Ailill. He spoke quietly. "Noll," he said with more authority, and the name seemed especially strange on his tongue, knowing that there was no need for him to pretend anymore that he'd known me better by my other name. He grabbed me by both shoulders and spun me around to face him, making me drop my search through the pages. "Please. I apologize. But you need to listen to me right now."

Looking into his eyes was a mistake, I knew that the moment I found myself staring into his dark gaze. I faltered under those pleading eyes, only remembering to grab his hands and pry them off of me a moment too late. "Are you going to tell me why you lied to me?" I said, looking at his shoulder instead of his face. "Because that's the only thing I want to hear right now."

"You are wrong about that." He took a deep breath and ran a hand over his hair. "I will tell you all I know about the kings and queens." He paused, waiting for me to try to stop him, but I found myself meeting his eyes again. "And the risk we took in coming to this place."

CHAPTER SEVENTEEN

A ilill chose the *perfect* time for another stroll through the gardens. He had me eagerly awaiting his words, but instead he broke away from me, choosing that moment to run his hand over the strange-flowered bushes around the edges of the garden.

I stood my ground, my arms crossed, refusing to move.

"Each of these bushes," said Ailill at last, his hand lingering on a bright yellow flower. "Represents a village." He paused, letting go of the colorful bloom.

I bit my lip, surveying the garden. There had to be at least two dozen bushes, each with a strange-looking flower. "The lilies," I said, lingering on the bush with the bloom I recognized from home. "Violet lilies dot our fields in the warmer months, so that one represents us."

"Yes!" said Ailill, like he was a tutor with a very smart student. I felt a little condescended to, but I didn't remark on it. He pushed aside the branches of the bush he stood by, revealing black roses. I winced, thinking of what even damaging one petal had done back home. "The roses you find beneath the outer layer of flowers match the rose bushes in each village's castle. Black for queens," he said, letting the branches fall back into place. He stepped back over to the violet lily bush and pushed those

570

branches aside. "White for kings." He frowned, staring at our village's bush before letting go of the greenery. "They have fought a long time over our village," he said. "It remains white for the kings because I am lord of it, but the power has clearly shifted from men to women a thousand years before."

"When I visited the village of the past." I swallowed hard. "When you first met me."

"Yes," said Ailill, and a flush spread over his face. He seemed paler than I remembered him since the rebirth. Nowhere near as pale as he was when I first knew him, but did he grow paler over time until he turned as white as a specter?

Ailill tossed his head back, ignoring the issue of what I had done in the past. "The point at which you met me, as the kings later told me, was precisely a thousand years into their game. And precisely a thousand years ago."

"*How* did I do that?" I asked. "Did the kings and queens send me there?"

Ailill shook his head. "They have no idea—or at least, they both claim to have no idea. I doubt the kings had anything to do with it. I am not as familiar with the queens, but I believe they had nothing to do with it, either."

I reached my fingers into my pocket and rubbed them across the coin. "I don't understand."

Ailill waved a hand and began to pace again through the garden. Instead of following the path in a circle, he merely walked a few steps back and forth. "Let us put that issue aside for now. As essential as it is to our fate and all that has happened to us, you must fully understand what I know first." He stopped walking and tucked his hands behind his back. "These people who live here in this barren place, they call themselves kings and queens."

I knew as much already. But there was a reason Ailill was reminding me of that now. "Like the made up stories," I said. "The ones that inspired me to think of myself as the 'little elf queen.'" I felt hot with embarrassment.

The corner of Ailill's lips twitched into a smile, like he genuinely was amused I'd said it aloud. "That is news to me," he said, and I realized I'd never fully explained my childhood delusion to him.

"Did you ever watch me as a child?" I asked. "Through the pages of the book?"

Ailill shook his head. "Not that I remember. I was in a bad place at that point. I hardly ever observed the villagers."

"Not that you *remember*?" I said, not willing to let that issue go. He frowned, realizing his choice of words, but I decided to save that conversation until this one was over. I sighed. "In any case. I used to pretend I was a queen who led retainers out on quests to slay monsters. We used sticks as swords—it never occurred to any of us that these things called 'swords' actually existed, let alone that they were holed up inside the castle."

"There was no need for them in our village anymore," said Ailill. "With the men's freedom of thought limited, there was no call for any tools that had no use."

I cocked my head. "Why is that, anyway? Why were women incapable of wielding swords? Why didn't they boss men around with swords at their sides, like the men did with them when you were a child?"

"I never said women were incapable of wielding swords. I thought you of all people would remember that, and the dagger my sister plunged through my brother's back." He winced.

I'd never spoken to Ailill about Elric. I wondered if even after all of these years, the pain of what the man had inflicted on him was still fresh.

"In any case, once those women died out, no even before that..." Ailill seemed lost in thought. "Women seem to find less use for them. Most women. If life is especially peaceful, their minds do not wander to violence."

"But men's do?" I thought of Jaron and Jurij, and whatever mischief they were up to now. I wondered if Elfriede was truly part of it.

"More often than women's. There are exceptions on both sides, but that is the general case. Something to do, I believe, with the natural state of man and woman, some piece inside men that women do not share."

I thought about that, but I was a terrible example. I'd spent my childhood whacking animals and stones with a stick, imagining the edge of a sword breaking through monstrous flesh. I'd goaded my friends, my *boy* friends, into the violence. They may not have had their complete freedom, but they had not yet found their goddesses, so they still had some minds of their own. Some were eager to take part in the pretend carnage, but others almost had to be forced into it. Jurij was one of them. Jurij, who'd hit me on the head with his sword's hilt…

"What about *these* men and women," I asked, deciding not to dwell on my own past just yet. "Are they prone to violence?"

Ailill laughed, and it wasn't out of joviality. He put a hand on his hip. "No, they will not take up a sword and stab each other, although they seem to desire it every waking moment of their existences. They agreed never to resort to violence in their war. No violence to each other, anyway. They leave that to the villages." He nodded at me. "Those stories you told each other as children, the ones that inspired you to playact as a violent queen? They are all the knowledge that remains of the kings and queens in the villages to all but the lords and ladies who rule over them. They are the history of a war between kings and queens that began long before the game ever started. Before the game, they were legion, and they took swords to one another's armies of subjects, thousands, maybe millions of people who once lived in places ruled by a king or queen. Now three of each such ruler remains, and they made a pact to fight through other methods."

"But *why*?" I asked, bewildered. "And what do you mean 'subjects'? What of these 'armies'?"

The corner of Ailill's lips turned up in a hesitant smile. "I cannot tell you for certain. It was long before my time. Over the years, between rebirths, the kings told me some of their history. There were many people in this land once. Many more than we know in our village."

I had to sit down. I went back to the table, reaching out behind me for balance as I lowered myself onto the bench. I couldn't keep everything straight. I didn't know what was important to know. "You come here between each rebirth?"

Ailill nodded, putting his hand behind his back and taking up his slow, deliberate pacing again. "We all come here when we pass." He paused. "This may be hard for you to grasp—I could not myself at first—but people are not meant to vanish at death. When they died here, long ago, in the age of the wars of kings and queens, they simply lay there, gone in spirit but not in body."

"What?" I cradled my forehead. "What do you mean?"

"Like livestock," said Ailill. He started pacing again. "No, that sounds terrible. But you know how the animals are still *there* after death."

"They have to be!" I grimaced at the thought of the farmers and butchers at work.

"They leave behind their flesh so we can eat it," Ailill added. "And so people, too, are meant to leave behind their flesh."

"So someone can eat it?" I nearly choked.

"No!" Ailill laughed softly. "No. No one eats them. They are just meant… to return to the land."

I let my eyes flit to the table behind me, to the open book. It showed a young woman I didn't fully recognize cleaning up the things that had tumbled over in her home. I let my fingers caress the pages, hesitating to flip through the book and pick up my search for Darwyn and Tayton, to check in with Jaron, Jurij and Elfriede. "They come here," I said. "And meet the kings and queens?"

"Yes," said Ailill. "The lords and ladies of the villages are given a golden token. A bangle from our village, perhaps something different from elsewhere. I have not met any others. I do know they are all allowed to go through the Never Veil and meet the kings and queens while still living when summoned—*if* they are summoned. For most, vanishing after death is their first time meeting them. And they do not remember them after."

I spun my head around. "What do you mean 'after'? Are you saying…" I stood, my heart thundering in my chest. "My father is alive?"

Ailill put a hand out and approached me. "No! No, you must not get your hopes up… *He* is not alive, you must understand."

I threw my hands up in the air. "I *don't* understand! You're telling me he—everyone who's ever died and vanished, Ingrith, Nissa's parents, your own family, your *brother*—came here at death and met the kings and queens. But they are not alive and do not remember. How can they 'not remember' if they are not alive?"

Ailill sighed and ran a hand through his hair. "They are reborn in their own ways. Not like how I was. There are a limited number of spirits, souls of the people who were once the subjects of the kings and queens when the games began, and the kings and queens reuse them for their game."

"'Reuse' them?" I could feel my face curling into a sneer at the repugnant way he described what was going on here.

Ailill gestured around him at the many bushes. "They are reborn—as infants, not as a newly-grown man as I am—in other villages, out of the reach of those who knew them before. They remember nothing of who they once were. Nothing. They cannot be considered who they were."

I didn't even feel my knees weaken before I was halfway to the ground. Ailill rushed in to steady me, but my knees clashed painfully against the stone beneath my feet before he could.

CHAPTER EIGHTEEN

Ailill had guided me gently to the bench at the table after my wave of dizziness, and we sat there now side by side in near silence. The kings and queens had yet to return, and Ailill seemed to think I was too overwhelmed to hear more of this bizarre fantasy—that I was too overwhelmed to handle my entire view of life and the village and everything torn down stone by stone. Perhaps he was right. I hadn't meant to fall, but my body clearly was less eager to learn than my mind was.

Still. Things made sense at last. The pain we experienced wasn't entirely my fault. And Father... was out there somewhere. No matter what Ailill thought, I considered him to be alive. That made me feel warm all over.

"Do you think your knees are bleeding?" Ailill looked down at my lap. "Or did you just bruise them? Is it all right if I..." He hesitated, his hands in the air above my knees.

We didn't have time to inspect for cuts and bruises. I grabbed his hands and laid them on my lap to draw his attention back to me. "Tell me more," I said, as hard and steady as I could.

"Do you think we should?" Ailill's gaze flicked to the garden door, but my eyes didn't follow. "You are not at full strength, and they could be back at any moment—"

"All the more reason." The touch of his hands on my thigh,

where I'd placed them myself, was light and awkward, almost as if he feared his hands lingering there. I decided not to press him on the subject of rebirths any further, at least not yet. "So the villages are a game for the kings and queens?"

"Yes," said Ailill with a sigh. "That chess game we played together... It is an analogy for the war of the kings and queens."

I raised an eyebrow. "Even though the queen pieces had all the power?"

Ailill smirked. "True. Yet the game marches on even if she falls. The whole thing revolves around the king. You stumbled upon one of the arguments between the kings and queens already."

"Okay," I said, feeling the clamminess in my grip on the back of Ailill's hand. I wouldn't let it go just yet. "It still seems a strange imbalance of power if the game is to establish whose rule is superior."

Ailill tilted his head slightly, his gaze fixed on the bushes a short distance in front of us. "Perhaps the rules are different in the villages where a lady rules instead of a lord. That is just how I know the game, and there have only ever been lords of our village, back to the start of creation."

"The lord—*you*—hardly played a role in the village for a thousand years. I'm not sure if that counts." I grimaced as I said the words, waiting for the rebuke.

"You are correct," said Ailill instead, attempting a smile. "Our village is a mystery to the kings and queens. They have argued for a thousand years which gender truly has the upper hand there."

"With men devoting their entire lives to women, and women having the power to kill unloved men with a glance? I'd have to say women ruled that one." I wiped the sweat on my palm off on my skirt.

"You sound like a queen." Ailill's hands lingered a moment longer on my lap, and he pulled them slowly away, twisting his torso away from me. "The kings argued that since no true lady presented herself to rule, that since I ruled and was immortal, the balance of power tipped in their favor."

I winced as my palm clutched at one of my sore knees. "And

now women certainly don't have an advantage over men regardless."

"You know," said Ailill quietly. "That has happened before. The kings and queens created an even number of villages, half ruled by lords and half by ladies. They sometimes tweak a village based on the outcome of a small skirmish or an idea to prove superiority. Over time, sometimes a lord and lady will rule side by side."

I met his eyes then and felt my face flushing, so I focused on my knees, which stung even beneath the skirt. "And what do these kings and queens think of those villages? Which gender is superior then?"

Ailill shrugged and clutched his hands to his own knees. "They never decide that. A lifetime for the pawn in their games is but a small time for them. Eventually, when free will reigns, chaos descends. Eventually one gender or the other takes power in a village, almost like a violent reflection of these kings and queens who silently rule over them."

"So what happened in our village during your childhood... Wasn't such an anomaly."

"There you are wrong." Ailill patted his hands on his knees a few times. "*You* made it different. No king or queen gave you permission to travel to the past. I do not even think either group can *do* that."

That was unsettling news. He was being so good at explaining the bizarre nature of everything that I was hoping he'd have some explanation for what was most bizarre about me. "I don't understand." I brushed that too-long piece of hair behind my ear, but it flopped back forward immediately.

"Neither do they." Ailill lifted a hand to my head and I flinched back instinctively. "I am sorry," he said, his hand faltering. "I only meant to..." Steeling himself, he reached forward and tucked that same strand of hair behind my ear. "This," he said, and I felt his soft fingertips dance across the top of my ear.

I almost died right then and there. It was like he was doing what I imagined doing to Jurij, to him—to the men of the village —whenever I stared too long at their pointed ears.

Ailill's touch was brief, and I felt both relief and disappointment as he pulled his hands back. I clenched my knees hard, using the soreness to snap myself back awake.

"You have ears like they do," he said.

I wasn't sure I was following. I resisted the urge to caress my own ears. "Like all women do?" I asked. "I noticed the kings here have ears without points as well as the queens, but surely that doesn't mean much."

Ailill stood up from the bench quickly, making me jump in place. "It means *quite* a lot." He gestured around him at the garden. "Every one of these villages is filled with pointy-eared pawns. Only the kings and queens have no edges atop their ears. They are quite proud of the difference, I must tell you, as if that small thing is enough to prove they are a superior race. They consider our people, these people they created out of their former subjects, 'elves,' although they call us 'pawns' or 'children' more than anything. Which is why you insisting you were a 'little elf queen' amused me." His voice drifted off. "I wonder how you even knew that term..."

I scrunched my nose up. "What are you talking about? Every woman in our village has rounded ears—"

"Because of *you*." Ailill bent over the table, reaching over my shoulder to grab something behind me. His gloves, which he'd removed for Adeyemi's healing. "The women in our village when I was a child had pointed ears. Do you not remember?"

He was right. I'd noticed it immediately, but it was soon forgotten when there was so much else to consider, especially when women often wore their hair covering their ears anyway. "But... What has that to do with me?"

Ailill slipped on one of his gloves. "That is something the kings and queens would like to know. When you made those proclamations about the rules of the village, they decided to go along with it and see what would happen." He tugged on the bottom of his glove and began pulling on the second. "They chose to send me back to our village each time I died. They caused the earthquakes when I left the castle or when a woman looked at it."

I frowned. "I'm surprised they would allow that, if I went back in time without their permission."

He tugged hard on the second glove. "They fought about that.

As they fight about everything. But they thought it different enough—*interesting* enough—to see what would happen."

"Even though I gave the women such an advantage?"

"In *every* village, one gender or the other has an advantage or two to see if it makes a difference in the overall war. They decide who gets to pick which advantage via games of chess, and then let free will of the pawns decide whether those advantages prove useful or not. In one village, the women are physically stronger than the men. In another, the kings tell me, the men can sing songs that lull those around them to sleep…"

I raised an eyebrow. *That* sounded terrifying.

Ailill noticed my expression and laughed a little. "Our village was initially meant to start the men off at an advantage. Each man was to be born incredibly beautiful, and with the power to heal—both of which you neutralized, by covering the men's faces and by ending their healing power."

So I wasn't just imagining those lovely faces… I blushed when Ailill caught me staring at him.

"I didn't mean to end the healing," I said, ignoring the distracting trail of my thoughts. "That would have come in handy. Wait—*I* neutralized? If *they* enforced my words, what does that have to do with me and the women of our village having rounded ears?"

"You made each woman a goddess. That word, another word you should not have known, was from the world as it was before the games began."

"I knew it because *everyone* knew it."

"Yes, but you created a paradox of sorts. No one would know what to call someone who is to be worshipped if not for you traveling back through the ages."

I frowned. "So are these kings and queens… goddesses?"

"*Gods* and goddesses, in a fashion. It's what they consider their race, but they prefer their titles of 'kings and queens.'" He sighed. "In any case, the women born after your decree all had rounded ears, and the kings and queens have not been happy with that."

"Don't they determine things like that? Didn't *they* enforce my decrees and make unloved men vanish whenever a woman caught sight of their faces?"

"No," said Ailill, quietly. He tucked his hands beneath his back and looked down. "They have no way of telling who loves whom. I do not think them capable of such a thing as love."

"But then what—" I cut myself off, my throat constricting. So I couldn't just blame them for what I'd done—it was me after all. Me who sent those men to their doom. "Tell me those men got reborn into other villages at least!"

"They did." Ailill frowned. "Still, the flames in men's eyes, those are not something the kings or queens gave them. They have no idea where that came from or how something was able to measure love and make these decisions for them. In fact, the queens hardly know whether or not to champion you, as they can hardly influence you themselves, and that might prove dangerous to them. But they have put their hopes in you so far, acquiescing to my frequent—frequent in terms of their life spans, that is—trips back here for rebirth because you yourself willed it. Otherwise, that is clearly a kings' advantage."

I laughed pitifully. "The kings hate me, don't they?"

"The kings and queens are no friend to anyone but themselves. But yes. The kings have argued that you have broken the rules of the games for a millennium now, and they wanted to take you out of the games entirely—but they couldn't until recently, until you were born. I do not think they recognized your spirit in any other form. I wonder even if your spirit existed in any other life before this one. They have not shared that information with me."

That was a strange thought. It was all strange. Was time a straight line to these unseen rulers? Did they see me appear in the past version of my village with no knowledge of who I was, or were they here with me in the present and there in the past simultaneously? It had to be a line, though, otherwise they would have been unable to account for my presence for a thousand years. I would never understand it. Maybe I didn't need to understand that much. Maybe I didn't want to.

And "recently," he'd said. I supposed almost eighteen years prior was recently enough for these immortals. "Yet the queens want to keep me alive?"

Ailill's brow scrunched together. "I would not trust them,

either. I think they fear your power but are loath to admit it to the kings."

"And they clearly are not *your* supporters."

"No, they are not. Noll, you are bleeding." He sat back down beside me and lifted my skirt without hesitation. I was too surprised to stop him, and if it weren't for the fact that he found my knees to be a bloody, bruised mess, I would have been embarrassed to think of him seeing so much of my legs.

Ailill reached for the bottom of his torn shirt again, but I put a hand out to stop him. "No. At my rate of injury this journey, you'll be half naked before sunset." I ripped the hem of my skirt and used it to dab the knees gently. The caked blood made the wounds look far worse than they were, but even so, I winced.

"Allow me." Ailill removed his gloves again and set them beside him on the bench. He gently cupped his hands around my hand clutching the bloodied scrap and my hand went limp, allowing him to swoop in and take over.

I watched him dab for a time, and then he stood up, dunked the scrap in the fountain and wrung it out before returning. Instead of sitting back beside me, he got on his own knees in front of me on the ground and proceeded to wipe the wounds carefully. His face was at a height just above my knees and I found myself pushing my hands between my thighs, desperate to make sure the fabric of the skirt kept everything from his view.

"It is not bad," Ailill said, his voice a bit shaky and his eyes carefully not lifting from where they looked down at my knees. "After wiping away the blood, I can see that most of it is already healed. I am sure the queens will heal you if we ask—"

I grabbed his wrist, keeping my other hand carefully plunged between my legs. "What am I?" I asked, not caring whether or not they healed my scratches, especially considering they might not let me go home or even live. "What am I, then?" I had to know.

Ailill's face twisted like I'd slapped him, as if it caused him pain to deliver the news to me. "You are Noll. Olivière, Gideon the Woodcarver's daughter—a Woodcarver herself. The woman who was once my goddess." He took the scrap of fabric from the hand I clutched and tossed it on the ground, grabbing my own wrist in his hand. "Beyond that, beyond all of that that makes you even more extraordinary, I do not know."

I blinked and felt tears dotting my eyes. I couldn't even explain why I was crying if he'd asked. "And what are *you*?"

Ailill dropped my wrist, and I dropped his. He stood and looked away. "Nothing special."

"That's a lie!" I spoke so loud, I startled myself. "You said yourself you're the only one who's reborn into the same life—"

"I am a pet of sorts of the kings', I must admit." Ailill put his hands on his hips. "I have seen them so many times, and I remember them—they're not used to that. I even spent a month here after you looked at my face before you loved me."

I nearly jumped in my seat. "That month when the village was so altered! It wasn't a dream! How—where were my parents then? Where was the castle?"

Ailill cocked his head and smiled. "They were all here. The castle was even here, out there in the canyon. Everything came here to this limbo between rebirths. No one was sent on their way because the kings and queens were waiting to see if you were going to do what they already knew you *had* done, and go back and finish what you'd started in the past. Just don't expect any of those lost during that time to remember. No one from the village but you or I seems to remember that month clearly, no matter where they were."

I felt sick and strange. There was so much to absorb. So much to finally understand. I fretted with my skirt anxiously, covering my knees again with the torn material.

Ailill sat back down beside me, taking my hand in his, running his fingers lightly over my open palm. "Olivière, whatever specialness there is about me, *you* gave it to me. I was a pawn. I was nothing. I was lost and in pain, and *you* made me special."

I met his eyes, smiling slightly. "You called me 'Olivière' again."

"Would you prefer I called you 'Noll'?"

I shook my head. "No. No... At first I didn't like that you called me that, but every time you've called me 'Noll' since, I missed it. My name sounds so lovely on your tongue. Like it belongs to this special woman who isn't me, but whom you believe to be me."

Ailill laughed softly. "There is no argument that you are a special woman, Olivière, or that you deserve your own name. I just worried my reliance on it when so many others call you by your name of choice would make you suspect..." He stopped, biting his lip.

It'd finally come back to this.

"Why," I said, taking my hand out of his, "if you remembered everything the whole time, did you wait to tell me any of this here? I know you said I'd have to have a golden token to know, but I've had one for weeks."

"I thought it best that you *see*. That you understand what we are up against."

"'Up against'? Are *we* at war with *them*—"

Ailill reached out to cover my mouth, his eyes darting to the garden door. "No. Not now. Not *here*."

"You waited until we got here to tell me everything else..." My sentence cut short. Ailill's eyes widened and I heard the creak of the garden door behind me.

I turned around to face whatever was coming for me.

CHAPTER NINETEEN

"We have come to a decision," said Jangmi. She entered at the same time as Adeyemi through the open garden door, the other kings and queens following in perfectly matched lines behind them. Marigold and Estavan shut the door behind them.

Why were there clearly leaders even among them?

Adeyemi clasped his hands together as he and Jangmi came to a stop in front of the bench where we sat. "We shall return you both to your village."

I felt a tension in my muscles that I hadn't even realized I'd had release. Even Ailill relaxed somewhat beside me, although his back was still stiff.

I felt I should thank them—but for what? I hadn't done anything *knowingly* against them. I hadn't known who *they* were. I couldn't help it if I'd broken rules I didn't know existed. I reached into my pocket to clutch my coin. "Thank you," I said stiffly. "But before—"

"However," said Jangmi, not acknowledging my gratitude. "There is one condition: Olivière is never to return here and never to travel through the Never Veil to anywhere, to any place—or time—ever again." She reached a palm out. "We could not agree whether or not what you possessed qualified as a token, but you are to leave that piece of gold here."

"Wait a minute!" I stood, ignoring Ailill's hand as it shot out to tug at my elbow. "Look, I have no *intention* of leaving the village. I never did. I don't know how I did so to begin with. Still, there may be reasons I should keep this token, problems that occur in my village—"

"There will be no *reasons*," snapped Estavan, taking a step forward. "You are not to assume the position of 'lady' in your village. You are not even to wed Ailill, nor bear him future lords." His snarling face was like a kick to the gut. Not that I'd been *thinking* of that. Not that I was ready for that, or sure how things stood between Ailill and me, but... My eyes traveled down to Ailill, who sat behind me, his hand letting go of my elbow, his eyes downcast. Estavan continued unabated. "You may live a life alone in your cottage or wed one of the other pawns, if you so choose, but you are to live within the confines of the rules of this game."

Adeyemi raised a hand and stopped him from speaking further. "She does not need to know anything more about the rules of this game. She will do her part as nothing more than a pawn or there will be greater consequences. Now please. The gold."

My eyes flit to the queens one by one, and I saw little evidence of emotion. They were confident, smug even. Not at all upset that I was to give over all semblance of power. Perhaps they'd decided that I was too unpredictable to have even on the side of women.

I brought my fist out of my pocket, but I didn't reach it out to Jangmi's waiting hand just yet. "My friends," I said.

"Olivi—" started Ailill quietly, but I continued.

"My family. The reason I was so eager to see you was because they are in danger at the hands of Ailill's servants for discussing Ailill's rebirth."

"As they should be," said Marigold, her nose wrinkling. "The last thing we need is pawns who know too much spreading rumors."

I clutched my coin tightly at my side. "It's not their fault they noticed his changes after his rebirth! It would be the same in any time in our village, if only Ailill had made himself known to the people there. They would have noticed he changed, especially if he died of natural causes as an old, pale man before reappearing as a dark, young one."

My plea for reason made no impression on them. "They know now, I trust, there are consequences to their actions?" asked Kin. I nodded. "Then they shall watch themselves and all shall be fine. You should be grateful we allow them to live even without them uttering a word."

"And yet Jurij—you let him know everything!" I shrieked. "You let him *come* here! What did you *say* to him?"

"I still do not like the idea of a new lord, either," said Chrysilla, ignoring the crux of my question.

"It is better than letting *that one* continue as he has been," interrupted Marigold. "Why was he allowed to come back, even after Olivière's curse was lifted?"

My curse. My chest tightened at the sound of that.

"We have already gone over this." Kin extended an accusing finger toward Marigold. "Ailill's resurrection was something *we all* agreed to. It was not connected to whatever it is that *this one* did. It was *we* who sent him back each time!"

"Why Jurij?" I demanded, not willing to give up until I had answers. "What do you have planned for him?"

"Will you look at her!" Estavan gestured toward me. "She keeps acting as if she were a player in this game!"

Jangmi, her palm still out toward me, raised her other hand toward the others to hush them. "She is not. She knows she is not," she said quietly. "Now give me the token."

"'Token'?" repeated Adeyemi. He watched Jangmi curiously. "I thought we agreed it would not count as a token."

"I misspoke," replied Jangmi, coolly. "I apologize."

Kin sneered. "Misspoke? I *told* you it was they who sent that coin, against the rules—"

"We did no such thing!" shouted Chrysilla. "And I will thank you not to lie like that again!"

"We have had this discussion," said Jangmi sternly. "The piece of gold, please."

I reached my fist out toward her slowly, still afraid to let this chance pass me by.

A rattling, shaking noise caught my attention, and I turned, looking at the garden door. Without even opening, the door went black, and the edges of a long black veil seemed to flow through it, fluttering like in a breeze. A woman stepped through the door, collapsing to the ground. I jumped in place and felt Ailill swoop in behind me, grabbing my shoulders. "Stand back," he whispered in my ears.

The kings and queens pushed past me, the coin still clutched in my fist forgotten. They gathered around the crumpled figure on the ground. She was young, *naked*, and she looked not at all like someone from my village. She had long, golden hair, and pointed ears. Her skin was as pale as Ailill's had been, or as Marigold's. She looked up at the kings and queens gathered around her, her eyes wide and frightened.

"Where... am I?" she croaked. "Dreaming...?"

"You are not dreaming," said Jangmi, and she bent down to wrap an arm around the woman's shoulders. "Your life has come to an end."

"What?" The woman allowed Jangmi to pull her up until she was standing, and her face flittered between all of the kings and queens around her, even stopping at Ailill and me. She seemed to be pleading with me to explain everything to her. Jangmi guided her to the bench and sat her down. The woman cradled her head. Noticing her nudity, she tried to cover her breasts with her arms and clutched her thighs tightly together, but there was no hiding her vulnerability.

"My child!" she said. "What happened to my child?"

Adeyemi turned to Kin and Chrysilla. "The tulip book. Quickly. To offer her some solace."

The king and queen grabbed hold of the door—now a plain garden door and no longer a dark veil—and stepped outside of it.

The woman was trembling. I turned around to face Ailill. "Your jacket," I whispered, removing it from my arms. "Please."

Ailill gripped my hands, stopping me. "No. You cannot," he said urgently. "Do not interfere, they will not be happy with you—"

"I'm not *interfering*," I said. I removed my hands from his grip and continued peeling away his jacket. "I just can't let her sit there like that with no comfort." This time he let me take it off, although he was frowning.

I stepped around Marigold to offer the woman Ailill's jacket, draping it around her shoulders. I didn't dare slip her arms into it for her, but just having the material over her exposed torso seemed to lift her spirits slightly.

"There." I smiled. "It's not much, but I hope it'll make you more comfortable." I couldn't imagine sitting on that cold stone bench without clothing. I had half a mind to tear my dress off and offer her the whole thing, the men present be damned.

"Thank you," the woman said, the pain evident even through her smile. "Who are you? I feel like I've met you before."

"*No one,*" said Marigold curtly, pushing me aside and behind her. Ailill quickly grabbed my arm and pulled me farther out of the way, but I hadn't missed the anger on Marigold's features. "*We* are your rulers, child. We six." She pointed to Jangmi and the remaining kings, to the open garden doorway as Chrysilla and Kin stepped back through it. Kin held a book, while Chrysilla had her hands positioned awkwardly behind her back.

"We found it," said Kin, flipping through the pages of his book. He held the open book out to the woman.

The woman looked at Kin curiously before her gaze fell to the book. She gasped, putting a hand to her mouth, the jacket tumbling open, exposing her chest again, but her shame was forgotten. There were tears in her eyes. "Helewise... Oh, Helewise—"

"Your child," said Jangmi calmly. She stood with her hands behind her back, displaying no emotion. She glanced at the page and nodded. "She survived the fall, even if you did not."

"Good," said the woman, and she reached out to touch the page. I wished I could see it. I imagined a child beside a cliff or mountain, the clothing the woman had left behind all that remained of her mother. "Good," repeated the woman. She sounded tired. "There's Bradyn," she whispered. "He wasn't far behind. You must be strong. Raise our girl well."

Jangmi nodded at Chrysilla, who stepped forward. I still didn't understand why she clutched her hands so high behind her back—and then I saw the sword she'd kept hidden there. She raised it above her head, holding it downward like a gigantic dagger over the seated woman.

"No!" I shrieked, and Ailill grabbed me tightly around the waist, pulling me back.

Chrysilla brought the sword down, piercing the woman through the base of her throat.

CHAPTER TWENTY

The jacket slumped to the bench, its wearer gone. Marigold glared at me for a moment, but I didn't care. My eyes were watering, and the strength in my legs was giving out.

"Watch," whispered Ailill. "Do not despair."

It was a strange thing to tell me. I was in such shock from the sight, but I blinked away the tears as Ailill's hands released me, his supporting grip shifting to my shoulders. I felt almost naked without his touch lately. When had it come to that? Chrysilla gently placed the sword down on the table beside the book that showed my village, just as Kin placed the woman's village's book on the table's surface. There was a violet light—a mist almost—in the air around the jacket, and Adeyemi and Jangmi stepped forward, their hands extended.

"Return, spirit, to your rulers," said Adeyemi and Jangmi in unison. The other kings and queens stepped back and Jangmi and Adeyemi stepped in tandem toward the fountain, their hands still clutching the light somehow between them. They paused before the fountain. "Return now, to the game. Find your way to your new home." They both extended their arms toward the trickling stream and the light vanished, almost like it was sucked into the movement of the water.

"The orchids!" called Chrysilla, and she stepped back so they could all stare at one of the bushes. It glowed bright with a violet light and rustled as if someone were shaking it. Then it stilled. Jangmi and Adeyemi turned to Chrysilla and Kin respectively and nodded, and both the shorter queen and king left through the garden door, taking the sword and book with them.

"She has been born again," said Ailill quietly. "As a different person in a different village."

I stepped away from Ailill, and he let me go this time. I wasn't at all comforted by the news, or what I'd seen. The woman had seen the sword coming for her. Her mouth had opened, her terror evident. She'd died violently *twice* within moments. I sat down numbly on the bench where she'd sat, noting the new rip at the neck of Ailill's jacket.

"It is a boy this time!" I heard Kin before I saw him coming back, a book in his hands. Chrysilla followed, frowning.

Adeyemi and Estavan exchanged a look of triumph. The disappointment on Marigold's face was evident, but Jangmi did little but nod her head toward the men. "Congratulations," she said. "May he bring you some advantage."

"Not likely in the orchid village," muttered Marigold, and she actually caused Jangmi to raise an eyebrow at her. "What?" she demanded, putting her hands on her hips. "It is a lady's village."

"And that could change at any moment," said Estavan.

I grew tired of all their bickering. I had no idea how Ailill had ever put up with them for his "frequent" visits. I had enough of them to last my entire life and then some.

All this time, even when I laid the jacket around the woman's shoulders, I hadn't let the golden coin out of my fist. Even now I clutched Ailill's jacket to my chest with two fingers.

"Back to the matter at hand," said Adeyemi, and all six of them shuffled back into place around me, Kin dropping the second book off on the table. Ailill hovered nervously behind the queens, now kept from me thanks to their semicircle.

I felt the coolness of the gold in my hand. "I'll give it to you," I said, taking note of Jangmi's extended hand. "And I'll stay away from the pool in the cavern and the hole behind the throne." My eyes darted nervously to Ailill's, and I could see he was pleading. Probably pleading for me to say no more, but was he going to accept what they demanded of me? Of him? Wasn't he worried about their plans with Jurij? I held my hand out toward Jangmi's palm, but I didn't drop the coin just yet. "But I refuse to allow you to dictate my life. I refuse to allow you to do whatever it is you have planned with Jurij."

Jangmi's usually calm and collected features twisted into a sneer. "You foolish child."

The other kings and queens broke out into chaos, each louder than the other, each repeating the same arguments I'd heard before. None were pleased with me, though. Even Chrysilla and Marigold implored Jangmi to do something "about me."

"She has outstayed her welcome, and she has overstepped her bounds for the last time!" Adeyemi walked to the bush covered in lilies. He reached inside of it with both hands and returned holding an entire white rose blossom. The other kings and queens went silent. Adeyemi stepped next to Jangmi and locked eyes with her, holding out the bloom for her to take.

My heart beat so quickly, I thought it was jumping up through my throat.

"Please," said Ailill, and he came around to the other side of the table. "She does not fully understand. This is *my* village more than it is hers, and if you punish it for her actions—"

"Quiet, Ailill," snapped Adeyemi, "lest you make more trouble for yourself. The kings are in agreement with the queens in this matter." He turned back to Jangmi. "Are we not?"

Jangmi took the bloom from him in the hand that had been held out for my coin and crushed it so hard I could see the muscles in her biceps bulging through her tight clothing. She slowly opened her palm, the dead, flattened petals dropping one by one to the ground, vanishing into a small burst of violet light before they reached it.

The harried turning of pages from behind me drew my attention. Ailill pored over one of the books on the table. His brow furrowed, his lips pinched thin, he stopped at one page and gasped.

I took a slow, careful step forward.

"Olivière, I should warn you..." Whatever else Ailill said, I couldn't hear him. I turned the book toward me to get a better look. Elfriede lay collapsed on the path through the woods, a panicked Jurij and Jaron beside her. They shouted something to one another, Jaron with one foot on the page, one off, Jurij with his arms wrapped around Elfriede's shoulders. I noticed there wasn't a single sword between them, and I wondered if they'd left them all in the cavern. Elfriede's eyes were closed, and Jurij shook her, but she didn't respond at all.

"What's wrong with her?" I asked, almost breathless. "She can't be dead, or this page wouldn't still be here."

"She is not dead yet," said Jangmi from behind me, "but she will be. And she is not the only one."

I flipped through the pages quickly, seeing woman after woman on the ground. Some were still standing—Roslyn, I noticed, and Mistress Baker—but too many had their eyes closed, their bodies splayed strangely. Alvilda was among them, Siofra and Nissa on the floor beside her, aghast. I couldn't find my mother—no, she was safe. She was there, distraught and holding Marden in her arms on the floor of the bakery, Roslyn and Mistress Baker rushing to join them at her side. What had *they* done? How had they decided this? I noticed no man in such distress. I finally found Darwyn and Tayton. They came out from the path through the woods that led to the cavern and joined Jurij and Jaron in their panic around the collapsed Elfriede.

"What have you done?" I asked, my throat constricting.

"This is the second time in your lifetime we have sent an illness to your village," said Adeyemi. He looked cool and composed through my forming veil of tears. "We did so the first time, after you first met Ailill in your lifetime."

The sickness that had taken some women's lives, and because they loved them, some men's with it. The sickness that had almost killed my mother, but for Ailill's long-fought efforts to stop it. Even so, there were so many *more* women collapsing this time! And for what? Because I dared to speak against the kings and queens?

"Why?" The coin practically burned into my palm. "Why?"

"It was then when we realized who you were," said Kin, referring to the earlier sickness. "And we had agreed long before, that once we found you, you would be made to suffer."

I fought the urge to scream. "Why not *me* then? Why the other people? And not just those I love—"

"Your village, your gender, your punishment." Estavan lifted his chin haughtily. "It was a shame that an equal number of men went with the women last time because of their devotion to them. This time, there will be no such collateral damage."

"But I didn't know what I was doing!" I pounded my fists against my thighs. "I hadn't even *done* anything then!"

"You knew at least that going to the castle as a woman was forbidden. Not that *we* made those rules, mind you." Marigold huffed. "However, we agreed you were somewhat ignorant then, and so we decided to keep the punishment minimal. However, now you know better. Now you go too far."

"No! No, I don't know better!" I walked forward on trembling legs and grabbed Jangmi's hand from where it hung beside her, shoving the coin into her palm. She arched an eyebrow and took the coin, taking a step back. I collapsed to my knees. "Please! I'm sorry! I'll do whatever you want, just please undo this."

Jangmi looked down at me over the tip of her nose. "What is done is done. Be grateful we shall still allow you to go back."

I don't know whether the kings or queens spared me another glance. I couldn't look up. I don't know how much longer it was before I felt Ailill's hands on my shoulders, and his strength attempting to lift me up. "We must go," he whispered. "They have opened the door. We can step through the Never Veil."

I wanted to fight back, but I was too in shock. I couldn't risk angering the kings and queens any further. I let him guide me toward where the garden door had been, where a black gauzy piece of fabric was fluttering out from a dark hole, as it had been when that woman had stepped through.

"Ailill," said Adeyemi at our backs. "Remember our decree. Do not get too attached to that one."

"Of course." Ailill let go of my shoulders and shoved me through. "I never was," I heard him say, as I collapsed into the Never Veil and silent darkness.

CHAPTER TWENTY-ONE

I should have taken a deep breath before I passed through, but I had no idea we were coming back this way. I snapped to life at the bottom of a pool of water, kicking violently to make it to the top through the blinding violet glow.

I felt Ailill's arm around my waist and with a few powerful kicks of his legs, we broke through the surface of the water. It took me only a moment of breathing to recognize the inside of the cavern, with Ailill swimming at my side, his arm still wrapped around me.

I wanted to shove him away, but I was too weak. Instead, I helped him kick us to the shore and then we climbed up onto the sediment. The water glowed red now, as if to remind me I was never to attempt to go back through it.

"That was rather nice of them to send us back through that passageway," said Ailill, and I wondered how he had become so acquainted with sarcasm. He went to run a sopping black glove through his hair and instead stared at it, shaking his head. "Considering we could have walked through the entryway behind the throne in the castle." He peeled it and the other glove off, tossing them on the sediment beside him. He must have left his jacket behind. His biceps glittered with the red light of the pool.

I had a feeling the inconvenience was intentional. And the

least of our problems. I wasn't in the mood to discuss it. Not just for that last parting comment, but for all of his lies. I stood on shaky feet and tried to get my bearings.

"Olivière," said Ailill from behind me. "Do your best not to get angry with me. I have no doubt they will be watching us quite closely for quite some time."

I froze mid-step toward what I realized was the stash of swords I'd seen the men gathering through the book. I turned my head around slowly. "It didn't occur to me to get angry," I said. "We have more important things to worry about."

"Yes." Ailill stood. "But I wanted you to know that last thing I said before I pushed you through the Never Veil... It was not true."

"Sure." I nodded, barely interested. He wanted casual, he wanted to put on a show for those who might be watching, so he could have it. I was done with him. "It's clear you do what they tell you. They wanted you not to care about me, so you had to make that clear."

"Yes," said Ailill, but he looked worried. I examined the pile of swords, grabbing my torn skirt and wringing what water I could out of it. "You cannot blame me for—"

"I can blame you for a lot of things," I snapped, facing him. He'd closed the distance between us and I jumped back. "You lied to me. Maybe you lied to them. Maybe this is you lying to me again. How can I trust anything you say?"

A muscle in Ailill's jaw twitched. "It seems to me that I am not the only man in your life capable of hiding secrets."

I let out a breath, exasperated. "That has nothing to do with this. You can't absolve yourself by comparing your behavior to others."

Ailill ground his teeth. "You are willing to forgive whatever he does, but not me?"

"I don't *forgive* anything. Do you think I've forgotten the clonk on my head? Or how his actions led to my father's death? Or how he stabbed..." I couldn't say the rest.

"Olivière, I had *reasons*, I *have* reasons for everything."

I pointed a finger toward his chest. "Reasons? All right then. I'll just accept that without question because this is *your* village and I'm just a nobody."

"That is not true! Olivière—"

I threw my hands out. "No. I don't need to know. If it won't help us make things right in the village, fine, I don't need to know." I cradled my head. "It doesn't matter. I'm not supposed to do anything but fade into the background. If I do anything else, they'll hurt the people more."

"They are *already* hurting the people. Hurting people you love."

Tears filled my eyes, making it hard to focus on Ailill through the water. "What can I *do*? You said they're watching right now. Maybe they weren't always watching before, but they're sure to be always watching now."

"I can help…"

I wiped the moisture from my cheeks—not that it mattered, considering I was soaked from the pool. "You shouldn't have let me go there. You knew what might happen. You *remembered everything* and yet you took me there."

"I did not think *this* would happen. Regardless, you were so insistent…"

I laughed pitifully. "Fine. Blame me. Everyone does. *They* even do."

Ailill pinched his lips. "I am not *blaming* you." He grabbed my hand in his. "Olivière, what I did, I did…" He pitched forward, releasing my hand and I caught him, digging my feet into the ground as much as I could. The ground beneath us was shaking. It took all my strength, strength I barely knew I had left, but I shoved him away so he wouldn't cause us both to tumble over. He fell back. I hadn't meant to shove him *that* hard. The ground stopped shaking.

"It doesn't matter. Ailill, it doesn't *matter*. I can't even… Apparently, we can't even touch each other…" I had to catch my breath. I hadn't expected to find the thought of not being able to touch him so painful. "I don't care anymore," I lied. "We have to go our separate ways."

"We can be smart about this." Ailill scrambled to his feet. "We will not touch each other, but I *must* see you. We can be discreet."

"*No.*" I started backing up into the darkness, not caring if I tripped over a rock. "There is no 'discreet.' It's over." I gestured to the pile of swords. "Please do what you can to make things better. Get rid of those. I'll try to talk some sense into them, if I can. But please... try to stay away from me if you see me."

"Olivière!" His voice echoed pitifully as I stepped into the shadows.

∾

MAYBE AILILL FINALLY UNDERSTOOD. Perhaps he stayed behind to throw the swords into the cavern pool. Maybe he went back to his castle to meet the specters and ask for their assistance. He didn't follow me, and I broke through the woods to the path where I'd witnessed Elfriede collapse. There was no sign of her, nor of any of the men I'd seen with her.

Our cottage is somewhat near. They must have taken her there.

The walk through the woods toward the village went incredibly slowly. I was shivering—the air was so much colder here, I'd nearly forgotten, and my clothes were soaked through. I was sick with worry, and my mind wouldn't stop thinking about what had happened, what I'd done. What *they'd* done. What they blamed me for.

My fingers dipped uselessly into my pocket. It was gone. I'd given it to them. Too late, but I'd done what they'd asked, and they still punished my village for it.

My heart was pounding when I approached the clearing, but it quickly sank when I noticed there were no signs of a fire or even candlelight in my family's cottage. Perhaps they were too panicked about Elfriede. I gripped my skirt and ran.

"Friede!" I said, pushing the door open. "Jurij, Jaron!" I stopped cold. There was no one there. No one. Where could they have gone?

I gripped on to the headboard of Elfriede's and my bed—of *Jurij's* and Elfriede's bed, I remembered, as I stared at it in the moonlight—to support me. *Calm down,* I thought. *Perhaps they saw no one was home and decided to take her into the village. But they could have fetched help and had someone stay with her. Why would they carry her limp body into the village?*

Forget it. I was trying to make sense of *Jaron and Jurij.* They made little sense these days. *The bakers. Mother is there. I'll start there.*

As scared as I was, I knew I'd do little good rushing into the village dripping wet and cold. I rushed to the chest at the foot of the bed and pulled out the dresses. Spurn and Scorn had brought me more of the ones I'd left behind and had barely worn at the castle, but the feel of their soft, refined material in my hands made me sick to my stomach. There were so many bad memories I'd rather not think about just then—and most of all, there was that commandment that I just become a "pawn" again, that I stop thinking I was anyone important. I used a familiar violet dress to wipe my wet body and grabbed a plainer brown dress at the bottom. I slipped it on—it was slightly tight at the waist, too large at the bust—*Elfriede's*—but I was long past caring. It wasn't so ill-fitting as to be uncomfortable. *It will have to do*, I thought, looking at the dark stains on my knees. I let Elfriede's skirt fall down over them. She'd taken the time to sew the outline of lilies into this skirt, her idle hands always wanting work even where there was none of import.

I shifted the material at the shoulders to tighten the bagginess at my chest and before resting a shaking hand over my nerve-wracked stomach. *There has to be a way through this*, I thought. *There has to be. I'll be a good pawn, and then they'll fix things. And if they don't...*

...I'll offer my life instead. I'll make them understand.

I took one of Elfriede's shawls, too, and wrapped it around my shoulders. It did a better job at hiding the bagginess. I thought about grabbing a lantern, but I wasn't in the mood to carry it. The moonlight was bright enough—I hadn't even known it was night yet until I stepped out of the cavern—and I knew my way around the village. I pulled open the door to leave, coming face to face with a specter.

CHAPTER TWENTY-TWO

He was so far from my mind that it took me a moment to realize I knew this specter. Even if he had somehow cleaned up his clothes—were there extras lying around?—and fixed his hair back into place.

"Spurn." I shut the door behind me. I clutched at the shawl at my throat and peered around him. There was no sign of any others. "I'm not... I'm not the lady of the village anymore."

Spurn nodded—that itself was a sign that he didn't fully understand that I wasn't the bearer of a golden token anymore. There should have been no sign of movement, no sign of acknowledgement in those hollow, black eyes.

"Well, you can attend to Ailill," I said. "I'm sure he has things for you to do."

He didn't move. I decided to ignore him. I started down the path to the village, walking so quickly my legs burned. I was most of the way there when I thought to look behind me. Spurn was several paces behind, ever my attendant. I stopped, panicked.

"Stay away from me!" I said. "They won't like it if you treat me differently."

He paused but didn't leave. I sighed, cradling my head. "If

you're following my orders then, I order you to go back to Ailill."
He didn't budge. "Or go on ahead to the Great Hall. Find some
way to be useful."

He still didn't move, and I gave up. I didn't have time for this.
Surely the kings and queens realized I hadn't asked this man to
follow me. I trudged ahead and jumped when the door to the
Tailors opened and a figure tumbled out.

He wasn't looking at all where he was going. Or more likely,
he wasn't expecting me. Luuk slammed into me, almost knocking
me over. Panic colored his face. "Noll!"

I placed my hands on his shoulders and pushed him gently
back. He was already my height somehow. "Luuk, where are
they? Where're my sister and Alvilda?"

"You've heard." Luuk took my hand in his. "Come on," he
said. I let him guide me.

We weren't the only ones on the roads despite the hour, but of
those we encountered, no one was simply going about his or her
business. When we turned one corner, a man carrying a sloshing
bucket of water nearly barreled us over, and he didn't even slow
down, just entreated us to get out of his way. A few paces past
him, a small girl cried on a doorstep in her nightshirt. My heart
went out to her—and I noticed the wooden squirrel she clutched
tightly against her chest. When we reached the heart of the
village, there was a crowd of harried figures around the well,
buckets dangling from their arms.

"Does water help them?" I asked Luuk, daring to hope. There
was such urgency to their movements, such impatience to get
their buckets filled, I thought they may have stumbled on an
answer.

"Nothing has worked," said Luuk, dashing all of my hopes.
He clutched something folded up in his other hand, something he
must have raced home to get. He stopped in front of the Great
Hall and let go of my hand. "But no one is willing to give up. No
one knows what to do." He laughed harshly and unfolded the
fabric in his hands. It was just a kerchief, a little worn and ragged.
"Mother sent me to Father's to grab this. She said it was the first
thing she made for Alvilda when they were girls—when Auntie
was actually the one helping the Tailor, my grandfather. Alvilda

taught Mother how to sew, although she herself never had much love for it. This was the first thing Mother made on her own, and Auntie gave it back to her the day she got married to Father." Luuk stared at the fabric in his hand, as if it might tell him something. "I suppose Auntie was angry with her, and Mother thought it too full of bad memories to take with her when she moved in with Auntie. But now… Now she's desperate. She seems to think that this *thing*, this piece of cloth, shoved in Auntie's hand might wake her."

"Luuk…" I wanted to reach out and wipe the tears forming in his eyes, but I saw anger there, too, and I didn't dare interrupt him.

Luuk clenched the handkerchief in his hands. "You have to do something." I followed his gaze to the open doors of the Great Hall, unable to make sense of the flurry of movement therein. There seemed to be collapsed bodies on the ground, with people flitting about, some shouting at one another while others sat on the ground beside those who had fallen. Had every fallen woman in town been taken here?

I took a deep breath and hitched my skirt up slightly, taking those first few steps toward the open doorway.

"I'll tell your mother you're here," said Luuk from behind me. I faced him, confused. "She's at the Baker's, with my mother and Nissa. Both Alvilda and Marden have fallen."

"What about Elfriede?" I asked, but Luuk had already turned and run.

I'd asked him to take me to them. Was Elfriede inside the Great Hall? Why wouldn't Jurij take her to Mother, if they hadn't left her in our cottage?

My eyes caught Spurn's. Of course, he was still a few steps behind me.

"Where are the others?" I asked, looking for a sign of white coats and white hair amid the village's hectic activity. Spurn didn't reply. As infuriatingly expected.

"Never mind." I headed inside.

No one seemed to be notice me at first. Men and women alike were barking orders to one another. People pushed past me with buckets in hand, sitting on the ground next to a sprawled-out woman, dipping a cloth inside the bucket and rubbing their foreheads. I could see even in the dying light the sheen of perspiration on the skin of all the collapsed women—even on the skin of those eager to help them, although theirs was probably from all the movement. The sick women must have been battling a fast-acting illness to be sweating so badly.

Mother and the women who perished after the first illness were still conscious for weeks, even months—Mother had lasted four months even before Ailill treated her. They were weakened, but not so visibly close to death's door so quickly. My eyes darted over the fallen women. I saw Vena among them, Elweard in tears at her side—almost as if this was before the curse was broken, and losing her might actually kill him too. I recognized a number of the fallen—perhaps not so much by name, as by occupation. I kept getting pushed aside. It wasn't until I was halfway into the room that the activity around me stilled, people nudging those still conscious around them until I drew almost every eye in the room.

I froze in place, realizing what Luuk had wanted of me. What any of these people expected of me. To lead. That was what I'd said I would be doing, after all. I hadn't yet told them otherwise, and I still had a servant dressed in white who wouldn't leave my side.

"What's happened?" demanded one man. I had no idea what explanation I could give him.

A woman with a young girl resting her head in her lap pointed at me accusingly. "Where were you? What have you done?"

I couldn't get my mouth to open. What had *I* done? She had no idea that it was my fault. But it was, in a way. They could blame me for everything.

I took a nervous step back, about to run away. I bumped into Spurn.

"Noll!" It wasn't Spurn who spoke, but I could tell that from the volume of the voice alone. Jaron shoved through the crowd from the place where Vena and Elweard had prepared the food.

My mouth fell open. I peered over his shoulder for signs of Jurij or Elfriede, but there were none.

Jaron smiled smugly. "I reckon you're surprised to see me here."

I latched on to his shoulders, shaking him. "Where's Elfriede? And Jurij?"

Jaron raised his eyebrows and gently pried my fingers off of him, taking a step back. "So you know. She fell, too."

"Yes, I know. I know the two of you—maybe even Darwyn and Tayton—have been rather busy since I last saw you. Now where are they?"

Jaron seemed fixated on Spurn behind me. "Jurij is with her. Darwyn and Tayton, too. They sent me to the Great Hall to see if we could find someone to help us." He gestured around the room. "And I come here to find... this. So many women have fallen ill. What's to be done to save them?"

I felt more than just the pressure of his question on me. I felt the pressure of every gaze in the room.

"I don't know," I responded quietly.

"What?" asked someone from behind me. He probably hadn't heard me.

I clenched my fists together at my side. "I don't know!" I said, louder. "I have no idea what the village needs, and I'm not even someone you should look to—I'm not going to be the lady of the village." My voice dropped. "I can't lead you."

The hall broke into shouts and whispers, curses and screams.

"I told you she couldn't help us—"

"I never cared for her anyway!"

"Trouble with the lord again?" said Jaron quietly beneath the uproar. When I didn't respond, he added, "The two of you sure like to keep your secrets."

"Why do we expect her or him to help us? We've never even seen the lord until recently, what good could he possibly do us?"

"You don't think... As soon as we see the lord, *this* happens!"

"No!" I said, spinning around to face the source of the accusation. I couldn't pinpoint who had spoken, so my eyes darted crazily between a large group of them. "It's not the lord's fault! I promise you that!"

Jaron surprised me by taking a step in front of me, gesturing behind him to shove me back. "On the contrary," he said loudly, commandingly, "I think the lord is responsible for a lot of the madness." The Great Hall quieted, the last echoes of the whispers fading into silence.

I was so stunned, it took me a moment to gather my wits about me. I stepped beside Jaron, shoving him back as he shoved me. "You're wrong! You don't know what you're talking about!"

Jaron shrugged. "That's right. None of us know what we're talking about. Only you and the lord seem to know anything."

My gaze darted between Jaron and the people watching anxiously around us. "There are things you have no need to know—"

"Do you or do you not know the reason for this illness?" demanded Jaron.

Lie, I told myself. *Just pretend you don't know.* I had a thought, then, that he would lay the blame at Ailill's feet if I refused to own up to it. Isn't this what the kings and queens wanted? Me to be nothing again, nobody's goddess, nobody's lady, nobody's anything? "I know," I said, biting my bottom lip. "It wasn't Ailill's fault. It was mine."

That brought the room back to a flutter, and I could hardly make out the screams and accusations hurled my way. A man jumped up from the ground and hurled himself toward me, his arms flailing. Spurn stepped in and held him back by the upper arms before I even flinched.

"Then *do* something!" the man said, and I realized the swollen and tear-stained face belonged to Elweard. Loyal Elweard, who loved Vena even when given the freedom to love freely, even though she took so long to love him back herself.

"I-I can't." My own tears were forming. "I want to—don't you know how much I want to? But I can't. I have to go. That's all I can do. I have to go." I bent my head down and hitched up my skirt, pushing past Spurn and Elweard, making my way to the door through the stunned crowd.

"Don't let her get away!" Jaron's voice was so halting, so angry, I froze.

I expected the people around me to block my path or shove me back toward Jaron to face their wrath, to face some sort of justice.

I felt two strong hands around my arms and looked down.

They were hands as pale as snow—the white hands of a specter. "Spurn!" I said, shocked. He didn't even look at me.

"This is what I've been trying to tell you," said Jaron, making his way through the crowd and to my side. When he reached me, he wasn't speaking to me, though. He looked out at the crowd, and the people nearest stepped back to give him space. "Our village suffers under this lord. Under his choice of lady." He gestured his hands above him. "He is not the only one meant to be lord. Jurij, Tailor's Son, Quarry Worker and Woodcarver, has been given the chance to lead us."

"What?" I said, although the kings and queens had told me as much. But to think that Jurij had actually went along with it, that he was—oh, goddess. He was probably in the castle right now, right where I'd sent Ailill. No wonder no other specters had come out to the village yet.

"It's true," said Jaron, and this time he looked at me. He clasped his hands together. "And Jurij promises us there will be no more secrets. There will be no more suffering."

I fought hard against Spurn's grip, but I had no luck. "Impossible!" I shook my head. "If he were to tell you what he knows, he would *cause* suffering—"

Jaron ignored me. "Jurij will get us through this!" he said. "He'll help us treat our loved ones. And if they should die..." He faced me. "It will be the last terrible affair at a terrible reign's end."

He looked above me, nodding at Spurn. "You know what your new lord has asked of you."

Spurn dragged me out the door, ignoring my attempts to dig my heels into the ground, dodging the kicks I sent back into his shins. A black carriage awaited.

A specter opened the carriage door.

"Noll?" The timid voice called out from within the carriage. Mother poked her head out. Her eyes were red, her face puffed.

"Mother!" I stopped fighting. Spurn used the chance to lift me and shove me inside. He slammed the door behind me.

I brushed the hair out of my face and scrambled to my feet, almost falling over as the carriage started moving, only avoiding injury because my mother stood up to catch me and guided me to the bench beside her.

"Your sister is ill," said a familiar voice across from me. I also heard the familiar crinkle of leather as he crossed his black-clothed legs. "Come back with me to the castle, and we'll do what we can to treat her."

I looked up and stared into the dark eyes of Jurij.

CHAPTER TWENTY-THREE

"**Y**ou." I launched myself over to Jurij, not sure what I was doing—was I going to slap him or choke him? All I remembered was wanting to just squeeze him—but it didn't matter. The carriage was moving faster than usual, and I took a tumble, falling not-so-gracefully into the seat beside Jurij.

Jurij patted my arm, and the golden bangle at his wrist slipped down toward his elbow like it was never intended to fit him. "Are you all right?" At least he hadn't donned Ailill's gloves, but the rest of his clothing... Oh, goddess, was this why Jurij had quit the quarry and taken a sudden interest in woodworking and sewing again? His outfit resembled Ailill's, but it wasn't quite the same. Instead of roses, Jurij had embroidered *swords* on his clothes. I could make the designs out at this close distance, through the bits of moonlight that filtered through the small carriage windows.

"Don't touch me," I snapped, recoiling backward.

Jurij let go. Something tugged at his face, something probably like pain, and he frowned. "Noll, I'm sorry about what I did back there—"

"You're sorry you hit my head until it bled and I lost consciousness, you mean."

Mother made a noise like a sheep being run down by Bow.

609

The thought of happier times with this man who'd inspired more anger in me than anyone—was it because I had once loved and trusted him? Is that why I felt my blood boil more intensely than it had with Ailill or even Elric?—made my face hot.

"I'm fine now, Mother," I said, looking at the wall. "No thanks to this man here."

"I panicked," said Jurij after a short while. "I really didn't want to hurt you. I just needed to get you away from him."

That was enough to make me face him once more. "Praise the goddess he got me away from *you* instead."

Jurij sighed and cradled his head in his hand. "This is hardly the time for this. I came to get you and your mother because something has happened to your sister."

"She's ill." Mother's voice cracked. "Jurij found me at the Bakers' and told me she was one of the ones who'd fallen." She lifted her apron to her eyes and started sobbing.

"I know." I crossed back across the carriage to sit with Mother. I wrapped my arm around her and folded her into an embrace. I glared at Jurij over Mother's shoulder. "I've been looking for her."

Jurij's lips puckered, his brow drawn suspiciously. "Did Jaron tell you?"

"You're not the only one who can look at a book," I said as Mother shifted back from me. She leaned into the seat, her lips quivering.

"When Marden fell, I just knew it wasn't something ordinary," said Mother, almost oblivious to the people in the carriage with her. "And then Nissa came in, distraught, letting us know Alvilda had collapsed in the streets, that she'd left her back with Siofra. Thea and Roslyn went to help carry her inside. When they came back..." Mother lifted her apron to her face again, her eyes welling. "They told us there were so many people fallen. So many *women*. I just knew then and there that one or both of my girls was among them. That it wasn't enough that I'd grown apart from Gideon, that I'd lost him before we could figure out what it was to love again, that I'd be alone completely soon."

She sobbed, and I rubbed her back, not sure what to say. Not sure what I *could* say. In a fit of terrible selfishness, I wanted her out of the carriage and at Elfriede's side already so I could talk with Jurij freely. Surely, even if they were watching, the kings and queens wouldn't punish me for that. He had a golden bangle, and he'd been where I'd been. They'd forbidden me to spend much time with Ailill, or did they mean with this "lord" as well? I didn't know if my anger was worth taking the risk, but I felt so helpless, and Jurij owed me an explanation at least.

"I'm here," I said, my conscience winning out over that darker part of me. I squeezed Mother's hand and this time she took me into her arms. No one else might need me. No one else might want me. But Mother would need me. Especially if... No. *If they'd wanted them dead, they could have killed them instantly.*

I just didn't know if this was enough to make them happy. I hadn't done anything they'd asked me yet—anything but push Ailill away—but surely they would allow me to see my sister? Or understand that it was this imposter lord who'd forced me into this carriage, away from the small shack at the north end of the village where I might end out my days?

I couldn't picture my days there anymore. Quietly carving, hardly speaking to anyone but to sell my wares. Even though now I should *want* to stay away from people. Even though now I could blame myself more than ever.

That's not true. I felt a pressure in my throat as I tried to bite back the heat rising throughout my body. *Now "they" have faces. You can blame them, too.*

"We're here," said Jurij, and the carriage ground to a sudden halt.

It didn't feel like we'd been in the carriage long enough to have reached the castle, so I was a little taken aback. It seemed nothing good came of what Jurij might have to show me, and there were only so many places between the Great Hall and the castle that might interest this imposter lord. Mother let me go as the door to the carriage opened.

"Mother, wait!" I didn't want her walking into whatever Jurij might have waiting.

Jurij stood, crouched over to avoid hitting his head on the roof. He might be a little taller than Ailill, I realized. So far from the little boy trailing behind me in his kitten mask in so many ways. He paused, looking back at me over his shoulder. "Come along."

I squatted to get a better look at the sight beyond the doorway. It was the castle gates, after all. I just must not have had a good sense of time, so enraged was I during the drive over. Mother followed two specters—the traitors, how could *they* possibly serve a lord who wasn't Ailill?—inside the castle doors. Jurij made to leave the carriage.

"Hold on," I said, and I grabbed his arm with both hands, wrenching it backward. Jurij stared at me, puzzled. "We have things to discuss!"

"Inside." Jurij shook himself free and jumped out of the carriage. "Don't you want to see your sister?"

I wanted to tell him it wouldn't do any good to see Elfriede. Not if she were unconscious anyway. And if she were conscious, she probably wouldn't get much comfort from me regardless. But Jurij was gone inside after Mother, and I was left alone in the carriage. Were it not for the fact that two specters remained standing at either side of the open carriage door, I might be free to leave. Yet I was unlikely to do any good anywhere else. And I'd promised Mother I'd be with her.

I jumped out of the carriage, ignoring the specter's proffered hand, particularly when I realized it was Spurn doing the offering. I swiped swaying hair out of my mouth. "Traitor!" I said, wincing, as the hypocrisy of me calling that former young boy a traitor wasn't lost on me. "You know this man isn't your lord. I doubt he even knows who any of *you* are." I kept having to brush hair out of my eyes as a cold wind whipped toward the castle. At one point, I thought I saw Spurn's mouth part, but by the time the wind died down, he was as still and silent as ever.

I marched into the castle, determined to stop Jurij and talk to him privately before he joined up with my mother and Elfriede. Maybe we could save her—save all the women—if we called a truce and put our heads together. He clearly had the kings' favor at the moment.

"Jurij!" There was no sign of him. The dining hall seemed as dark as ever, so I was about to ascend the stairs where they'd surely taken Elfriede to a bedroom. I'd just grabbed hold of the banister when a creaking sound commanded my attention.

The garden door flew open and a gust of chilling wind

slammed across the entryway and over to me. *The garden. He's gone to our garden.*

"Jurij!" I called again, stomping over to the open door. "Jurij, we need to talk, and I can see Friede after..."

It wasn't Jurij who sat at the stone table in the garden. I thought it was a specter for a moment. It was Ailill, slouched over, his arm across a game board. Chess pieces were strewn across the table, the bench and the ground around him.

"Ailill!" I shrieked, scattering fallen white petals from the rose bushes as I ran to his side. I bent over him—he was pale again, almost as pale as he had been the first time I'd seen him—and latched on to both of his shoulders. "Ai—"

The ground shook beneath my feet and I screamed, falling backward, a couple of rose bushes cushioning my fall. My arms were scratched, and a thorn wedged itself into one of my palms.

I can't touch him even now? When I just want to make sure he's still breathing? I could barely see through the haze of tears as I ripped the thorn out. *I never asked for this. I never asked to upset you, unseen kings and queens—why are you doing this to me?*

"Olivi... ère..." His voice was quiet and slow, but there nonetheless. A cascade of breath I didn't realize I was holding flew out through my lungs.

I jumped back to my feet, the soreness from the scratches be damned. "What happened to you?" I asked, at once both demanding and pleading. "Who did this to you?"

Ailill seemed to strain with the effort of moving his head slightly. His hair had grown paler, too—a light brown instead of black. "Watch... out..."

"Jurij's wondering where you've gone," said someone from behind me. I spun around to find Darwyn running a hand over the back of his head. Tayton stood behind him, a grimace on his lips and his arms over his chest.

"You two!" I tried my best to stand between them and Ailill. "Did you do this to him?"

"No!" said Tayton, and his puckering lips looked especially sour and rounded. "He just sort of... collapsed." He lifted an eyebrow as he peered over my shoulder, my height not enough to shield Ailill from him. "He and Jurij played some odd game on that board and it only went on for half a minute, I swear, before Jurij won and this lord got as pale as one of the servants."

He wasn't *that* pale. Not yet, anyway. But I wasn't about to debate the smallest details. I spread my hands out to either side, like it might do some good and protect Ailill. "I don't believe you," I said, remembering my own chess matches. Even if Jurij knew how to play—and really, had the kings managed to teach him that? Was that as important to an imposter lord as it seemed to be to the real one?—there was no way he'd beat Ailill. There was no way the game would be over in a handful of moves.

Unless the kings *had* taught him something. Some way to win quickly. And yet that would be cheating, wouldn't it? Would the queens allow that?

I thought they already agreed they both won this village! Why are they so involved in everything still?

Darwyn shrugged. "Believe it or not, I don't care." He nodded his head behind me. "I bet he could tell you what happened, but he doesn't seem to be moving."

I spun back to check on Ailill. His eyes were still open, but his eyelids were drooping. His back moved just slightly with the rhythm of breaths, but I wouldn't expect Darwyn to be able to see that—not if he didn't care for Ailill like I did.

Ailill nodded ever so slightly. I had to wipe tears that had trickled down my cheeks, tears I didn't want any of them to see. "Then I just don't understand," I said. Defeating a lord in chess made you lord and practically killed the last one? I faced Darwyn and Tayton, who both had scabbards in full display at their waists.

"Why, you little bastards!" I tried to grab Darwyn's hilt to get the blade away from him—I'd already seen what "good" blades did in the hands of my *friends*. He stepped back to avoid my movement easily.

He rolled his eyes. "Come on," he said, gripping my bicep not too lightly. "Jurij is waiting for you upstairs. He thought you might have had something to do with that earthquake we just experienced."

I ripped my arm away from him. "I'm not going anywhere until someone helps Ailill."

"Who?" asked Tayton.

I grit my teeth and gestured behind me. "Your *lord*. The only person in this garden who's currently halfway to unconsciousness."

Tayton puckered his fishy lips. "Jurij's lord now. And he said to leave him until we've done all we can for the ill women. Their health is priority."

"There's nothing you can do for them!" I spat. "Only *they* can decide." I bit my lip, hard. "You can at least take Ailill to a bed. Keep him warmer."

Tayton and Darwyn exchanged a glance. "If you care so much, why don't *you* take him?"

"I... I can't," I said, remembering what had happened both times I'd touched him since returning to the village.

Tayton sighed and stepped around me. I instinctively went to block him and he jumped back, both hands in front of him. "Whoa! I'm just offering to help." I stepped back and kept a careful eye on him as he stared down at Ailill. He wrapped an arm around Ailill, picking him up halfway. Tayton stared at me. "Grab his other side already!"

"I can't!" I took a step back. My gaze caught Ailill's and I could feel the hot tears running down my cheeks.

"Well, *I'm* not helping out," said Darwyn from behind me, and I spun around, about ready to launch myself at him. He must have read that in my face because he held his own hands out in front of him like Tayton had. "Don't get so mad at me. *You're* the one who told us never to help a fallen comrade if it means you can't hold your sword. Or your stick."

"I was a child!" I clenched my fists. What a benevolent leader I'd made. "That was a game! Get over here and help him!"

Darwyn cupped his chin. "Hmm," he said. "Adamant enough that we ought to help him, but not adamant enough to help yourself?" He lunged forward and I jumped back, but it did no good as he grabbed hold of my wrist and twisted it.

I screamed in pain, and Darwyn looked taken aback. "I'm sorry, I just want to test something," he said. He didn't let go, instead dragging me over to Ailill. I dug my feet into the ground, determined not to let him bring me toward him, but there was no way I could stop Darwyn. Even though I clenched my fist, he managed to touch my knuckles to the top of Ailill's head. My heart beat thunderously as Ailill looked up at me in pity.

The ground beneath us shook and Darwyn dropped my hand. Tayton growled and tipped sideways a few steps, almost, but not quite, dropping Ailill. Darwyn stepped back, his eyes darting everywhere, and his hand on his sword's hilt, like that would help him in an earthquake. It was over before it'd hardly begun—stopping almost the instant Darwyn let go of my hand and I'd pulled it back from Ailill.

Darwyn kept his gaze locked on the sky. "Well, I'll be. Jurij will be glad to learn about that, I'm sure." He nodded at Tayton. "Leave him. We'll have Jurij send some of the servants to take him."

Tayton shrugged one shoulder and bent down to put Ailill back on the bench. At least he was as gentle as his tall, bulking frame would allow. I couldn't fully reconcile these men with my friends or with the menacing men I'd met in the past. They were somewhere in between, and I didn't understand how to feel about them anymore.

Darwyn gestured toward the door. "After you," he said, half bowing, "my elf queen. The lord awaits."

I spit at his feet and hitched my skirt up, striding toward the open door.

CHAPTER TWENTY-FOUR

I stopped at the first specter I saw, who was standing on the staircase, and folded my arms. "Your lord needs you. Take him to a bedroom." It wasn't Spurn. I didn't know how I'd come to tell him apart from the others even when he was being a traitorous, lifeless servant, but I did know this specter wasn't him.

When the specter didn't move, Darwyn stepped in front of me and put a hand on the specter's shoulder. "She means the former lord. Yeah, go ahead and take him to a bed. I don't think Jurij would mind."

The specter started moving, and he was joined soon after by another specter at the bottom of the stairs. They headed off toward the garden together. When I looked at Darwyn in disbelief, he shrugged. "Jurij told them to follow our orders."

I grabbed the banister and brushed past him, my nose in the air. "Yours, Tayton's and Jaron's, I take it? Or is Sindri back among you?"

Darwyn took two steps at a time to catch up to me, while Tayton lagged behind. "He's still recovering," he said, a hint of sourness in his voice. "We barely got to check on him before all of this happened."

"Alvilda and Siofra told us about being careful with what we say," Tayton said from behind us. Darwyn eyed the line of specters as we came to the second floor. They let us walk past without so much as blinking. Tayton took his place at my other side, so I was trapped between the two of them. "We wanted to see if Jaron knew anything more about it."

I stopped, causing the two of them stop with me. "Didn't they tell you I was going to discuss it with the lord?"

Tayton scratched his elbow and exchanged a glance with Darwyn. "Well, yeah. But…"

"We don't exactly trust that lord," said Darwyn. He glanced over my shoulder at the specters behind me. "For obvious reasons."

"But you trust this one."

"Well, yeah." Darwyn's nose twitched. "We grew up with him. Or you and I did, anyway."

Tayton, a little older than us, hadn't joined the group until recently. And he'd moved quite quickly from friend to Darwyn's love. Men and their freedom. It certainly resulted in interesting reactions—both of love and of violence.

I almost didn't bring it up. It might serve them right if they attracted *their* attention. Even after how angry they'd made me, we'd had enough of death and violence. "You know, though, not to discuss what you know about the previous lord. No matter if you 'trust' this new lord or not."

Tayton scratched his cheek. He was growing a patchy beard. "We figured. Just to be safe."

"All right. Where is he?"

Darwyn cocked his head. "Your mother and Elfriede are in a bedroom at the end of the hall."

"No," I said. "Not yet. Where is Jurij? Is he with them?" There was movement at the foot of the stairs. A specter climbed up the landing backward. After he took a few more steps, another specter made an appearance, with a dark figure—Ailill—prone between them. I started walking toward them before I even realized what I was doing.

A gentle pressure on my arm stopped me. "He's upstairs," said Darwyn, tugging me backward. "In the throne room."

Of course. Somehow I should have known I'd find him there.

∼

DARWYN AND TAYTON escorted me to the throne room door—what was I going to do? Poke around in the prison cells?—saying nothing. I stopped in front of the open kitchen doors, startled when something soared through the air. It was Arrow, who had jumped up to catch a flank of meat a specter had thrown. He munched on it beside his mother, who stretched out luxuriously in front of the fire. A specter chopping meat on the table beside the fire looked up briefly. He'd fed Arrow—or had at least let him steal a snack. Leave it to Jurij to be concerned about the animals' welfare, even with so much else going on around us.

"You know the rest of the way." Darwyn wove an arm through Tayton's to stop him.

I nodded, and the two left. I straightened my shoulders and clenched my fists. I had to do this. A couple of specters flanked the door as I approached, but I found none of them inside the room. *Good. He won't have anyone to help him if he gets out of hand.* That was a lie, I knew. With just a snap of his fingers, the specters —the *Ailills*—would come running if needed.

"Why aren't you with your mother and sister?" Jurij was sitting on the throne, the stand on which the book usually sat moved so he could easily look at it from his seat. The room was well lit with torches, and I saw at once that he'd actually forgotten about one sword. Elgar still hung over the throne, although it'd lost its violet glow.

"Why aren't *you*?" I asked, coming closer. "Why aren't you out there in the village pacifying people if you're so eager to play at being lord?"

Jurij jerked up from looking at the book. "I'm not *playing* anything."

I was at the dais now, and I took the step up slowly. "It seems like it to me."

Jurij sighed and bounced his leg, looking away. "I sent Jaron out to check on the people. I'll watch them from here."

"A lot of good that will do."

"It's more than the last lord did the last time women fell ill in the village."

"That's not true," I said. "You know it was he who healed my mother."

Jurij scoffed. "If only there were healing magic now, I could do the same."

I looked over my shoulder, but there were no signs that Darwyn and Tayton had returned. "You could talk to *them* about it."

It was like I'd slapped him. "Don't you think I've tried? The veil behind here doesn't lead to anywhere. The tunnel ends in a red light."

They didn't want to see Jurij even? After all that talk about how he might be the new lord? "How did you know to beat Ailill in a game of chess? I didn't even realize you knew what chess was."

"I didn't." Jurij ran a hand over his face. "The kings told me how to win. Quickly."

I frowned. "But I've beaten Ailill before," I said, but then I stopped, a pain in my chest. No, I hadn't actually. Both Ailill and Elric had stopped the game before I could actually win. I'd attributed it to stubbornness, but maybe it was more than that.

"You need one of these when you play," said Jurij, rubbing the ill-fitting bangle at his wrist.

So maybe those two actually were just stubborn.

It didn't matter. I was letting myself get distracted. I gripped my palms on my skirt, feeling the sweat soak through the material. "Why are you doing this?" My voice was quieter than I intended it to be. I cleared my throat and spoke louder. "Why are you trying to be the lord?"

"I *am* lord now," said Jurij harshly, although his brow soon softened. He sighed and stood up, gesturing behind him. "Maybe you better have a seat. This might take a while."

Cautiously, I slipped past him and took the proffered seat—the throne. I felt my blood run cold as I gripped the uncomfortably hard armrests. Would this upset the kings and queens? Did they think I was pretending to be the lady by sitting here?

There was no earthquake, so I had to assume they'd let this go for now. To be safe, though, I unclenched my hands from the armrests and folded them in my lap. Jurij paced back and forth in front of me on the dais, preparing himself to say whatever it was he felt he had to—and then he suddenly stopped.

"Those are Elfriede's clothes," he said. "I recognize the…" He gestured at me and turned away.

I looked down and found the material at my chest poorly sagging, my shawl not quite covering things up as I'd have liked it to. "I was in a hurry." I adjusted the material and ignored the flush at my cheeks. "You know Elfriede's things by sight? I wasn't aware you had any good memories of your time with Friede."

Jurij laid a hand on the book stand. The book was open to a page showing his mother, father, Luuk and Nissa crowded around a bed on which Alvilda rested. "On the contrary. I remember feeling happy. Ecstatic. I don't think I've ever felt anything like it since."

I stared at my hands in my lap. "The freedom to feel comes with the freedom to feel unhappiness, too. To feel anger."

"I know. I understand that now." He dropped his hand off the stand and began pacing again. "I especially understand resentment."

"I'm sorry," I said, although I still felt he had a lot to apologize for. "I never meant for any of this to happen."

"Do you mean the way life was in the village before? The way it is now?" He swallowed. "Or do you mean how things are between you and me?"

"All of it," I answered. I finally felt brave enough to look up and meet his eye. "You have to understand. I didn't know what I was doing when I cursed the village. And I thought I was doing the right thing when I gave Ailill the right to un-curse it."

"So it was him who undid it." Jurij broke away, resuming his pacing. "But how?"

"Since you've obviously been given more of their blessing than I have, I'll assume it's safe to tell you. But you have to understand that you put anyone else in danger if you discuss this with them."

I waited for Jurij to stop pacing, and he did. I took a deep breath and spoke. "When I went back to the distant history of this village, the men treated women like animals. Worse than animals. They were led by a lord whom I thought—whom I *mistook* for Ailill."

"Because you hadn't yet seen his face? Even so, why did you assume the man you knew was alive then?"

"He *was* alive then. I didn't fully realize I was in the past at that time anyway. It seemed like the village, but not the village. And I had seen his face by then. I got so angry after you were hurt after your wedding that I... I asked him to show me."

Jurij put his fingers to his temple. "The kings and queens sent you to the past?"

I shook my head. "No. No, in fact, they don't know how I went through the entryway without crossing through the Never Veil. They don't know how I got to the past."

"Then how did you?"

"I don't know! The first time, I didn't mean for anything to happen. I just wanted to get away from Ailill because he'd frustrated me. I heard voices calling my name. The second time, I wanted to go back. I thought I could visit Ailill in the past and help the women whom I'd met there and who needed some guidance."

Jurij lifted a hand to stop me. "All right. You don't know how. *They* don't even know how. Tell me about the men then, the ones who led you to... do what you did."

I wrung my hands together. "They were violent. Wicked. Worse than the monsters we used to pretend were our foes. They looked like us, but they acted so terribly. They made women do all the work in the village. They hurt women. They forced their grotesque version of love on them. They tore babies from their mothers, raised boys to treat women like lesser things—" I stopped and jumped as Jurij sat on the armrest beside me. There was pain on his features, his injured eye the punctuation to that misery.

"So the story was true. I always thought it was just a story. I... I actually never thought about it at all. Women as nothing but laborers, as bearers of children." He ran a finger over the figure of Alvilda on the page, over his mother. "Why?"

"I don't know. It was all our village knew for a thousand years. The kings used our village as part of their game, showing how things could be when men had the advantage over women."

"And they thought this showed men *favorably*?"

"I can't say. I suppose it showed men having more power."

Jurij rested against the tiny portion of the throne behind the armrest. "They told me that men once had power in this village. They encouraged me to take it back."

I leaned back in the throne with him. "The queens would probably like to know that. Seeing as how the two groups decided to call our village a draw between the genders. But that was after they last spoke to you, I suppose."

Jurij shifted his head to face me, and for a moment I felt like we were just spending time together like we once had. That no one's lives were in danger. That no ill will had ever passed between us. "You said Ailill undid the curse?"

"Yes, well..." I took a deep breath. "The lord I thought was him was his brother. They had similar features, and I was so eager to hate Ailill. To hate the 'lord' who took me away from my life. But it wasn't really him I was angry at. I was angry about the whole village."

"And yet you said yourself you became the first goddess, and started the village on its path of goddesses and their men."

"Yes." I squeezed my hands together tighter, trying to slow my rapid heartbeat. "The men were so terrible, I thought they deserved it. *They* did deserve it."

"What changed your mind?"

"When the other lord died right in front of me, I realized he wasn't the lord I knew. And somehow, at once, I knew it was Ailill, who was only a boy then. Yet at that point, I'd already cursed the lord of that time to a thousand years of suffering— only the lord, when I uttered my curse, was the innocent boy."

Jurij frowned. "I'm confused."

I straightened back into the seat. "So am I. Just know that I regretted dooming Ailill to this, and I tried to give him the power to undo it one day. If... If he forgave me for what I'd done."

"That was quite a risk you took," said Jurij, and there was a sharp stab in my stomach.

He was right. "Yes, but I didn't really know if it'd work. I didn't understand anything. That was part of why I shut everyone out after the curse broke."

"So the lor—*he* forgave you?"

"I guess he did." I clenched my fists until my knuckles turned pale. The paleness reminded me of Ailill's skin, and how losing the darkness in his skin seemed to signal his path toward vanishing. "But then he didn't. He sent me away when I came to him—that made my choice to live alone clear. I knew I had myself to blame, and I was tired of being responsible for everyone's pain."

Jurij nudged my arm. "You're being too harsh. You weren't responsible for everyone's pain. You tried undoing what you did, and it worked. Besides, giving men back their freedom—something they claim they wanted now—might not have worked out for the better." He leaned forward and flipped through the book again.

"The sickness wasn't you," I said. "It was me. The kings and queens were angry with me."

Jurij froze. "It was me who made your Ailill sick." He surprised me by taking my hand in his, and I surprised myself by not immediately ripping it away. "I'm sorry. I didn't realize winning would hurt him."

Tears started forming in my eyes, and I fought hard to ignore the pressure that built up in my head. "You left him lying there in the garden."

"I was more worried about the women." Jurij grimaced. "And I was angry at him, Noll. I've been nothing but upset about your love for him since I realized I loved you, too."

I pulled my hand away, but slowly and gently, without malice. I didn't know what to say.

Jurij did. "So this is how you felt. When you loved me as more than a friend, as more than a brother, and I kept turning away."

"You had no choice," I said, after a moment's silence.

"Maybe," he said. "But I wouldn't wish *this* choice on anyone. This choice to love where love isn't wanted—"

I grabbed his chin. His mouth fell open in the shock. "I will never not want your love." I leaned forward, blinking back tears, pushing away my thoughts of anger. I bent his head lower and kissed him on the forehead. "I just want you to love someone else more, to be happy with someone who will love you like I once did." I put my forehead to his, shaking my head slightly. "No. More than I ever did. More selflessly than I ever did."

"I doubt I'll find that." Jurij took both of my hands in his, not leaning back. "You rewrote the world for me."

I clenched my teeth together. It had started out that way. I had gone to meet Ailill, breaking one of the cardinal rules of the village, because I wanted to free Jurij. In the end, though, it was more than that. I'd done it out of anger. I'd done it out of hate. I hadn't even been thinking of Jurij because by then all of my thoughts were consumed by—

By Ailill. And now, even after so many of the world's mysteries had opened up to me, after I came to know so much, I'd lost the ability to be with him, to even touch him. Him and his stupid lies be damned, I wanted to hold him again. I started sobbing.

Jurij dropped one of his hands from mine to rub my back. "Noll…" he said, soothingly. "Oh, Noll. I'm sorry. Why did I ever listen to Jaron, to any of them? What have I done?"

He clenched the back of my dress hard, and my sobs choked to a stop.

CHAPTER TWENTY-FIVE

I wrestled my hands free and pushed Jurij back. "What do you mean? What else have you done? Tell me!"

Jurij blew out a deep breath. "Where do I start?"

I thought about Elfriede in a room somewhere in the castle, about Alvilda, and all the women out there, ill. And Ailill, too. Was there anything I could do for any of them? Was demanding the truth from Jurij bound to make it all worse?

So far they hadn't done anything terrible to punish me for talking to Jurij, even though I knew they were watching from when I'd touched Ailill. I'm sure they didn't know what we were saying. I made a decision; I had to know. I couldn't go back to the cottage, forget about everyone else, until I was certain Jurij wasn't about to ruin everything worth sacrificing everything for. "From the beginning," I said. "From the night in the cavern."

Jurij stood, stepping back from the throne. "There isn't much to tell about that time. Not for a few days at least."

"Really?" I fought the urge to roll my eyes. "A whole few days?"

Jurij held a finger out. "No, listen. I was upset for weeks. I barely did anything."

"Alvilda told me you'd taken to sewing and woodwork."

"Only because I certainly didn't feel like going back to the quarry. And you know her, she wouldn't let me sit idle for more than a few days, no matter if I'd stabbed someone and inadvertently caused the tavern fire along with the rest of the group. *Especially* since there was so much work to be done." He ran a hand over his face. "Look at me, complaining about my aunt when she's lying there, dying…"

"So you never saw Jaron?" I said, getting him back on track. The truth was, I felt uncomfortable spending too long thinking about those women. "Or Darwyn, Sindri and Tayton?"

"I saw Darwyn and Tayton. I guess I saw Sindri, too." Jurij started pacing again. "I don't remember."

"What about Luuk? Your father?"

Jurij stopped, shaking his head. "They're not involved with any of this this time. Please don't think ill of them. They shouldn't have ever been involved. Father was just so angry with Mother and Alvilda…" He sat down on the step of the dais, his back to me. "Yes, I saw them. They were pretty shaken up, too. And they'd hardly played a role in what we'd done."

I got up from the throne and slid onto the floor, sitting on the dais beside Jurij. I could never picture Ailill treating the throne room so casually. "I imagine Siofra and Alvilda wouldn't have let Luuk out of their sights after that."

"Or me, neither," said Jurij, wrapping his arms around his knees. "They forgave Father, though. We spent the first few days all under one roof, with Nissa, too, like a strange, wedged-together family."

I nudged Jurij with my arm. "Not *like* a family. That is your family."

"Yeah." A small smile flittered onto his face. "I wasn't in good shape those first few days. I just sat there, carving. Sewing. Doing whatever Mother and Alvilda tossed in front of me."

I gestured at his clothing with my elbow. "Did you sew that while you were at it?"

Jurij ran a hand over his sleeve, over the bangle that got caught halfway up his forearm. "It was a purchase," he said. "The lor—*he* asked for more clothing when he… came back."

Oh. So it was him who wanted a new design, to go along with his new life.

"That doesn't look like it would quite fit him."

"No." Jurij touched his cheek, fingering the slight scar that remained across his eye. "I adjusted it myself. Without realizing, I think."

You "think"? I decided to let that one go. "You must have met with Jaron at some point. What was he doing, 'turning himself in'?"

Jurij hugged his knees. "He dropped by Mother and Alvilda's one day, along with Darwyn and Tayton. They'd all three been displaced by the tavern fire—"

I blew air through my lips to show how little sympathy I felt for that, but Jurij kept going.

"—and Darwyn and Tayton, who'd been staying with Darwyn's brother, went one day to your cottage—Ingrith's old cottage, that is. They felt bad about the roles they played that night. But instead of you, they found Jaron."

I laughed, and not kindly. "Really? He indirectly killed my father and Ailill, then he decides to move into my house?"

"He'll move into one of the new commune homes eventually."

"Good. Back where he belongs." I felt a tightness in my stomach even as I said it, and I hugged my own knees to my chest in a reflection of Jurij. "It's not going to be a bad place anymore, anyway," I added, quietly.

"Yeah," said Jurij. "And besides, you don't need the cottage anymore. You have your family." His lips pinched almost as soon as he said it, probably thinking of Elfriede. My own heart clenched. Just because I hadn't visited her yet didn't mean I could deny the fact that she was ill, and it was my fault. "Sorry," said Jurij after a moment. "I wasn't thinking."

I tucked my knees under my cheek, resting on them. "Was Jaron the one with the plan again?"

"There wasn't a *plan*, not right away." Jurij tapped his hands together in front of his legs. "They just all felt so... lost. They thought I might, too."

"How many men were in on the first plan? You talk about men being unsatisfied not knowing why they were ever cursed or how the curse was broken, like it was all or at least most of the men who were on your side."

"Jaron tried to rouse them. For weeks. Months even." Jurij

leaned back, putting his hands out on the dais behind him to support himself. "Maybe some were on the verge of paying attention, but too many of them were lost in the joys of drink. Of women—women they weren't forced to love. Women they could just have fun with—multiple women."

My eyes widened as I sat back up, and Jurij laughed. "Sorry. That's not what you asked. I think they would have gotten there. If Jaron had waited just a bit longer—but he felt sure you were keeping something from us."

"And now you know I was. Now you understand better *why.*"

"I'm not sure I do."

"But—"

"No, I understand why you kept quiet." Jurij stood back up, grabbing the book from the stand, and sat back down on the dais beside me. "I just don't understand why *they* make us stay ignorant of them." He flipped through the pages. "Don't they want to be worshipped?"

I checked the door for signs of any of the specters, but there were none. A couple had to be posted outside the door at least, but we seemed to be far enough back that they weren't hearing this. Either that, or they gave Jurij a freedom I never had. "I guess not," I admitted. "I think they care more about what they think of each other, and think very little of us." My voice was quiet, but I couldn't stop my heart from hammering, my eyes from watching for a listening specter. I stopped Jurij from flipping through the book. "But don't let them suspect you're thinking too hard about their reasons. I dared to ask a few questions—I just wanted them not to hurt anyone who might talk about what they knew—and they did this." I looked down at the book, at a woman in bed I didn't recognize. "They punished all of them because of me."

Jurij let the book fall to his lap and took my hand in his. "It's not your fault."

I tore my hand away and went back to hugging my knees. "So this time. You said Jaron didn't have a plan. What did he want from you?"

Jurij laughed sourly. "To know what I knew. They figured out you'd told me some things I hadn't told them." He paused. "Why was I allowed to know, anyway?"

"Maybe the kings had you groomed for a replacement lord

629

even then." I shrugged. "Or more likely, they couldn't hear me speak to you when I told you some of what I knew in the woods. They didn't know to punish either of us yet, and then you pocketed one of the golden bangles you found in the dining room, and that made it okay for you to know." I frowned. "There were a lot of those bangles there. Ailill got one every time he was reborn, and he started using them to hang the curtain that used to be there."

Jurij shut the book. "I remembered that. I—well, you have to go back. You have to understand how desperate Jaron still was to know, to make the sacrifices worth something."

"None of this was worth my father's death! Or the others'. Or the sense of uneasiness that permeates the village now."

"Since none of that can be changed, it's better for it to be worth something than nothing at all, right?" Jurij smiled haltingly, hesitatingly. "At least that's what we thought."

"So," I said, putting on my own false smile to help disperse some of the anger I was feeling, "Jaron wanted to get back into the castle, and he figured the only way to do that was to 'turn himself in.'"

"Yes," said Jurij. "And I was supposed to come along later to free him. Darwyn and Tayton were to follow if I didn't come back."

"Free him and what?" I threw my hands out to the side. "Explore the secrets of the castle? Enter the hole behind the throne? Gather more swords to cause more trouble?" The scabbard Jurij wore around his waist was empty. Like he was ready to take up a sword if he needed to but confident enough to walk around without one until that moment.

Jurij seemed to realize where I was looking and patted his empty scabbard. "I left it in the cavern. After I got back, after I realized what I'd done to you... Did they heal you?"

"Yes," I snapped, rubbing the back of my head. There was no evidence of Jurij's betrayal, besides what I would always know in my heart. "I wonder if you tossed it in the cavern pool to wash the blood off."

Jurij grimaced. "Most of the swords are in the pool now. I watched you and Ailill return from here, and I saw him throw our pile into the water after you parted."

"Good. Maybe at least if you jump in to get them, you'll fall through the Never Veil and leave our village in peace."

Jurij sighed and traced the cover of the book with his finger. "I didn't want to hurt you."

"Funny. Because when I asked the same thing about Ailill that night in the cavern, you seemed to imply that accident or not, you wouldn't have minded hurting Ailill."

Jurij clenched his jaw. "That was different."

"Not to me."

"I really did not mean to hurt him then, okay?" Jurij sounded exasperated. "I wasn't thinking straight. I thought maybe Jaron had you again and I... All I was thinking about was saving *you*."

I couldn't look into his eyes for long. "You left him at the garden table."

"And you had him brought to a bed." Jurij's face twisted. "I don't know what else to do for him, Noll. I thought it was some sort of lord ritual. I had other things to worry about." I could see the slight twitch of his jawline.

"Like Elfriede," I said for him.

Jurij didn't comment on that. "I didn't know what I know now about Ailill, after what you just told me." The name sounded strange and foreign on his tongue, and he made a face like he had a distaste for it. "I thought he'd treated you poorly. I thought he was keeping the truth from us all for no reason." He was half right with both ideas. "Jaron whipped us all up into a frenzy! If anything—if I shouldn't forgive someone, it should be Jaron, for using you like that. Or even me—I shouldn't forgive myself."

We'd gotten off track again, and I needed to know if there was anything left that I ought to add to my pile of worries. "And what was your plan with Jaron this time?"

"It was less involved than a 'plan,'" said Jurij, shifting uncomfortably. "We did want to get to the hole behind the throne. We did want to remove all those swords from the castle—Jaron worried the servants would take them up and use them against us, now that we knew they were there."

"And you believed him?" I snorted. "After he convinced you all to wear them at your hips like a king and his retainers?"

"Jaron is *not* interested in leading. He just wanted peace. He wanted the truth—he needs that for peace."

"Sure." I sighed. I took the book from Jurij's lap. He didn't protest, and I hesitated for a moment, wondering if looking at its pages—if being the one to turn the pages—without my golden token was a sign of defiance to the kings and queens. Yet they'd let Ailill send out those pages before, let a group of us discover the secret of the moving reflection of life in black and yellow.

"We thought at some point there might be fewer servants," said Jurij, letting my sarcasm slide. "And that the lord himself might be out, thanks to the rebuilding efforts. But he didn't leave the castle as much as he originally seemed to indicate he would."

Because he was staying away from me. Although now that I knew he was only pretending to be shocked to discover his "lady" was the woman from his childhood who'd doomed him to this existence, I had to wonder why he still hated me enough to stay away.

"The agreed-upon night came, the last night we were willing to wait." Jurij paused. "I was supposed to volunteer to turn myself in, maybe wrestle the keys away from a specter—"

"That doesn't sound very smart."

"—but instead, I heard my name coming from the cavern." Jurij grabbed his knees again and stared blankly in front of him. "It was almost like I had no choice. I had to go."

"And then you wound up there." I still hadn't opened the book. My pocket felt dangerously bare without the coin, and I wondered how I was allowed to speak about any of this without making them angry. Was the specters' distance my only salvation? "You don't have to tell me what happened there," I said quickly. "In fact, perhaps you better not." I stood up and placed the book back on the stand without flipping it open. I stood there a moment, thinking. "But I need to know: Why are you doing this? Why are you trying to become the lord?"

Jurij grimaced and stood, closing the distance between us with a few short steps. "I *am* lord now, Noll." He got uncomfortably close, and I tried backing up, but the stand dug into my back. "But I may not always be." He took a deep breath and put his hands on his hips. "Jaron was right. They have a right to know. So I let him take them."

There was something I didn't like dancing behind Jurij's eyes. "Take what?"

Jurij gripped the bangle at his wrist. "The rest of the golden bangles. If you have one, you can know... And you can rule this village." He turned to face the door. "Come in!" he shouted.

Two specters appeared before us, their arms extended toward me.

CHAPTER TWENTY-SIX

I took a step back, shoving the bookstand between me and the approaching specters before crouching behind it.

"Noll, what are you doing?" Jurij looked between the specters and me. He waved a hand at the specters and they both stood still, lowering their arms.

I straightened up a little. "Weren't you going to make them take me somewhere?"

"I thought it was high time you visited your sister," said Jurij. One of the specters broke away and whispered something in Jurij's ear. In *Jurij's* ear. I still had to remind myself that he had stolen Ailill's place.

A faltering smile flickered on my face. "So you know they talk now—to the lord of the village."

There was a flash of embarrassment in Jurij's expression as the specter pulled away. "That was a strange revelation. In any case, your mother has been asking for you." He shoved aside the bookstand and put a hand on my elbow while he grabbed the book and tucked it under his other arm. "I'll escort you there."

The sword hanging over the throne caught my eye as he dragged me down from the dais. I swore I saw the slightest violet glow for a moment, but it was gone as soon as I blinked. Jurij

634

took us past the specters, and I checked to see if either was Spurn, but I didn't think he was among them.

I pulled my arm from his grasp and walked a few steps away from Jurij. He looked slightly affronted, but I couldn't care less. "Why was Elfriede with you?" I asked, eyeing the book under his arm. There was no way all the specter told him was that my mother was looking for me. "After you came back from that place, when you met up with Jaron in the cavern?"

Jurij stopped abruptly in front of the kitchen. "You saw that? How?"

The specters were at work in the kitchen, and I practically felt their non-existent breath behind me. "Don't ask me that," I whispered.

Jurij looked over my shoulders and quickly took my meaning. "Of course. Well, she... She said she was looking for him."

She was acting strange when we last parted, and I didn't understand why she was so concerned with Jaron, even if they'd briefly courted one another. "Here?"

Jurij put a hand behind my back, pushing us both forward. "No, the cavern. She said she was also looking for me."

Naturally. Even after all they'd been through, her looking for Jurij made more sense. "But she found Jaron first?" I asked as we descended the staircase.

"He got out with the help of a servant, believe it or not."

I stopped, two steps from the second floor. "What?"

Jurij kept us moving down the hallway. "Maybe the kings let them know I'd want him free."

"But you weren't even lord yet," I said, realizing it was the first time I was admitting it, even if my heart still didn't believe it.

We stopped a few yards from a room where Darwyn and Tayton were chatting. Jurij lowered his voice. "I don't know, Noll, but that's what he told me. After he talked to you, one of the servants came back and let him go. A strangely disheveled servant at that."

Spurn. What *was* that specter up to? The queens and kings alike insisted they hadn't sent me that coin, but Spurn had claimed they had. *Is he capable of deceit? Who am I kidding? He's the shade of Ailill, of course he is.*

"How's it going, your lordship?" Darwyn placed one hand

over his shoulder and bowed slightly. The devious smile on his lips made it clear he thought this was a game. And here I thought he'd evolved past childhood into someone a bit less exasperating.

Tayton watched Darwyn and echoed his posture, bowing more deeply, the subtle subversion of the gesture clearly lost on him. "Lordship," he said brusquely.

Jurij let go of my back, adjusting the book under his arm. "We must go," he said. "We're needed in the village."

"Why?" I searched for some telltale sign among the three of them. Darwyn's jaw twitched slightly. I grabbed Jurij's arm. "What's going on in the village?"

"Illness and unrest, of course. You know that." Jurij glanced over my shoulder and I turned around to see the two specters standing there. "You stay here with your mother and sister. Stay in this room."

Darwyn and Tayton headed for the stairs that would take them down to the entryway. Just before they turned the corner, a glistening at their waists caught my attention. Golden bangles were woven through their belts, and they shone as they passed the torchlight. I hadn't noticed them before because they were at their backs. Jurij moved to follow them.

"Jurij!" I squeezed his elbow tighter. Our eyes met, and for a moment I saw the flicker of firelight within those dark irises. But it was just the reflection of a nearby torch. "You aren't meant for this."

Jurij took my hand in his tenderly and moved it away. "Maybe not. But I can try. If being lord allows me to protect you from them, then I must." He followed Darwyn and Tayton. "She stays here," he said, over my head.

Protect me from them? What had the kings and queens promised him? "Wait!" Intending to follow, I took one step toward him, but the two specters' hands were soon around my arms, dragging me inside the room.

~

IT COULDN'T HAVE BEEN that long since Jurij, Darwyn and Tayton left to do only-they-knew-what in the village with Jaron. It felt like ages. I paced in front of the fire lit in the room given to

Elfriede—the same room I'd lived in over the course of a few months when I felt like a prisoner in these walls, but Jurij had no way of knowing that. It didn't feel real to be here again under such different circumstances.

"I wish you would stop doing that," said Mother, quietly. "Elfriede... Elfriede needs her peace and quiet." Mother lifted Elfriede's still hand to her lips for what must have been the hundredth time since I'd entered the room and started crying again.

"Peace and quiet won't help her now." I leaned against the mantle, staring at the flickering of the flames. My heart was still racing, my foot still tapping.

"Don't say that. You don't know that. You don't even know what's wrong with them."

I bit my tongue, letting Mother's sobs fall into murmurs, eager not to agitate her further. Even if Elfriede was beyond my help, Mother's fragile state of being actually was affected by my movements.

The crackling of the fire was the liveliest sight in the room, and it drew my gaze like it was a goddess and I was her man. I couldn't get Elfriede's quiet, restful face out of my head, but I didn't want to keep looking at it. *I did that to her. She'll die because of me, and we'll never have forgiven each other for Jurij and how we let that man come between us.*

There was also the fact that on the other side of the wall, I knew Ailill was lying in a bed much like Elfriede's—at least that was where I'd seen the two specters carry him. It wasn't his room when I lived here—that was upstairs, I assumed, in one of the rooms I'd yet to explore. I could imagine how agitated I'd have felt if I was sleeping just a wall's width away from him back when I hated him, and when I uttered the curse that brought us together. His illness was something of a different kind than the women's—he'd been conscious, if just barely. I could do more good at his side. I could say my farewells...

No. Don't think about farewells. He isn't going to die.

The most good I could do would be to round up all one hundred and some—how many specters had Ailill said there were?—golden bangles, and throw them all into the cavern pond because I thought I now knew what Jurij and Jaron were up to. I hit my forehead against the mantle, not even caring about the pain. *What were they thinking? Giving men bangles gives them the right to know—but there couldn't be over a hundred lords of this village. They'll kill each other. By playing that stupid chess game or just outright stabbing each other.*

If I did anything—if I *could* do anything considering Jurij demanded I stay here—the kings and queens were sure to be more than displeased. What else did they expect of me? Was I supposed to suffer quietly in a room away from it all, just watching my sister die? Was I supposed to sit by and let Ailill die, while Jurij and the other men tore each other apart?

Did they even care about our village now that they'd agreed it was a "draw" in their game? Were they just toying with us? Were they hoping we'd all die, so they could send us off to populate the villages that were calmer?

The door opened, and a specter stepped inside with a tray full of food. He set it down at a small table beside the bed. Mother, her head on the bed beside Elfriede's, didn't even seem to notice him.

"Wait." I crossed the room and put a hand on his arm. It was so cold, I nearly ripped my fingers away like they'd been burnt. "I need to see Ailill."

The specter gave little sign of acknowledging me. He moved his arm out of my reach and stepped outside the room, his hand gripping the handle behind him.

I shoved my body through the open door before he could fully close it. The two specters posted at my door joined the one who'd dropped off the food in staring at me.

I took a deep breath and tossed back my shoulders. "Jurij said I was supposed to stay 'here.' Everywhere in the castle is 'here,' isn't it?" Without waiting for the reply I knew would come in the form of hands on my arms, dragging me back into the room, I strode to the room next door. I put my hands on the handle, waiting for the specters standing there to challenge me, but they didn't. I pulled.

I'd gotten the door halfway open and seen the darkness of the room before I felt the cold hands on my arms.

"I'm allowed to be here!" I snapped, looking from one specter to the other.

They both let go of me at once. I didn't wait to see why they'd changed their minds, and I scrambled inside the room. I saw a prone form on the bed, felt the chill of the air, and spun on my heels, pointing at the fireplace behind me. "This should be lit! Do you have no concern for your own self?"

My rant died on my lips when I saw the specter who'd followed me inside the room.

"Spurn?"

He turned his head and nodded at the specters behind him, and they went to work, piling wood from the corner of the room into the fireplace. A fourth specter stepped inside with a torch and lit the pile.

I met Spurn's eyes and saw them burst to life in the flicker of fire, but I had other pressing matters on my mind. Ailill's almost lifeless body was on the bed, lying on his stomach. The specters had basically thrown him there without tucking him in for adequate warmth.

"Ailill?" I quickly pulled my hand back after I found myself reaching toward him. I turned to Spurn. "Help me get him under the blankets," I snapped. "It's the least you could do after all the trouble you caused me." As soon as I spoke, the irony of that statement wasn't lost on me, but I had other things to worry about just then.

Spurn moved into motion, shifting Ailill so I could pull the blanket out from under him before rolling him on his back to the center of the bed. I threw the blanket over him, careful not to let my fingers brush him as I did—dying to let my fingers brush him as I did.

Ailill breathed in and out, his eyelashes fluttering. That was more movement than I noticed in Elfriede, who might be completely gone if her body wasn't still there.

Bodies used to not vanish when we died. Spirits used to not get reborn.

But she'd been breathing. Just barely. I sat down at the edge of Ailill's bed, careful not to even let my backside brush against his leg beneath the covers. Perhaps they'd let me get away with that level of touching, but I didn't want to risk it. Not after everything. Ailill deserved some peace and quiet at least.

I gave it to him for quite a while, Spurn the only specter who remained in the room with us. Ailill did nothing but breathe as I cleared my mind, thinking of what could be going on in the village at that very moment. I didn't even notice that Spurn must have left the room at some point or at the very least met another specter at the door because eventually he held a mug out toward me, steam from the open cup looking like mist in front of his black eyes.

Taking the mug from him, I let out a single laugh despite myself. It was a brownish liquid, a little bitter on my tongue. I shuddered but drank again. It was better than eating and drinking nothing. When was the last time I had had any appetite? I hadn't eaten much when the kings and queens offered.

"Is this, my goddess, a dream?"

The mug almost slipped out of my hands. "Ailill!" I moved to touch him but quickly patted the bed beside his prone form instead. I gave him half a smile. "You're not dreaming, but if you still think of me as your goddess, I wonder if you're still half asleep."

Ailill took his arm out from under the covers and reached toward me. I recoiled, bringing my hand out of his reach.

"Not a dream," said Ailill. He grinned slightly. "In my dreams, you never shy away from me."

I cradled the mug with both hands, letting the warmth of the liquid bring life to my numb fingers. "You're not fully awake. You'd remember."

Ailill shifted up, sitting with his back against the headboard. He frowned. "They said you could not be with me."

"I can't even touch you, remember? The last few times I tried, they made the ground shake."

"They do not want you with me," said Ailill, his voice a little hoarse. "Yet they do not seem to want me as lord anymore, either. If I am to be a nobody, what difference does it make if we are nobodies together?" There was a slight upturn to his lips. "Not that I think you could ever be a nobody, as much as they want you to be."

I tucked my hair behind my ears. "Maybe they just don't want me to be happy."

"Would that make you happy? Being with me?"

I opened my mouth and then shut it the moment I looked into

his eyes. The firelight continued to play tricks on me, dancing an echo of the magic that once shone across his irises. When I spoke again, it wasn't with the affirmation he seemed eager to get from me. I had to know first. "Why did you lie? About not being able to remember?"

It was as if I'd kicked him in the stomach; his face looked so twisted with pain. "My intentions were never to hurt you."

I wondered if my own face was similarly marred with pain. "Well, you did. At least once I realized you were lying. Once it struck me how much you wanted to forget."

"I never wanted to forget!" Ailill slammed his fist against the headboard behind him and I almost dropped my mug. He ran a hand through his hair and struggled to smile. "I apologize. There I go again. That is exactly why I wanted to start anew—and if I could not actually start over, at least pretend I could."

I set the mug on my lap. "You wanted to start anew?"

"Yes." Ailill bit his lip. "I wanted you to see me as someone you could love."

I do love you. I loved you months ago. I tried telling you. It was right there on the tip of my tongue again, but I couldn't say it. I couldn't just let his mistakes go. "You thought I could love someone who lied to me?"

Ailill got lost staring at the fire. "Better than someone who frightened you. Or was cruel to you."

I tapped my fingers against the mug, listening to the clank of my nails on the metal. "You didn't frighten me—especially not since I realized my trip to the past wasn't a figment of my imagination. When I realized you'd started as a good person, that it was my curse that twisted you—"

"Do not blame yourself. It took me a long time to realize it. I cursed my fate, rallied against my feelings for you even when I knew you were the one who had cursed me to it. Maybe I needed to see you again, to sit with my freedom at last. Eventually I did realize it. You never meant me harm. You meant harm to the man who had hurt me more than anyone, who deserved it more than anyone. You meant to save me, and to save others from him."

"I did," I said, after a moment. "But it's still my fault for not thinking things through."

"It is not." Ailill laughed softly. "Despite the loneliness, despite the long years of living without hope, I am grateful you cursed me. I would have never seen you again otherwise. I would have never realized the love I felt for you was something of my own choosing."

"I don't know why." The words practically caught in my throat. "I've rarely been kind to you, either."

"That is not true." Ailill shifted in the bed beside me, taking a deep breath and wincing as he did.

"You're in pain—"

He held a hand out. "No. I am fine. I just need time."

"Why is your skin lightening again? Are you so weak because Jurij beat you?"

He laughed sardonically. "I do not know. I have never had a successor, and I became lord only when my brother died. There was no need to fight for the title over a game of chess while wearing a golden bangle."

I gripped the mug tighter to stop myself from touching his leg. "Will you die?"

"Because of this?" Ailill gestured in the air. "I think they would have killed me immediately if they cared enough to see my death to its conclusion."

Unless they wanted you to suffer first—or me to suffer. To feel the full impact of their edict that I can never even touch you, nor comfort you as you're dying.

"Olivière. You were unkind only when I was unkind to you. I deserved it."

"Not always," I said. "You were kind to me—the kindest anyone has ever been to me—the first time I met you. Then, I didn't come to see you until I wanted something from you."

"That is all right," said Ailill. "You were not unkind to me, just afraid to accept I had found the goddess in you. You did not feel as strongly for me as I felt for you—you did not feel anything for me. You could not have. With the freedom of my own heart, I understand that now."

My nose twitched. "I kissed Jurij on his wedding day."

"You were not happy with me then. I had kept you against your will here, when I knew, even then I knew, you had the right to send me the commune."

"'One does not send the lord of the village to the commune.'"

Ailill scoffed. "So I said. Would you expect any different of someone eager to save his own skin?"

"I wonder how that would have worked anyway," I said. "Seeing as how I banished you to the castle regardless."

Ailill shrugged. "I would have caused an earthquake when I set out, but it would have stopped shortly after. It is not as if the ground would not stop shaking the entire time I left the castle."

Not like what happens now whenever I touch you. I shook my head. "I guess I didn't think that command through."

"We have already established you did not realize the kind of power you were playing with." He smiled. "But see, I could have come out to join you all after a brief earthquake. I was just too bitter to."

"And after your rebirth? You were out and about among the people, like a real leader."

"I told you I wanted to start anew."

I sighed. "Then you pretended to realize I was the woman who had cursed you and pulled away from me. Away from everyone again."

"I still went to the village. But yes. I was surprised to find out how awkward being out among so many people made me feel, and well, then I had an excuse to spend more time back in the castle. I was still helping and sending out the Ailills." He bit his lip. "That was not the only reason. I thought pretending I was surprised to discover who you were was going to work out in my favor. When you saw how kind I could still be to you, that I could forgive you far easier than I had before, I thought…"

"Ailill, do you remember when you were a child, and I covered you with a shawl, telling you to protect your face from women?"

"Of course. How could I forget?"

"Perhaps things were too chaotic for you to fully realize, but men were vanishing when women looked at them. I—a woman not related to you—looked at your uncovered face, and you went nowhere."

"Because the magic…" Ailill sat up straight abruptly. "Because you loved me! Even then? Why? How?"

I couldn't look at Ailill's pleading eyes for long. I stared instead at the mug in my lap. "I don't know. I didn't even realize it then. I guess when I found out you were the same as that boy—when somehow I could start thinking over all that had happened in that light—I felt something for you I couldn't even acknowledge yet." I brushed a tendril of hair out of my face. "I think I loved you even when you kept me here, but I was too angry with you to realize it."

Ailill kicked off the sheets and scrambled over toward me, surprising me so that I barely had time to jump off the bed and out of his reach. The rest of the liquid, long gone cold, spilled onto the ground and over my feet as the mug cluttered to the stone floor with a clang. "I do not care." He reached toward me. "Let the ground shake. Let me hold you just this once."

"No!" It came out sharper than I meant it to. Spurn crouched in front of me—I'd almost forgotten he was still there—and produced a cloth from his inner jacket pocket, which he used to mop up the fallen liquid.

Ailill collapsed back onto the bed, moaning, staring at the ceiling. "And then you came back to me, despite my stubbornness, and I pushed you away. I was too blind to realize my own feelings, too foolish to understand my own role in the terrible blood between us."

Ailill's skin shined with the flicker of the firelight, and I worried he was soaking in sweat. I clutched my skirt with my clammy palms even as Spurn patted my boots gently with his cloth. "I don't want to fight with you anymore, Ailill."

He rolled his head slightly to look at me. "I do not wish to ever fight with you again, either."

I let out a deep breath. "Whatever your intentions when you lied to me, I want you to know, it hurt me. I... I don't know if I can ever fully trust you again."

Ailill held his hand out toward me, but I wouldn't stand close enough to let him touch me. "I was wrong," he said. "Please forgive me. I did so much that was wrong, and I wished so badly for a new start. I should have just asked... I should never have deceived you."

"We were already almost there." I stopped as Spurn stood and blocked the sight of Ailill from me. He bent over one last time to grab the mug and stepped away. "I thought I felt something more honest between us, that day you died."

"You were right. I felt it, too." Ailill rolled slightly, cradling his head in his hand as he pushed himself to sit upright on the bed. "I was a fool to doubt it. After all I had done, I never believed you could forgive me. That you could feel even a tiny flicker of the passion I felt for you."

I could feel the heat rising on my cheeks. "I forgive you, Ailill. If you can forgive me."

Ailill leaned his head against the post of the bed, wrapping his arms around it as if embracing it gave him strength. "Do you not remember? My forgiving you was necessary for the curse to end."

"That's right." I practically wrung the fabric of my skirt in my sweaty palms. "Thank you."

"Thank you," echoed Ailill, his eyes fluttering shut. He struggled to keep them open. "Thank you."

"It doesn't matter now, does it?" I said, my voice a whisper. "It's too late."

"Not too late." Ailill slunk back down to the bed, his voice nearly exhausted. "Never too late. Help me stand... against them..."

He spoke about fighting against the kings and queens back in their garden. How? Why would he even think that was possible?

I stepped forward, about to touch him.

A hand clamped on my arm to stop me. I looked up to meet the eyes of Spurn, and he wasn't looking past me. He looked at me, and then he tugged me after him.

CHAPTER TWENTY-SEVEN

Spurn dropped my arm as soon as we left the room, and I peered through the door as he shut it closed behind us.

"See that he's made comfortable again," I pleaded.

Spurn nodded. He grabbed my hand in his and dragged me to Elfriede's opened door.

"Where are we..." I stopped. The peaceful breaths from Mother at the chair beside Elfriede's bedside were what drew my eyes at first. But that was forgotten by the slight movement under the blanket draped over Elfriede's feet.

"Friede!" The name was hoarse in my throat. I didn't even recall crossing the distance between us or lifting her hand and grabbing it in mine. It was ice cold to the touch, but I kept squeezing.

Elfriede's eyelashes fluttered open. "Noll?" Her voice was barely a whisper.

The smile I found on my lips was so rare, so out of place as of late, it felt like it was tearing through my skin. I didn't care; I could hardly stop myself if I wanted to.

"Mother!" I coughed, choking on the well of tears that leapt to my face. "Moth—"

Spurn's hand clamped down on my shoulder and I jumped in place. He shook his head, nodding back toward Elfriede.

I knew without being told that this was an anomaly, something meant for just me—which meant it couldn't last. Which meant they were playing with me.

"How do you feel?" I asked quietly, now determined not to wake Mother, to keep Elfriede awake and speaking with me for as long as possible. Elfriede's forehead was as cold as her hand, which was worrying. Heat would have at least meant she was alive, that she was fighting something.

"Is this a dream?" Elfriede's head rolled toward me. "Are you a dream?"

"No." It was strange to be asked that twice in one night. "No, this isn't a dream."

"I feel like... I've been dreaming. Where's Jurij?"

The smile on my lips was nothing but a memory now; the dread in my chest was all that pervaded. "He's... fine." I brushed a bit of hair out of Elfriede's face, remembering how I once envied its bright and cheery color. It would have looked out of place on me. It was better framing the face of a delicate little bird. "You've had us worried."

"What happened?" Elfriede's eyes seemed to flicker in and out of awareness, but it may have been the reflection of the firelight. "Where's Arrow?"

I laughed. I'd forgotten the dogs. "He's in the kitchen," I said, remembering the eager way he chomped into the flank of meat one of the specters had tossed him. "Jurij wouldn't forget them."

"Where are we?"

"The castle."

"Why?"

"Friede, I know you're confused and probably scared, but I need to know what happened between you and Jurij and Jaron. What you last remember—what you were doing in the cavern."

Elfriede found the strength to wrinkle her nose. "Not in the cavern. Not with Jurij. Swords and red water. Water and..."

She wasn't making sense, and I desperately needed her to. I glanced at Mother, making sure she was still asleep. I took Elfriede's hand in mine. "You said you were going to look for Jaron. You found both him and Jurij in the cavern, remember? They were standing with a pile of swords in front of the pool."

"Yes," croaked Elfriede. "I didn't like that. I told Jurij, but he was already upset with Jaron. I didn't know Jurij would be there. I hoped he would be... He was wet."

"You argued with them? Was Jurij trying to stop Jaron or—"

"Do you know what I think?" Elfriede's eyes grew slightly wider, but there was no masking the haze that plagued them. "I think you still love him. Jurij."

I took a deep breath. "Friede, I don't know how long we have before you fall back asleep—"

"You love him."

"I don't." It was true enough. "Not like that. Not now. I used to, but now I..." I searched Elfriede's face, determined to see if I could convince her to talk about more important things. The way she stared at me, the way she seemed barely with me, even though I held her hand in mine, made me realize this was all she'd woken for. The kings and queens may have woken her to tease me, to show me how little control I had over what they did, but this was all Elfriede would stay awake for. This was all she cared to discuss, and the only reason why she could finally speak it was because she was so weak—too weak for pride to halt her tongue.

"Friede. I know you'll find this hard to believe, but I tried to stay out of your and Jurij's way. I did."

"No." Elfriede tugged feebly on her hand and I let it fall to her side on the bed. "You were always there between us. Always."

"Always? I was always between you? What about when I was kept here, like a prisoner, for most of a year? What about..." I clamped my mouth shut. This wasn't the time.

"Before then. Before the Returning."

I cradled my head in my hands. Were we really doing this right now? "I seem to remember he was always eager to spend more time with you. I don't know if he told you, but you accidentally commanded him to be my friend, so there was no need to be jealous."

"It wasn't an accident." Elfriede coughed so delicately, there was no danger of her waking Mother up. "It was at first, maybe, but... I figured it out."

"And you were too upset about accepting Jurij as your man to do anything about it. You liked having him out of your hair."

"No, I didn't. I was nervous." Elfriede squeezed the blanket hard.

I understood her nervousness now. I understood not wanting to accept that someone you hadn't wanted to find the goddess in you was eager for your love.

Elfriede opened her cracked lips. "Also... I just didn't want you to be alone."

The way her eyes flicked quickly to mine, she seemed so earnest. I reached out to grab her hand again and she let me take it. "You probably expected my man to find me with a year or two. You must have expected I wouldn't be alone for long."

"Maybe." Elfriede smiled slightly.

"But I wasn't alone. I wouldn't have been, even if you'd rescinded your order to Jurij." I pulled her hand closer to me. "I had you."

"I couldn't offer you the kind of friendship Jurij could. I know that."

Mother drew a sharp intake of breath and I tensed, unsure if my hunch would prove right—that Elfriede would drift back to nothingness the moment we had a witness to her waking. But Mother's head rolled back in her chair and she kept sleeping.

"Friede, I'm sorry." I took a deep breath. "It was never my intention to hurt you. Ever. I know I did, but I was a different person then."

"I don't know," Elfriede croaked. "You still push me away."

I didn't say anything for a moment, feeling the pain of the fleeting seconds of our time together slipping through my fingers. "I thought you wanted me away."

"I wanted..." Elfriede sighed. "I wanted you with me, but I was too blinded by envy and too upset to accept Jurij for who he became after he was free to love who he wanted." I didn't interrupt to explain how different Jurij was now and how little he had in common with the man who'd once been her husband. Elfriede's lax grip on my hand grew tighter. "You're my only sister."

"And you're mine." I gently put Elfriede's too-cold hand beside her and tucked her entirely beneath the blanket, hoping it'd keep her warmer. "If we were closer, if we could coexist in peace like we did back when you watched me play among the lilies on the hill, I'd have told you so much. I'd have convinced you I was in love with Ailill."

"It's still so strange to hear the lord addressed by a name." Elfriede's eyes fluttered shut, and I didn't dare correct her when it came to calling Ailill "the lord." "But I knew. I knew since the cavern you loved him. I just thought... Maybe you loved two... Maybe Jurij had to apologize to you for hurting Ailill, and you'd forgive him, and the three of you would leave me behind."

I would have laughed if there wasn't so much that was unbearable about the situation right then. Elfriede had been imagining I'd wind up with two men—how either of them would feel about sharing me with one another, I couldn't even fathom— as if I could hurt them both by never choosing one over the other, as if such a thing were even possible, even acceptable. I did laugh then, just slightly, as the idea that it *was* possible, it *could* be acceptable, entered my mind. It wasn't with those two partners. And it wasn't what I wanted.

"I'd never leave you behind," I said. "Not if I knew you were alone. I wouldn't hurt you like that. I won't let anyone else hurt you."

Elfriede's eyes fluttered shut as her head rolled back further into her pillow, and I jumped with a start as Mother snorted and sat straighter. "Noll? Did Elfriede wake?"

My gaze caught Spurn's. "No."

Mother bent over and patted the back of her hand against Elfriede's forehead. "I must have been dreaming. I thought I heard her voice."

Spurn headed out the door, and I paused, allowing myself one last look at what remained of my family, knowing Mother would stay with Elfriede no matter what happened, that she would never be alone again, before I left them behind.

I HAD to run to catch up to Spurn, struggling to keep up with his furious pace as we climbed to the third floor, passing the kitchen. I spared a glance inside, but there was no activity, no movement but the slight breathing of the two furry lumps curled up in front of the fire.

"Spurn! Where are you leading me? I can't..." My gaze fell on the throne—at the hole behind it. "I can't go through there."

Spurn ignored me, going by himself to the throne and climbing on top of it to grab Elgar. He held it out to me with both hands.

I shook my head vehemently. "They're watching," I said in a hushed whisper—like the volume of my voice made any difference. "They taunted me with Elfriede just now. If I do something foolish..."

Spurn shoved the sword against me until I felt like I had no choice but to accept it. He walked back toward the throne as soon as I did. The blade glowed faintly in the dim light; I hadn't been imagining it. I wanted to drop it, to show whoever might be watching that I'd have no part in this, that it was the fault of this strange, rogue specter and no other.

Spurn pushed the throne aside, the heavy metal grating across the stone floor.

"What are you doing?" I hissed, crossing the room to join him. "I can't go there! I—certainly not *alone*."

Spurn produced a parchment from his pocket. I tucked the sword under my arm awkwardly and took it from him:

Go now, read the note. *We hope you enjoyed speaking with your sister. We thought it wise to show you she can still be saved—they can all be saved. We have instructed this shade of a spirit to allow you passage. We have the kings distracted.*

I had no idea who could have written the note—other than the queens—but it had to be a lie, right? They hated me as much as the kings—or maybe not. Maybe a little less, since I was of their gender, but Ailill said never to trust them.

We sent the golden coin to you.

Those liars, I thought. They either lied to the kings then or lied to me now. What were they plotting?

I hesitated in front of the dark hole, not sure I wanted to play any part in it.

The light glowed violet deep in the back of the cavern.

I was startled as a pair of hands wrapped around my waist.

Blushing at the absurdity of this older shade of Ailill, especially one I knew as a child, caressing me so, I jumped back, but it was Spurn tying a belt around my waist. A belt that included Elgar's scabbard.

Did they send that back, too? The sword and the scabbard should have disappeared into nothingness, having served its purpose in a loop of impossible visits through time.

I slid Elgar into its sheath.

I didn't trust them. I didn't think what lay on the other side of the Never Veil would be inviting. But it was my one chance to get back there. It was my one chance to save the women of this village—to save the men.

I stepped through the dark, feeling nothing but cold air until the caress of the black veil.

When I finally untangled from the fabric, I couldn't breathe. I was in water. I kicked hard, trying to get my bearings. I blinked and through the violet haze, I thought I saw a pile of glistening iron from beneath my feet.

The light faded from violet to silver. I pushed hard until I broke through the surface of the water, gasping for air.

Once I reoriented myself, I recognized the cavern. The cavern, not the land beyond the mountains. Not a castle, not a barren canyon. They'd tricked me again, forced me through the Never Veil into another spot in my village. But I'd been fooled before. Was I even still in the same time in my village?

I swam to the sediment and climbed out, bending over and spitting out some of the water I'd swallowed. Elgar still hung around my hips, clanging against my leg with each heave.

I wrung out my skirt and shawl with shaking hands before abandoning that annoyingly-frequent task and setting out for the mouth of the cavern. I stopped almost the moment I set off. There were still a small number of swords beside the rock where Jaron and Jurij had left them, which made me think I'd traveled a distance, but not to the past. I turned around to gaze into the water, trying to ignore the red glow. There were swords at the bottom of the pool, I could tell, but not enough for the pile to have near fully depleted. The sediment around the pool was too upset, and the image of many feet trudging around here, each to grab his own sword, came vividly to my mind. Perhaps Jurij had caught up with Ailill long before he was able to toss the entire pile into the water. Maybe the men had dived for the rest. Whatever the reason, I felt sure I was in my own village, and that once I stepped out there, I'd find more than a hundred men with golden bangles and swords.

I squeezed the water out of the long parts of my hair and threw my shoulders back. The queens or Spurn or both had simply given me passage past the other specters. It was ridiculous, thinking of what any of them might plan by this. How long could the queens keep the kings from watching me? Why would they feel any need to?

Because over a hundred men will be competing to lead the village, and not a single woman will be among them. Not just because of the illness that attacked only women, but because Jurij and Jaron wanted the *men* to hold the gold, so they'd have the right to know —and what they'd do with that knowledge hardly bore thinking.

I pushed aside the idea of why the queens should even care as I made my way through the cavern and onto the path. This village was supposed to be a draw between the genders. Besides, even if the men rose to power, they had always been the ones to rule because of the lords in this village—and there were other villages for the kings and queens to worry about. Maybe it was me. Maybe I'd so altered their plans that neither the kings nor the queens were really willing to let our village be. Maybe they thought this village played a role in declaring a victor for the games they played with our lives.

I didn't even pause as I passed my dark and empty house, even if I was sure to find another change of clothing inside. Streams of sunlight were making their way over the horizon behind me; they would have to do for drying me. I had no idea how much time I had.

The thing that worried me most as I approached the village was the silence of it. It was dawn, and most people rose at that time to begin the day's tasks. The illness of the women had distracted everyone, to be sure, but there were no longer people running around in a panic, grabbing buckets of water or handkerchiefs or other things that would do nothing to help them.

If I can't get back to the kings and queens, I can do nothing to help them, either. I'd gone through the Never Veil without a golden token. But if the queens had wanted me to have one, surely they would have tasked Spurn with it since they seemed to have him at their beck and call. Unless, they wanted me to take one for myself. They'd had my sword sent to me—they must have wanted me to take it through violence.

The thought made me queasy as I remembered the blade through Elric's chest. I was little comforted by the idea that he should be out there, alive, perhaps a hundred times over by now, in another village.

Although... who said he'd be in another village? There were far fewer than a hundred flower bushes in that garden. Even if he cycled through all of them, perhaps he'd been given a new life here in this one again and again. I shuddered. Even if he didn't remember his past villainy, surely a spirit that tainted didn't just start anew.

"Noll!"

Without realizing it, my feet had taken me past the bakery. If this were any other situation, I would have headed there first, eager to check on Alvilda and all the rest of them. Nevertheless, this wasn't any other situation and I could feel the ever-advancing threat of passing time.

"Noll!" the quiet voice repeated again. A hand rested on my elbow.

"Nissa." I crouched down and embraced her, unable to bear the sight of her trembling lips. I grabbed her by the shoulders, pushing her back. "Alvilda?"

"Still asleep," replied Nissa, and I realized at once that was a more accurate description of what had happened to the women. They were fading like Mother had during her illness, but they didn't cough or get sick. They were simply with us one moment and gone the next, asleep in their own little worlds. Nissa frowned. "Marden, too. Roslyn is beside herself, between that and the men leaving—"

"Leaving?" I almost asked for more details, but I figured they were all headed to see Jurij—and where were they likely to go? They weren't back at the castle. The Great Hall afforded the most room, if the men were willing to trample over all the fallen women's bodies. "Even Sindri?"

Nissa nodded. "He was doing better. Luuk almost stayed

654

behind, but Master Tailor urged him to go with him." Nissa ran a trembling hand over her cheek. "Darwyn and Tayton stopped by. They told us Jurij was the new lord, and he called for all the men to gather in the village square. That only a hundred could enter the Great Hall at once, but that they should all be there. They would all get their turn." She grimaced. "What are they talking about?"

I patted Nissa's shoulder and stood, noticing her gaze locked on Elgar at my hip. "Go back inside," I said. "I'll try to send Luuk and Coll back to you. I don't want them caught up in this."

"Caught up in what?" Nissa's eyes widened. "Are you going to fight them, like you fought the unseen monsters? By yourself?"

I shook my head. "I won't fight them." *I won't.*

"You can't go alone."

"I must." I stood back. "Please go back inside. *Please.*"

Nissa hesitated, but she did as I asked. I waited until the door to the bakery shut and waited a moment more to make sure she didn't peek her head back out. Satisfied, I headed toward the heart of the village and the Great Hall.

Nissa was right. There were men as far as the eye could see packed in all corners of the center of the village, spilled into the connecting pathways. I had to slink against the wall and push past them to make any progress toward the Great Hall, and I didn't like the look many of the men gave me as I made my way past.

I could feel the tension in the air. Like the men were just one moment away from violence, and I didn't even know why. I didn't know if they knew why. *I don't know if they know who their foes are, or if they care.*

At the very least, none of them held weapons or wore swords at their hips. None of them until Darwyn and Tayton. They stood in front of the doors to the Great Halls, their hands on their sword hilts—who were they threatening to use them on?—their eyes poring over the crowd gathered before them. I crouched as soon as I realized they were there, hiding behind taller men, and drawing a few strange stares as I started crawling between their legs. I didn't want Darwyn and Tayton to see me coming just yet.

"What's taking so long?" a man from the front of the crowd shouted.

"There's a lot to explain." Darwyn held a hand out to stop the man from advancing. "You'll all get your turn, but we have to do it in groups. No more than a hundred can fit inside."

"My wife is in there!" said another man. I was surprised to find a man talk about a wife, considering so few had remarried—although it was entirely possible his wife wasn't originally his goddess.

"The women are safe," said Tayton. "Part of the reason everything is taking so long is Jaron asked those invited to help move the fallen women to the back of the Great Hall, out of the way of the meeting."

I froze. Elgar poked obnoxiously into my sopping thigh. Would the women be in danger if they were present for Jurij's reveal of the truth, even if they were unconscious? *Jurij, you fool.*

A man raised his foot and stared down at me to let me pass. He startled me as he crouched down beside me and whispered, "Noll? What are you doing?"

It was Luuk. A "man" indeed. He was certainly tall enough to be one. "I thought you'd be inside," I answered.

Luuk furrowed his brow. "Father went inside. He was worried about Jurij. He told me to go back to the bakery, but I..."

"You're worried about them." I tucked my legs underneath me and sat down, my progress halted. My eyes danced over the Great Hall, which never had a single window built into it, seeing as how it used to be a safe place for men and boys to gather without their masks when the danger of women looking at them loomed. There was just that one door Darwyn and Tayton were guarding.

"You need to get inside." Luuk studied Darwyn and Tayton at the door through the legs of the men in front of us.

"I have to try to stop them." I noticed the immediate effect my words had on Luuk, the way his shoulders tensed, as if I were confirming his fear about the situation. "And you must stay out of there. It's not safe. Promise me."

"I promise." Luuk met my eyes and looked away, sheepishly. I could see the features he shared with his brother, ones that had somehow evolved in the past few years from boyish to breathtakingly handsome. "But I'll help you get in there."

"How?"

Luuk screwed up his features into an echo of his brother's recent determination. He stood and adjusted his jerkin. "Leave it to me."

He pushed forward through the men in front of us and made his way to the Great Hall door.

CHAPTER TWENTY-EIGHT

"Jurij claims to be our new lord." A hush fell over the crowd as Luuk walked toward Darwyn and Tayton. I crouched slightly as I continued to push my way past a few more men who stood between me and that door. "Why should we believe him?" Luuk said loudly.

I was close enough now to see Darwyn's stunned features. He spoke with a softer voice than Luuk had, but I was just one row away and I could hear him. "Luuk, what are you doing?"

Luuk gestured to the crowd of men, like a leader before an audience. "Where is our *real* lord? He came down to visit us after our tragedy; he helped us get this village built again. Were we dissatisfied with him? I don't think so! Why is Jurij presuming to take his place?"

A number of men began murmuring to one another, and Tayton stepped forward to lay a hand on Luuk's shoulder. "Why are you acting like this?" He seemed worried, afraid even. "He's your own brother!"

Luuk spun on him. "Yes. He's my *brother*, not my *lord*!"

"Yeah!" said a man from the crowd. "Who made *him* lord?"

"What happened to the old lord? If he wanted Jurij to take his place, why isn't he out here telling us that?"

"I thought he was marrying the Woodcarver woman!"

Darwyn stepped in front of Luuk. "Calm down now. You'll all get a turn to ask your questions."

"Why are we waiting out here anyway?" said one man. "Why did they get to go in first?"

Tayton rolled his eyes and blew out a breath. "They weren't singled out. We let in as many as would fit, as many as could wear the bangles—"

Darwyn cut him off with a hand to his chest. "Be patient. You will be allowed in soon."

"Why should I be patient? My wife is in there!" It was the man who'd spoken about his wife before. "I dared to go back home for a blanket for just a short time, and now you won't let me back in!"

Darwyn stepped down the step toward the man. "You'll be able to go back in again—"

"No!" The man shoved Darwyn, and he fell on his backside, wincing as the scabbard twisted uncomfortably between his thighs.

"Darwyn!" Tayton let go of Luuk and ran after his love, tugging at his sword as he did. It got stuck and his hand fumbled, but eventually he pulled it all the way out.

"What is *that*?" asked a man standing near Tayton. He took a step back, his eyes transfixed.

"Tayton, put that back." Darwyn rolled over onto his knees, about to stand up. "They said not to brandish those about like toys."

"It's worse than the tavern!" screamed a burly man. "I was there!" His eyes went wide and he cradled his head with his hands. "That's like a huge knife! Men stabbed other men with their knives, the knives they'd used to cut the meat on their tables!"

"This isn't like the tavern," said Darwyn quickly, using Tayton's arm to scramble to his feet. He held his hands out toward the man. "Now I just need you to calm down."

"Noll," hissed Luuk in my ear. At some point he'd crossed back toward me, the men in front of me pushing him aside to get closer to the conflict. Luuk grabbed my wrist. "Come on!"

"But…" We used the shifting crowd for cover and managed to get up the stairs and to the door behind the line of men advancing on Darwyn and Tayton. I ripped my hand out from Luuk's as he reached for the door. "No! Luuk, these men could hurt each other. They could hurt Darwyn and Tayton. I didn't want this—"

I was cut short as Luuk stared pointedly at the sword I carried at my waist.

"We need it," said Luuk grimly. "We need this distraction. I'll try my best to calm them," he said, "but you must get inside."

"That's a sword!" shouted a man from somewhere behind us. "Like in those tales—do you remember? The tales of kings and queens and battling monsters?"

"Do they think we're monsters?"

"They both have one!"

"I saw Jurij with one, too. And Jaron!"

"Get those away from them!"

"Ow! It cut me!"

"Tayton!"

Luuk had already opened the door, and he put a hand on my back. "Inside!" he said, and before I could protest, I fell forward and the door shut behind me.

A room of a hundred men went silent and turned around to face me.

My eyes roved over all of them, over the shapes of the fallen women strewn out far in the back of the Great Hall, over Jurij, Jaron and Sindri, who stood before them.

"Noll?" Jurij's voice echoed loudly in the silence of the Great Hall.

As the echo faded, I could make out some of the grunting from outside.

I pointed to the door behind me and gritted my teeth. "There's trouble out there! It may lead to more violence!"

Jurij's face went ashen, but Jaron was hardly bothered by the news. He turned and whispered to Jurij, who turned to two specters standing behind him. "See to it," he said. "Summon as many of the others as you need. Keep everyone calm and stop them from harming one another."

I moved as far from the door as the crowd would allow to let the two specters past, afraid one or both of them might grab me and take me back to the castle while they were at it.

Why had he left so many specters behind at the castle? I hadn't noticed a single one outside. And if he was trying to keep what he said secret, why have the two with him? Did Jurij really want them to overhear what he was telling these men and report back to the kings and queens?

I strode forward, pushing into the gap the crowd had made to let the specters pass. "Jurij! You've put all these men at risk!" My eyes fell on the women behind him as I came to a stop in front of the crowd. "All these *people* at risk!"

"It's not our intention to harm anyone." Sindri rubbed his bruised neck. I wondered if that was intentional or a subconscious reminder of the harm he'd experienced himself. I noticed a golden bangle dangle from his wrist.

"Intentional or not, you haven't thought this through." I eyed Jurij and Jaron, waiting for either to dare to contradict me. I faced the crowd of men. "Whatever they've told you, did they also tell you that wearing those golden bangles is the only thing keeping you from harm?" I pointed behind me at Sindri. "Some of you might have seen what happened to Sindri here the other night. A lord's servant attacked him because he discussed something he shouldn't have when he wasn't wearing that golden bangle."

"We know that now," said Jaron smugly. "We've told them once they remove the bangles, they can't talk about what we've told them."

"And you expect them to be able to keep quiet?" I stared at Sindri, thinking of hundreds of men with specters' hands around their necks.

"I don't really get why we have to keep quiet!" shouted a man from the front of the crowd. I watched him rub a hand over the bangle at his wrist. "Or why we have to give these back."

"We went over this," said Jurij, stepping forward. "You pass them on to the next wave of men to come inside, so they can hear what you've heard—"

"Sounds pretty ridiculous and complex to me," spat one man. He nodded toward Jurij. "And why just the men? What if I want the woman I love to know all this?"

Jaron joined Jurij closer at the edge of the crowd, pushing him back with a hand to his chest. "Because women didn't really have to suffer through all those years of the curse, did they?"

The man raised both eyebrows. "I don't agree! My Mariah suffered plenty, forced to be with some dolt she didn't care about—"

"Hey!" snapped a man several rows over. "I *was* that dolt. I mean, that man! Although I should thank you for taking that bitch out of my life."

"Watch your mouth!" The first man shoved through several others to get toward his lover's former man. He slowed down as he got nearer, the men between the two attempting to stop the man from advancing.

"We aren't here to discuss women!" shouted Jaron over the noise of the crowd.

"*I* am!" said a man from beside Jaron. "I don't care about any of this—I want to know what you're doing to save my daughters!"

Jaron looked as if the man had slapped him. "You don't care? You don't care that we were cursed to be women's slaves because of the whims of the first goddess?"

My eyes caught Sindri's warily, eager to see how he reacted. He noticed and bent toward me, whispering slightly. "We haven't said anything about you in particular. Although Jaron objected— he's quite adamant we share all we now know. But Jurij insisted we keep your name out of it."

I let out a breath I didn't even realize had caught in my throat. I studied Jurij and Jaron as they moved around the front of the crowd. Jaron burnt with so much more anger than Jurij. So much more righteousness. Jurij was practically his helpless, quiet child-hood self beside the bossy leader. The leader Jurij was convinced had no interest in leading.

Sindri nudged me and I looked up to see him studying me like I was a brand new species of cow. "I *still* can't believe that about you, by the way—"

I lay a hand on his arm to stop him. The man upset about his daughters shook the bangle off his arm with a flourish and slammed it to the ground. It echoed so loudly, the crowd went silent. "No, I don't care! I don't care about what happened—I care about my daughters! I care about my former wife!" He gestured at the fallen women behind us. "I care that there are women in our village who can't wake up!"

"Speak for yourself!" said one man. "I want to know what happened!"

"Now isn't the time," said another. "We have to work together."

"What can we do?" Jaron clenched his fists. "For the women? Nothing. Except accept this as a sign that maybe it's time for the men to take charge of this village again."

"Take charge?" Jurij put a hand on Jaron's elbow. "What are you talking about? This is just about sharing the truth."

Jaron spun on his heel, shaking Jurij's hand away. "Yeah, well, the truth ain't pretty. And I've had enough—"

Jurij raised a finger and Jaron went quiet. They both strained their heads slightly, and it took me a moment, but soon I heard it, too: roaring from outside the Great Hall, like a crowd in anger. A sound I hadn't heard since my time spent in the past, only this crowd was filled with deeper voices. I felt sick.

Coll stepped out from the crowd. I hadn't even noticed him in the front row. "Luuk!" he said, pushing through the crowd to get back to the Great Hall door.

"Father!" Jurij ran after him.

Master Tailor threw the door open. I heard the gasps of men in the crowd before I saw it. I couldn't make it out well from where I was standing, but the village center was a flurry of movement. A flurry of white movement, dotting the masses. The specters were in the middle of the crowd, *fighting*.

I didn't care who started it, or if the specters were only trying to quell rising violence. Luuk and I had given way to that violence, and I'd never forgive myself if anyone else got hurt. Or worse. I ran forward, hitting the back of the crowd as it spilled out into the village center. Before I was even halfway there, though, an arm flew down over my head, grabbing me across my shoulders.

"This is familiar." I recognized Jaron's voice at once, along with the stance. Sure enough, he drew his blade and held it out in front of me.

"These are rather inconvenient. They ought to be designed to be shorter." He sighed and started pulling me back, away from the merging crowds. Jurij and Coll had passed through and were beyond my sight. "Come on, first goddess. We have a few things to discuss."

"Jurij!" I screamed, but I didn't know if he heard me.

CHAPTER TWENTY-NINE

"What are you doing? Are you mad?" Sindri stormed up to us as Jaron dragged me back toward the fallen women.

"Relax," said Jaron as he shoved me to the ground near a woman I didn't recognize. "I kept quiet about her to the crowd, didn't I?" He pointed the tip of his sword at me. "That doesn't mean I think she shouldn't be willing to talk to me."

Sindri looked about ready to rip his hair out. His eyes darted toward the door, as the last of the men interested in leaving made their way out to see what was going on. A few of the men had rushed to the back of the hall and now held the hands or stroked the foreheads of some of the women lying near me. None of them seemed to pay us much mind, but I noticed the man who had removed his bangle among them. And then I checked—there was a golden bangle unclaimed where he'd tossed it to the floor.

Either my eyes gave me away or Jaron thought much the same as I did at the same time. He stomped over toward the bangle and picked it up, sliding it on the hand without one. "Does this make me twice as worthy?" he asked to the sky. He knew about those who were watching, then.

Were the kings still distracted? Had they made the specters fight with the men? Or was it simply the specters defending themselves and the other men from the anxious crowd? Or were the specters on the side of the queens, or was it just Spurn? I couldn't keep my mind from racing.

I did find strength of mind enough to scramble to my feet, pulling out Elgar as I did.

Sindri stepped back as if I'd slapped him. "Goddess save us, that thing is glowing!"

Jaron stomped over, his own sword held clumsily with both hands. "The Goddess won't save us. *She's* the one threatening us with a sword."

I looked between Jaron and Sindri, unhappy to find Sindri's own hand clutching the hilt of his sword. "I'm not threatening anyone," I pointed out. "I'm defending myself against you."

With the doors open, the noise of the crowd outside was even more uproarious. I couldn't spare a moment to glance at it with Jaron and even Sindri staring me down. I backed up, my backside hitting against something—probably the table on which Vena and Elweard had prepared meals not so very long ago.

Jaron moved closer, and Sindri stepped between us, one hand on the top of his hilt, the other against Jaron's chest. "Now's not the time for this." He gazed over Jaron's shoulder. "We've got to calm them down—and get those bangles back!"

"No." Jaron shoved Sindri's hand aside. "Now's the perfect time for this. Jurij would never let me question her—" A high-pitched scream from the Great Hall door cut Jaron off. Sindri's face paled. Leaving me to face my would-be attacker alone, Sindri sprinted for the door.

Roslyn tumbled inside the Great Hall, clutching her arm. Sindri crouched down beside her, gathering her in his embrace.

The clack of Jaron's sword on mine snapped my attention back to my predicament. Even though I'd encouraged women to arm themselves with farm tools, even though I'd had stick-blade battles, I had never really heard the sound of sword on sword. It wasn't at all the elegant cling of metal on metal that I expected— more like the hollow whack of an axe on a tree.

I gripped my sword harder and Jaron failed to knock it out of my grasp as he'd intended. At least, I hoped that was what he intended. "Do you want to kill me?" I spoke loudly so my voice could be heard over the roar.

"Kill you?" Jaron lowered his sword just slightly, but it was no longer at level with my own. "Kill Aubree's daughter? She'd never forgive me. I don't *want* that."

"I'd like to think you wouldn't want to kill me, no matter whose daughter I was. Besides, my mother is in no mood for forgiveness since you indirectly caused my father's death."

"She never loved him."

"Yes, she did!" It was strange how despite everything that was going on, such a comment could still cause my knees to tremble.

Jaron let go of his sword with one hand to point at his chest. "She loved me!"

I opened my mouth before quickly snapping it shut. Mother had said as much. "That doesn't mean she didn't love Father, too."

Jaron shrugged. "I don't care. If things had been different, she wouldn't have. I could have returned the feelings of a woman who actually cared about me."

I scoffed. "How do you even remember my mother's childhood affections for you? Weren't decades of your life since consumed with thoughts of Alvilda?"

It was the wrong thing to say. Jaron's handsome face twisted, and a dark cloud passed over his features as he went back to gripping his sword with two hands. "Exactly. And whose fault was that? Yours, I discovered."

"I didn't mean for anyone to suffer." I wanted to stand my ground, but I found myself leaning even further back into the table. I had to drop a hand from Elgar to put it on the table behind me to steady myself. "Not anyone who didn't deserve it, anyway."

Jaron rolled his eyes. "So an entire gender? Every man deserved it?"

"No." A flurry of movement from far behind Jaron drew my eyes over his shoulder. "But the way you've been acting since you got your freedom, *you* might."

He roared and raised his sword again toward mine, jabbing at me like a boy poking a sheep with a stick. I wasn't much more skilled, but I managed to move sideways and roll my sword around his. I started making my way along the edge of the table, eager to put it between us. But it was a long, long table. "What is wrong with you?" I demanded. "I thought you were happy courting all the women in town!"

Jaron advanced on me, one slow step at a time. "Yes, a few months of fun makes up for a lifetime of torment." He thumped at his chest. "I want to experience the kind of love promised to me as a man who worshipped a goddess. The perfect love. A life-time of happiness. I did nothing wrong! I should have been judged worthy."

"You can't blame Alvilda for that." I reached back to see how much more of the table I had left. "She loved someone else."

"Then I can blame the one who cursed me to be that way."

I finally reached the corner of the table. "That wasn't real love anyway." I slipped slowly around the edge, hoping he wouldn't notice. "Real love isn't all happy. It's full of pain and disagree-ments and it *hurts*." I clenched the damp shawl at my chest and finally succeeded in putting the table between us. "It hurts, but it's worth the fight. It's worth coming to a true understanding of yourself and what you're willing to give up." Hot tears burned my cheek and I blinked hard so I wouldn't lose sight of the man across from me. "You're wrong if you think anyone deserves a perfect love."

"Enough of your squirming!" Jaron lifted his sword high above his head. "Put that thing down and tell me why! Tell me why you did this!"

The sword came down and I rolled, tossing Elgar to the floor beneath the table and coming to a stop when I bumped into a woman lying prone on the floor. Jaron's sword made a racket as it clanged against the table again and again. The racket stopped with a sudden thunk. I scrambled to my feet to see the tip of his sword stuck in the wood of the table.

"What are you doing?" Jurij appeared at Jaron's side, and he wrapped his arms around the shorter man's torso, ripping him away from his stuck sword. Jaron fought back, grabbing at the table, knocking down a lot of the plates and utensils and souring food that Vena and Elweard must have left when Vena fell ill. Jaron spread his hands out over the table, trying to grip it, but Jurij pulled him to the ground.

I scrambled to pick up Elgar before I jumped back up and

took in the scene. Jurij and Jaron rolled as one on the ground with Coll, Luuk, Sindri and Roslyn looking on in horror.

"Get off him!" Roslyn clutched her arm. A makeshift bandage made of cloth was dyed red. I had no idea which wrestling man she was speaking to.

Coll bent down and grabbed Jaron's shoulders when he rolled on top. "You need to calm down!"

Sindri patted Roslyn's hip and joined Coll in peeling Jaron away from Jurij. Jaron looked like a bull in heat, his face flushed and his breath labored. Jurij's false-lord clothing was torn, his hair sticking up in all directions. He stood, staring at Jaron like the man had bit him. Maybe he had.

Jaron took a deep breath and ripped his arms out of Coll's and Sindri's grasp. He huffed but said nothing.

"Darwyn's hurt," said Sindri, his voice cracking. "Pretty bad. We can't find Tayton."

"There are men's clothes out there!" Roslyn burst into tears. She couldn't mean—had men *died*? Again? My heart pounded. "They made such a racket, I had to come and find out what was going on, to see if Sin—if any of you were injured, and I couldn't even walk through the crowd without someone shoving me over and another man trampling me."

Sindri's throat bobbed as he watched Roslyn, and I wondered how they'd gone from acquaintances—former family, I suppose, since they'd married each other's siblings—to a couple in love in such a short time. It wasn't even like a young man finding his goddess. There was something more harrowing, more real about the way the two of them looked at one another.

"What is going on exactly?" The voice came from behind me. The man concerned about his daughters had joined a couple of the others who'd stayed behind. Together, they approached our group. Their faces paled as they looked out the Great Hall doors. "This is worse than the tavern!"

One of the men got ahold of himself pretty quickly. He marched over to Jaron and jabbed him in the chest. "This is because of you! Because you insisted we know these things! What are we supposed to do now that we know? How does that help us? How does that save our women?"

Jaron flicked the man's finger away. "Knowing the truth is

always better than living in ignorance. Hang the consequences. Hang your daughters."

The man raised his fist, drew it back and slammed it into Jaron's jaw. Jaron staggered back and cradled his jaw, and everyone else went still.

When Jaron spit, it was the color of blood. "You don't care about how we got to be cursed? Fine. You care about how your daughters got sick? It was her." Jaron's eyes narrowed as he looked at me. "Noll was the cause of both problems."

The man turned on me. "Is this true?"

"Jaron!" Jurij gripped Jaron by the front of his jerkin, nearly hanging the stocky man in the air a few inches. "I told you to leave her out of it."

"Why?" said Jaron, not seeming to mind in the least that Jurij was snarling at him. "She doesn't love you, you know."

"I don't care!" snapped Jurij. "That isn't why! I love her. She's my friend. My dearest friend." He spared me a quick glance in the midst of all this anger. I smiled despite myself. "And I love her sister, too. I don't care if they don't love me anymore. I won't let you do anything to harm either of them."

"Ha!" Jaron turned his head and spit blood again. "You're nothing but a man besotted by goddesses, even with the freedom to choose otherwise." He grabbed Jurij's wrist and their two bangles clanged together. "You don't deserve this." He shook Jurij's too-loose bangle.

Jurij opened his mouth and choked out a gurgle a moment later. I didn't understand what had happened, but I recognized the pain on his face.

"Jurij!" screamed Coll and Luuk as one, and they pushed Jaron back to give Jurij space. Jaron held Jurij's bangle between his fingers. He slid it over his arm, his other hand splotched with... blood.

Elgar slipped from my grip. I watched in horror as Jurij grabbed hold of the handle of a meat knife that stuck out of his abdomen and pulled it out, falling to his knees and then face forward into the ground. His hand moved slightly toward me before he vanished into nothingness.

CHAPTER THIRTY

"Jurij!" I ran around the table to the flattened pile of black clothing, skidding and stumbling to my knees. I patted the clothes with both hands, like he was hiding somewhere beneath them.

"What have you done?" I clenched my teeth and tried to stare at Jaron through the tears. He was nothing but a formless lump above me.

Jaron spoke quietly, but the Great Hall had gone so silent, it was easy to hear him even over the din of the outside fight. "I made myself the lord of the village."

"That's not how it works!" I screamed. "You can't kill the lord and become him."

The ground shook, and I tumbled, falling onto Jurij's clothing. I inhaled Jurij's scent and images of lying together in the fields overwhelmed me. *He can't be dead. He can't be.*

And Elfriede would soon follow. And Ailill—but even if he lived, I could never spend time with him again. Even though they'd granted me my life, the kings and queens would leave me nothing to live for. The shaking of the ground would not cease, and I wanted to melt into the floor and be swallowed up by the movement.

Were the kings no longer distracted? Was this them ripping up petals because I was here, even if I wasn't acting like a leader? Was this them angry because of what Jaron had done? Did they only realize there was something amiss in the village once Jurij showed up naked in their garden—

Jurij was in their garden. He wasn't dead. Not really. He never would be. And there was a chance he could be given life right here again.

As a baby. As a new person.

No. I shot up, not caring that my legs were wobbling. *They'd keep him long enough to talk to him—he was the lord for a time, after all, and he'd be worried about all of us. They'd gone out of their way to comfort that woman a little before they sent her to a new life. He's still there.*

And I will get there. I will save him, Elfriede, and Ailill—everyone. Even if it's the last thing I do.

The quake ceased and I tumbled, but Luuk shot out to catch me. His face was lined with tears. "This is my fault," he said. "You warned me not to make the crowd violent."

"*No.*" I pulled away from Luuk. "No. It's not your fault. They were already agitated. And I'm going to make it right."

"How? Jurij's dead!"

I ignored him and stepped over the broken plates and strewn food to get back to the other side of the table, to put Elgar in my grip once more. The men who'd been at the women's sides rolled the shifted women onto their backs, checking for breathing, their faces panicked. I left them to it and walked past the gawking group gathered around Jurij's clothes to the Great Hall door.

"Where are you going?" sneered Jaron from behind me. "I order you to get back here!"

"You shut your mouth!" said a quaking, deep voice.

I paused just long enough to look over my shoulder, to see Coll gripping Jaron by the jerkin, much as his son had moments before. Coll was even taller and bulkier than his son, so he really did lift Jaron up off the ground. "You killed my son!" screeched Coll. "You were never right, not since you got your freedom! You never understood that we all suffered in our own ways, that it wasn't just you and the others who'd been in the commune!"

"You think I care about that? You think I care about—" Jaron didn't get to finish. Luuk appeared around his father's side and then Jaron's mouth opened and he vanished. Coll was left holding his empty clothing and he tossed them to the floor as the three golden bangles went rolling. Luuk threw down the same knife Jaron had used on Jurij on top of the clothing just as two of the bangles came to a stop at my heel.

I stared at them, then bent down and picked them both up, sliding them over my wrist.

Luuk has killed, I thought as I stood. *A killer made him a killer.* I limped forward, only just aware of the throbbing in my knees—I must have bruised them again in the fall when the ground started shaking—but I kept moving, shuffling forward, dragging Elgar along the ground at my side. *I can undo this. I can even make sure Jaron is reborn somewhere else. Somewhere he won't be so unhappy. I can give Luuk that solace. And I can bring Jurij back.*

I just had to make my way through the throng of specters and men fighting to get there.

~

I GOT SHOVED A FEW TIMES, but getting through the rabble was less problematic than I pictured. It was almost like I was invisible, dragging my glowing, violet sword along the ground. While fights happened on one side or the other, the men and specters somehow gave me enough berth.

The closest I got to injury was when a man threw a specter onto a vegetable stand in front of me, breaking the stand and sending pieces of wood flying. I thought the specter was bleeding, but it turned out to be squished tomatoes.

The specter met my eyes and I laughed bitterly. It was Spurn.

"Thank you for encouraging this problem." I shook my wrist with the bangles, letting them glitter in the midday sunlight. "Feel like answering to this candidate for ruler of the village or one of the hundred or so behind me? I need your help getting back to the castle."

Spurn stood, brushing the front of his coat with his hands in vain. The back of him was dyed red with tomatoes. I took that as a sign of his agreeing to follow and moved on, dodging the last of the crowd and avoiding the road that led to the bakery, lest I bump into Siofra or Nissa.

The village was quiet the farther away we got from the heart of the village. I blinked back tears even as my head pounded. I couldn't think about whether or not the specters and villagers would stop fighting. Whether or not there were piles of clothing and more dead villagers in the wake of what had happened. The kings and queens were aware of it now, were aware of my coming, for sure. I couldn't stop. I wouldn't stop.

We ran into no one between the edge of the village and the woods. I laughed as the idea of changing clothes once again danced through my mind as we passed the empty, dark cottage that was my home. I may as well not. I was about to jump into that pond again anyway.

Except that before I could even put a foot off the path, Spurn grabbed my arm. "This way," he said, each word slow and with emphasis. "Through the throne."

I almost forgot I had the bangles on, and that meant he could talk to me. He let go of my arm as I changed direction. "Won't the specters—the other servants there stop me?"

"Gone," replied Spurn, that voice scratchy again. "To the village."

"To fight the villagers." I picked up my feet. "I can see Ailill."

Spurn spun me to face him. "Gone, too."

I felt like he'd reached into my throat and twisted my heart. "Where? Not to the fight?"

"Faded away. Vanished."

My knees buckled. I would have fallen to the ground and banged my knees again, but Spurn was there to catch me.

"Not reborn yet." Spurn tugged to pull me up. "Still at that place."

Ailill's spirit was with the kings and queens, but they'd been no help to him while alive. What could they possibly want with his spirit now?

"All right." I straightened my shoulders and slid Elgar into its sheath at my waist. "All the more reason for me to go."

Spurn followed me silently through the first set of stairs in the castle, past the room where I'd left Elfriede and my mother. I paused, my hand on the door. I didn't have time to comfort Mother just yet, to explain what was going on. "Are they all right?" I asked Spurn instead.

"Still there," replied Spurn. "Woodcarver's wife not eating. Both sick in different ways."

I removed my trembling hand. I kept walking. *Everyone is dead. Everyone is dying. I'll be left alone in this place. Maybe that's what they wanted.*

When we passed the kitchen and arrived in front of the throne room, I faced Spurn. "Will you come with me?"

Spurn gazed at the throne room behind me. "I cannot."

"Haven't the queens been contacting you? They sent you that note, correct?"

"Yes," said Spurn. "It appeared through here." He opened his coat and showed me his inner pocket. The pocket that seemed to have an endless supply of whatever was needed with each servant, except perhaps for the things that were too big to fit in there. "The gold coin, too. And the feeling that it needed to get to you."

The queens *were* behind it. They were cheating at their own game, surely risking the kings' wrath. Had they lied about it all? Had they orchestrated my travel through time, too, or was Ailill right that the queens didn't trust me because I'd done things on my own, things they couldn't affect?

"Is there anything else in there?" My tears should have dried — at least until I'd given up all hope and despite how hopeless things were, I hadn't given up hope yet—but I had to blink them back as I studied the haggard appearance of my red-stained servant. As I pictured Ailill that older age, with me at his side, and how I was likely to never see it. As I pictured that scared boy who'd become this shadow again.

The inner lining of Spurn's jacket softly glowed violet and he stiffened. I wondered how I'd never seen it before or if you couldn't see the color through the outside of the coat.

"Yes." Spurn reached into his pocket. He pulled out a folded parchment and handed it to me.

My hands shook as I unfolded it, recognizing at once the type of paper that filled the book allowing you to watch over the village. I knew looking at the one in the throne room would show me nothing of Jurij and Jaron—nothing of Ailill—if they were all there in that other place. The kings and queens had their own such books in their castle, though, and I wondered if the same rules applied.

Apparently not. The drawing I saw was of Ailill, his wrists bound to a wall with chains. He was slumped over, and I recognized the place where he was: the prison—only I knew for sure I wouldn't find him down the hall from where I was standing. He was in the prison in that place, in one of the mirrored castles of the kings and queens.

The note at the bottom made that all the clearer.

Here his spirit lies for eternity, out of reach of all men.

"The queens?" I asked, sure that the kings wouldn't have imprisoned their own favored spirit, even if they had experimented with Jurij taking his place.

Spurn nodded as his coat pocket glowed violet again. He reached inside and pulled out a small knife, no larger than what one would use to peel vegetables. Along with the knife, there was another parchment, and Spurn handed that and that alone to me.

"Why the knife?" I said, leering at it. I took the paper with cautious fingers.

I kept watching Spurn as I unfolded it, not ready to totally trust he wouldn't stab me the moment I looked away.

Yet I had to see what they wanted me to know. This drawing showed Jurij, with Jaron next to him, in the garden on the bench. The kings and queens were there—at least some of them were; the others may have stood beyond the page's point of view. The note at the bottom of this one was in a different handwriting than the other.

"When I was lord," said Spurn. "I dreamed of you."

You shall be left alone, for all that you have done, read the message.

"Farewell, my lady."

Spurn plunged the knife into his chest.

CHAPTER THIRTY-ONE

I trampled over Spurn's white clothes, stained red with tomatoes that reminded me of blood—blood that would have been there, had Spurn been anyone but a specter, a shade of a man that once was. The servants had all vanished with Ailill in the cavern after Jurij stabbed him, but they hadn't vanished when Ailill had this time, nor when Jurij had—if the vanishing was tied to whoever was lord. The kings and queens seemed to have lost all sense of fairness and rules at the moment, ignoring whatever it was they'd decided would be the servants' fate—forcing Spurn to put on a show. I could see the anger on their faces even in the drawing in my hands—the one where they stood around Jurij and Jaron, taunting me to come and save them. To come and face them.

It was hard to push the throne aside without help, but I managed, summoning a strength in my arms from the anger coursing through my entire body.

I didn't even hesitate to step in. I didn't expect to encounter any resistance, any red glow. They wouldn't have taunted me otherwise. They could have simply killed me where I stood.

The edge of the cave glowed violet as I approached the Never Veil, and I stepped through it, hesitating only to touch Elgar's hilt.

No. I won't step in, my sword out and ready. These are creatures of non-violence, who enjoy making others do their violent work for them. I won't give them the satisfaction.

I stepped through.

~

I CAME out through the door to the shared entryway of the kings' and queens' castles, not directly into the garden where they were with Jurij and Jaron, as I'd expected to.

Whether that was by accident or on purpose—or if I'd taken fate into my own hands—I wasn't about to throw the chance away.

Jurij and Jaron are there to tempt me to them, but the queens showed me Ailill for a reason.

I glanced up the stairs to the left—the ones I'd seen the queens descend—and tucked the two parchments into my pocket. No one came out from the garden to stop me, so I made my way up.

There was a black veil at the top of the stairs, and I hesitated for a moment, worried that stepping through would take me somewhere else, but I had no other ideas.

No. You'll make *it so you step through to the queens' castle. It doesn't matter what anyone else might have in mind.*

I filled my mind with images of Ailill and stepped through. Nothing appeared to have happened. It was just like I'd passed through a curtain with no greater power threaded through it at all.

The hall was empty. Torches lit the way along the wall. I didn't know how long it would take before the kings and queens were after me, so I picked up my skirt and ran.

I came quickly to a halt as I passed an open room. There were three black thrones at the back of a long room that looked almost exactly like Ailill's throne room, but for the fact that there were three seats instead of one. I was already on the floor that mirrored Ailill's castle's third floor, even though I'd just stepped onto the second.

Well, the queens surely have no need for so many bedrooms.

I tried hard to think of what the castle had looked like from the outside, how I thought it was like two of Ailill's castles merged and mirrored into one. I'd missed that there was no third floor.

I suppose this way the throne room and the prison are closer to the ground floor, like they were in tales of kings and queens we used to play to. But they'd never be on the ground floor here, not if that was shared space. Now that I was closer, I wanted to be sure I would indeed find a door to the prison waiting for me beyond the throne room. It was there. I let out a breath caught in my throat and ran toward it.

The door opened so easily in my grasp.

"Ailill!"

There was no answer as I tumbled into the room. No light but the dying flicker of a single torch on the wall. I grabbed it and swung the light toward the first cell. Nothing. I tried the second. Nothing still. *They deceived me.*

My breath hitched as I stood before the third cell. Ailill was there, his hands chained above him as they had been in the drawing. The thought flickered through my mind that he ought to be naked—like this was the time to worry about that—if his spirit had come here, but someone had clothed him in specter garb—the lord's outfit pale as snow.

"Ailill!"

Ailill's slumped-forward head lilted slightly.

I grabbed hold of the prison door, not sure why I assumed I'd find it unlocked. I shook the bars to no avail. "Argh!" I'd come too far for this. I stepped back, drew Elgar out from my sheath and slammed it against the keyhole, like that would make a difference.

It'll make a difference, I told myself, as I slammed the sword against the keyhole again and again, watching the violet glow in the near-darkness. *Because I decide it does.*

Lo and behold, the door swung back. I didn't even bother to marvel at it. I was through the door, Elgar tossed aside, and my hands on Ailill's cheeks as I lifted his head up. "Ailill, can you hear me?"

His eyelids fluttered open. "Noll...?"

I smiled. "I thought we agreed I liked it when you called me Olivière."

The very corners of Ailill's lips twitched. "Too much… to say. Can't speak… Queens' castle… bad for men."

He was speaking in contractions. He was definitely dire.

I stood, reaching for the metal around his wrist. There was a keyhole on each of those, too, and they wouldn't budge. I picked up Elgar and swung it up.

Ailill's head lolled forward a little. "No sword! No… Just you. Just you."

I laughed despite the terribleness of the situation. I expect he worried I might miss. I sheathed Elgar and decided to trust him.

I grabbed one metal bangle in both hands. *Release him*, I thought. *Release him and open. Let him go.*

My hands glowed warm and violet light appeared from my fingers. I jumped back and let out a yelp as the bangle broke open, and Ailill's arm fell down, free.

He tipped his head up slightly and smiled. "See? Just you. Special."

I scrambled back to my knees and did the same for the other bangle, then caught Ailill around the chest as he fell forward.

"The queens' castle makes you weak?" I asked, not sure how a spirit who was neither truly dead nor alive could be weakened by anything. I positioned myself so one of Ailill's arms wrapped around my shoulders.

"All men." Every word caused Ailill strain, like there was a pain somewhere in his abdomen. "Including kings."

I struggled but managed to stand, bringing us both to our feet. "Where can I bring you that you'll be safe?"

Ailill let out a raspy sound that might have been a laugh. "Nowhere. But I will be stronger past veil. Back in entryway."

"Save your strength, then," I said, and we began the slow journey out of the prison and down the long hall.

No one disturbed us, although I feared a king or queen—just a queen, I supposed—would appear from one of the rooms we passed every few paces. I hadn't for certain seen them all on the page they'd sent me, and in any case, they were bound to start looking for me by now. They must have expected me. The page hung heavy in my pocket. Perhaps I could check to be sure. As soon as my eyes passed over Ailill's face, though, I knew I had to get him toward the veil, no matter what awaited me. I would face them eventually regardless.

Ailill's weight seemed to get less heavy as we approached the veil at the end of the hallway. He still leaned on me, but it wasn't like he was hanging off me anymore. His back straightened somewhat. His head lifted higher.

"Let's stop." Ailill leaned against the wall beside the fluttering veil. I wondered where the flow of air came from.

He's still speaking casually. I leaned against the wall beside him, putting myself between him and the veil in case we had visitors. "Are you feeling better, though?"

"Better." He laid his head against the wall. "As soon as we pass through there, I'll be fine."

"Then why stop here?"

"You need to know a few things before we go out there."

I thought of Jurij and Jaron, and the parchment in my pocket. "You do, too."

Ailill rolled his head back and forth. "I'm not dead."

The corner of my lips twitched. "I can see that."

"No, I mean, I didn't die in our village and vanish. Is that what you thought?"

I frowned. "Yes. Well, that's what Spurn told me."

"Who?"

I felt my cheeks flush at the stupid name. "One of the servants. The... first one, actually. It's just a name I gave him."

Ailill's jaw tightened. "I had a feeling they were developing a little too much personality." He hit his head softly against the wall a few times.

"Just the one," I said. "That I noticed anyway." I'd wanted so badly to find Ailill in Scorn, but it was clear now he was nothing but an empty shell of the man.

Ailill leaned his head toward the veil. "It was them. The queens."

"Why?"

"It happened at the end of the life two lives ago... The life before the one you first knew."

"Do you remember that life?"

Ailill clenched his fist together and rapped it against the wall behind him. "Yes. I mean, I can only remember so much of any life, just like you can only remember so much of yours, but there are snippets of memories of all of them. I'm sorry I lied about that."

I smirked. "You're talking in contractions."

Ailill unclenched his fist. "I'm still a bit weak. It helps save my breath perhaps." He rolled his head slightly and glanced at me. "Besides, I'm not lord anymore."

I scoffed. "I refuse to believe a chess game is all it took."

"That and a bangle." Ailill rubbed a hand over his wrist absently.

I opened my mouth to speak but snapped it shut again, holding up a finger. I strained to listen past the veil to the entryway below. I thought I heard movement, but after a few moments of silence, the tension in Ailill's body relaxed and he resumed talking.

"Before we were reborn to the life you first knew, just as were about to step through the Veil, reborn yet again as a young lord… I saw the queens take that shade of me aside." He shook his head. "I don't know how. They must have sufficiently distracted the kings for long enough. He's been working for them ever since—at least he has been since they've been interfering with us over the past few months."

I tried to remember if I recognized Spurn in any of my memories from my time in the castle, but I could hardly tell them apart back then. Besides, kings and queens in another castle were so far beyond my imagination at the moment; I wasn't looking for traitors amidst the stoic servants. "Do you think he willingly helped them? The first you?"

"Who knows? If so, perhaps he thought it the right course of action. Perhaps he was tired of the kings always bringing us back to life… I know a part of me thought that every rebirth. And he'd been with us the longest, seen the most suffering. Shade or not, that must have impacted him."

Ailill let out an exhausted breath and continued. "In any case, earlier, after you left, he guided me to the hole behind the throne room. He practically had to drag me up the stairs. If only the most important rooms weren't on the third floor of the castle."

"I've wondered about that." Although now was hardly the time. "There are two floors here, but still, why the throne room and the prison on the upper floor? Why not on lower floors, and leave the private rooms to the upper ones?"

"The kitchen, too." Ailill nodded toward the row of doors on the wall. "They keep those next to the throne room. In case they feel like dining without the kings. Or on the kings' side, without the queens."

"So they want the important rooms away from the other gender?"

"I suppose," said Ailill. "And since their guests rarely stay long, they had no need for additional bedrooms beyond that which one floor could provide."

"And the castles for the lords and ladies in the villages do?"

Ailill smiled slyly. "Perhaps those leaders are more social than the lord to whom you were accustomed."

"You're speaking formally again."

Ailill's cheeks darkened just slightly. "The villages' castles simply echo the ones here. The most important rooms are high up, out of the reach of enemies. The prison, too."

"Makes it harder for someone to break your enemies out, I suppose."

"Apparently not. Not with an Ailill going around releasing my prisoners."

I leaned one of my feet flat again the wall behind me. "So Spurn led you to the throne room?"

Ailill pursed his lips. "I went through the Never Veil and instead of arriving in the entryway or the kings' throne room, as I usually do, I came out here." He jutted his chin forward. "Through the queens' throne room."

"Better than in some canyon leagues away, I guess."

"Not if you grow weaker the farther you are from this veil."

I stared at the veil, watched it flutter like someone was on the other side, running her hand across it. Maybe someone was. "So I should steer clear of the kings' castle."

Ailill stood at my side. "You should avoid being there alone, in any case."

"I'll remember that—assuming I can ever go back."

He tugged on my arm. "You might be able to pass through the Never Veil behind the center throne in the queens' throne room. That's where the connection is in the kings' room."

"What about you?"

He bit his lip. "I do not think I could make it through. I will try the kings' side."

"Why did they make Spurn their traitorous servant?" I asked after a moment's thought.

"You, I suspect." Ailill took one of my hands in his. "When they turned him into their pawn, they must have known you were coming soon." His eyebrows cinched together. "Actually, you would have already been there, as a young child. I suppose they recognized you somehow."

"Wait, I was... older than you in your last life?" I cocked my head. In a sense, I was older than this Ailill, too, since he was "born" as a young man when I was already eighteen. So that must have been the case before. He was born as a young man already grown and then had lived as the Ailill I knew for what— ten or so years? So had he died an old man before that in the days since I was born? What if I'd met him as an *old man*, what if I'd been expected to fall in love with him when he looked as if he could have been my grandparent? It was maddening to think about.

Ailill laughed. "I don't think you've ever been or ever will be 'older' than me."

"I was when you were a boy."

Ailill paused and laughed again. "So you were." He traced an unseen pattern on the back of my hand. Whoever had dressed him—even if he hadn't vanished and died, someone *had* changed his clothing—hadn't given him a pair of gloves. I was struck by the bareness of his wrist.

"You don't have a golden token anymore," I said. "So why did the queens draw you here?"

"I am certain they wanted to draw you here again."

I raised an eyebrow. "Despite threatening everyone in my village if I ever dared to think of returning?"

"They said that to make the kings think they were working with them, I suspect."

It didn't make sense. Who ordered Spurn to kill himself? The kings? Because they knew what the queens had done? The queens because they were done with him? "You know what? I don't care. I don't care anymore." I watched Ailill's fingers as they moved over my hand, felt the familiar shiver run up my spine at his touch. I put my other hand on top of his. "I'm tired of their game, Ailill. I'm not going back."

The look of panic on Ailill's face was enough to make my confidence waver. "You have to!" he said.

I turned Ailill's hand in mine so we were holding each other again, palm to palm. "No. They have Jurij and Jaron out there, in the garden, right now. They're waiting for me. Suspiciously patiently." I dropped his hand and slid one of the bangles from my own wrist over his. "But I want you to go."

"Absolutely not!" The volume of Ailill's voice made me flinch.

"The queens think you're here. The kings seem to have forgotten about you entirely. If you come with me to the garden—"

"We'll take them by surprise. Perhaps." A faltering smile appeared on Ailill's face. "We go together."

I wanted to say no. I wanted to shove him through a hole in the wall, but there was no way I could send him somewhere he'd be out of the kings' and queens' reach.

"All right." I straightened my shoulders and stood at his side. "Together." We stepped through the veil to the staircase.

CHAPTER THIRTY-TWO

Marigold waited FOR us at the bottom of the stairs. Estavan stood as her reflection at the bottom of the kings' staircase.

"We have awaited your arrival," said Marigold. She gestured to Estavan beside her. "The kings did not think it fair that any of us should go see what delayed you in our castle, since they cannot witness it themselves."

Ailill dropped my hand to pat my arm as he took the lead, crossing over in front of me. "Did you know they had locked me up in there?" he asked Estavan.

Estavan studied Marigold, who refused to acknowledge him. "We have been discussing that. We agreed to let Olivière remove you from the queens' castle as soon as we discovered it, since we could not do so."

"You brought Ailill to your castle many a time out of our reach," said Marigold curtly. "You did not find us complaining about it."

Estavan's lips curled into a sneer. "That was different, and you know it."

I gave Marigold a wide berth as I shuffled toward the garden door. I was tired of the petty arguments between these selfish figures. "Are Jaron and Jurij still there?"

Marigold looked like she was holding in a sneeze. "They are." She clasped her hands together in front of her. "They could not have peace in their new lives until they knew what became of those in their old ones."

They won't have peace in their new lives because I'm sending them back to their old ones. Somehow. Even Jaron. Maybe.

I ran to the garden door and tugged it open.

"Olivière, wait!" Ailill's urgent cry went unheeded.

I blinked twice as my eyes adjusted to the bright sunlight. This land where the kings and queens dwelled was hot and dry and harsh, and it was far brighter than home.

"Noll!" The sound of Jurij's wavering voice was so like his old self. I ignored the standing figures to sit on the bench next to him, wrapping my arms around him. He hugged me back, and it was like all of the terrible things between us, all of the awkward moments, were gone. I pulled back, feeling his face, wondering at the physical form his spirit had in my hands. He had no scar over his eye and cheek now, as if vanishing to this place took all of the hurt from the old life away.

My eyes were drawn to the shifting figure seated behind him and I dropped my hands. "Why did they seat you next to *him*?"

Jaron sat bent over, his elbows atop his legs spread slightly apart, his arms dangling down between his knees. "Hello to you, too, Noll."

"Here are your answers, Jaron." I faced the kings and queens. Marigold and Estavan joined the other four, just as Ailill appeared at my side beside the table. "I hope you were as kind to them as you were to us when you were demanding them."

"I told Jurij I was sorry." Jaron's voice was gruff, with just a hint of the emptiness I remembered from his time in the commune.

"And you accepted his apology?" I asked Jurij.

Jurij rubbed his palms together, his eyes flickering quickly toward the standing figures in front of us before looking down at the ground. "It doesn't really matter now, does it?"

"I disagree." I felt my face go hot as I realized both Jaron and Jurij were naked. I'd just hugged Jurij while he was *naked*. I'd been so glad to see him I hadn't even thought about it. "Ailill, spare your jacket?"

Ailill shrugged out of his white jacket, half a smile poking at his face. "I should really get you one of your own. But then, you would not keep that one, either." He took to the task rather awkwardly, turning away from the kings and queens and then keeping one hand behind his back as he finished. The hand with the bangle.

I grabbed it from him and put it around Jurij's shoulders. I didn't look down. I refused to look too closely at his lap. Jaron could spend eternity in the nude for all I cared.

"Are you finished?" asked Adeyemi. "You have a lot to answer for."

"All right," I said, eyeing Jangmi. "I will be happy to give you all of your answers."

Jangmi stepped in front of Adeyemi, her hands clutched in front of her abdomen. "We agreed," she said to him. "No more discussions with her. We shall decide her fate as a group. She is here. She will stay here until we have decided."

Apparently the queens were still eager to conceal the full extent of their involvement.

"There is far more than that to discuss," said Kin. "Do not think we will let your abduction of Ailill go. You violated the rules."

"You had already selected a new lord for that village by then," Chrysilla remarked dryly. "I see no rules broken."

Jangmi held up a hand. "We shall discuss it all. Let us adjourn to the dining room."

"Very well," said Adeyemi. He nodded toward me. "She must give up her stolen token."

Jangmi held both hands out and I didn't hesitate to slide the bangle off and give it to her this time. I wasn't going to risk their wrath again, and besides, I didn't care if I never went back. I'd stay until I fixed everything.

Ailill moved closer to me, laying his hand without the bangle on my shoulder. No one spoke as the three kings and three queens stepped through the door back to the entryway of the castle. No one spoke for a moment more after the door shut, either. I wrapped my hand around Ailill's wrist with the bangle and smiled up at him.

He turned and slid it off, putting it into my hands.

"Didn't they tell you to give that to them?" Jaron seemed to have woken up from his stupor.

"This is a different one." I stood. "And we'll have to act fast." I ran over to the garden door and started gently probing it. I was afraid of making too much noise, that trying too hard to turn it into a portal would attract the kings' and queens' attention. And the door seemed to be in no mood to turn into the veil.

"Act fast to do what?" Jaron was incredulous. I tried not to look at him much, though. Not just because I was angry at him, but because I had no interest in seeing him nude, no matter how lovely the men of my village were. I didn't like noticing that about someone who'd done so much harm to those I loved.

I gave up on the door and ran to the bush with the purple lilies and caressed the fragrant flowers. I spoke to Ailill, ignoring Jaron. "If breaking one of these blooms causes illness in the village, what can I do to undo it?"

Ailill frowned as he approached. "It is simple to destroy, to cause damage. I do not know how one can repair it. Only the natural rebirth of the flowers can lead to good, I would assume."

Panic seized my throat. We had such little time to get this right. I had little confidence I had any power to do it. My eyes darted over the fountain and I gasped. A glinting flitter of gold sparkled from beneath the still water's surface. I bent down, dunking my hand under the tepid water, and withdrew my gold coin, holding it up to the light. "They left it *here*! They just left it here... And they left me here with it!"

Ailill put a hand over my fingers clutching the coin, lowering my arm. "I would not trust that. They must have left it here on purpose."

"I don't care. It gives us a second chance." I slid the coin into my pocket, my fingers brushing the parchment I'd nearly forgotten about stuffed in there. I brought both pieces out. *The hole behind the throne. It showed even when the throne covered it. If there's a secret to this garden...* "Ailill, stand here." I maneuvered him in front of the lily-covered bush. I unfolded the piece of paper and saw Jurij and Jaron on the bench, staring forward— probably staring at me, but I was off page. There were no hidden holes on that paper, so I tucked it beneath the other one.

The parchment showing Ailill depicted the exact scene I was

looking at. I frowned. The *exact* scene. There was nothing promising.

"What are you doing?" asked Jurij. I pulled his parchment out to keep an eye on where he wandered throughout the garden, too. He stood, looked down, and quickly slid off the single piece of clothing he was wearing, tying it like a loin cloth in front of him with the arms of the jacket behind his waist. I nearly choked and checked to see if Ailill had noticed me. I hadn't witnessed it directly, full color and all, but I could tell from the mischievous look on Ailill's face that he knew what I'd seen on the parchment.

"Looking for something," I said, not turning my head. "Could you walk around the garden?" I looked up. "Both of you?"

Ailill nodded and headed one way, while Jurij stood still, his mouth slightly open. "Like when we saw the hole behind the throne."

"That's the idea. Please. Our time is limited."

He nodded and went the opposite direction of Ailill. I held both parchments out, eager to find anything odd about either of them. I was soon disappointed.

"Nothing?" asked Ailill as he crossed paths with Jurij and the two came to a stop in front of the lily-covered bush.

"Nothing." I sat down between the lily-covered bush and its neighboring one on the lip of the fountain. I let out a sigh of frustration and stared up at half-naked Jurij. "When you came here the first time, where did you appear?"

"You mean on the other side of the Never Veil?" Jurij frowned. "I don't remember actually. It was like I was drowning... And then I came to here—in the garden."

Ailill sat beside me and jutted his chin toward the garden door. "The Never Veil's doorway must have led through the garden door, just like it did when we left last time."

Jurij nodded slowly. "I was wet."

"Wet from the cavern pool," I said, like it was obvious. We sure spent a lot of time wet thanks to that place.

"Or maybe...?" Ailill turned around and ran his hand through the water in the fountain behind us.

"I don't know what you're bothering yourselves for," said Jaron sourly. "These people have the power to do anything to us. There's no hope in fighting them. They said we get to be reborn in other villages, so there's that. As soon as all those women die, we'll have our 'peace of mind' and can get on with things. Them, too. That's good enough."

"No, it's not!" I looked up at Jaron despite myself. "I want to save the people I know. The people I *love*." I was so upset I hardly noticed as Ailill grabbed the parchments from me. "No one else has died yet, since you two came here?"

Jaron eyed the door. "I guess not. Perhaps those kings and queens put a stop to death while they debated. Too many spirits to process at once."

"But that fight with the men and the servants—"

Jurij lifted a finger and went back to the table, picking up a book and bringing it over. He leafed through the pages until he found one and then flipped it over, showing it to me. "That's over. Father and Luuk managed to put an end to it somehow. We've been watching them like little pantomime figures on these pages. I don't know what they're saying, but the men have stopped. They're treating the wounded."

"What about the bangles?" I asked, rubbing the one Ailill had returned to me.

"The servants collected them all," answered Jurij.

"Is that what they were doing?" I sighed and pushed some hair out of my face. "It looked to me like they were in a battle."

Jurij smiled slightly. "A battle with monsters?"

"Who knew then that people could be the monsters," I replied. I gave him a faltering smile back. "That's not true. There's no such thing as a completely heartless monster." My eyes darted to Jaron, who was still slumped over on the bench.

"Olivière, I've found something."

Ailill handed me the paper with the image of his back on it. He leaned forward, almost tipping into the fountain but stretching an arm out toward the stone to steady himself. I was afraid he was going to fall in.

"Look at the parchment," he panted. I did as I was told and saw the paper now showed the fountain as if I were looking down at it and Ailill from the sky.

There was a black hole in the bottom of the fountain, just large enough to fit a person though.

CHAPTER THIRTY-THREE

"That's it!" I wrapped my arms around Ailill's torso and pulled him to an upright position. He tumbled into me as we stood. Our eyes met and I was so happy I could have kissed him—but then I was suddenly overwhelmed with the idea that I'd *almost kissed him.*

I pulled back. *Is that disappointment on his face? He couldn't have known what I'd almost done.* "We can send you back." I turned to face Jurij. It was he I wanted to send back first.

Jurij looked from me to Ailill and back again. "How? I died. It's not the same as wearing a bangle and walking through a veil."

"I'll make it so." I slid the bangle off my wrist and grabbed Jurij's hand, sliding it over his. Jaron's face was incredulous. "I will."

"Noll, how?" Jurij shifted some of my hair behind my ears, a strangely tender gesture in the midst of all of this. "You're not a king or queen."

"I'm the elf queen." I laughed. "Remember?"

The lump at Jurij's throat bobbed. "Noll, I appreciate it, but even if you could send me back—"

"Which I can—"

"Even if you *could,* I don't want to go back. I don't want to go back to a village full of illness, knowing the only people who could do something about it are here, and I left them behind."

I bit my lip and looked back over my shoulder at Ailill. Ailill stepped forward and took the book from Jurij's hands and opened it.

"When someone is reborn into a new village, a new flower blooms." He flipped through the pages. "It's not that that individual life is tied to the individual bloom—there would be hundreds of roses buried beneath the flowers of each bush if so. But the new birth gives an added jolt of magic to the village, and more opportunities for the kings and queens to make an impact on the village." He paused when he got to the very back of the book and frowned, running his finger over the inside of the cover slowly. "I think rebirthing a soul into a village may give Olivière the power she needs to wish the women well again."

"There you go." I stared at Jurij before hugging him, ignoring the strangeness of having my cheek rest against his bare shoulder. It was like what I imagined getting too close to a naked brother might feel like, so I couldn't let us linger for long. "I'm sending you back."

Jaron scoffed from his entirely unhelpful position over at the bench. "They told us we'd be born again as infants when they sent us to new villages. That we wouldn't remember any of this—that we'd been reborn many times before."

"That is when you go to a new village." Ailill still studied the inside cover of the book, his finger and eyes moving down and then back to the top again. "That is why they never send spirits to the same village twice in a row. Not just for fear someone still living there might recognize something of the essence of the spirit in a new child, but because you will grow to remember your past lives. Perhaps not in detail, but well enough." His finger stopped suddenly and his eyes snapped up. "If you take a golden bangle with you, as I did each time I was reborn, you can even stay the same exact age you were when you died, with no loss of memory at all. Or you can choose a younger age. The kings recommended I be reborn at the age at which I became a man, again and again." He shut the book closed. "I agreed because I would be that much closer to my latest demise." His voice softened. "It seemed a small comfort at the time."

A flutter in my stomach told me that Ailill wasn't just being sorrowful at the thought of his past selves, that he had seen something in the book he was keeping from me, something important, but if he chose not to share it just then, then I would have to wait to ask him.

"Jurij, please." I wrapped my fingers around the bangle I'd given him. "Please. I need you back there. I need to trust someone is there, someone who will look after my mother and Elfriede."

"You speak as if you're not planning on coming back."

I placed a finger over his lips. The last thing I needed was an argument from him that he would stay or the promise that he would come back if I didn't show within a certain amount of time. "I will," I lied, not feeling at all bad about it. "But you must give me time, and you must do what you can do for me—and that's agreeing to a rebirth. Give me the flower I need to work with to make the women well again."

Jurij grabbed my hands in his and squeezed them. He looked over his shoulder at Jaron.

"Don't look at me," said Jaron. "You want to risk their wrath, you're welcome to it. Besides, you deserve another chance. I had no right to take your life from you."

Jurij's gaze flickered to Ailill. "Promise me you'll keep her safe."

Ailill slipped an arm around me. "I live for nothing else."

I slipped my own arm around Ailill's waist, knowing it might give Jurij the courage at last to leave me behind. He watched us a moment and nodded. We stepped aside and let him pass through. Jurij lifted one leg and put it into the fountain slowly, testing to make sure he wasn't about to fall into it. He looked back at me. "Can I keep the jacket? Or should I go nude?"

Ailill laughed, and the sound was so strange coming from him. It was genuine, not at all tinged with derision. "Keep it. Please. They let me wear clothing each time I went through."

Jurij's jaw twitched and he put his other leg into the water. He stared down at it. "I can see a bit of red," he said. "Like there's a circle here, but it's red, not violet."

I grabbed Ailill's hand and we approached the fountain together. I reached into my pocket and clutched the coin hard.

694

Send him home. I closed my eyes. *Send him home, as he once was. As Jurij. Send him home!*

"It's violet!"

I opened my eyes to see Jurij stick one foot forward. He almost fell down but stopped himself. "It just looks like stone, but there is a hole here."

"Hurry," I said, still repeating the line in my head. *Send him home.*

"All right." Jurij hesitated. "Goodbye, Noll. I loved you." He walked forward and then vanished into the ground.

"Quick," Ailill said, and he clutched both my shoulders. He guided me to the lily-covered bush. "Make it happen, Olivière. I know you can."

I leaned in front of the bush and reached in, gently moving the outer layer inside until I saw the white roses. *Send him home.*

Parchment crinkled from somewhere behind me. "He's there!" said Ailill. "The same Jurij, just as we hoped!"

The bush began to glow. A small, violet sphere appeared on a branch, the light rippling like a veil at the slightest touch.

I clasped my hands together over the coin and stared at that forming magic. *Make them well,* I thought. *Undo the sickness in my village. Make them well. Make them well.*

The sound of papers shuffling—Ailill flipping through the book. "The women are stirring! Keep wishing it, Olivière. Keep going!"

Make them well!

The white rose burst into life, scattering the violet light in all directions.

"They're awake!" I got to my feet and spun around, still so unused to hearing casual speech on Ailill's tongue. I wasn't used to the sheer joy that decorated his features, either. "I knew you could do it, Olivière. I knew you had it in you."

I laughed and embraced him, book and all. I don't know how long we stayed that way. I do know that the first thing to disturb us was Jaron's gruff and unpleasant voice.

"Well, now you've doomed us all."

I pulled back, my eyes darting to the garden door, expecting the kings' and queens' arrival, but there was nothing, not yet.

They had a lot to discuss, and their perception of time must surely run much more slowly than ours.

I stomped over to Jaron, feeling the weight of the coin in my hand. I don't know when I made the decision, but it came out of my mouth, like it was the only thing to do. "I'm sending you back, too."

Jaron looked at me as if I'd proposed marriage. "Oh, no. No, you're not. You sent the bangle back with Jurij, remember? Doesn't that make it easier for you to send people?"

I jumped as a white shirt flew over my shoulder to Jaron's bare lap. At least now the most embarrassing parts were covered from my sight. Although then I realized that meant Ailill was wearing nothing on his top half.

I didn't realize I could almost faint from embarrassment without even looking at something. I steadied my feet and tossed the coin atop the shirt.

"You'll go back with this."

Jaron stared at me, not even picking up the coin. "You trust me?"

"No. But I trust my friend. The one who existed before he wanted all the answers."

Jaron grabbed the coin and picked up the shirt. He stood, and I looked away as he put his arms through it. He was shorter than Ailill, so I hoped it'd reach beyond his thighs. The next time I dared to look, I saw that it did. He shook his fist. "What if I don't want to go back?"

"Where else would you go?" asked Ailill, slipping in beside me. Just looking out of the corner of my eyes, I caught sight of his bare chest and I had to bite down on my lip hard to stop it from trembling.

Jaron gestured to the bushes all over the garden. "Somewhere I won't remember the things I did."

"We want you to remember," said Ailill stiffly, as if he'd known all along I'd send this terrible man back to our people. "We do not want men to forget their propensity for violence. No more than we want women to forget that men's freedom to love should be equally respected."

I spoke, adding my own reasoning. "Plus, your death made

Luuk a murderer. I won't let that be true." Aillil slid an arm around my shoulders, and I found myself leaning into him.

"All right," said Jaron as he brushed past us. "If you're sure."

I nodded and broke away from Aillil, following Jaron to the fountain. He got in quicker than Jurij, more surefooted.

I turned back to face Aillil, my treacherous eyes drinking in his thin but defined chest before landing on his face. "Can I do it without a token of my own?"

Aillil smiled and nodded, and that was all the encouragement I needed.

I clasped my hands together and shut my eyes. *Send him back,* I thought. *Back as he was.* I hesitated. *Perhaps a little nicer.*

Send him back.

When I opened my eyes, he was gone.

CHAPTER THIRTY-FOUR

Ailill, bare-chested and practically shining in the sunlight, walked back to the table and flipped the book open as he sat at the bench. He smoothed the two pieces of parchment torn from it and lay them on the table beside it.

There was still no sign of movement at the garden door. I slid in beside Ailill, resting a hand on his shoulder. His skin felt like fire—in a good way, like comforting, warming, lively fire. It sent pinpricks to my fingers.

Ailill squeezed my hand, shooting the pin pricks from my fingers to my toes.

"Is he back?" I asked.

"I don't know." Ailill began flipping through the pages. There were people I only somewhat recognized and familiar faces —*Alvilda* awake, Siofra and Nissa embracing her—but every page was a good one. There was no worry or violence; only happiness and rest and respite from all that had happened.

Ailill came to a stop on a page that glowed as it wove from the binding, from nothingness into being. As the light faded, it showed Jaron breaking through the surface of the cavern pool and let out a breath. "He is back," he said, speaking slowly. His shoulders relaxed visibly.

I traced my fingers over the length of his back, finding the muscles between his shoulder blades to be as sharp and defined as if they were sculpted out of a large block of wood. Oh, how I missed carving. I wished I'd thought to carve some more after Father's death. I didn't realize I would never again seem to find the time and strength of mind for it.

...I was comparing Ailill to a hunk of wood. They may have both brought me joy, but that might have been the dumbest thing I had ever thought. My cheeks burned.

"You talk less formally when you're happy," I teased, making my fingertips brush his skin even more lightly.

Ailill shivered under my touch. "No, I don't." His face grew flushed. "All right," he admitted. "I suppose I do."

I wrapped my hand around his side and squeezed him into me, ignoring the poke of Elgar's sheath in my side as I did. But I didn't let myself get too distracted. "Okay, we set out to do what I wanted. We saved the women. We saved both Jurij and Jaron." I rested my chin on both hands on the table. "Without any golden tokens, I don't think we can go back. I wanted to send you back—"

"I will not go back. Not without you."

I smiled and let it go. I understood. If he had sent me back but stayed behind... Well, I couldn't bear to think about it.

"How do we stop them?" I asked. "From undoing what I've done?"

Ailill laughed and I turned to see what he was looking at. Elgar was still sheathed to my waist. "They took your golden bangle away," he said. "But since they will not use weapons themselves, they hardly seemed aware of that."

I raised an eyebrow. "You propose we... fight them? With a sword?"

"They will not expect it."

"I suppose not." I ran my fingers over Elgar's hilt. "I... I don't know if I have it in me again. To hurt people with violence."

Ailill slid the book closer to me. Jaron, dripping water, exited the cavern for a moment, but Ailill flipped past that page, past all the pages—Elfriede! Awake and embracing Mother!—until he reached the back.

He was looking at whatever was there before, and I knew even then he wasn't happy with what he found there.

699

"Do you know what this is?" asked Ailill.

It was a series of names, an almost endless list, written in the smallest possible handwriting. I squinted and looked closer. "I can't really read it. But names?"

Ailill nodded. "The names of everyone who ever lived in our village. It is not a feature the book they gave me shares. I have never been alone with this version of the book long enough to get a clear look."

My eyes widened as I pointed at the page. "Everyone? No wonder it's so small." I peered down again. "Even so, it seems like there should be more."

Ailill ran a finger from one side of the book to the other. "They repeat, and you will find the secondary names of each spirit right there next to the first one. Once a spirit has been reborn in all of the other villages, it returns back to this one."

"Really?" I didn't think anything else could surprise me about how everything worked, but I was wrong. "Does it say who I once was?"

Ailill grinned and tapped a name in the last column at the very bottom. I squinted. It was my own, and there were no other names by it. "Just you. I told you you were special."

"What about you?" I asked.

Ailill laughed and ran his finger over names toward the beginning, in the second column. His name looked strangely empty, but there were a couple of names before it. "Apparently I was reborn in that village two times, before my strange never-ending rebirth as Ailill." He gestured behind him. "But that means I had lives in all of these villages, too."

My eyes wandered up above his name, catching sight of Avery. There were a number of names after hers, and the last one was Alvilda. I gasped. "Your sister was reborn as Alvilda! I thought they were alike."

Ailill coughed and tried to grab the book back from me. "My sister died," he said. "She lived so many lives since, I could hardly consider her current incarnation the same person. In fact, I am surprised there's any similarity at all."

"I'm not." I tugged back on the book, not letting Ailill take it away from me. "The spirit was the same, so how could they not share—" I stopped. The name "Elric" stood out like it was jumping up at me.

"Olivière, I was not sure you should know…"

I let my finger follow the trail of names I didn't recognize from that spirit. Without even seeing the last one, I was sure I was going to find Jaron's name there, but I didn't.

It was Jurij's.

~

GETTING past the dining room without making a sound was one of the most difficult things I'd ever done. I thought for sure they would hear the pounding of my heart as I did: thunderous, loud and echoing in my ears.

Ailill signaled for me to join him at the end of the entryway. The door to the dining room was open, and instead of seeing the kings and queens debating or eating in there, we found them each playing a game of chess with one from the other team in near silence. Each second it took to pass the room was agony. I was afraid they'd look up and see me, but they didn't.

The fact that the garden door was unlocked—I hadn't tried opening it when I tried to see if I could summon the portal there —made me nervous. Like they were expecting us to walk past.

"I need a weapon, too," said Ailill. "The kings and queens each keep one hanging over their thrones. As a testament to how things once were."

"A testament to violence?" I asked incredulously.

Ailill shrugged. "Whatever the reason, I need to get to the kings' throne room to grab one. I can't… go through the queens' again."

I reached for Ailill at the door. He took my hands in his. "Here we part," he whispered. "Take the queens' swords, just in case they decide they want to use them, and meet me back here."

He started climbing the staircase to the kings' castle. I followed. He stopped halfway up the stairs. "What are you doing?" he hissed.

"I'm coming with you," I hissed back.

"You cannot!"

"I must." I steeled myself for the argument. "I will. We're doing this together, right? I won't get separated from you again."

Ailill gestured behind him, glancing down to the entryway. "But the veil will do the same to you that the queens' veil did to me."

"I don't care." I tossed my shoulders back. "I have you. You'll protect me."

Ailill bit his lip and grabbed the railing behind him. "Perhaps we should go to the queens' throne room, then," he said. "I can put up with it and grab one of their swords."

He stopped. The creak of a door widening made us both freeze in place.

"It shall be done," said Adeyemi, some distance below us.

I planted both hands on Ailill's back and shoved him up, pushing him quickly, getting us both past the veil to the kings' castles and out of their sight.

As soon as the veil stopped moving behind me, I felt it at once. I tumbled, shocked that Ailill had managed to put up with this for so long.

Ailill swooped in beside me, catching me before my knees hit the floor again. "We have to go back."

I forced my head up and did my best to send him a reassuring smile. "No. I need your help. We need another sword."

He stood, supporting me with his arms around my waist. I shuffled after him, intent on keeping up a faster pace. I worried that I'd made a mistake, that I slowed him down and had proven a burden to him.

He froze. "May I carry you?"

My first instinct was to say no. My first instinct was to be his equal, to stop him from giving me more than his due, but I'd done my best to support him in the queens' castle. Just because I didn't have the strength to carry him didn't mean I wouldn't have had the option been available to me.

I nodded my assent, even the word "yes" proving to be too much just then. He wrapped my arm around his neck and bent down to place one hand under my knees, the other resting carefully at the small of my back. I shifted Elgar slightly so it would hang from the side away from him.

"See?" I said. "Women can be here. They just need to be friends with a man."

"I hope that by now, we are far more than friends." Ailill

bounced me in his arms before taking his next step, closing the distance between us and the throne room at a far brisker pace.

"Jurij killed your mother." The words came harder to me the farther in we went, but at least we weren't headed as far as the kings' prison.

"He did not."

We reached the throne room, which had enough torches to light our way. Ailill hesitated a moment but plunged us inside.

It was like someone was sitting on top of me the moment we crossed the threshold into the room.

"Argh," I said, then, "I'm fine" when Ailill froze in place.

Ailill grit his teeth and kept carrying me forward. "Do you know how many lives that spirit has lived since then? He is not my brother."

I thought of Avery and Alvilda, and how the two reminded me of each other. There was nothing in Jurij that reminded me of Elric. I'd always associated Elric with the more stubborn version of Ailill I knew at the start. There was this way that Elric had looked at me, full of longing, that I'd seen in Jurij, first with Elfriede and then with me... *No. Jurij has so much kindness in him, even when he's doing things that aren't kind.*

We arrived at the dais and Ailill put me down in the left throne. The dark metal felt cold and lifeless beneath my arms, even through the dampness of my skirt. I sunk my head back into it, sure I could never summon the strength to get off the chair again.

Ailill leaned on the center throne and pulled the sword hanging over it down. He placed it on the arm of the throne I was sitting on and did the same for the sword above my head. I stared at the two swords beside me and felt the slightest bit of warmth coming from that direction. I was too tired to be sure, but I thought I saw a glimmer of violet.

Ailill was leaning on the third throne, his hand on the sword hanging over it, when the shadows of figures at the end of the room danced across the torchlight.

"Halt! You traitor!" Adeyemi stormed into the room, followed closely by Estavan and Kin.

Ailill climbed down from the throne, the sword in his hand. "I have done nothing to betray you—"

703

"On the contrary!" Estavan appeared before me, his hands on my arms before I could even think to fight back. He flung me to the ground in front of the throne, the swords cluttering to the ground along with me. "You put a woman on my throne! A woman!"

Ailill crouched beside me, pulling me closely to him. "Are you all right?" he whispered.

I nodded slightly, the movement sending a hammering echo to my head.

"Where are the two spirits from your village?" asked Kin.

"Why are you asking us?" said Ailill, the slightest hint of a sneer in his voice. So I wasn't the only one he spoke to in that tone.

"The queens took the lily village book," spat Estavan. "I shall assume they are back there."

Kin bent forward and grabbed Ailill's wrists and then mine in turn. "Where are they? Have you been hiding golden tokens from us?"

"Not us," I said, fighting to speak. It was partially a lie, but I didn't care. "Maybe you should ask that of the queens."

Kin's head snapped up and he stared at Adeyemi and Estavan. "They have lied to us. Again."

Adeyemi held a hand up. "We have no proof."

"Proof? We have had enough of that." Estavan scowled and bent down to grab one of the fallen swords. "We have had enough of these games!"

They were talking about the queens lying to them, not Ailill and me. I hoped.

Adeyemi put a hand on Estavan's arm. "Do you know what you risk by picking up that sword?"

Estavan laughed sourly. "There are only three of them."

"And there are only three of us."

Kin picked up the second sword, and Ailill clutched the one he'd taken tighter against him in case they tried to take that, too. Instead of keeping it, Kin held out the sword to Adeyemi with both hands. It made sense. Adeyemi seemed to be a leader, and that sword had come from the center throne.

Adeyemi stared at it. "We give them one chance. One more chance."

"What?" asked Kin.

Adeyemi looked us over. "We tell them what she did. We remind them of what they agreed to, should she upset the games again."

He ran his fingers over the hilt of the blade and took it from Kin, turning it over in the torchlight. "All of the women in the lily village must die."

CHAPTER THIRTY-FIVE

"N o!" I found the strength to scream that word, no matter how much agony I was in just trying to breathe. "You can't!"

Adeyemi did something I never expected him to do—he crouched down beside Ailill and me. "It is because you have defied us again and again."

"That doesn't matter!" I almost choked on my own breath. "I'm here! Punish *me*. You can't... You can't..."

Ailill embraced me tighter. "Your Majesty. Without women, the men of our village will die out."

Adeyemi stood slowly, dropping the sword to his side. "We have never had a village that was all one gender." He exchanged a look with Kin and Estavan. "Even if no other men can be born without women, perhaps they shall at least know true happiness before they die out."

"No!" I said again. "No. There's more to it than just being able to have children. Men and women... We are a village. We are family. Friends." I rolled my head toward Ailill, not caring about the effort it took. "Lovers."

Ailill touched his forehead to mine before pulling back and facing the kings. "She is right. We are not at war with women, and they are not at war with us. We exist together. Even when women love women and men love men, there is still a need for each other that goes beyond birthing new villagers. We keep the village alive together. We are all just… people."

"*People* you are not." Kin shoved Ailill back to grab the sword that rested on his lap and Ailill's head slammed against the center throne. "You are only experiments. Elves. Our creations." His eyes lingered angrily on my ears, which I knew set me apart from the rest of their spirits. "And we have long been tired of the women of your village being born with ears a mockery of our own."

His words were lost on me. It was all I could do not to scream, but I felt the urge rise in my throat. He had to be alive. He had to be. I didn't see blood. It was just like when Jurij had hit me over the head. He'd wake and soon. Until then, it was up to me.

The three kings towered over us with their swords at their sides. They held so much power over us, over all that we loved, and the weakness I felt in every inch of my body only accentuated the fact. Still, I didn't regret coming here, even knowing I would weaken. I would never part from Ailill again, if I could help it.

Although the movement felt like I was tearing through muscles, I rolled to my knees and pulled Elgar out of its sheath, pointing it toward them. I wanted to stand. I wanted to hold the sword higher, but it was all I could do to keep this position. The blade shook terribly in my fingers.

Kin laughed. "What is this? Did she bring that from the queens' throne room?"

Estavan leaned closer but quickly shrunk back. "Perhaps. I do not think we can get too near it."

Adeyemi waved a hand. "No matter. She has no strength to wield it here. Let her stay there until she collapses from the fatigue coursing through her body. She is no threat to us."

There was a loud scraping from behind me, a sound that echoed in my ears as loud as thunder.

"*I* might be." The deep voice carried loudly across the cavernous throne room.

I slunk back down to the floor. It was all I could do to close my eyes and give in to the exhaustion.

I forced them open again and watched as a man approached from behind the center throne.

Jaron.

I slumped over, still clutching my blade.

I DON'T KNOW if I ever expected to open my eyes again. Or if I did, I never expected to see what I saw.

I rolled over. The queens were in the kings' throne room, visibly weakened and each holding a sword. Jangmi did the best job of standing straight—Marigold and Chrysilla both slouched slightly, their swords a heavy weight—but even Jangmi's limbs trembled slightly.

Estavan couldn't stop laughing. "You fools. You fools! You bring your swords here, to our castle? We will not even have to fight you. We simply can lock you in here and leave you to die."

I felt Elgar's weight still in my hands and took a deep breath, slapping one of my palms out against the cold stone floor and pushing, pushing so hard to sit back upright. No one seemed to take notice of me. I searched the room. Ailill was no longer lying against the throne, and I panicked, but his clothes weren't there, either. The throne was moved, a black hole behind it, the edges of a billowing black veil visible through it.

I looked around for Jaron, but there was no sign of him, either. Nor of any empty clothes to signify he had died.

We gave him a golden token. That meant he might have swum out of the cavern pool and walked right into the castle, right through the entryway behind the throne. Right back here. But why? After all we'd done for him.

"You will not kill Olivière," spat Jangmi, with far more strength than I would have had standing like that.

"You admit you have been helping her, then," said Kin.

"She is a woman," Marigold sneered. "We are allowed to let her be our champion."

"You lost the game!" snapped Estavan. "You agreed she would be dealt with."

"The game means nothing." Chrysilla lowered her sword and then grunted, pulling it back upward. "We shall win the war."

Adeyemi took a few casual steps forward. "If you want to save her, everything is off. The games are over. We shall have war again—we shall have bloodshed."

Jangmi stared at him. "We would rather your blood shed than hers."

Estavan howled and ran forward, his sword drawn. Marigold parried it despite the weakness in her limbs. I'd never seen people actually fight with two swords so deftly. It was different than I imagined in the stories. Faster and with no fumbling. Graceful and not at all awkward.

"Men are clearly the superior gender," roared Kin, and he lifted his sword, diving at Chrysilla, but she flipped over, swinging the sword in a circle, and he missed.

How can she do that? I can barely stand.

"If that were true," said Marigold between panting, "you wouldn't need the advantage of our weakness before you finally attacked."

I stuck Elgar into the thin line between stones on the dais and grabbed hold of the hilt. *If they can stand, so can I.*

"You brought yourselves here. You presented us with this chance." Estavan lunged forward and Marigold barely made it out of his way. She breathed heavily and slammed her elbow hard down on his back, making him cry out. He jumped back, menacing. "If you had not come, we would not have attacked you. Would you have attacked us, even if we had no swords of our own?"

"You had swords of your own," barked Chrysilla. "As soon as we got here, you already had swords in hand."

Jangmi and Adeyemi had yet to actually join the fight. They simply walked around in a circle, staying at opposite sides. Jangmi barely seemed affected, but as I used Elgar to stand on my own two feet, there was a slight wobble in her step.

"That was not us." Kin dodged one of Chrysilla's thrusts and managed to roll her sword in a circle with his, out of his way. "She had them when we got here. And then that lost spirit appeared."

Jaron? Ailill? Had they escaped through the portal? How, if Jaron was the only one with a golden token? I didn't believe Ailill would voluntarily go with Jaron, so he must have still been unconscious.

"What lost spirit?" spat Marigold. "Some other trick to help you do battle with us?"

Estavan scoffed. "No. The second spirit we kept in the garden. That man, Jaron."

Chrysilla panted, her sword lowering to the ground. "He appeared here, in your throne room? You must have invited him then."

"A lie," said Adeyemi, his eyes widening slightly. "Surely you must recognize that. What advantage would we gain from that? He was nothing."

"Perhaps when the other new lord failed you, you thought he would have to do," said Jangmi. "You might be creating a new king-like spirit of your own, to match the queen-like spirit that is Olivière."

Adeyemi paused and lifted his own sword in echo. "So you admit you played a role in her creation?"

Jangmi shook her head. "We did not. But you have always been envious of her. You would not take her existence as a sign that women are clearly superior."

I removed Elgar from the floor and started walking toward the wall, first one foot and then the other. I would get through this long enough to do what I could to stop these mad kings and queens. I sunk into the shadows between lit torches. There were no eyes on me, no eyes on the pawn, even if they seemed to recognize her chances of becoming a queen.

"A lie!" Estavan roared, swinging his sword over his head. "We have known from the start. It is the men who are superior! The women are nothing but charlatans."

Marigold tried lifting her sword. She screamed as she did, as if the sound would give her the strength to block the sword in time.

It didn't.

The sword came down at her neck, and a shower of blood spurt out from it. When Marigold fell to the ground in a heap, the blood soaking her golden tight outfit, I marveled at how she could still live after losing so much blood. Then I realized she wasn't alive. She hadn't vanished, but she wasn't alive either.

People didn't always vanish when they died. Their bodies remained behind and melted into the earth.

"Sister!" screamed Chrysilla, but Jangmi didn't so much as flinch. Her eyes were locked too hard on Adeyemi in front of her.

Kin shot his sword out before Chrysilla could make her way to the fallen Marigold. She brought her own sword up in time, but she groaned with the effort, her perfect hair falling over her face.

Estavan kicked at Marigold's body with his boot, his back to me.

A short distance from me.

I hated violence. The sight of Elric's blood—of the screaming, vanishing men—sickened me, but they would kill all of the women in my village. There was no going back for me. At least let me even the odds again.

Biting my tongue to stop myself from grunting, I tasted blood in my mouth as I lifted Elgar higher, aiming the point right at the bottom of Estavan's back. I hesitated only a moment, and then I struck.

The king gurgled, and Elgar dripped with blood. I yanked the blade out, and Estavan fell, lifeless, on top of Marigold.

Chrysilla's and Kin's swords stopped clashing, and all eyes in the room were on me.

CHAPTER THIRTY-SIX

"She killed Estavan!" Kin's mouth fell open as he lowered his sword. "She killed him!"

Chrysilla, bent slightly forward with exhaustion, glanced at him out of the corner of her eye. Without saying a word—her teeth clenched together—she pointed her sword upward, driving it straight up and under Kin's rib cage.

His open mouth filled with blood and he fell forward, bringing Chrysilla with him to the ground.

I collapsed back against the wall, breathing hard, struggling to keep my feet from sliding in the blood. I fought to keep my eyes open because if this was the end for me, I would see it all. I would go into rebirth—or nothingness, if that's what awaited me —knowing if my loved ones were still in danger.

Chrysilla's arms shot out from under Kin and she roared, trying to shove the fallen king off of her. Her hands were dyed in blood—whether her own or Kin's, I couldn't be sure. Chrysilla made an anguished cry and reached out toward Jangmi. "Sister!"

Jangmi stared down at her. She did nothing as Adeyemi walked over toward the two and drove his sword through Chrysilla's neck.

He turned back to Jangmi and me, flicking his sword and

sending droplets of her blood to stain the floor. "I have no brothers left, and now you have no sisters."

Jangmi must have given something away in her face—she had her back to me and I couldn't see it—but Adeyemi's eyes turned instantly to me. "No," he said. "No. She will not be queen! She cannot be queen!"

He didn't cross over to Jangmi right away, instead resuming their slow circling, his path taking him farther away and toward the door. "You are both weakened here," he said. "And you have no help. I let that wandering spirit go in exchange for taking Ailill along with him. You will find no help here."

Jangmi readjusted the sword in her hands. "Ailill? Help us? We have no use for a man. You are mistaken, and you do yourself no favors by sending a man away."

"Wrong," I said, only the second word managing to make it past my lips. I rolled my shoulder into the wall, dragging Elgar with me. "You're... wrong."

Jangmi gave no indication that she'd heard me, so I found the strength to move and ran my sword through her back in the same place I'd pierced Estavan.

Jangmi fell forward, and this time, I let Elgar go with the body as it crashed to the floor. I fell to my knees, already realizing I'd made a mistake. If this was the last bit of strength I had, I should have saved it until I had a chance to attack Adeyemi, should have waited until he'd fallen before turning my attention to the lone queen. But I wasn't sure I'd ever have another chance to end Jangmi's rule, to put a stop to her games of toying with the lives of people she saw as pawns, and I would just have to hope it was enough—that Adeyemi would be satisfied to be the lone ruler.

I was wrong.

"That was foolish, but I suppose I should thank you." Adeyemi strove closer, his sword casually at his side. "Not that I required the assistance."

I said nothing. It was all I could do to stay seated, to face my end head-on. *Ailill...*

Adeyemi raised the sword over his head. "If you think this favor will save the women of your village, you are mistaken. Now there is no one to stop me from ending women in all the villages. Men may perish, but we shall live lives of glory before the end." He brought the sword down.

He fell forward on top of Jangmi, the sword cluttering harmlessly to the ground beside him. He had a blade sticking out of his back.

I could barely lift my head. The white was blinding. "Spurn...?"

"He's gone, remember?" Ailill swooped in beside me to stop me from falling over. "It's far past time for people to lead themselves, to help themselves. I asked all the Ailills to embrace their final end."

I settled comfortably into Ailill's arms and ran my fingertips across one of his cheeks. "Not *all* the Ailills."

"No, not this one. This one will never leave you again." He leaned forward and rested his forehead against mine. "This one should have never left you to begin with."

I found a bit more strength and wrapped a hand around the back of Ailill's head, bringing it forward so his lips would meet mine.

He stopped me, a mere hair's breadth from the kiss. "No."

"No?" My hand fell limply to the floor. My eyes couldn't stay open, but beneath my eyelids, I could feel the tears. "Suppose... I deserve that..."

Ailill snorted and I felt his arms under my legs and behind my back again, felt him lift me up as he stood. "If anything, it is I who deserves your rejection. No. No, we'll do this where we're equal."

I was so close to slumber, his gentle footsteps felt like someone rocking me to sleep.

～

STRENGTH COURSED BACK through my body, and by the time I felt the soft fluttering of a veil over my face, it was like I was entirely reborn. My eyes jolted open, like I had been slapped awake.

"You're wet," I blurted. He was.

"You're not completely dry, either." Ailill laughed as he carefully descended the stairs with me still in his arms. "I came back through the cavern pool and the garden fountain."

"What happened?" I asked, struggling slightly so he would understand to put me back on my feet. "I passed out, and when I came to, you and Jaron were gone."

Ailill was still. "Do you mind if I still carry you?"

I stopped struggling, my face hot. "What?"

"I know that we are equals here." He nodded his head around us at the entryway. "But I ask that you grant me this boon just once. I like the feeling of you in my arms."

I couldn't look at him. I might have mumbled my acceptance, my hand resting comfortably on his bare chest.

He started walking again. "I was still unconscious when Jaron came back. Otherwise, I never would have let him take me with him."

"But how did you both get back? You only had the one coin between you."

Ailill grimaced as we finished descending the stairs. "According to Jaron, he asked the kings to give him a rebirth, or he would fight them. He told them he would rather die than go back. They certainly considered him no threat, but they promised him they would grant his request if he first brought me back to our village with him one last time. They granted him a bangle so I would have a token to wear as I made my way through."

We reached the garden doorway, which was open, the dying light of twilight streaming in through the garden.

I looked around as we stepped inside. "So where is he?"

"Here," came a voice from behind me. "I've been making a number of trips. Making sure we brought all but one of these."

I pushed harder on Ailill's chest and he lowered my feet to the ground. I smoothed my still-damp skirt and hair nervously, embarrassed at being caught in his arms.

Jaron—with pants on to match Ailill's shirt, I was relieved to see—was seated on the bench in front of the garden table, a shimmering pile of golden bangles behind him. He stood up. "Wish I'd been able to bring you back instead of him. You would have been easier to carry. This fellow's got more heft to him than you'd think, just looking at him."

I glared at Jaron. "You came back."

Jaron shrugged. He was wet, too. "I wondered why you trusted me."

715

"But you helped us." I looked to Ailill for confirmation. "You helped Ailill cross back through the cavern pool, so he could take the kings by surprise."

"Only because he practically wrung my neck when he woke up in the wrong castle. He promised me you could do what I asked the kings to do for me, so I may as well be on the right side. For once."

I grinned at Ailill and wrapped my arm around his, leaning into his shoulder, not caring that we had an audience.

Jaron clenched his jaw and walked to the table, grabbing the open book and showing it to me. "Your sister is doing well. Your mother, too."

The drawing showed Elfriede dancing, a huge grin on her face. She ran back and forth in front of our cottage, fluttering her arms about with something that might be a shawl catching in the wind, passing by so many recognizable faces: Mother, who had happy tears on her face, and Thea at her side; Roslyn, hand in hand with Sindri; Darwyn and Tayton sitting against our cottage wall, Tayton's head wrapped in bandages, but a smile on both their faces; Siofra leaning into Alvilda; Nissa nudging sour-faced Luuk and managing to get a small smile to appear on his features; Coll looking on and clapping as Arrow yipped at his heels, Bow panting happily on the ground at his feet.

And then Elfriede halted, and I could see the flush on her cheeks even though the page was devoid of color. A man came tumbling into view on the page—a man, I realized, who'd been chasing along after her. Jurij grabbed Elfriede around the waist and lifted her up above him, looking like he wanted to devour her with his gaze.

I guess he figured out his true feelings at last.

Jurij put Elfriede down and leaned forward to kiss her.

Jaron must have seen my face because he pulled the book back and examined it. "Oh. Yeah. Jurij is doing well, too. He was so glad to see Elfriede well again, and she sort of melted into his arms in tears, telling him she never stopped loving him." He scratched his head and shrugged. "I don't know. I only saw part of it. I passed through the castle to get to the other entryway to this place and I met them on their way out. They wouldn't let each other go the whole time."

I guess after enough lifetimes, even a spirit as wicked as Elric's could learn to love.

I eyed Jaron thoughtfully. He wasn't always this way, I was sure of it. He wouldn't always have hurt me, or killed Jurij, or caused the death of my father. "You really want to be reborn in a new village?"

Jaron shut the book closed hard. "I do. You may think I need to live with my pain, but I beg you." He got down on his knees. "I beg you to show me mercy. I did as he asked. I made sure I took all of the bangles here, as many as I could carry each trip, leaving only the one Jurij had on behind."

I looked at Ailill. "You left one with Jurij?"

Ailill smirked and put an arm around me. "He was lord of the village when we left it. They may as well have one leader. A real leader. Someone born in this time. Someone who knows the people well."

I thought about that, and what kind of leader Jurij might make. The lord of the village would lose a lot of his mystery, and if the specters were all gone, he'd need to invite some people to live with him and help him. But Ailill was right—a lot of people knew Jurij. They might trust him more when it came to rebuilding the fragile state of the village—if they could get over the incident at the Great Hall, and if they never learned of his indirect involvement in the fire at the tavern, maybe.

But I couldn't see Jurij doing that, either. Starting his rule with lies or hidden truths. Who knew what the future really held for my village.

"Don't do that," I said to Jaron, who was still kneeling. "Don't bow to me." I threw my shoulders back. "If I can, I'll do it."

A huge smile broke out across Jaron's face. "Thank you!" He got up to move forward, seemed to realize he still had the book in his hand, and quickly dropped it off at the table. Then he grabbed my hand in his. "Thank you."

I felt the warm weight of the coin transfer from his palm to mine.

"All right." I stepped back and lead the men toward the fountain. I ran my fingers lightly over the lily-covered bush and stopped at the next one, covered in yellow blossoms I didn't recognize.

717

"Daffodils," said Ailill, as if reading my mind.

"I'll send you here." Jaron stepped in front of the yellow-covered bush and I frowned, turning to Ailill. "Will this work if he came here alive, and not as a spirit?"

Ailill saw something greater in my visage than I could ever believe existed, like the beauty of a setting sun over the mountaintops. "Olivière, you can do anything. I'm sure of it."

I bent down on my knees in front of Jaron, clasped my hands together over the coin, and closed my eyes. *Give Jaron rebirth in this village*, I thought. *Give him a new life. Give him happiness.*

There was something there, something I was just about to access, but I was afraid to grab it. "I can't."

"You can." Ailill kneeled down beside me, his hands on my shoulders and his eyes closed. He must have been thinking it, too. *Give Jaron rebirth in this village.*

Set him free.

The warmth shot through my hands and traveled everywhere. I could feel it pulsating up Ailill's arms and back through me, like we were one living being.

I opened my eyes just in time to see the clothing Jaron had been wearing crumple to the ground, to see the violet light burst into life on the daffodil bush.

I laughed. "We did it!" Without even finding the book for that village, I knew. The proof was the golden bangle on my wrist, the coin no longer in my palms. It'd somehow changed into the more traditional token as it spread the power of my wish all throughout my body.

I turned to face Ailill, and I saw that same thing in his eyes that he must have seen in mine. It was more beautiful than flickering fire in irises. It was like the entire sun was reflected in those eyes.

He took both my hands in his and we stood, as one, at once. I was so mesmerized by the sun in his irises, at the fire it seemed to ignite in my body, that it took the glowing golden light from the top of his head for me to tear my own eyes away from his.

I gasped. "There's a crown! On your head! Like the kings wore! Only..." I tilted my head. "It's far lovelier than anything they wore." His crown was made of blossoms of countless different colors, as if a flower from each village's bush had woven together to anoint him their new king.

Ailill laughed and squeezed my hands, bringing me closer to the water fountain. "You have one, too."

I reached up and where I expected to feel nothing, my fingers brushed against soft petals. I bent over to look at my reflection in the water. A crown fit for a queen rested atop the thick black hair I once found so difficult to tame—hair that was far longer now than I remembered. When had it grown so long? Was that part of the magic, too? I felt like it was. That it was a sign that I was no longer just nobody's goddess or nobody's lady—the girl who cut her hair when she wanted to be left alone. I was no longer alone, but I was nobody's pawn. My tresses looked wild even now, but it suited the crown. It suited the woman who looked up at me.

Although Elfriede's wrinkled hand-me-downs certainly didn't.

"So we're the ones who must watch over the villages now." I chuckled as I pulled away and patted my clothes. "We won't have to wear those very tight suits, will we?"

Ailill grinned. "We can wear whatever we please. But perhaps now that my shirt is once again free, I should at least wear *something*." He bent down to pick it up.

"Wait!"

Ailill froze, his hand on the shirt, his eyebrows raised. "Wait to put on my shirt?"

I blushed. "Yes."

"All right." Ailill straightened up. "May I ask why—"

I interrupted him with a kiss.

AUTHOR'S NOTE

Official The Never Veil Series art by masart.tumblr.com.

Thank you, thank you, thank you to everyone who has stuck with Noll, Ailill, Jurij, Elfriede and everyone else for three whole books. I hope you're satisfied with their own version of happily ever after, as strange as it might be. I especially appreciate those of you who shared a review and/or who reached out to me to tell me what you thought of the books! You've made this author's day over and over again. You needn't think of Noll's journey as over, although I've finished telling it. Her real life and her true purpose have just begun.

ABOUT THE AUTHOR

Amy McNulty is an editor and author of books that run the gamut from YA speculative fiction to contemporary romance. A lifelong fiction fanatic, she fangirls over books, anime, manga, comics, movies, games, and TV shows from her home state of Wisconsin. When not editing her clients' novels, she's busy fulfilling her dream by crafting fantastical worlds of her own.

Sign up for Amy's newsletter to receive news and exclusive information about her current and upcoming projects. Get a free YA romantic sci-fi novelette when you do!

Find her at amymcnulty.com and follow her on social media:

amazon.com/author/amymcnulty

bookbub.com/authors/amy-mcnulty

facebook.com/AmyMcNultyAuthor

twitter.com/mcnultyamy

instagram.com/mcnulty.amy

pinterest.com/authoramymc

LOOK FOR MORE YA SPECULATIVE
FICTION READS FROM SNOWY
WINGS PUBLISHING

Snowy Wings
PUBLISHING

725

CROWN OF ICE

VICTORIA GILBERT

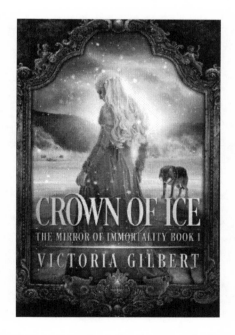

Snow Queen Thyra Winther is immortal, but if she can't reassemble a shattered enchanted mirror by her eighteenth birthday she's doomed to spend eternity as a wraith.

Armed with magic granted by a ruthless wizard, Thyra schemes to survive with her mind and body intact. Unencumbered by kindness, she kidnaps local boy Kai Thorsen, whose mathematical skills rival her own. Two logical minds, Thyra calculates, are better than one. With time rapidly melting away she needs all the help she can steal.

A cruel lie ensnares Kai in her plan, but three missing mirror shards and Kai's childhood friend, Gerda, present more formidable obstacles.

Thyra's willing to do anything—venture into uncharted lands, outwit sorcerers, or battle enchanted beasts—to reconstruct the mirror, yet her most dangerous adversary lies within her. Touched by the warmth of a wolf pup's devotion and the fire of a young man's love, the thawing of Thyra's frozen heart could prove her ultimate undoing.

ALL THE TALES WE TELL

ANNIE COSBY

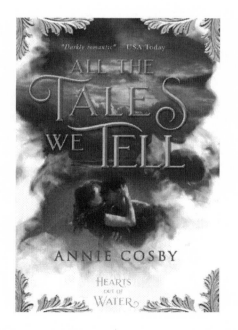

She's filthy rich. He's not. It'll take patience, an old woman who thinks she's a selkie, and one salty-sweet summer on the beach to make them realize what's between them.

When Cora's mother whisks the family away for the summer, Cora must decide between forging her future in the glimmering world of second homes where her parents belong, or getting lost in the enchanting world of the locals and the mystery surrounding a lonely old woman who claims to be a selkie—and who probably needs Cora more than anyone else.

Through the fantastical tales and anguished memories of the batty Mrs. O'Leary, as well as the company of a particularly gorgeous local boy called Ronan, Cora finds an escape from the reality of planning her life after high school. But will it come at the cost of alienating Cora's mother, who struggles with her own tragic memories?

As the summer wanes, it becomes apparent that Mrs. O'Leary is desperate to leave Oyster Beach. And Ronan just may hold the answer to her tragic past—and Cora's future.

READ MORE FROM AMY MCNULTY

FANGS & FINS (BLOOD, BLOOM, & WATER SERIES)

A dapper vampire. A sullen merman. Two heirs to a great conflict—and each needs to claim a beloved to become his kindred's champion.

High school senior Ember Goodwin never had a sister, but after her mom's remarriage, she now has two. The eldest is no stranger to her—Ivy is a witty girl in her grade who's almost never spoken to the shy bookworm before—but she's surprised to find the popular girl quite amiable. Their burgeoning friendship is tested, however, when Dean Horne, a pale, besuited charmer, shows interest in them both and plans to reveal his appetite for blood to the one who'll stand by his side.

Seventeen-year-old Ivy Sheppard is tired of splitting her time between her dad's and her mom's, particularly when her dad uproots their lives to move them in with his new wife and step-daughter. Used to rolling with her parents' whims, she tries to make the best of it and befriend her nerdy new step-sister. Her hectic life grows more unwieldy when she catches the eye of junior Calder Poole, whom she swears she sees swap well-toned legs for a pair of fins during a dip in a lake. Now she's fending off suitors left and right, all while trying to get to the bottom of the strange happenings in her town.

The first book in the Blood, Bloom, & Water series sets family against family and friend against friend as an epic, ancient war comes to a head in a supposedly sleepy suburb.

BALLAD OF THE BEANSTALK

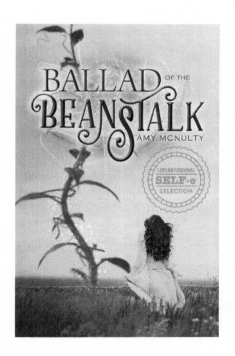

A Library Journal Self-e Selection.

As her fingers move across the strings of her family's heirloom harp, sixteen-year-old Clarion can forget. She doesn't dwell on the recent passing of her beloved father or the fact that her mother has just sold everything they owned, including that very same instrument that gives Clarion life. She doesn't think about how her friends treat her like a feeble, brittle thing to be protected. She doesn't worry about how to tell the elegant Elena, her best friend and first love, that she doesn't want to be her sweetheart anymore. She becomes the melody and loses herself in the song.

When Mack, a lord's dashing young son, rides into town so his father and Elena's can arrange a marriage between the two youth, Clarion finds herself falling in love with a boy for the first time. Drawn to Clarion's music, Mack puts Clarion and Elena's relationship to the test, but he soon vanishes by climbing up a giant beanstalk that only Clarion has seen. When even the town witch won't help, Clarion is determined to rescue Mack herself and prove once and for all that she doesn't need protecting. But while she fancied herself a savior, she couldn't have imagined the enormous world of danger that awaits her in the kingdom of the clouds.

A prequel to the fairy tale *Jack and the Beanstalk* that reveals the true story behind the magical singing harp.

FALL FAR FROM THE TREE DUOLOGY

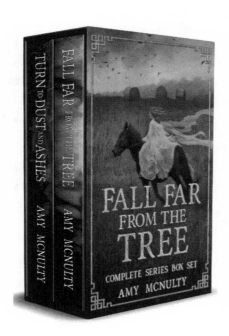

Terror. Callousness. Denial. Rebellion. How the four teenage children of leaders in the duchy and the neighboring empire of Hanaobi choose to adapt to their nefarious parents' whims is a matter of survival.

Rohesia, daughter of the duke, spends her days hunting "outsiders," fugitives who've snuck onto her father's island duchy. That she lives when even children who resemble her are subject to death hardens her heart to tackle the task.

Fastello is the son of the "king" of the raiders who steal from the rich and share with the poor. When aristocrats die in the raids, Fastello questions what his peoples' increasingly wicked methods of survival have cost them.

An orphan raised by a convent of mothers, Cateline can think of no higher aim in life than to serve her religion, even if it means turning a blind eye to the suffering of other orphans under the mothers' care.

Kojiro, new heir to the Hanaobi empire, must avenge his people against the "barbarians" who live in the duchy, terrified the empress, his own mother, might rather see him die than succeed.

When the paths of these four young adults cross, they must rely on one another for survival—but the love of even a malevolent guardian is hard to leave behind.

Made in United States
Orlando, FL
22 January 2022

13883902R00443